ALL THAT MATTERS

SUSAN X MEAGHER

Being deeply loved by someone gives you strength; loving someone deeply gives you courage.

—Lao Tzu

ALL THAT MATTERS

© 2006 BY SUSAN X MEAGHER

EDITED BY ANNE BRISK

COVER DESIGN AND LAYOUT BY CAROLYN NORMAN
ISBN 0-977088-56-1

THIS TRADE PAPERBACK ORIGINAL IS PUBLISHED BY BRISK PRESS, NEW YORK, NY 10011

FIRST PRINTING: SEPTEMBER 2006

Dedication

My dear friend Anne edited this book during the last months of her life. Her illness, ALS, had rendered her hands almost useless, but she was determined to finish the project.

I have memories, both immeasurably proud and deeply sad, of her efforts just to move the cursor. The small movements required, expended all of the energy and focus she could bring to bear, but she never gave up.

Because of our collaboration, this book will always hold a special space in my heart. I wish with all my soul that we could have worked on many more books together, but fate wasn't kind to her.

The world is diminished by the loss of each human being—particularly, in my view, of this one.

Acknowledgments

Many people have helped edit and proofread this manuscript. I'd like to thank Aquila, Di Bauden, Tracy Bricker, Catherine from France, Kay Davis, Day, Emelyn East, LMG, Judy McCormick, P. Mitchell, Elaine Mulligan, Noirin, Steve P., Shana, Jen Stamey, and Tena.

Carrie designed the cover, formatted the text, did at least ten "final" proofs, and put up with my obsessive need to look at the manuscript just one more time. Her patience is nearly limitless, and her love exceeds her patience. The luckiest day of my life was the day I met her.

By Susan X Meagher

Novels

Cherry Grove

All That Matters

Arbor Vitae

Serial Novels

I Found My Heart in San Francisco:

Awakenings

Beginnings

Coalescence

Disclosures

Entwined

Fidelity

Getaway

Anthologies

Undercover Tales

Telltale Kisses

The Milk of Human Kindness

Infinite Pleasures

To purchase these books go to

www.briskpress.com

Chapter One

"*H*oney, this isn't an orthopedist's office."

"What?"

"If you squeeze my hand any harder, you're going to break it, and I'm not sure these doctors know much about repairing broken bones."

The joking comment pulled David Spencer from his anxious state and made him chuckle mildly. "I bet they know plenty about boners," he said just as the door opened, making him jump.

"Good morning." A pleasant-looking, middle-aged man stuck his hand out towards David. "Jonathan Greene." He snuck a very quick look at the chart in his hand and asked, "Mr. and Mrs. Spencer?"

"Yes," David said. "I'm David, and this is my wife, Blair."

The doctor shook Blair's offered hand and sat down behind his desk, now looking at the chart more carefully. "Let's see now…you've been working with a Doctor Coughlin."

"She's my gynecologist," Blair said.

He looked at the pair and commented, "Not to turn away a patient, but why are you here? You're less than halfway through the usual screening tests for infertility."

David started to speak, but Blair placed her hand on his arm and said, "My husband is the prototypical A-type personality, Doctor Greene. When he learned that his sperm count was a little low, he couldn't rest until we called out the big guns."

"We don't have any time to waste," her husband said, eyes wide. "Her eggs are almost thirty-five!"

She indulgently patted him again, discreetly rolling her eyes at the doctor and then speaking quietly, acting as if her husband couldn't hear her. "Sometimes, I hate the Internet. David's been researching every infertility site imaginable, and he's learned it's much harder to conceive once the woman's past thirty-five. He seems to think that, on my thirty-fifth birthday, my eggs are going to seize up and refuse to have anything to do with sperm again."

The warm smile that settled on the doctor's face showed how much he appreciated hearing a humorous take on a very common problem. "It's true that it becomes more

1

difficult to conceive naturally as our bodies age. But there's no firm cutoff date. Let's not let other people's experiences color our perceptions too much, okay?"

David nodded so quickly that it was fairly obvious the doctor's advice hadn't really reached him. "Right…I just want to make sure that we don't waste another minute. We want to have a baby, and I don't want to look back in three years and feel like we let the chance pass us by."

Doctor Greene nodded. "We'll do our best to not let that happen." Looking at his notes, he asked, "It says you've been trying to conceive for a year. Is that correct?"

"Yes," Blair said. "I stopped taking the pill last August. After we didn't get pregnant right away, we started being a little more deliberate about it. I started taking my basal body temperature to make sure we were having intercourse whenever I was ovulating."

"So, you've been having well-timed intercourse for how long?"

"About six months."

"Well…" He leaned back in his chair, not speaking for a minute. "That's not a very long time. Most doctors recommend waiting a year before you even consider seeing an infertility specialist."

"We're not most people," Blair said, casting a sidelong look at her husband. "We're results-oriented." She gave the doctor such a charming smile that he seemed to mimic it involuntarily.

"I can see that. Well, in that case, let's see if we can give you a little help." Reading the specifics in their chart, he commented, "Your sperm count *is* low, David, but not remarkably so. We generally consider twenty parts per million low, and you're at twenty-one." He smiled at him and said, "Remember, only one of them needs to meet its match."

"I know that," he said, "and I'd generally love those odds. But we've been trying for months now—"

"I realize that," Doctor Greene interrupted. "But all we know at this point is that your count is borderline low. We don't really know much about Blair's reproductive capacity. I'd feel much more comfortable going forward if you would have the routine tests done."

"We had the postcoital test done, as well as the sperm mucus penetration test," she said. "But I was reluctant to have the more invasive tests done yet. I think we're jumping the gun since we've only been trying hard for six months."

"But your eggs—" David said.

"If you call my eggs 'old' one more time, your sperm won't have the opportunity to visit them…ever." Blair's expression was just as calm and loving as it had been a minute earlier, but something in her tone gave the impression that she meant every word of her threat. David just nodded, clearly knowing when to back off.

Turning to the doctor, she said, "I know it's premature to see you. But my gynecologist hasn't been able to convince David that some simple things could increase his fertility. I thought that a reproductive endocrinologist might be able to persuade him to make some lifestyle changes. That might be all we have to do."

"I assume you have some changes in mind?" the doctor asked, not even trying to hide a smirk.

"I've done a fair amount of Internet searching myself," she said, "and I think that David could win the 'How to lower your sperm count' competition. He smokes, he drinks, he wears briefs, he sits in a hot tub, he's under a tremendous amount of stress, and he drinks more caffeine than any man on Earth." Patting her husband's thigh, she smiled and said, "I know caffeine is more of a fertility inhibitor for women than men; I just want him to quit caffeine so he won't be so crazy."

"You make me sound like a chain-smoking, drunken head case!"

Tilting her chin, she regarded him with deep affection clearly visible in her green eyes. Her shoulders shrugged slightly as her smile grew wider. "I still love you, sweetie."

The doctor couldn't help but chuckle at the look on Blair's face. David obviously wasn't able to resist her charms, either, since he smiled and took her hand. Looking back at the doctor, he said, "I don't think I drink too much, but my beloved wife doesn't agree with me. However, I do chain-smoke, and I suppose all of her other claims are valid, too. But I read on the Internet that lifestyle factors don't really have that big an impact."

"I disagree," Doctor Greene said. "In a case like yours, where your count is marginally low, stopping smoking and cutting down on your drinking could really have an effect."

With a near-pleading look, David said, "Look, Doc, I work in a very stressful job. The only way I can sleep at night is to have a few Scotches when I get home. I sit in the hot tub after dinner to relax, and I just don't think I can stop that."

"That's up to you, David," Doctor Greene said, "but if having a baby means a lot to you, you might want to consider doing whatever you can to increase your odds."

David turned to his wife. "I'll make you a deal: if you'll have the other tests done, I'll start wearing boxers, and I'll stay out of the hot tub."

Blair narrowed her eyes and thought for a moment. "No dice. I'll only do it if you cut down to one drink a night. You're up to three, David, and it's starting to worry me."

He gave the doctor a helpless shrug and said, "Five years, and I haven't won an argument yet." Extending his hand, he and Blair shook on the deal.

Blair asked, "Should I go back to my gynecologist for the remaining tests?"

"That makes sense," Doctor Greene agreed. "You already have a relationship with her. Once we see how your tests come out, we can chat again and determine whether you should return here or continue on with Doctor Coughlin."

"Sounds good to me," Blair said. "If we come back, will we see you again? Doctor Coughlin said that all of the doctors here work together."

"That's true," he said. "Each of us has an area of expertise, so before we come up with a treatment plan, we all meet and discuss the details of a case. That lets everyone have a voice, so you get four specialists for the price of one. As long as you're here, why don't I see if the other doctors can pop in to meet you?"

"Great," Blair said, but David looked decidedly uncomfortable. Blair leaned over and whispered something to him, and eventually, he nodded his head and took her hand, looking as if he were expecting a firing squad.

Doctor Greene pressed the intercom button and asked, "Marcella? See if you can round up Doctors Martini, Novachek, and Mackenzie and have them come into my office to meet some new patients." He released the button and said, "I think they're all in the office this morning. We usually consult about new cases over lunch on Mondays."

"You specialize in male infertility, right?" Blair asked.

"Right. Doctor Martini's field is in vitro fertilization, Doctor Novachek works primarily with artificial insemination cases, and Doctor Mackenzie is a reproductive surgeon."

"I hope we don't have to work with him," Blair said, her eyes growing wide.

"Doctor Mackenzie is—"A gentle knock on the door accompanied Doctor Greene's reply. "Well, here she is now."

A woman poked her head in the door, gave Doctor Greene a wide smile, and asked, "Does somebody need a doctor?"

"Come on in," he said. "Mrs. Spencer was just saying that she hopes she never has to meet you."

"Well!" The woman perched on the edge of Doctor Greene's desk and looked at Blair for a moment. "People generally don't start disliking me until we've met. Is it the name? Are you anti-Scottish? Were you frightened by plaid at a young age?"

"No," Blair said, laughing. "I just don't want to have to go under the knife. Anybody's knife." She reached out and offered her hand. "I'm Blair Spencer—knife phobic."

"I don't blame you, Blair." Doctor Mackenzie smiled, her eyes reflecting the warmth of her grin. "I only like the blunt end of the scalpel myself."

"We're a long way from discussing a surgical option," Doctor Greene said. "The Spencers haven't even completed all of the standard screening tests."

"Impatient sorts, eh?" Doctor Mackenzie said. "Me, too. I can play a minute waltz in fifty-two seconds."

Blair regarded the woman, noting the incredibly attractive smile that had settled on her face as though it were her usual expression. She tried not to be jealous of the doctor's curly, chin-length hair, self-consciously brushing her own straight locks from her collar.

There's something vaguely familiar about her. I wonder if I've ever seen her at an open house.

In short order, Doctors Martini and Novachek entered, and the four doctors chatted with the Spencers for a few minutes. Doctor Greene stood and shook both of their hands, and then the other doctors did the same. "Make those few changes we talked about, and I think there's a good chance we won't have to meet again," Doctor Greene said. "But if we do work together, I'm confident we can help you two have the baby you want."

Blair took David's hand and said, "The baby *I* want is delivered to the house with my dry cleaning. But I'm willing to do it the hard way for David." Once again, her smile and teasing tone belied the fact that her words were deadly serious, and Doctor Greene briefly wondered if the Spencers were equally committed to the long process that likely awaited them.

The next afternoon, Blair came dashing into the house, shopping bag in hand. "I just have a moment, sweetie. I'm meeting a client at my office at 5:00, and then I'm going to a play in NoHo."

"North Hollywood will always be North Hollywood, no matter how artsy you try to make it sound," he said, chuckling softly. "What have you got in the bag?"

"Your new underwear." She dumped the contents of the bag onto his lap and then dug in her large black leather carryall and produced a few pieces of paper. "This is your membership to Clank, the only gym on the Westside that doesn't have a hot tub, and this is a certificate that entitles you to a dozen massages at that nice spa on San Vicente—where that supermodel you like goes."

"I don't *like* her. I just mentioned that a guy at the office saw her being wrapped in seaweed there."

"Yes, dear," she said. "And there was no other reason for your wanting to go there that weekend for your very own seaweed wrap." She leaned over and kissed his cheek. "By the way…straight guys don't get wrapped—in anything."

He gave her a wry smirk and looked at the cards she'd handed him. "So, is it gay to get a massage? I don't want to give the supermodels the wrong idea."

"It's massively straight. And I just know your little guys will thank you for finding a new way to calm down in the evening. I don't want to see you and the fellas in the tub until we get pregnant."

Looking down at his lap, now covered with packages of boxer shorts, he commented, "Hear that, guys? No more hot tubs." He snaked his arm around his wife's waist and pulled her onto his lap, causing her to let out a little yelp when she slid over the arm of his chair. "The guys were just thinking they'd like to visit. Spare a half-hour?" He started to nuzzle his face into her strawberry-blonde hair, sniffing delicately to take in the scent. "How do you manage to still smell so great at the end of the day?"

"Well, selling real estate isn't akin to tarring roofs. And since I didn't get out of my jammies until noon, it's hardly the end of a long day."

"I envy you," he said. "It must be nice to stay up like an adult and get to watch David Letterman."

"I don't watch David Letterman," she reminded him, "but I have to agree with you. I could never switch schedules with you. Going to bed at 9:00 and getting up at 4:30 would make me lose my mind."

"It just makes it hard to perform my stud service," he said. "I've gotta catch you when you're in heat."

"Well, I'm not in heat today, so you and the boys rest up." She clambered off his lap and adjusted her clothing. "Maybe we'll get lucky this month and I'll be ovulating on the weekend."

"We can dream." David smiled wistfully. "Of course, we can still only have sex every other day. This scheduling crap takes all the spontaneity out of it."

"True. But we could always adopt and never have to worry about any of this stuff again." She leaned over and slipped her hand behind his head, drawing it forward until his face met her breasts. Shaking her shoulders, she nuzzled his face into her chest. "These would stay perky a lot longer, too, sweetie."

He pulled back just a few inches and placed his hands on the sides of her breasts, compressing them slightly. "I do love them just like they are now. But I don't mind sharing them with David Jr."

"Have it your way," she said, patting his hands. "But don't fall in love with that 'David Jr.' thing. Not gonna happen." She kissed him gently and said, "I'll do my best not to wake you tonight. Your boys need their rest to build their ranks."

He reached behind her and palmed her ass. "Feel free to wake us if you're in the mood to..." He gave her a sexy look and twitched an eyebrow.

"Will do. It's always cute to see how quickly I can make you go from sound asleep to ready for action."

"I'm putty in your hands, baby. And I'd give up sleep any night of the week for you."

⟶

Blair stood close to a stone wall, her view that of the entire west side of Los Angeles. A strong, moist breeze ruffled her hair in the warm evening, and the hint of ocean breeze that snaked up to the top of the Santa Monica Mountains, near the Sepulveda Pass, was very welcome. A handsome blond man appeared next to her, nodding his head towards the sea, clearly visible as the sun sank into it. "Can you imagine how horrible a place this would be without the ocean?"

"Yes, I've been to Phoenix," she said, not taking her eyes from the magnificent vista.

Blair heard a woman's voice from over her shoulder say, "There you are." Turning, she cocked her head and thought for a moment, finally deciding that she recognized both the voice and the woman. "Uhm, Doctor...?"

A warm smile bloomed on the woman's face, and she handed one of the drinks she carried to the man so that she could shake Blair's hand. "Mackenzie. I remember meeting you, but names aren't my forte."

"Blair Spencer." Suddenly, the man was gone, Blair not having seen him depart. She looked around and asked, "Where did...?"

"Oh, Nick makes himself scarce whenever I run into a patient. He's a psychologist and is more paranoid than I am about revealing confidential information."

"Well, I'm not really a patient. And luckily, I won't ever be *your* patient."

"I really do good work," the doctor insisted. "You might want to have me take something out or move something around just for kicks."

"I'll take your word for it," Blair said, smiling at the doctor's easy familiarity.

6

"I take it that there's some reason behind your determination not to let me see your internal organs?"

"Well, many reasons, actually. But besides being pain averse, there's one big reason. I don't know how much of our situation you're aware of—"

"I don't normally admit to this, but I don't know a thing," the doctor said, adding a wink. "I didn't even glance at your chart."

"Oh. Well, my husband's sperm count is a little low, and the concentration is on the low side, as well. I just finished all of my tests, and it looks like I check out fine." She gave her a wry smile and added, "I had that perfectly delightful endometrial biopsy and the equally pleasant hystero-blah-blah-blah."

"Hysterosalpingogram."

"Gesundheit! Anyway, all systems are go for me, so we're going to keep trying."

"Excellent," Doctor Mackenzie said, her smile nearly blinding. "I hope it works out for you."

"So do I," Blair said, sighing a little. "I'm dreading going any further than this." She twitched her head towards the shining white buildings of the Getty Museum and asked, "What brings you here tonight?"

"The chamber music recital. How about you?"

"The same. I'm up here every Thursday evening during the summer. I love the variety of the programs."

"Are you a big fan of the arts? I ask because you seem very familiar to me. I thought so when we met at the office."

"I thought the same thing. I assumed I'd shown you a house. I'm a real estate broker."

"No, I don't think that's it," the doctor said. "I haven't been in the market for a house in a very long time. Do you go to many plays?"

"Constantly," Blair said, rolling her eyes. "My husband says I'm a thespian wannabe."

"Were you by any chance at a Bertolt Brecht play at the New Wave not long ago?"

Blair's eyes widened. "Yes! *The Mother*! That's why I recognized you! I think the play was just a day or two before we met at your office." She started to laugh and said, "How many people were there? Ten?"

"Yeah, about ten before the curtain went up, but only six managed to hang in there until the bitter end. Nick was ready to leave, and he likes *everything*!"

"I envy you," Blair said. "I have to go to most plays alone. My husband would rather walk on hot coals."

Seeing her companion lurking about, Doctor Mackenzie twitched her head, signaling him to come over. "Nick, this is Blair Spencer. She's happily not a patient, so you can meet her," she said, laughing a little. "Blair, this is Nick Scott, normally a big Brecht fan, but even he has his limits."

"That's why you looked familiar," Nick said. "You were at that water torture at the New Wave. By the end of the play, I was studying the other patrons, trying to figure out why they were still there. I assumed they were homeless!"

"It was like watching a car wreck," Blair said. "You knew you shouldn't look, but you couldn't turn away!"

"Apt…very apt," Nick agreed. He checked his watch and said, "The concert will be starting soon. We should go find seats."

"Blair's here for the concert, too," the doctor said. Looking at Blair, she asked, "Would you like to sit with us?"

"Sure, if you don't mind. I usually call clients during the intermission. It might be nice to chat with people I can see." She looked at Nick and said, "I just mentioned to Doctor Mackenzie that I sell real estate. My cell phone is my lifeline."

"Kylie," the doctor said, giving her that heartwarming smile. "You can only join us if you call me Kylie."

"I think I can manage. Kylie it is."

⤶

"So, Blair, does your husband really not mind your hanging out with the artistic set?" Nick asked during the intermission.

"No, he doesn't mind. He knew all of my quirks before he married me. Besides, he goes to bed by 9:00 every night. If I followed his schedule, the only cultural event we'd go to would be the Easter Sunrise Service at the Hollywood Bowl."

Nick's brow furrowed, and he said, "By nine? What is he, a dairy farmer?"

"No," she said, chuckling. "He's an industry analyst for Fortune Funds. He's the guy who decides which banking and financial services stocks the fund should buy."

"And he lives in California?" Kylie asked. "Has he noticed that there aren't any major banks headquartered in the entire state?"

"He has," Blair said. "He travels quite a bit, but his firm is based in L.A., so this is where they prefer he work."

"Could be worse," Nick reminded her. "Your accent suggests you're a transplant, right?"

"I am," she said. "From Chicago."

His pager went off as she spoke, and he reached for his waistband to grasp it. "I'll go return my call. I have a feeling the litany of Chicago wonders is about to begin."

Looking to Kylie, Blair cocked her head.

"Northern suburbs," the doctor said. "You?"

"Near North. Close to Lincoln Park."

"You grew up in the city?" Kylie asked, rather wide-eyed. "I've never met anyone who said they were from Chicago who actually was!"

"I've never spent a night in a Chicago suburb. But I know most of them. Which one spawned you?"

"Lake Forest," she said and rolled her eyes when Blair made a face. "We lived in a perfectly modest home. We were practically on food stamps."

"Uh-huh." Blair nodded agreeably. "The wealthiest suburb in all of Lake County. What did your father do, only run a *Fortune 1000* company?"

"He's a doctor. A pediatrician. But I don't think he made his first million until he was fifty."

"Oh, my God! Did the town run a food drive for you? Were you on the free lunch program?"

"No, but I really was pitied in high school. I was the only kid who didn't have her own car in my social circle."

"Ooh...did you have to bear the shame of having the butler drop you off?"

Kylie giggled, the sound at odds with her sophisticated appearance. "My dad obviously made a good salary, but I was the baby of seven, and we didn't have the money to live very luxuriously. Education was where our money went."

"Wow, seven kids! Your parents obviously didn't have a problem with fertility."

"No, I guess not. Although, who knows? Maybe they wanted to have ten kids," she said, chuckling. "How about you? Any siblings?"

Blair shook her head. "No, I'm an only child. Actually, my parents were infertile. I'm adopted."

"Oh." Kylie waited for a minute to see if Blair would provide further information.

"My birth mother didn't have any trouble popping 'em out, though. She had four."

"So, you've met?"

"Uh-huh. I was her second child, and she had me when she was barely seventeen." She made a face and said, "She was obviously very much in favor of sex and very much opposed to birth control. My biological grandmother agreed to raise the first child, my older brother, but she put her foot down when I arrived, and they put me up for adoption. Lucky for me," she said with a smile. "My birth mother had two more kids by the time she was twenty. Her mother must have been more flexible, or she liked the next two better than me, 'cause she let her keep them. But not long after the fourth child was born, my grandmother died, leaving my birth mother alone to raise three kids."

"A twenty-year-old with three kids? That must have been an adventure."

"I guess so. She didn't do very well, and all of the kids were taken away by the state."

"Wow," Kylie said, wide-eyed. "Have you met them?"

"No. Eventually, they were adopted by three different families, and my birth mother is only still in contact with my older brother, Morrison."

"Morrison? That's a unique name."

"Unique is the word for it. She named him after Jim Morrison. Mom was more than fond of sex, drugs, and rock and roll. It's amazing I don't have three legs or fins."

Kylie looked at her and felt a wave of compassion for this self-confident woman, who was obviously still deeply wounded from her birth mother's rejection. "What about your other two sibs? Have you met?"

"No. I don't really care to," she said, shrugging her shoulders. "My bio-mom doesn't know where they are, and I'm not interested enough to spend the money to find them. I grew up as an only child, and I'm happy to keep it that way. Actually, I didn't want to meet my birth mother, but my mom really encouraged me to do it. I guess I'm glad that I met her, just so I could get some medical information and things like that. But I think of her as an egg donor. She's not my mom."

Kylie was nodding enthusiastically. "Your mom is the woman who loved you and changed your diapers. That has nothing to do with genetics."

"That's what I've been telling a certain someone," Blair said. Nick came back just as Kylie was going to ask her to elaborate, so the surgeon chose not to pursue her question.

＊

After the concert, Kylie asked, "You mentioned the Hollywood Bowl earlier. How would you like to go to the closing concert next week? Nick can't make it, and I'm really a sucker for the fireworks. It's not as much fun to 'ooh' and 'ah' all alone."

"Don't tell me; let me guess," Blair drawled. "Tchaikovsky, maybe a little Irving Berlin, John Philip Sousa?"

"Ditch the Berlin, and you hit it," Kylie agreed. "Too lowbrow for you?"

"No, I'd like to go. I've always said that a symphony is missing something if there aren't a few Roman candles thrown in."

＊

On the following Wednesday afternoon, Blair was driving down San Vicente Boulevard, going to visit a new client. The broad, six-lane road was one of the few in Santa Monica that was bisected by a wide greensward, making it the most popular jogging venue in the area—despite the steady stream of cars that zipped past, spewing pollutants. Since the 45-mph speed limit was blatantly ignored, it seemed as though everyone was in a terrific hurry to get somewhere, either by foot or car. Her cell phone rang as she pulled up to one of the infrequent stoplights. "Blair Spencer," she announced through the phone mike clipped to her blouse.

"Hi, Blair, it's Kylie Mackenzie. Still on for tonight?"

Blair replied by singing the well-known and concussive strains of Tchaikovsky's *1812 Overture*, adding a thumping *boom-boom* to represent the cannons. "You bet. Want me to stop and buy some food?"

"Uhm, yeah, that'd be great." The doctor cleared her throat, sounding a little hesitant. "I have something to tell you. *I* don't think this is a big deal, but I wanted to bring it up just so everything's out in the open."

Blair heard the slight discomfort that colored the woman's voice. "What is it?"

"Since I didn't look at your chart or examine you, I don't consider you to ever have been my patient, but if you feel that you were, then we—"

"Oh, don't worry about that," Blair said. "You didn't get your scalpel anywhere near me. I've had more intimate connections with the guy who fixes my car."

The doctor's tone lightened immediately, taking on what Blair was beginning to understand as her typical jocularity. "Oh, so you trust a guy with a wrench to look under your hood, but you won't even let me have a peek inside."

"Kylie, you're never going to see what lies beneath my skin. Get over it."

"I know when I'm fighting a losing battle. There's one more thing though…"

"Yes?" Blair drawled.

"This isn't a big deal, either, but I thought you should know that I'm a lesbian."

There was a period of stark silence. Then Blair, her concern evident, asked quietly, "Does Nick know?"

"Huh?" Kylie let the question sink in and then started to laugh heartily. "Yeah, he knows. Though he wouldn't be interested in me even if I were straight. Actually, you're more his type. He's a sucker for blondes."

"No dice. I like 'em tall, dark, and handsome. Rich doesn't hurt, either."

"If my memory serves, I'd say that you've done pretty well for yourself. Your husband is taller than I am and could pass for a young Omar Sharif."

Blair laughed and then stepped on the gas when the impatient man behind her honked for her to clear the passing lane. "You know, with a moustache…"

"Yeah! That's all that was missing."

"Well, David is half-Armenian, so he's a little on the swarthy side. He's just started to gray at the temples, and I think it's incredibly sexy." She paused and added, "But you shouldn't have noticed that—being a lesbian and all." She could hear the doctor squawk in complaint and said, "Gotcha!"

"Okay, okay, you got me. You know, I never do this. I hate to make my sexuality a big deal. But I've been in situations where a woman has been uncomfortable with me once she finds out I'm a lesbian, so I try to go for full disclosure."

"Well, let me reciprocate," Blair said. "The only kind of person with whom I don't like to associate is one who's close-minded or too full of herself. Though I'm *pretty* sure you're not close-minded…"

"Hey! I'm not…well…okay, I guess I am a little full of myself," she said. "But just a little—really. It's an occupational hazard. You've gotta be pretty cocky to be a good surgeon."

"Then you must be a great one," Blair said, laughing. "I'll pick you up at 7:00, Doc. Speak now if there's anything you won't eat."

"I'm more partial to vegetables than meat, but I'm pretty easy to please."

"I doubt that, but we'll just have to see," Blair said, switching off with a silly grin on her face. *Gotta love a woman you can be a smart-ass with.*

⌒

Kylie's seats at the Hollywood Bowl were in the highly coveted garden boxes, located right next to the orchestra. The pair made their way down the narrow aisle, and Kylie hefted the picnic basket, which Blair had brought, over the railing. They had to maneuver a bit to enter the stunningly small box, but they managed. Sitting on the tiny, folding café chair, Blair commented, "It's hard to believe they get away with providing such uncomfortable seats."

"It's a joke," Kylie agreed. "Especially when you have long legs, like I do."

"The first time I saw you, I was jealous of your height and your curly hair."

Kylie smiled, looking a little surprised. "That's funny. I've always wanted straight hair. Thick, straight blonde hair is my favorite."

Blair reached behind her neck and slowly moved her fingers through the length of her hair, letting the heavy locks spill down. "Jealous?" she asked in a dramatically sexy voice.

"A little, yeah! But I've resigned myself to my curls. You're right to be jealous about being tall, though. It rocks."

"Maybe, but I'm more comfortable." Blair playfully stuck her tongue out. "And I can fly coach and not have to go to a chiropractor."

"I thought you were the one who was jealous of my height?"

"I am, but once it becomes competitive, I have to win."

"Boy, you would have fit in perfectly with my family," Kylie said. "Everything is a competition."

They managed to eat the small assortment of crudités and cold appetizers that Blair had provided, but they had to put each course on the tiny table separately. As soon as they'd finished eating, they moved all the way to the top of the huge amphitheater so they could continue to talk during the concert. "You know, I really prefer the cheap seats," the doctor commented once they were settled. "Do you know these seats only cost a dollar for most performances? Best deal in town."

Blair looked around, noting that each seating section grew less crowded as the price dropped. "Typical L.A. People only want to go to things that cost a lot. If they raised the price for these and said there was a waiting list, there'd be a line to get the tickets."

"Most likely."

They were quiet for a while, listening to the orchestra as it launched into "Stars and Stripes Forever." Kylie leaned against the wooden bench and tilted her head back to stare into the star-filled night. "I can't believe how beautiful it is here. If it weren't for the parking nightmare, I'd come every night."

Blair nodded, a happy smile on her face. She looked out at the steep, dark hills that surrounded the Bowl, taking in the faint smell of dry chaparral, dust, and smog that was the distinctive perfume of Los Angeles. A few homes were visible in the distance, their lights golden and glowing. There was just enough light to detect a single red-tailed hawk circling overhead, probably wondering what had caused such a large crowd to flock together. "You know, you could sit up here all the time and stretch out. Why pay the big bucks like all of the other conspicuous consumers?"

Kylie jutted her chin out while narrowing her eyes. "Well, I'm a fairly well-known Westside surgeon, doncha know? I can't afford to look like the common rabble." The air she adopted was definitely upper crust, the transformation so opposed to her usual mien that Blair couldn't help but smile.

Blair curled her finger, indicating that Kylie should come close. The doctor's soft, dark curls brushed Blair's lips, and she whispered, "How do you think it looks to not only be with the common rabble, but to sneak into their seats?"

The doctor leaned back and gave her companion a slightly baffled look. "Huh. I never thought of that." After a moment, she snapped her fingers and said, "I could always claim that Nick made me do it. We share these tickets, you know."

"What's the deal with you and Nick? Not that you're an unpleasant companion, but wouldn't he rather bring a date to these events? He couldn't possibly find it hard to hook up."

Kylie started to nod, but then her expression turned to one of outrage. "Hey! Are you implying that *I* can't get a date?"

Blair shrugged, smiling at the doctor. "You tell me."

"I could get a date if I had to. I might have to call an escort service, but I could get one." Blair patted her friend's leg, sympathizing with her obvious exaggeration. "But Nick's my best friend, and we both like to make sure we have a good time when we go to a play or a concert."

"You don't have to sell me on that idea. I coerced David into going to a few museums when we first started to date. I quickly decided it was more fun to go alone than to have him looking at his watch."

"Hmm…museums, plays, concerts. You're quite the aesthete, Ms. Spencer. How did you develop your appreciation of the arts?"

"My parents. Both of them love to spend the day at the Art Institute, and they started taking me when I was barely able to walk. As for music, my dad plays the cello, so he helped me develop my musical tastes. My theater jones comes from my mom. She's a dramaturge."

Kylie blinked, shook her head, and then said, "I've met a lot of people in my life, but I've never, ever met the child of a dramaturge."

Blair smiled back at her. "I've never met anyone in L.A. who knew what a dramaturge was." Narrowing her eyes, she queried, "You do know, don't you? This isn't just one of those 'I'm a surgeon, and I can't admit to not knowing something' things, is it?"

Acting as though she was reading from a dictionary, Kylie cleared her throat and said, "A dramaturge can be responsible for any number of things in a theatrical setting. She might choose the productions, get the script in shape, translate a script from another language, or write notes on the production for the playbill. The list can be endless, depending on the needs of the theater company and her talents." Wrinkling her nose, she asked, "How'd I do?"

"Not bad. Not bad at all. In fact, you get an A. So, how did you develop *your* taste for culture? You're obviously not a poser."

"I came to it fairly late. I went to the U of C," she said, referring to the University of Chicago by the shorthand that a fellow Chicagoan would undoubtedly recognize, "and I had a very highbrow friend whom I was dying to impress."

Blair's eyebrow lifted. "Impress?"

"Have sex with," Kylie corrected amiably. "Anyway, I threw myself into every possible artistic pursuit. We went to plays and the opera and the symphony. I read up on all of them just to impress her. Alas, she was always more interested in culture than she was in me. She had an affair with a grad student in the classics department and broke my little heart."

"Poor baby."

"Nah. It was just as well. If she'd succumbed to my charms early on, I never would have taken the time to learn about drama and music. Her hotshot grad student didn't last half a term, but I've had a lifetime of pleasure from the things I learned."

"Ah…so you knew you were gay in college. Is that when you figured it out?"

"A little earlier than that," Kylie said. "I was a senior in high school, just about to graduate, when it finally clicked for me. I was on a date with the guy that the entire female population of my school was hot for, but while we were making out, I kept angling him so I could get a good look at the girl being pawed in the backseat. I used that poor guy as a shield so I could fantasize about committing all sorts of lewd acts with her." She shrugged and said, "That's when my powers of denial were finally overcome."

"When did you finally…what's the term?" Blair asked.

"For what?"

"Don't be coy, Doc."

Blinking her eyes ingenuously, Kylie supplied, "Have sex?"

"No…I mean, yes," Blair said, shaking her head. "I'm not sure how lesbians refer to having sex for the first time. Do you call it 'losing your virginity'?"

"If you do it right, you can," Kylie said, grinning wickedly. At Blair's quizzical look, she said, "I'm just teasing. I've never heard it called 'losing your virginity.'" She looked puzzled and said, "Actually, I don't think we have a term for it. But whatever you call it, shortly after I decided I was gay, I was no longer a chaste woman."

"Please go on," Blair said, seeing that Kylie didn't mind opening up.

"I was a counselor at a science camp that summer, and I fell in love."

"No one who goes to science camp has sex, Doctor Mackenzie. You must be mistaken."

"No, no, I'm pretty sure it was sex. I took a course on sex in medical school, and I'm certain we met all of the requirements."

"Well, well, that's quite an accomplishment for a science nerd. How long did the romance last?"

"Until we both went to college in the fall. She didn't want to be gay, so she decided she was going to date guys when she got to MIT. I lost track of her after that."

"So, lesbian relationships don't have a better success rate than straight ones, huh?"

"Not if you use me as the example. My longest is three years."

Blair's expression showed her surprise at this revelation. "Huh. I never would have guessed that. Something about you says that you'd be a good partner."

Kylie's even teeth gleamed brightly in the moonlight when she smiled. "Why, thank you. I like to think I am. I just haven't found anyone who fits, ya know?"

"I do." Blair nodded. "If I hadn't met David when I was twenty-five, I'm sure I'd be single now."

"Don't remind me," Kylie moaned. "The older I get, the harder it is for me. I haven't had a date that means anything since I broke up with my ex, Stacey, two years ago."

"If you don't mind my asking, why did you break up?"

"I don't mind," Kylie said. "I suppose it was mostly because we didn't share the same goals. She was a fitness nut. She maintained a strict vegan diet—never touched alcohol, caffeine, or sugar, either. We went to Italy on a trip I'd been looking forward to for years. I wanted to hit every art gallery, visit every notable church, eat as much as I could handle, and make love until I was cross-eyed." She smirked wryly and said, "She wanted to make love, which was great, but she wanted it to be after hiking up the nearest peak. She honestly wanted to rent bikes and ride from one end of Italy to the other." Her eyes grew wide as she said, "That's why they have trains!

"We were sitting in a café one afternoon after I'd persuaded her to go to St. Peter's with me. I remember how antsy she was after doing nothing more energetic than looking at art and architecture all day. She was sipping her plain, steamed skim milk, still a little pissed that no one carried soymilk, while I was drinking this marvelous concoction of sparkling wine, peach nectar, and fresh peaches. And then it finally hit me. I didn't want to share the rest of my life with an ascetic! I wanted to be with a woman who wanted to experience life, not regulate it. I mean, she had a fantastic body, and that was because she worked at it so hard, but how does that fill your soul?" Shaking her head, she said, "We broke up right after we got home."

"I'm so sorry to hear that," Blair said, her empathy showing in her eyes. "I hope you find someone, Kylie."

"I'm happy with my life. I love my work, I have great friends and a huge family with more nieces and nephews than I can count, and I have enough money to go to every cultural event that interests me. All that I don't get is sex." Shrugging, she added, "It's a tradeoff that I've been willing to make. I'd rather be celibate than give up the things that touch me emotionally."

"There has to be a smart, cute, cultured lesbian out there just waiting for you."

"Well, the minute you find her, send her my way. There's a significant finder's fee involved."

"I can really hustle for the right commission," Blair said. "You'll be married by the end of the year."

"It's September. I don't like to rush into anything."

"Okay, then next year," Blair said, amending her offer. "You'll be happily married within fifteen months."

Extending their hands, Kylie and Blair shook on the deal. "You can be my matron of honor. I hope you'll be pregnant and look just awful in the dress I make you wear."

⌐

"Bad news." Blair dropped her bag and collapsed into a chair.

"What's wrong?" David asked. He looked up from the magazine he was reading and gave his wife a quizzical look.

"I got my period."

With a resigned sigh, he looked back to his magazine.

"No comment?" she asked, her hormones making her ready for a fight.

He put his magazine down and stared at their mantel, saying, "I don't want to argue."

An image of David as a small child, crossing his arms and saying no to his mother, appeared in Blair's head. Normally, she didn't like to argue, either, but she couldn't stop herself from responding. "About what?" she asked, her tone a little harsher than she'd intended.

He sighed again and shook his head, still not looking at her. "I'm not sure you're having orgasms."

"Pardon me?"

The tone of her voice showed that she was ready to take up arms, but he continued. "You don't act like you used to in bed. I've been thinking that you might be faking orgasms just to make me think you're trying to get pregnant."

She looked at him for a moment and felt all of the fight drain from her body. Wearily, she said, "This isn't right, David. It's just not right." Leaning her head back, she muttered, "We don't even think of it as making love anymore. We're 'trying.'" She got up, walked over to his chair, and sat on the arm. "I don't want to 'try' anymore. I want to express my love for you, and that's what I want you to do, too. If we have a baby from that union, fine. But if we don't…then we don't."

He took her hands in his, and she looked into his brown eyes. "I thought we'd agreed," he said quietly. "Don't you want children?"

"Yes," she said. "I *do* want children. I just don't care how we get them or who they look like or how old they are. I want a child to love and nurture, David—any child."

"I know that's true for you, but I don't feel that way. It really means something to me to have a baby that I'm related to. I know it's selfish." His eyes closed as he admitted the truth. "But I've got to be honest. Having a child of our own…is worth a lot."

She started to remind him that any child would be theirs, so long as they lavished their love on him or her, but she'd made the point many times before to no avail. She clambered onto his lap and rested her head upon his chest, sighing and tucking her arms around him. "I know it is," she said. "We'll keep trying."

⌐

To reciprocate for Kylie's taking her to the Bowl, Blair offered tickets to a performance of the Kodo drummers at UCLA. Kylie accepted enthusiastically, and they agreed to meet at Royce Hall on the following Sunday.

When Blair approached the building, she found Kylie sitting on a low wall, her head thrown back as she gazed up at the bright-blue afternoon sky. "Contemplating your place in the universe?" Blair asked quietly.

The usual smile quickly took its place on the doctor's face. "A little. I was trying to remember back eighteen years to when I first set foot on this campus. It seems like a very, very long time ago."

"You went to school here?" Blair asked. "I assumed you stayed in Chicago for med school."

"Nope. UCLA has one of the top training programs, and quite frankly, I wanted to strike out on my own. I have two older brothers who are doctors, too, and I wanted to go someplace where no one had ever heard of the many Doctors Mackenzie."

"Makes sense. Is that why you stayed in L.A.?"

"Nope," she said, grinning. "Once I got here, I realized that I never wanted to hear the words 'lake effect snow' again."

Blair raised her hand, and Kylie slapped it hard. "Amen, sister!"

Their ears were still ringing when they emerged from the auditorium. "That was intense!" Blair decided. "I really liked it, though."

"Oh, I did, too!" Kylie enthused. "Maybe I should get one of those to relieve stress."

Gazing at her curiously, Blair said, "Maybe it's just an act, but you don't seem like the type who stresses much. Do you?"

"Honestly? No. I've always been pretty easygoing, and I wanted to make sure I stayed that way. That's why I chose the field I did."

"Being a surgeon is a low-stress job? Since when?"

"Hey, how about some ice cream? The student union's right over there."

"I'm game," Blair said.

They walked across the quad, and Kylie said, "I'm an odd mix. I'm very goal-driven, and I love to challenge myself and win. But I'm also very placid emotionally. So, I decided to do something where I had to be at my very best, but for a limited amount of time each day. The kind of surgery I do is just perfect for my personality. The women and men I work with aren't ill. They have a functional problem that I believe I can correct. When I'm right, and the surgery works, they have the ability to have a baby." Looking contemplative, she said, "It's not strictly a matter of life and death; though, in another sense, it is. I can help a woman create life when she would have had no chance without intervention."

Blair mirrored her smile. "That must feel wonderful."

"It does. Now, granted, many people never conceive. I fail much more often than I succeed, but I do my best to give my patients every possible chance."

"That means everything to some people, doesn't it?" Blair asked, her eyes clouding over with what looked like sadness.

"It does." They reached the student union and wound through the halls to find the ice cream, pausing in deep concentration before determining their preferred flavors. Taking their cones, they went back outside to enjoy them. After taking a few long, slow swipes with her tongue, Kylie looked at her new friend and asked, "Having a child doesn't mean everything to you, does it?"

Blair's head shook, the sun making her hair appear more red than blonde as it moved gently across her shoulders. "No, it doesn't. It does to David, though."

In a calm, nonjudgmental tone, Kylie asked, "Do you want to have children at all?"

"Yes, very much so, but I'd be just as happy to adopt. David, for reasons I don't comprehend and he can't explain, doesn't feel that way, though. It means a lot to him to have the child be genetically related to both of us."

"That's not at all uncommon," Kylie said. "Of course, my sample self-selects for people who feel that's important."

"We took statistics at Northwestern, too."

"Northwestern?" Kylie asked, eyes wide. "Maybe you shouldn't have a baby. That's the shallow end of the gene pool up in Evanston, you know."

"If you didn't have on such a pretty dress, I'd drop this cone in your lap," Blair said, wagging a finger. "And don't think I wouldn't."

"I don't doubt that in the least," Kylie said. Turning serious, she said, "How about talking to Nick?"

"About...?"

"I'm sure I mentioned he's a psychologist." Blair nodded, and Kylie continued, "He could help you with a referral so that you could get some of these things out in the open."

"I don't think so. David's not a therapy fan."

"It can be very helpful. In fact, that's how I met Nick. I worked with a couple who'd been seeing him, and after I noticed how helpful he was, I started referring more and more patients to him. We finally met and hit it off right away." She paused a moment to catch up with her cone and added, "By the time people get to me, they've usually exhausted their options. It's a rare couple that doesn't have problems with their relationship somewhere along the way. Trying to overcome infertility can be very, very hard on a marriage, and if you're not both equally committed, it makes it that much worse."

"I agree," Blair said, nodding energetically. "This is the first major thing that we can't seem to agree on. If we don't get pregnant, I'm sure he's going to want to have in vitro fertilization, and I'm not going to do that."

"You don't sound like you're willing to budge on that issue."

"I'm not," she said, her gaze assured. "There are too many things that can go wrong, there are too many side effects for me, and the chance of success isn't high enough to risk it. Besides, it seems *so* self-involved to spend over $50,000 just to have a genetic copy of yourselves. I can see that it makes sense for some couples, but not for us. We're young enough to adopt, and we should be able to get a child fairly soon, especially if we're not adamant about having an infant."

"I don't want to offer unwanted advice," Kylie said, "but you'll be doing your marriage a favor if you can agree on this before you get much deeper. I've seen women change their minds thirty seconds before the anesthesiologist puts them under. And believe me, that's not a fun talk to have with an anxious husband in the waiting room. Once it gets to a certain point, it's hard to pull back."

"I appreciate your advice, Kylie. Really, I do." She nudged her friend with her shoulder and said, "Once again, I'm glad you never got your scalpel-wielding hands on me. If you had, we couldn't be friends."

"That's only if I operate on you professionally," Kylie said. "If we're just goofing around in my rec room, nobody need be the wiser."

Giving her a warm smile, Blair said, "You have a very unique sense of humor."

"Pray that you never meet my entire family. I'm the most normal one in the whole bunch."

"It'd be interesting to hear your siblings' take on that point."

"Well, now that you mention it, they might see it the other way around," she allowed, grinning.

⌐

By Christmas, Blair and David were still practicing well-timed intercourse, and both were beginning to give up hope. "It's been a year, honey," he reminded her when she got her period just before the New Year. "You're thirty-five; I'm forty. I don't think we can wait any longer."

She was lying in bed, a heating pad under her back. She wasn't sure if it was psychological or physical, but her formerly mild cramps were now painful enough to knock her out for an entire day—reminding her on a monthly basis that she was, once again, not pregnant. "One more month," she begged. "This time, let's give it our all. We'll wait four days before we have sex. I'll lie on my back with my hips elevated for an hour. I'll have two orgasms after you come, just to give the boys a boost."

"I know you must talk about this with your doctor buddy," he said. "What does she think our chances are?"

"Well, she hasn't offered an opinion on us, but she did say that if it hadn't happened after a year, the odds weren't good for its happening without help."

"I think it's time to see the gynecologist again, Blair. I think we should try a few rounds of artificial insemination."

She nodded, feeling sick to her stomach. "I'll call and make an appointment. It'll take a while to get in, so we can try the usual way in January." Rolling over onto her belly to try to ease the cramps, she let her worry have its voice. *This is as far as you're willing to go. And that's why you're so afraid to take this step. If this doesn't work, it's either adoption...or no children.*

⌐

Blair got her period right on time in January, and after a few days of stalling, she called the doctor to make an appointment for an artificial insemination. "Let's see..." the receptionist said. "The doctor can see you at 8:00 a.m. on Friday. Your husband will have to be here early enough to provide a sample, so you can come anytime after 7:30, when we open."

"Can't he do that at home?"

"No, it has to be fresh."

"Oh, he's not going to like this," Blair said, imagining the argument that would ensue.

"No one does," the woman agreed. "Tell him that men come in here every day to do this. He's not gonna stand out in the crowd. We have magazines to look at, and you can be with him if that helps."

"Thanks," Blair said. She hung up, feeling the all-too-familiar knot in her stomach that accompanied every step down this slippery slope.

⌐

That night, Blair made one of David's favorite dinners and plied him with Cabernet before she mentioned the matter. "Honey, I got us an appointment with the gynecologist for Friday morning. We're gonna see the doctor at 8:00, so we have to be there early enough for you to..." Her eyebrows twitched a little, and she looked pointedly at his lap.

His eyes closed for just a second, and she could see the tense set of his mouth. She prepared herself for a laundry list of complaints, but he just said, "Right." David got up and poured another glass of wine, drank it without pause, and then walked by her on the way to the bedroom. "I'm turning in. See you tomorrow." He gave her shoulder a quick squeeze, obviously a substitute for his usual kiss.

⌒

On Friday morning, Blair accompanied David into a small room at the gynecologist's office. "Are you sure you want me here?" she asked. "I think I'd need privacy."

"You're not me," he said, giving her a strained smile. Unzipping his slacks, he removed them, folded them neatly, and then took off his boxers.

"You get undressed? I'd think you'd just—"

"Hey, a guy's got a routine. This isn't the day to screw with it."

"But your routine doesn't usually include me," she reminded him, sparing a teasing smile. "I thought all bets were off."

"Are you gonna help me or not?"

"Of course. Name it."

He looked around the room, seeing nothing but a table with some well-worn "men's" magazines and a molded plastic chair. "Maybe we should have gone to a sperm bank. They have videos." He was in a sour mood, and Blair could see how tense he was. He'd smoked four cigarettes in the car on the way over—something he never did with her in the car—and the doctor's office was only fifteen minutes away. "Well, I guess we should start kissing. That never hurts."

It was difficult for either of them to find the atmosphere conducive to arousal, but Blair gave it her all. She wasn't fond of David's smoking, but the smell didn't normally bother her much when they were being intimate. Today, when the whole setup was not only clinical, but also contrived, the odor was all she could think about. Nonetheless, she kissed her husband lasciviously, trying to block out everything but his body and the softness of his lips.

David was the best kisser she'd ever experienced, and she let his technique help her crank up the heat. Despite her best efforts, David's penis knew this was a command performance, and it was experiencing stage fright. After a long time, she pulled away, noting that very little was happening.

"Why don't you let me give you a hand, honey?" she asked, wrapping her fingers around him.

He shrugged his agreement and then looked around the room again. "I need lotion or lube."

She did a double take. "You do?"

"I'm a lube guy. Can't do it dry."

"We've been having sex for ten years, and I had no idea."

With a thin smile, he said, "I'm a man of mystery."

It was clear that David didn't want to chat, so Blair looked around for supplies, quickly seeing there were none to be had. "I'll go ask for some K-Y Jelly. They always have that in a gynecologist's office."

"No!" He grabbed her by the arm. "They'll know why you need it!"

"Uh-huh." She nodded slowly, not understanding his point.

"Everybody will know I'm having trouble," he said in a stage whisper. "This is embarrassing enough!"

The knot in her stomach returned with a vengeance. Giving David a look that she hoped was filled with understanding, she went to her oversized bag and rooted through it for a moment. With a flourish, she pulled out a small bottle of hand lotion. "How's this?"

He took it and made a face. "Lavender? I'm gonna smell like lavender?"

This'll never work. Let's get it over with right now. Giving him as sexy a look as she could manage, she sat on the chair, grasped him again, and pulled him to herself. Bending over a little, she heard him groan when she took him into her mouth. Her efforts were almost immediately rewarded, but she couldn't stay focused. Her mind began to wander while she worked. *Yes, Son, your conception was a beautiful thing. I took your daddy into a room the size of a phone booth and blew him, he shot into a little cup, and the doctor had all of the boys washed to get rid of the poor performers. Then she put a few million of your brothers and sisters into a long syringe and injected them all the way up into Mommy's uterus. That's past the vagina, Son, through the cervix…up, up, up there. Then Mommy got to lie on a table with her hips elevated for an hour, just so your sweet little sperm self could meet one of Mommy's eggs. It was so moving, Son. True poetry. Not a dry eye in the place.*

⌒

An hour later, the doctor came in and gave them the okay to leave. David had been reading some articles he'd brought, and Blair had been lying on her back, making calls to clients. She felt as emotionally invested in the whole procedure as she did when she had her teeth cleaned. David was hours late for work, so he didn't bother going into the house when he dropped her off. Blair kissed him on the cheek and said, "We'll forget all about this when we have our baby, honey. I guarantee it."

His mouth twitched, turning into a reasonably warm smile. "Thanks," he said. "I know this isn't how you want it."

"I want to have a baby with you, David. That's what I want. The details aren't important."

"You're being a damn good sport. You know, I've always had a little nurse fantasy. If we have to do this again, will you wear a uniform?"

"With a garter belt and a push-up bra if that trips your trigger."

His smile grew brighter, and he reached out of the window and gave her a one-armed hug. "Thanks. See you tonight."

As soon as Blair entered the house, she put in a call to the North Side Repertory Theater in Chicago. "May I speak with Eleanor?" she asked when the phone was answered. She waited a few moments, then felt her body flush with relief when she heard her mother's voice.

"Hello?"

"It's me, Mom."

"Blair, I thought you might call today. Did you see the doctor yet?"

"Yeah, we just finished. This is so strange," she sighed. "Statistically, I have the best chance of getting pregnant that I've ever had. Within forty-eight hours, I might be carrying a child, but this whole experience feels so sterile and mechanical. This isn't what I dreamed of."

"Oh, sweetheart, try not to feel that way. I guarantee that once you get pregnant, all of these details will fade right out of your mind. Don't let the circumstances ruin this for you."

"That's what I just told David," she said. "But I'm not sure I believe it. I just wish we could go back to making love."

"Honey, there's no reason you can't. You can go back to normal. You can only try insemination once a month, right? The worst that can happen is you get pregnant by mistake."

Pausing a moment, Blair decided to be completely frank with her mother. "We don't normally talk about things like this, Mom, but would it upset you to hear some pretty personal details?"

"Well…no, honey, not if you need to talk about something."

"I do. I wish I didn't, but I do. The thing is…David doesn't have much interest in making love anymore. If we're not doing it on a scheduled day, he doesn't seem to care."

"Is this a big change?"

"Yeah. Very big. We're…well, we were as into each other as we were when we met, Mom. This really has me worried."

"Try not to worry so much. This is hard for you both. Don't let the stress make you see things that aren't there. David's a fine husband, and I know he'll be a fine father, too. Once you get past this rough patch, I guarantee things will get back to normal."

"I hope you're right, Mom, 'cause I want a husband more than I want a baby."

Blair didn't have a meeting scheduled until 11:00, so she sat down to read the paper and listen to Bach's Concerto in A Minor for Harpsichord, Flute, and Violin, hoping that it would calm her and improve her mood. The first movement had barely finished when the phone rang. "Hello?"

"Blair? It's Sadie."

Fuck me! I could kill David for telling his mother about this! She took a breath to hide the rancor that was starting to bubble up inside. "Hi, Sadie. How are things?"

"You're the one who has things to tell. So, tell!"

"Well, it wasn't fun, but it's over. Nothing out of the ordinary. Do you want me to have David call you?"

"No, you know how men are. He never tells me anything."

He tells you more than he should! "There really isn't much to say, Sadie. I'm sure you've been surfing the Web. It was just like the sites say."

"Did David have any trouble? I don't think Bruce could have performed in a doctor's office, God rest his soul."

Jesus! Why couldn't I have a mother-in-law who'd blush at the mere idea of her son kissing a girl? "No, David's very…versatile," she said, not quite knowing which adjective to use. "Everything went just fine."

"Are you lying down? The sites I read say you should lie down to make sure the sperm get to your uterus."

"Yes, I'm lying down," Blair said as she scooted around and dropped onto the couch. "I want to make sure this works."

"This is very, very important, Blair. This is our last chance to continue the Hagopian line, even if we can't continue the name."

Don't snap at her. You'll be paying for it for years. "But your sister Alice has a son. Michael's not even married yet. He can carry on the line, too."

The older woman's voice lowered into a conspiratorial whisper. "Don't tell anyone you know, but Michael's adopted. He's not Armenian."

"David never mentioned that," Blair said, ignoring the hurtful part of the message.

"Oh, he doesn't know. Alice and Lou didn't want anyone to know. Michael doesn't even know. They thought it'd be better for him if he thought he was really theirs."

Blair nearly bit through her lip to avoid lashing out at her mother-in-law's insensitivity. Even greater than her anger was an overwhelming sense of empathy for her husband. *Oh, baby, I'm starting to understand why adopting is gonna be hard for you, if that's the kinda message you got from your parents. I hope to God it doesn't come to that.*

⌒

In early February, just after Blair had learned that the artificial insemination hadn't worked, she received a call from Kylie. "David's out of town this weekend, right?"

"Yeah, he is, but you still can't come over and operate on me."

"You're such a stick-in-the-mud," Kylie said. "One day, you're gonna beg me to fillet you like a salmon, but it's gonna be too late. I'm not gonna leave this offer open forever."

"Did you want something other than to harass me? I'm busy not being pregnant right now." There was a fairly long silence. Then Blair said, "Sorry. I don't mean to sound like a jerk. It just comes naturally."

"Hey, you're disappointed. I would be, too."

"Well, that still doesn't give me the right to snap at you. I don't know you well enough to let you see my evil side."

"No, and I don't think I want to," the doctor said. "So, before Evil Blair comes out again, I'll get to the point. I want to buy a house, and I thought this weekend would be the perfect time to start looking." She paused and asked, "You can still be my friend if we work together, can't you?"

"If that's what we are, I can," she said, her joke sounding more mean than funny. Trying hard to inject a happy timbre to her tone, she said, "We're good friends, Kylie, and I'd love to work with you. What do you have in mind? Another condo?"

"We just got the numbers from our accountants," Kylie said, her excitement obvious. "We had a wonderful year, and I'm gonna buy a big-ass house! And since I am, by your description, a conspicuous consumer, I refuse to look at anything south of Montana."

"Kylie," she said, "I know you're trying to cheer me up, but you don't have to focus on the most expensive neighborhood in Santa Monica."

"I love ya, Blair, but I'm *not* buying a house north of Montana to snag the Mother Teresa award. This is for me, baby! Me! Me! Me! You're just along for the ride."

"And the commission."

"And the commission," Kylie agreed.

On Sunday, they spent over eight hours looking at every property that fit Kylie's geographic demands, but the pair decided that none of the listings were quite right for the doctor's needs. "I'm hungry and bored," Kylie said. "Let's have an early dinner."

"Okay. Go out or eat in?"

"In. I wanna take off my shoes and relax."

"Done."

They stopped at the market, and as soon as they got to Blair's place, Kylie said, "I volunteer to be in charge of everything that involves slicing, dicing, or filleting."

"You don't have a scalpel on you, do you?"

Smiling, Kylie shrugged her shoulders and said, "As a matter of fact, I do. I have a few in the bag in my car. But a chef's knife works better on most vegetables."

"Do you cook for yourself?" Blair asked while she organized the ingredients.

"Yep. I'm actually pretty good at it, too. I like to pamper myself with a great meal."

"I cook, but I wouldn't say I enjoy it. It's more of a necessity than anything."

"Then you just sit on that chair," Kylie ordered. "Put your feet up and relax while I cook for you. Where's your stereo?"

"You don't have to do this," Blair insisted, but Kylie guided her to the chair and held her in place until she sat.

"Doctor's orders. Want a glass of wine?"

"I shouldn't," she grumbled. "I quit drinking over a year ago when we started trying to get pregnant."

"A glass or two won't hurt you. Especially since you can't be inseminated for a couple of weeks."

"All right. Set me up."

"First, I need that music," Kylie said. Blair pointed to the living room, and a few moments later, she heard the doctor comment, "Got enough CDs of the Chicago Symphony Orchestra? This must be their whole catalog!"

"It is," Blair called back. "One of the perks."

"Of?" Kylie asked, popping her head around Blair's shoulder, startling her.

"Of having your father be a member of the CSO. He sends me a CD every time they put one out—which seems to be weekly."

Kylie's eyes nearly bulged from her head. "You didn't tell me your father was in the Chicago Symphony!"

"I'm sure I told you he was a cellist."

"I thought you meant he played the cello like I play the piano! You know, like in his spare time."

Blair smiled proudly. "Nope. He's a pro. He started playing when he was just a tyke."

"Damn! I've never known anyone connected to a major symphony orchestra. That's so cool!"

"I don't think I've ever seen you this excited about anything," Blair said.

"It's just so cool!" Kylie repeated. "You and I were probably both at a bunch of their performances when I was in college. I wish I'd known you then."

"That would have been nice. I never had anyone in my life who understood what music meant to me. I would've loved a friend I could've shared that with."

Leaning over her slightly, Kylie gave her a warm hug, holding on for a few moments. "You have one now."

As Kylie pulled away, she squeezed Blair's shoulder, and the blonde realized that she'd quickly become comfortable with Kylie's affectionate nature. "You know, for a Chicagoan, you're pretty tactile. Have the Californians influenced you?"

"No, I love to touch." A slightly troubled expression crossed her face. "Doesn't bother you, does it?"

"Bother me? I've gotten used to hugging nearly everyone I meet. The guy who cuts my hair hugged me and kissed me the first time we met. I'm getting comfortable with being more affectionate. One more good thing about California," she said. "Lowers your physical barriers." Blair brought the glass to her nose and inhaled deeply, savoring the bouquet. "Damn, I miss a good glass of wine. One of life's small pleasures." She took a sip of the wine, rolling the liquid around in her mouth before swallowing. "Nice, very nice."

"You sound like you're going to seduce that poor glass," Kylie said. "You've got that 'Do you come here often?' voice."

Blair nearly did a spit-take with her wine, and her shoulders shook with laughter. "Oh, that's good. I haven't laughed in two days."

Concentrating on preparing the vegetables they'd bought, Kylie said, "Let's have a purely fun night—nothing depressing or upsetting."

"Deal, Doc." Blair felt some of the tension start to leave her body while she watched the surgeon operate on a red pepper. Kylie's hands were sure and competent, moving with an effortless grace that was mesmerizing to watch. Blair was so enthralled that she barely heard her friend when she spoke. "Huh?"

"Dozing on me?"

"No, no, I was just watching your hands. You cook like a surgeon."

"Mmm…you ought to see me hem a pair of slacks. I could make a living as a tailor if my nerves ever go."

"I know you said something before, but I missed it."

"Oh. I was just wondering if you play an instrument. I'd think your father would have bought you a tiny cello when you were in diapers."

Blair shook her head, took another small sip of her wine, and set the glass down on the marble counter. "No." She stretched, getting the kinks out of her back. "He wasn't that kind of dad. Neither of my parents pushed me to do anything that didn't capture my interest."

"You weren't interested?"

"I love music, Kylie, but I saw how professional musicians live. My dad's been playing for over sixty years, but he still practices every day. He plays in a chamber music group, too, so he's working or practicing all the time. I decided that I wanted to appreciate music, not live for it."

"Interesting." The self-appointed chef was quiet for a few minutes, her knife nearly a blur as she diced an onion. "I can see that. I always wonder what makes people choose their professions."

"That's easy for me," Blair said. "By the time I was in high school, I was pretty sure I wanted to have a career in sales."

"Really? I don't know why, but that seems kinda odd."

Blair gazed at Kylie until the doctor made eye contact with her. "Think about why it seems odd," she said, obviously miffed.

"Oh! Not weird or anything," Kylie said quickly. "I…I just seem to remember that my friends all talked about doing something that required grad school. I can't recall anyone saying she wanted to have a job. They all wanted professional…" She trailed off, her cheeks coloring pink with embarrassment.

Blair's eyes were boring into her, and Kylie tried to bail herself out. "Not that you're not a professional! Really! It's just that…" Kylie looked at Blair, nearly pleading with her eyes.

"Go on," Blair said, twirling her finger in a small circle. "You're being very eloquent." Her expression was impassive, but her eyes were fixed on Kylie like a hawk following a mouse.

"Damn it!" Kylie walked over to her and put a hand on her shoulder. "I'm sorry that came out that way. There's nothing wrong with being a salesperson. I just don't know many, to be honest. I've got a…"

"Prejudice," Blair supplied.

Nodding, Kylie said, "Yeah, I guess I do. But it's only because I'm hounded by pharmaceutical salespeople. They'd be in my office all day if I'd let them."

"The nerve! How dare they try to make a living when you're saving lives?"

"Oh, shit." Kylie sat on the other stool and put her hands on her knees, lips pursed in thought. "I can't take back what I said. So, all I can do is ask you to forgive me for being so…"

"Superior."

Kylie's brow shot up. "I don't feel superior. Really."

Finally smiling, Blair patted her leg. "It's okay. I know you'd never intentionally insult me. But you did hurt my feelings."

"I'm sorry," Kylie said, sincerity dripping from her words. "Truly."

"It's all right. You probably didn't grow up knowing any people with real jobs."

"Sure I did."

"Like who?"

"My teachers, checkers at the grocery store…"

"That's it?"

Coloring slightly, Kylie nodded. "Everyone we knew was a doctor. My friends' fathers were all lawyers or doctors or CEOs or stockbrokers."

"Stockbrokers are salespeople."

Kylie's expression brightened. "Really? I knew a couple of them."

"You're a regular plebeian."

"I can't help that I grew up in a pretty homogenous place, but everyone I've dated has had a normal job."

Blair's head tilted. "Really? No other doctors?"

"No. Never."

"Interesting," Blair said slowly, imitating Kylie's earlier comment and facial expression.

"Not really. I always wanted to be with someone whose day wasn't like mine. I like learning about other things."

"That's pretty open-minded, Doc. I'll stop torturing you now."

Kylie wiped her brow dramatically. "Thank God! Now, will you enlighten me about how and why you wanted to be a salesperson?"

"Sure. But it's not very interesting. A lot of the people in the apartment building where I grew up were in sales. My parents were friends with some of them, and their jobs sounded kinda cool."

Kylie smiled mischievously. "That's not very interesting." She scampered away, just avoiding Blair's hand reaching out to slap her.

"The truth, Doctor Mackenzie, is that what matters is doing something that appeals to you and doing it well. Selling real estate is perfect for me. I'm my own boss, and I can make a lot of money if I'm willing to work hard."

"Seeing you in action today showed me that you're good at what you do. You seem to enjoy it, too."

"I do. Oh, clients can be a pain in the ass, and every once in a while, I want to commit homicide when a seller acts like he owns Versailles, but I really do like it. I'm happy with my choice."

Kylie looked at her for a moment and then smiled. "It's nice, isn't it?"

"What?"

"Being happy in your career."

"I guess I don't think about it a lot, but I am happy. I lucked out and chose well."

"You know, people always complain about getting older, but it's so nice to feel confident and settled in your career. I really like the way my life is going—except for the celibacy thing," she added.

"Celibacy and I wouldn't get along," Blair said, laughing. "I love being married. I'm independent, but it's so nice to have a person to come home to at night, especially when he's ready and willing to have sex at the drop of a hat. Any hat. Any hat anywhere in the world. When a hat drops in China—"

"Got the picture!" Kylie said, laughing.

Blair shifted in her chair, picked up her glass and took a sip. She reached up and ran her fingers through her hair, a gesture Kylie had seen her make when something was troubling her. Quietly, Blair said, "That was the old David. Now he's much more interested in my basal body temperature than he is in the rest of the neighborhood."

"I understand. But things will go back to normal."

Letting a thin smile show, Blair said, "I know I shouldn't complain. He's a great guy and just the kind of guy I need. It took me a while to find him, and I'm gonna keep him. Being married is good for me, even when things aren't going well. I hated dating. Ya know?"

"I do," Kylie said. "I'm sure I could have hooked up by now if I went on every blind date my friends try to arrange, but I hate spending the evening with a dud. I'd rather cook myself a nice dinner, put on something classical, and read a book."

"You can *wear* something classical?"

"Oh, har-dee-har-har," Kylie moaned.

"How long has it been since you've had sex?" Blair asked. "'Cause you might have forgotten how much better it can be than a book."

Kylie looked at her and let her mouth slide into a slow smile. "Oh, I remember. Besides, I didn't say what kind of books I read."

"Ooh…bodice rippers?"

"No, no bodices in the things I read. I wouldn't pick up a book that had a muscle-bound hunk on the cover, anyway. I like tanned blondes, but I like them with breasts and a nice curve at the waist."

"Oh, right." Blair blinked and said, "You know, sometimes, I forget that you're a lesbian."

"Don't you dare forget that," Kylie said. "I want you to keep me in mind every time you meet a single woman. You don't mind asking every woman you meet if she'd like to hook up with a surgeon, do you?"

"Does she need to be a lesbian?"

"Mmm…no, but she'd better be at least bi-curious. I don't want to have to start from scratch."

"Got it," Blair said. "I'll keep my ear to the ground."

Kylie started roughly chopping some Roma tomatoes, and Blair noticed that the doctor didn't seem to have the capacity to work and talk at the same time. Waiting until Kylie was finished, Blair said, "You seem to enjoy doing this."

"Cooking?"

"No. More than that. I mean…doing something nice for me. I think you have a big heart, Kylie…Mackenzie. I was gonna use your middle name, but I don't know it."

The taller woman gave her an adorably shy smile, looking as if she were going to say, "Aw, shucks." "I do like doing things for my friends. I'm not very self-absorbed, to be honest. I get a lot out of giving, rather than taking. And for the record, I don't have a middle name. My parents thought fourteen letters were enough for anyone." She cocked her head. "I don't know your full name. As a matter of fact, I've always been a bit surprised that you took David's last name. You seem like the type of woman who would want to keep her own."

"I would have," Blair said. "I was already starting to build a reputation when we married, but I think I would have changed my name no matter what David's was."

"Really? How bad was yours?"

"Bad. Very bad. Brace yourself: it was Schneidhorst."

Kylie snorted. "Schneidhorst? Really?"

"Yes. Blair Schneidhorst. Stop laughing, please. It's a perfectly respectable name."

"It is," Kylie said, unable to stop herself from laughing. "It's just…a mouthful."

"Try pronouncing it with a lisp like I had when I was a kid."

"A sibilant 's'?"

"Yeth. The name wouldn't have been so bad if my parents had named me Helga or Elke. Then I'd just sound like a German national. But giving me a WASP name like Blair totally ruined the flow."

Kylie was obviously at a loss for words. "God. Schneidhorst." Looking mildly frightened, she asked, "Do you have a middle name?"

"Yeah. It's nice, though. Anne."

"Blair Anne Schneidhorst. My parents would say you were over the reasonable letter allotment."

"No argument. I love David, but I might have married him just for the name."

"No one would have blamed you, Blair. No one at all."

⟿

After her third failed artificial insemination, Blair lay in bed, curled up in David's arms. She'd been crying for a long while and had felt his tears on her cheek merging with her own. "I'm so sorry, sweetheart," she sobbed. "I'm so sorry."

"It isn't your fault. You're not the one with the defective sperm."

"Your sperm isn't defective," she said, pulling away to focus. She wiped at her tears and said, "Please, David, can't we drop the whole thing and go back to how it used to be? Every time it doesn't work makes me feel like a failure."

"I'm the failure," he said softly. "I didn't tell you this, but I went back in and had them do another sperm count. It's even lower than it was before. The doctor says it's probably from stress, but I don't know how to calm down."

"Sweetheart," she soothed, "this is starting to hurt our marriage. There's nothing wrong with either one of us. We just haven't gotten pregnant yet. There's no shame in that."

"I want you to be inseminated with donor sperm," he said quietly, not looking her in the eye.

"What?" Blair sat up. "Why would you want to do that?"

"Because this isn't going to work. I want to have a baby soon, and if we keep wasting time, we delay the whole timetable."

"David, if we're not going to use your sperm, there's no reason not to adopt."

"Sure there is," he said. "If the baby can't be ours, I want it to at least be yours. Besides, I'm worried about taking a baby when we don't know the mother. What if she was using drugs or drinking or smoking? We'd have no way of knowing that. I want to do everything we can to make sure we have a healthy baby, and having you bear it will do that."

"David, there aren't any guarantees. I know nothing about my biological father's genetic profile. He might have been a drug-crazed, psycho killer. Hell, knowing my birth mother, it's likely!"

"I know you don't see it this way, Blair, but I want to be part of the entire process. I want to see your body change. I want to be there when you give birth. I can't do that if we adopt. I'm really afraid that I'll feel like a complete outsider if we don't give birth to the child."

"Can't we try a few more cycles with your sperm?"

His head shook decisively. "I'd really rather not. I know you'll say that I shouldn't feel this way, but I don't want to have another AI using my sperm. I'm afraid of how the baby will turn out. I'd never forgive myself if it had some awful birth defect."

She stared at him, mouth agape. "What are you talking about? We've been trying to get pregnant with your sperm for months and months. Why would it be defective now?"

His eyes didn't meet hers, and he looked small and vulnerable. "I don't know. There's something about the whole process that seems so…artificial."

Blair tickled under his chin, trying to make him smile. "That's why they call it 'artificial' insemination, honey. But it's only the insemination that's artificial, not the sperm. They process it to make sure it's extra healthy."

"I don't like it."

"Okay." She racked her brain, trying to think of a way around his irrational reasoning. "How about this? Why don't we have sex as much as we can?"

He looked at her warily, and she tried to pump up her enthusiasm for the pitch.

"We'll do it like we did when we were first together. We'll have it in the shower and the yard and the dining room." His smile was clearly reluctant, but it was peeking through his frown. "Remember that time we got in the backseat of your car and practically had to go to a chiropractor afterwards?"

A short laugh bubbled up. "Yeah. That was after we went to a club, and you made me so hot dancing with you."

"I can still make you hot," she said, giving him the look guaranteed to make him respond with sexual interest.

He smiled—the full, sexy one she loved. "You always can. And I guess it couldn't hurt to keep trying the old-fashioned way." David put his hands on Blair's shoulders and looked into her eyes. "But I still want to make plans to use donor sperm. I've got no confidence in myself, and I don't want to waste any more time."

His smile and his self-esteem seemed to evaporate at the same instant. Blair knew she had to do whatever it took to bring both back to the man she loved. She wrapped her arms around his body and soothed him as best she could. "All right, David, all right. We'll try it and see what happens."

⌒

Since she knew her mother woke with the sun, Blair snuck out of bed at 4:00 a.m., not having slept more than twenty minutes at a time. After relating the events of the previous evening, Blair asked, "Do you think this is the right thing to do, Mom?"

"Honey, I can't tell you that. This is your business."

"I had a feeling you'd say that," she said, sighing. "Maybe you should put Dad on; he's never afraid to give me advice."

"You never take it," Eleanor reminded her. "That's why it's safe for him."

Laughing softly, Blair said, "I wish I lived closer. I really need to see you."

"I'd tell you to come home for a few days, but you need to be with David now."

"I know. Besides, I'm determined to have sex as much as humanly possible. Maybe we can reconnect emotionally by connecting physically." She sighed. "This has been so hard on him, Mom. He honestly feels like less of a man just because I haven't gotten pregnant."

"It's your job to support him through this. This is a critical point in your marriage. You've got to let him know that you still rely on him."

"I do," she insisted. She ran her hand through her hair and said, "I hope I don't live to regret this, but I'm going to go ahead and plan to use donor sperm. Part of me believes that he really needs to be a parent at this point in his life and that he'll resent me if he doesn't. Once the baby gets here, he might be able to put this all aside and just focus on what we have, rather than what he doesn't have."

"That's the spirit, honey," her mother urged. "I think you're making the right decision."

"You always say that after I make it," Blair chided her. "Is that in the mother's handbook?"

"It is. And I promise to send you a copy as soon as you get pregnant."

Chapter Two

S itting at her desk one afternoon, Blair realized she'd been staring into space when her assistant walked into the office and said, "Is everything all right? You've been acting…distracted lately, and that's not like you."

Blair started to do what she normally did at work: say that everything was fine and change the subject. But she'd been working with Mandy for almost three years, and they'd become more than just co-workers during that time. They didn't socialize much, but that was mostly because of their partners' schedules. Mandy's boyfriend was in dental school, and they stayed in most evenings, while David was asleep when Blair was ready for dinner. A smile crossed her face when Blair realized that she didn't feel like Mandy's boss anymore and that the younger woman would probably want to move on fairly soon to strike out on her own. "Something *is* bothering me," she said. "Do you have time to talk?"

"Sure." Mandy closed the door to the office and sat down, giving Blair an expectant look.

"I'm having some problems at home," Blair said, stalling a bit while she tried to get comfortable with revealing details about her personal life.

"Is something wrong with David?"

"No, not really, but…oh, I'm just gonna spill it. We're trying to get pregnant, but not having any luck."

Mandy winced. "I'm sorry to hear that. I know how hard that can be."

"You do?"

"Yeah, my older sister was infertile."

"Really? Did she ever get pregnant?"

"No, but it worked out all right for her. She'd just entered an MBA program when they started trying. She thought she'd get pregnant, spend a year with the baby while she was in school, and then get a job."

Blair smiled ruefully. "You can't always make your body follow your plans."

"Right. I learned from her experience; I'm gonna start trying next year."

"That's great!" Blair reached across the desk, and they exchanged high-fives.

"We're excited about it. Although it'll probably be hard for my sister if I get pregnant."

"Is she really bitter about it?"

"No," Mandy said thoughtfully. "She seems happy now. She got a great job after she graduated, and she told me, not long ago, that she's happy she doesn't have to worry about childcare and all of the other things that go with having kids while you're working."

"Did they go through a lot?"

Mandy rolled her eyes dramatically. "Oh, yeah. My brother-in-law's a doctor, and he wouldn't rest until they did everything possible. They did a few rounds of in vitro, and when that didn't work, she had assisted hatching." She made a face and said, "Doesn't that sound like something you'd do to a hen?"

Blair made a gurgling sound and laid her head on her desk. "How long did they try?"

"Years," Mandy said. "They started when she was…oh, thirty-eight or so. They didn't give up until she was forty-three. They spent well over $100,000."

"My stomach's in knots," Blair mumbled. "Please tell me she's still married."

"Oh, sure she is. She said that all the struggles they went through made their marriage stronger. I think she's really happy now, and her husband seems happy, too. They're able to go on nice vacations, and Rick just bought a new Audi TT, something he'd never have been able to do if they'd had a baby. Things seem good between them."

"Well, that's a relief," Blair said, lifting her head. "I'm worried that this is gonna wreck my marriage."

"David's crazy about you!"

"Yeah, he is, but he's not crazy about himself right now."

"Ooh…is he the one with the…problem?"

"The doctors think so. He's not handling it very well."

"My sister was the one who had problems," Mandy said. "Maybe that made a difference."

"I wish it *were* me. Then David might feel sorry for me rather than feeling inadequate."

"God, that sounds horrible," Mandy said. "Just horrible."

"You know, I don't admit this to many people, but it *has* been horrible." Blair was surprised to find herself feeling a bit better now that she was getting some of her worries off her chest. "It's affected our whole relationship. Our sex life has suffered. We're not as patient with each other. Everything's…off."

"How's David in the communication department?"

Blair shrugged. "Not great. He's not the type to show me his soul, ya know?" She laughed and said, "Not that I show my soul very often, either."

Mandy laughed along with her. "You are a little guarded."

"Only Child Syndrome. Sadly, David's an only, too. Neither one of us is very good at sharing our deepest feelings."

"I don't know what to tell you, Blair, but you can talk to me anytime you need to. I'm a good listener."

"I know that, Mandy," she said. "That's why, other than my mom, you're the only person I've talked to about this. I trust you."

⌐

One Friday evening, Blair, Kylie, Nick, and his date, Kathy, were at Disney Hall, listening to the Los Angeles Philharmonic perform a program of Chopin, Liszt, and Rachmaninoff. When the concert was over, Nick and Kathy went out for a late dinner, and Blair drove Kylie home. "I'm sure glad you two subscribed for four tickets," Blair said. "I'm going to the Philharmonic more than I have in years."

"When we did that, we both had hopes that we'd have dates to use the extra tickets," Kylie said. "It's worked out much better for Nick than it has for me."

"Well, you've got me now, Doc. I'm sure you'd rather have a date, but I'm better than an empty seat."

Kylie looked at her and laughed. "You're a lot better than an empty seat. I really enjoy being with you. Of course, I'd like it better if you wanted my body in the most lewd and lascivious fashion, but you're still pretty good."

"I don't think I'm your type," Blair said, giggling. "Girls don't make me hot."

"Then you're definitely not my type. I prefer women who start drooling the minute they lay eyes on me."

"Many of those come along?" Blair asked, smirking.

"They're out there. I know they're out there, and some day, I'm gonna find one of 'em."

Blair was still smiling when she said, "You haven't changed your mind about telling me how to live my life, have you?"

"No, I struggle with my own decisions. I really can't take on a boarder." She looked at her friend and saw the smile fade. "Wanna talk about it?"

"Same old thing," Blair said. "I told David I'd use donor sperm, but I can't bring myself to make the phone call."

"It's a big step. You're smart to think it through."

"But I'm not thinking it through," she complained. "I'm just going around in circles. I don't want to do this, but I'm afraid that David will never forgive me if I don't."

Kylie gave her a look filled with concern. "That's not a very good reason to have a baby."

"No, no, I want to have a baby; I'm sure I do. I just wish that David would agree to adopt. But he's not going to, so I might as well stop whining."

"Hey, just because *he* won't give in doesn't mean that you have to."

"I know, I know. I don't always give in. Actually, most of the time, David is the one who caves. My mother thinks I take advantage of his good nature."

"Don't you love that? My mom thinks it's all my fault that I can't find a girlfriend."

"Well, *she's* right, but my mom's totally wrong," Blair said, managing to really laugh for the first time all day.

"I wish I had the answer for you. I really do. But all I can do is recommend a good sperm bank. I'll even make the call for you if you want."

"Thanks," Blair said. "I'll make it. I think."

⟶

Once she'd decided to make the call, Blair checked with David to see when he was available to go with her. "Honey, I was thinking of going to Westside Cryogenics this week. What afternoon's good for you?"

"Huh?" He put his drink down and immediately picked up his cigarettes. He tapped the end of the pack and put one in his mouth, motioning for his wife to follow him.

When they married, Blair had promised that she'd never complain about his smoking so long as he never smoked in the house. She'd noticed that he was spending significantly more time in the backyard lately, but she forbade herself to bring up the topic. As his contribution to the baby's health, David had promised that he'd quit smoking the minute Blair got pregnant, and she thought she'd best leave it at that.

He lit his cigarette the moment he hit the back steps. Walking through the cloud of smoke, Blair said, "If we want to get moving, we have to choose a donor. Westside Cryogenics sounds like the best place."

"Can't we do that over the Internet?"

Blair blinked at him and then said, "I didn't think to ask." She placed her hand on his waist and asked, "Don't you want to be a part of this? Picking the donor is a big deal."

"Yeah, yeah," he said, sucking on his cigarette as if it provided life-sustaining oxygen. "I just don't want to have to go in person. I just...I don't want to." He stubbed out his cigarette and shoved his hands in his pockets. "Wanna go for a walk?"

Knowing that David was more voluble when he was walking, Blair readily agreed. A few minutes later, they were strolling along the streets of their Santa Monica neighborhood. They didn't speak at all until they were a good twelve blocks from home. Finally, David said, "We'd better turn around."

Blair rolled her eyes, but didn't comment further, knowing David didn't react well when pressed to communicate. They passed their street, still without saying a word. When they reached the ocean, David sat down on one of the benches overlooking the cliffs that dropped to the sea. They were about eighty feet above the water, making the usual roar of the sea a mere whimper. A cool breeze blew in their faces, and Blair felt chilled even through her sweater. She scooted over, and David picked up on her cue and wrapped an arm around her shoulders. Cuddling closer, she rested her head on his chest, and after a long while, he said, "I know you're trying, but you don't understand how humiliating this is for me. I...I can't do it."

"Can't do what, honey? Have you changed your mind about using a donor?"

"No. I still think that's what we should do. But I can't go to the place."

"Okay," Blair said, patting his stomach. "I'll go check things out and see if I can do a first cut. Then we'll see where we stand."

"'Kay." They spent another hour sitting on the bench, both of them staring into the black sea, not even a moon to illuminate the inky depths.

⤶

Blair's first visit to Westside Cryogenics lasted nearly two hours, and when she returned home, she was dismayed to see Sadie's car parked in front of the house. *Good Lord, did David ask her over tonight? Or does she have a sixth sense for the worst possible time to drop in?*

Blair walked into the house and was immediately met by two pairs of dark-brown eyes. "Well?" Sadie asked. "What did you learn?"

"Hi, Sadie," Blair said. She walked over to the older woman, gave her a hug and a kiss, and then did the same to David. "David didn't tell me you were coming; I would have made dinner."

"Oh, honey, you know I don't like to cause a fuss. I only wanted to see if you're going to continue with this thing."

"Thing?"

"This sperm donor thing," Sadie said, her hands anxiously fluttering like a pair of wings.

"Well, David and I have to talk it over," Blair explained. When David didn't say a word, she continued, "Do you want to know what I found out?"

"Sure," David said. "I'd like a drink. Mom?"

"Oh, no, it's too early for me. You go ahead, though."

David gave Blair a relatively discreet head twitch, and she said, "I'll help you, honey. I could use a cold drink, too."

The pair went into the kitchen, letting the door swing closed behind them. "I'm sorry, baby," David said. "I talked to her on the phone this afternoon and mentioned that we were thinking of using a sperm donor. By the time I got home, she was sitting in her car in front of the house."

"Why did you tell her?" Blair asked, her voice rising despite her efforts to remain calm. "There's no reason anyone has to know about this."

Looking away, he said, "I tell her everything important. Since my dad died, she's been so dependent on me. I can't shut her out while she's struggling to rebuild her life."

"Okay, okay," she said, patting him on the waist. "If you want her to know about this, it's okay with me."

"I don't," he grumbled, "but she'd kill me if she found out later. It's easier to get it over with now."

"She's your mom. You're the one who has to decide how to handle her."

"Thanks." He kissed her on the cheek and gave her a squeeze.

"No problem," she said, but she knew there were going to be problems galore now that Sadie was part of the decision-making team.

⤶

The trio sat at the dining room table, looking over the brief donor profiles that Blair had brought home with her. Sadie dismissed most of the men immediately, but one donor—a man of Russian and Armenian descent—intrigued her. "If you're going to go through with this, then this is the fellow," she declared.

David looked at the profile and nodded. "Grad student in electrical engineering, on the water polo team in college, baseball team in high school, sports fan, doesn't want the child to be able to contact him—he looks good to me."

"Only one thing I don't like," Sadie said. "He says he has no religion. I don't like that."

"Our child will have whatever religion we practice, Sadie. Why does it bother you that the donor isn't religious?"

The older woman shrugged in a way that was clearly a dismissal. "You never know."

Blair often ignored her mother-in-law's comments, but something about this one bothered her, and she couldn't let it go. "You never know what?"

"He might be hiding his real religion. It might be something funny."

"Funny?"

"He could be anything," Sadie said. "I'd like to know what his people are before we commit."

"Fine," Blair said, not having the strength to push the issue.

"You can't be too careful. He might be…Muslim or something," Sadie blurted out.

"I'll check," Blair said, pasting a smile on her face. "Any other religions that would bother you?" She felt David's hand on her thigh and saw the set of Sadie's jaw. "They said they'd call the donor with specific questions."

"Thanks," David said, obviously grateful to her for agreeing to consider Sadie's favorite candidate and for giving up on the argument.

"I'll make the call for number 1051, but I like *this* guy," Blair said, pushing another profile across the table.

David picked up the sheet and read it quickly. "National Merit Scholar, graphic artist." He started to laugh, looking up at Blair. "His favorite hobby is reading. How weak is that?"

"One of my favorite hobbies is reading, honey," she said, smiling thinly.

"Right!" His expression froze for a moment, and she could almost see the gears turning in his head. "And since you've got that covered, there's no sense in asking for more of it. I want this kid to be well rounded."

"Good recovery," she said under her breath.

"I think you're making a mistake with this donor thing," Sadie said. "A big mistake. But if you insist on doing this, you've got to go with number 1051."

"I agree," David said. "I think he's ideal."

Blair sat back in her chair and said, "I know when I'm outvoted. I'll call and have them ask about his religion. They'll also need to make sure they have enough of this guy's sperm for a second go, in case the first time doesn't take."

Sadie got up from the table, her broad-shouldered bulk looming over both of them. Suddenly, Blair felt like a child about to be lectured by the teacher. "Just because I like number 1051 doesn't mean I agree with this whole thing. Why are you two giving up so easily on conceiving your *own* child? I read about a technique where they can fertilize an egg with just one sperm. You have millions, David! Millions!"

David looked a little small, too, but he took in a breath and held his ground. "We're not giving up easily, Mom. But to do that, we'd have to use in vitro fertilization, and they usually want to fertilize several eggs. We don't want to run the risk of having triplets or quads. Besides, the doctor says that the risk of passing on genetic defects might be higher using the single sperm technique."

"I read the same things you do, David. They can do an amniocentesis to make sure the baby doesn't have any chromosomal abnormalities."

"Jesus, Mom, how do you think I'd feel if we went through all of this crap and then had to abort the baby because of my defective sperm? I'm not gonna take that chance."

Sadie sighed and then looked at her son, her dark eyes like twin lasers. "I don't like to tell you what to do, David, but this is wrong, and you're going to live to regret it."

Blair looked at her husband and saw him swallow. She knew how much his mother's opinion meant to him, and she wished that she could rewind the last minute of the conversation and hit the delete button. *Dear God, please don't ever let me guilt trip my child like that.*

↩

"There's not a chance in the world you'll tell me whether or not you think I'm making a mistake, is there?"

"Nope." Kylie stood by a sparkling, aquamarine swimming pool, trying to imagine if the house they were investigating was the right one for her. "I'll never do that. Only you and David know if using a donor is the right choice for you."

"But you have so much experience with couples who've been in our situation. Can't you give me anything?"

Kylie gazed at her friend for a few moments and then nodded her head. "I'll give you one piece of advice: if you're conflicted about it, you should spend some time talking about this in couples therapy. This is a life-changing decision, and once you're in, it's tough to go back."

Sighing deeply, Blair let her head drop back and the sun warm her face. "David's antagonistic to therapy. He's not the kind of guy who likes to analyze his motivations for things. He's all action, no reflection. I've suggested therapy, but he's refused."

"That's my best advice. I wish I could be more help, but I don't have a clue if this is right for you. All I know is that you're going to be a great mom, no matter how you become one."

"I think I will," she said, a small frown wrinkling her forehead. "And I know that David will be a good dad. We just have to get through the preliminaries and get a baby in the house."

"You'll get there, Blair. You're a very determined woman."

"I am," she admitted, "but you don't get some things by determination alone."

↩

On the morning she started to ovulate, Blair and David rode in silence to the doctor's office. Neither made mention of the canister of donor sperm resting on the floor of the backseat. David had not even been able to refer to it by name, asking his wife if she wanted him to carry the 'thing.' She fought down the voices that continually questioned her, deciding that all women would be worried about conceiving if they had to do it as deliberately as she did.

When they entered the office, the nurse came in and explained that they would have to sign consent forms before Blair could be inseminated. She briefly explained the content of the forms and then left them to read the paperwork and sign. "Why do we have to do this?" David asked. "It's not like we just wandered in off the street."

"The donor's not on the hook, honey. Since we're married, we have to acknowledge that if I get pregnant, you're the father."

He read the form twice, took out his pen, and then signed. Blair watched him carefully, seeing how coiled with tension his body was. "There," he said, handing the papers to her. "Not one chromosome from me, but I'm the father. I'm sure the baby's gonna buy that."

"Hey!" She grasped him by the shoulders and looked into his eyes. "We agreed we weren't going to tell anyone." She bit her lip to keep from reminding him that he'd broken that agreement by telling his mother. "There isn't any reason for our child to know that he or she was the product of donor sperm. It's just a technicality, David."

"Technicality?" He shoved his hands in his pockets and kicked at the vinyl baseboard. "Eye color, hair color, height, bone structure, blood type, talents, fears, diseases, life expectancy." He turned back towards his wife, and Blair was sickened by the sorrow she saw in his mournful, dark eyes. "If those are technicalities..."

"David, David." She put her arms around him and hugged him as tightly as she could. "No one is forcing us to do this. If we have a baby this way, *you're* the father— not the wad of gunk in this tank!"

"Right." He pulled away and stared out the window again.

Blair went to him and forced him to look at her. "If we don't talk this out, I'm leaving, and you can't do much here without me."

"All right." He sounded bone-tired. "What?"

"I want you to look me in the eye and tell me that you'll love the baby we have, no matter how we get it."

His answer was immediate, and she could see that he was telling the truth. "Of course, I will. Jesus, I'm not a heartless bastard!"

"David, I never implied that you were. I just don't want you to spend your time thinking about who contributes what to create the embryo. Parenting doesn't start until our baby is resting in our arms." She softened her voice and pulled David close. "I want to raise a child with *you*. The guy who provided the sperm isn't going to help us raise this baby. After today, his contribution is over, while ours is just beginning."

He held her close and rocked a bit, kissing and nuzzling against her neck. "I'll do everything in my power to give this baby all of my love."

"Save some for me," Blair whispered. "Mommies need love, too."

The soft chuckle that David let out rumbled against Blair's ribs, reassuring her thoroughly. "I have more love for you than I'll ever be able to tell you, sweetheart. You'll always be my sweet baby."

A knock on the door startled both of them. The nurse picked up the papers, looked at them, and said, "Mrs. Spencer? You didn't sign."

Blair signed and then handed the papers back to the nurse. "Great," the woman said. "I'll take the sample and warm it. The doctor will be in soon."

They were both still nervous, and Blair tried to make conversation. "I wonder what makes a guy decide to donate sperm."

"The money," David said immediately.

Something about his tone made her look at him, and she asked, "How do you know that?"

He walked over to the window, looking out towards the ocean. "That's why I did it."

"*You* did it? You donated sperm?"

He whirled around and glared at her. "Yes, *I* did. I used to have a full supply."

"I didn't mean it like that. At all." She put her arms around him and felt the tension in his body. He stood motionless, so she pulled away, trying to give him some space. "I was only surprised because you seemed so…I don't know…judgmental about the donors."

"I'm not judgmental," he said, turning back to the window.

"When did you do this, honey?"

"When I was in college," he said, still staring. "A bunch of my frat brothers did it, and it seemed like an easy way to get a few extra bucks. We'd go over on Friday afternoon, make a deposit, and then hit the bars. It gave me spending money for the weekend, and if I did happen to get lucky, I could last a lot longer since I'd already knocked one out."

Blair approached him and placed her hand on his back. "How'd you feel about doing it?"

Laughing mirthlessly, he said, "I didn't feel anything. I was twenty-one years old, and it meant nothing at all to me. I knew I had an unlimited supply, and this just seemed like a good way to get rid of the excess. I jerked off every day, anyway. Why not make $50 while I was at it?"

Afraid to hear the answer, Blair still asked the question. "How do you feel about the guy who donated the sperm we're going to use?"

David gave her a sad smile. "I feel like he's a lucky asshole who doesn't know how lucky he is. When I was his age, my biggest worry was getting a woman pregnant. I couldn't imagine a worse fate. Now, almost twenty years later, I still worry about the same thing…from the opposite angle."

"Do you ever wonder about the children you might have…"

"I didn't used to, but in the last few months, it's been on my mind a lot. I know a couple used my sperm because the sperm bank called me to ask if I'd come in and make another deposit. That time felt kinda weird. I felt like a cow being milked. But even then, I didn't wonder if that couple was successful. Until now," he added quietly.

She wrapped him tightly in her arms and asked, "Are you absolutely certain this is what you want?"

He nodded. "I want to have a baby with you. This is the only way."

A quiet knock on the door signaled Doctor Coughlin's entrance. "Good morning," she said brightly. "Ready to make a baby?"

⟶

"I just had one of the strangest days of my life," Blair said. She had her telephone headset on and was sitting outside in the cool, dry evening, drinking a glass of lemonade. "It was like the worst possible one-night stand. No dinner, no movie, and the worst kind of sex possible. All I have to show for it are a few cc's of semen from a guy I'll never see again."

"Blair, honey, we've had this discussion before. There are some parts of your life that you should keep private. I'd really rather not know that you ever had anonymous sex."

. Laughing, Blair said, "That was a hypothetical, Mom. You know I was perfectly chaste when I met David. Our wedding night was such a shock! If only I'd known…"

"I'm glad you didn't go into acting, honey. You would have starved to death," her mother said dryly. "And you know I'm teasing you. I was just trying to cheer you up, sweetheart. You sound so…lethargic."

"I didn't sleep well," Blair said. "I can't imagine that every married woman who goes through this doesn't have decidedly mixed feelings about it."

"I think so, too. Do you want to tell me more?"

"Mmm…just…just that I almost chickened out."

"Was it that bad for you? Oh, Blair, there are times when I wish you'd never left Chicago. I could have been with you."

"That's okay, Mom. Having Doctor Coughlin in the room during my attempted conception was freaky enough. I don't think I could have had my mother there and stayed sane."

"Tell me about it. What happened?"

"I still don't know if we should have gone through with it. David told me some things that make me wonder more than ever if he's in the right frame of mind for this. Hell, I'm still not sure that we picked the right donor!"

"Maybe you just have cold feet," Eleanor said. "I almost had to tackle you to keep you from leaving the church before your wedding."

"Funny. Everyone wants a funny mother."

"I'm sorry, Blair. Come on now; tell me what's on your mind."

"I'm really snappish today. Don't mind me. And I'm sure that you're partially right. I do have cold feet. But David was so ambivalent today. He's totally focused on the fact that he won't be making a genetic contribution. Try as I might, I can't understand that! I was thinking that maybe because I'm adopted, I have more insight into what real parenthood is, but now I'm not so sure."

"How does David feel about your being adopted? Does he think of us as your parents?"

"Yeah…I mean, I think he does. He's never said anything that would make me think otherwise." She sighed heavily and reclined in her lounger. "Maybe that's part of the problem. Maybe David can't understand why this isn't like an adoption. I don't think of this guy as being the birth father. My sperm donor had a relationship with my egg donor. He shared in the decision of whether or not to raise me. If things had been different, he and my egg donor would have been my parents. That's not the situation here. This donor may have had charitable motives, but he also might have just wanted to make an easy $75 while watching porn! I don't know him; I never will. I can't tell my baby anything about him, other than what's in his profile. That's why I liked that the donor didn't want us to contact him. If I'm pregnant, it's my baby and David's— legally and morally. I don't want my baby to know about the donor."

"Are you sure that's wise? I don't want to give unwanted advice…"

"Go ahead. I always want your advice."

"Well…" Eleanor hesitated for a few seconds and then said, "Why would you want to keep this a secret? Doesn't your baby have the right to know who the birth father is? I suppose I thought you'd be in favor of full disclosure."

"I would be if I were married to anyone else," Blair grumbled. "I don't want to give David any more ammunition for not feeling like the father. I just thought it would be easier for him if the baby didn't know."

"But your father and I know, and now Sadie knows. She's not the most discreet person—"

"Don't remind me," Blair moaned. "David's telling her screwed everything up. Sadie'll never be able to keep this a secret."

"You'll deal with it when and if you have to. If you're pregnant and there's a glimmer of a chance that he or she will find out, you'll tell the baby yourself."

"Yeah, we will." She paused for a moment and then said, "I hate to say this, but I hope I'm not pregnant. David and I are going to have a very long talk before I agree to do this again. I think we were too rash."

"Now, honey, it's too late for thoughts like that. No matter what happens, you and David can work it out."

"Yeah, you're right. If I'm pregnant, I'm sure I'll be happy. I just hope my happiness is delayed until I'm more certain about the whole thing."

⤚

Just a week after being inseminated, Blair was planning to meet Nick and Kylie for a film noir festival at a West Los Angeles theater. She'd left work early, getting home well before David.

Taking the opportunity to pamper herself, she doffed her clothes and filled the tub in the master bath. Adding some of her favorite bath salts, she climbed in and turned on the jets. *I hope David doesn't come home soon,* she thought as the bubbles tickled under her chin. *I know how much he misses his hot tub. He might just throw off his clothes and jump in here with me, and this is definitely not a tub for two. Mmm…come to think of it, he can jump back in the tub anytime he wants. We obviously don't plan on using his sperm since he thinks each of them is some sort of mutant.*

She'd had a busy and stressful week, much of the stress courtesy of a house falling out of escrow. There'd been a nagging suspicion in the back of her mind about her buyer, but she didn't feel good about having been right, especially since she'd had to spend hours on the phone placating the seller's agent. Even though it occasionally happened to everyone, it irked Blair that her buyer had flaked on her. She prided herself on representing well-qualified, reliable clients, and she felt that having a house fall out, once it was in escrow, reflected badly on her.

I probably could have gotten all of that idiot's earnest money back if I'd sold my soul to Harriet Glickman, but I was not going to hang myself out to dry just because Mr. Paranoid read an article in the paper saying that Santa Monica could be washed away if a tsunami ever hit. She slapped at the bubbling water with the flats of her hands, the situation still annoying her. *If I'd been concentrating at work, I would've seen the warning signs earlier. When he insisted on having a geological inspection done on a perfectly flat piece of land, I should have sensed that he wasn't sure about it.*

The bath helped a little, but she was still out of sorts when she lay down for a nap. Her brow furrowed, and she slipped her hand into her robe and cupped her breast, giving it a squeeze. *It made sense when I was in the hot water, but why are my tits still tingling? It feels like a teeny, tiny electrical current passing through them.*

Turning onto her side helped take her mind off the annoying sensation, and she was nearly asleep when a familiar feeling in her uterus nudged her awake. *Oh, fuck, I'm getting my period.* She flopped onto her back and pressed gently on her abdomen. *Huh. It doesn't feel like it normally does. It's not cramping; it just feels…full and a little heavy. Huh.* Lacing her hands behind her head, she allowed herself to fantasize for a minute, but then dismissed the errant hopes. *It's been a week! No one can feel pregnant in a week. Just go to sleep and forget your delusions. You'll probably have your period by the time you wake up.*

———

After the first feature, Nick went to buy snacks, and Blair leaned over and whispered, "I know I'm probably insane, but could I possibly feel pregnant already?"

Kylie produced the biggest grin imaginable, and her hand immediately dropped onto Blair's belly. Her fingers slid up and down the soft cotton of her khakis. "Really? Do you really? Tell me exactly how you feel. Include *everything.*"

Blair patted her friend's hand, and Kylie immediately pulled it away, staring at it for a moment as though she didn't recognize it. "Damn, I'm sorry for touching you like that. I lost my head for a minute there."

Reaching over to take Kylie's hand and give it a squeeze, Blair smiled and said, "It's cool to see how excited you are. You're really into this, aren't ya?"

Kylie nodded enthusiastically. "I am! As many women as I've helped, I've never been involved past the surgery. Plus, I know how much this means to you and David, and I really want it to work out." Her smile increased a few lumens, and she said, "I'm really charged!"

"Well, like I said, it's probably all in my head, but I just feel different. My breasts feel a little like they do when I have PMS, but they're even more sensitive. It actually hurt to have the shower spray on them this morning."

Kylie's expression grew sober, and the thought ran through Blair's mind that this was her friend's doctor persona coming out. The intense, intelligence-filled eyes gazed at her carefully, Kylie's attention completely focused on her face.

"I also almost vomited when I opened the refrigerator at work earlier today. There was nothing particularly noxious about it—just too many smells." Blair shivered briefly in memory.

"Anything else?" Kylie asked, her tone low and soft.

"That's mostly it."

The gaze sharpened. "Mostly?"

Her expression was so penetrating that Blair heard herself admit to something she'd sworn she was going to keep to herself. "Again, I know I must be imagining this, but at the moment the doctor injected the sperm, I got this funny kinda rush. It's impossible to describe, but it was a very different feeling than I got the other times." She raised her hands and put her palms up. "I know it's weird, but I feel pregnant."

Kylie impulsively leaned over and brushed her lips across Blair's cheek. "It's not weird at all. Many women detect subtle signals very early, especially if they're attuned to their bodies. It's possible that you're pregnant, and if you are, I'm totally buzzed to be the first to know." She giggled and said, "I know that shouldn't make me so happy, but I love to know things before other people do."

"Must be from being the baby in a big family," Blair said, giving her friend a little pat on the cheek. "I'm not going to say anything to David yet, since I don't want to get his hopes up. But I'm gonna have that EPT test in my hot little hands on exactly the fourteenth day. I can't wait! I told my mom that I hoped I wasn't pregnant, since I think David and I still have some things to work out. But the mere thought that I might be is making me ridiculously happy. Just goes to show that you're never sure what your reaction is gonna be until it happens."

⌐

When Blair returned home, David was asleep, and she stood in the doorway of their bedroom for a long time, just watching him. Needing to be close, she slipped off her clothes and climbed into bed, receiving a small grunt in response. Placing soft, moist kisses along his back, she reached around him and tickled up and down his belly.

He woke slowly, mumbling, "Tired."

"You don't even have to wake up. Just let me love you."

Rolling onto his back, he sighed and wrapped an arm around her, nuzzling his face into her shoulder.

She was incredibly aroused, her burgeoning belief that they were finally pregnant making her nearly mad with desire for him. He was still half-asleep, so she unbuttoned his pajamas and started to stroke him.

Surprisingly, he touched her arm, stopping her. "Kiss me," he said. "I want to feel your lips."

Sliding her hand out of his pajamas, she propped herself on her elbow and leaned over him. "You'd rather kiss than...?"

"Uh-huh. I would."

She looked at him for a few moments, seeing the love reflected in his eyes. "Why?" Her voice was soft, her eyes questioning. "Don't you like to make love to me anymore?"

"Of course, I do!" He grasped her and pulled her to his chest, hugging her tightly. "I love you. Very, very much." He said this with such fervor that she felt chills run up her back. "But we've been so...I don't even know what we've been, but I wanna start over. I want...I want it to be like it was when we just started to make love. Damn, do you remember how much time we spent kissing?"

"I do," she whispered, her mind filled with memories of lying in bed for hours, doing nothing more than kissing David and staring into his eyes. "It was wonderful."

"Let's make it wonderful again. I know we can." He rolled onto his side, taking her with him. He caressed her face, barely touching her skin. "You're so beautiful. The most beautiful woman I've ever kissed."

She felt herself melt into his arms and his lips touch hers. After the briefest touch, he pulled away and brushed the hair from her forehead, looking deeply into her eyes. "I love you."

"I love you, too." She kissed his chest and rubbed her chin and cheek on the soft black hair that covered his upper body. Looking up at him, she smiled and murmured, "Kiss me."

↪

Kylie picked up the ringing phone on Sunday afternoon, muttering a curse. "Hello?" she called out from what sounded like a distance. "Hold on a sec!"

Moments later, the volume of the stereo at a manageable level, she picked up again. "Hi. Who's this?"

"Did you skip the class in medical school where they tell you how easy it is to damage the human eardrum?" Even though the words were teasing, Kylie could hear the edge in the caller's voice.

"Hi, Blair," she said, her voice low and warm. "I did attend that class, and loud noise would more likely damage the hair cells in the cochlea, but I get your point. I was out on my deck, so the noise wasn't as loud out there. Actually, it's your fault if my hearing goes. If I hadn't come inside to answer the phone, I'd be just ducky. So, what's up?"

Blair took in a deep breath and then asked in a shaking voice, "Wanna come over and celebrate?"

"What's wrong? Are you crying?"

"Yes, I'm crying," she whimpered. "I...I...I'm pregnant...and David's not coming home tonight like he was supposed to."

"Oh, you poor thing." Kylie paused a second and then shouted, "You're pregnant!"

Despite her disappointment, Blair couldn't help but smile at her friend's enthusiasm. "Yeah. I'm pregnant," she said, the words sounding odd as they rolled off her tongue.

"That's awesome! I'm so excited for you!"

"I am, too," she said. "But I'm also sad. I…I…I was gonna make David a special celebration dinner…and I…I'm lonely…"

She started sobbing, and Kylie spoke soothingly to her. "Do you have the food you wanted to prepare?"

"Uh-huh."

"Unlock the door. Then go lie down and put a cool cloth over your eyes. I'll be there in an hour."

"You sure?"

"You couldn't keep me away. If the door's locked, I'll break it down."

Blair hung up and followed the doctor's orders, lying down on the couch, a smile starting to build as she thought about Kylie's exuberant reaction. *I think she's more excited than my mother's going to be.*

⌒

It only took Kylie forty-five minutes, and by the time Kylie slipped in, Blair was dozing on the couch. Kylie half sat, half reclined on the floor, folding her long body between the coffee table and the sofa, just to be near her friend when she awoke.

Some time later, Blair blinked her eyes open to find a dark head resting against the cushion. Kylie was contorted into a remarkably uncomfortable-looking position, and when Blair ran a hand through the doctor's hair, she groaned in pain. "It's been a long time since I could take a nap in that position and not pay for it."

"You must have been awfully tired," Blair said, her voice low and a little raspy from sleep. "Hot date?"

"Uh-huh. Hot from a fever. I had a patient who developed an infection last night. I spent the night at the hospital keeping an eye on her."

"How is she?" Blair asked, sitting up.

"She's fine now. I stopped by and checked on her on my way over here. That's what took me so long."

"So, you were up all night?"

"Pretty much. They called me at 1:00, and I wasn't completely satisfied until 9:00 this morning. I spent half of the time reassuring the poor woman's anxious husband. He and I sat in the cafeteria, drinking coffee until it was coming out of my ears."

"You didn't have to do that, did you?" Blair asked, giving Kylie's hair an affectionate mussing.

Intentionally misunderstanding, she said, "I guess not, but it's more socially acceptable to drink coffee than inject myself with amphetamines. Don't know why, but that makes people skittish."

"Don't try to dodge a compliment, Doctor Mackenzie. You know full well what I mean. Not many surgeons would hang out for hours to reassure a family member. I know you've got some little space at the hospital where you could have taken a nap."

Turning slightly to be able to look into her friend's eyes, Kylie said, "I wasn't able to perform microsurgery on this patient. I had to open her up. I made the incision that allowed bacteria to invade her bloodstream. Granted, it wasn't my fault that she got the infection, but I'll be damned if I'm gonna put a woman's life at risk and then go hide while her husband worries himself sick."

Blair leaned forward and kissed the top of Kylie's head. "You're such a sweetheart that part of me wishes you *were* my doctor. But I'd never want to give up our friendship."

Kylie got to her feet with some difficulty and then stretched for a moment, wincing when some of her joints crackled noisily. "I'm really glad we didn't work together, too. You're a good friend, and you're going to be a world-class mom." She extended a hand and helped her friend to her feet. "If David were home, he'd be pampering you silly tonight. So, since I'm standing in for him, I'm gonna do the honors." Folding Blair into her arms, she hugged her for a long time, murmuring, "I'm so happy for you. It's all gonna work out just like you want it to."

"Thanks," Blair said, wiping her tears with the back of her hand. "I have a feeling I should start carrying a handkerchief. I haven't cried this much since *I* was a baby."

"You're allowed. You'll hardly recognize your own behavior from all of the hormones you've got coursing through your bloodstream. But the baby needs every one of them, so you get a free pass to be a complete lunatic."

"That's something to look forward to," Blair said, starting for the kitchen. "I don't think my clients will agree, but at least you do."

"Oops…I almost forgot." Kylie went to the door and, stepping outside, said, "I'm glad you have a covered porch." She reappeared in a moment, trying to herd a bunch of balloons into the house. There were six pink and six blue, and they were partially weighted down by a cuddly-looking brown teddy bear that clung to them. "I know you'll have to deflate them before David comes home, or the surprise will be ruined, but I had to do a little something to commemorate the occasion."

"You're wonderful," Blair sighed, hugging her tight. "You've made me feel so much better."

"Glad I could help. You're going to feel even better after I cook you dinner."

⌒

Blair had to admit that she did feel even better after dinner. They'd dined well, listened to a Rachmaninoff symphony that Blair was particularly fond of, and were now sitting in the living room, waiting for dinner to digest so they could eat dessert. "I get to do this all again tomorrow night," Blair said, grinning. "How lucky am I?"

"Very." Kylie scooted around on the couch, trying to get some of the stiffness out of her shoulders. "Can I ask why you didn't wait for David to get home to do the test?"

"Sure. I want to make this a big celebration to help him let go of the fact that we couldn't use his sperm. But there was no way I was going to take that test with him home and have it be negative. I'm very protective of him lately, and I didn't want him to be disappointed."

"He's a lucky guy to have you. I bet he knows it, too."

"Usually, he does. Up until now, we've had a very good relationship. Oh, he has his little shortcomings, but so do I, and our quirks fit together really well. I just hope he welcomes this baby with as much joy as I'm feeling."

"I didn't want to say much before, but you're very lucky to have been able to conceive this way, especially on your first try. Very few women do."

"I know we're lucky," Blair said. "I read all of the statistics, and I knew the odds were against us." She looked at her friend for a moment and then asked, "You've never talked about having a baby. Have you ever considered it?"

Kylie nodded. "A lot. I've been trying to figure out a way since I was about thirty. It's just been in this past year that I've begun to reconcile myself to the fact that it isn't gonna happen." She looked at her friend and said, "Honestly, that's part of the reason I'm so ecstatic about your pregnancy. After deciding I'd never experience it, it's a gift to get to watch a good friend go through it."

"Are you unable…?"

"I have no idea. I think the odds are good that I'm fertile. Neither my mom nor my sisters had any trouble. But I've never been in the right situation. When I was young, I considered having a child alone, but I had so many loans to pay off that I couldn't have afforded a live-in nanny. Now that I can afford it, I don't want to take the time away from my practice. I'm at the point where I have my career where I want it, and I worry about dividing my loyalties. I know how I am, and I'd never let a nanny take over if my child were ill and needed me. And I don't have the kind of job where I can call in sick. When a patient gets up the courage to schedule surgery, I'm not going to make her do it again because my baby has a bad cold." She rolled her shoulders and said, "Besides, the older I get, the less I want to hire someone to raise my child. If I can't do it and really experience the joys of parenthood, I think I should give up the dream."

"But you'd feel different if you were partnered?"

"Yeah. I have enough money for my spouse to be a stay-at-home mom. That would be ideal."

"You've been thinking about this for ten years. Have you ever come close to doing it?"

"Not very. Stacey and I talked about it, but she was ten years younger than I was, and she didn't want to consider it until she was thirty-five or so. We probably would have done it if we'd stayed together, but she was gone long before she hit thirty-five."

"Well, I can't give you this one, or David will be pissed, but I can make you a godmother." Blair paused. "How's that?" She got up and walked over to her friend, took her hand, and placed it on her belly. "Meet your godmother, Baby."

Kylie's expression turned to one of pure astonishment. "Really? *Really?*"

"Yes, really. You're my closest friend."

Blinking back tears, Kylie patted the flat belly and said, "I feel the same about you. Well, Nick's my closest boy friend, but you're my closest girl friend. Of course, I have some good friends from med school—"

Blair covered Kylie's lips with her fingers. "You're blathering." The doctor looked up at her and nodded. "Now, say hello to your godchild."

"Hi, Baby," Kylie said, her voice breaking on the word. "I can't wait to meet you."

"He or she wants to meet you, too. I have a feeling that Baby Spencer is gonna be spoiled senseless by Godmother Mackenzie."

"No doubt." She looked up at Blair and said, "Isn't it mind-blowing to think that you have a tiny, little person growing inside of you? In my book, this is one of the best parts about being human—having conscious knowledge of our gestation and being able to plan and dream and experience all of the joys that go along with anticipating birth. What a cause for celebration." She leaned over and placed a soft kiss on Blair's belly. "I hope you don't mind, but I'm compulsive about touching pregnant women. That's the only thing I don't like about my job. I never see my patients once they get pregnant."

"I'm sure I'll have to lower my normal personal space barriers, but for you, I'll take 'em all the way down. You have to leave my skin intact, but other than that, you can thump me like a melon."

Kylie gave her a playful pat and said, "That's the right attitude. Your tummy won't be your sole property for the next nine months. Strangers will come up to you and cop a feel. It's a lure that women can't resist."

"I don't think I'll mind," she said. "I was so excited I almost told the neighbors today. But then I decided that I should tell David first." She grinned and said, "After you, of course. Girl friends know everything first."

"He's gonna be on cloud nine."

With the briefest flash of worry, Blair said, "I hope so. I really hope so."

⌒

The next day, Blair cleared her calendar for the afternoon, stopped by the gourmet market, and purchased prepared foods for their celebration. *I was willing to cook last night, bud, but you missed it.* Her last stop was the drugstore where she picked up another pregnancy test kit. She didn't think she was a particularly good actor, but she was so genuinely excited and so wanted to share her joy with David that she was confident she could pull it off.

He had arrived home moments earlier and was still in his suit and tie. "Hey, sweetie," he said upon seeing her. "What brings you home so early in the day?"

"A few things." She put her bags down and went to kiss him. "One, I missed you. I hate it when you travel over the weekend."

"I do, too," he murmured, his face nestled in her hair. "These ridiculous conferences never help me do my job. Just a bunch of stuffy guys trying to blow smoke."

"Well, you were missed. The second reason I'm home is that this is the fourteenth day since the procedure," she said, using the most neutral term she could. "I haven't gotten my period, so we can safely do a pregnancy test."

His eyes went wide. "Is that wise? Isn't that something the doctor should do? I mean, we don't wanna get a false reading."

"The test is just as reliable as the one the doctor does, honey. Really."

"You're sure this is the right time?"

"Yes. You remember that Doctor Coughlin said we might be able to get results after ten days."

"But it's just fourteen days. Maybe we should wait a few more just to be sure."

She folded her arms around his waist and rested her head on his chest. "We can do it today. All of the tests are reliable at fourteen days. It'll be okay."

"I'm...I'm really nervous about this, Blair."

Looking into his eyes, she soothed, "It'll be okay, David. Trust me."

He nodded, but when she removed the test from the bag, he looked at it as if it were set to explode. "I...I'll wait here."

"No way. I want you with me. You've seen me in more humiliating positions than this in recent weeks. Peeing on a stick is nothing!" He followed along fairly compliantly, but she had to tug on him a bit to get him into the bathroom.

"Don't you want to change? I think I'd like to change."

"I pee while wearing a suit every day, David. Besides, I don't think there's a special 'watch your wife pee on a stick' outfit, is there?"

Turning quickly, he mumbled, "I'm gonna put some jeans on. Be right back."

Rolling her eyes, she removed her skirt, then her nylons and panties. When he came back in, she was wearing her silk blouse and a slip, and his expression was so pitiful that she finally asked, "Do you have a phobia about being in the bathroom while I do this, or are you just nervous about the results?"

He shifted from foot to foot. "Maybe both. I've, uhm, seen people doing some pretty weird things to you lately, not all of them good. There are still some things I wanna keep a little mystery about."

"Fine." She hitched up her slip and sat down, shaking her head when he scampered out of the room. Deciding not to waste the money, she snuck out the side door and retrieved the positive test she'd taken the day before. *These things are too expensive to waste! I'll take the unopened one back tomorrow.*

Now that she'd been talking about it, she really did have to pee, and when she was finished, she went back into their bedroom and changed. With seduction on her mind, she put on a seriously sexy teddy that David had purchased for her not long after they were married. He was quite fond of sexy lingerie, and this piece was his favorite. She'd taken to privately calling it her "gettin' lucky" outfit. She slipped a long, silk robe over it, just to avoid showing her hand, and then returned to the living room.

David was just taking the last sip of a Scotch, and when she entered, he hopped up and poured another. "Want a drink?"

"Mmm...I believe the instructions on the test say 'not to be taken with alcohol.'"

He didn't get the joke; he just nodded and poured an especially stiff drink. Returning to his chair, he gave her a speculative look and asked, "Where is it?"

"In my pocket. We can't look for ten minutes." He sat back down, and she sat on the arm of his chair, leaning heavily against him. "Wanna talk about how you're feeling?"

"Tense," he said, his single word making that abundantly clear.

"About?"

He looked at her as if she were insane and said, "I'm worried that you're pregnant, and I'm worried that you're not." With a shake of his head, he asked, "Do you really not get how big a deal this is?"

She grasped his chin and turned him to face her. "If I'm pregnant, it means that I'm voluntarily going to put on forty or fifty pounds, have a thing the size of a basketball contort my belly past all reasonable limits, have a heavy weight resting on my bladder while I try to sleep, have my tits blow up to twice their normal size—only to later have them deflate to less than I have now—and in nine months, when the baby is as big as I can make him, expel him from my vagina." She shook his chin roughly. "In case you didn't hear that last part, I said *my vagina*. That perfectly cozy little space that feels quite full when you put your penis inside it. Last time I checked, your penis didn't weigh nine pounds, and it wasn't eighteen inches long." She shook him again and said, "Yes, David, I do get it, and I'm scared shitless! But we'll get through this together because we love each other and want to share our love with a child." She scowled at him and asked, "Now, do you want to know if we're pregnant or not?"

He nodded almost mechanically, and she gentled her expression and kissed him.

"Are we doing the right thing, Blair?"

"It's too late for second thoughts. If we're pregnant, we're pregnant. If not, then we can revisit this. I'd just feel a hell of a lot better to hear you say you're certain we made the right choice. 'Cause if this stick is blue, there's a baby inside of me."

His eyes closed, and he took in a deep breath. "We did the right thing," he said, obviously trying to make himself sound confident.

She reached into her pocket and took out the stick. Handing it to him, she said, "Take off the cover."

"What color do we want?"

"We want blue," she said. "You went to Michigan. Go Blue!"

"Yeah. Go Blue," he repeated. His hands were shaking more than they had been on their wedding day, but he managed. The stick, as she knew, was a bright, robin's-egg blue. His eyes went from it to her, back to it, and then finally settled on her. "You're pregnant," he gasped.

"*We're* pregnant," she whispered, drawing him into a bone-crushing hug. "We're pregnant. You and I are going to have a baby."

❧

After enjoying dinner, which Blair had provided, and toasting repeatedly with sparkling apple cider, David looked at his watch. "Damn, it's already 8:30. Who put me on this schedule, anyway? I went to bed later when I was in grade school."

Blair rose and stood between his legs, starting to loosen the tie to her robe. "You know what you need?" she asked in her sexiest voice. "You need the proper motivation. Going to bed early can be fun." When her robe was open, she performed a quick striptease, baring one shoulder, then the other, and bending forward to brush her lace-covered breasts against his stunned face. "We don't ever have to make love on a schedule again. We can go back to normal and just enjoy each other." She knelt astride him in the wide, upholstered chair and twitched her hips. "Come to bed and enjoy me." When he didn't respond immediately, she said, "Or we can stay right here. I love to ride you while you sit in a chair. Whatever you want, David. Make your dreams come true." Reaching down, she took his hands and put them on her breasts. It was when she met his eyes that she detected nary a hint of arousal.

Deeply wounded and more than a little humiliated, she climbed off the chair and settled her robe on her shoulders. Seeing the expression on her face, he jumped to his feet and held her in his arms. "Hey, why the face? I was just making up my mind. You gave me so many choices, I got lost in the fantasy."

"Really?" Her expression was so fragile, so wounded, that it would have broken the heart of the most callous man.

"Of course! Come on; let's go to bed." Reassuring her with a warm smile, he led her by the hand, and when they reached their bed, he slipped her robe off and nuzzled his face against her neck. "You look so hot," he murmured, his voice sounding a little forced to her ears. His hands slid up, and he caressed the sides of her breasts, pressing them together slightly.

"Ow!" she winced. Stroking the backs of his hands, she said, "They're way past sensitive, honey. They feel like they're about to burst."

He gave her a curious look and asked, "Already? You're only two weeks pregnant."

"I know, but it's not my imagination. They're as tender as they've ever been." She slipped the straps of her teddy off and let the material drape around her waist. With a caress that barely pressed the skin, she trailed her fingertips across the flesh of her breasts. "Can you do it like this? Touch 'em lightly…"

Watching her face, he tried, giving her a good effort, but looking at his earnest expression made her lose whatever interest she had left. He looked like an underling trying to impress his superior, and since Blair was most aroused when David was the aggressor, she realized they weren't going to get anywhere that night.

Kissing him lightly, she said, "There're going to be a lot of changes for us, David. We need to spend some time getting used to the new landscape. Why don't we spend a long time investigating each other this weekend?"

"Okay," he said, looking a little relieved. "I'll bring you breakfast in bed."

"It's a deal, Dad," she said, giving him as broad a smile as she could manage. "You do want to be called Dad, don't you?"

"It's awfully early to make those decisions, isn't it? So many choices: Daddy, Dad, Pop, Poppa. Besides, they don't talk when they come out, do they?"

"No, it takes them a few weeks to speak." Pushing the dark hair from his forehead, she asked, "Are you really happy?"

"You're having a baby! Of course, I'm happy." He led her to her side of the bed and carefully tucked her in. Sitting on the edge, he bent over and kissed her. "I love you."

"I love you, too," she murmured. As he got up and went around the bed to slide into his side, she noted with a growing sense of discomfort that he hadn't once put his hands on her as Kylie had done. *Is Kylie right? Do only women have the urge to do that?*

⌒

On Monday, after showing a very nice house to a very obnoxious woman, Blair returned to her office. She started to pull her desk chair out, only to find a large box resting upon it. Catching her assistant's eye, she asked, "Mandy, do you have any idea what this is?"

"No. It was on your chair when I got in."

There was no return address, but her name was clearly written in a firm hand, along with the word "CONFIDENTIAL" in bold red letters. Puzzled, she used her letter opener to break the seal and then started to laugh when she saw the contents.

·Mandy started to walk over to her. "What is it?"

Quickly closing the box, she tried to lift it, finding that she had to strain to do it. "Oh, it's nothing. Just some things a client wanted me to read. Could you help me put it on the floor?"

Mandy tried to lift it herself, finding that she was unable. "Someone sent you a set of encyclopedias?"

"No," Blair said, laughing, "just books on some topics she and I have been discussing."

"Do I know this client?"

"No, I suppose you don't. You'll meet her if she gets serious about buying."

After helping wrestle the box to the floor, Mandy went back to her own desk. Blair didn't feel able to examine the contents thoroughly, since she wanted to keep her pregnancy a secret for as long as possible, but she did peek one more time and found a card:

> To Blair and Tenant,
>
> I don't know about you, but I need to read everything written on topics of particular interest. Here are a few titles that my sources tell me are good.
> Enjoy!
>
> Godmother Mackenzie

Blair sat back in her chair, a big smile on her face. *I have a feeling that the good Doctor Mackenzie is going to help make this pregnancy a lot of fun.*

Still smirking to herself, she dashed off an e-mail:

> Dear Godmother Mackenzie,
>
> Aren't you the people who always tell pregnant women not to lift heavy objects? Just kidding, Doc. I can't thoroughly investigate the package right now, but I'm immensely grateful for your thoughtfulness.
> Why not come over after work and help me get the box into my car? David is going to the Lakers game tonight, so I could treat you to dinner. Let me know.

⌒

Kylie walked into the real estate office and spoke to the receptionist for a moment. Blair happened to glance up and watched her friend approach, letting out a quiet whistle when Kylie entered her office. "Boy, you look great."

"Thanks," Kylie said, a half-grin on her expressive face. "I was in the office all day, and since I have to wear scrubs on surgery days, I like to dress up when I'm seeing patients."

"You wear dresses a lot, don't you?"

"Uh-huh. I like 'em, but I'll admit I started to wear them for practical reasons. Where are we going, anyway?"

"Not sure. Let's walk down Montana and see what strikes us." They headed east, and as they walked along, Blair said, "Tell me about your practical reasons for wearing dresses."

"Oh. Well, when I was first starting out in my residency program, one of my mentors was a woman—one of the best eye surgeons in the country. She took me aside and looked me over from head to toe and told me that to be successful, I needed to make myself as unimposing as possible, since my natural style was a little...fierce."

"Well, that's sexist," Blair said, eyes narrowing.

"Sure it is, but so's medicine. She gave me good advice, and I took it. I'd be most comfortable wearing my scrubs all day, but I've found that it intimidates people to meet their surgeon and have her wearing scrubs. It looks like you're going to whisk them into the operating room at any moment."

"Okay, I can see that you don't want to meet a new patient with scrubs on, but why not wear slacks?"

Kylie laughed warmly. "I think I have nice legs." She stuck one long limb out and pointed her toe, flexing her calf muscle. "Don't you agree?"

"They're fantastic," Blair said, giving her a wry smile. Continuing her appraisal, Blair said, "You really do look nice in dresses. Of course, it helps that you're thin and nine feet tall, but don't think I'm jealous."

"Jealous? You think it's easy to walk around when you're nine feet tall? I can hardly count the number of times I've hit my head on…"

Blair scowled at the teasing, and Kylie gave her a slightly apologetic look and continued, "The only part I'll never get used to is the shoes. I wear flats, but still, I long for tennis shoes at the end of the day."

"Then let's go into the next place we see," Blair offered. "I don't want your tootsies to be mad at me."

⌒

"So, how did David take the news?" Kylie asked once they were seated.

"Well." Blair paused and corrected herself. "Pretty well." She thought for a moment and said, "It's hard for him. We were talking last night, and he kept making comments about the baby being a water polo player and running marathons."

"Huh?"

"Oh, the sperm donor is a jock. David's focused on the things the sperm donor does—all things David doesn't do, of course. He wanted the donor that was a jock, even though David's a real couch potato himself. He watches sports fanatically, but he'd hurt himself if he ever tried to participate. It seems like he's jealous of the donor and thinks the baby will be just like the guy." She snapped her napkin open and continued, "He doesn't get that his contribution to the baby's development will be a thousand times more important. It's like he believes that the male role in the process is now complete, and some other guy did it!"

"That's not uncommon," Kylie said, frowning. "You know, fatherhood is tough on men, and it's even worse when they're infertile. There seems to be a primal need to reproduce to carry on the line, and when that role's taken away, a lot of guys struggle. I really think some very old forces come into play here that make men need to prove themselves through reproducing."

"So, how do I reach him?"

"I'm not sure. I don't know David, so I can't even hazard a guess. But as time goes on and more and more attention is properly focused on you, I'm afraid it might get worse. Guys start to feel left out during a pregnancy, so I'd urge you to do everything you can to prop him up for a while. Really make him understand that he's important to you."

"He is," she said, her expression earnest. "He means the world to me. He used to know that, but lately, I'm not so sure."

⟶

Saturday morning found David, as promised, making breakfast in bed for Blair. His efforts were modest, but she praised them nonetheless, eating the frozen waffles with gusto. "You did great, David." She smiled and reached over to dab at his mouth with her napkin. "Got a little syrup there. Hold on." Scooting over, she put her hand behind his head and pulled him to her, removing the droplet with her tongue. "Mmm...you are one sweet-tasting man."

"Why, thanks." He reached out and picked up the syrup bottle from the bedside table. "Want me to pour some of this on any other spots?"

"No, I like you all natural. The syrup would just disguise your perfectly delicious self." She rubbed her face against several spots on his body, murmuring, "You smell so wonderful. So sexy."

He looked at her, the tiniest hint of a question in his eyes. "You really love to have sex, don't you?"

Sitting up to get a good look at him, she said, "We've been lovers for ten years. Is it a newsflash that I like sex?"

"No, no, of course not. I just...I wonder how you'll feel when you can't have sex anymore. Won't it bother you?"

Scrunching up her nose, she asked, "Do you know something that I don't know? 'Cause I'm not planning on giving it up."

"Well, we won't be able to do it when you're really pregnant."

"I'm really pregnant now, David, and there isn't a reason in the world we can't be having sex up until the baby's born. Granted, I won't feel like it all of the time, and I guarantee you're not coming near me for months afterward, but other than that, it should be business as usual."

"No," he said, although he sounded uncertain. "You can't really...you wouldn't want to...would you?"

"I wouldn't want to what...have sex? Just because I'm pregnant?"

He nodded, looking even more unsure of himself.

"You know Jeanne in my office, right? She's one of my team members?"

"Yeah," he nodded. "Sweet little thing, kinda shy and quiet."

"That's her," Blair agreed. "When she was pregnant, her husband threatened to hire prostitutes—for her! I caught her leering at the UPS driver one day when she was about eight months along. I swear, David, we all kept an eye on her so she didn't start humping men when they came in the door!"

"No! Really?"

"Yes, really. Women in my office talk about these things, and from what I've heard, most women want sex a whole lot more or a whole lot less when they're pregnant. I think some of it has to do with how difficult your pregnancy is and things like that, but if I'm healthy, I think I'm gonna be in the 'want it more' camp. I'm already itching for you, and it's only been a few days." She chose not to acknowledge the whole truth: they hadn't had sex since she'd been inseminated—the longest gap they'd ever had.

He still looked puzzled, but some compelling things she was doing with her hand captured his interest. "I can barely keep up with you now," he gasped when she hit a very sensitive place.

"You'd better take your vitamins, big boy." She forced him to his back. "You're gonna need 'em."

⌐

An hour later, she lay on her back, knees raised, feet flat on the mattress. Pushing some strands of hair from her damp face, she murmured, "That was absolutely awesome! Damn, you haven't gone at me like that for ages." She rolled onto her side and rested her head on his chest, hearing his heart still hammering away. "I think you're just hitting your peak."

He laughed softly and turned his head to kiss her. "I think you might be able to hit another peak. Wanna try?"

"Like I ever say no to that." She took his hand and slid it between her legs, guiding him so he touched her gently. "'Atta boy. Keep it nice and slow and soft." Wrapping her arm around his neck, she pulled him to her and kissed him with gusto. After just a few minutes, he was ready for action again, and she urged him to enter her. "God, I love not worrying about birth control or getting pregnant. It's so nice to be able to just have sex again."

His dark eyes were bright with desire as he slid inside. He hovered above her and bent to kiss her again, sliding his tongue into her mouth. Coming up for air, he asked, "Can we do everything we used to do?"

"Yeah…everything."

He gripped her legs and slung them over his shoulders, easing in and out of her for what seemed like hours, keeping her just on the edge of orgasm. With her hands on his hips, she tried to pull him into herself harder, but he grinned playfully and held back, making her want it all the more. It wasn't until she groaned in frustration that he gave her the cadence she wanted, and once he did, she came noisily, moaning and thrashing around on their big bed. He followed quickly, and she held him tight, loving the feeling of him pulsing inside of her.

David stayed inside for a few moments, since he knew Blair loved having his weight on top of her. But he rolled off quicker than usual, saying, "I don't want to hurt you. I know you're sensitive." He snuggled up behind her, draped an arm around her waist, and they both fell asleep immediately.

Nearly an hour had passed when David groggily opened his eyes. But he woke completely when he saw the look on his wife's face. "What's wrong?"

Her hands went to her abdomen, and she pressed her fingers against a few places. "I…feel a funny cramp."

"Where?" he asked, his voice getting higher.

"Not sure. It feels like my uterus or maybe an ovary."

"That's all that's in there!"

"I have a few more things," she said, palpating her belly. "I'm a human as well as a woman."

"Does it still hurt?"

"It's been thirty seconds, David. Give me a minute."

She rolled out of bed and went into the bath, mainly to get away from her husband's contagious anxiety. Looking into the mirror, she saw the tense set of her own jaw and decided she needed to at least speak to her doctor. She hadn't yet picked an obstetrician, so she had to call her gynecologist. Just as she turned to leave, a cramp hit her, and there was no doubt about this one. She sank to the edge of the tub, her legs about to give out—more from anxiety than pain. For an instant, she had an image of her tiny baby dislodging itself from her uterine wall and floating down towards her cervix. "No!" she cried, causing David to burst into the room, eyes wild.

Shaking and pale, she demanded, "Call Doctor Coughlin. Tell her I'm having cramps and ask what we should do."

"We should go to the hospital!"

"David, please do as I asked. Please," she begged, sending him flying.

Moments later, he was back, portable phone in hand. "Her service says she's unavailable. There's a Doctor Jablonski on call."

"I've never heard of him or her," she growled. "I'm not gonna waste time listening to a stranger tell me what to do!" She took in a few deep breaths, knowing that she was panicking. "Give me the phone." He handed it to her, and she dialed Kylie's home. When the machine picked up, she paged her and then got up to splash some cold water on her face. "I'm gonna get into the shower and clean up in case we have to go to the ER. If Kylie calls, tell her what's going on and see what she thinks we should do." He nodded mutely, his skin the color of flour. She kissed him gently and tried to summon her courage. "It'll be all right. I'm sure of it."

⟶

After her shower, Blair walked into the living room, seeing that David was on the phone. "Here she is," he said, obviously relieved to hand the device off.

"Hi," Blair said. "Did David tell you what's going on?"

"He did," she said briefly in full doctor mode. "Describe your symptoms for me."

"I got a slight cramp that felt like it was in my uterus. Then I got up, and when I did, I felt another one, much stronger than the one before."

"Have you felt cramps like this before?"

"Not since I've been pregnant, but I'd say the last one reminded me of the kind I get when I start my period."

"How are you feeling now? Have the cramps subsided?"

"Yeah, I just have an achy feeling in my lower back. Nothing too intense."

"Any spotting?"

"No."

Kylie's tone sharpened, and she asked, "Are you certain? Have you checked?"

"Yes. I just took a shower. There was nothing there."

"Were you sleeping when the cramps started?"

"Yeah," she said. "Uhm, I guess if I'm gonna use you as a doctor, I have to tell you the whole truth. We'd made love and fallen asleep when the first one woke me."

"You made love *right* before this happened?"

"Uh-huh. Is that a problem?"

"No, not at all. Did you have an orgasm?"

Blair would normally have teased Kylie about the privacy invasion, but she was too worried to tease, and Kylie was acting completely businesslike. "Yeah. I had two. The first one was very intense."

Kylie sounded relieved. "That's probably it."

"I shouldn't have sex?" Blair asked, hoping that David's fears had been groundless.

"No, no, but sometimes, intercourse can bring on a little cramping."

"Does that mean we shouldn't…?"

"No, really, having sex is a good thing for you. It keeps your uterus nice and toned. But your body's going through some pretty significant changes. You might experience a few funny sensations, but they aren't anything to worry about."

"Do you think I should go to the ER?"

"No, I don't. If you're not spotting and the cramps are down to an ache, I wouldn't. Just monitor how you're feeling, and if things change significantly, you'll want to take some action. Did you call your gynecologist?"

"Yeah. She's unavailable. Somebody I've never heard of is covering for her."

"Well, that won't do you much good. Whoever it is probably won't have access to your chart. I think you're fine, but just to be safe, you should get busy and choose an obstetrician. That's who should be seeing you, anyway."

"I meant to ask you about that. I got a list of names from Doctor Coughlin, but I don't know a thing about any of them."

"Tell you what. A good friend of mine from med school practices in Santa Monica. She's an excellent obstetrician, and I guarantee I can get you in to see her tomorrow. What do you say?"

"Sold. What's her name?"

"Monique Jackson. I guarantee you'll love her."

"Thanks, Kylie. We were on the verge of going mad here. You're a lifesaver."

"Well, yeah," she drawled, back in friend mode. "That's why I make the big bucks. I'll call you later tonight after I get in touch with Monique. You go put your feet up and lie on a heating pad for a while. Don't forget that you can't take any pain reliever, okay?"

"Yes, Doc, I remember."

"And if you feel worse, page me, and I'll go with you to the ER. I know how to go to the head of the line." Her voice grew somber again, as she added, "I'm teasing you only because I'm sure you're fine. Got it?"

"Yep, I got it. Talk to you later, and thanks again."

"You owe me dinner. No such thing as a free consultation."

"Done."

"And Blair, don't let this freak you out. It's common, and it shouldn't make you afraid of having sex. Do your best to make David believe that, too."

"That might be a harder sell," Blair admitted, "but I'll try."

She hung up and clambered onto David's lap. "I assume you got the gist of the conversation?"

He wrapped his arms tightly around her. "Yeah, I did." Placing soft kisses on her face, he murmured, "I'm so sorry, honey. I know how freaked you were."

"We may as well get used to it, David. Being a parent is all about being scared out of your wits half the time."

⌒

Kylie was true to her word, and the next afternoon, Blair was sitting in Doctor Jackson's office, talking to her before they began the exam. The intercom buzzed, and the receptionist said, "Doctor Mackenzie on line one. She says it's urgent."

Doctor Jackson rolled her eyes. "All of her calls are urgent. Surgeons," she muttered good-naturedly. "Do you mind if I use the speakerphone, Blair? I'm sure she's checking on you."

"No, not at all."

Monique hit the button. "This had better be an emergency, Doctor Mackenzie; I'm in a consultation with a very important patient. She's listening in on the speakerphone, by the way."

"Hi, Blair," Kylie said. "I just wanted to make sure Monique hadn't scared you off with her dreadful bedside manner."

"Listen here, Shakes," Monique interrupted. "I've got better things to do than play games with you. Go practice your sewing."

"I really called to thank you for seeing Blair, Monique. She's a good friend, and I know you'll treat her well."

"Thanks, Kylie. I'm sure we'll enjoy working together. Now, you go make some tiny little incision and charge $25,000 for it and let me get back to work."

"I'll call you later, Blair, and we can gossip about Monique," she managed to get out before Doctor Jackson hung up.

"Shakes?" Blair asked quizzically.

Doctor Jackson held her hands out and made them shake violently. "That's what we called her in med school once she declared she was going to be a surgeon. It just stuck."

"I like it," Blair said. "A lot. I'll have to use it."

⌒

After receiving a clean bill of health from Doctor Jackson, Blair spent the next week trying to prop up David's self-esteem. It was only after she had unsuccessfully tried to get him to make love for the third time that her suspicions were confirmed. "Do you think you caused me to have that little cramping episode?"

"Well, didn't I? We were way too energetic. We can't do things like that anymore."

"David, I explained this to you. Kylie said it was good to have sex. Monique said we should continue to have sex. Monique said that if anything, it was my orgasm that caused the cramps, and I'm not giving up having those—period!"

"I feel funny about it. I can't get it out of my mind. You looked so scared, honey. I was afraid of losing you!"

"Come on now," she said, enfolding him in an embrace. "You're not going to lose me. And we're not going to lose the baby. We have to go along just like normal."

"I'll try, but I'm just not in the mood right now. How about a foot rub?"

"Great," she said, pasting on a wan smile. *Just what I've always wanted—a nice, hot, sexy foot rub!*

He got some lotion and rubbed her feet so lovingly that she didn't mind not having sex. He had such a gentle, yet firm, touch that she loved to have his hands on her body—in every way. "You know," he said, "you've got two women giving you advice on our sex life, and I don't know much about them."

"True," she said. "Would you like for me to have Kylie over for dinner? I think you'd like her if you got to know her a little."

"Nah," he said, "I know you like to have your friends all to yourself."

She laughed. "That's just because you know I don't have many friends, and I don't like most of yours."

"You don't mind when I have my friends over to play cards."

She patted his cheek, smiling at him fondly. "So gullible. I've never been home when you have your friends over. That's why I don't mind."

Scrunching up his face, he nodded. "I guess you're right. I suppose we'd better keep our separate friends separate. Then I won't know if I hate Kylie." He continued to rub her feet, pressing his thumb down the center of her arch, making her moan with pleasure. "You haven't said much about Monique. What's she like?"

"She's nice," Blair said. "Pretty irreverent, just like Kylie. They went to med school together at UCLA, and I think they rubbed off on each other."

"UCLA, huh? That's reassuring. I like my doctors to go to good schools."

"I think she's well-educated, honey. I was in her office and saw her undergraduate diploma: summa cum laude from Howard."

"Isn't that school mostly black?"

"Yeah. She's mostly black, so I suppose she fit right in."

"You didn't tell me she was black."

"Didn't seem important." She gave him a curious look and asked, "Doesn't bother you, does it?"

"Nope. You just didn't mention it."

Hmm...I also haven't mentioned that Kylie's gay. I think I'll keep that to myself. David is pretty open minded, but I'm not sure he'd like my best friend to be a single, great-looking lesbian. I'll tell him when he's acting more like himself. I can never tell what's going to upset him anymore.

That Sunday, bubbling with excitement, Blair called Kylie. "Who do you consult before you make a major decision?"

"No one. Why?"

"Surgeons," Blair muttered, making Kylie laugh.

"Well, you asked. Why?"

"Because I'm going to show you a house that you're gonna want to buy, but you need to make an offer today, or you'll never get it. So, I want you to come with whomever you need to help you decide."

"Well, when you put it that way, I guess I'll bring Nick. He's good at helping me ferret out any deep, dark emotions luring me into making a poor decision."

"You sound pretty calm for a woman who'd better be buying a house in a couple of hours. Aren't you excited about this?"

"Oh!" Kylie took an audible breath. "I was in my 'I'm stunned, but have to maintain my composure because I'm a surgeon' persona. I'm very, very excited. If you're sure I'm gonna like it, it's a done deal."

"That's the kind of talk I like to hear. Meet me at my office at 2:00. I should be able to get the keys by then. Oh—bring your checkbook...and binoculars."

Kylie hung up, looked at the phone, and said, "Huh?"

They met at the office, and Blair quickly filled Kylie and Nick in on the details. "Okay, the owner of this place is a well-known actor, and he's decided that he needs more space for his growing family. He owns this property and the one next door. He wants to tear down both houses and build on the property next door because he likes that view better. I sold him the other property, by the way."

Kylie watched her friend speak, noting the professional, organized air she projected, tempered by a youthful enthusiasm that she found herself quite taken with.

"Anyway, I'm trying to talk him into buying a much bigger place further up the hill. He wouldn't have to do a lot to the new property, and I think it would suit his purposes much better. He hates the thought of going through the hassle of selling both houses, but I've promised him I can sell each of them with one viewing. This will be the easier one to sell, since it's so much less expensive, but I need to sell it today. This is the only opportunity you have. If you like it, make an offer. If you don't, you're insane, and I lose both listings." She gave her friend a sickly-sweet-looking smile.

"Thank God there's no pressure," Kylie said, feeling a little ill. "Well, let's go take a look. I guess I'll either own a house or lose a friend by the end of the day."

"Don't be silly," Blair said. "You could easily lose more than one friend today. I bet Nick won't like you, either, if you don't bite on this house."

They got into Blair's E-class Mercedes, Kylie allowing Nick the front seat to accommodate his slightly longer legs. "If you only have one chance to sell this, you must be pretty confident of your buyer, Ms. Spencer," Kylie teased.

Shooting her friend a look over her shoulder, Blair said, "I am. I don't mean to put pressure on you, and I swear I won't hold it against you if you don't buy it, but I'm risking a pretty hefty commission on the conviction that I know what you want."

"I think you do, too," Kylie said, squeezing her shoulder.

They pulled up in front of a large wooden gate, and Blair rolled her window down and buzzed. "Blair Spencer," she announced when someone answered. The gate swung open, and as they pulled in, Kylie muttered, "I'll take it."

Her voice filled with excitement, Blair said, "It's wonderful, isn't it?"

Kylie nodded mutely, too impressed to speak. They all got out of the car and started to look around, Blair hanging back while Kylie and Nick took in the setting.

The sprawling, Spanish-style home sat perched on the side of a steep canyon. Just outside the massive stucco wall that surrounded the property, wild canyon plants predominated. "There are homes all around here," Blair said, "but the vegetation is so dense that you can only see them at night when you can catch a glimpse of their lights."

"What are we on in terms of soil?"

"Granite," Blair said. "The house is very secure. The seller is a real worrywart, and he had two geological surveys done before he was satisfied."

"Sounds great," Kylie said. "I'm not a worrier, but I'd hate to go down this hill in an earthquake or a mudslide."

"If you're inside the house, you're not going anywhere," Blair assured her. "Did you bring your binoculars?"

"Yep."

"Well, pull them out and look down and to the south when we stand on the porch."

Kylie did so, asking, "Is that Riviera?"

"Yep. From the private garden off the master suite, you have a very good view of the country club. You can watch the L.A. Open while you sip a nice drink, get on your cell phone, and harass people who live someplace cold."

"Speaking of cold, my brothers are gonna be so jealous." She grinned widely. "Nothing better than making your brothers jealous."

"Never too late for a little therapy, Kylie," Nick said. "You should've resolved your sibling rivalry by the time you're forty."

"Too late now," Kylie said, sticking her tongue out at her friend's teasing.

Blair led them to the entrance, and a friendly young woman answered the door. "Hi, you must be Blair," she said, extending a hand. "I'm Nicole. They said you'd come over this afternoon. I'll just run over to the main house to give you some time to look around."

When she left, Blair informed them, "The nanny and the housekeeper live in this house, and the kids hang out here a lot of the time, too. This property's completely walled in and has a big play area in the back, so it's a little kid-centered. But you can get rid of the kid stuff without too much trouble."

The home wasn't huge by Hollywood standards, but it was good-sized by anyone else's. It contained three bedrooms, three baths, a home office, and a large family room that was set up as a home theater.

They took their time in the house, examining every room carefully. The place had clearly been very well maintained, with windows newly installed and wide-plank wooden floors throughout. Kylie was particularly impressed with the master bath. It had been remodeled in just the last year with a bidet, artisan-made stainless-steel double sinks, and a huge, enclosed, multi-head shower. "They took out the tub to make room for that shower," Blair informed them. "They needed the big size to wash the dogs." She giggled and shrugged her shoulders. "Hollywood."

Nick's eyes grew wide, and he gave Blair the "cut" sign. "Don't even get her started on dogs! That's the only reason she wants a house."

"Is it really?" Blair asked, turning to Kylie. "I had no idea."

"Well, I usually keep my secret desires secret," she said, wrapping her hands playfully around Nick's neck. "Some therapist."

"I'm not *your* therapist," he joked, giving her a one-armed hug. "I can gossip about you all I want."

"We always had dogs when I was growing up, and I really miss having one. A house with an enclosed yard like this is just what I've needed."

"She'll be breeding them in the backyard in no time," Nick said.

"Yeah, this neighborhood is just the kinda place where a hand-lettered sign in the front yard announcing 'Free puppies' would be very much appreciated," Kylie said, laughing heartily.

"The neighbors would hang you—and I don't mean in effigy," Blair said. "We can revisit the dog issue later. Now it's time to look at my favorite element." She opened the sliding doors of the media room and watched as Kylie and Nick walked onto a long, deep, covered veranda.

"Good Lord," Kylie said, her smile growing. "Why do you need a house when you have such a beautiful space?"

"I love the veranda, too," Blair said, "but this play area is a real work of art. Obviously, you can have it all taken out..."

Kylie gave her an astonished look and said, "You must be mad! This is where Baby Spencer and I will while away our afternoons."

The built-in playground equipment was of a quality never seen in public parks. Blair commented, "He spent over $100,000 on this setup. There's almost a foot of shredded rubber under this surface. I don't think you'd kill yourself if you jumped from the top of the slide and landed on your head."

"Nice to know," Kylie said, obviously not paying attention. Her gaze was sweeping along the tall, spiky, native plants that nestled along the property line. In the rear corner of the yard stood a huge wooden doorway, which bisected the white stucco wall separating the residences.

"That's how they go back and forth between the houses," Blair indicated. "You'd obviously have that taken out and extend the stucco."

"Right. But it's such a nice door, I might leave it."

Blair smiled as she watched her friend. Then she caught Nick's eye and mimicked snapping her wrist and reeling in a fish. He laughed, covering his face so Kylie didn't see him. "The yard's nice, isn't it?" Blair asked, now standing next to her friend.

"Duh! Built-in gas grill, granite prep surface…uhm…some kinda stone deck."

"Arizona flagstone," Blair said. "And it's planted with curly thyme so you get a little cushioning as well as a nice scent when you walk on it."

"That's what that is!" Kylie said, her smile brightening. "I love details like that." She turned completely around, slowly taking in the property again.

"God is in the details," Blair said.

"I love it." Kylie turned to Nick and cocked her head. "Doctor Scott? Do you have an opinion?"

"Of course, I do. Do you want to hear it?"

"Yes, Nick," Kylie said, slightly exasperated.

He looked at Blair and winked. "Isn't it fun to torture her?"

"It's my favorite hobby," Blair agreed.

Kylie pursed her lips, but her eyes were still smiling. Nick said, "It's the nicest house I've ever seen, and I know you'll love it here." He turned towards the house and shook his head. "My mother always told me I'd regret not going to medical school. For once, she was right."

"You love your job," Kylie scoffed.

"Yeah, but I'd like your salary."

"Well, I like the women you get. Life's unfair."

"I don't mean to rush you, but I've gotta pee," Blair said.

Kylie grinned at her. "You know damned well that I'd buy this place if it were just the yard. The house is a bonus. A big damn bonus!"

Blair grabbed her arm and gave it a squeeze. "I knew you'd love it!"

"I just wish it had a pool. It'd bug my brothers more if it did."

"There's a pool," Blair said, scoffing ostentatiously. "Right this way." They walked to the side of the house where a long, narrow lap pool had been installed. It was tightly covered by an automatic pool cover, and Blair pointed to the surface and said to Nick, "Walk on it."

"Are you nuts?"

"No. Go ahead. You can't hurt it."

"You want me to break an expensive pool cover owned by one of the biggest action heroes in the world?"

"He's not a *real* action hero, Nick," she said, laughing. "He just plays one in the movies. If you break it, I'll pay to fix it."

Giving her a suspicious look, he stepped gingerly onto the surface, amazed when it barely moved under his one hundred ninety-five pounds. "There's no possible way for a child to get under that cover," Blair said. "He had it specially designed because his kids are very…oh, shall we say…inventive?"

"I've gotta have this place. It's absolutely perfect. I just have to make one call," Kylie said. She took her cell phone off the waistband of her jeans and hit a speed dial number. "Alan? It's your baby sister." She paused for a second and said, "Yes, it's Doctor Baby Sister. Listen, I need some help. I found a house I want to buy, but I have to make an offer today. If I fax you the contract, will you take a look at it for me?" Pausing again, she nodded. "Sure, I'll trade you a vasectomy for your opinion, if you don't mind having me take a scalpel to your…" She trailed off and then giggled. "It's not as effective to tell Mom on me anymore, Alan. Besides, she knows I routinely slice and dice on men's… All right, all right, I'll stop. I'll fax the stuff to your house, okay? Give my love to Annette and the kids."

Switching off, she gave Blair a broad grin and said, "Let's go to your office and buy me a house."

"Don't you want to know how much he's asking?"

The question hit Kylie like a bucket of ice water. She blinked as her mouth dropped open and then closed again. "I…I don't care how much it costs," she said, her voice rising into whine range. "I've gotta have it!"

"It's within your range," Blair said, drawing out the suspense.

"How much? Not that it matters. I'll start selling my body if I have to."

"A million six," Blair said, waiting for the reaction.

"I told you my range was up to a million five. Five's less than six."

"Yeah, yeah," Blair said. "What's $100,000 when you're up at this level? Besides, you pre-qualified for one and three quarters million. Quit whining." She turned towards the house, and Nick followed her.

Kylie lagged behind, shoving her hands in her pockets and sticking her lower lip out while mumbling, "I said a million five."

⟶

Kylie took pity on Nick, and rather than make him hang out for the rest of the afternoon, they dropped him off at his home before returning to the office. Watching him walk up the path to his condo, Blair said, "He's a very good catch. I wish I knew someone who was single and looking."

"I don't think he's looking," Kylie said. "He likes being single. He wants to get married some day, but he swears he won't be tied down until he's forty."

"How old is he?"

"Thirty-five."

"Mmm…my age." Blair nodded, watching his butt when he climbed the stairs. "Dark-blond hair, slightly curly. Such a nice face. Great jaw. I love a man with a good jaw, don't you?" she asked wistfully.

"Oh, yeah. I never date a man without a good jaw," Kylie said, her teasing answer ignored.

"Good body…nice, broad shoulders. Why do guys like him always want to wait to marry?"

"It's easy to say you're going to wait, but when the right one comes along, you forget all of your vows."

Blair turned and smiled at her friend. "He could make me want to forget my vows, but now probably isn't the best time to start cheating on my husband, is it?"

"Not ideal," Kylie agreed. "Timing is everything."

⌒

When they reached the office, Blair took out a standard offer form and poised her pen over the space where it read, "Offer price." "Okay," Blair said. "He's asking one million six, but he didn't say it was a 'take it or leave it' price. What do you feel comfortable offering?"

Kylie rubbed her face with her hands. "I hate stuff like this."

"What? Making decisions?"

"Nah. I don't mind making decisions. But I hate guessing what the other person wants. That's part of the reason I refuse to buy a new car."

Blair put her pen down and gazed at her friend for a moment. "I'm representing both you and the seller, so I can't tell you things I might know about his price. But you're my friend and I don't want you to overpay."

"But what's overpaying?"

"Overpaying is paying one dollar more than you think it's worth. In my experience, both the seller and the buyer are happy if they negotiate a little…but just a little."

Kylie cocked her head, staring into Blair's eyes. Her own lips were slightly pursed, and she looked as if she were trying to read Blair's mind. "Put down one million four. If he refuses, I'll hang myself. But I think I'd be pissed at myself for offering the asking price."

Without showing a glint of emotion, Blair wrote the number on the contract. "Done," she said.

Showing a little insecurity, Kylie said, "Would you tell me if you thought I was gonna ruin this?"

Blair gazed at her thoughtfully. "Probably. But if you offered something ridiculous, like a million flat, I might not. That would show me that you were going to be difficult, and I'd rather have him tell you that." She smiled, showing her teeth. "I'd rather have you mad at him than at me."

"So!" Kylie said triumphantly. "You don't think I'm gonna ruin it."

"Not necessarily. He might tell you to take a hike." She put her head down and filled in a few lines of the contract. "But given my hormones, I'd probably be ticked off if I was sure you were wasting our time." She looked up and gave Kylie a big smile. "Do I look pissed off?"

Kylie leaned over and gave her a hug. "I really like you, Blair. You're a darned good egg."

⟶

It took much longer than Kylie thought it would, but at 9:00, Blair reached over, shook her friend's hand weakly, and let her head drop to her desk. "You've got yourself a house, Doc."

"Fantastic!" Kylie looked remarkably fresh, given the long day of ups and downs. "I'm really happy to have gotten it for the exact price I was willing to pay. I'm just bummed about one thing," she mused. "It's kind of a shame to have his attorney sign the papers. I wanted to have his signature. If the house loses value, I thought I could sell the contract."

"That house won't lose value," Blair assured her. "Actually, I'm sure I could have sold it for a couple of hundred thousand more."

Kylie blinked at her and said, "But…that's money out of your pocket—and his!"

"It's worth it to him not to have to deal with people. He doesn't want a bunch of strangers trooping through his house. Heck, he doesn't want people to know he lives in L.A. Selling the house in an afternoon is worth a lot to him."

"But what about you? You get a percentage of the sale. Selling for less than the max comes out of your pocket."

"Look," Blair said, her tone businesslike, "I know what I'm doing. Now that you've bought the smaller nanny's house, he'll *have* to sell the main one and buy another. My guess is that I'll sell him at least $10 million worth of real estate this year. Given that I make anywhere from 2 to 4 percent…" She waved her hand dismissively. "I'm not crying over the commission on a couple hundred grand."

"But if you know you have clients who'd pay more—"

"Kylie, I called you first; then I called every client I thought might be interested. If any of them had been ready to bite, I would have stuck them in the car with you and let you fight it out."

"You would have?"

"Sure. I'd never harm my seller's potential profit. But I also know him pretty well. He wanted to get things done in a hurry. I knew you trusted me enough to believe me when I told you that a geological survey wasn't necessary. Most of my other clients would have wanted to dicker around with things like that, and the seller hates that crap. He wanted a quick deal, and I knew you'd be decisive."

"Damn! You're really good at this," Kylie said, her admiration evident. "And you must make a shitload of money if you get 2 to 4 percent!"

"Well, last year, you beat me, but two years ago, I made more than you did," she snickered. "Don't forget, I've seen your mortgage application."

"I went to school for seven years and worked for almost nothing for another seven to be able to make this kind of money!"

"I took a two-month-long evening school course to get my license," Blair said, getting up and doing a little satisfaction dance. "I don't even need my high school diploma! Who's the smart one? Nah-nah-nah-nah-nah-nah!"

"You are," Kylie agreed, laughing. "Without question, you are." As they left the deserted office, Kylie draped an arm around her friend's shoulders. "But I do get to play with knives."

～

The next night, Blair was at home when David arrived. She was out in their yard, half reclined on a chaise. She wasn't reading or listening to music, and she looked like she was asleep. But when he slid the glass door open, she turned around and greeted him.

"I thought you were asleep." He walked over to her and sat on the edge of her chair. "Whatcha doin'?"

"Nothin'." She put a hand on his shoulder and pulled him down for a kiss. "I've been sitting here letting myself feel good."

"Is that something you do…often?"

She smiled at his puzzled expression. "No, honey. I'm usually filling my mind with something every minute. But having this baby is making me slow down—a lot."

He ran his fingers through her hair, smiling when she leaned into his hand like a happy puppy. "It makes you tired, too. That must be hard for you. You're such a high-energy woman."

Smiling languidly, she said, "I've gotten used to it. Actually, I've grown to like it. I'm slowing down and trying to appreciate every day."

"Are you reading those Oprah books? You're sounding awfully touchy-feely."

"Maybe I am. But Oprah isn't influencing me. Being pregnant makes me feel different. It's hard to describe, but it's very different."

"Try," he said, cocking his head and giving her an inquisitive look. "I wanna know."

Blair sat up excitedly and put her hands on his knees. "I'm so glad you want to know things like this."

He frowned at her, looking irritated. "Of course, I want to know. Damn, you make it sound like I don't care about you."

"I never thought that, honey. I know you care about me, but you don't ask many questions about the baby."

"I'm asking now," he said, his expression softening.

"You're right. Okay…how do I explain this?" She thought for a minute and said, "Some of the pregnancy books say that a lot of women get depressed when their hormones start going wild. But it feels like the exact opposite to me. I feel…I guess the word is euphoric. Yeah," she said, nodding, "that's it. I feel euphoric. Like everything is good and the baby's healthy and we're in love and the world's a kind, gentle place."

"Damn, I wish I could get pregnant," he said. "I think everyone's evil; some people just haven't shown it yet."

She rubbed his close-cropped hair briskly, making him laugh. "You're not that cynical."

"No, I'm not that bad, but you and I used to have the same worldview. How am I gonna handle being with an optimist?"

"Oh, this too shall pass," she said. "I'll be back to my old self one of these days."

He leaned over, kissed her again, and then held her head still and started to probe her mouth with his tongue. "I like happy Blair."

"Happy, horny Blair," she said, giving him a sultry kiss.

"I like horny Blair, too. Although you've always been pretty willing to be my love slave."

She put her hands up over her head and crossed her wrists. "I'm yours," she said, her swollen breasts showing through her thin tank top.

His eyes narrowed, and she could see him take in a breath. "Right here?" he asked, his voice deep and smoky.

"Anywhere, David. Anywhere you want me."

In a flash, his tie, his shirt, and his pants were tossed onto a spare chair. He moved another chaise next to Blair's and stripped off his briefs. She watched him closely, loving the way his angular, smoothly muscled body moved. "You look hot in your snuggies," she said. "I'm glad you've changed back."

He put the back of her chaise down flat and then slipped off her loose shorts. Kneeling down, he put one leg between hers and the other on the second chaise. She reached out and touched him, moving her hand from his knee to his chest. Then she wet a finger and traced one of his nipples, watching the hair on his arms stand up in reaction. "Let's frighten the neighbors, David. Make them think we've brought two wild dogs into the yard." Lowering himself onto her body, he tried to get comfortable, but found himself worried about hurting her. "Hey," she soothed, "what's wrong?"

"I don't want to lie on your stomach."

"It's okay, David. You can't hurt the baby. He's very well protected."

He didn't look convinced, and after fidgeting for another few moments, he stood up and tossed one of the cushions on the ground. "If we're gonna growl like dogs, we may as well lie on the ground."

She nodded and got up. He put her cushion next to his, making a thin, but wide bed. Blair reached up to take off her tank top, and he stilled her hands. "Leave it on," he said, huskily. "You look like you're gonna pop out of it any minute." At her raised eyebrow, he added, "It's hot."

Getting back into the mood quickly, Blair soon found herself on her hands and knees, with David stroking her ass and hips with his hands. "Damn, you look great. Such a sexy ass."

She twitched her butt at him, and he growled and started to kiss her everywhere. They made love, their tall privacy fence screening out any prying eyes.

Twenty minutes later, Blair lay on her side, David plastered up against her back. He was sweating and panting, his chest moving rapidly against her. "Animal control should be here at any time," he rasped out.

"Mmm…that was some fine lovemaking." She reached back to pat his hip. "We don't do it that way very often."

"If we want the neighbors to think we have dogs, we have to do it doggy-style," he said, laughing.

"I like variety. But you have to work extra hard when I'm on my hands and knees. I can't help much."

He kissed a line across her shoulders, his warm breath making her sigh. "You come so easily now. I don't need much help."

"You've never needed much help. You've always known just how to touch me."

"I do my best."

"You just keep thinking of new tricks, Mr. Spencer. You're the idea man around here."

"I've got one now," he mumbled. "Sleep?"

"Sure." She turned over and put her head against David's chest, listening to his heart calm to a slow, steady beat.

"Mmm…remember my mother's coming over tonight. She won't be here till 6:00, though."

"Fuck!" Blair was upright immediately. "I forgot! I don't have any food in the house."

"We can order out," he said lazily. "Lie down with me and cuddle. Since I can't smoke, it's the least you can do. God knows how I loved to have a cigarette after sex."

"You're mad," she said, getting to her knees and then standing. "Besides, you're still smoking."

"I'm down to ten a day. That's progress."

"Yeah, it is. You can rest as a reward. I'll shower and pick up the newspapers lying all over the living room. And when you get up, you'd better check those cushions, buddy. Your mother likes to sit outside, and the thought of her sitting on our—"

"Got it," he said. "A tiny nap, and then I'll get right on it."

He was almost asleep by the time Blair reached the backdoor, but she didn't mind the inequity. It felt so nice to make love and be close that she decided to reward him with a long nap. *Even Sadie can't bring me down today*, she thought, her euphoric mood making her feel as if she were floating into the house.

⌒

Sadie arrived fifteen minutes early as she was prone to do. Blair was used to her mother-in-law's habits by now, however, and just assumed that she would always be early and figured that into the invitation.

The couple had decided to withhold the big news until Blair had visited the obstetrician, but now that she had, they were ready to make the announcement. Blair would have preferred to wait a while—like nine months—but she knew that wouldn't fly. She had called her own mother the moment she found out, but that seemed like a perk Eleanor was due.

"Sadie, how are you?" she asked, giving the older woman a kiss on both cheeks.

"Fine. I'm fine. The question is how are you?" Sadie was looking her over like a mare up for auction, and Blair was glad to feel David walk up behind her and interrupt.

"Hi, Mom." He kissed his mother and took her by the hand, leading her to a chair. "We've got good news."

"You're pregnant!" Sadie screamed.

"Yep, she is," David said, smiling as he hugged Blair.

Sadie was up in a flash, hugging each of them ferociously. "That's wonderful! Just wonderful! Oh, David, your father would have been so happy, God rest his soul. I wish he could be here today." She started to cry, and Blair went to get the tissue box, giving Sadie a moment alone with her son.

When she walked back into the room, David was holding his mother in his arms, both of them crying. She stopped and watched for a moment, her mind wandering. *I hope our baby loves us and shows affection as easily as David does. In that area, I hope our child is just like his daddy.*

Chapter Three

*T*wo weeks later, Blair sat in Monique's waiting room, making calls and updating her Palm Pilot to pass the time until the doctor returned to the office from her morning's delivery at the hospital. She normally refused to wait for a doctor who scheduled appointments poorly, but she understood that an obstetrician couldn't plan her day as carefully as many others could.

She was so tired that she considered stretching out on the all-too-comfortable leather loveseat and taking a nap. She started to fantasize about sleep, feeling her eyes close once again. *Oh, that's bad. Now I'm feeling a sexual tingle when I think of a big, fluffy bed. Times have changed. I used to have to imagine a big, hunky man in a bed to make my heart pound. Now the man's optional.*

When Monique's nurse called her in, Blair put on a gown and waited impatiently. No sooner had the door opened than she started in on her main complaint: "Does the baby actually grow in my bladder? Should you take an x-ray or something just to check?"

Smiling at her patient's hyperbole, Doctor Jackson said, "Hi, Blair. How are things?"

"Good, except I'm tired—although that's not nearly a good enough word to describe my exhaustion—and I have to pee every thirty seconds."

Monique nodded. "Besides the fact that I'm sure the baby's in the right place, x-rays aren't a good idea right now." She patted Blair's shoulder and reminded her, "This is perfectly normal, and regrettably, it'll get worse as your pregnancy progresses. There isn't much you can do about it. You really need all of the water I've urged you to drink. This is one of those 'only seven and a half more months' kinda things."

"This date thing is strange. I know the exact moment that I was inseminated. It's been four weeks. Why am I supposed to say I'm six weeks pregnant?"

"You can *say* anything you want," Monique teased. "You can say you're sixty-six weeks pregnant, but we always count from the first day of your last period."

"Doesn't make sense." Blair's lips pursed. "I don't like it."

"Other than being unhappy with the nomenclature and being in just a tiny bit of a bad mood, is everything else all right?"

Laughing, Blair said, "Yep. I actually feel wonderful. I still have that euphoria thing going, and I feel sexy all the time. Life is pretty sweet. Now, if I could just stay awake to enjoy it…"

"No more cramps after sex?"

"Every once in a while, but I'm not worried about it now. It just feels like the cramps I used to get with my period. I figure that if I'm not bleeding, there's nothing to worry about."

"You're pretty calm, aren't ya?"

"Not usually," Blair admitted, "but I'm happy, and I know the baby's perfectly fine. I don't know how I know, but I know."

"I'm glad to hear that," Monique said, patting Blair's knee.

"It's funny. I must be growing less sensitive because I feel less pregnant than I did at first."

"Oh, you're more pregnant. Your body's just adjusting to the increased hormone levels." Monique laughed and said, "Don't complain about not noticing you're pregnant. Some women have a lot of reminders throughout the day."

"No, not me. I'm just tired and have a pea-sized bladder."

"I'm sure you know that being tired is a universal complaint, but are you getting enough rest to be able to function?"

"Yeah. I can't stay asleep for the entire night because of the peeing thing, so I take naps a lot. A *whole* lot. I go to my car and take a twenty-minute nap if I have to be in the office for long, and I fall asleep within five minutes of getting home at night. My husband has to throw me over his shoulder to get me into the dining room for dinner."

"Any chance of your husband coming in soon? I'd like to meet him."

Blair gave her an embarrassed smile and said, "He travels a lot, Monique. He wanted to come with me, but he's out of town again. He comes home tonight, but…"

"It's not a big deal. But if he has questions or concerns, urge him to come with you next time. Coming to your regular appointments will help him feel like he's involved."

⌒

That night, Blair stood in the kitchen, starting to prepare dinner for David. She was dreadfully tired, but she'd been slacking off so badly that she felt she needed to prepare a meal at least once a week. Just as she put some broccoli in the steamer, her stomach decided that the smell of the stuff was a very, very bad thing. She ran past David so quickly that his newspaper folded over from the air current. "Hey, where's the fi—?" he started to ask, but his question was answered when Blair reached the guest bathroom and begin to retch violently.

"Are you all right?" he asked quietly a minute later, barely sticking his head into the room.

She was sprawled out on the floor, leaning heavily against the toilet, waiting for another attack. Evil Blair, as she had taken to calling her hormone-ravaged self, wanted to ask him if it was possible to come up with a stupider question, but she wisely bit her tongue. *If you die, you'll need him to call your parents. Don't piss him off.* "I'll be fine," she mumbled. "Just a little morning sickness."

"But it's six in the evening," he said reasonably, yelping as a forcefully thrown wicker wastebasket caught him square in the chest.

⌐

"Hey, Kylie, it's Blair. We need to get together and talk about getting your condo sold. Let me know what's good for you. Oh, and would you mind hooking me up to an IV? 'Cause I'm never going to put another thing in my poor stomach, and I'm gonna need some form of nourishment."

Kylie didn't get back to her until nearly 5:00. "Sorry for the delay," the doctor said, sounding exhausted. "I've been in surgery since seven this morning."

"Working on one person?"

"No, I had two procedures of my own, and I was ready to leave the hospital when I got called over to UCLA to assist on some poor soul who…" She paused and said, "Given the comment about an IV, I'm gonna assume you have morning sickness."

Blair's tone sharpened, and she said, "That term is intentionally misleading and should be abandoned by all who fear for their lives, but, yes, I do. Why do you ask?"

"Because I just realized that you won't want to hear how I spent my afternoon. Let's change the subject, okay?"

"I'm not that fragile."

"Trust me on this one," Kylie said, her tone serious. "Anyway, all I've had to eat is a protein bar between procedures. I'm nearly faint from hunger. Wanna talk over dinner?"

"I can't risk it, Kylie. The smell of food being cooked is lethal."

"Okay, how about this? I'll stop and pick something up, and you and I can walk down to the ocean and eat at a picnic table. You should start going for walks every day, anyway."

"Are you sure? You could just stop and eat and then meet me later."

"No, I'd rather make sure you have something in your stomach. I have a feeling you're going to need to be closely monitored by a doctor during your pregnancy," she joked. "Do you have casual shoes?"

"Sure do. I'm just doing paperwork today, so I'm in my jeans. I can't button the top button, by the way, which makes me even grouchier."

"I can handle you," Kylie said. "Anything in particular you can't bear the thought of?"

"The list of things I *can* tolerate is much shorter. So far, that's only animal crackers."

"Oh, you *are* going to need supervision. I'll be there in an hour. Do you mind if I don't stop to change?"

"Nope. Come as you are, Doc."

⌐

A little over an hour later, Kylie arrived, carrying a shopping bag, which Blair fervently hoped contained nothing but animal crackers. Taking a long look at the doctor—noting her indigo-blue scrubs, her haphazard hairstyle, and the bluish

74

smudges under her red-rimmed eyes—Blair commented, "I hope I don't look as bad as you do."

Giving her the same treatment, Kylie shook her head and said, "Hate to break it to you, but you look worse. You're not wearing Kabuki makeup, are you?"

"That wasn't even close to being funny. I'll have you know that I looked fairly decent until I heard the local news on the radio. Seems that a team of doctors at UCLA surgically reattached a man's penis this afternoon." The words had no sooner left her mouth than she leapt to her feet and flew to the restroom, leaving Kylie to gaze after her sympathetically.

When Blair returned, looking even worse, Kylie said, "I told you it wasn't something you'd want to hear."

"Well, when you figure out how to filter the newscasts, let me know. I think I'm gonna start listening to one of the Spanish stations. At least I won't understand most of what they say."

With a tired smile, Kylie asked, "Did they mention my name on the news? I'd love to be famous."

"Not unless you've changed your name to 'team of doctors.'" Giving Kylie a nervous glance, she asked, "Those aren't the scrubs you wore while you were operating, are they?"

"God, no! Those were covered with…uhm…candy!" she said, grinning goofily. "I…uhm…had a big box of chocolate, and you know what a pig I am when I eat, and I—"

Blair placed a hand over her friend's mouth and said, "I appreciate the attempt to avoid the word *blood*, but you're starting to sound like a fucking lunatic!" She took a portfolio from her desk and clipped her cell phone to her waistband. "Let's go. I need some fresh air." Once outside, she asked, "Now that I have absolutely nothing in my stomach, tell me about your surgery."

"No, really, Blair, it's not something a woman with a balky tummy wants to hear about."

Blair stopped walking and placed a hand on her friend's arm. "The news report made this sound like a very big deal. I can't imagine you're not proud of what you did. I'd like to share that with you."

Giving her a charmingly shy grin, Kylie said, "I *am* pretty excited. Do you really want to hear about it?"

"I do."

"Okay," she said. "The media makes a bigger deal of this kind of thing than it really is. In a city of this size, there are body parts reattached all the time. It's only when it's a child or a…particularly kinky injury that the news picks up on it."

Blair gave her friend a hip bump and ordered, "Stop deprecating your work and tell me what happened."

"Okay, okay." Blair watched Kylie's face transform rather remarkably as the fatigue disappeared, replaced by a wave of enthusiasm that threatened to burst from her. "This guy had partially severed his penis with a circular saw. Luckily, if you can ever call a guy who cuts his penis half-off lucky, the cut was just behind the corona. He was fairly incoherent, but managed to say something about gym shorts and no underwear and...well, he was particularly gifted in the length department. I guess it just got in the way." She gave Blair a careful look and asked, "How ya doing?"

"Good," she said. "I'm focusing on your words and your excitement rather than the details."

"Great! Well, he cut just halfway through, and it was a fairly clean cut. Regrettably, he severed his urethra, and that's why they wanted me."

"You're the go-to guy for urethras?"

"Actually, there aren't many of us in L.A. who do microsurgery on the reproductive tract. I work on a lot of scrotums, but not that many penises. I'm usually working to reverse vasectomies rather than open up a urethra, 'cause that's not a common reason for infertility. Anyway, they had a couple of vascular surgeons and a plastic reconstruction surgeon who'd all been working for hours. The vascular guys could have done it, but they were toast by the time they called me in. So, I stitched up the urethra while a bunch of other people looked over my shoulder." She gave Blair a grin and added, "Surgeons love to kibitz behind your back while you're working. What an annoying bunch of people we are."

Blair was gazing at her with an expression bordering on awe. "I...I don't have any idea how you could possibly do something like that. How can you even see something so tiny?"

"With a microscope," she said. "I use a special microscope that makes everything appear pretty darned big."

"But it isn't big," Blair insisted. "It's tiny, and you have to go in there and sew it up with what I assume must be tiny, little instruments."

Kylie laughed softly. "Well, it's not like I use instruments from the Doctor Barbie collection. My tools have normal-sized handles. They just have really teeny blades. It's pretty cool."

They were waiting at a stoplight, and Blair took Kylie's free hand and examined it curiously, saying, "I know I tease you about what you do, but I have a tremendous amount of respect for you. These are such talented hands." She released her friend and tucked her own hand around Kylie's arm. "I'm proud to know you."

Walking the rest of the way in silence, Kylie seemed deep in thought. Just before they crossed Ocean Avenue, she said, "Every once in a while, I step back and consider what an impact my work can have on people. Like when a couple gets pregnant after years of trying and they take the time to let me know. But honestly, I don't get a lot of feedback. I clean out a pair of fallopian tubes, and after a brief follow-up visit, I never see the woman again. Doing something like I did today is really rewarding."

"You did good, Doc." Blair smiled up at her friend. "You're one hell of a 'team of doctors.'"

⟿

"You know, you did pretty well for yourself in picking this food," Blair commented a while later. "How'd you get so smart?"

"Just an educated guess. When my stomach's queasy, I prefer cold foods to hot and vegetables and starches to animal products."

"You eat pretty well most of the time, don't you?" Blair noted. "I don't think I've ever seen you eat junk."

"Yeah, I do eat pretty healthily. Since I'm on my feet all day, I like to stay lean to put as little stress on my legs and feet as possible. I don't exercise, so eating well is the only way to do it."

"You don't exercise? At all?"

"As little as possible. That's part of the reason I want a dog. If I get into the habit of walking a dog, I'll at least get my heart pumping a little bit."

"Well, we'd better get you into that house quickly! I want that heart to keep pumping."

"I'm ready to go," Kylie agreed. "Can you sell my condo?"

"Well, condos are a little beneath me," she sniffed, "but I'll make an exception for you. Actually, I think I have someone who'd like it."

"Already? I don't even know how much to ask for it."

"I do," Blair said, giving her a small scowl. "One of my team members sells condos, and she loves your building. She tells me that your unit is worth about $450,000."

Kylie's eyes widened. "I paid $150,000!"

"One fifty, huh?" Blair's eyebrows knit together briefly. "You bought it in...'89 or '90."

"How did you know? My parents bought it for me when I came out here for med school. I had to pay them back, of course, but they let me slide until I started to practice."

"I sold condos when I started out. I know the market backwards and forwards."

"So it would seem."

"Here's the straight scoop: I think Mandy is right, and your place is worth about four fifty. But that doesn't mean that's all you can get for it. We might be able to squeeze out a few thousand more. If you want to, we'll list it, have Sunday open houses, and show it to every potential condo buyer on the Westside. I don't mind doing the work, Kylie. But if that doesn't appeal to you, Mandy will buy it for four fifty, if you can afford to carry a little paper."

"How much is a little, and where do I have to carry it?" Kylie asked, wrinkling her nose.

Blair gave her a playful punch, something she did often with the mischievous doctor. "Mandy qualifies for a $400,000 loan. So, if you could carry a $50,000 note for say...five years, she'd either be able to refinance to pay you off or sell the place. My guess is she'll want to sell within five years, anyway. She and her boyfriend are going to get married when he's finished dental school, and they'll probably outgrow your condo."

"I'd much prefer to get this over with," Kylie decided. "I don't want to have to keep the place pristine and clear out every time you want to show it. I can easily carry a $50,000 note. Actually, I can go higher if she needs it. I assume she's a good risk?"

Scowling, Blair said, "Would I ask you to make her a loan if she weren't?"

"No. I'm a little slow today. My brain's still back in the operating room."

"That makes sense," Blair said. "Not to worry. I have my broker's license, and in the five years I've worked for this company, I've never asked them to let me broker a property on my own. So, I told them that I wanted to broker yours. After a little moaning and whining, the owner of the company gave in. So, you, my friend, are going to save 6 percent. No commission."

"No way, Blair! I wouldn't dream of taking advantage of you like that."

"You wouldn't be taking advantage of me, Kylie." Blair's face grew serious as she said, "I don't let people take advantage of me, and I sure as hell don't volunteer for it."

"But this is how you make your living. You deserve to be compensated for it."

"I agree, but I also don't want to take advantage of you. On a $450,000 sale, the usual commission is $27,000. So far, I've had two short conversations about this house—one with Mandy and this one with you. Is that worth $27,000?"

"Yes," Kylie said decisively. "If that's what you normally make when you sell a house of that value, then it most certainly is."

"Look," Blair patiently explained, "I want you to buy the new house. I want to make sure your old house sells because if you pull out of the deal, I stand to lose a lot more than $27,000. I'm not going to take your money, so if you won't agree, I'll just let the firm broker your condo. The owner of the firm will get $13,500 for doing nothing, and Mandy will get the rest. If you're gonna do that, you might as well drop the price of the place by ten thousand. It'll save Mandy money since she won't have to pay income tax on the commission." She shrugged and added, "Seems dumb to me, but that's the way to do it."

"I'm not comfortable with this," Kylie said. "I'm not even sure why, but it feels like someone's getting screwed."

Blair pursed her lips and thought for a minute. "Okay, how about this? Give Mandy your refrigerator and your stackable washer-dryer. That stackable will be wrong for your new house, and you'll already have a built-in Sub-Zero refrigerator. In return for that, Mandy will do all of the paperwork, relieving me of doing anything at all."

Giving her a warm, affectionate smile, Kylie shook her head briefly. "I've said it before, but I'll say it again: you're good at this."

"Sure am."

"I love hanging out with people who're good at what they do."

"Me, too. And if I ever get my penis cut off in an industrial accident, you're the first one I'll call."

⁓

The next night, Blair curled up next to her husband on the couch. "You busy?" she asked.

"Not too busy for you." He put down the book he was reading, took a healthy sip of his Scotch, and gave her a warm smile. "What's up?"

"I wanna talk about ultrasound."

"I don't think I have much to contribute to that topic, honey. I'm not even sure what an ultrasound is."

"You would if you'd read some of the books Kylie gave us."

"I have to read so much for work," he complained. "I keep trying to read your books on the weekend, but the time…"

"I know, but that's not what I want to talk about. When I saw the doctor, she said that she'd be happy to perform an ultrasound during my next visit."

"Uh-huh," he said, nodding for her to continue.

"I don't think I want one yet, but I'm willing to have one if you think I should."

"Me?" He looked at her as if she were a complete stranger sitting next to him on a bus.

"Yeah, you. Who else would I discuss these things with?"

"Well…me. But I don't know what we're talking about, so how can I help?"

"An ultrasound is just a test where they bounce sound waves off my belly and get a grainy picture of the baby. I'm sure you've seen them before."

"Oh! Yeah, guys at work have had them. I know what you mean."

She tickled under his chin, making him giggle. "Such a smart boy." She climbed onto his lap and tucked her arms around him, savoring the faint, musky smell of his body. "Doctor Jackson wants to do one during the second trimester, but it's up to me if I want to have one earlier."

"Is it dangerous?"

"No, they don't think so, but it's a little inconvenient. Most doctors do them in the office, but Doctor Jackson uses a specialist for them. I'd have to have it done at the hospital."

"What's the purpose?"

"At this point, I think they'd only be able to see if something was horribly wrong. The baby's still too small for them to be able to discern much detail."

He shifted, wrapping his arms tightly around her body. "Are you worried?"

"No, not really. I'm not much of a worrier about things I can't control, and for some reason, I'm sure the baby's healthy. It's just a feeling I have."

"Your feelings are usually pretty accurate," David said. "I think you should stick to your first instinct and not have it done."

She looked a little embarrassed and admitted, "I know I'm being a little weird about this, but I don't want to disturb the baby."

"Disturb?" David asked, giving her a look that showed just how little he understood her point.

Wriggling a little on his lap, she said, "I told you it was weird, but I think the baby deserves privacy. I don't want to be bouncing sound waves off his or her house if I don't have to."

"I think that's cute," he said, giving her a fond smile. "Very cute."

"You won't mind having to wait to carry around a tiny, indistinguishable picture in your wallet?"

"I can wait," he said, kissing her on the lips. "You know what I can't wait for?"

"No, baby. What?"

"I can't wait to lie down next to you and touch you. You look so pretty tonight." He caressed her cheek with the tips of his fingers, smiling when she shivered. "You're so sensitive...so beautiful."

She drew his head forward and kissed him, lingering for a long time. Luckily, her newly sensitive nose barely noticed the smell of pepperoni pizza and Scotch on his breath, but the lingering odor of his last cigarette made her stomach turn. "Honey," she said, looking him in the eyes, "you're gonna have to stop smoking, or we're gonna have to stop kissing. I can't bear the smell."

He looked like he wanted to argue, but after a pause, he nodded. "I'm trying. I really am. But I've been smoking since I was sixteen."

"I know you're trying," she said, alternately stroking his cheek and outlining the dark stubble with her finger. "But you're gonna have to quit if you want to be close. I can smell it on your breath when you face me in bed."

"Okay," he said, blanching a little at the thought. "I'll stop on Monday morning so that I have one last weekend to indulge."

"All right," she said. "But don't even think about kissing me until you purge yourself of the smell."

"How about your neck?" he asked, kissing all over her sensitive skin.

She slapped at him, giggling the whole time. "You know that tickles!"

"I've gotta kiss you somewhere."

"Top of my head?"

"Oh, that's sexy."

"Motivation, baby. You need the proper motivation. When the smell of smoke leaves, my lips come back."

"If anything will motivate me, that will," David said, kissing his wife on the top of her blonde head.

⟶

A week later, Kylie went to Blair's office around lunchtime to sign some papers concerning the sale of her condo. The always-perky receptionist smiled at her and held up a finger when the phone rang. "Potter, Higgins, and Hale... Yes, he's in. I'll put you through." She smiled up at Kylie and said, "Blair's waiting for you. Go on back."

Kylie knocked softly and opened her friend's door, smiling when she saw Blair with her shoes off and her feet propped up on the open bottom drawer of her desk. "Close the door, will you?" she requested. "Clients are always walking by, and I don't want them to see my tootsies."

They took care of business quickly, and Kylie turned the conversation to personal matters. "You mentioned you're alone all week. Where's David?"

"I think he's in Cincinnati...no, wait...Cleveland. Yeah. Cleveland...I think."

"Has he always traveled so much?"

"Yep. His busiest times are April and May and again from October to December. Most financial institutions have a year-end in either June or December, so he hits the road to do a lot of legwork before they close the books. It's good that he's traveling now since he can provide me with my fix."

"What's that? Tiny bags of peanuts?"

"Unh-uh. Barf bags."

"Are you serious?"

"Sure am. I told him not to bother coming home if he can't steal me at least a dozen of 'em."

"But why would you want to use a bag?"

"Because I can't spend the day cleaning the toilet at work," she said, grimacing. "The mere thought of putting my face near the spot where everybody else has had his ass makes me retch. Plus, I drive around a lot during the day, and I'm not going to stick my head out the window of my car. The last time I did that was in high school when I had too much cheap wine." She laughed. "David thinks I'm mad, but I make him clean the toilet every time he uses it. I caught him peeing in the bathroom sink last night, just so he didn't have to get the scrub brush out again."

"The thought of *that* makes me retch," Kylie said, wrinkling her nose. "I'll never use your bathroom again."

"He's been properly chastised," Blair assured her. "He's been banished to the guest bath."

"Uhm, isn't that the bathroom *I* use when I visit?"

Blair nodded, trying to hide her smirk. "Better go at home."

"I think I will. So, how *are* things at home?"

Blair shrugged and said, "David's doing his best, so I'm trying to be patient with him. He's clueless about pregnancy in general, and I have to explain every little thing. If I didn't know how bright he was, I would think I'd married a moron!"

"Oh, right, he's an only child. He probably hasn't been around a lot of babies."

"I don't think he's ever held one!"

"He's gonna have fun the first few weeks." Kylie laughed. "You'd better make sure he has supervision until he gets comfortable."

"If my mood doesn't stabilize, I'm gonna be divorced by then! Either I'm the happiest woman on Earth, or I snap at him for tiny things. I'm really trying not to, but sometimes, I can't control myself."

"It's gotta be hard. Some of the most placid women I know become tigers when they're pregnant."

"I've never been one of those wives who bitches her husband out about everything, but I can see how you might get into that habit during pregnancy. Sometimes, I feel like I've got a baby inside of me and another one sitting in a chair in the living room."

"What do you need from him? Is there anything I can do?"

Blair smiled and reached across the desk to pat her friend's arm. "No, it's pretty husbandy stuff. For example, I'd like it if he'd make dinner, so I didn't have to smell it. But his response is that we should get carryouts."

Frowning, Kylie said, "Maybe he doesn't want to cook after a long day at the office."

"You're right; he doesn't. But I don't want to eat pizza and burgers and all of that junk food. I'm not asking for a lot. I just want some wild rice or pasta or a baked potato. Nothing fancy."

Giving her a very serious look, Kylie asked, "Are you eating right? 'Cause if you're not, I'm going to start bringing you dinner every night."

"I think I am. I'm eating yogurt, fresh and dried fruits, and some raw carrots during the day just to keep a little something in my stomach. Then I have starches and grains in the evening. I get sick in the evening more than the morning, and having a plain baked potato or something like that helps. Then I munch on dry cereal if I need something before bed."

"That sounds okay if it's all you can manage. You'll be fine if you just eat cereal for a few weeks, but you'd better be taking your pregnancy vitamins if you're not getting a balanced diet."

"Pregnancy vitamins," Blair scoffed. "Who invented those horse pills? They're huge!"

"I know, but you need some of those vitamins at this stage of your pregnancy. It's also a good idea to try to work in a little protein. Can you handle some cheese and crackers?"

"Maybe," she said. "But cheese doesn't sound very good these days."

"Keep tinkering. I think you're doing pretty well for a woman who's having morning sickness."

"Thanks for caring," Blair said quietly.

Something about her tone made Kylie ask, "Do you think that David doesn't care?"

Blair shook her head. "No, I'm sure he does. He just isn't showing it as much as I want him to. He never asks me what I'm eating." She smiled wistfully and said, "I had this fantasy about how involved he'd be, and it's not turning out that way. He doesn't even get out of his chair when I'm in the bathroom, retching my guts out. If I'm loud enough, he looks up from what he's reading and asks, 'You all right?'"

"Maybe he's just not that kinda guy. Some people are better at comforting than others."

"But he used to be good at it. Before, when I was sick, he'd call me so often that I couldn't get any rest. He was very connected to me physically, and now he's…not. That's what has me stumped."

"You both have a lot of adjustments to make," Kylie said, "but I'm concerned about you. When does he come home?"

"Friday."

"Okay, for the next three nights, I'm either making dinner at your house, or you're coming to mine. I'm confident I can tempt your tender taste buds."

"Kylie, you don't have to do that," she said, making a face.

"I know I don't; I want to. I have to make sure Baby Spencer has nice strong bones so we can play on my swing set together. I have completely selfish motives."

"Don't you have plans?"

"Just for Thursday. Nick and I are going to the symphony. But we don't leave until 7:30, so I have plenty of time to get you fed."

"Okay, I know when I'm beat. My house tonight?"

"It's a deal. Just clean the bathroom sink before I get there—twice!"

Late Friday afternoon, Blair came into the house not long after David had arrived. She was pleased to see him dash out of the bedroom, clad only in his shirt and loosened tie, pants and jacket missing. "Is that you?"

"Yeah," she said, trying to sound perky. "Welcome home."

He caught her as she was coming down the hall. While folding her into a hearty embrace, he kissed her head repeatedly. "I missed you so much. I was dreaming about you on the flight home."

"Were you really?" she asked, delighted by his affection and interest.

"Sure was. In my dream, you were wearing fishnet stockings and a black bustier. Really hot," he growled, wrestling with her a little.

"I don't think I have a bustier. You didn't buy me one at the airport, did you?" she asked, leaning back in David's arms and tapping his chin with her finger.

"No, they don't have those at the airport newsstands. You have that black satin tank-toppy thing with the thong…"

"Ew, honey, that would look downright nasty. The tank top fits too snugly, and I'm completely losing my waist. The thong might still work, though. Wanna try it?"

As she spoke, his smile dimmed and changed until it began to look forced. "Sure. That'd be fun. Let's go out and have some dinner first, though. I'm really famished."

She started to ask why his obvious ardor had cooled so quickly, but she decided to let it pass, hoping she could tempt him after dinner.

They settled on a small restaurant close to their house. Livorno had a few outside tables tucked up on a still-sunny deck, and they were there early enough to find one. To Blair's delight, a helping of mashed potatoes went down and stayed down, and she was able to eat several bites of David's roast chicken.

They talked about his trip, about the weather in Cleveland, and about how nice his hotel had been. She told him about having Kylie come over to cook for her and a few details of the house she was in the process of listing. It felt good to have things be so normal, and she felt remarkably happy that David was home. After dinner, they walked all the way to the ocean—a distance of almost two miles—while he told her of his travel plans for the remainder of the summer. They caught the sun just disappearing before turning for home.

On the way, Blair held on to David's arm with both her hands, leaning against his shoulder. "I'm so happy to have you home. Actually, I'm just plain happy."

"I'm happy, too," he said, smiling at her. He stopped and placed a tender kiss on her lips, saying, "Let's go to bed and have a little 'welcome home' party."

She looked at him for a moment, a smile on her face. "I don't know… Only nonsmokers can party with me."

"I don't know if I'm a nonsmoker," he said. "That sounds like a permanent kinda thing. But I didn't smoke when I was away. Not even one," he said, waving a solo finger at her.

"Oh, sweetie, I'm so proud of you." She hugged him tightly. "This means a lot to me, David. I know how hard this is for you."

"Oh, I think it's easier to quit smoking than it is to have to throw up half the day. I'm getting off easy."

"Speaking of easy, I think you could have me tonight...if you wanted to," she said, giving him her most overly dramatic, sexy look.

"Let's go," he said, his smile bright. "I've missed you, and I can't wait to see you naked. Very naked."

"Sounds good to me. As usual, I'm as horny as a toad."

"You say that like it's a bad thing. I say the more the better."

"Ooh...that's not gonna be true when it comes to buying new clothes." She made a face and said, "I did some window-shopping online, and the things I'm gonna have to buy are just hideous! The thought of wearing those massive pregnancy panties turns my stomach. It's gonna be tough for you, Mr. Sexy Lingerie."

He just nodded, his attention fixed upon a house that was being renovated.

They continued to walk, with Blair mildly chiding herself. *When are you ever gonna learn that men don't care about clothes? You're wasting your time trying to get him to care about the yucky things you have to buy, especially when his inner construction worker gets tweaked.*

When they arrived home, she was so tired she could hardly put one foot in front of the other. He helped her get undressed and stood behind her, holding her up while she brushed her teeth and muttered how she hated being so tired. Tucking her into bed, he bent to kiss her, and she mumbled, "We didn't get to play dress-up."

"No rush," he said, smoothing her hair. "Plenty of time for that."

She fell asleep as if she'd been clubbed, her last thoughts how patient and loving David had been and how much she'd missed him.

⌒

The next morning, David was up two hours before Blair was, and when she finally forced her eyes open, she called out, "David? Can you get me some Cheerios?"

"Sure, honey. Milk and sugar?"

"No. Just the box, please. I don't even need a spoon." He came into the bedroom wearing only a pair of briefs, carrying a box of Frosted Cheerios. "I need the plain ones, babe," she said as patiently as possible. "Those are yours."

"Oh." He looked from her to the box, saying, "You sure you want the plain ones? These are really good."

"I'm sure. Can you shake a leg, please? I can't sit up until I have something to eat, and I'm about to wet the bed."

He shrugged and went to get the proper box, returning with it moments later. Sitting next to her on the bed, he said, "I never thought you were going to get up. I was forced to make myself breakfast. I tried to make eggs like you do, but the first one had something weird sticking out of the yolk. Kinda like a tiny beak or something... Honey? Are you okay?" he called to her fleeing form.

She had to vomit into the wicker wastebasket, since she knew she'd pee all over the floor if she delayed another second. Putting the receptacle outside the door, she called out, "David, come get the wastebasket and throw it away, will you, please?" and closed the door again. She got into the shower and spent ten full minutes reminding herself that just because he wasn't sensitive to her dietary phobias didn't mean that he was the spawn of Satan.

Coming back into the bedroom, she saw him sitting on the bed, looking guilty. "Uhm, it was stupid to talk about the beaky eggs, wasn't it?"

With her eyes nearly popping from her head, she cried, "Don't you dare do that again!" She grabbed the Cheerios box and started shoveling handfuls of the cereal into her mouth. After getting enough in to calm the storm in her stomach, she sat down next to him. "Have you ever had a really horrid hangover?"

"Yeah, sure. Dozens of 'em."

"What's the worst one you ever had, and what were you drinking?"

"Senior year. Spring break. Rum punch," he said, grimacing in memory.

"Have you had rum since?"

"Nope. Never will, either. The mere thought of it..." He nodded, getting her point.

"When my stomach's upset—which is most of the time—almost any food is my equivalent of rum. I'm sorry to be such a baby, but this isn't fun for me, either. It should pass within a month or so, but these next weeks are going to be challenging, and I need some help from you."

"Okay," he said, nodding soberly. "What can I do?"

"You can be in charge of dinner. If you don't do it, Kylie will, and I don't think you want that."

"No," he said, laughing. "I'd rather be alone with you in the evening. But I'm such a lousy cook, baby. Doesn't it make more sense to get carryouts?"

"Yes, it makes sense, but no, I don't want that. You can bring home carryouts for yourself, David, but I need something blander than that most of the time. All I need for you to do is throw a package of wild rice in some boiling water or stick a potato in the microwave. You don't have to do a thing to it—just put it on a plate. I know it sounds crazy, but I can't be around food while it's cooking."

"But nobody wants to eat that," he argued. "Don't you need me to do something fancy to it? You used to make potatoes with that gooey cheese—" He clapped his hand over his mouth. "Shit, I almost did it again, didn't I?" he asked when he saw her widening eyes.

"You were on the edge of the cliff," she said, gobbling another scoop of cereal.

"I'm sorry," he said quietly. "I don't mean to be an idiot, but I don't get sick very often, and I forget what it's like."

"I know," she said, stroking his leg. "I know you're trying to be supportive."

"I need some remedial training," he said, smiling at her. "Treat me like a dog trying to learn a new trick. Repetition is the key."

"Damn," she yawned, "I haven't been up for a half-hour, and I need a nap. I'm gonna brush my teeth, pee an ounce, and go back to sleep." When she was finished, she lay down, and he lay next to her, letting her cuddle up to his chest. "Just a quick nap," she mumbled. "Don't let me sleep all day."

"Okay," he said, kissing her forehead. "I promise."

⟵

Blair opened her eyes and blinked for a moment, smiling once she saw David gazing at her. "You're so pretty when you sleep," he said. His fingers trailed along her cheek and then followed the planes of her face. "So pretty."

"C'mere, you handsome thing," she said. He placed a hand next to each of her shoulders and braced himself on his hands. They kissed for a long time, each of them trying to crank the heat up slowly. "I love Saturdays," she murmured.

He swept her hair away from her face and kissed her again. "Me, too. No rush, neither of us in a hurry…very, very nice."

Their eyes met, and she gazed at him for a long time. He looked at her with a question in his eyes, and she nodded slightly. His dark, soulful eyes blinked slowly, and she tilted her chin to be able to kiss his enviably long black eyelashes. The late-morning sun burnished his skin with golden hues, highlighting his olive coloring. She kissed the tip of his nose, thanking her lucky stars that he had inherited his father's straight, nicely shaped one. His eyes were deep set, and she liked to tickle around them with the tip of her tongue. The tiny cleft in his chin got the same attention, and he pulled back and smiled at her. "Love me?" he asked.

"Oh, yeah," she sighed. "I love you every day, but I love you best of all on the weekends. You're…more you when you haven't been at work."

"More me, huh? How would you like all of me…right now?"

"I can handle you, big talker. Let's see what you've got."

"Just lie there and let me have fun," he said. He started to undress her, rolling her onto one side and then the other. When he had her naked, he took his briefs off, put her on her side, and then got behind her. He lavished attention on her body, kissing her from the back of her neck all the way down her legs. "God, you've got a beautiful body," he mumbled. He continued to kiss and nibble on her pale skin, trying to elicit the soft moans she always uttered when he hit a sensitive spot.

"Come inside me," she said. "I'm so ready for you."

He was more than ready and urged her onto her belly. She gasped in surprise when he pushed one of her legs up and went into her from the rear. "Mmm…nice," she purred after a few seconds. "You've been watching porn in your hotel again, haven't you?"

"Nope." He latched on to her neck, sucked in a bit of skin, and bit lightly. "Don't need porn. Just need you."

⟵

The following Thursday, Nick wasn't able to make one of his regular Philharmonic dates with Kylie, so Blair stood in for him. "If I can swing it, I'd love to go with you guys next year," she said as they traveled down the Santa Monica Freeway in Kylie's ancient Honda Civic.

"Swing it?"

"Yeah. I'm not sure how we'll handle babysitting duties."

"If you don't mind a piece of unsolicited advice, it's important to do things you like once the baby's here. It's a big mistake to let him or her be the sole focus of your life."

"I know that—conceptually, at least. I'm just not sure how willing David is going to be to change his habits." She stretched a bit within the confines of her seatbelt and said, "Oh, well, we can afford a babysitter."

Kylie shot her a look. "You seem down today. Feeling puny?"

"No, I feel fine. I'm...I...oh, never mind. I'm sure you're sick of hearing me complain by now."

"Blair," Kylie gently chided, "you don't complain. We're friends, and you share things that are bothering you. I do the same thing with you."

"Not nearly as often," she grumbled, making a pouty face.

"Things are going really well for me right now," Kylie reminded her. "You should've heard me when Stacey and I were about to break up. Every day brought some new revelation of how incompatible we were. Nick was about to charge me by the hour just for having to put up with me."

"I doubt that. You're the most upbeat person I know."

"Not when things in my personal life are upsetting me. I'm a regular depressive. Now, tell me what's bothering you—if you want to, that is."

"Okay." Blair sighed and said, "Something's been bothering me, and today, it dawned on me that David must think I'm having puppies instead of a baby."

"I don't know what you're getting at, but if you do have puppies, I'll take one."

That comment earned a rather sharp slap to her leg. "I'll give you a puppy," Blair muttered.

"Come on; get to the point. I've never known you to beat around the bush."

"I'm a little embarrassed," she said quietly. "This is about sex, and I'm not sure how comfortable you are talking about it."

"I love to talk about it," Kylie said, grinning widely. "Lord knows I don't have it, so I might as well talk about it."

"Okay, but this is pretty personal."

"I operate on people's reproductive organs, Blair. I'm not squeamish about sex. Really."

Blair sighed again. "All right. It's bothering me, so it might help to talk about it."

"'Atta girl," Kylie said, giving her a smile.

"Here goes." Blair took in a deep breath and said, "We only have sex doggy-style ever since I started to show."

Kylie's lower lip jutted out, and her expression grew thoughtful. Blair was afraid that she was seeing her friend's discomfort, but soon realized that the doctor was merely giving the issue her full consideration. "That's not uncommon. Many pregnant women prefer that position. As you get bigger, you might find that's the only way he can even reach you. Side entry or rear entry are the only games in town in the third trimester."

"It's not my idea. It's his. I've never been a big fan."

Kylie shot her a look and blinked. "Oh, and you're not satisfied…"

Annoyed, Blair shook her head. "I knew this was gonna sound stupid. I *am* enjoying it. A lot. I get excited more easily now, and I reach orgasm more easily, too. I used to need to have a free hand, if you know what I mean, but I don't now."

Giving her a smile, Kylie said, "I'm the world's foremost expert in all of the intricacies of self-pleasuring. I know exactly what you mean."

"It's not that the position isn't good," Blair said, "and it isn't that I'm not satisfied. We've been having sex a lot, and we're enjoying it more than we have since before we started trying to get pregnant." She let out a final sigh and said, "One of the things that really connects us is sex. I hate to complain now that we're connecting again."

"But something's bothering you. What is it?"

"I don't think I'm imagining this, although God knows it's easy to hurt my feelings now." She looked out the window, knowing she was on the verge of tears, and tried desperately to fight the urge. After biting her lip for a moment, she said, "It feels like he doesn't want to face me while we're having sex."

"Oh, Blair, that can't be true!"

Blair felt some of her anger well up, and her voice shook. "This is a big change, and it doesn't seem like a coincidence to me."

"Maybe he's in a little rut. Maybe you did it that way one day, and it felt so good he doesn't want to change."

"Well, we did have a great time one day…" She shook her head and said, "No, that's not it. Damn it, he doesn't touch the front of my body, even during foreplay. He gets behind me in bed and caresses my back and my butt and my thighs, but his hands never gravitate to my breasts or belly. And before now, he was most decidedly a breast man. You'd think he'd be all over them since they're significantly bigger!"

"You'd think so," Kylie said slowly, looking puzzled. "Jesus, that's where I'd be living!" She paused for a moment. Then her mouth dropped open, and she quickly turned to Blair before looking at the road. "I can't believe I said that! I didn't mean it like it sounded!"

"Tell me how you meant it, and I'll tell you how it sounded," she said, giving her friend a puzzled gaze.

"I didn't mean I'd be on *yours*. I just…I'm very…" She blew out a breath that made her lips flutter noisily. "Okay, I guess I have to tell you more than you want to know to get myself out of this one." She took in a deliberate breath. "I think pregnant women are incredibly hot, and if my partner were pregnant, she'd probably need to get a restraining order to keep me off her." Kylie was blushing—a deep pink flush that colored her entire face and even took in the tips of her ears.

Blair giggled quietly. "Well, I guess we both revealed something personal tonight. Are you okay?"

"Uh-huh," Kylie said, clearing her throat. "I just don't want you to think that I think about you like that. I swear I don't."

"At this point, I'd welcome your attention. I love to have my breasts played with, but even more than that, I wanna look him in the eyes!"

"Damn, I wish I could help you out," Kylie said, giving her a lascivious look. "We could both get our needs met. I love breasts like bees love honey."

"Funny." Blair slapped her thigh. "It's really nothing to laugh at. I don't feel attractive anymore. David's always been so hot for my body. He's made me feel like the prettiest woman in the world. Now I feel…" She slumped down in her seat and put a hand on her belly. "I feel fat and frumpy."

Kylie glanced at her and then nodded her head slightly as if she'd made a decision. "I wouldn't normally say this to a friend, but I have to be honest with you. From a purely objective standpoint, you're an uncommonly beautiful woman. And you grow prettier each day." She reached over and placed a hand on Blair's knee, giving it a squeeze. "I mean that sincerely. You're prettier than the day I met you, and that's no easy feat. I think the changes in your body have added to your appeal—tremendously." She let out a nervous, obviously embarrassed giggle, sounding like a young girl caught doing something naughty.

Blair tapped her on the leg with the flat of her hand and then softly asked, "Would you mind writing that down and giving it to David? I'd love to hear that from him, even if it wasn't an original thought."

"Are you sure I didn't offend you? I'd never want to upset you."

"No, not at all. It'd make me uncomfortable if I thought I filled your fantasies, but I don't think that's true…is it?"

Kylie laughed, sounding relaxed and playful. "No, I'm complimenting you from a purely objective standpoint. I'm sure I *could* fantasize about you, but I'm pretty happy with my current stable of luscious beauties."

"You need to get a human girlfriend," Blair teased. "You'll never meet a woman as good as the ones in your fantasies."

"I'll make you a deal. I'll stop fantasizing about gorgeous women when you get me a date."

"I'm working on it," Blair said. "Just be patient."

"Patience isn't my thing. Get busy! If you don't get something going for me, I'm gonna have to start playing with your breasts."

"Promises, promises," Blair said, sticking her tongue out at her grinning friend.

❧

On the way home, Blair sat in the passenger seat, trying to control her temper. "I can't believe you let me do that!"

"I didn't *let* you do anything," Kylie said, trying to keep the edge out of her voice. "We've been over this four times already. The woman didn't mind. We made eye contact, and she gave me a signal to tell me not to wake you."

"Kylie, I slept on a woman's shoulder during the performance. I *drooled* on her!"

"She had on cotton," Kylie said, wincing when she heard how weak it sounded.

Blair slapped the doctor on the leg and said, "Don't ever let me do that again! It was mortifying!"

"I'm sorry. It just seemed like the prudent thing to do. She was a nice old lady. Heck, she said she'd had four kids of her own. She knew what it was like to be pregnant."

Taking in a deep breath, Blair tried to let her temper seep out. "I'm sorry for snapping at you. You didn't do anything wrong. I'm just lashing out." Giving her friend a contrite smile, she asked, "Forgive me?"

"You don't need to be forgiven. Remember, you get lots of leeway while you're pregnant. Just don't snap at me after the baby comes, or I'll cut you."

"And you could!" Blair said, a smile peeking out from her scowl.

—

When they reached the house, Blair looked at Kylie and asked, "Wanna come in?"

Kylie turned in her seat and asked, "For?"

"Just to talk. I'm...kinda lonely."

"Is David out of town?"

"No, but he's in bed by now." She looked away and said, "It's no big deal. Forget it."

"No, no." Kylie gave her friend a concerned look. "Let's go in and talk."

"Really?"

Blair looked about ten years old. Kylie had never seen the woman look so vulnerable or unsure and found herself nodding enthusiastically. "Really. I don't have a tough day planned for tomorrow, so I can stay up late."

"I'm not usually like this, but I don't feel like being alone tonight. I want you to come in, but only if you're sure you want to."

"I'm positive. Let's go."

They walked into the house, and Kylie noted that all of the lights were out. "David's asleep, huh?"

"Oh, yeah. He's never up this late."

Kylie looked at her watch. "Right. It's...gosh, almost 10:30." She smiled and asked, "How do you do it? It must have been quite an adjustment when he started going to bed so early."

"Want a drink?" Blair asked.

"Sure. Have any Scotch?"

"Uh-huh. That's David's drink. Single malt or blend?"

"I think I'll have a wee dram of your single malt. Neat."

Blair poured a couple of ounces of Glenmorangie into a rocks glass and handed it to the doctor. She led the way into the living room and immediately kicked off her shoes. "Now, you said something about having to adjust?"

Kylie took her shoes off as well and then sat on the couch, tucking her feet up under herself. "Yeah. Wasn't it hard when David went on this schedule?"

"No. It's always been this way."

"Really? How'd you date?"

"Oh. Well, he used to stay up later on Friday and Saturday nights since he didn't have to work the next day. But we never saw each other during the week. I didn't mind."

"Huh." Kylie scratched her head, looking as if she were going to speak, but instead, she stared at her drink for a moment and took a sip. "Good. Very good. David has good taste."

"Something's on your mind, Doc. Spill it."

"Oh, it's nothing. Really. I was just thinking how hard it would be for me to partner with someone if I didn't see her in the evenings."

Blair stuck her lower lip out and considered Kylie's comment. "I like having my own time. Always have. You're not like that?"

"God, no!" Kylie laughed at herself. "I'm a leech!"

"Oh, you are not," Blair said with a laugh. "You're very independent. I think you're a lot like me."

"Not by choice," Kylie said and then wished she could retract the comment when she saw her friend blink. "I mean, I'm not really very independent. I just have to entertain myself since I don't have anyone around much of the time. I don't like it. I don't choose it."

"Wow. That was one of the reasons I was drawn to David. I think the same is true for him."

Kylie took another sip and then asked, "Why were you attracted to David, if you don't mind my asking? I always like to hear what brings people together."

Blair stretched like a cat, arching her back and then shivering. "Mmm...I was attracted to a lot of things. He's very tactile...very affectionate. I like to sit in his lap and play with him. He's like my big doll."

Kylie smiled. "That's sweet."

"He is sweet. He's usually thoughtful and complimentary. And he's very nice to his mother. I like men who love their mothers. But what's kept us together is how well we get along. I don't think we've had three big fights since we've known each other. It's so nice to be with someone who doesn't irritate you very often."

Kylie blinked. "You never fight?"

"Not never, but not very often. Why would you fight with someone you love?" Blair's expression showed her confusion.

"Damn. Stacey and I fought all the time. The emotion was so high." Wrinkling her forehead, Kylie asked, "Don't you know what I mean?"

"Unh-uh. It's never been like that for us."

"Not even at first?"

"No. It's kinda like my parents. They never fight, either."

"How long have they been married?"

"Oh...forty-two years, I think."

Kylie nodded, her brow slightly furrowed. "What else do you love about David?"

Blair's smile looked a little suggestive as she said, "There's the obvious. We've always had a great sex life."

"But doesn't that calm down after a few years?"

"Not for us," Blair said, a note of pride in her voice. "I'm just as hot for him now as I was when we met. His actions show he feels the same…up until now, at least." She looked thoughtful for a moment and then said, "I'm pleased that we've never become an 'old married couple.' I think part of the reason we have such a good sex life is because we don't spend a lot of time together. It always feels fresh."

"How much time *do* you spend together?"

Blair thought over the question, counting on her fingers. "We see each other for two or three hours a day when he's in town, unless I have a client meeting. We always have our Saturday mornings together. That's our special time—no other plans allowed. But I work a lot of Saturday afternoons, so we don't count on that. We usually go out for dinner on Saturday night, and we spend Sundays together, unless I have to work. But David watches sports all day, and I hate sports, so I usually read or listen to music if I'm home while he watches his games."

Kylie sat patiently, waiting for more. When nothing more was forthcoming, she couldn't stop herself from asking, "That's it? You don't do anything together? No hobbies? No other interests that you share?"

"No. Not really. Why? Isn't that enough?"

"Well, it is if you like it that way, but that structure would never work for me. Gosh, when I first met Stacey I wanted to move in—to her body!"

"Oh, David's in my body a lot." Blair smiled contentedly.

"No, no, I wanted to be with her every minute. I was very attracted to her, and we had sex a lot, but I wanted to be with her…to *do* everything with her. Just watching her eat fascinated me."

"Ugh! I couldn't stand that," Blair said, the edges of her mouth pointing down. "I was so happy when I met a guy who didn't mind my having my own life. Most guys are so needy." She gave Kylie a guilty smile and said, "Of course, I practically begged you to come in tonight. I sounded like a guy who was completely desperate to get a woman into his apartment."

"Nah." Kylie smiled at her. "I like to be with you. It's never an imposition."

Blair stretched again, massaging her lower back with her hand. "So, what are you looking for, Doc? What's your dream girl like?"

"Mmm…I want to meet someone I'm rabidly attracted to and then proceed to study her, one inch at a time. I'd like to know someone inside and out and have her feel like a little something was missing if she didn't see me that day."

"I was never like that," Blair said. "Not in college, not in high school."

"I was worse before," Kylie admitted. "I tended to suffocate my lovers."

"Did you have to put a pillow over their faces to stop them from screaming for help?" Blair was quite amused by her own joke, and Kylie nodded her acknowledgment, but her usual smile was absent.

"I mean it," the doctor said. "I'm learning that I have to back off a little bit, and I think being alone for the past two years has helped me. It was hard for me to find my equilibrium after investing three years with Stacey, but I hope my next lover benefits from my burgeoning independence."

"But you're so smart, so introspective, so interested in things. Why do you need someone to be with you all the time? Isn't your own company enough for you?"

"I like to have people around me. I don't consider that a weakness. And it doesn't have to be *all* the time. I just want someone whose day brightens up when she sees me."

"Mine does," Blair said, smiling. "Does that count?"

"Of course, it counts. It doesn't get me laid, but it definitely counts."

"I'm gonna get you a date. I'm gonna find you a girlfriend just as good as the house I found for ya."

"You've got your work cut out for you, pal. That's one kick-ass house!"

⤙

Blair spent all of the next day assuring herself that all couples had some sexual miscommunication during pregnancy, reminding herself that they could get through anything if they were able to talk about it honestly. Thinking that it was best to discuss the issue outside of bed, she waited until they'd eaten dinner to allow time for her food to digest. It never had the chance to, though, and departed her belly not twenty minutes after she ate. When she was fairly sure her stomach was going to behave, she laced up her running shoes and said, "Let's go for a walk, okay?"

David looked like he wanted to refuse, but he turned off the television and took her hand. They walked through the quiet, residential streets of their neighborhood, speaking little for quite a while. "David," she began, "I'm worried about us."

His hand tightened briefly. Then he asked, "What about us?"

"I'm concerned about how we're relating to one another. Especially in bed."

"But we've been having sex all the time. I know I was a little reticent at first, but not now."

"It's not the frequency; it's the way we're being sexual. I don't know if this is conscious or not, but we're not treating each other like we used to."

He stopped and jammed his hands into his pockets. "You keep saying 'we,' but I know you mean me."

She turned and put her hand on his chest. "Why do you already have an attitude about this? You used to like it when we talked about sex. You used to be concerned with how I experienced our lovemaking."

"I still am. It's just…it's just hard for me. I have to concentrate so hard now."

"Concentrate?"

"Yes, concentrate. I have to forget about the time that you had cramps. I have to try to ignore the fact that there's a little, tiny baby trying to sleep just a few inches from the tip of my cock. I have to be careful not to squeeze your breasts because they're so tender. I…I'm always afraid I'm going to do something wrong or hurt you." He stared at the ground and kicked at a stick near his foot. "Sometimes, that takes the spontaneity out of it. I feel like we've had to do one thing or not do another for over a year now. I want things to be like they used to be."

She felt her temper flare immediately, but then a wave of sorrow swept over her. Not trusting herself to speak, she slipped her arms around his waist and hugged him as tightly as she could, hoping his embrace would ease the pain.

"I'm so sorry I said that," he mumbled. "I never want to hurt your feelings." He kissed the top of her head, saying, "It just doesn't feel like we're alone in bed anymore. There's another person there, and it feels like he's watching."

"David, that's our baby! He's not watching!"

He released his hold on her, looking sheepish. "I know that intellectually. But sex isn't about intellect."

She knew she was asking a loaded question, but she did it anyway, needing to know the answer. "Do you like my pregnant body?" His eyes closed, and he waited so long that she knew the answer without his saying it. "That's what I thought." She turned her back to him and started to walk home, going as fast as she could.

"Blair!" He trotted after her and grabbed her hand. "I'm getting used to it. It's just taking me a little while."

"What did you think was going to happen? You're the one who wanted me to carry this baby! I specifically remember telling you that my body would change— permanently!"

"I know, I know, but I didn't know I would *feel* like this! Everything's different. Your whole body's changing, and I guess I didn't think it would be this noticeable so soon. Besides, Chet's wife had a baby last year, and he said they hardly ever had sex. I just thought…"

"You're saying you wish I didn't feel like having sex?"

"Well…no, I just thought that's how it'd be."

She stared at him as if he were an alien, finally asking, "Are you just turned off by pregnancy in general, or is it me?"

He shook his head briskly. "I don't know." He spent a moment thinking, knowing he was on very thin ice. "It feels really, really weird to have sex with a pregnant woman. It's…it…feels kinda wrong."

"Wrong?"

"I know that's stupid. But I can't help it! You don't seem like my hot wife anymore. You seem like somebody's mom!"

Once again, she felt her anger rise, but she tamped it down. Forcing herself to stay calm, she took in a breath and started to walk, putting her hand on her slightly protruding abdomen as she unconsciously did so often these days.

They walked home in silence, neither able to put their feelings into words.

⟶

On the weekend that followed David's revelation, Blair was sitting out in their small backyard, reading a book and sipping a glass of lemonade. David had been watching the NBA playoffs, and he came out after watching the Laker victory, filling his wife in on all of the details while she did her best to appear interested. "What are you reading?" he asked.

"Just one of my many baby books," she said. "I'm still only halfway through the ones Kylie gave me."

"Oh." He stood and started to walk back into the house, but she called him back.

"Guess what our baby has now."

"Gosh..." He paused, looking guilty. "I have no idea."

"It's been ten weeks since we conceived, and the baby is starting to look like a person."

"Wow. Ten weeks, huh? I guess you're right. It was in April, wasn't it?"

"We did the pregnancy test on April 20. But March 21 was the first day of my last period. That's when we count from."

"That doesn't make much sense."

"I agree, but it's the convention, and they're not gonna change it for us. What I wanted to talk about was that the baby has sex organs now. If it's a girl, she has a tiny labia and a clitoris. And if it's a boy, he has a penis and a scrotum. I think we can start making some plans."

"Like?" He sat down in his usual chair, scooting it close so he could rest a foot on the arm of Blair's chair.

"We can start telling more people, for one thing. You can tell your work buddies."

"Okay," he said, giving her a strangely emotionless smile.

"I thought it would be a good time to start thinking about names, too. I'd like to have some ways of referring to him or her."

"We don't know if it's a boy or a girl. Let's wait until we do."

"I'm not sure I want to know. I'd prefer to be surprised. Do you want to know?"

"I guess it's not a big deal. If you don't want to know, that's okay with me."

"All right, Mr. Easy." She pinched his toes through his Topsiders. "It's not that much trouble to come up with two names, is it?"

"I guess not."

"Actually, we only have to come up with one," she said, a gentle smile forming on her face. "If it's a boy, I want to call him David." She got up and sat on the arm of her husband's lounge chair. "He'll be a lucky little guy if he takes after his daddy."

He gave her a look of total wonder. "But you always said there was no way you'd name the baby David."

"That was before I was pregnant," she reminded him. "Now that I am, I feel different about it."

"I don't think it's a good idea," he said, shaking his head. "I, uhm, think it's a burden on a kid. He should have his own identity."

With difficulty, she controlled her voice, keeping the incredulity from it. "I know you, David, and you weren't kidding when you told me you wanted your son to be a junior. Why have you changed your mind?"

"You changed yours; I changed mine. It was a fantasy before, but it's real now, and I think he should have a nice, unique name that'll be his alone."

She stood and looked at him. Then she put her hand under his chin and forced him to look into her eyes. "Why don't you want him to be called David? Tell me!"

He tried to control himself for a moment, his fists clenching and unclenching. His attempt to pull his chin away was unsuccessful. Blair had him in a death-grip, and she wasn't going to let him evade the question. His lips pursed together as he tried to force himself to stay silent, but eventually, he lost the battle. "Because he's not mine!" he spat, lunging to his feet and stumbling. He stood there and glared at her, his anger nearly uncontrollable. "You're trying to create this fucking little fantasy world! Naming him after me says I had something to do with it! I didn't, God damn it! It's…not…mine!"

She grabbed him by the shirt and leaned into him, shaking him with all of her might. "It *is* yours, God damn it! If this baby isn't yours, he isn't anyone's!"

"He's yours," he said, tears rolling down his cheeks. "He's your baby."

She shook him again, wishing she could smash his head on the stone patio where they stood. "Tell me you're happy we're having this baby! Tell me you want him!"

His eyes locked upon hers, and an eternity passed between them. She could hear the blood pounding in her ears, and she felt her fingers tighten on his shirt. Taking a steadying breath, he gasped, "I'm not. I'm so fucking sorry, Blair, but I'm not happy."

Releasing him, she somehow found her way back to her chair and sat. She bent from the waist and held her head in her hands, moaning piteously. Her tears started to flow, accompanied by heaving sobs. Kneeling at her feet, he tried to get his arms around her, but she wrenched away from him, pushing so hard he landed on his seat.

Blindly, she took a few lurching steps forward, stopped, and vomited on the ground, slowly sinking onto a low garden wall. Wiping her mouth with the back of her hand, she looked at him and asked, "What do you want, David? Do you want me to have an abortion? Is that it? Do you want me to kill our baby?"

"No," he insisted, sitting next to her. "Of course not. I just…I just wish we hadn't done this. I wish to God we hadn't done this."

She put her hand upon her belly and said, "This is a human growing in here. It's not some appliance we thought we wanted and then decided we didn't need."

"I'm not asking you to have an abortion, Blair. That's ridiculous. I'm just trying to explain why I'm not…into this yet. I have to get used to this. I need more time."

"Into this? *Into this?*" she choked out incredulously. "You've had ten weeks! What do we do if you never get into this?"

"I don't know," he said quietly. "That's what keeps me awake at night." He put his arm around her shoulders and said, "I'm so sorry. I know it doesn't help, but I realize this is all my fault. I go over it again and again in my head, and I know we wouldn't be in this fix if I hadn't insisted on going forward."

She looked at him carefully, her mind unable to grasp the full weight of his words. He actually looked like a stranger to her, and she couldn't bear to have him touch her. She got to her feet, waited for the slight bit of vertigo to settle, and then went back to her chair. "So, what do you want to do? Give the baby up for adoption? Tell our families that it was stillborn?"

"I…I hadn't considered that," he said softly. "Could you do that?" He looked completely puzzled, but his puzzlement lasted only a few seconds.

She got up and went to him. Bending over so that they were nose to nose, she said, "If you had a loaded gun pointed at my head, you couldn't get this baby away from me. It's not a mistake. It's not anything but the expression of our love." Turning abruptly, she dashed into the house to let her empty stomach have its way again.

David went into the house and saw that Blair was in the bathroom. Knocking softly, he asked, "Are you all right?"

"Go away! Just go away."

"No. We have to talk about this."

"What is there to talk about? You don't want our baby!"

"I didn't say that." He tried the knob, knowing the door would be locked. He slid down the doorjamb, propping his feet against the opposite wall. "I said I wasn't happy. That's not the same as not wanting him."

"It is to me! It is to the baby, too!"

"Can I tell you why I wanted to have a baby with you?"

She didn't answer right away. He heard water running, and a few moments later, he heard her sneakers squeak when she must have climbed into the tub. Her voice echoed a little when she said, "If you must."

"I know this is stupid, but from the time my dad got sick, I wanted…I needed to have a baby. It would have made him so happy." He was quiet for a moment, trying to stop himself from crying. "When Dad died," he said, his voice breaking, "the urge got even stronger. I wasn't sure what was happening, but I've been thinking about this so much that it's finally became clear."

"Go on," she said tiredly.

"I wanted someone who'd feel about me the same way I felt about my dad. I guess it didn't occur to me that I'd have mixed feelings about the baby…if it wasn't mine."

"If you say that one more time, I'm gonna bash your head in with the first heavy object I can find. I'm…not…kidding. I could easily kill you. Easily."

"I know." He tipped his head back against the jamb. "I don't blame you." He paused for a few moments, waiting for her to speak. When she didn't, he said, "I should have realized I had my head up my ass when I was so adamant about not adopting. I'm surprised you agreed to go forward when I said that."

Her voice was low and lethal sounding. "If you so much as *try* to shift the blame—"

"No, no, no. This is all…*all* my fault. I felt a void that I wanted to fill. I thought having a baby would do that."

She sighed so heavily that he heard her. "I should have said no when you refused to adopt. It's not all your fault."

"You're being very generous, and I don't deserve it," he said. "It is my fault."

"How do you feel about my being adopted? Do you think I'm my parents' child?"

"Yeah, yeah. I guess I do." She didn't say a word while she waited for him to think through his thoughts. "If I'm totally honest, I've always felt a little sorry for you. I hate the fact that you don't know and love your birth parents."

"Everyone should be as lucky as I am," she said, her voice cold and hard. "I'd take my parents over..." She paused, unwilling to bring his mother into the mêlée. "Anyone's."

"I know you love your parents. And I know how much they love you. But it's not the same, is it?"

"David," she said, her voice thin and weary, "you don't know jack shit about being adopted. Don't try to act like you do."

He was quiet for a moment and then said, "I, uhm, know a little bit. I've never told you this, but my cousin Michael's adopted."

"Really?" she asked, not revealing that Sadie had already told her.

"Yeah. I was about five at the time, and I remember my mother telling my father that my Aunt Alice was crazy for adopting. I specifically remember her saying it was like going to the pound to pick out a puppy. You never knew if the puppy would be vicious or sickly and would have to be put down. Not long after that, she finally let me get a dog. We had to go to a breeder because she said you couldn't be too careful when you adopted a dog." He started to cry, and Blair closed her eyes against the pounding anger she felt towards her mother-in-law. "Every time I saw my cousin, I looked him over, trying to see if he was sick or mean. I was afraid he'd bite me." He was sobbing now, and in a matter of seconds, Blair came out of the bathroom and was at his side, torn between holding and strangling him.

They cried together, both of them terrified and desperately sad. "Michael knows he's adopted," he said when he could speak. "My aunt and uncle didn't tell him, though. He found his original birth certificate and his adoption papers. He's never felt like he belonged to anyone." David burrowed his face into his wife's neck, crying hard. She fought the urge to push him away, knowing that it would hurt him terribly to be rejected when he was so vulnerable. "I don't want our baby to feel like that—and now he will."

Blair pulled back and looked at him, seeing only the top of his dark, close-cropped hair. "That's not true! I don't feel like that. Your aunt and uncle should have told him, David. He just feels that way because it's such a fucking secret."

"We weren't gonna tell our baby about his sperm donor," he said, looking at her carefully.

"Jesus fucking Christ! We've been over this."

"I know. But why didn't you want to tell him if you weren't worried about his knowing?"

"God damn it, David," she said tiredly. "I didn't want him to know because I didn't want you to have to acknowledge it to him. I thought you'd bond better if you didn't have to tell him that he didn't share your genes."

"So, you were gonna lie to him for me?"

"Yes. There was no reason in the world the baby would have to know. It's a lie that wouldn't harm him. The donor has a much healthier family than you do. It's not like there's some dangerous disease lurking in the background that he'll have to be tested for."

"It's still a lie," David said, not budging an inch.

"Fine, but it's a lie we're never going to have to worry about. Your mother knows, and that's the same fucking thing as putting a banner headline in the *L.A. Times*." She shook her head so roughly that her eyes ached. "The only thing that really matters is that he knows he's loved."

He looked at her, his dark eyes filled with pain. "How can we be sure he'll feel loved? How can he feel like he's wanted when I'm not sure I want him?"

Her head dropped into her hands, and she let out a primitive wail. "How can you say that? How can you?"

"I don't know. I just feel...disconnected." He leaned back and banged his head softly against the doorframe. "The last time I spoke to my dad, before he went into the coma, he said he could let go because he knew I'd still be here, carrying on for him." He looked at Blair and said, "I have my dad in me. When I was little, I'd put my hand on his and dream about when I'd grow up and have hands like his. And now I do! I put my hand on his that day, and I almost fainted. My hands looked just like his. He's inside me. I carry his blood."

"Jesus Christ, David, that's not why you loved him."

"It was part of it," he maintained. "I can carry on for him now that he's gone."

"What the fuck does that even mean?"

David looked sheepish and said, "I don't exactly know, but it was really important to him."

"I'm carrying a baby because of some deathbed nonsense that your father, in his morphine-addled state, said to you? Was he some feudal lord who could only pass his title on to his rightful heir? Jesus, David, he was a mattress salesman!"

"I know that. But I can't stop feeling this way. Don't you think I've tried?"

She grabbed two handfuls of her own hair and yanked hard. "I'm insane! I'm the one who's crazy! How did I not know this about you? Have you always been this fucking shallow?"

"I guess so," he mumbled. "If feeling this way makes me shallow, then I guess I am."

"Great! You admit that you're shallow. How in the hell does that fix anything? We're having a baby. We're having it because you insisted that I carry it. You insisted that we use a sperm donor. You and your mother ganged up on me and talked me into using a donor I didn't really want. And now...now that we've created a human being, you decide that you don't think you can love him. I've never heard of anything so totally fucked up. So morally indefensible!"

"I know, I know," he said, sounding defeated. The whining tone of his voice made her sick, and she got up and ran to the toilet to throw up again, gagging bile because her stomach was so empty.

For a change, David was right at her side, stroking her back and pushing her damp hair off her forehead. "I'm so sorry, Blair. I'm so sorry."

She turned enough to be able to rest her back against the tub. She was pale and shaking, her skin clammy. "How does that help our baby?"

"It doesn't. I know it doesn't." He got up and wet a washcloth. Wiping her face and neck, he said, "I'll do anything, Blair, anything to make this right."

"I could hang myself," she muttered. "I can't believe I went through with this. How could I have been so stupid? This isn't like me!"

"Don't be so hard on yourself. You were trying to make me happy."

Bitterly, she spat out, "Are you happy, David? Did the experiment work?"

He hung his head, obviously ashamed. "No, it didn't."

"Do you have any idea how you're going to learn to love our baby? Any idea at all?"

"No. I've...run out of ideas."

Sighing, the weight of the world on her shoulders, Blair got to her knees and then stood. "I've got to be alone. I need some space."

He didn't say a word. He simply watched her walk into their room and close the door.

↬

A long time later, David entered their bedroom tentatively, expecting to find Blair crying her eyes out. Instead, he was treated to a display of Business Blair. She was placing neatly folded garments into a suitcase, and when she saw him, she said, "I'm going to stay at a hotel. It's not good for me to be this upset, and I refuse to put the baby at risk while we settle this." She took off her shorts and T-shirt and put on a blouse, jacket, and slacks that she normally wore to work. "I'm not sure where I'll stay, but you can reach me on my cell phone. If you want to save our relationship, you'd better think of a way to change your attitude. You're this baby's father, and until you believe that, we have nothing more to talk about."

She ran a brush through her hair, added a touch of lipstick, gave him one final, incalculably sorrowful look, and then walked out.

Chapter Four

K ylie was sitting at a card table on Sunday night, glaring at the hand she'd just been dealt. Her pager went off, and all four doctors reached for theirs. Kylie shot a look around the table while taking the device from her waistband. "This one's mine, although I don't know who could be paging me. I don't have anyone in the hospital this weekend."

"Rub it in," Monique grumbled. "I'm on call, and I haven't had two uninterrupted hours in a row."

"Yeah," Eileen, a pediatrician, agreed. "You'll get no sympathy here, Shakes. Your hours are more regular than a banker's."

"I'm not complaining," Kylie said. She looked at the display. "Oh, it's not the hospital. Just a friend. Be right back." She went out onto the porch and dialed Blair's cell. "Thanks for calling," she joked when Blair answered. "I'm playing poker tonight, and I'm about to lose my shirt."

There was a moment of silence. Then, in a rush of words so rapid that Kylie had to focus intently to decipher them, Blair said, "I think I'm losing the baby. You told me once that you could get me into the ER quickly. Can you?" The terrified woman gulped in a breath of air, and Kylie thought she detected the warning signs of hyperventilation.

"Hold on," she said, trying to sound both soothing and in control. She stuck her head into the house again. "Monique! C'mere. Hurry!"

Her friend got up and dashed outside, taking the phone when Kylie extended it towards her. "It's Blair Spencer. She thinks she's miscarrying."

All business, the obstetrician said, "Blair? Monique. Tell me what's happening."

Slightly puzzled to be talking to her obstetrician, but not wanting to waste time asking why, Blair said, "I've got a little cramping—about like I described the first time I saw you." She gulped in air. "I've been struggling with them all day, and I kept telling myself it was only stress. But I just took a bath, and I'm bleeding."

"Describe the blood. What color is it?"

"I don't know!" she cried on the verge of panic, her breathing growing even more rapid.

"Come on, Blair. Take a deep breath and let it out slowly. Again," she said, listening carefully to make sure her patient was following her instructions. "Now think. Was it pink, bright red, rust colored…?"

Kylie saw the concern on Monique's face and went into the house. She grabbed her bag and took Monique's as well. "Sorry, guys," she said to their friends, "but we've got to run. See you next month."

"You're just trying to get out of losing this hand!" Jocelyn said.

"I wish that were true," Kylie said as she ran back outside. Monique handed her the phone, hitting mute as she did.

"I can't tell what's going on. She was in the tub, and the water started to turn red. It's possible the water made the blood brighter than it would have been if she'd just seen it on her clothing. But if the blood's bright red, I'm worried. I'm also concerned because she can't be sure if there were any clots."

"Are we meeting her at the ER?"

"Damn, I hate to do that to her. It's probably nothing…"

Kylie gave her a penetrating look. "You can't be sure of that."

"Well, no…" she began, and before the words were out of her mouth, Kylie was telling Blair, "We're just wrapping it up for the evening. We're gonna swing by and take a look at you."

"Oh, Kylie, I can just go to the ER. That'd be faster."

"Are you worried?"

"I'm fucking terrified," she whispered. "I've never been so frightened."

"Have you ever been to the ER?"

"No," she said, sounding like a little girl.

"It's no fun. Just relax for a few minutes, and we'll be right there. Have David make you some herbal tea."

"Uhm, Kylie…I'm not at home. I'm at the Spinnaker Hotel. Room 315."

"Okay," she said, not wanting to spend time asking what was going on. "We're on Marine, so we're just a few blocks away. Be right there."

Monique gave her a narrowed glance, but Kylie told her, "I'll make it up to you. Promise."

"Oh, without a doubt, Shakes. You definitely owe me. I haven't made a house call since my sister was pregnant. And I only made that one to avoid my mother's wrath!"

❧

Monique had driven Kylie to the card game, and when they pulled into the valet zone of the hotel, Kylie hopped out and instructed, "We're physicians on an emergency call. Keep the car close."

"Yes, ma'am," the red-jacketed man agreed as Kylie pressed $10 into his hand.

The two doctors knocked on Blair's door a few minutes later. "C'mon in," she said. "It's open."

Kylie walked in and quickly looked around, her brow knitted. "Are you alone?"

"Uh-huh," her friend said, adding nothing. Blair looked down and saw that both women carried bags. She cleared her throat and weakly joked, "Don't you even think about using whatever you have in there, Kylie. I'm sure it's full of scalpels."

Kylie gave her a half-smile, trying her best to act as if everything were normal. "Don't worry; Monique'll keep an eye on me."

"I promise I won't let Kylie open her bag," Monique said. "She just likes to bring it so she looks like a doctor." Her tone turning more professional, she said, "I'd like to take a peek at you, Blair. Would you mind lying on the bed while I give you a quick exam?"

"Sure." But she stood right where she was, looking slightly embarrassed.

"Want me to wait in the lobby?" Kylie asked.

Blair took in a breath and gave her friend a tremulous smile. "No, don't be silly. I'd like it if you stayed." She went into the bath and got a clean towel, spreading it out on the bed. She was wearing a large T-shirt and a terrycloth bathrobe. Taking off the robe, she lay down while Monique went into the bath to wash her hands. "Do you think you could hold my hand?" Blair asked Kylie quietly. "I'm about to jump out of my skin."

"My pleasure." Kylie sat on the edge of the bed and chafed her friend's icy hand while they waited for Monique to get organized.

The exam was very brief, and as she removed the disposable speculum, the obstetrician said, "Everything looks completely normal. Your cervix is closed up tight just like it should be. I think you're absolutely fine," she said, giving Blair a reassuring smile. "Check carefully the next time you urinate. You probably won't bleed again, but if you do, check to see if the blood's bright red or has clots in it. If it does, go to the ER immediately. But I truly don't think that'll happen. This isn't uncommon at all. I had some bleeding with both of my kids. It scared me half to death, but it was nothing at all."

"It has to be something," Blair said. "It's blood!"

"Honestly, having a little spotting or bleeding is very, very common, and it doesn't indicate that anything is wrong. I wish I could tell you exactly why it happened, but I'm afraid I can't. It just happens."

Blair sighed and said, "This isn't an exact science, is it?"

"Not by a long shot. But I'm confident you don't have anything to worry about."

"Thanks so much for coming," Blair said, her relief obvious. "Thanks to both of you."

"Just to be safe, you might want to stay in bed tomorrow or lie outside in the shade and read a good book," Monique suggested. "I'm sure the baby's fine, but you're looking awfully wrung out."

"I am," Blair said. "A day off sounds like a very good idea."

"Ready to go?" Monique asked Kylie.

"Do you have your car here, Blair?"

"Sure. Why?"

"I'm gonna send Monique home. I'll drive myself home in your car and come back to get you in the morning. I want to make sure you're settled."

"But Kylie..."

Kylie took a twenty-dollar bill from her wallet and handed it to Monique. "That should cover parking. Thanks for everything, buddy."

Monique took the money and said to Blair, "Don't argue with her. It's a waste of time. See you soon."

As soon as the door closed, Kylie turned to her friend. "What happened? Where's David?"

"At home. I needed some time to myself."

Once again, the doctor felt a little unsure. She shifted her weight and nervously rubbed her earlobe. "I don't know what's going on here, and I'm feeling a little out of my element. Do you want me to leave? Is it okay that I sent Monique home?"

"Yeah. Of course." Blair got to her feet and put her robe back on. "We had a fight, and I needed to be alone. Actually, I needed to be away from David. I'm really happy to see you."

Kylie walked to her and bent over just enough to look directly into her friend's eyes. "Need a hug?"

"Desperately." She tightened her arms around Kylie's waist and clung to her for a long while.

Blair's robe was open, and when she stepped back, Kylie looked at her and asked, "Can I say hi to the baby, too?"

A bright smile bloomed on Blair's lips. "We'd like that. We've really had a tough couple of days."

Kylie dropped to her knees and placed one hand on her friend's abdomen, leaning in close to say, "Your mommy's having a rough time right now, Baby. It's time for you to calm down and stop scaring her, okay? She needs her rest tonight, so I want you to stop with the cramps and the bleeding, too. Just be a good baby and go to sleep. Oh, and stay away from her bladder tonight." She drew even closer and rested her cheek against Blair. "Okay, yeah, I'll tell her."

Kylie stood and said, "The baby said he or she was sorry to worry you. He or she isn't sure what sex he or she is yet, and he or she apologizes for the excess of pronouns."

Falling into her arms, Blair let herself cry, the tears that had been flowing for two days nowhere near depleted. After a while, she calmed down enough to talk and said, "David and I are in real trouble. He doesn't want the baby."

Gripping her by the shoulders, Kylie held her at arm's length. "How can that...he must have been...he couldn't have meant that!"

"No, no, he did. This happened yesterday afternoon, and he hasn't retracted it, so he obviously meant it."

"You've been here since yesterday? Why didn't you call me?"

"I didn't really want to talk. When I'm upset, I like to be alone." She looked up at her friend and said, "No reflection on you. I knew you'd be there if I needed you. Just like you were tonight." She shivered and drew her robe tightly around herself. "I needed to be alone to think."

"You can always count on me to be there for you. However you need me."

"Thanks," she said, patting her gently. "I'm exhausted. My keys are on the dresser there. Bring the car back whenever you want. I'm not going anywhere tomorrow."

"I'm not leaving," Kylie said. "I have surgery at seven, so I'll need to leave here at six, but I should be finished by noon at the latest. When I get back, we'll decide what to do next. Do you have another T-shirt I can borrow to sleep in?"

Blair sighed, sounding completely drained. "Kylie, don't worry about me. I'm fine. Go home."

"Don't waste your time arguing. I'm not going to leave you alone after the day you've had. Get over it." She wore her usual calm expression, but in her eyes, there was a determination, which convinced Blair that she meant business.

Going to the dresser, Blair pulled out another T-shirt. "This might be small on you, but it's the best I can offer."

"Don't worry about me. I can sleep in my shirt. You hop into bed now." She went into the bathroom and came back out with Blair's moisture lotion. "I'd like to rub your back, but only if it won't make you uncomfortable. It should help with the cramps," she said, continuing to explain.

Blair put a hand out and touched her arm. "You never make me uncomfortable, and I'd love a little human contact. I've never been so lonely." She bent over and held herself, her shoulders shaking as she sobbed.

Kylie sat on the edge of the bed and held her, letting her cry herself out. They didn't talk, even though Kylie was desperate to learn everything that had happened with David. But it was clear that Blair was too worn out to keep her eyes open. Kylie urged her onto her stomach and then pulled her T-shirt up and began to thoroughly soothe the tight muscles.

"You have great hands," Blair mumbled.

Kylie laughed, her voice low and soothing. "That's an entrance requirement for a surgeon."

"Feels better. Cramps all gone. Sleep now?"

"Good." Kylie pulled the blanket up, tucking it around her friend.

"I'll never be able to thank you for this. I just don't know how to…" Before her sentence was completed, Blair's eyes fluttered closed, and she began to breathe heavily. Kylie smiled at her and then took off her pants, getting into the other bed and falling asleep nearly as quickly as Blair had.

⌐

Kylie returned to the hotel room just after one, finding Blair still in bed, the curtains drawn. Blair stirred and moaned, rolling onto her side and pulling a pillow over her head.

Not an afternoon person, Kylie thought. *I wonder if she's missing any appointments. I hate to do it, but I know she wouldn't want to flake on her clients.* She walked over to the bed and gently touched her friend's arm. "It's after one. Do you have any meetings today?"

"No," she mumbled and then added, "Go away."

"Okay," Kylie said, the rebuff stinging. "I'll be down by the pool, having lunch. See you."

Before she got to the door, Blair flung the pillow from her face and asked, "Did I say that 'go away' part out loud?"

"Loud and clear," Kylie said, managing a half-smile.

"I'm sorry. I'm just so fucking depressed that I don't want to see anyone."

"I can understand that," Kylie said, even though she really couldn't. "I'll just take a cab home. Call me when you feel like talking, okay?"

Blair sat up a little more and gazed at her friend. "Don't be mad. I just…I can't be nice today."

"I'm not mad. I just don't know how to be."

"Be gone," Blair said, her voice much more gentle now. "Just let me feel sorry for myself. I deserve a day to wallow in despair."

"If that's what works for you, be my guest. But this happened a couple of days ago. It's easy to get into something you can't get out of."

Blair slid out of bed and walked over to her friend. "I know you mean well, but I won't die if I sleep for another twenty-four hours. I don't like to be supervised. Especially when I feel this bad. I promise I'll call you by tomorrow, okay?"

The dark head nodded, even though it was obvious that the doctor wasn't happy about being sent home. "I'll wait for you to call me, but I won't stop worrying about you until you do."

"That's playing dirty, Doc," Blair said, unable to keep from smiling.

"I do what I have to do." She hugged her friend, gave her a smile, and then left her alone.

↩

Blair called that evening. "I don't want to talk, but I don't want you worrying, either. How's this for a compromise?"

"Pretty good," Kylie said. "Have you had dinner?"

"No babying me," Blair said, her voice only slightly playful.

"I'm just making conversation."

"Uh-huh. That's the thing I don't wanna do. I'll call you tomorrow. And I'm very glad that you care about me. Just let me handle this my own way."

"I don't think I have a choice," Kylie said, laughing wryly.

↩

At 8:00 p.m., Blair glared at the door, hoping that whoever was knocking could duck. "Who is it?" she barked, surprised to hear herself sounding so angry.

"It's David."

"Which one?" she asked. She got up and opened the door, staring right into his eyes. "The one I thought I married or the one I did marry?"

He looked like a beaten dog, all of his usual self-confidence vanished. "I don't know. I'm just a guy who wants his wife to come home."

She walked away, but left the door open, and David took this as an unspoken invitation. He followed her into the room and sat down on the second bed when she crawled back into the one by the window. "State your business," she ordered.

"Damn," he grumbled, "do you have to treat me like shit?"

"Yeah, I do. What do you want?"

He looked like he wanted to get up and leave, but he collected his thoughts and said, "I know you're a very practical person, and I know you've been thinking about your options."

"That's true. If I weren't sure that the neighbors heard us arguing on Saturday, you'd be coroner's exhibit #387 right now. No one would have suspected me, and I'd have your life insurance policy to live on."

"Jesus, Blair, I know I screwed up, but thinking about killing me is kinda harsh!"

"Count your blessings. I think about dismembering you, too. In my fantasies, you *beg* for a quick death."

"Have you always been this vengeful? God damn it, I've known you for ten years, and you've never even yelled at me."

"Then I'm overdue," she said. "Do you have a point?"

"Yes, of course, I do." He looked at her for a moment and then said, "If you divorce me, you'll have to raise the baby on your own."

"Brilliant. You're very good at math."

"Stop kicking me in the ass long enough for me to make my point, okay?"

She looked at the sparks of fire in his eyes and actually felt more comfortable with him. She hated wimps, and when David acted sorry for himself, she truly wanted to kill him. "Fine. Go on."

"You're a very attractive woman, and I know that you'll meet some guy who wants to be with you if you leave me. If that happens, he'll be the baby's stepfather."

"Uh-huh." She gave him a blank look.

"If you could let another guy be the baby's stepfather, why can't you let me try to be a real father? I'm not sure I can do it, but I know I'd be better than a stepfather would. I might never think of the baby as mine, but neither would the guys you date."

"Is that the best you've got? 'Cause it ain't much."

He nodded. "Yeah, that's the best I've got."

Her legs slid over the side of the bed, and she rested her weight on her forearms. "Look, David, there's a big difference here. You *are* the baby's father. The fact that you can't believe that is what would make you a horrible father. You have some brainless notion that you'd feel more connected if your genes were in this baby's body. But you wouldn't. If you think of this child as something you own..." She shook her head. "That's just too fucked up to discuss."

"Okay, okay," he said. "Let's agree that I'd be the world's worst father. I haven't been a bad husband. I know that, Blair, and you know that, too. So come home with me and let me be your husband. My being in the same house won't hurt the baby, will it? Let me help you through this pregnancy. Please!"

"So far, you've sucked more than I can tell you, David. Why should I believe you'd be better now?"

"I know I have," he said. "I know that. That's because I've had all of these feelings tearing me apart. Now that they're out, I can act more like myself. I don't have to hide how I'm really feeling and censor myself every moment."

She flopped back onto the bed and let out a weary sigh. "I don't know what that would buy me. What if your feelings for the baby don't change?"

"You could leave me then."

"And you think that would be easier for me? I don't think I could go through this twice. It would kill me."

"But you need someone to help you. You can't live alone during this."

"Yeah, I think I can," she said. "Lots of women do."

"But how many of them have a husband who wants to be there to support them? I wanna be there for you. I really, really want to help."

She sat up and stared at him. "If you really want to help, you'll figure out what's stopping you from loving your child. You have thirty weeks left, David. Go to therapy three times a week, and you can change if you try hard enough."

"Shit, I'm no good at that stuff. You know I don't have that introspective thing."

Giving him a blank look, she let her shoulders raise and drop. "That's my best offer. I'm not going to get back together with you until I'm confident you can be a good father. Doing it the other way would make me insane."

He got up and then sat next to her, letting his body lightly touch hers. "Our marriage isn't important to you? I'm not important to you?"

She reached out and took his hand, holding it tightly for a minute. Starting to cry again, she brought his hand to her lips and kissed it, rubbing it gently across her face, wishing for some of the old magic to return. "You're more important to me than you'll ever know. I loved you enough to do something I knew might not be right. Something I really didn't need or want to do. Adopting would have been the right thing. I got pregnant because it meant so much to you. But the baby comes first, David. That's all there is to it. The baby comes first."

He put his arm around her, and she leaned against his chest. "I'm worried about you," he said. "It drives me crazy to think of your lying here alone, crying your eyes out. Isn't there anything I can do?"

"Change the way you think. It's the only way." She yawned and then rubbed her eyes.

He looked at his watch. "It's still early."

"Not to me. I'm tired. I've never been this tired." She slumped down, collapsing onto the bed. "I feel like all of the energy's been drained out of me."

David sat on the edge of the bed, watching as his wife's eyes fluttered closed. She tried to open them, but they didn't heed her command. In just a few moments, she was breathing slowly and steadily, and he saw the lines of tension leave her face.

He reached out and stroked her face, marveling at how beautiful she was. Her face was a little rounder than normal, but the extra weight had filled her features out, making her look a little like she had when he'd first met her. "So pretty," he whispered. "Such a pretty woman." She purred a little under his gentle touch and then rolled onto her side, her usual sleep position.

Should I stay? She's been so sad, and I miss her so much. I think she might like some cuddling. He stood up, took off his pants and shirt, and then gingerly lay down next to her. She reached behind herself and took his hand, tucking it between her breasts, just like always. He buried his face in her hair, feeling tears stinging his eyes once again. It felt so good, so familiar, and so right that he wouldn't let himself sleep. He lay awake for hours with his hand resting on her belly, trying to feel something—anything—for the child that grew inside her.

↩

Blair woke to the pressure in her bladder. She was thoroughly disoriented, not sure why she was lying on the wrong side of David. Stealthily taking his hand from her waist, she sighed and sat up. She stood and waited for her balance to settle when it hit her like a body blow. She felt desperately sad, wishing there were some way to get her life back. *Did I ask him to stay? I was so tired I might have.* She went into the bathroom and sat down, letting her head drop into her hands. *How did we get here? How did it all go so wrong?*

She went back into the bedroom and stood next to the bed for a moment, gazing at David. Still torn between the feelings she'd had for him for ten years and her desire to strangle him for screwing things up so badly, she let her instincts take over. Doing her very best to sink into denial, she climbed back into bed and sighed heavily when David immediately sought out her warm body. *I wish this were enough. Dear God, I wish this were enough.*

↩

On Wednesday, Blair called Kylie early in the day. "I have to go to work today, so I'll be in your neighborhood. Wanna have dinner?"

"Sure. Where do you want to go?"

"I was thinking your house. All I want is some pasta with a little Parmesan on it. Can you handle that, Doc?"

"Yeah, I think I can manage. Will it bother you if I put some vegetables on mine?"

"Not if you cook 'em before I get there."

"I'll try to time things properly, but if I don't, you can always sit on my deck. We can eat out there, too. What time should I expect you?"

"I'm free after seven. Is that okay?"

"Perfect. See you then."

Kylie hung up and looked at her cell phone for a moment. *You're a handful, Blair Spencer. A real handful.*

↩

Dinner passed without complaint or much conversation. Kylie was afraid of pushing her friend, and Blair was still very close-mouthed. All they managed was polite "How was your day?" talk that sounded very lame given the circumstances.

Kylie insisted on cleaning the kitchen, and she gently suggested that Blair sit outside while she worked. The doctor finished neatening up and then went outside, surprised and pained to see her friend crying hard. "Oh, Blair, please tell me what's going on."

She squatted down in front of her, looking into her red-rimmed eyes.

"I told you," she said, her voice shaking. "David doesn't want the baby. Now the question is…do I?" She collapsed against the table, giving her head a fairly good whack.

Kylie was at a complete loss. She'd learned that Blair didn't like to be smothered, or even prodded, when she was upset, but she couldn't stop herself from pulling the shaking woman into her arms. "Tell me" was all she said.

"Would you hate me if I didn't keep the baby?"

Blair looked so fragile that Kylie felt her head begin to shake. "Of course not! You're my friend. I'd never judge you." She waited a second and then said, "If you want to abort, you don't have much time left."

"Abort!" Kylie was sure the neighbors heard the shout, but she didn't care much at that moment. "How could you even say that?"

Shaken, Kylie said, "I thought that's what you meant."

"Then you don't know me very well, Kylie Mackenzie. You don't know me very well at all!" She stood up, looking like she was going to leave. Instead, she touched her belly and said, "It's not this baby's fault that his parents are a couple of idiots! He's not going to suffer because I had my head up my ass when I got pregnant!"

"Blair!" Kylie approached tentatively, afraid that her friend might swat her away. "Why are you saying things like that? You got pregnant very, very deliberately."

"Yeah," she said, her words venomous. "I got pregnant because I thought my husband knew what love meant! Did he become heartless, or was he always that way?" She sank into her chair, sobbing so hard that her body shook violently.

Kylie didn't have anything to say, partly because she didn't know what had happened between Blair and David. So, she knelt and tentatively put her arms around her friend, rocking her gently. "Sh," she soothed, "Sh, now."

It took a long time, but Blair finally calmed down enough to speak. "Can I tell you what happened?"

"If you don't, I'm gonna explode." Kylie took Blair's arm and helped her to get up. "It's getting chilly out here. Let's go inside. I'll make you some decaf tea."

They walked inside together, and a few minutes later, Blair told the whole tale, the events so burned into her memory that she didn't omit a thing.

⟻

Kylie was curled up on one corner of the sofa, her head dropped back against the upholstery. She had an empty glass in her hand, the Scotch now stinging her stomach. She sat up, wiped at her eyes, and said, "I don't know how you've managed to keep this inside since Saturday. Have you told anyone?"

"No."

"Not even your mom? I know how close you are. I thought—"

Blair's response was immediate and sharp. "No. I don't want her to know. If I decide to give the baby up for adoption, I'll tell her, but on the off chance that David and I get back together, I don't want her to know about this whole fucking mess."

Kylie looked at her friend, but then her eyes shifted, and she focused somewhere in the middle distance. She seemed uncomfortable, and Blair stuck her foot out and tapped her friend's thigh. "Sorry I'm being so bitchy. I just feel like my head's gonna burst open. I talked with a client today, and when he was complaining about some minor thing, I wanted to strangle him with my bare hands and say, 'I might have to give my baby up for adoption! How can you carry on about a pool not having a big enough filter system?'"

"Do you wanna talk about it?"

"No. I told you I wanted to kill the last guy who wanted to discuss filter systems." She didn't smile, but Kylie saw that her friend was just on the verge of one.

The doctor didn't say another word. She just left her question on the table. Blair stretched and moved around on the couch, trying to get comfortable. "Can I put my feet up? I had to wear heels today, and they felt like tourniquets."

"Toss 'em over here," Kylie said, patting the cushion that separated the women. "I give a good foot rub."

Blair did as she was told, and a moment later, she began to purr. "Oh, God, why aren't you married? Do the women you date know you can do this?"

"Maybe not," Kylie said. "Maybe I should change my approach."

"Damn!" Blair shook her head and said, "I could fall asleep. Of course, it helps that I've been getting about an hour of sleep at a time. I wake up in a cold sweat, seeing a nurse take my baby from me while I'm lying in a bed, covered with blood."

"Tell me about it," Kylie said. "Tell me why you're considering putting the baby up for adoption."

"All right." Blair looked at her friend and said, "I can't decide if I'm thinking of the baby's best interests or if I'm trying to punish myself and David. Of course, I guess all three things could be accomplished at the same time."

"Why do you need to be punished? What have you done wrong?"

"I created a life with a man who wasn't ready to have a child. I knew...I knew we were making a mistake, but I talked myself into it. I gambled with a human life. And I lost."

"You did not!" Kylie said, her voice rising. "Things aren't working out like you'd planned, but you didn't act rashly. Things happen!"

"I should have been certain that David could handle this. I had doubts!"

"Okay, so you had doubts. That makes you want to give your baby away?"

Blair looked at her for so long that Kylie feared the woman was trying to figure out if her hands would fit around the doctor's neck for an efficient strangulation.

But to Kylie's relief, Blair wasn't angry. "No," she said with an extraordinary amount of determination in her voice. "I don't want to give my baby away. I love this child with every bit of my heart. I would only give him up if I thought he'd be better off with parents who *both* loved and wanted him."

"Oh, Blair," Kylie said, starting to cry. "That's such a loving act."

"He's my baby," Blair said, crying along with her friend. "I'd do anything in the world to make sure he had the best life possible—including giving him up."

"That's the best example of a mother's love I've ever heard." She squeezed Blair's feet and said, "You don't have to give the baby up to make sure he has a wonderful life. You can provide that. With or without David."

"I can?" Blair asked, looking hopeful.

"Yes. I'm sure of it."

"But it's better to have two parents." Her eyes filled with tears, and she looked like a small, frightened child.

"What if David wanted the baby, but died right before you gave birth?"

"That might happen. Don't give me any encouragement."

"No, really. Would you give up the baby then?"

"N…no, I guess I wouldn't." She paused and shook her head roughly. "Of course I wouldn't. The baby would be all I had left of David." Her chin quivered, and she started to cry again.

Kylie patted her friend's feet, stood up, and walked to the other end of the couch. Squatting down, she said, "You don't know what's going to happen. You can't guarantee an adoptive couple would do better than you would alone…or than you and David would do together. It's a crapshoot. But millions of single people have babies and do very, very well by them. You have enough money to work fewer hours and spend time with the baby, and I'm sure David will want some role, even if he doesn't think he does now."

"I swing back and forth between the depths of despair and knowing that everything will be all right. Sometimes, I dream of how it will be when David holds the baby for the first time. In my fantasies, he's in love with him as soon as he lays eyes on him."

"Yeah," Kylie said, seeing a glimmer of hope in her friend's eyes. "That could definitely happen. It probably will." She touched Blair's chin, moving her head up until their eyes met. "But if it doesn't work out, you won't be alone. I know I can't take David's role, but if you divorce him, I promise you that I'll help you in any way I can. You can depend on me. Hell, I'd gladly watch the baby every weekend so you could have some time to yourself. We can work this out."

"You'd do that…for me?" The pale-green eyes filled with tears once again.

"Of course, I would. Just promise me one thing: don't give up someone who means so much to you. He's your baby," she soothed, putting her hand on her friend's tummy. "Don't give him away unless you're *sure* you can't give him a good home."

"But what if someone could do a better job?" the blonde asked, still looking terrified.

"I've got news for you. Someone can always do a better job." She patted her friend's thigh. "Your baby doesn't need to be raised by a perfect parent. He just always needs you to try to do your best—as you see fit. Seriously considering giving him up for adoption shows you're already doing that."

"It does?" she asked, her jaw quivering again.

"It does," Kylie said emphatically. She wrapped her arms around Blair, holding her tight. "You're gonna be a great mom. I'm sure of it."

⁓

A little while later, Blair gathered her things and prepared to return to the hotel. "I'd really like it if you'd stay here," Kylie said. "I'd like to keep an eye on you."

"You don't have a guest room."

"I have a sleeper sofa in my office. It's a good one—really. I don't mind sleeping there."

"No way. Your job is too physically demanding to have you tossing and turning all night long. Besides, you're moving this weekend. You must have a million things to do."

"Oh, God, don't remind me! I haven't done a thing."

"Kylie, what are you waiting for? The movers will be here on Saturday morning!"

"I know, I know. I just hate to pack. And even worse than that is unpacking. I hate to be a prima donna, but my hands are too critical to my livelihood to risk hurting them."

"Let me take care of it for you," Blair offered. "You won't have to do a thing."

"Oh, sure, I'm gonna let my pregnant friend do the work I'm too much of a baby to do. That's gonna happen."

"I'm the last person who would pack or unpack a box. I have a crew that works with me to move my wealthy clients. They're going to be at Mr. Action Hero's house tomorrow. I think I can have them squeeze you in on Friday and then unpack you on Saturday."

"Will it cost a lot?"

"Of course! But how much are your hands worth? Remember, I know how much you earn, Doc. You can afford it." She waited a beat and then added, "Besides, you don't have any other options, you big dope."

"I guess you're right," Kylie admitted sheepishly. "But we still have to figure out what to do about you."

"I'm not going to sleep on your couch, I'm not going to let you sleep on it, and I'm not going to sleep with you. We're not in grade school anymore. We're too old for sleepovers."

"Fine," Kylie said, "but I have two guest rooms in my new house. You'll move in with me on Saturday and stay until you decide what to do."

"You still won't have a spare bed."

"Sure I will. I'll buy one tomorrow. You can come with me to make sure you like it."

Blair sighed and gave her friend a wry smile. "If I had another choice, I wouldn't impose. But I can't afford that hotel for much longer, and I won't consider going back to David until he decides he can't live without this baby."

⌒

On Friday afternoon, Blair was sitting in her office, staring out the window. She had work to do—plenty of it—but she couldn't summon the energy to make or take a phone call. The receptionist had buzzed her three times, but Blair ignored the always-annoying sound, knowing that it would stop eventually. She was vaguely aware of her door opening, but she thought it was one of her assistants, just dropping something off. She jumped when she heard her mother-in-law's voice. "Blair?"

"Oh! Sadie!" She turned her chair around to face the older woman, surprised when Sadie leaned over and hugged her.

"How are you, sweetheart?"

"Not good," Blair said, her words slightly muffled by Sadie's boucle knit suit.

Sadie released her and sat on the edge of a chair. She looked at her daughter-in-law with deep concern and said, "I just heard that you've moved out. What in the world has happened, honey?"

"What…what do you know?"

"I know what David told me. He said that you'd had an argument about the baby and that you were staying in a hotel." She leaned over the desk and said, "Tell me what happened. This isn't like you."

Stunned at her mother-in-law's calm tone and apparent empathy, Blair said, "I don't want to betray David, Sadie. This is between us. If he wanted you to know everything that'd happened, he would have told you."

The older woman sighed and then sank back into her chair. Blair looked at her, noting how defeated Sadie appeared. Normally, she was a regular cyclone, her large, boxy body always in motion. It seemed that even her features had softened. She had a large, nearly triangular-shaped face with a very prominent nose and a sharp chin, but today, she didn't look as fierce as usual. Her dark eyes still flashed, though, and Blair was still a little wary of her. "He told me enough," Sadie said quietly. "He said he didn't think he could love this child as his own." She looked down at her hands, the fingers nervously linking and unlinking. "How could he say that?" She looked like she was going to cry, amazing Blair.

"I don't know, Sadie. I was astounded, then angry, and then desperate. For the last two days, I've considered giving the baby up for adoption…" Sadie gasped so loudly that Blair jumped. She shook her head, saying, "A friend helped me see that wasn't a good idea."

Sadie reached across the desk and took Blair's hand, squeezing it firmly. "I'm so sorry, honey. You must be losing your mind."

"I am," she said and then started to cry. Sadie got up, came over to Blair's side of the desk, helped her up, and then enfolded her in a hug. Amazingly, the hug felt wonderful, and Blair wanted to stay in the woman's arms all day.

"He'll come to his senses," Sadie said. "He's just frightened. Most men are frightened when their wives are pregnant."

"He's not frightened. He's thought this through. He doesn't feel connected to the baby, and he doesn't think he can ever be."

"Good Lord!" Sadie sat back down and slapped her open hand on the desk. "How can he be so stupid? God knows I didn't think this was a good idea, but once you've made the commitment, you can't just change your mind!"

"Apparently, you can when you're not the one carrying it," Blair said wryly.

"Give him some time. He'll realize how much he loves this baby. Don't give up on him."

"Sadie, I love David so much…" She crossed her arms and laid her head upon them. "I miss him so much. But I can't be in the house with him. It's bad for the baby to have me so upset. I can't spend every minute of the day crying."

"Come to my house," Sadie said. "You can stay with me until things are back to normal."

"No, no, I need to be close to Santa Monica. I'd be driving all day if I stayed with you in Glendale. I'm gonna stay with a friend who just bought a house in the Palisades. But thanks for your offer. I really do appreciate it."

"Blair, I know I can get on your nerves, but I think of you as family. That's my grandchild who's growing in you. Please take care of yourself and the baby."

"I will," Blair said, misting up again. "Thanks for caring, Sadie."

"I care very much. And no matter what happens, that won't change."

Blair gazed at her mother-in-law for a few moments, trying to get up the nerve to ask a very loaded question. Figuring she had little to lose, she finally said, "I think part of the reason David's so screwed up about this is because of you."

"Me? What did I do?"

"He remembers being a little boy and hearing you and his dad talk about someone adopting a baby. He says that you thought it was a bad idea and that it was like taking in a stray dog from the pound."

"I never…!" Sadie began, but then softened. "He says I said that?"

"Uh-huh."

"Dear God." Sadie tilted her head back and blew out an audible breath. "The smartest thing a parent can do is have a soundproof room in the house. That's where you can go to have a conversation that your kid won't hear and torture himself over for the rest of his life." She looked at Blair and said, "I'm sure he's talking about my sister, Alice." She closed her eyes and looked like she was on the verge of tears. "I didn't know he knew about Michael."

"He knows," Blair said. "So does Michael."

"God damn it!" Sadie bellowed, her voice booming against the walls. "I was twenty-five years old and talking nonsense! And David's gonna let one stupid remark ruin his marriage and his relationship with his child? What kind of idiot is he?"

Surprisingly, Blair felt her hackles rise. It was one thing for *her* to call David an idiot and quite another for Sadie to do so. "He was a little boy. It frightened him, and he obviously didn't think he could tell you about it."

"Damn me," she said, her face red with anger. "How can I fix this?"

"I don't think you can. David's got this belief that he's not related, so he's not connected."

"I don't understand that," Sadie groaned. "Of course, he wants his own baby, but he can't have that! This is the only alternative for him, and it's almost the same. The baby is *yours*, not some stranger's. That has to be enough."

Blair stared at her mother-in-law, too stunned to speak.

"It's like my friend, Annette. Her son is a homosexual. Now, Annette doesn't want him to be one. Who would? But he's her son, and she still loves him. Just because he's not normal is no reason to stop loving him."

"Right," Blair said, wishing she were alone so she could start weaving a noose. She was fairly sure she could hang it over the door and kick her desk chair away…

"I'll go talk to David," Sadie decided. "I'm sure, between the two of us, we can knock some sense into him."

"You start," Blair said. "Let me know how it turns out."

Sadie got up and hugged Blair again. "We'll fix this. You just wait and see."

"Oh, I'll be waiting," she said, forcing a smile. "I'll hold my breath."

On Saturday afternoon, Blair and Kylie sat on the veranda of the new house, drinking lemonade while they listened to the movers bang furniture around inside. "I haven't moved often," Kylie said, smiling at her friend, "but this is clearly the best moving experience I've ever had." They'd been at the house for about two hours, occasionally going inside to supervise the moving crew. "Are you sure you have enough sun block on?" Kylie asked. "Your skin is more sensitive to the sun now."

"I'd like to know what part of me isn't more sensitive," Blair complained. "There isn't one part of me that feels like it used to. My hair's even different. How can that be?"

"Extra protein," Kylie said. "It looks great, by the way. Really thick and shiny."

"Yeah, it's so ironic. My hair looks great, my breasts are bigger, I'm horny as hell, and I chose this moment to leave my husband. Poor planning on my part."

"You haven't left him; you're just taking some time out."

"It's our anniversary, Kylie. Our sixth anniversary, and I'm spending it staying at a friend's house. That sounds like some pretty significant time out, doesn't it?"

"Damn, I didn't know it was your anniversary. That really sucks."

"Well, pregnant women are well known for their tendency to cry for no reason at all," she said. "At least I've got a reason."

Kylie got up from her chair and went over to offer a hug. "I'm so sorry," she said as she held her friend. "I just hope that David comes to his senses soon."

"I do, too," she said. "I lie in bed worrying half the night about what I'll do if he isn't able to get past this. I mean, I told him that I'd divorce him before I'd live with a man who doesn't love our baby. But do I have the guts to *do* that? Jesus, Kylie, I love him! Up until now, we had a really good marriage. How in the hell did this happen?" Kylie increased the strength of her embrace and let Blair cry herself out. It took a while, since her hormones were really raging, but she was finally able to collect herself.

"It's not exactly the same, but I think I felt a little like you do when Stacey and I broke up. It was devastating for me, and I wasn't pregnant. I really can empathize."

Blair looked at her friend for a second and then said, "I didn't know it was that hard for you. When you've talked about her before, you made it seem like just another relationship that didn't work out quite right."

"Oh, no," Kylie said soberly. "She was…I was…it was a major blow. I thought we'd be together until the end."

"Damn, Kylie, I didn't know." She looked at her friend, seeing the sadness in her expressive eyes. "Tell me how you felt."

"I felt like I'd lost a piece of myself," Kylie said, her eyes misting over. "My hopes, my dreams, my heart…all broken."

"But why...I mean...you said you broke up because you didn't share the same interests. Was that all there was to it?"

"Yeah. That was really it. In every other area, we were really good together."

"Tell me about her. Tell me all about her."

"We don't need to do this now," Kylie said. "You've got your own problems."

"Your problems are just as important as mine are. Let me in."

The doctor paused a moment and then gave her friend a half-smile. "Stacey used to say that. She didn't think I was very good at talking about things that bothered me."

"You're not," Blair said, smiling at her. "Unless your life is as perfect as you've led me to believe, you really kinda suck at it. You're not a good complainer."

Kylie laughed. "Complaining wasn't allowed in my house. I never got into the habit."

"It's never too late to start a habit. Give it a try."

"Okay, but don't blame me if I start crying on your shoulder once an hour."

"I can handle ya. Give it up, Doc."

"Okay." Kylie sat in her own chair and rolled her shoulders a few times, her expression a look of deep concentration. "Stacey was almost perfect for me. I was incredibly attracted to her, I respected her, and she made me a better person than I was before I met her."

"That's a lot on the plus side."

"Oh, there's more," she said, tucking a leg up beneath herself. "She was very kind and thought about other people a lot. She had more energy and enthusiasm than I did. She was always upbeat and ready to go."

"But...?"

"But we didn't like to spend our time doing the same things."

"That's it?"

"Yep. That's it." Kylie stared out at the yard for a minute, obviously thinking. "I've been wondering if we didn't make a mistake."

"A mistake? How do you mean?"

"Well, I see how you and David were able to have a happy marriage while each enjoying your own interests. Maybe I wanted too much. Maybe it's not possible to have one person fulfill all of your needs."

"I've never found anyone who could. But I've never looked for someone to, so I'm not the ideal person to ask."

Kylie looked at her with a question in her eyes. "You haven't?"

"No, not really. One of the things I liked about David was that he needed alone time as much as I did. My other boyfriends were always so needy. They wanted more than I was willing to give."

"Huh." *In my entire life, I have never heard a woman complain about her boyfriend being too needy. It's usually just the opposite.*

"They were always pushing me into making a commitment, and I pull away if I feel too much pressure. Before David, I went with a guy whom I really liked, but he was always talking about marriage. I was too young for that kinda talk. It really turned me off."

"Huh." *I've gotta think of something to say, or she's gonna think I've been struck mute!*
"Are you like that, too?"

"Uhm, no, not at all. Just the opposite. I broke up with a woman I loved because she didn't want to go to the symphony with me. I hated not being with her on the weekends, so I stopped going to the things I liked. Then I started to resent her."

"Wow. I can't imagine that. I mean, I thought it would be nice to have David love the arts, but I would never deprive myself of something I loved just because he didn't like it. Don't you enjoy your own company?"

"Yeah, I guess I do, but when I love someone, I want to be with her. That's the whole point, isn't it?"

"I guess it is, if that's how you are. But it seems to me it would be easier to find someone to go to the symphony with than to find someone to love."

"Yeah. You might be right," Kylie said thoughtfully.

"Tell me how you felt when you broke up," Blair said. "How did it affect you?"

"Oh, damn, I was so depressed. I had dreams of growing old with Stacey. We'd planned to have kids, and I used to dream of how much they'd look like her and act like her. She was such a beautiful person, Blair." She sniffed a little and wiped her eyes with the back of her hand. "She got me out of my shell—got me to start doing volunteer work. She made me care about the world in general, not just my little corner of it."

"She sounds fantastic! What did she do for a living?"

"She was, and still is, the development director for a nonprofit corporation that's trying to create disease-resistant, indigenous crops for Third-world countries. Part of their agenda is to help native people make enough money to resist the lure of cutting down more of the rainforest. It's a big job, but she's really making a difference."

"And she got you involved, too?"

"Yeah." Kylie smiled fondly. "We took a couple of trips to South America for research. I loaded myself up with some simple medical supplies and played doctor in some remote villages while Stacey talked to the people about proper crop rotation and biodiversity. Those were some of the most rewarding weeks of my life."

"Kylie, it sounds like you lost so much."

"I did," she said. "That's why I have some idea of what you're going through."

"Jesus!" Blair said. "I don't think I lost half of what you did." Her mouth dropped open at the same time Kylie's did, and both women stared at each other. "I can't believe I said that…but it's true." She started to cry again, and Kylie went to her and tucked an arm around her waist. "I miss David, but I miss him because we got along so well. It was so easy to be with him." She looked at Kylie with her red-rimmed eyes and asked, "Do you know what I mean?"

"No. It was never that easy to be with Stacey. We worked on our relationship all of the time, trying to find ways to get our needs met."

"I meet my own needs," Blair said. "How can you expect someone to do that for you?"

"How can you not?" Kylie asked, truly puzzled. "Why be in a relationship if you're not going to try to fill your partner's needs?"

Blair looked at the doctor for a long time, finally saying, "Do you think I love David?"

"Huh? Jesus, Blair, I don't have any idea. You certainly sound like you do, but I don't know what goes on when you're alone." She leaned over until she could look directly into her friend's eyes. "Why ask a question like that? Do you have doubts about your love?"

"I didn't until now," she said softly. "Your relationship sounds so much...deeper than ours. I don't know," she said glumly. "Compared to how you felt about Stacey, David and I sound like roommates. And you broke up!"

Kylie gazed at her friend for a moment, thinking, *Thank God you said that 'cause I sure didn't want to.* "Your relationship is what it is, Blair. Don't try to judge it against other people's."

"I know, I know," Blair said. "But it sounds like you two were really part of each other. David's more of a...I don't know...maybe a companion."

"Whatever he is to you, you miss him. That's what matters."

"I do miss him," she said. "I think I'll go over and see how he's doing. You can manage without me for a while, can't you?"

"Yeah," Kylie said. "I think I can carry the load. You just take it easy and try not to get upset. Baby Spencer likes everything to be cool."

"I'll call before I come back. I can pick up something for dinner, okay?"

"Do you mind stopping at the market? I really wanna cook tonight. I'm anxious to break in my new kitchen."

"It's a deal."

⌒

When Blair returned, Kylie was sitting in the backyard, sipping an iced tea while she read a book. "Hi," Blair said, her voice weary.

"Hey, how ya doing?" Kylie asked, getting up. "Have a seat and let me get you some tea. It's herbal."

"I should insist on getting it myself, but at this point, I'd choose to die of thirst rather than walk all the way into the kitchen." Given that they were about twelve feet from the room, Kylie had a pretty good idea of how tired her friend was.

The doctor moved one of the chaise lounges into full shade and said, "Lie down right here and relax. I'll be back in a sec." Blair did as she was told and was nearly asleep when Kylie returned moments later.

Handing her the tea, Kylie observed, "Those are some pretty swollen eyes you've got there. Tough day?"

"Incredibly. David cried more than I did, and he's not even pregnant. We're both so sad, Kylie, but neither of us knows how to make this right. I just pray that he's able to make some progress in therapy." She yawned heavily and said, "Part of me knows that's unlikely, though. He has zero respect for the whole process. He thinks therapists are snake oil salesmen." She looked at her friend and asked, "Mind if I take a nap?

This new furniture is lethally comfortable."

"Let me lower the back for you." She did and then pulled a chair over and sat next to her friend. "I know things are going to be very hard for you. Just know that I'll help in any way I can. I can't substitute for the love you're missing, but I care for you. I really do."

Lower lip quivering, tears rolling down her cheeks, Blair just nodded and then managed to croak out, "I know. And that means so much to me. It's only been a week, but I'm so lonely. I miss him so much."

"I understand," Kylie whispered, moving to hold her friend in her arms. "I really do."

"Oh, David said my mom called earlier. Remind me to call her back, will you? My mind's like a sieve nowadays."

"I'll remind you. Now, you go to sleep, and when you wake up, we'll have a little dinner."

"I bought everything on the list you gave me," she said through a yawn. "Don't let me sleep out here all night, 'kay?"

"You got it." Kylie reached down, unlaced her friend's running shoes, and then tugged on the toe of her sock. "See you later."

"Kylie?" she said softly. "Thanks for being my friend."

"Thanks for being mine."

⟶

Two hours later, Blair woke slowly, and Kylie did her best not to laugh at the creases on the woman's face and the drool that darkened her salmon-colored knit shirt. "Did you slip knockout drops into that tea?" Blair grumbled.

"Nope. You're just taking the usual coma-like nap of pregnancy. Get used to it, buddy."

"I hear that a lot from you doctor types. Every time I complain about something to Monique, she tells me to get used to it."

"Actually, I don't say that at work. I always say, 'Hell, yes, I can fix that!' Obstetricians pull that helpless act; surgeons are women of action."

"I'd hate to think of how you'd surgically render me less tired," she said, "but you probably have some ideas."

"I'll think about it while you call your parents. Can I bring you the cordless phone?"

"No, I'll use my cell. My parents have Caller ID."

"You still haven't told them, huh?"

"Nope, and if I can manage it, they'll never know. My father would be on the first plane out here. He's very protective normally, and now that I'm pregnant, it isn't pretty."

"Well, I hope you never have to tell them."

"I normally tell them everything, but I don't want them to think badly of David."

"I understand," Kylie said. "I'll go inside and start dinner. You stay out here and chat for as long as you like."

"I will as soon as I pee. I can't miss an opportunity."

⏤

"You're gonna make some woman a damned fine wife, Doctor Mackenzie," Blair decided an hour later as she asked for a second helping of the delicious risotto that Kylie had prepared.

"Got you to eat your green vegetables, didn't I?" the doctor teased. "And you said you didn't like spinach."

"I like it plenty when it's hidden in this delicious rice. Are you sure you're not Italian?"

"Nope. All Scottish. We're known for our cuisine."

"Uh-huh," Blair said, nodding. "I haven't enjoyed a meal this much in well over a month."

"Glad to oblige. This is a very critical period for the baby, you know, and we want to give him plenty of nutrients to form his central nervous system."

Blair patted her stomach. "You build a good one, baby. We're counting on you." She pushed her plate away, adding, "I hope I gave him enough nutrients 'cause I can't put another bite into my mouth."

"You did very well," Kylie said, obviously pleased. "I'm gonna fatten up those cheeks before you leave here."

"Oh, I'm sure I'll be plenty fat before this is all over. As soon as my all-day sickness passes, I'll be chowing down big time."

"You can come over and help me walk my dog."

"That reminds me," Blair said, "I have a housewarming present for you. Let me go to my room and get it."

"I should say, 'Oh, Blair, that's not necessary,' but I love presents. Go get it right now!"

"Such a child," Blair clucked. "I can't believe people let you come at them with a scalpel."

"Time's a wastin'," Kylie reminded her, tapping the face of her watch with her finger. "Presents now, jokes later."

Muttering to herself, Blair walked down the hall and organized all of the little things she'd bought. She affixed the bow to the biggest of the presents and put the others in various pre-wrapped boxes. The bundle was ostentatiously large, and as Blair waddled back down the hall, Kylie exclaimed, "Good God! What do you have there?" In moments, she removed the gifts from her friend's hands and carried them into the living room.

"Just a few things you're going to need."

Kylie looked down at the fluffy, sheepskin-covered dog bed, wrapped in a wide ribbon with a big bow attached. Next, her eyes traveled to two large boxes. "Uhm, Blair, are there air holes in one of those boxes?"

"Of course not!" she chided, bumping her friend with her hip.

"Well, I know you've been really forgetful, and I thought that maybe—"

"Kylie, I did not buy you a dog! That's like buying you a girlfriend!"

"And the problem with that is…? I have no objection to your bringing in a great big box with a cute little lesbian in it. I don't even mind if she bites."

"Will you open your presents? I know I promised to find you a girlfriend, and believe me, I'm working on it. But I'm not going to have one delivered to the house."

"I'm a busy woman," the doctor maintained. "I'm really not very picky. I trust you."

"Open your presents," Blair repeated, eyes narrowed.

"Oh, all right." Kylie sat down on the dog bed and scooted around a little. "Nice. I'm sure the dog will sleep with me, but this'll look good to people who don't know what a softie I am." She opened the first box to reveal six paperback books, all on the proper way to choose and welcome a puppy into a home. "Cool! I love to read up on stuff before I make a decision."

"I know that," Blair said. "I've been paying attention, Doctor Mackenzie."

"Indeed you have," Kylie said, smiling broadly. She dug into the box again and started to pull out dog toys, revealing chew rings, bones made out of compressed cornstarch, and some made of ground carrots.

"Those seemed ucky to me, but the guy at the pet store says that puppies love 'em."

"Maybe I could get you to eat the carrot ones when your stomach's queasy."

"That doesn't even deserve a response. There's more; keep digging."

Further investigation produced the world's tiniest nylon collar, a six-foot leather leash, a pair of adorably decorated ceramic bowls for food and water, and a bag of puppy dog food. "Goodness, Blair, there's everything here but the dog!"

"That's where you're wrong." She pulled out a card that had been hidden in one of the books and handed it to her friend. "I believe this takes care of everything." Inside the card, which pictured at least twenty-five different puppies, Blair had written:

> Dear Kylie,
>
> As soon as you make up your mind, I'll buy you the dog you desire. It's not the girlfriend I promised, but it's a start.
>
> Thanks for everything, but especially for being my friend when I really needed one.
>
> Blair

"Aw, now you've made me cry," Kylie protested, wiping her eyes with the back of her hand. "That's no fair."

Blair helped her friend to her feet and gave her a robust hug. "I always buy a client a housewarming present, but I'll admit this is my first housewarming dog. Happy new home, Kylie."

"My friends all have nice houses, and their real estate agents gave them bottles of wine or a gift basket with cheese and crackers."

"Well, you're a special client. Very special."

"Thank you, Blair. Thank you so much. This means more to me than I can tell you."

"You just sit down in the kitchen and start reading those books while I do the dishes. I have a feeling you're the type who likes to yell things out while you read."

"Doesn't everyone?" Kylie asked, confused. "I wouldn't read at all without an audience."

↵

It might have been the new house or the new bed, but whatever the cause, Blair had a very difficult time getting to sleep and staying asleep. She had to meet a client at 8:00 a.m. and knew that part of her problem was her obsessing about sleep, which only guaranteed that she was unable to relax. There was a bath adjacent to her room, so she was confident, at least, that she wasn't keeping Kylie up with her frequent trips to the bathroom. After her third trip, at 2:00 a.m., she decided to get up and have some warm milk. Padding through the living room, she noted that Kylie's light was on. Assuming that her friend had left the light on when she fell asleep, Blair knocked softly.

To her surprise, the knock was met with a "C'mon in," so she opened the door and poked her head in. Kylie was lying atop the covers, resting on her stomach, head braced on her hands. All six of the books that Blair had given her were spread across the surface of her king-sized bed, and a legal pad lay amidst the jumble as well. A pen was tucked between her teeth, and when she looked up at Blair, she furrowed her brow and mumbled, "Well, it's down to an Italian greyhound, Tibetan terrier, soft-coated wheaten terrier, bichon frise, or a bulldog."

Eyes wide, Blair asked, "Do you have any idea what time it is?"

"No," she said absently. "I don't work tomorrow, so I can sleep in." With her scowl growing, she said, "I've got to get this figured out. I want to get the dog tomorrow, you know."

Blair marched over to her and extended her hand. "The pen." Giving her a curious look, Kylie took it from her mouth, wiped it dry on the sheet, and handed it over. Blair stuck it behind her ear, then picked up most of the books, and put them on the dresser. The legal pad and the remaining books were whisked away as well, and when the surface of the bed was clean, she ordered, "Get up." Still compliant, Kylie got up, watching as Blair folded the covers back. "Lie down." Once again, Kylie did as she was told, smiling tentatively when the covers were tucked up under her arms—after she had been ordered to lift them, of course. "You are not buying a dog tomorrow. You may dream of dogs while you sleep, but that's the best I can offer. When I get back from my meeting, we'll talk about this, but you have to do more research than just read a few books. I won't have you making a rash judgment about this. Understand?"

The dark head nodded guiltily. "Yes, ma'am."

"Now, go to sleep. Two insomniacs in one house is one too many." She leaned over and kissed the top of Kylie's head, and by the time Blair hit the door, she could hear the soft breathing that characterized her friend's sleep. *Oh, that's cruel, Kylie Mackenzie. That's beyond cruel.*

↵

Blair's meeting lasted the entire morning, and by the time she got home, she was ready for bed. Kylie was sitting at the kitchen table, dog books spread in front of her, also looking like she could use a long nap. She looked up when Blair entered, cocked her head, and asked, "Breakfast? Lunch? Brunch?"

Walking by her, Blair ruffled her friend's disordered hair and said, "I had a bagel and some fruit an hour ago. I'm fine." Walking over to the sink, she picked up her bottle of vitamins and shook a pair of them into her hand. "I think I'll even be able to keep these babies down today." She took them with water, making a face as they went down. "Now comes the countdown. If they stay down for fifteen minutes, the odds are good that I'll keep 'em." Coming back over to the table, she took a seat and gave Kylie a mildly sheepish look. "Sorry to be grumbling already. I'm awfully bitchy when I don't sleep."

"You're not so bad. I'm a little grouchy myself, to be honest. I was planning on lying around and napping all day. Wanna join me?"

"Sure. Sounds like my kinda Sunday." She picked up a book and said, "Sorry about last night. I'm not usually so autocratic. It just pissed me off that you could sleep and were choosing not to!" She chuckled at herself. "I'm so envious of people who can sleep through the night it amazes me."

"Hey, don't apologize. I didn't mind a bit." She looked mildly embarrassed and said, "I've lived alone for too long. It felt great to have someone care about me." With a pensive look, she continued, "It reminded me a little of my mom when I was young. She'd always come into my room and confiscate my portable stereo or a book that I was trying to finish. When I get into something, I have a hard time putting it down. I kinda need some supervision."

Seeing the sad look in her eyes, Blair reached out and covered one of her friend's hands. "Are you lonely? You seem so self-sufficient that I forget you don't like living alone."

"I hate it," she admitted quietly. "I grew up with eleven people in the house: seven kids, my parents, and my father's parents. We always had a couple of dogs, and my oldest sister had two cats. I really like having people around. It doesn't feel like home when I'm alone." She shook her head. "I'm sure you noticed that my condo looked like I was just passing through. I lived there for eighteen years, and I didn't even bother to decorate it. I always thought that I'd fall in love and buy a real home that my partner and I would decorate." She closed the book right in front of her and turned away from Blair to gaze outside. After a moment, she said, "I had to admit defeat to get myself to buy this house. I can't wait my whole life for something I'm not going to get."

"Do you mind talking about this? I don't want to dig into your personal life if you'd rather keep it private."

"No, I don't mind," she said, turning back and smiling gently. "I don't have secrets from you."

Blair looked down at the table, collecting her thoughts. "Why do you think it hasn't happened? I can't imagine a more appealing woman."

"Thanks," Kylie said, a nervous laugh accompanying the word. "I don't mean to be immodest, but I think I'm a pretty good catch, too." She thought for a few seconds. "I think it's mostly a matter of timing. Most people want to partner up when they're young or at least younger than forty. It sounds trite, but most of the great women around my age are taken."

"You never cared for anyone before Stacey?"

"Not enough to partner with permanently. Remember, I didn't get out of medical school until I was twenty-six. Then I spent seven years doing my surgical residency. I barely had time to shower, much less date. The smart guys were the ones who married right out of college or med school. Then they had someone to take care of them during the horrors of the residency program. I used to envy those guys, having a woman waiting at home for them after a seventy-two-hour shift on call."

"Did you have a girlfriend in college?"

"Not a steady one," she said. "I had to work my butt off in college. This was during the time when medical schools were turning away piles and piles of qualified applicants. If you didn't have a 4.0, you didn't even bother to apply. And getting out of the U of C with a 4.0 took a lot of work. But even if I'd had time, I didn't want to be tied down at that point, since I knew I wanted to go to California for med school. And once I got to California, I...I really enjoyed being young and free and..."

"Good looking and charming and sexy as all get out and a great catch..." Blair impishly supplied.

"Well, I did have a couple of years there where I was having a fair amount of success with women. It was a pretty heady time. I mean, one of the things that makes you a good surgeon is a certain bravado, and I had that in spades."

"You still do," Blair said. "You just don't show it much once you let your guard down."

"Maybe," Kylie said, looking a little uncomfortable. "But that all stopped abruptly when I entered my residency program. I don't think I had two dates in seven years. When I hit the sheets, all I wanted to do was sleep—alone."

"What about after that?"

"I started to date again as soon as I began my practice, and I met some nice women, but no one really clicked. I met Stacey when I was thirty-five, and since then—nothing. My friends try to fix me up, but it's not like they all have a bounty of available lesbians hanging around. I play cards and go to family events with my doctor friends, I socialize a little with the guys in my practice, and I monopolize a lot of Nick's time going to cultural events. If he ever finds a steady woman, I'm going to have to start hiring an escort."

"Aren't any of your doctor friends lesbians?"

"Nope. All straight. All married."

"Do you have any lesbian friends?"

Kylie shook her head. "Not by choice, but no, I don't. Stacey got all of our mutual friends after the divorce."

"Really? That amazes me."

"Nah. It made sense. She's much more social than I am. She used to call our friends and ask them to dinner. She was always our social director. I've just never taken the time to seek out new friends since Stacey left."

"Isn't that kinda…funny?"

"It's not that I don't want gay friends. I just don't do the things I'd have to do to hook up with women. I don't belong to any social groups or clubs. I don't like to exercise or go on nature hikes or any of that stuff. I do volunteer work, but only as a surgeon. There are women at the hospital I could date, but I don't want to do that. I like to keep my private life separate from my professional life."

"Well, real estate is full of gay men, and some of them have to have lesbian friends. God, my list of things to do just keeps getting longer and longer. I have to find you some lesbian friends; then I have to get you a girlfriend." She shook her head. "Let me see that list of dogs you like. I have a feeling I'm gonna have to do that, too," she teased playfully.

⟶

By the time dinner was finished, the pair had narrowed the list down to two. "I think it's between the wheaten and the bichon," Kylie decided. "My books say they're the best with kids and strangers."

"They both have to be groomed professionally," Blair mentioned.

"That's okay. I don't mind paying to have the dog groomed. Neither one sheds, which is worth a lot to me. I don't want to hire a housecleaner, and I don't want to be vacuuming every day."

"No housecleaner? Are you mad?"

"No," she said, shaking her head, "I don't really like having strangers in my house. I've always cleaned my own place."

"You've never had a home this size," Blair reminded her. "When you change your mind, I'll ask Isabella if she wants to take you on. She's wonderful."

"All right," Kylie said and then continued with her dog analysis. "Which one do you like best?"

"I'm not sure I've seen either one up close. Let's do what that one book suggested and find a dog show somewhere around here. Then we can see a bunch of them."

Giving her a bit of a pout, Kylie said, "I'm not gonna get a dog next weekend, either, am I?"

"Not likely," Blair said. "But I guarantee you won't regret your decision when you do get one. Isn't that worth waiting for?"

"Surgeons don't like delayed gratification. We're a special breed."

"I understand how special you are," Blair teased. She kissed the top of her friend's head and then stood and said, "Now, get your special butt over here and help me with the dishes."

⟶

When Kylie came home from work on Monday, Blair's door was closed. *Must be taking a nap*, Kylie assumed. By dinnertime, when her friend still hadn't appeared, Kylie went to the door and knocked, hearing a mumbled, "Yeah?"

She opened the door and saw Blair lying in bed with a pillow over her face. "You'll never get to sleep if you nap all night," warned Kylie. "I have dinner just about ready."

"I'm not napping. I'm still in bed."

"Blair!"

The pillow was lowered, and Blair focused as best she could. "I don't wanna be an asshole, but I can't stay here if you try to mother me. I told Mandy that I was pregnant and that I've been having dreadful morning sickness. She's gonna cover for me this week. So, I plan on lying in bed and indulging myself in any way I see fit. Please let me make my own choices, Kylie."

"I'm sorry," the doctor said, feeling like she was about to cry.

Blair saw the look on her friend's face and immediately regretted her words. "C'mere," she said, patting the bed. Kylie walked over and sat down, trying to make her face follow Blair's instruction to smile. "I'm sorry for snapping at you. But I feel like I've lost control of my life. I'm pregnant and, from the looks of things, well on my way to being a single mother—something I never would have chosen for myself. The baby's sapping all of my energy and my concentration, and he's ruined my stomach. I just want to have a week where I'm not responsible for anything or anyone." She took Kylie's hand in hers and squeezed it. "Can you understand that?"

"Yeah, yeah, I can."

"I like being here, and if we were both just starting out, I'd love to share a house with you. But as much as I like you, I had to leave my husband to be here. I'm sad. Sadder than I've ever been. If I weren't pregnant, I'd go to my doctor and demand some Prozac. But I can't do that. I just have to fight through this, and I have to do it on my own."

"No, you don't. You could find someone to talk this through with, Blair. You don't have to do this on your own."

"Look, Kylie, normally, I'd agree with you. But I don't have some deep-seated psychological stuff going on. I'm going through a crisis, and I don't have control over most of the elements. Seeing a therapist isn't going to do much for me at this point."

"I still think that you could benefit—"

Blair squeezed Kylie's hand and said, "I know you care. But you can show you care by letting me do this my own way."

Kylie nodded, fighting the urge to argue her point. "I do care." She leaned over, kissed Blair's forehead, and then got up. "My offer of dinner holds, but I won't bug you about it."

"Thank you. I could use one thing, if it's not too much trouble."

"Anything."

"Would you be uncomfortable lying with me for a little while? I'm so lonely, and I miss human contact."

Kylie kicked off her shoes and then took off her skirt and blouse. She was wearing a very pretty black full slip, and when she climbed into bed, Blair sighed, feeling the silky fabric against her legs. "You feel nice. Soft," she said, cuddling up to her friend's back. "Very nice."

Kylie patted the hand that rested on her waist and slid her fingers through Blair's. "Sleep now. Try to forget your troubles. Just sleep."

"Thanks...for everything," Blair said through a massive yawn. "You're the best."

⟶

When Blair woke, she spent a few moments trying to get her bearings. She slept so deeply during her naps that she often felt disoriented upon waking. But being pressed up against Kylie's body had her even more confused for a few seconds. Kylie must have felt movement, for she said, "You awake?"

Blair rolled onto her back and said, "Yeah. Barely. I was just trying to recall how you wound up in my bed."

Kylie flipped over quickly and said, "You invited me!" Her eyes were wide with alarm, but her expression calmed when Blair smiled.

"I remember now. I was just confused at first."

"This is kinda odd," Kylie said, her eyes darting to the tiny space that separated them. "I don't think I've ever been in bed with a thoroughly straight woman."

"Thoroughly straight?"

"Yeah. I slept with a woman who was vacillating between men and women, but never with one who was certain she was straight."

"You have now. There's never been a question in my mind. But you're very nice to sleep with. You're very cuddly and soft. Kinda maternal." She looked at Kylie and said, "I can't imagine feeling sexual with a woman. Even though you're very nice to sleep with, I can't see how being with someone like yourself turns you on."

"I can't see how being with someone so different turns you on. I love men, but they're so..." She made a face. "Hard and rough and hairy. I wouldn't want to sleep with someone who could overpower me."

"Oh, God, that's the best! You've never had that?"

"No. No way."

Kylie looked so repulsed that Blair asked, "You...haven't had a bad interaction with men...sexually, have you?"

"No, not at all! I just love the softness and suppleness of a woman's body. Thinking of having a big, strong man hold me down gives me the willies."

Blair groaned sexily. "There's nothing better. Trust me. I love to feel overpowered. To have a man hovering over me, holding me in place. It's such a turn-on to know he can do whatever he wants, but trust him to take care of you." She shivered roughly. "Sooo sexy."

"Well, I'm not switching." Kylie patted Blair's leg and started to get up.

"I'm not, either, but I'd love those maternal hugs and cuddles every once in a while." She gazed at Kylie rather shyly. "Is that too much to ask? I don't wanna impose..."

"I don't feel maternal with you. More like we're...sisters. And I slept with my sisters until they forcibly threw me out of their rooms."

"Sisters it is," Blair said, extending a hand for Kylie to shake.

"Anytime you need some comfort, you just let your adopted sister know. I'll always be there for you."

On Wednesday afternoon, Blair dragged herself from bed at 2:00, took a long shower, and then dressed in the coolest thing she owned—a pale-blue, Oxford cloth shift. Normally, she wore a T-shirt under it, but the weather was so hot and sticky that she didn't bother. She drove to her home, her heartbeat picking up when she saw David's BMW in the driveway. She rang the bell, feeling odd doing so. But it seemed like David's house now that she was officially staying with Kylie. After a minute, she realized he must be in the back, so she walked down the driveway by the side of the house. She heard the spa motor whirring and smiled, thinking of how happy David was when he could relax in the hot tub after a stressful day. As she expected, he was sitting in the tub, an unhealthily large glass of Scotch in one hand and a lit cigarette in the other.

Blair stopped so quickly that her neck hurt a little. He must have seen some motion out of the corner of his eye because he turned to face her. He tried to look relaxed, but she could just see his mind working, trying to think of a way to remove himself from her glare.

She walked over to him and sat down on the chair that held his towel. For a moment, she busied herself by neatly folding the towel and placing it on her lap. The few moments this took allowed her to compose herself and speak in a calm voice. She twitched her head towards his hands, asking, "How long did you stay smoke-free?"

He looked so guilty that she almost felt sorry for him. "Couple hours after you left."

She exhaled loudly. "After the pain you went through to stop? All of those weeks of anguish?"

"I was upset," he said. He took a drink and then another drag on his cigarette. "I don't know any other way to calm down."

"That isn't a way to calm down, David. Drinking as much as you do is just a way to avoid feeling—anything."

"Hey!" His dark eyes were filled with anger, shocking her completely. "You can't leave me and still tell me what to do! If you're gonna boss me around, you have to live here to do it."

"Boss you around?" She stared at him, dumbfounded.

"Yeah. You heard me. You boss me around. You always have." He took another drink, gulping down nearly a third of his Scotch, and then gave her an insolent glare. "You lost your right to do that when you left."

She put her elbows on her knees and dropped her head into her hands, unable to stop herself from crying. He didn't say a word or move a muscle. He just continued to stare at her. She cried quietly, angry with herself for showing him how upset he'd made her. When she felt like she could drive, she got up and started to walk away.

"Hey! Don't you dare leave!"

"Why not?" She swung around and looked at him as if she'd be happy to shoot him right between the eyes. "So I can sit here and have you insult me? So you can blow smoke in my face?"

"My whole world is coming apart," he said, his teeth clenched together. "I've lost my wife, I'm never going to have a child, and now you've turned my mother against me! Why don't you just cut my balls off, too?"

"Don't tempt me," she spat. Wiping her eyes, she took in a breath, squared her shoulders, and strode back down the driveway, ignoring his shouts. She was able to guide her car a few blocks away; then she turned it off and rolled the windows halfway down. Turning on the classical station, she lowered her seat and cried until she fell asleep.

⤙

When Blair walked into the house, Kylie was in the kitchen, making a dinner that normally would have had Blair salivating. She was so upset, though, that she couldn't bear the thought of eating or conversing.

"Hi!" Kylie called out in her normal cheery manner. "Did you go to work today?"

"No." Blair walked into the kitchen and up behind Kylie. She put her hand on the doctor's shoulder and said, "I went to see David, and it was horrible. I don't want to talk about it, or anything else, for that matter, so I'm going to bed."

"It's only 6:00," Kylie said. "Are you sure?" This last sentence was directed at Blair's back, and Kylie only received a nod in reply.

⤙

On Friday morning, Blair came out of her room just as Kylie was leaving for the hospital. "Hey, how ya doin'?" the doctor asked.

Blair looked horrible. She hadn't washed her hair since Wednesday, and it stuck out at odd angles all over her head. Her eyes were bloodshot and puffy from crying and bore smudges of a purplish-blue hue on her lower lids. She was wearing lovely salmon-colored silk pajamas, but they were formfitting, and the last button wouldn't fasten, allowing her tummy to show. "I'm great," she said, her sarcasm dulled somewhat by a wry smile.

"Other than staying out of the way, can I do anything to help?"

Blair walked over to the refrigerator and stuck a glass into the dispenser on the door, watching it fill with water. "Why've you been home every night this week? You usually go out."

Kylie gave her a puzzled look and replied, "I didn't feel like going out. I like my new house and don't want to leave it."

Leaning against the counter, Blair crossed her ankles and gave the doctor a long look. "Bullshit."

"Pardon?"

"That's bullshit. You always go out. Sometimes once, sometimes twice, more likely three times a week. You're hanging around here because of me."

Exasperated, Kylie said, "Well, Jesus, do you blame me? For all I know, you're committing suicide in there! I've never known anyone who was so withdrawn when she was upset."

Blair put her glass down, walked over, and stood right in front of Kylie. "Can I have a hug?" Blair put her arms around her friend and held on tight.

"Sure you can," Kylie said. "Anytime." They held each other for a long while, and Kylie could feel Blair's body shake as she started to cry.

"I'm so lonely," she sobbed. "But I don't want to talk. I just want to make it all go away."

"I know you do," Kylie said. "I know that."

Blair looked up at her friend, green eyes filled to overflowing with tears. "Can you make it go away, Kylie? Make things like they used to be?"

"I wish I could," Kylie said, tears forming in her own eyes. "I'd do anything in the world to help you through this, but I don't think I can change the past."

"That's why I want to sleep through the future," Blair said. She released Kylie, patted her on the side, and shuffled back to bed, closing the door behind herself.

◡

That night, Blair was lying in bed, watching a three-hanky DVD and crying as usual. To the gentle knock on her door, she said, "Come on in, but it ain't pretty in here."

Nick stuck his head in, making Blair leap to pull the covers over herself. "Jesus! Where'd you come from?" she demanded.

"Sorry," he said, blushing a little. "I should have announced myself before I came in."

"No, no, that's all right," she said, obviously flustered. "I thought it was Kylie. I'm not dressed for company." She ran a hand through her hair and then gave him a suspicious look. "Did Doctor Worrywart send you?"

"Not directly. I've been asking about you, and Kylie keeps saying that you're depressed. Are you doing anything to feel better?"

"Sleeping all day?"

He smiled at her and sat on the edge of her bed. "That's one of the symptoms of depression, not a remedy for it."

"Nick, I can't take any drugs—"

"I know that," he said. "But there are other ways to fight your way out of this."

She put a hand on his arm, giving it a squeeze. "It's not that I doubt your abilities, Nick, but I don't want a therapist."

"I couldn't be your therapist if I wanted to be, so that's not an issue. I'm your friend, and I care about you."

Nodding, she said, "I'm your friend, too. But I don't want a referral, either."

"How about a non-therapeutic conversation? No harm in that, is there?"

She gave him a slight scowl. "You're very persuasive, Doctor Scott." She put her hands behind her head and lay back against the pillows. "Whaddya wanna know?"

"Well, as a friend, I'd like to know how you've been spending your days. Kylie tells me you didn't work much last week and not at all this week."

"Stoolie," she grumbled. With a sigh, she said, "I've been lying in bed, watching sad movies so I can cry about someone else's miserable life."

"Have you been crying about yours, too?"

"Yeah. Of course, I have. It's been a rough year, Nick," she said, giving him a wry smile.

"So…sleeping and crying, huh? Is that all? Have you been talking to friends or family or making any plans?"

"No. Just sleeping and crying." She shook her head, looking annoyed. "But I only sleep during the day. I'm up almost all night, worrying and wishing I could turn back the clock." She hit the bed with her fist. "I know I should do…something…but I can't make myself."

"I'm not criticizing you, Blair. Far from it. I just wanted to know what's going on."

"Short story. Daily agenda: cry, sleep, worry, and repeat ad infinitum."

He smiled and rubbed her knee. "I can't imagine how hard this has been for you. I mean that. I can't begin to understand how devastating this must be."

Seeing the empathy in his eyes, she started to cry again. "Damn it, Nick, I thought I was done for the day."

"How about a suggestion?"

"Sure." She took the tissue he offered and wiped her eyes.

"I know how insidious depression can be. And yours is mixed with grief. But you're not going to get better by lying here every day."

"I can't make myself do anything else. I've tried."

"How about this?" He looked at her for a moment, obviously thinking of a plan. "Your schedule is going to be screwed up unless you make yourself get up and stay up during the day. I can understand if you're not able to work, but you have to get up and get out of here. You can go for walks, visit with friends, talk on the phone, listen to music, go to movies…whatever gets you out of this bed."

"Okay," she said, nodding. "You're right. I've got to stop feeling sorry for myself."

"No, no, no," he said quickly. "You need some time to feel your grief and your anger. But you need to schedule that time."

"Schedule it?"

"Yeah. Set aside an hour or even two hours a day where you let yourself feel whatever comes up. Your sorrow and your anger and your depression are real, but you don't have to let them take over your life. Keep them contained, but don't deny them."

"How do I do that?"

"Do you have a laptop?"

"Sure."

"If I were you, I'd sit down at a designated time, not near bedtime, and write my feelings down. You don't have to keep the notes; you never have to read them again. Just write. Don't edit what you put down, and don't worry about spelling or grammar. Let your feelings out."

"I'll try," she said. "That's not my style, but I'll try."

"Okay. If you get up and move around, you'll start to feel better. I'm sure of that. But you might need a little extra help at night."

"Yeah. Like a fifth of vodka."

"That would work, but it might have some side effects," he said, smiling at her.

"How about trying this? Sit down at your computer again and write down the things you worry about at night. Don't leave anything out."

"How's that different from the other thing you want me to do?"

"The other thing is much more inclusive. I want you to feel your feelings as you do it. All of them. But at night, I only want you to name your fears. Write down the things that haunt your dreams. The things that make you afraid to lie down and close your eyes."

She gave him a look. "Who told you?"

"No one," he said with a laugh. "When people are depressed, they're usually afraid, too. That's one of the biggest reasons people have insomnia."

"I don't see how this can help. I hate to be afraid, and thinking about it'll just make it worse, won't it?"

"No, it won't. I know it seems counterintuitive to put names to your fears, but I've seen it work—often."

"Okay, okay. I'll try anything at this point."

"One last thing," he said. "I want you to try some visualization."

Her head dropped back, thunking softly against the wall. "Oh, God, this is therapist talk."

"It is, but it works."

"Hit me," she said, looking pained.

"I know you're stuck in the present, but I want you to visualize the future. I want you to think of your baby—your happy, healthy, chubby little baby. You're holding him in your arms and feeling his soft skin against your body. Imagine how completely happy you are now that your child is with you. You can think about nursing him, if you're going to do that, or giving him a bottle. Think of the peace and serenity you'll feel once he is here."

Nick's voice was soft and deep and seemed to reach inside Blair's heart. She found herself hearing every word as if it were handed down from on high. "Focus on that," Nick said. "Imagine every precious sensation. His smell. The way his head is shaped. His little hand grasping your finger. The way he looks at you with those deep-blue baby eyes. Keep those images in your head until you fall asleep. I guarantee that you'll be able to sleep if you can keep those pictures in your head."

She was crying again and found herself wrapped in his arms. "I've been afraid to think of him," she sobbed. "I'm afraid I'll lose him somehow or he'll be stillborn. It feels like nothing good can come of all this pain."

"That's not true," he said, his voice sure and calm. "That's just not true. Your baby is fine, and he is gonna be very, very happy to meet you."

"I love him so much," she whimpered. "So very much."

"I know you do. He knows that, too. Things will get better. I know they will." He pulled away and then brushed her hair from her eyes. "Now, take a shower and come out and have dinner with us. Kylie's cooking, and then we're gonna watch a happy movie."

"I don't remember how to smile," she said, looking a little panicked.

"Yes, you do." He cupped her cheek and looked into her eyes. "We'll help you. We're your friends, Blair. Let us be involved in your life."

"I will," she said, sniffling again.

"No more crying tonight. It's not on your schedule."

⌐

Later that night, Blair helped Kylie clean up the kitchen, both women bustling around the large space, neither speaking. They were nearly finished when Blair took a dishtowel from Kylie's hands and started to dry. "I was pretty angry with you for dragging Nick over here tonight, but talking to him did help me."

"I know I should have stayed out of it, but I knew you weren't eating regular meals and—"

Blair put a hand on her friend's arm. "It's all right. I would have done the same thing if you were depressed. Sometimes, you have to do what feels right."

"I'm glad you're not mad at me. I hate to be in trouble," the doctor said, looking charmingly juvenile.

"You're not in trouble. I can't imagine staying mad at you, anyway." She crossed the kitchen to put the towel away and said, "Nick gave me some suggestions that I'm gonna try. But one thing I thought of during dinner might help, too."

"What's that?"

"I'm gonna try to make myself believe that David's on a really long business trip. It's so hard for me to walk around and act like nothing's wrong when he's only a few minutes away. I'm gonna tell myself that I can't reach him and put him out of my mind."

"Can you do that?" Kylie asked. "I don't think I could."

"Well, I can't fool myself, but I'm not going to ask him when he's traveling. I'm just gonna assume he's gone. And I'm gonna tell him that we can only talk or see each other once a week. And I want that to be on the weekend, so I can lie in bed and cry if it doesn't go well. I refuse to have this ruin my work."

"I think that's a good idea," Kylie said. "Limiting contact is probably a good idea, too."

"Yeah. The last time we saw each other was horrible. I can't afford to have scenes like that very often. I have to think of what's best for the baby, and having this much stress isn't good."

They walked into the den, and Kylie turned on the TV. Watching the evening news with half of her attention, the doctor said, "Wanna tell me about what happened when you went over there?"

"There's not much to talk about. He acted like an asshole and then apologized the next day. I forgave him, of course, but it really…I don't know…I guess it made me wonder again just who he is. He was so angry with me, Kylie, and he accused me of things that I never did to him. He was so fucking self-involved, and that's not how he used to be."

"Really? I didn't think you could hide something like that for ten years."

"I know! That's my point! That's part of the reason I think he might get over this.

He's not acting like himself. I've known this guy for ten years, and I'm sure I know him well. I'd hate like hell to split up and then have him go back to being the guy I love."

Kylie stared at the television for a long time, obviously thinking. She finally turned to Blair and said, "Ten years is an awfully long time. I wouldn't give up easily, either."

"Thanks," Blair said, patting her leg. "It's nice to hear that you don't think I'm being an idiot for hanging on."

"I don't," Kylie said. "I promise I don't. I think you'd be an idiot to give up on a guy you love, especially when he's acting irrationally. Hell, maybe he should have a thorough checkup."

"Not every problem has a disease behind it," Blair said, giving Kylie a teasing look.

"No, but if he does, I can just open him up and take it out." She smiled and added, "Nick works with people for years. I could never do that. I like problems I can fix with a scalpel."

"I think Nick's a better doctor for our problems," Blair said, "but I wish you could fix this one quickly. I'd even let you operate in the kitchen."

"The lighting *is* really good," Kylie said wistfully, trying to imagine her home surgical theater.

⌐

When Blair came home from work the following Wednesday night, she plopped her briefcase down by the front door, went over to sit next to Kylie on the sofa, and announced, "You've got a date for Saturday."

"I do?" she asked, wide-eyed. "With whom?"

"Remember my telling you about Sheila, who works for me?"

"Uh-huh. Your secretary, right?"

"No. That's Jeanne. Sheila and Mandy are both agents."

"Oh. Right." Kylie waited a beat and then said, "I thought she was married."

"She is, silly. But she has a lesbian cousin who's gonna be in L.A. for a job interview on Friday. She wants to see the sights to help her decide if L.A. is right for her. Sheila was moaning about the fact that she has to work both days of the weekend, and she wasn't wild about giving her cousin her car since the poor woman doesn't know a thing about L.A. So, I volunteered you to be her tour guide."

"A tour guide, huh? Can you tell me anything about her, other than she sleeps with women and doesn't know how to read a map?"

Looking slightly crestfallen, Blair asked, "Aren't you excited? I am."

"Of course, I am," Kylie insisted, even though she hated the thought of going on a blind date. "I'd like to know a little something about her so I can, uhm, make sure I take her to places she'd like."

"Oh." Now Blair's smile widened, and she said, "I'll ask a bunch of questions tomorrow. What do you want to know?"

How early can I drop her off if she's a dud? Kylie wanted to say, but she advised her friend to ask the usual questions about the woman's likes and dislikes.

⌐

"Big weekend coming up, huh?" Blair said with enthusiasm when she got home on Friday night. "A date with Amanda tomorrow and a dog show on Sunday. We're making progress here, buddy."

"We sure are," Kylie said, smiling warmly, touched by Blair's obvious concern. "You know, I've been amazed at how good your mood was this week. You seem almost like your old self."

"Well, I'm not," Blair said, "but Nick's suggestions have really helped. I'm still sad and lonely, and I miss the David I used to know, but I'm able to contain my feelings. I spend some time being sad every day, and that lets me spend the rest of the time feeling like my old self."

"I'm glad it's helping. Baby Spencer's probably happy, too."

"That's where my focus has to be. I have to look to the future."

⌐

When Blair woke on Sunday, she splashed some water on her face, brushed her hair, and grabbed her robe, practically running to find Kylie. She slid across the kitchen floor on her stocking feet, eyes bright with excitement. "How'd it go? It must have been pretty good for you to be gone so long."

Kylie took a long sip of her coffee, just to prolong the torture. "You, my friend, can pick my dates any old time you want. It went very well, and if she moves here, I'm going to pursue her with abandon."

Blair started to jump around the kitchen like a kid on a pogo stick. "Yeah!" she cried. "That's so great!" She reached down and hugged her friend roughly. "Tell me everything. Don't you dare leave one detail out."

Kylie blinked up at her impishly. "Sure about that? For all you know, we had wild sex all night long, and she just left."

"Oh!" Blair sat down heavily on a kitchen chair. "Well, uhm, I don't…I mean…"

Laughing heartily, Kylie caught her friend's nose between her thumb and index finger and gave it a tug. "I kissed her good night, Blair. Granted, it was a helluva kiss, but that's it. My date was entirely G-rated."

"I knew that," Blair said, looking happy. "You don't seem like the type to sleep with someone on the first date."

"Well, I have, but it's not my norm. Actually, it's rare for me to kiss someone on the first date, but Amanda's…well, I wanted to let her know I was most definitely interested."

"So tell me about her!"

Kylie looked at her watch and said, "I'll tell you about her on the way to Santa Barbara. It's 9:00, and the dog show only lasts until 2:00. We've got to get moving."

"Damn!" Blair got up and said, "Get in the shower with me so we can talk while we get ready." Kylie blinked at her, her mouth not moving when she tried to speak. "Got ya back for that 'she just left' comment," Blair teased, capturing Kylie's nose victoriously.

136

Kylie agreed to drive after Blair declared that she had a tendency to pull over and take a quick nap when she was behind the wheel for very long. At Blair's insistence, they took her car since she had little confidence that Kylie's could make it to Santa Barbara and back. They hadn't driven two blocks before Blair began her badgering. "I've been the very soul of patience. Now tell me everything!"

"Okay," Kylie said. "I picked her up at noon, and we went over to the Third Street Promenade since it was such a nice day."

"Back up," Blair demanded. "What'd she look like? What was she wearing?"

"Uhm, she looked kinda normal. Nothing all that distinctive."

"Oh, please. I want some details."

"This isn't what I'm best at."

"That's becoming painfully obvious. Don't look at me," Blair commanded. "What color is my hair?"

"Kinda red, kinda blonde. More blonde when you're inside, more red when you're in the sun."

"Excellent. It's called 'strawberry blonde,' in case you're interested. Eyes?"

"Green mostly, but a little hazel in dim light."

"See?" she said triumphantly. "I knew you paid attention. Now describe Amanda."

"Okay," Kylie sighed, obviously thinking hard. "If I had to compare her to someone, I'd say Jodie Foster. She's thin and kinda slight. Looks like a good wind would knock her over."

"Jodie's cute," Blair beamed.

"Now, she doesn't look exactly like Jodie. She's the only person I could think of who was even close."

"But Amanda's cute, right?"

"She not...un-cute," Kylie said, wincing a little. "She isn't my usual type, but I'm not gonna let that bother me. Amanda has appears to have all the qualities I want in a woman. That's what matters."

Blair looked at her friend for a moment and then said, "How bad was she?"

"She wasn't bad! She was just...plain. Nothing about her was eye-catching. Like her hair. It's not really blonde and not really brown; it's kind of a medium color."

"There's no such thing as medium color. Try again."

"This is hard!" she complained to no avail. "Okay, I guess it's mousy brown, but that's such a nasty term for hair."

"How does she have it cut?"

"I don't know," Kylie said, looking puzzled. "It looked like Jodie's. Straight, about to here," she said, indicating her shoulder. "I think she parted it on the side. Nothing special. Just hair."

"Did it have any body?"

"Body? You mean thickness?"

"Not really, but that'll do."

"Uhm, no, not really. It was kinda thin, and you could see the shape of her skull."

Blair made a face that Kylie couldn't see. "Eye color?"

"Good lord! I don't need to be able to identify her in a police lineup, do I?"

"Eye color," Blair insisted.

"Brown. But real pale. Kinda the color of her hair, I think. And her skin was pale...the same tone as her hair, come to think of it. She was kinda...beige."

Blair winced. "Beige?"

"Yeah. But beige is nice. Neutral, but not bad."

"How was she built?"

"Fine," Kylie said. "Nothing jumped out at you, but she was just fine."

"Nice breasts?"

"Blair! I didn't feel her up!"

"Oh, come on," she chided. "You've already told me you like breasts. Don't try to act like you didn't check 'em out."

Kylie mumbled something that Blair couldn't catch and then shrugged her shoulders, saying, "There wasn't much to check. She was very modestly endowed. Actually, she was completely flat. But that's not a deal breaker for me," she insisted. "I'm not overly swayed by a woman's body. I've dated lots of pretty women who made me want to hang myself rather than spend another minute on the date."

Beaming, Blair patted her thigh. "I like you, Doctor Mackenzie. I knew that's how you'd be."

Winking at her, Kylie said, "Don't get me wrong. If I could find a cultured, literate, kind, funny, gorgeous woman with a C cup, I'd be delighted. But the gorgeous part and the bra size are clearly at the bottom of my list."

"Understood. You're looking at the inside first, outside second."

"Well, I am a surgeon," she playfully reminded her. "I love the inside of a woman."

Blair pinched her on the waist, saying, "I assume that Amanda was cultured, literate, kind, and funny—even though she was beige and had small breasts—correct?"

"Well, I'm not sure about the kind part," Kylie said, "but she had the cultured, literate, and funny parts nailed. She was here to interview for an assistant professor's job in the English department at UCLA. She teaches poetry and creative writing."

"Wow, that *is* literate."

"Yeah. She's thirty-three—which is well within my preferred age range—she doesn't have a lot of emotional baggage, and she's not averse to having children."

"You asked her that?" Blair gasped.

"No, Blair, I didn't say, 'You look like good breeding stock, Amanda. How are your fallopian tubes?'"

"Well, how do you know she's willing to have kids?"

"We were talking about our past relationships, and she said she'd recently dated a woman with a child and found that being with a toddler appealed to her. She said she thinks she'd like a child of her own. She's waiting until she's settled into a job that seems permanent before she considers the matter more fully."

"She sounds perfect for you, Kylie. Heck, you could even give her breast implants!"

"Hmm...I'd never thought of that. I could turn my woman into a Victoria's Secret model."

Chuckling, Blair said, "I'm happy now. I think I've gotten everything out of you that I'm gonna get, so I'm taking a nap. Wake me when we get there." She pulled her handy pillow from the backseat, lowered her chair, and twitched around until she was in a good position.

When Blair was minutes from sleep, Kylie said softly, "She can't dance a lick, but she kissed like she knew how to use her tongue."

"Behave!" the blonde giggled. "If I don't get a nap, I'll be barking at those dogs."

⌐

Kylie was as excited as a child on Christmas morning. "Do you think anybody will be selling puppies?" she asked as they parked the car at the fairgrounds.

"No, I don't, and if anyone is, we're not buying one today. We're here to let you see a large sample of all the dogs you think you like so you can be sure you like them in person."

"When I was a kid and we wanted a new dog, we went down to the pound and picked the one that looked like it needed a home the worst. Why can't I do that?"

"You can, but you've been talking about getting a purebred dog. And if you want to go that way, I want to make sure you get the one you really want."

"You're gonna be a good mom, Blair; you've got the drill down cold." She reached down and captured her friend's hand, partially to help her across the uneven terrain and partially to avoid another pinch.

⌐

By 2:00, not only had the quest for the perfect dog not been resolved, but also the number of dogs Kylie was interested in had mushroomed to over a dozen. "I thought this was supposed to make things easier," she said. "Now I want dogs I've never even heard of!"

"We're gathering information today," Blair reminded her. "Looking at dogs was only part of my plan."

They walked along the line of tents where vendors were selling every type of dog product. They found a very talkative and opinionated man at the big grooming care booth. Kylie started up a conversation with him, telling him that her biggest concern was finding a dog that loved children, and he gave them his personal opinion on each of the breeds on Kylie's expanding list.

"How old are the kids you're talking about?"

"Well, I want a dog that likes all kids, but the one I'm most concerned about isn't going to be born for five and a half months."

Stealing a discreet look, he winked at Blair and said, "I'd go with the Norfolk terrier."

Kylie's surprise was obvious. "A terrier? Really?"

"Yeah. It's a great little dog, and it hasn't been overbred like some of the dogs on your list. They're very good-natured, very loving, and very active. We had small terriers when my kids were little, and it was great. The dog entertained the baby, and the baby entertained the dog. Kept them both busy," he said, laughing.

"Do they have any here?" Blair asked.

"Sure. As a matter of fact, I have a friend who has his RV set up not far from here. Go down this aisle, turn left, and stop at an RV with a spare tire cover that says 'Gideon's Norfolks.'"

"Thanks a lot," Blair said. "You've been a lot of help."

The pair wandered around until they found the RV, and Kylie started to squeal when she saw a portable, wire-mesh enclosure holding a female with a litter of puppies, all four of the pups nursing peacefully. Blair hoped fervently that the puppies were not old enough to wean since she knew they'd be taking one home if they were. Kylie's expression was positively enraptured, and she dropped to the ground like a rock, murmuring sweetly to the little dogs.

The owner came out of his RV and, luckily, was not put off by a stranger drooling over his puppies. Blair spoke to him while Kylie was held in thrall, barely cognizant of her surroundings. She finally responded to a persistent tugging on her shirt. "Time to go, Kylie," Blair said. "The puppies have to go home now."

"But they just finished eating," she said, eyes riveted.

"You can't have any of them. They're all spoken for. It's time to let go now."

Kylie looked up at her friend with the saddest eyes Blair had ever seen. "I can't have one?"

"No, but the nice man gave me some good suggestions on how to get you one of your own."

Kylie got up slowly, brushing her slacks off when she stood. "I can pay twice whatever he's getting for them," she said quietly.

Blair took her by the sleeve and tugged her away from the space. "Kylie! People have entered into contracts to buy those dogs. You can't try to steal them out from under them."

"Why not?" she blinked.

"Because it's not right, and you wouldn't like it if someone did it to you."

"You are such a mom," she said, laughing. Draping an arm around Blair, she admitted, "I was just pulling your leg. I wouldn't really try to outbid someone."

"I wouldn't put it past you," Blair said, snuggling into her friend's hug. "You looked like you were deeply in love with those pups."

"I am," she sighed. "I've gotta have one. As soon as I go home and research every site that talks about them, that is. I can't bear to make a mistake about such a big decision."

"If this is the right breed, you give me a little while, and I'll use the ideas that breeder suggested. We'll get you a great dog."

"At this rate, I'll have a girlfriend before I get a puppy." She caught herself saying that and asked, "Am I gonna bitch about that?"

Chapter Five

*D*avid volunteered to see a therapist, and with referrals from Nick, he started to go once a week. Blair was still trying to limit contact with him, but she found herself calling him after every therapy session. He always seemed so down that she wanted to try to prop him up a little, and a phone call was the only way she felt safe doing it.

She'd been out of the house for three weeks when she told him, "It means a lot to me that you're working so hard. I know this isn't something that comes naturally to you, and I appreciate that you're going out of your comfort zone."

"Blair, I told you I'd do anything to get you back, and I meant it. But to be honest, I don't think it's helping. We don't even talk about the baby. This guy is totally focused on my infertility, and it's driving me nuts!"

"He is? That's what you talk about?"

"Yeah. I finally asked him why we keep going over the same stuff, and he said that he thought I had a lot of unresolved conflicts about my inability to get you pregnant. Jesus, did he have to go to school to learn that?"

"I'm sure he knows what he's doing," Blair said. "Nick says he's very good."

"Well, his only advice to me was that if I don't think I'm making progress, he can see me more often. He wants me to come three times a week. I think he is trying to save up for the down payment on a house and has decided to use me rather than go to a bank."

"Maybe he's right. He *is* a pro."

He sighed. "All right. I'll consider it. I guess I don't have anything else to do with my evenings. I might as well spend them with *Charles*."

He said the name like an insult, and Blair asked, "Do you dislike him?"

"I don't..." He paused for a second, and Blair could just imagine him rubbing his hand over his short hair, one of his nervous habits. "I don't *dislike* him. He just seems like such a know-it-all. He sits there and looks like he knows what I'm thinking. I hate that."

"Keep working at it, David. It's too early to tell if you're going to click with him. If you really don't like him, I'm sure Nick can find someone else for you."

"No, no, I've bared my soul once. I don't wanna have to go through that again."

"Okay," Blair said. "It was only a suggestion."

"I'm sorry," David said quietly. "It's just frustrating. Shouldn't something be happening by now?"

"I don't know, honey. I've never been in therapy. If you can think of another way to change how you feel, go for it. But this is the only way I know."

"I guess you're right," he said, sounding very defeated. "If it's possible to change the way I feel, I guess this is the way to do it."

⤙

Later that night, Kylie was sprawled out on one end of her new extra-long sofa with Blair curled up on the other. They were watching a movie. Rather, Kylie was watching a movie, and Blair was asleep and drooling, her shirt wet and her head at an impossibly uncomfortable angle.

Trying to get up with as much stealth as possible, Kylie eased herself off the butterscotch-colored leather, grimacing as it creaked noisily. She snuck over to Blair and gently slipped a hand under her face, trying to place her head back onto the cushion. Pale eyes blinked open, and the sleepy woman muttered, "Getting fresh?"

"Yeah," Kylie said, smiling at her. "The only way I ever get lucky is to sneak up on a woman while she's asleep. You woke up before I could get your clothes off."

Blair looked down at her herself. "Was I drooling on the new furniture?"

"Like I care about that. Besides, that's why I bought leather. I knew you were a drooler, and I figured my new dog might be one, too."

Blair rose up on an elbow and smiled at her friend. "You have a strange sense of humor. I guess that's why I like you."

"I like you, too," Kylie said. "That's why I was trying to sit you up a little—so your neck didn't cramp."

"I think I'd rather go in the other direction," she said, dropping back down and scooting a little so her head was on the seat cushion.

Blair forced an eye open and saw that she was taking up most of the space. When she started to get up, Kylie urged her to stay. "Go right ahead and stretch out. You can rest your feet in my lap. I don't mind."

"Sure?" she mumbled sleepily. "I could just go to bed."

"I like the companionship." Kylie sat back down and put Blair's legs across her lap, giving her friend's feet a rub. By the time Kylie had expended ten minutes of attention on Blair, she had started to snore, and the doctor reached for the TV headphones that were a requirement once Blair started sawing logs. "Sleep tight," she whispered, continuing her gentle patting.

⤙

The next week, David called Blair after his Wednesday afternoon therapy session. After some small talk, she commented, "I go to see my obstetrician next week. I told her I'd make up my mind about amniocentesis before I came to see her."

"I've been reading that book you left me," David said. "Is amniocentesis where they stick that great big needle into…?" He paused and then asked, "Talking about this doesn't make you sick, does it?"

"Well, yeah, a little. Thanks for asking, though. And yes, this is where they take a sample of amniotic fluid to test for some heavy-duty birth defects. Monique hasn't pushed it, but she thinks I should probably do it. I'm sure you remember I'm right on the cusp of a high-risk pregnancy."

"Then why waste time worrying about it? Just let her do it."

"It's more complicated than that. There's a risk to the baby's health."

"Oh. Is it a high risk?"

"Well, no."

"What else is bothering you?" he asked. "You sound like you're worried."

"I am. If the results come back showing a major genetic defect, we'd have to make some choices."

"Like…?"

"Abortion, David. It doesn't make sense to even have the test if I'm not considering the option of an abortion if something horrible is wrong."

"Well…would you?" he asked tentatively.

"I wouldn't make that decision without your help. This is our baby."

"I can't…I couldn't…" He took in a breath and said, "I don't think I'm the right person to help you with that. It's your body."

"And *our* baby," she said for the millionth time. "I would never make a choice to terminate the pregnancy without you."

"Blair, please don't ask me to get involved. You know how ambivalent I am right now. If I thought you should have an abortion, you'd always worry that I did it because I didn't want the baby. I know you'll make the right decision if it comes to that, and I'll be there for you. I promise I will. Just don't ask me to help make the decision."

"All right," she said tiredly. "I'm bushed. I've got to take a nap."

"I love you, Blair. I really do."

"I know. I know you do."

She hung up and sat in her room, crying for a long while, but she didn't follow her instinct to isolate herself. Instead, she went in search of Kylie and found her in the den, watching *The Magic Flute* on PBS. "You're home early," Blair said. "Mind if I join you?"

"Love to have you."

Blair dropped onto the sofa. "I just need some company. I'm feeling awfully lonely."

"Wanna talk?"

"Actually, I'd love to have a foot rub. It makes me feel grounded. If it's not too much—"

"One foot rub coming right up," Kylie said, giving her a welcoming smile. Blair slumped deeper into the sofa and swung her feet up, putting them carefully in Kylie's lap. Kylie began to rub Blair's bare feet, sneaking occasional glances at her friend. As expected, the sandman arrived in just under ten minutes. *I get better all the time*, Kylie thought. *One of these days, I'm gonna break the five-minute barrier.*

A half-hour later, Blair's soft moans made Kylie start to stroke her friend's leg, trying to reassure her in her sleep. Suddenly, Blair sat bolt upright, eyes wide, a fine sheen of sweat covering her face. She started to pant, and Kylie leapt up and knelt in front of her. "You had a bad dream. Everything's all right. Just calm down and take a deep breath."

Leaning heavily against her, Blair did as she was told, and after a moment, she caught her breath. "God, that was a bad one," she moaned.

"Wanna talk about it?"

"No, no, this one was too real." She wiped her hair away from her face and said, "Nick told me to write down all of my fears before I go to sleep, but I've been passing out so easily that I haven't been doing it. Damn!" She shivered and hugged herself tightly. "I've been having this one a lot when I nap."

"It might help if we talked about it. Sure you won't try?"

"No, I don't...I can't," she said shakily. She tried to slow her racing heart by breathing slowly. The television was on, but Blair couldn't convince herself to listen to it. All that she could focus on were the images from her dream, still assaulting her. She looked at the television. "Are you watching this?"

"Nope." Kylie switched off the set.

"I don't wanna talk about the dream, but I can tell you why I'm having it." She took in a calming breath and said, "I'm worried about having amnio."

"Oh." Kylie nodded and looked contemplative. "I was wondering when that would come up. Are you worried about the test or the results or what?"

"All of the above. I'm sure I'm worried about more things, too, but that's all I can think of at the moment."

"Tell me what's going on. I know *I'd* be worried about it."

Blair sat stock-still, trying to gather her thoughts, and then said, "I guess my real issue is whether to have the test at all."

"I can understand that. It'd be hard for me, too."

"You wouldn't be in the mood to tell me what to do, would you?"

"No, that's not what you need," Kylie said. "You need someone to support you no matter what you do. That's my job."

"That's my husband's job, too," Blair grumbled. "Actually, it's his job to help me make this decision, but he won't."

"Tell me what the issues are for you. Maybe I can help you sort them out."

"Issues? I'm too screwed up to organize my thoughts. I'll just tell you what I'm afraid of." She sighed heavily. "I'm afraid of hurting a perfectly healthy baby by having the test."

"That's a possibility, but it's not very likely. What else?"

"I'm obviously worried about finding out something horrible. Given my age, there's a real chance that I could have a baby with a genetic defect."

"Yeah, there's a chance. Again, it's not likely, but there's a chance. How would you feel if you *didn't* have the test and your baby had a genetic defect?"

"I can't be sure," she said thoughtfully. "I don't think anyone knows how she'd react in that situation."

"What's your guess?"

"I'm afraid I'd hate myself for not having been able to prepare for the news."

Looking at her with an expression of warm concern, Kylie asked, "How would you *ever* prepare yourself for that?"

Blair rolled her head slowly, trying to work some of the tension from her muscles. "I don't have the slightest idea." She looked at Kylie and said, "I told you I wasn't thinking clearly."

Kylie shook her head. "No, no, you're doing well. Just think about it for a minute. If you knew the baby had a genetic defect, how do you think you'd react?"

The room was completely silent, but Blair was sure she could hear her own heart beating. The question she'd been avoiding was finally on the table, and it scared her to death. "I guess I might have to decide to abort if the birth defects were severe enough."

"Would you?" Kylie gave her a penetrating look, holding her gaze for a long time. "Would you be able to make the decision to abort if the baby had a severe problem?"

"No," she said immediately, surprising herself. "I guess I could withhold treatment once the baby was born if he didn't have brain function or something horrible, but I can't voluntarily decide to kill my baby." She shuddered roughly and shook her head. "I can't."

"Then don't have the test." Kylie blinked and said, "I just told you what to do!"

"You sure did," Blair said, tears welling up in her eyes. "Thank you, thank you so much." She leaned forward and brushed her lips against her friend's, holding on to her for a long hug. "This is the right decision for me. Thank you, thank you for helping me make it."

"Anytime." Pulling away, she got to her feet and tugged Blair up with her. "Time for dinner." She walked with her to the kitchen and stood in the doorway for a moment, looking pensive. "Let's make a pact. Let's both believe that you have the healthiest, happiest baby in the whole world growing inside of you. Belief can make things happen, Blair, and I'm a believer."

Blair looked at her, seeing the quiet confidence she radiated, and allowed herself to feel its infectious power. "I believe, too, Kylie. I do."

⌒

On Friday night, Blair came into the house and found Kylie in the den, reading. "I've got great news," Blair said.

Her delivery was so unenthusiastic and her expression so flat that Kylie said, "You look pissed off. That's never good news."

"Oh. I sat in Monique's office for two hours before I finally gave up and left. I had to psyche myself up so much to make the decision about not having the amnio, and now I'm bummed that I have to wait to tell her." She walked over to Kylie, threading her hands through her friend's hair and giving the curls a little fluffing. "I wanted to get it over with so I could stop worrying about it."

"Aw, that sucks. And I know how you hate to wait. You must have been pissed off, too."

"Yeah. Even though I understand her schedule is bound to be unpredictable, I'll never like it." She made a face and then tried to look happier. "I shouldn't make a big deal about it. I'll just go next week."

"Well, I hate to be the bearer of bad tidings, but Monique's only gonna be in the office on Monday and Tuesday. She's going away for a long weekend."

"Then it'll be the week after that," Blair said. "I can't let a little delay bring me down."

"So, what's the great news?"

Blair stuck her hands out and took in a deep breath. She opened one eye a little bit and said, "I'm trying to get excited." Another deep breath, a little running in place, and then she opened her eyes and raised her voice to a higher register. "I think I've found you a puppy!" She jumped up and down as much as her changing body would allow, looking like a happy child.

"Let's go get it!" Kylie cried. She scrambled to her feet, grabbed Blair's hand, and headed for the garage.

"Wait!" Blair pulled the eager woman to a stop, letting her own enthusiasm all drain out in a moment. "That'll take a little work. It's in Boston."

"Boston! The only Norfolk terrier in the country is in Boston?"

"Well, no," she said, looking abashed. "There's a litter in Pacific Palisades."

"Blair, I could walk to Pacific Palisades! Why on earth would I go to Boston?"

"'Cause the one in Boston needs you more," she said, batting her eyes at her friend.

"Come sit down here and give me the whole story 'cause I want to go to Pacific Palisades right now and get a puppy!"

"Okay." Blair took a deep breath and told the whole truth. "I want you to take in a dog that's been rescued. I've been trying to find one that was abandoned."

"Because…?"

"Because it's the right thing to do. People give away so many dogs that it just seems wrong to buy one from a breeder. You don't want to make it into a show dog, and you don't want to breed it, so why not take a dog that someone else didn't want?"

Seeing the hopeful look in her friend's eyes, Kylie nodded agreeably. "Okay, I see your point. But I want a puppy. I want to make sure the dog's socialized properly when it's young so that it's good with the baby. Besides, the book says that the breed can be tough to potty train. I don't want a dog that someone gave away because it peed all over his house."

"I *found* you a puppy," Blair said. "Some family bought a puppy from a breeder, and when the children didn't feed it and walk it like they'd promised to, the parents took it to the pound." She narrowed her eyes and added, "To punish the children."

"Christ!"

"Yeah. Sound like nice people, don't they? So, a woman in Boston rescues Norfolks, and she took him in. He's sixteen weeks old, and she said he's just perfect. He needs a home, Kylie. Don't you want to adopt him?"

Something about the way Blair said the word "adopt" nearly made Kylie cry. She found her head nodding decisively. "Let's call; I want him."

Blair started to cry as she threw her arms around her friend, sobbing pitifully. "I knew you'd want to take him. I just knew it." And suddenly, Kylie felt as proud of herself as she had at any time in her life.

⌐

"Hi, Linda. This is Blair Spencer. My friend, Kylie, definitely wants the puppy."

"Oh, that's good to hear, Blair. When can she come to Boston?"

"She has to come? I thought you could just send the puppy—"

"Oh, no. I'd never do that in a rescue situation. This dog has been through enough turmoil having to change homes twice in the last four weeks. I have to make sure Kylie is going to be a good owner."

"I can understand that, but Boston is quite a trip."

"I'm sure there will be a dog on the West Coast at some point. If it's too much for her to get away, she'll just have to be patient."

Kylie frowned at the look on Blair's face and signaled for the phone. Blair asked Linda to hold for a second and put her hand over the speaker, saying, "She needs you to come up there. She wants to make sure you're a good bet."

Scoffing, Kylie took the phone. "Hi, Linda, this is Kylie Mackenzie."

"Hi. Blair tells me it'll be tough for you to get out here. I wish I could help, but I can only wait another week. Blair called first, but I've gotten a dozen calls since then."

"It's not a problem," Kylie said. "I can be in Boston on Thursday, if that works for you."

"That's great. If you give me your address, I'll e-mail you all of the details."

Kylie finished with Linda, turned in her chair, and shrugged. "I guess I'm going to Boston."

"Can I go, too?"

"Sure. We can go on Wednesday night since Thursday is the Fourth of July. We could come back later that day or stay over and come back Friday." She went to her wallet to pull out a credit card, but stopped on the way back, pausing to tap her nose with the card for a moment. "How close is Boston to Maine?"

"You could drive it easily. Why…oh, I know," she said. "Someone wants to pay a visit to Professor Amanda, lesbian poet."

"Well, I'll be right in the neighborhood. It'd be rude not to stop by. I've always wanted to see Maine, you know. Actually, it's a life goal." She was grinning, and Blair gave her a pat.

"Tryin' to dump me, huh?"

"Well, not dump exactly, but…"

"Go ahead, Doc. Call her and pitch the idea. You *do* have her number, don't you?"

"Why, I believe I do," Kylie said. "But since this trip will cost me an arm and a leg, I think I'll send her an e-mail. Much cheaper."

⌐

Amanda was happy to have a guest, and Kylie was able to rearrange her schedule, so she was able to make the trip guilt-free. But her clear conscience didn't extend to Blair.

On Tuesday night, Kylie said, "I don't like the idea of your being here all alone. I think I'll have Nick come stay with you. I'm sure he wouldn't mind."

"Kylie, I haven't needed a babysitter since I was ten. I certainly don't need Nick to watch me. If I have any trouble, I can call David; he's five minutes from here."

"But who's going to keep you company at night? Who's going to rub your feet?"

"Some pregnant women go an entire nine months without one massage. Rumor has it that the experience doesn't leave lasting scars. Now, I want you to go, and I want you to have fun doing whatever you people do on a second date."

"You people?" Kylie said, blinking.

"Just trying to get your goat, Doc. Now lighten up. Give me a nice backrub tonight and make it extra special to compensate for the ones I'll be missing."

"You got it."

⌐

Kylie had already left for the airport by the time Blair got home from a dinner meeting on Wednesday night. Sitting in her friend's usual place on the sofa in the den, Blair found a pillow, nearly the size of Kylie, with a note taped to it:

Hi,

> Cuddle up with me while you sleep in front of the TV and then take me to bed with you. I know I'm really big, but that means you can drape a leg over me, and that might help take some of the strain off your back.
>
> I'm no substitute for Kylie's magic fingers, but that's understandable since she's godlike. She'll be home on Sunday night, and she said to tell you that she misses you and Baby Spencer already.

Puffy

Damn, she must have some very scary hidden quirks to still be single. Maybe she forces her girlfriends to undergo "minor" surgical procedures once she gets 'em alone. Blair giggled for a moment, wishing Kylie were there to hear her joke. *Well, there's nothing else to do around here; it's time for a nap.* Smiling, she kicked off her shoes, slipped off the skirt that had been digging into her belly all evening, and curled up with Puffy, barely remembering to turn the TV on before she fell asleep.

⌐

Kylie had not recruited Nick for babysitting duty, but Blair wasn't surprised in the least when the psychologist just happened to call her on Thursday afternoon and ask if he could take her to dinner. "Did she coerce you into this, Nick? 'Cause I'm all right."

"No, it was my idea. I've wanted to try a new place on Montana, and I thought you'd be the ideal date."

"Sold," Blair said, knowing he was lying a bit, but not minding. "Drop by my office whenever you're free. I have tons of work to do, so just get here when you can."

"It's the Fourth of July!"

"Real estate agents work when there's something to be done. And lately, I've had a hell of a lot to do."

Nick arrived quite early, just after 5:00, and Blair was very happy to see him. Sitting at her desk for a long time was hell on her back, and she loved the idea of a nice walk to help her get the kinks out. "How far is this new place?" she asked.

"It's at Montana and 22nd Street," he said. "Is that too far to walk?"

"She told you to make me walk, didn't she?" Blair asked, eyes narrowing.

"Well," he drawled, "she mentioned that if we happened to go out, it might be best to make sure we got in a nice, long walk. You know, dinner *was* my idea, but Kylie made me promise to take you for a walk on the Palisades this weekend."

"She watches me like a hawk," Blair said, laughing. "Is she like this with all of her friends?"

He hesitated for a moment and then shook his head. "No, actually, she's not. She doesn't mother her other friends at all." He gave Blair an appraising look and said, "I've known her for quite a while, and I'm surprised by how generous and concerned she's been with you. You bring out a side of her that only Stacey got to see." He smiled and said, "You've gotten beneath her façade, and that's not easy to do. You're lucky," he added. "It's very nice behind the façade."

⌒

They were nearly at the restaurant when they passed a café with an outdoor seating area. Blair was speaking when she suddenly stopped mid-word and stared at a couple as if she'd been turned to stone. Nick put his hand on her shoulder to see what was wrong, and she managed to gasp out, "My husband!"

He whirled and saw a man and a woman, laughing and sharing a platter of oysters, and then looked at Blair again. Her normal demeanor slowly returned, and without looking at Nick, she said, "I'll be right back," stalking away before he could move. She approached the railing that separated the diners from pedestrians and tapped the man on the shoulder. David's eyes nearly popped from his head when he turned and saw her.

"Blair!"

"David," she said briskly. Extending her hand, she faced the woman and said, "Blair Spencer. David's *wife*." She said the word *wife* with as much emphasis as possible, feeling some satisfaction when the woman looked more than a little abashed.

"I'm Kimmy Reynolds. David and I work together," she managed to get out. "We were just, uhm, talking about work. We're having a...meeting."

David looked too stunned to speak, and after a moment, it became clear that he wasn't going to.

"Ah…the Fourth of July is always a good time to *meet*," Blair snapped. "Although it's hard to hear each other over the fireworks." She twitched her head at Nick and turned in the direction whence they'd come, marching away like an army of one.

⌒

It took almost three blocks for Blair to stop shaking violently and then another quick side trip to let her vomit against the curb. Nick had never been so cognizant of the lack of public transportation or cabs in his home city, but there were none to be found, and Blair and he were forced to walk the entire fifteen blocks.

When they reached her office, he said, "I'm gonna take you home. You're in no condition to drive."

"Look, Nick, I know what I'm capable of. I can drive home, and I'm going to."

"Blair, I don't think that's wise."

She put her hand on his shoulder and squeezed it. "I've been through worse traumas in the last few months. I'll be fine."

She entered Kylie's house at 6:30 and spent the next half-hour cursing David's name, wishing she'd never met the man, hoping that some catastrophe befell him in the immediate future, and thanking God that her baby would not share one single chromosome with the cheating bastard. She was just about drained of her anger and well on her way to the depression she knew would follow when the front doorbell rang. Assuming it was Nick checking up on her, she went to the door and peeked out, surprised to find David standing on the porch. "Go fuck yourself!" she shouted through the closed door, kicking it sharply to emphasize her point.

"Come on, Blair; open up! I can explain!" he shouted.

"If I open this door, I might kill you!" she yelled back. "Still wanna come in?"

"Yes!" he hollered. "I want you to know the truth."

She flung the door open, looking as horrid as she'd ever allowed herself to look in his presence. She hadn't gained much weight, and no one at work had noticed the changes in her body. But her waist had thickened, making her short, tight skirt look positively obscene once her jacket was off. Her eyes were red and bloodshot, her nose was running liberally, and her expression was one of pure malevolence. "Go on. Explain!" she shouted, hands balled into fists.

"She's just a co-worker. Really. I've never touched her."

"I've met your co-workers," she said. "Every person you work with is at least ten years older than that woman. Damn it, David, every one of your co-workers is a man!"

"She's new," he explained. "She doesn't know her way around yet, so we went to dinner to talk about office politics. That's it. I swear."

"What does she do at your firm?" Blair asked, one eyebrow raised.

"She's, uhm, she's a receptionist."

"Well, that makes sense," she sneered. "I'm sure you have many techniques to share with her about how to answer the fucking phones properly!"

"Look, you don't have to believe me, but I have never touched her. Never."

"How many times have you been out with her?" she demanded, sensing from his tone that this was not the first time he'd socialized with the woman.

Even though he was digging himself in deeper, he appeared to tell the truth. "We've had dinner or lunch together four times."

"I've been out of the damned house for six weeks," she yelled, "and you've had four dates!"

"They were not dates. I don't pay for her. We just have a meal together or go to the movies. We're just friends. Is it wrong to have a woman friend?"

"Yes. It's wrong to have a woman friend when your pregnant wife's living away from home, while you're supposed to be making some changes so she can come back. Yes, in that case, it's wrong to have a woman friend."

"You were with a man."

Tears flowing, she sniffed, "That was Nick, Kylie's friend. She's out of town, so she forced the poor guy to baby-sit me. She's just my friend, and she cares enough to make sure I'm taken care of—even when she's gone. You, on the other hand, are spending all of your energy on making sure Kimmy can answer a phone. What in the fuck kind of name is Kimmy, anyway? Adults aren't named Kimmy!"

"I didn't name her, and *you're* the one who didn't want to see me. *You're* the one who made that rule, not me." He glared at her and added, "But that shouldn't surprise me since you've made all of the rules."

"I *have* to set down rules because you're so fucking helpless. All I hear from you is that you're not connected and you don't know how to change."

"I don't!"

"Have you made any progress at all in therapy?"

He looked down at the ground, silent for a moment. Finally, he said, "No. I haven't."

"In six weeks, you haven't made any progress at all?"

"No." Again, he stared at the floor, infuriating her.

She grabbed him by the tie, yanking hard. "What have you been doing? I'm a third of the way through this pregnancy, and you haven't made one bit of progress!"

He glared at her while prying her fingers from his tie. "I've been humiliating myself. Three times a week, I go and tell *Charles* how it feels to be half a man." He got right in her face and fumed, "You want to know why I like talking with Kimmy? I like her because she doesn't know my dick doesn't work right. I feel like a real man when I'm with her. Like I used to feel before this whole God damned mess started!"

Blair turned and walked down the hall, headed for her room. She didn't much care if he stayed or left. She just had to get away from him and get out of her constricting clothing. Tossing clothes haphazardly, she reached into her dresser and pulled out the cozy flannel nightshirt that Kylie had recently bought for her. It was a message shirt, and she'd delighted in it until tonight. Now it seemed positively ironic, but she didn't have many other things that fit her and kept her warm in the cool evenings. Tugging the navy blue garment into place, she glanced at herself in the mirror, nearly shocking herself with how truly awful she looked. "Baby under construction, indeed," she snarled at her image before returning to the entryway.

The front door was closed, and she assumed David had left. She actually let out a startled yip when she saw him sitting stiffly in the living room. "What do you want?"

"We were having a conversation—" he began, but she cut him off.

"What do you want to do about us?"

"I don't know. I *do* know that I want to quit therapy. It's not working, and it makes me feel worse and worse."

"Fine. Quit," she said without emotion. "My question remains."

He sat back heavily and scrubbed his face. "Do you have any liquor? I could use a drink."

She had to think, but then said, "Look in the cabinet over the sink. That's probably where she keeps it."

He got up and looked, and she could hear him say something to himself. A few moments later, he came back, a stiff-looking drink in his hand. "She has some very nice Scotch."

"She's Scottish. Maybe she makes it herself." Giving him a pointed look, she repeated, "What do you want to do?"

"Could we go outside? I need a cigarette."

"I need a husband. My baby needs a father. Everybody needs something, but nobody's gonna get what he wants tonight."

He stared at her for a moment and then shook his head and sat down. "I want you to come home, and I want to try my best to be a father. I can't promise to be as enthusiastic as you want me to be, but I'll try my best. That's all I can do. I can only try my best."

"What if your best isn't good enough? What if our baby knows he isn't wanted? Is that just the breaks?"

"I don't think that'll happen. I'll probably be crazy about him or her once it's here. And even if I'm not, I can't imagine the baby would know that."

"And what about us? How do I get over the fact that *I* would know? How do I regain the respect I used to have for you? How do I get the man I used to know back? The one who would never create a child and then decide he wasn't able to love it. Where's that guy?"

"He obviously didn't exist," David said quietly. "I'm the same guy I've always been. You just want someone better."

"I don't think that's true. I think you're a giving, caring man who's trying *not* to love this child. I think you're afraid to take the risk. I think you're afraid to open your heart."

"I've tried, Blair. I swear I've tried. I wish I were the man you think I am, but I'm not. I'm just a guy who loves you and very much wants you to come home. I've loved you for ten years," he said, "and in just a few months, you're ready to walk away from me forever. How much could you love *me* to be able to do that?"

"We obviously have some sort of communication gap," she said. "You don't understand how parenthood changes you. Your focus naturally goes to your child. The baby I carry is my top priority. I think of it before I think of my own needs, and yes, I think of it before your needs. This child is what matters."

"Not to me," he said firmly. "You're my priority. Our marriage is what matters to me. Even if it were my baby, I'd feel that way. I chose you. You're the one I want to spend my life with." He cocked his head and gazed at her for a moment. "Why don't you get that?"

"That's not how I'm made. I didn't make a decision to put the baby first. But I can't imagine being any other way."

"I can't, either," he said with just as much determination as she had. "If you love me as much as I love you, you'll come home and try to work this out with me. I promised to love you for the rest of my life. Children weren't even mentioned in our wedding vows."

"Jesus! Our vows didn't mention a lot of things."

He stuck his chin out, glaring at her. "They said you'd love me until you died. You took a vow."

Crying softly, she nodded. "I do love you. But I can't live with you if you can't love our baby."

He gestured at the house, clearly frustrated. "You're living in a strange house with a friend. I've gotta be as supportive as she is!"

"That's where you're wrong. I get total support from Kylie. She cares for this baby as if it's critically important."

"I know that Kylie's the world's most perfect person, but you didn't marry her. You're stuck with me. Besides, maybe she has an advantage because she's a woman. Being supportive might be something that women are programmed to do."

"No, that's not it. She simply realizes that this is vitally important to me, and since she's my friend, it's vitally important to her. Shouldn't the same be true of you?"

"I wish it were true," he said quietly. "I wanted a child more than you did. This meant more to me than I can ever explain to you. I've had to give up my dream to have a child of my own, and I don't think that's something you can ever understand."

Feeling exhausted, she sank back against the cushions. "You're right. I can't understand that because I think it's wrongheaded. Your idea of fatherhood seems to be passing on your genes. Well, what makes your genes so fucking wonderful? Your genetic contribution is nothing compared to what you could give this child in love and nurturing and guidance. A real man could make that contribution. So, maybe you're right. Maybe you are half a man. But it's not your sperm that makes you that way." She stared at him until he met her eyes. "It's your heart."

He leaned his head back as he drained his drink. He got up, and she assumed he would leave, but he returned with another drink of the same strength. Sitting down, he stared at her for a long time. "It's your turn," he said. "I told you what I want. What do you want?"

"You know full well what I want, but I'm not going to get it. I'm *willing* to live apart and hope that you change your mind. You might have some epiphany when you hold the baby for the first time and realize that you're the only father he'll ever know. He either has you or no one."

"Maybe," he said, looking unconvinced. "And if I don't have some major revelation when the baby's born?"

"Then I'll divorce you," she said without emotion. "I've got to be honest. If I knew you felt this way about non-biological children, I never would have married you. Hell, I wouldn't have dated you." She shook her head and said, "There isn't a better father in the world than mine. And there's no doubt in my mind or in my heart that he's my father—my real father. The jerk who had an orgasm in my egg donor is nothing to me. Our baby will always know that you're his father, even if you don't recognize him as your child. That's a burden you're going to have to bear, David."

"I've offered you the best that I can do. I want to be your husband. I want to try to be a good father to your baby. I wish I could live up to your standards, but I can't. Sometimes, loving someone means that you have to accept a person with his flaws."

"Sometimes, you do," she agreed tiredly. "And sometimes, you don't." She stared at him for a full minute, the time ticking by like hours. "I'm gonna ask you an important question, and I want the truth."

He looked her right in the eye, waiting for her to speak.

"You've been in therapy for six weeks. Have you given it everything you have? Or did you just do it because I made you?"

He didn't even blink. He looked at her with his head held high and said, "I did it because you made me. Therapy is a waste of time. It's like throwing money down the toilet."

She nodded and then said, "That's what I thought. I'm not going to wait until the baby's born. I'm gonna file for divorce right now. You don't deserve to be this baby's father or my husband."

He stood and looked at her, his mouth moving, but no sound coming out. She gazed up at him as if he were a stranger, and after seeing that her resolve didn't waver, he set his glass down, turned, and walked out the door.

⌒

On Friday afternoon, the phone rang, waking Blair from her afternoon coma. "Blair? It's Kylie. I wanted to check to see how you're doing."

"Fine," she mumbled, trying to make her voice work.

"Did I wake you? It's noon there."

"Oh, I'm just taking a nap. Didn't get much sleep last night. So, how are things?"

"Good…great, actually. I spent most of yesterday with the breeder. She's really nice, although she missed her calling as a police interrogator. She knows more about me now than my mother does."

"Tell me about the puppy," Blair said, her excitement starting to build as she woke up.

"He's a doll," Kylie said. "A real little comic. The people who gave him up must be psychopaths."

"Are you going to take him now?"

"No, no, I'm on my way up to Maine. I'll come back here on Sunday and then go to the airport. I've got to buy a traveling crate and a few other things."

"Are you excited?"

"Very. I'm so excited that part of me that wants to come home right now. But then I slap some sense into myself and remember that I might be able to kiss a real live woman before the weekend's over. So, I'm off to Maine. Wish me luck, buddy."

"Don't do anything I wouldn't do," Blair said.

Kylie was quiet for a moment. Then she said, "I've got about twenty comebacks to that comment, but I'm not sure if they'd offend you. For the time being, let's just say that the most fun parts of being a lesbian are doing the things you wouldn't do."

"I want to hear every one of your dirty comments when you get home," Blair said. She could feel herself misting up, but she was determined not to let Kylie know what had happened with David. "I miss you, Kylie. Baby Spencer misses you, too."

"I miss you both, but I'll be back soon. You two get your rest and be ready to have fun when I come home. The house will never be the same."

Blair spent all of Sunday showing a client around, and when she poked her head in the front door that night, she paused for a moment, listening for puppy sounds. "Kylie?"

Her friend came running into the room. "Hi!" she said brightly. She went to the door, pulled Blair in, and then kissed her gently. "Missed you."

"Where is he?" Blair asked, looking around. "Oh, I missed you, too," she added, slipping her arms around Kylie's waist and giving her a big hug.

"Won't be long," she said. "We were playing in the backyard." As predicted, a fluffy, brick-red ball of energy appeared on cue, scampering across the tile so quickly that it slipped and skidded right into Blair's feet.

"Oh, my God! He's adorable!" She bent and picked him up, cuddling him, and then tucked her hands under his front legs and held him up in the air. "Uhm, Kylie, he's not a he."

"I know," she said. Just then, another ball of fluff flew into the room. "But he is."

"You got two?"

"I had to," she said. "They needed me the most." She scooped the other pup into her arms and held him up for Blair's inspection. "Meet Nick and Nora. They're just seven months old, and they're siblings."

"But I thought you didn't want an older dog. And why in the hell did you name one of them after your best buddy?"

"I didn't, and I didn't," she said. "The dogs already had names, and I didn't want an older dog, but only because I wanted to be sure the dog, or dogs in this case, would be good with kids. I'm completely satisfied that these two will be."

"Let me go change. I want to hear the whole story." She looked at her friend and said, "Come with me. I can't bear to wait."

"Okay. Do you two want to go watch Blair change?" Giving her friend a grin, she advised, "They're in."

When they got to her room, Blair started to take off her suit, and Kylie couldn't help but note that the time had arrived for maternity clothes. Even though Blair wouldn't have been showing in casual clothes, her work clothes were not at all casual. She always wore a skirt or a dress, and most of them were very formfitting and short, highlighting every spare pound. "Wanna go shopping this weekend?" Kylie asked as tactfully as possible.

"Smooth," Blair grumbled, seeing through her comment. "Actually, I'm *sure* I'll be going shopping this weekend. With my mother."

"Your mother?"

"Yep," she said, plopping down onto her bed. "That's something we need to talk about. My parents are coming to visit for the weekend…actually, maybe a little longer than that. I thought I'd put them up at—"

"They'll stay here," Kylie interrupted. "We have another guest room. We'll just go buy another bed."

"Oh, Kylie, I don't want to impose. I'm just a guest myself."

"Not if I had my way. I want you and David to sell your house and move in here. I love having you. It's gonna be so hard for me when you leave."

Unwilling to start revealing her bad news until Kylie had told her all about the dogs, Blair tried to hold back her tears. "I love it here, Kylie. I…I…don't want to leave. I don't have anywhere to go." By the time she finished her sentence, she was bent over at the waist, crying her eyes out.

Kylie went to her and held her in her arms, stroking Blair's body to calm her. The dogs became agitated as well and started to scamper all over her, licking her face and whimpering.

"I'm upsetting the puppies," she sobbed, crying even harder.

"They're fine," Kylie assured her. "They just want you to feel better, and so do I." She kissed her friend's head repeatedly, rocking her gently and murmuring into her ear, "Tell me what's wrong. Why are you so sad?"

"D…D…David and I are getting a di…divorce," she choked out, a fresh stream of tears accompanying her words.

"Oh, no," Kylie gasped, holding her even tighter. "Oh, God, what happened?"

"A lot of things. It all began when Nick took me to dinner on Friday, and we saw David with another woman."

The shock that immediately covered Kylie's face quickly turned to an expression of abject sorrow. She started to cry as well, and soon, Blair found herself comforting her in return. "How could he do that to you?" she sniffed. "Stupid fucking bastard!"

"It's all right," Blair soothed, stroking Kylie's back. "He claims he isn't sleeping with her. He just likes to hang out with her because she makes him feel like he used to." With an outraged expression, Kylie started to speak, but Blair placed a finger on her friend's lips. "I know it's ridiculous, but it's how he feels, and I don't have any way to reach him anymore. He hates therapy; it humiliates him to have to talk about being infertile." She shook her head. "He isn't going to get to where I need him to be. I decided that the baby would be better off with no father than with one who didn't love him with all his heart."

Kylie's eyes were filled with both tears and fierce determination. "I know it's not the same, but I'll fill in for him in any way I can. I'll be there for you every step. I swear."

"I believe you. I knew it without even asking." They held each other for a few minutes, both of them slowly calming down. Once neither woman was crying, Nick curled up across Blair's thighs with his head leaning against her belly. Nora took a similar spot on Kylie, even though her pillow wasn't as pronounced as her brother's. "The puppies are tired," Blair yawned. "Me, too."

"A nap sounds great," Kylie said. "We've been running around since 3:00 a.m.— California time."

"Lie with me?" Blair asked, a touch of shyness inflecting her voice. "I don't want to make you uncomfortable, but I'd love it if you'd hold me. I feel so broken today, Kylie."

"I could never be uncomfortable holding you. Never. It makes me feel good to have you ask me." She tucked Nora up under her arm and scooted into position. Blair took Nick along and then lay on her side next to Kylie, putting her blonde head on the nearby shoulder.

"Is this okay?" Blair asked. "Not too close?"

"It's perfect." Nora moved down to lie on Kylie's belly, while Nick draped himself across Blair's hip. "I'd love to get a picture of this," Kylie chuckled. "We must look like quite the group."

"I don't care how we look. All I know is that I haven't felt this safe in ages. Thanks."

"You're very welcome," Kylie murmured. "You're welcome to cuddle with me anytime you want. Cuddling is addictive."

"A nice addiction," Blair sighed. "Feels good."

❧

Blair woke before Kylie, nuzzling tightly against her friend, needing the warmth of her body to help feel grounded again. As soon as Kylie felt the movement, she was awake, eyes bright and alert. "How do you wake so quickly?" Blair asked.

"Training. When you're a surgical resident, you might be sound asleep one minute and expected to make a perfect incision ten minutes later. When you have people depending on you for their lives, you learn how to wake up quickly." She stretched and said, "But my training also taught me how to fall asleep quickly. If you have twenty minutes to yourself in a twenty-four-hour period, you don't want to waste precious minutes falling asleep. I can sleep in any position for any length of time."

"If I could only learn one thing from you, it would be that," Blair said enviously. "I waste so much time trying to wake up and then trying to go back to sleep during the night. I've got to learn to be more efficient."

"Once the baby comes, you'll be amazed at how quickly you wake. You'll pick up my talent all on your own."

"Looks like the dogs are more my style," Blair observed, seeing the two limp puppy bodies.

"Nah. They're just like me," Kylie said. "Watch. Who wants dinner?" she asked excitedly.

In a flash, they were awake, hopping around the bed, jumping on top of Blair, scampering across Kylie in a rush to get their evening meal. Blair giggled at their antics, deciding, "No, they're like me. I haven't had all-day sickness since Friday, and the thought of dinner makes me drool. Let's go, guys!" She slid off the bed, and both dogs followed her, running in circles around her bare feet.

"Wait for me," Kylie called after them. "I'm the one who cooks!"

⌐

Blair wanted to help, but Kylie insisted that she wanted to cook. "You sit down and get acquainted with the babies."

Blair put Nicky on the breakfast bar and petted him. "Tell me all about them. I'm all ears." She giggled as Nicky nibbled one of the ears in question.

"When I got there on Thursday, I met the puppy, and he was just as cute as you could imagine. But the breeder did have a long list of people who wanted him. These little guys had only been with her a few days, but she didn't have any takers yet. She says it's harder to place a pair of dogs, so she expected it might take a while."

"How do you know they'll like kids?"

"Ooh, it's a sad story. Sure you want to hear it?"

"I can take it. I'm all cried out, anyway."

Kylie glanced over at her, but continued. "The guy who owned the dogs was a breeder in the Boston area. Martha, the woman who rescued them, knew the guy pretty well. He was an older man, and he found out he was dying of an inoperable cancer. So, he started to give his older dogs away to other breeders he knew. This pair was from the last litter his dogs had produced, and he kept these two just because he couldn't stand to be without any dogs at all. He had them spayed and neutered, mainly because he wasn't sure what would become of them and didn't want them bred indiscriminately. Anyway, he started taking them to the hospital when he went in for treatments. The hospital he went to had a pet therapy program, and the dogs took to it. So, for the last few months, these little guys have been going to the pediatric department every week, cheering up sick kids. Apparently, they were a big hit and learned how to be around kids of every age."

"Oh, Kylie, that's so sad." Blair reneged on her promise not to weep. "Did the owner die?"

"Yeah, he did. Just a week ago. So, the puppies are understandably sad. They need some extra care until their little broken hearts heal."

At that, Blair lost it and started to cry in great, wracking sobs.

"Hey," Kylie soothed, "we'll make them feel loved. They won't forget their daddy, but now they've got two mommies."

"I can be a mommy, too?" she asked, looking up at her friend while she sniffled.

"Of course, you can be."

Blair looked at the sweet, inquisitive face of the pup and asked, "Can I be your mommy, Nicky?" At the sound of her voice, Nora started to cry. Kylie swept the other dog up and put her on the counter as well. Nora licked Blair's face, pushing her brother out of the way to get full access.

Kylie put one arm around Blair while herding the pups close to each other. All four faces were huddled together, tiny dog tongues furiously licking human faces. "No one can have too many mommies," Kylie said, sputtering a little between licks. "The puppies need all the love you can spare."

Blair pulled out of the huddle and wiped her face. She grabbed Kylie with both hands and pulled the doctor into a ferocious hug. She was still sitting, so her face was nuzzled against Kylie's stomach. "You make me feel so good," she said. "I've been so sad since you left, but now…now I feel as happy as I have in months."

"It's the puppies," Kylie said. She ran her hand down Blair's back, gliding from her shoulder to her hip.

She could feel Blair's head move as it shook slowly. "No, it's you. You know how to cheer me up. You make me feel needed. Like the puppies need me, too."

"That's not something I try to do," Kylie said. "It's just the truth. I need you, and so do Nicky and Nora."

"Well, the truth is that being with you makes me happy." She looked at the dogs and said, "I have a feeling you two could cheer up Ebenezer Scrooge." On cue, they licked her face, their tongues making her giggle. Blair thought of a question she'd forgotten to ask. "Are they named after the couple in *The Thin Man* movies?"

"Uh-huh. Nick and Nora Charles. The owner loved old movies. I thought we could call the puppy Nicky just to be a little different. I don't want Nick to come running when I call the pup."

"I think Nicky and Nora are cute names. Cute names for very cute dogs."

⌒

When they sat down to dinner, the dogs lay at their feet—one head on Blair's foot, another on Kylie's.

"It's very generous of you to let my parents stay here, Kylie. Luckily, they both like dogs, although I can't imagine who wouldn't like these two. One condition, though: you let me buy the bed. You've spent so much money on furnishing this place that even your ample resources must be tapped out."

"I'm a long way from looking for a second job. You don't need to furnish my house. I just haven't gotten around to furnishing the guest room. This'll spur me into action."

"Well, can I buy the linens and the pillows? I'll feel bad if I don't contribute."

"Sure. It's a deal."

"You know, we've been home for hours, and I haven't heard one word about Maine."

"Well, we were a little busy," Kylie reminded her. "But if you're interested, I can fill you in."

"Of course, I'm interested. Tell me everything."

"'Kay." She put down her fork and leaned back in her chair, something Blair had noticed her friend always did when she was telling a story. "We had a nice day on Friday. She showed me around the campus, which is one of the most gorgeous places you could imagine. If I'd seen this place when I was considering schools, I would have gone there for sure. Then Amanda made dinner for me at her apartment." She smiled and said, "She's a decent cook. Nothing too fancy, but she's very competent."

Blair tsked and gave her friend a mock scowl. "Such a critic."

"Well, you asked for everything." Kylie wrinkled her nose and continued, "We just sat around her apartment for the rest of the evening, talking. It was nice. I got to know her a little better, and I told her all about myself. Around 11:00, I was too tired to move, so I went to my hotel and collapsed."

"You stayed at a hotel?" Blair asked, surprised.

"Well, yeah. She didn't offer to have me stay with her, and she only has a one-bedroom apartment."

"Have you ever heard of making a move?" Blair asked. "Do I have to teach you everything?"

"No," Kylie laughed. "I know how to make a move, but…it didn't seem right."

"You're pretty cautious, aren't ya?"

"Yeah, I guess I am. I don't want to get too close too fast. She might not even wind up living here."

"Do you have to be in love before you sleep with a woman?"

"I think so. I didn't feel that way when I was a kid, but as I've gotten older, I've decided that sex doesn't mean as much to me as being intimate. I can please myself sexually—and I do a much better job than a stranger would. Luckily, Amanda feels the same way. We both decided that we should keep this very casual until she decides to move here."

"So mature," Blair said, grinning and batting her eyelashes.

"Cautious is more like it. I'm not sure she's the woman for me, even if she does move here. I don't need the complication of sleeping with her before I know it's right."

"Do I detect a cooling of interest? You don't seem as excited as you were before."

"No," she said thoughtfully, "I like her a lot." She paused a moment and then said, "Well, you might be right. I hate to resort to such a cliché, but I don't feel any chemistry with her. She seems more like someone I'd rather hang out with than date."

"You don't think like can turn into love?"

"I guess it can, but it never has for me. Amanda seems a lot like me—emotionally, at least—and I'm not usually attracted to people who are too much like me."

"Opposites can attract," Blair said, adding a sad smile. "David and I were opposites in some ways."

Kylie nodded. "I know what you mean. Stacey was my opposite in so many ways. You know, she's one of the first people I'd ever seriously dated who knew how to handle me."

"Are you tough to handle?" Blair asked curiously.

"I don't think so, but only Stacey and you seem to know how to keep me from running roughshod over you."

Blair blinked, totally surprised. "You don't try to do that to me."

Kylie blinked back, puzzled. "I…I guess I don't, do I? That's always been the number one complaint from my serious girlfriends."

"You must have changed, Doc, 'cause you're the easiest person to get along with that I've ever known."

Grinning widely, Kylie said, "That's what I kept telling them. I knew those women were psychos!"

＜━

Blair was so tired that she didn't even pretend to watch TV with Kylie and the puppies. She gave her friend a hug and went to bed not long after 8:00, falling into a stupor in minutes.

The dogs wandered around the house for much of the evening, occasionally getting onto the couch with Kylie, cuddling for a while, and then roaming again. It was obvious they missed their former owner and their routine, so she decided to let them settle in at their own pace. She'd left the door to the backyard open a crack, and they immediately figured out that was where they were expected to relieve themselves. Just before bed, she decided to take them out and wait with them until she was sure their bladders were empty. After locking up, she looked around the house, unable to find them. Padding down the hall, she snuck a peek through Blair's open door, finding Nora lying between Blair's breasts and Nicky curled up at the apex of her thighs, his head pillowed on her belly.

The pups know who needs them more, she decided, blowing a kiss to the trio.

＜━

When Blair got home the next night, she spent a few minutes sitting on the floor with the dogs. They perked her up so much that she was almost cheerful by the time she went outside to say hello to Kylie. "You've got some very cute antidepressants here, Doctor Mackenzie."

"They do make you smile, don't they?"

"Yeah, and I had a hard time doing that today." Blair unzipped her skirt and tugged it off, draping it over the back of a chair. "You don't mind if I just wear my slip, do you?"

"Nope. I'm used to greeting complete strangers who're wearing disposable paper gowns. You're a little overdressed for me."

Blair sat down on a chaise and then let her head sink back. Nicky jumped onto her chair, so then Nora had to follow, both dogs trying to occupy her lap. "There's barely room for one of you," she said.

Kylie snapped her fingers. "Nora, come." The dog cocked her head and then jumped from Blair's chair to Kylie's, looking at her expectantly. "Good dog," she praised, scratching Nora under her chin. "Lie down, baby." The dog did so, giving her brother a haughty look.

"Sibling rivalry, huh?" Blair asked. "I guess that's one more reason to be glad I'm only gonna have one child. It'll also let me get by with a two-bedroom apartment."

"Apartment?"

"Yeah. Our deal was that I would stay until David and I resolved things. Well…they're resolved. I'd like to stay another couple of weeks if you don't—"

"I don't want you to move!" Kylie was staring at her friend with an alarmed expression. "I don't!"

"But this is your house. You don't want a roommate."

"I do, too," she said. "I didn't know it until I got one, but now that I've had the experience, I've decided it's just what I need."

"But why?"

"Look," Kylie said, "I've told you several times that I don't like to be alone. Part of the reason I'm not going out as much as I used to is because of you, but not because I'm babysitting you. I like you, and I enjoy being with you. You're a lot more fun than some of the movies and plays that used to occupy my evenings. I really like having you here."

"You do?"

"Yeah, I do. I cook more, I read more, and I'm listening to music more often. It's been great for me. I mean that. I don't want it to end." She looked at her friend for a moment and then said, "Oh, shit. I didn't mean to put you on the spot. You probably need your privacy."

Blair returned her gaze and then felt a smile form. "I usually do, but it's been nice for me, too." She reached over and took Kylie's hand, giving it a squeeze. "You're fun to live with. I find myself perking up when I pull through the gate and see that your car's here." She shook her head. "It's surprising for me, but I like being here. I mean, I knew I liked you, but I never thought I'd prefer living with a woman to being alone—and I think I do."

"Then it's settled," Kylie said, her full, bright smile in place. "We'll live together until one of us doesn't like the arrangement."

"That's what the marriage contract should say," Blair grumbled. "That'd save a lot of attorney fees."

"Thank God we don't need an attorney. We can cement our deal with a handshake."

"Okay, but we have to work out the financials. How much rent do you want?"

"Rent?" Kylie looked at her like she was crazy. "I don't want money from you."

"Then I can't stay. You know I make good money, and I don't want to feel like a charity case."

"Money has to be an issue for you," Kylie said. "It's gonna cost money to get divorced, not to mention having to sell your house."

"House? Oh! I don't own a house. David owned our place before we got married. I didn't contribute to our housing expenses."

"You didn't?"

"Nope. We kept our finances separate. He paid for the house, and I paid for groceries and utilities. He paid more than I did, but he owned the place, so that seemed fair."

"You kept your finances separate?"

"Completely. I have a rough idea of how much money David makes, but I don't know how he spends it, and I don't have a clue how much he has saved. That's his life."

Kylie just stared at her friend for a moment, seemingly unable to think of a return comment. "Well, even if you don't have a lot of expenses, I still don't need for you to pay to live here."

"Whether you need it or not, I need to pay."

"Fine. Why don't we do it like you did with David? You pay the utilities and buy most of the groceries. Now, I don't want us to nickel and dime each other, so if I go to the store, I'll pay. But I'll let you shop most of the time."

"Sounds more than fair since you cook all of the time," Blair teased. "It's obvious I'm getting off too easily, so I'll just have to make myself the world's best roommate to compensate."

"You already are."

"Yeah. A pregnant woman, who cries most of the time, won't communicate when she's upset, can't cook, is prone to snappishness, and lies on the sofa napping all night. You've picked a winner, Doc."

"I know I have. We're gonna get along fine. As for the money, if it was good enough for David, it's good enough for me."

"David was compensated—very well, I might add—in ways that you won't be," Blair said, giving her friend a sexy smile.

Kylie stared at her, her eyes darting all around Blair's face. "Yeah, well, I'm taller than you are," she finally said, looking proud of herself.

"You weren't on the debate team, were ya, Doc?"

"Secretary of the science club," she said. "I'm just a nerd."

"You're a very lovable nerd, Kylie Mackenzie, and I think we're gonna be very good roommates."

⟶

Blair had a business meeting the next night, so Kylie called Nick and convinced him to come over for a barbeque. "The place is looking great," he said after he'd wandered around the house. "You've had to spend a lot of money to furnish this space, haven't ya?"

"Yeah, but Blair's helped me out a lot. She arranged to have some guy on La Brea make my leather sofa at about 30 percent of what I would've had to pay in a store. And a carpenter she knows built the entertainment center. I'm pleased with the job he did, too. I think it looks like it's been here since the place was built."

Nick walked over to the rustic-looking shelving in the den and rapped his knuckles on it. "To be honest, I thought it was here when we looked at the place. How did he do this?"

"He's from Mexico, and he has a big stash of mesquite down in his home village. He doesn't like to give it up, but he loves Blair, so he agreed to do this for me. It matches the front door so well that it looks original, doesn't it?"

"It sure does," he said. "I'm gonna have to have Blair help me furnish my place better."

"She's your woman," Kylie agreed. "She knows everyone."

Nick took his beer and walked out onto the veranda. He looked all around and said, "This is such a great place. I'm so happy for you."

"Thanks, buddy," she said. She put her arm around his shoulders and pulled him in for a hug. "I'm happy now that I have Blair and the puppies and a baby coming by Christmas."

He gave her a puzzled look and said, "You make it sound like Blair's staying. Is she?"

"Yeah, she is," Kylie said, beaming. "I didn't think she'd want to, but she likes living here."

Nick didn't say anything for a minute. He took one of the rubber balls that were lying on the veranda and tossed it, watching both dogs run for it and wind up in a ball, tumbling across the lawn—the toy forgotten. "Good retrievers," he said, laughing.

"They're terriers," she sniffed. "Throw a bunch of rats out there, and they'll have them cornered in no time."

"Do they have the run of the house when you're gone?"

"Oh, sure," Kylie said. "I have a house full of new furniture, so I thought it would be fun to bring two puppies home and let 'em chew on it. You know how I love to live on the edge." She laughed at her cautious nature. "I keep an eye on Blair, Nick. You never know when she's gonna put a glass down and not use a coaster."

"Well, you're being kinda wild lately. I thought that might extend to the dogs."

"Nope. They have a big wire crate that they've had since they were born. They seem to like it. I think they feel safe there. I make sure they eat early enough so they have time to go to the bathroom before I leave in the morning, and they're fine until 2:00 or 3:00. Either Blair or I can at least swing by the house by then, even if we have to go back to work. Actually, she's often home until 10:00 or 11:00, so the dogs don't have to be crated for more than four hours at a time."

He sat down and watched the dogs gambol around the yard. "Sounds like you two have things all worked out."

"You're using your shrink voice. Spill it."

He sighed, hating that she could always read his mind. "Are you sure it's a good idea to have Blair stay?" He didn't look at Kylie, and his tone was very neutral, but she knew what he was getting at.

"Nick, I can make my own decisions."

"I know you can, but you've just gotten to the point where you're ready to date again. I know you, and if you have someone waiting for you at night, you won't want to take the risk of dating."

"I went all the way to Boston to see a woman this past weekend. Blair was here then. As a matter of fact, Blair's the one who fixed me up."

"I'm not saying you'll close yourself off," he insisted. "But we both know you have a tendency to…"

She let her head drop against the back of her chair. "I know I cling, Nick. But I'm not doing that with Blair." She laughed. "Mostly because she won't let me."

"That worries me. I don't want to see you get so involved with someone who can't return your affection. You'll wind up getting hurt."

"I know I'm a delicate little flower," she said sharply, "but it's not like that with Blair."

"Answer one question for me?"

"Sure. Give me your best shot 'cause you're not getting another."

"Do you have feelings for her?"

"Yeah," she said immediately. "I love her like a sister. Actually, I like her better than I like my sisters. I care for her a lot, Nick, and I want to help her through a very tough time."

Nick was quiet for a moment and then asked the question he was a little afraid of posing. "You're not in love with her, are you, Kylie?"

"That's a second question, but I'll answer it anyway. No, Nick, I'm not *in* love with Blair. I love her very much, but I don't want to sleep with her." *Well, that's not entirely true, but I don't think of her as a potential sex partner. He doesn't have to know about the cuddling. A guy would never understand that.*

Chapter Six

The next afternoon, Kylie got home early, changed clothes, and packed the dogs into the car. She drove down to San Vicente Boulevard, one of the main jogging streets on the Westside. It wasn't an ideal place to run, since the path was in the middle of six lanes of speeding traffic, but the day was cool and breezy enough to blow most of the exhaust away. Kylie knew the dogs liked to socialize as much as they liked to walk, and San Vicente was always so filled with people that she knew the pups would get all of the attention they craved.

The dogs had a tremendous amount of energy, but Kylie was a neophyte in the land of physical fitness. She knew they'd be happier if she let them off their leashes so they could run round her in circles, but she wasn't about to risk their safety. "I'm sorry, guys," she said when they looked up at her at a stop sign. "I know you can go much faster than I can—even though my legs are about twenty times longer than yours—but you've got to give poor Mama Kylie a break. This exercise stuff isn't in my nature."

She heard a pair of feet slapping the ground behind her and hoped that the runner hadn't heard her speaking aloud to her dogs. Thankfully, there was a break in traffic, and the woman blew by her, not giving her another glance.

Kylie watched the woman for a moment, liking the way her hips moved when she ran. "You guys should be with her," she said to the dogs. "She knows how to run." They started off again, and Kylie tried to pick up her pace a little bit. Several people stopped to exclaim over the pups, making all three of the walkers happy.

They'd managed to do about a mile when Kylie told her canine companions that it was time to turn around. She turned, and Nora went right with her. But Nicky darted between her legs, continuing towards the ocean. When he saw that he was alone, he ran around Kylie's left leg, nearly tripping her in the process. She started to hop on one foot while she kicked at the leash, trying to get it off her leg. Both dogs thought they were playing a new game, and they gleefully joined in. They jumped and barked, as Kylie became twisted more and more in their leashes. She was finally reduced to sitting down and working her way out of the mess that had developed. When she was finished, she got on all fours to rise and was unable to avoid looking at a pair of terrifically long legs directly in front of her.

"Need a hand, Doctor Mackenzie?"

The voice, and then the legs, triggered her memory, and she gasped in surprise. "Julie!"

The woman extended a hand and helped Kylie to her feet. "What have you got here?" Julie asked. She got down on the ground and let the dogs make a fuss over her. "Are these yours?"

"Yep." With her mouth slightly open, Kylie looked down at the woman, marveling at her.

Julie looked up and asked, "Something wrong?"

"I'm...I'm amazed. Your hair is the same color as the puppies'!"

Julie laughed and then grasped one dog in each hand, holding them up to her face. "You callin' me a dog?"

"Far from it," Kylie said, her voice softening. "I don't think I'd ever noticed how beautiful your hair is. It's really extraordinary."

Julie put the dogs down and got to her feet. "You okay?"

"Yeah, yeah," Kylie said, nodding. She fidgeted a bit, looking decidedly uncomfortable. "I'm just...I hope...I wish things hadn't ended like they did."

The woman put a hand on Kylie's arm. "I knew you weren't involved in my firing. It was all Doctor Greene. We never got along."

"Well, I wasn't in favor of firing you. I thought you were the best office manager we'd ever had."

"Thanks, Doctor Mackenzie. That's nice to hear."

"Hey, please, I was never comfortable with your calling me 'Doctor.'"

"You were the only one," Julie said, laughing. "And if I had to call the men by their titles, I certainly wasn't gonna call the only woman by her first name."

"It wouldn't have bothered me."

"That's why I liked you," Julie said. "You didn't act like you thought you were God."

"Well, I do," Kylie laughed, "but only my closest friends know that."

"I think you're lyin'," Julie said, smiling the smile that had always innately attracted Kylie. "Wanna have a cup of coffee so I can judge for myself?"

"Yeah," Kylie said, surprising herself.

"Okay. I live right off Montana. Wanna come to my apartment?"

"Well, my car is the other way." Kylie waited for a moment and then proposed, "Come to my house. I have to take the dogs home, anyway."

"Sounds great, Kylie. Give me your address, and I'll come over after I go home and shower."

"We'll be waiting." She took a small leather note holder from her pocket and wrote down her address.

Julie took the note and smiled. "Still working on the original notes?"

Kylie looked down and said, "Oh, right. You gave me this, didn't you?"

"Yeah. I tried to find Christmas presents for you guys that'd be personal but not too personal."

"I obviously liked it," Kylie said. "I still carry it with me every day. And you'd be surprised how far a thousand cards go."

"That's how I make sure people remember me," Julie said. "Give 'em a huge supply of personalized note cards."

"You should've put *your* name on them."

"Not a bad idea. I'll do that in the future." She waved to Kylie and the dogs and took off in the opposite direction. Kylie gazed after her for a moment. *I was staring at Julie's ass when she ran by us at the stop sign! How could I forget that butt after staring at it for three years?*

They started to walk towards the car at a fast clip with Kylie's mind moving even faster. *Was she coming on to me? I didn't know she was gay. She sure doesn't look gay.* She nearly slapped herself for her own stupid comment and then started to worry again. *Maybe she wants to talk about old times at the office. Hell, maybe she wants to sue us! The other guys'll kill me if I reveal anything to her about why they fired her. Of course, it's not illegal to fire someone just so you can hire your cousin. It ought to be, but it isn't.*

But she sure was friendly. And not just co-worker friendly. More like lesbian friendly. She looked down at the dogs. "Mama Blair says I don't have a good first move. Let's go prove her wrong."

⌒

Kylie raced home and spent a few minutes picking up the newspaper she'd left on the table that morning. Then she sorted the mail and put Blair's in her room. The dogs were on her heels the whole time, knowing she was excited and not wanting to miss anything. When the house was neat, she went to her room, washed her face, and combed her hair. She looked at herself carefully and then decided that she didn't like her hair. She put some styling gel on her hands and worked it through, arranging her curls to her satisfaction. "How does this shirt look?" she asked the dogs. "Do I look as good as that pretty lady we saw today?"

The dogs didn't have an opinion, so she decided to stay as she was. She was too nervous to sit still, so she went outside with the dogs and threw their stuffed football for them. They were getting better at fetching, even though there was always a brief wrestling match involved. After what seemed like hours, Julie arrived.

Kylie jumped when the bell rang and then ran for the front door. She paused for a moment, so she wouldn't sound out of breath, and then opened the door. "Wow," she said, "you look great." *Damn! Do I have to say everything I think? Hold back a little, Mackenzie!* She showed Julie inside and took her on a brief tour, pleased when Julie was so complimentary.

They reached the backyard, and Julie exclaimed, "What a great place, Kylie! This is the backyard I've always dreamed of."

"Thanks. It was what made me buy the house." She realized that she hadn't extended any hospitality at all, so she asked, "I usually sit out here in the late afternoon and vegetate. Wanna have a drink and veg with me?"

"I'd love a drink," Julie said. "What've you got?" They walked inside together, and Kylie recited the options. Julie chose cranberry juice with a little vodka, and Kylie joined her—adding less than an ounce of vodka to her own drink. Julie watched the surgeon work, commenting, "Do you have a patient in the hospital?"

"How'd you know?"

"I'm used to doctors. The good ones have child-strength drinks when they might be called in."

"I try to be a good one. Besides, with the cost of my malpractice insurance, I can't afford a drinking problem."

They went outside and sat down, and soon, both dogs were on Kylie's lap. "They seem pretty fond of you," Julie said.

"Oh, they are." Kylie laughed and said, "But they think my roommate is their mommy. I'm only a stand-in."

"I assume your mortgage is astronomical, but I never figured you for the roommate type." She gave Kylie a long look. "A girlfriend, yes, but not a roommate."

"Nope, no girlfriend. My friend Blair's living with me. She's in the process of getting divorced, and being roommates is working out really well. We're good buddies."

"Divorced…from a man?"

"Uh-huh." The dogs ran for the front door, and Kylie said, "You'll get to meet her. My early-warning devices are never wrong. They bark when anyone comes close to the house, unless it's Blair or me."

Seconds later, Blair's voice called out, "Kylie, I'm home!"

"I'm outside. Come on out; we've got company."

Blair walked outside, dogs flanking her. She gave Julie a pleasant smile and said, "This looks like a fun way to spend the afternoon."

"It is," Kylie said. "Blair, I'd like you to meet Julie Holland. Julie and I used to work together. She was our office manager. Julie, this is Blair Spencer."

"Pleased to meet you," Blair said.

"Same here," Julie said. "Kylie was just telling me about you."

"Oh, God," Blair said. "Has she told you she's opening a home for pregnant divorcees?"

Julie's eyes widened. "I didn't know you were pregnant. Kylie said you were getting divorced."

"Well, just because Kylie doesn't have a big mouth doesn't mean I don't." She laughed and said, "I'm gonna change and go for a little walk with the pups. While I'm gone, I'll think of a few more embarrassing things to tell you about myself, Julie."

"Don't worry if you can't think of anything," Kylie said. "I've got a million of 'em."

She turned to her former co-worker when Blair left and asked, "So, where are you working now?"

"I'm managing the office of a laser eye surgeon in Beverly Hills. It's much easier to work for one doctor."

"I'm sure that's true. Are you still a big theatergoer?"

Julie gave her a warm smile. "I'm surprised you remember that. Yeah, I am. A friend and I are going to New York on Thursday to see a few plays. I go at least twice a year."

"Cool! I never do that, and I really should. I go to almost everything here, but I never get off my butt to go to Broadway."

"You should come with me sometime," Julie said. "I bet you'd be fun to travel with."

"I can be fun," the doctor said, giving Julie a sly smile. "Who do you normally travel with? You used to talk about what you did for fun, but you were always very circumspect about your personal life."

Julie nodded and took a sip of her drink. "I don't give my employers any reason to dislike me. You never know when someone won't like your religion or your hobbies or your sexual orientation. I thought it would be okay if I was out at work since you were, but I didn't want to take the chance."

"Huh. I never had a clue," Kylie said. "I guess my gaydar isn't very good."

"Come on!" Julie stared at her for a moment. "You didn't know?"

"No. Really. No clue."

"I guess I'm better at hiding my life than I thought I was. I was *sure* you knew."

"You should never assume I'm aware of anything," Kylie said, laughing at herself. "I'm in my own world at work. I pay attention to my patients, but everything else is kinda like white noise."

"That's how you seemed," Julie said. "Unless I caught you first thing in the morning, you always had a sort of vacant look in your eyes."

"That's concentration!" Kylie protested.

"That's what I meant," Julie said. "You always had a mask of deep, studied concentration on your face."

"That's better. I've got a reputation to maintain."

"You have a great reputation, and I think you know it. I think you're a pretty confident woman, to be honest."

Kylie studied Julie for a moment and then decided to give her an honest answer to what clearly was a teasing comment. "I'm confident about a lot of things, but I'm starting to lose confidence in my ability to find a partner. I've been single for two years now, and I'm tired of it."

Julie gave her a suspicious look. "Are you only considering twenty-one-year-old supermodels?"

Laughing, Kylie shook her head. "I'm sure there are some wonderful women who model, but that wouldn't be my preference. I'm just looking for someone I click with, but I haven't had much luck."

"Where are you looking? 'Cause I know a lot of single women who'd chew off an arm to date someone like you." She brought her forearm up to her mouth and began to act as if she were gnawing on it. "One person in particular comes to mind," she added, her mouth filled with her own skin.

Kylie gave her an intentionally sexy smile. "Hey, I don't want you to lose an arm. We'd better make a date before you do any damage."

Julie released her hold and gave Kylie an open, guileless smile. "I'm not even gonna act like I have to squeeze you into my schedule. I'm available anytime you want to get together."

"How about Monday? I would ask you for this weekend, but Blair's parents are gonna be in town, and I said I'd help entertain them."

"Gee, you're helping to entertain your roommate's parents? Are you sure you're human?"

"Positive," Kylie assured her. "But I can be sickeningly thoughtful."

"You can make me sick anytime, Doctor Mackenzie. You can start on Monday night."

⤙

Blair and the dogs walked in as Julie was leaving. They all said their goodbyes, and when Kylie and Blair went into the house, the doctor started chanting, "I've got a da-ate. I've got a da-ate."

Stopping in her tracks and whirling around, Blair said, "Get out! That woman's a lesbian?"

Kylie laughed and nodded. "I hate to admit this, but I was surprised, too. I worked with her for a couple of years, and I had no idea."

"Wow, she must be really closeted for the gossip mill not to have spread that around."

"I don't know if she's closeted or careful. She said she doesn't want to give her employer any reason to dislike her."

Blair thought about that for a moment and then nodded. "I guess that makes sense. Did she do a good job?"

"Yeah, I thought so, but Greene never liked her. He convinced the rest of us that she wasn't doing a good job for *him*, and two weeks later, his cousin became our new office manager. I'm still pissed about that."

"Sounds like a jerk."

"I think his mother might have put pressure on him. So, even though I don't think he's a jerk, he's a mama's boy."

"Speaking of just such a creature, I got a call from David today, telling me that he told his mother about us and that she'll probably be showing up on the doorstep soon. So, if you see a stocky, dark-haired woman who looks like a human tornado—bar the door."

"I'll do my best, but I'm kind of a wimp when it comes to physical confrontations. If she yells at me, I'm giving you up."

"Nice to be able to rely on you," Blair said. She gave her friend a rough, one-armed hug, and as they went into the kitchen together to start dinner, she captured Kylie's cheek in a healthy pinch. "A date!" she said, squeezing a bit for emphasis. "My little girl is growing up!"

Kylie giggled and slapped ineffectually at her.

"Let's hear all about it, and don't leave anything out. God knows I hate to threaten such a vulgar, despicable method…but I'll pinch you if I have to."

⟶

The new bed, dresser, and night tables were delivered on Thursday afternoon, and Blair washed the new linens before Kylie got home. After dinner, they got the room ready, even making up a little guest basket for the dresser. Everything was ready by 10:00, and as usual, Blair got ready for bed as soon as they'd finished. "I know we're gonna be busy this weekend, so I want to catch up on some sleep while I can."

"Hmm…I'll join you. It's no fun to stay up when you're not hanging out."

"I don't know how you ever lived alone, Kylie Mackenzie. You, my friend, are a people person."

"That's me. I'm pleased as punch to have more company. I might ask your parents to move in, too."

"They've never been crazy about California, but this might be the time they feel the magic."

⟶

The next day, Blair took the afternoon off to pick up her parents from the airport. Nicky and Nora accompanied her, resting in the backseat in their wire crate. The dogs had traveled everywhere with their original owner, and she wanted them to feel that they were getting back into their normal routine.

When she reached LAX, she pulled up to the arrivals level and parked, trying to look busy so the police wouldn't force her to leave. Luckily, her parents were right on schedule, and by the time they reached her, she was in tears.

"What's wrong, sweetheart?" Werner Schneidhorst asked, his eyes wide with alarm.

"I'm pregnant, Dad. I cry all day long. Seeing my parents for the first time in months is a guaranteed gusher."

"My poor baby," Eleanor Schneidhorst said, wrapping her daughter in a hug.

"Are you sure you're all right?" Werner asked again, his concern obvious.

"Yeah, I'm fine. I'm so glad to see you both. Wanna meet the kids?"

Eleanor chuckled and said, "Try and stop us. Your father talked about the dogs during the entire flight."

Blair opened the back door, and two very excited terriers ran to meet her. "This one is Nora, and this one is Nicky, or at least that's my best guess. We've taken to putting different colored collars on them. Saves having to lift them up to look."

"They're adorable," Eleanor gushed. "Aren't they cute, Werner?"

"Very. But is it a good idea to have them so close to you while you're pregnant? Can't they transmit…something?"

"Other than fleas, I don't think so," she said, smiling at his concern. "Believe me, if there were any risk to my health, Kylie would have the little guys in quarantine. She's more of a worrier than you are." She wrapped an arm around her father and kissed his cheek. "You'll like her."

"Well, I should think we would," Eleanor said. "She must be a very generous woman to welcome you into her home."

"She is that," Blair said. "She's become a very close friend. Just like a big sister."

By the time Kylie got home, the threesome was sitting outside in the warm afternoon sun, one dog on Werner's lap and the other on Blair's. "Well, isn't this a happy-looking group?" the doctor said, her grin wide. Both dogs leapt from their respective perches to circle her, both sitting up and pawing at her legs. "Those are expensive nylons, guys; let's watch it." To Blair's parents, she said, "Hi, I'm Kylie Mackenzie."

"This is my mom, Eleanor, and my dad, Werner."

Werner stood and shook Kylie's hand. "Pleased to make your acquaintance."

"The pleasure is mine. I've been spending the last month listening to your entire catalog. The CSO has always been one of my favorite symphonies, Werner, and I can't tell you what a thrill it is to meet one of its members."

"It's rare to meet someone your age who even knows of the symphony," he said. "Are you sure that Blair didn't force you to listen?"

"Don't get him started, Kylie," Eleanor warned. "He'll talk your ear off if he thinks you're really interested."

"I am! Actually, that's how Blair and I met. We found that we went to the same cultural events. The first time we really talked was at a chamber concert, remember?"

"I do," she said, smiling at Kylie. "At the Getty."

"Oh, I'd love to go to the Getty," Eleanor said.

"Great. That'd be fun," Blair said. "We can shop a little, spend a day at the museum, and then you two can go home. I know you wanted to check on me in person, but I also know that this isn't when you'd scheduled your vacations. I bet you're missing a concert in Grant Park this weekend, Dad."

"The second chair cello can use the increased exposure," he said, smiling slyly.

"And I know you're in the middle of getting the fall season lined up at the theater, Mom. Once you see what good care Kylie takes of me, you can go home and rest easy."

"Well, you do look absolutely wonderful, Blair. I thought you'd look ten years older after all you've been through."

"It's been tough," she said, "but I'm being very well taken care of, and Kylie makes sure I'm eating well. Having the dogs really brightens my spirits, too. So, given what's happened, I'd say I'm doing remarkably well."

Werner, his eyes narrowing, said, "I'd like to pay a visit to David while we're here. I want to have a man-to-man talk with him."

"No way, Dad," Blair said. "You and Mom are not getting in the middle of this. This is our issue."

"What kind of man would leave his pregnant wife?" he demanded, his face turning red.

Kylie leaned over slightly, muttered, "Hear, hear," and went into the house, asking, "Anyone for a little snack?"

⤶

A few minutes later, Blair went into the kitchen, giving Kylie a swat on the seat. "You're not allowed to aid and abet my father. You're supposed to be neutral."

Kylie turned to her and gave her a very serious look. "I could never be neutral about you. Never."

Blair tucked her arms around her friend's waist and held on tight, fighting tears once again. Eleanor came into the house just then and blinked her eyes in surprise before discreetly walking down the hall to find the bathroom on her own.

⤶

Blair was bed-bound by 9:00, the emotional reunion with her parents having thoroughly drained her resources. Her mother went to sit with her while she got ready for bed.

"Kylie's such a lovely woman," Eleanor said. "You're awfully lucky to have met her."

"You don't have to tell me. I know how lucky I am."

Eleanor watched her daughter brush her hair. "Why don't you let me do that? I haven't brushed your hair since you were a girl."

She turned and gave her mother a smile, nodding. "I'd like that." Blair sat on the edge of the bed and let out a contented hum when she felt the brush sliding along her scalp. "Good lord, that feels good. I'm afraid I'm gonna have to add that to the list of things Kylie already does for me."

The brush paused for a moment. Then Eleanor asked, "What else does Kylie do for you?"

"I'm embarrassed to say the list is endless." She laughed softly. "If I had to pay someone to do everything Kylie does, I'd have to find a second job."

"Like?"

"I don't want it to sound like I take advantage of her. But she offers to do so many things that I find myself saying yes more than I should. She cooks for me every night that I'm at home, and I have to fight her to clean the kitchen."

"Who could resist that? I hoped you'd inherit your grandmother's love of cooking, but I'm afraid you got stuck with my love of dining out or ordering in."

"Yeah, that's my idea of fun, but it's so nice to have a home-cooked meal. We've been eating outside every night, and most nights, we stay out there until it's fully dark. We're watching less TV, which is really great, too. It gives us more time to talk." She was quiet for a moment and then said, "I know more about Kylie's work than I did about David's, and David did something that I understood."

Her mother didn't respond to that comment. She just kept brushing.

"Kylie usually rubs my feet or my shoulders when we're outside, and I've gotta tell you—I've never experienced such tranquility. Sometimes, we're completely silent for an hour with Kylie just rubbing my feet. You can hear all the sounds of the neighborhood and the little nocturnal animals coming out. Of course, seconds later, those little animals are running for their lives," she laughed. "Nicky and Nora are two ferocious little hunters. Thank God they haven't had their first kill yet."

Eleanor laughed. "Those sweet little things don't seem like hunters."

"The chipmunks don't know that."

Continuing to run the brush through Blair's hair, Eleanor asked, "So, what are your plans? Are you going to stay here until the baby's born?"

"Yeah, at least that long."

"At least? You aren't planning on living here permanently, are you?"

"I don't know," she said thoughtfully. "I mean, I'd like to meet someone at some point, and Kylie wants a partner, too. I've been just the tiniest bit worried because she's met someone. If she and Julie hit it off, I guess I'd have to leave."

This time the brush stopped completely. There was a brief pause, and then Eleanor asked, "A woman?"

"Yeah, Kylie's gay."

Eleanor's voice didn't change much, but her expression was one of intense surprise. "Oh. You didn't mention that."

"Mmm," Blair nodded. "I don't think her being gay is one of the most notable things about her. I have a long list of attributes that I'd comment on before talking about her sexual orientation. Besides, to tell you the truth, I forget she's gay sometimes. She's just my friend."

"I suppose I forget that some of my friends and co-workers are gay," Eleanor agreed. "I doubt that they ever forget it, though."

Blair turned and gave her mother a puzzled look. "What do you mean by that?"

"Oh, nothing really. I was thinking of something one of the artistic directors at the theater said to me once. He said that straight people stop thinking of him as gay once they know him. But he never stops thinking of himself that way."

"Hmm...I don't know how Kylie feels about being gay," Blair said thoughtfully.

"Are you sure that Kylie's not...interested in you, honey? To be honest, you two act like you're more than friends."

Blair nearly fell off the bed. She got up and gave her mother an indignant look. "Because we care for each other?"

"No. I'm glad that you have a friend like Kylie. But she's a lesbian, honey, and she might be looking for more from you than you're able to give."

Blair said, "Not everyone is looking for something when she offers her friendship. I love Kylie, Mom, and she loves me, but our love is *entirely* platonic."

"Honey." Eleanor got up and put her arms around her daughter. "I can see I've upset you, and I hope you know I didn't mean to. Maybe I'm not used to your being this close to a woman. You have to admit that this is very different for you. You've never been much for women friends."

"That's only because I'd never met a Kylie before," Blair said, putting an end to the discussion.

A few minutes later, Blair tossed and turned in her bed. She'd been relaxed and half-asleep while her mother brushed her hair, but now she had a jolt of adrenaline coursing through her body. *She can say so much with a few careful questions. She can get inside my head without even trying.*

I've never given a second thought to the way Kylie and I interact, and now Mom has me obsessing about it! She thumped her pillow like a punching bag, annoyed that she was letting her mother's casual comments get under her skin.

I've never thought that Kylie was being too familiar, but we do touch each other nearly as much as David and I did. Is that normal?

She looked back on their relationship, considering how their physical affection had progressed. *I don't think that Kylie has ever touched me in a way that I didn't ask for. I asked her to cuddle with me in bed after she got home from Maine. I've asked her to hold me when I'm sad. I started kissing her head when I come home. Hell, I'm the one who tosses my feet in her lap at night. She doesn't come sneaking into my room, trying to rub my feet when I'm asleep!*

Her analysis was starting to take effect, and Blair felt herself begin to relax. *Kylie's a wonderful friend who offers me all the affection I want. There is nothing in the world wrong with that. Just because I haven't done this with other women simply means that Kylie and I are closer than I've ever been with my other friends. That's all there is to it.*

⌒

The next day, Eleanor and Blair made plans to go shopping for some of the necessities that Blair had finally agreed to buy for her changing body. "Any chance of your coming with us, Kylie?" Blair asked.

"No, I think I'll hang out with your father. He should be back from his walk with the puppies soon. I thought we could chat about music. Of course, I'll make you a sumptuous dinner. All you have to do is call me when the mood strikes you for a particular thing, and I'll have it ready when you get home."

At Eleanor's surprised expression, Blair commented, "Now I know why men want wives." She got up and stood behind Kylie, bending slightly to kiss the top of her head. Looking up, Blair caught the look on her mother's face and then put her arms around Kylie's neck and hugged her, refusing to change her own behavior because of her mother's suspicions.

⌒

The Schneidhorst women were driving from one maternity store to the next, so far only choosing some panties and a couple of supportive, expandable bras. "I've never bought such unattractive underwear in my whole life," Blair grumbled. "Underoos were sexier than these things."

"You won't have to wear them for long. As soon as you don't need them, you can burn them."

"I'm not sure they *will* burn. They might just melt. I swear the panties are made from recycled soda bottles."

"I didn't know you were so particular about your underthings," Eleanor said, smiling at her child.

"Well, I am, and being with David all these years made me worse. He was definitely a lingerie guy."

"Do you want to talk about David, honey?"

Blair glanced quickly at her mother and said, "I don't particularly want to, but I will. What do you want to know?"

"I suppose I don't want to know about David, to tell the truth. I'm much more concerned about you and how you're taking all of this."

"I'm fine, Mom; I really am. I'm moving on with my life."

"I see that," Eleanor agreed. "I just don't understand how you can do that so…easily."

The look Blair gave her mother this time wasn't particularly kind. "Easily? You think this has been easy?" She pulled over to the curb at the first opportunity and put the car in park. Knowing that she was on the verge of snapping off a sharp comment, she tried to calm down. She opened the sunroof, took a few deep breaths, and then said, "It might seem sudden to you and Dad, but this has been going on for months. From the time I got pregnant, I knew that there was something seriously wrong with our relationship."

"You did?" Eleanor's voice was thin and sharp with surprise.

"Yeah. I did." She was quiet for a few seconds, trying to remember the chain of events. "It's like the people in Malibu who lose their houses to erosion. The house might only move an inch or two a month, but they know they can't rely on the foundation to save them. It's only a matter of time before they slide down the hill." She let her head drop back against the headrest. "I knew that our foundation wouldn't hold. I knew it almost from the start."

"But, honey, you never said—"

"What could I have said? I wasn't about to worry you and Dad with my troubles. There was nothing you could do about it. Besides, I thought there was a ghost of a chance that David could try to pull it out."

"A ghost of a chance? That's all?"

Blair nodded. "I know him like a book. He has many good qualities, but he's not a very flexible guy—especially emotionally. He gets something in his head, and I swear it turns to stone. I didn't think he was going to be able to change, but I wanted him…I needed him to try."

Eleanor grasped her daughter's hand and held it to her chest. "Why…why didn't you tell me sooner?"

"You know how I am. I'm not good at sharing my troubles. I like to wait until I know where I stand before I start talking about things like this."

"That's not good for you, sweetheart. And it puts the whole weight of the situation right on your shoulders."

"I know that, but I don't know how to be different. I went through a very, very hard time, but I worked my way out of it. I'm looking forward now and focusing on my baby."

Eleanor gazed at her child for a few moments and then said. "I know you're not going to like this, but I've got to admit that I'm worried about your staying with Kylie."

"Worried? What is there to worry about?"

"What if she falls in love with someone and you have to move? Wouldn't your life be more settled if you found a place now?"

"Well, yeah, I guess it would be more settled, but I don't want to do that." She stared at her mother for a moment. "What is it? Do you think she's gonna make a move on me?"

"No! I don't think anything of the sort! I'm just concerned about you. About your security. I thought you'd be more secure if you had a place of your own."

"Mom, I love living with Kylie, and I don't want to leave until I have to." Blair was quiet for a moment and then said, "Even though she's starting to date someone, I have a suspicion it won't work out. She's always saying she wants to find a partner, but she hasn't been very proactive. I still can't figure out why."

"There's usually a reason for everything, honey."

"What's that supposed to mean?"

"Nothing. I simply meant that it's hard to know what someone really wants. Maybe she prefers being single."

"No, that's not true. She wants to be loved. She has a real need to be connected to another woman. I'm sure of that."

Eleanor gave her daughter a puzzled shrug. "I can't venture a guess about her desires. Only Kylie knows why she's single."

⟿

Kylie and Blair dropped the Schneidhorsts off at the airport on Sunday evening, and as they drove away, Kylie shook her head. "I'm gonna miss that guy."

Blair beamed at her. "You two were as thick as thieves. How late were you up last night?"

"I don't even know. We started talking about the difficulty of getting audiences to listen to newer symphonic works, and before I knew it, I was half-looped. I haven't had that much to drink in years!"

"My father loves a good bottle of Scotch. He doesn't drink often, but he can't resist an excellent single malt."

"Well, my single malt is gone," Kylie said, "but it was worth it. I had a lot of fun. They can visit anytime."

"They were really serious about inviting you to visit, you know. Dad really wants to take you on a thorough backstage tour of the symphony."

"Hey, I'm going home in two weeks. Why don't you come with me? You'll still be able to fly then."

"Two weeks, huh? I think I can make it, and I'd like to visit Chicago before winter. Are you going for any particular reason?"

"Yeah. My birthday. My family is having a big party for me."

"Oh, your forty-first birthday."

"No. My fortieth."

"But you've been telling me all year that you're forty," Blair said, giving her a puzzled look.

"This is the year that I turn forty. I always click my age up in January. Then I don't have to remember what month it is."

"You're an odd one, Mackenzie. But I can't resist the lure of meeting a whole house full of your clan. Will all of your brothers and sisters be there?"

"They'd better be," she said. "How often does Doctor Baby Sister turn forty?"

—

The next morning, Blair was up when Kylie came into the kitchen. "Hey, what's got you up so early?" Kylie asked, tousling Blair's already tousled hair.

"Just nerves," she admitted. "I'm going to see Monique today, and I'm nervous. I'm always worried that she's not gonna hear a heartbeat or something equally horrific."

Kylie sat down and gazed at her for a moment. "I thought we had a deal. It doesn't do much good if I'm over here being all positive while you're thinking bad thoughts. You're gonna cancel out all of my good vibes."

"I know," she moaned. "I can't help it." She shook her head. "I used to be such an optimist. But ever since I've been pregnant, I have these horrid dreams and wake up certain that his spinal cord isn't going to close or that he doesn't have a brain." She shivered. "It scares me half to death."

Kylie reached out and took her hand, stroking it until Blair met her eyes. "That's not going to happen, bud."

"I know it probably won't. But I worry. I wish I could feel his heartbeat when I'm lying in bed, worrying about him."

"Have you noticed that you refer to the baby as 'him' almost all of the time?"

"I guess I do. He's always seemed like a boy to me, but I kept forcing myself to say 'he or she.' I've given up the ruse."

"Why does he seem like a boy?"

"I'm not sure. It's a feeling I have."

"Do you want to know? I mean, if Monique does an ultrasound and gets him in the correct position, she'll be able to see. His genitals are formed by now, you know."

"I'm kinda ambivalent, to tell you the truth. Part of me really likes not knowing. But if he's gonna be an exhibitionist, I guess I won't have much choice, will I?"

"Nope, not unless you don't want to look."

"Oh, sure, like that'll happen. I'll make sure she gives me the little printout so you can see, too."

"Are you going this morning?"

"No, 3:00."

"I should be at the hospital then, checking on patients. Page me when you leave, okay?"

"Will do, Doc. Now, you'd better get going. Nobody likes to be kept waiting in an operating room."

"Big day," she said. "I've got two vasectomy reversals and a pair of fallopian tubes to clean out." Bending, she picked up the dogs and let them lick her face. "You two be good today. Maybe Mama Blair will give you a new toy to fight over before she leaves."

"Mama Blair sounds so darned funny."

"Hey, they sleep with you, so they must think you're their mama." She kissed the top of Blair's head. "They know a good mama when they see one."

⌒

Blair was only halfway undressed when someone knocked on the door of the exam room. "You can come on in if you don't mind watching me strip."

"You never make that offer at home," Kylie's low voice teased. "Do you like Monique better than me?"

"Kylie!" Blair whirled around, clad in her bra and panties, and threw her arms around her friend. "Damn, I'm glad to see you."

"I heard that Baby Spencer was going to be on TV, and I had to be here for his big performance."

Blair squeezed her tight and then pulled away. "I've got to get undressed. I don't wanna keep Monique waiting."

Kylie took the paper gown and held it in front of her friend so she could have a modicum of privacy.

When Blair had the gown in place, she held up the panties she'd just removed and showed them to Kylie. "Have you ever seen a less appealing pair of panties? This is the new sexy lingerie that my mother insisted I buy."

Eyes wide, Kylie said, "I have to admit that those wouldn't get my engine running, but then again, I've never dated a pregnant woman. If the woman in the panties made me hot, I guess that before long, the panties themselves would make me hot. I'm very adaptable."

"I wish more men thought like you did," Blair grumbled.

"I'm not most men—thankfully. I've seen how temperamental their equipment is, you know. They break down too easily."

With a soft rap on the door, Monique entered and then paused to give Kylie a look. "Don't tell me I'm gonna have you in here from now on."

"'Fraid so," Kylie shrugged. "The AMA has asked me to keep an eye on you."

"Are you sure about this, Blair? Your care might actually be compromised by having Shakes in here looking over my shoulder."

"I'm most certainly not going to be looking over your shoulder," Kylie said. "That's a view I don't think Blair wants me to have, anyway."

"No, I'd rather you were near my head. There are some things only your doctor should have to see." Blair thought for a second and decided to tell Monique the truth. "The bad news is that my husband and I are getting divorced."

"Oh, Blair, how awful that must be for you." Monique sat on her rolling stool and gazed at her patient with sympathy. "How are you handling it?"

"I'm okay," she said. "I moved out of the house and moved in with Kylie."

"Kylie? You moved in with Kylie?" The sparkle was back in the doctor's warm brown eyes. "You poor, poor thing."

"She must not show you her best qualities if you think that, Monique. Doctor Mackenzie is the best roommate I could ever hope to have."

"Well, well, Shakes has hidden qualities," Monique teased.

"Not very hidden," Kylie insisted. "You haven't been looking." She stuck her tongue out at her old friend and said, "If Blair doesn't mind, I thought I'd come to some of her appointments. But don't you even think of keeping us waiting," she warned. "I'm a very busy woman."

"I'll pay you fifty bucks to lie to her about your appointments," Monique said to Blair, adding an aggrieved look.

"She'll be good," Blair promised. She turned and looked at the surgeon. "Won't you?"

"Yeah, I'll behave."

"We'll see," the obstetrician said. She turned around and washed her hands, put on a pair of examination gloves, and sat down again. Monique looked at Blair. "I want to talk about some pretty personal things today. Are you sure you don't mind having company?"

Blair's eyes grew a little wide, and she shook her head. "No, I want Kylie to be here." She stuck her hand out, and Kylie was there immediately, holding it.

"My heart's pumping here, Monique. Is something wrong?" Blair asked anxiously.

"No, nothing like that. But I want to talk about genetic testing, and I know that's a sensitive issue for almost every woman."

"Oh." Blair let out a breath, profoundly relieved. "Kylie's the one I've talked to about this. She's been a tremendous help, Monique. She knows exactly how I feel about the testing."

"Great," Monique said. She gave her friend a smile. "You really do come in handy every once in a while, don't ya?"

"Not often, but I remember every time," Kylie said, smiling thinly.

"Well, we talked about amniocentesis last time, Blair. What are your thoughts about having it?"

"I don't want to have it." Kylie felt her friend's hand squeeze her own. "The results wouldn't make me terminate, and the risks are too high just to have the information."

"Okay," Monique said. "We don't need to discuss it anymore. What about the multiple marker blood test? It's not as accurate as amnio, but it's completely safe."

"I think I'll have it," Blair said. "There's a part of me that wants to know if something's wrong—to prepare."

"That sounds like a wise decision," Monique said. "So, let's do that and do an ultrasound."

"Transvaginal or transabdominal?" Kylie asked.

"Vaginal," Monique said, narrowing her eyes at her friend.

"Is that good?" Blair asked.

Monique gave her a noncommittal shrug. "Some women prefer the transvaginal; some like the transabdominal. I like the transvaginal because the image is a little crisper since the probe is in your vagina."

"Mmm…probe…vagina. Sounds like fun," Blair decided, making a face.

"I'll give you a quick exam first and then draw some blood and send you over to the hospital, okay?"

"Hospital?" Kylie asked. "Why don't you do it?"

"Because I read the studies that the National Institute of Health puts out, Shakes. Using the same set of patients, 13 percent of women had abnormalities show up in the doctor's office. But 35 percent of those same women showed abnormalities when given the test by a registered sonographer."

"Thirty-five percent?" Blair blanched. "Thirty-five percent!"

Shooting Kylie a lethal glare, Monique said, "That doesn't mean that 35 percent of women have problems. The number is far, far smaller than that. Most abnormalities are easily explained away."

"Sorry," Kylie said quietly, looking completely chagrined. "I'll keep my big mouth shut."

"I'll believe that when I hear it," Monique said.

"If I could ask just one more tiny question…?" Kylie asked, holding her hand up like a schoolgirl.

"Yes?" Monique replied, quirking an eyebrow.

"Don't you normally do ultrasounds at every appointment?"

"We used to," Monique said, "but Blair wasn't in a hurry to have one, and her insurance only pays for one, so I didn't want to do it too early. Twenty weeks is a great time. We can see a lot now. Anything else, Doctor Mackenzie?"

Kylie shook her head and walked over to the window to stand by Blair's head. Monique got Blair into position and started to perform the exam, asking, "How are things going in general? Anything bothering you?"

"Not really." Blair's brow furrowed, and she bit her bottom lip. "I got a very sharp pain in my side today when I bent over to pick up one of the dogs. Is that normal?"

"Probably. Did the pain go away quickly?"

"Yeah. As soon as I stood up."

"The ligaments around your abdomen are starting to stretch, and they don't really want to. Having a pain or two like you describe is nothing to worry about. Just let me know if it lasts or gets worse."

Giving her friend a stern look, Kylie said, "Call me when things like that happen. I'm a doctor, too, ya know."

"Kylie, you were in surgery. I'm not going to page you and worry you like that. Monique's my doctor; you're my roommate."

"I'm Doctor Roommate," she insisted, "and I want to know when you have unexpected pain."

"Yes, ma'am, Doctor Roommate. I'll keep you informed henceforth."

Monique finished the exam and removed her gloves, disposing of them before she moved over to stand next to Blair's head. "Everything looks perfect. Just what I'd expect at this stage. Do you have any questions?"

"No, I can't think of anything."

"I have a couple," Monique said. "Are you sleeping well?"

"Much better. I'm only getting up once a night to pee now that Kylie's started to restrict my fluid intake in the evenings. That really helps."

"Things do tend to calm down here in the second trimester. You seem like you're feeling pretty spry."

"I am. Actually, I'm feeling quite good. No more morning sickness, my breasts aren't tender anymore, and I'm sleeping better. As soon as I can feel the baby kick, I'm gonna feel fantastic."

Monique looked at her curiously and asked, "Is that worrying you?"

"Yeah, a little." She cleared her throat. "Okay, a lot. My books say I should start to feel him at sixteen weeks, and here I am at twenty—and nothing!"

"You'll feel movement soon. I'm certain of it. Now, let's draw some blood; then you can go have that ultrasound. You'll see some movement during the test, even if you can't feel it. That should make you feel better. I'll have the technician come and get you as soon as she's ready to draw your blood." Giving Kylie a smile, she said, "I'll see you Saturday, Shakes. Can't wait to see your new house and your new dogs."

"Blair will be there, too," Kylie reminded her. "Maybe we can make her sit in for a few hands."

"No way," Blair said, shaking her head. "I'm not a card player. I'll play hostess, though."

"Sounds great," Monique said as she stood. "See you both then."

As soon as Monique left, Kylie started opening cabinets, peeking into each one curiously. "What are you doing?" Blair demanded. "Get out of there!"

"Ah…here they are." She took out a sterile glove and blew it up, tying off the top like she would a balloon. "Have I ever showed you the proper way to milk a cow?" the doctor asked, making Blair giggle.

"No, I don't think you have," she said, reaching out to pull on the faux udders.

"You'd better watch it," Kylie teased. "You don't want the nurse to think you're as odd as I am."

"I've lost all sense of decorum," Blair said. "I guess that's what happens when there are so many people poking around between your legs that the hookers are jealous."

"Braggart," Kylie said, earning a well-placed pinch.

———

While they walked the short distance to the hospital, Blair looked up at her friend and asked, "How in the heck did you have time to be with me? Don't you have surgical patients you check on in the afternoon?"

"Yep. Before I came over, I got the two men checked out and sent them both home. The woman is going to stay overnight, so I can pop in on her anytime. I thought I'd go by after we were finished. Going to the hospital will make it easy for me to check on her, so this is great for me."

"I've never been to your hospital," Blair said. "Will you show me around?"

"Sure. I might even be able to let you peek into an operating room if any are vacant."

"I don't know about that. Being with you, unsupervised, in an operating room might be more temptation than you can handle."

"I'll check my scalpels at the door."

When they reached the radiology department, Kylie gave her friend a wink and said, "Give me your insurance card, and don't disagree with anything I say, okay?"

"I can't guarantee that. God only knows what you'll say. What's going on, anyway?"

"Trust me; I'm a doctor," she insisted, taking her hospital ID out of her purse and clipping it to her dress. As she had expected, the room was bursting with patients. Walking up to the window, she smiled and said, "Hi, I'm Doctor Mackenzie here with my partner, Blair Spencer. Monique Jackson sent us over for a transvaginal ultrasound." She reached down and picked up her beeper, shaking her head. Turning to Blair, she said, "Honey, I'm not going to be able to stay for long. I have a surgical emergency." Giving the woman at the desk a winning smile, she whispered, "She's very nervous about the procedure. Is there any chance you could squeeze us in before I have to leave?"

"Well..." The woman looked down at the list in front of her and said, "Transvaginal, right?"

"Right," Kylie agreed.

Keeping her voice low, the woman said, "If you can be on the table in about two minutes, we can do you right now."

Kylie beamed a smile at the woman. "You're a goddess. Through that door?" she asked, twitching her head.

"Yes. Someone will show you to the proper room."

"Here's her insurance card," Kylie said to the receptionist. "We'll pick it up on the way out." Placing a hand on her "partner's" back, Kylie said to Blair, "Come on, sweetheart. We have to hurry."

Walking down the hall, Blair gave her an elbow in the ribs and whispered, "That's cheating! All of those other people were waiting patiently, and you cut in line!"

"I didn't spend eleven years in training to sit in a waiting room. I don't get many perks, but getting cuts is one of 'em. Now quit complaining and get undressed."

"No wonder you don't get any dates if that's your best line," Blair grumbled, but still doing as she was told.

By the time Blair was up on the table, the technician came in, ready to get to work. "Hi," she said. "Had one of these before?"

"No," Blair said. "I'm a little nervous."

"It's really not a big deal," the woman assured her. She picked up the probe and showed it to Blair. "See? This is actually a little smaller than a tampon. I put a sterile condom on it, lube it up a little, and place it in your vagina. The only discomfort you should feel is from my needing to hold it against your cervix." She made her preparations and then approached Blair, placing a hand on her thigh for a moment. "Ready?"

Blair nodded and gripped Kylie's hand firmly, noting that her friend was watching the technician like a hawk. "Uhm, not to be a big baby, but could you hold on to my forearm?" the doctor asked. "I really need those fingers to work."

"Sorry," Blair winced. "It's uncomfortable, and I'm nervous."

All thoughts of discomfort and anxiety vanished when Kylie turned towards the monitor and said, "Look! There he is!"

There, on the screen, was a picture of the baby, his little body floating around peacefully in his cushiony bed of amniotic fluid. "Oh, my God, Kylie! Look at him!"

"Do you two see something I'm missing?" the technician asked. "I can't tell it's a he."

"She has a feeling," Kylie informed her, giving the woman a pointed look. "Besides, his hand is between his legs."

"I don't care what he is!" Blair cried. "He's moving! Look at him, Kylie! Look how perfect he is!"

Kylie wiped a tear from her eyes and then leaned forward and kissed Blair's forehead. "He's absolutely perfect," the doctor murmured. "See how well his little heart's pumping?"

"That's not too fast, is it?" Blair asked worriedly.

"No, no, it has to pump fast. That's perfectly normal."

"Yes. His heart looks just great," the technician said. "Want me to see if I can get him to move a little? I might be able to get him to move his hand."

"No," Blair decided immediately. "He can do whatever he wants as long as he's moving." The baby's other hand reached out, and the trio watched, transfixed, as he grabbed the umbilical cord and gave it a robust tug.

"He's putting on a show," the technician said. "He's a very active little guy today. You picked a good day to come in. We're almost done now," she advised. After the technician took the probe from Blair's vagina, she handed them the little pictures and left the room, promising that they'd hear from their doctor with the results.

Blair stretched a little while her friend handed her a few pre-moistened wipes. "You might want to get rid of that lubricant," Kylie said. "You certainly don't want to ruin those sexy panties first day out."

Trying to scowl, but ending up with a half-grin, Blair commented, "That was a very strange experience. It felt like a fifteen-minute-long Pap smear, but I never wanted it to end. Can you bring one of these machines home?"

"Sure. The baby will be driven mad from being pinged with sound waves, but that's a small price to pay to see him every day."

Blair sat up and tugged her gown back in place. That's when it hit her that her friend had seen her naked and then some, given that Kylie had watched the technician insert the transducer. "It doesn't make you uncomfortable to have me so blatantly exposed before your very eyes, does it?" Blair asked.

Kylie chuckled and said, "Uhm, please don't take this the wrong way, but I didn't really notice."

"How could I possibly take that the wrong way?" she asked, quirking a grin.

"It's a doctor thing," Kylie insisted. "I mean, if we were at home and you took off your pants and spread your legs apart, I'd see your vulva." She shook her head and corrected, "I mean, I'd see *your* vulva. But in a clinical setting like this, it doesn't connect for me like that. I'm not looking at my friend Blair; it's only an exam. It doesn't have any emotional resonance for me. I was watching to see if she knew what she was doing. I wanted to make sure she'd done one of these procedures before. If she looked nervous, I was gonna take over," she said, sounding completely serious.

"I'd prefer you let the poor thing do her job," Blair said, "but I appreciate that you care. I find it odd that you could probably have taken over for her and not felt like you were looking at me or touching me, though."

"You have to be like that," Kylie insisted. "I mean, I have my hands in more than my share of vaginas, but when I'm in a clinical setting, the vagina is just about as erotic as a uterus or a vas deferens. But when I'm with a woman that I care for, I get a real thrill from touching her inside. It's a completely different experience for me, odd as that sounds. I mean, thank God it's that way! How horrible would it be to put my fingers inside a woman and think, 'No gross abnormalities, the walls are smooth, no noticeable lesions…' Yuck!"

Blair giggled at the look on her friend's face. "I always wondered about that. I thought that a gynecologist might be unable to get a thrill from being with a woman after seeing so many of them."

"I can't speak for them, but that's never been a problem for me. I honestly feel like I haven't touched a woman in almost two years, even though I most definitely had the better part of my hand in a woman's vagina this morning."

"Speaking of which, you'd better go check on that woman before she calls in a missing person's report on you."

"I'll go collect your insurance card while you get dressed. If anybody's mad that we got cuts, I'll let them take a swing at me rather than you. See you outside."

⌒

They were chatting quietly as they walked down the corridor, and as they got close to her patient's room, Kylie commented, "You'd better wait by the nurses' station. I think I'm going to have a problem here."

The room was one down from the nurses' station, and Blair stopped obediently to give her friend some privacy, but the man approaching Kylie didn't seem to mind who heard him.

"Where've you been?" he demanded in what was about one decibel short of a yell.

"What's the problem, Mr. Hart?"

"My wife needs attention, and she's not getting it from these nurses! We paid good money for this surgery, and I expect the surgeon to be here to check on her."

"I'm here now," Kylie said patiently, trying to guide him into his wife's room. "What do you need?"

He roughly shook her hand off. "I want to see you here before 5:00 at night! Her surgery was at 8:00 a.m.!"

"I didn't see you when I came out of surgery, Mr. Hart, and you weren't here at noon when I stopped by again," Kylie said, still patient and calm. "I've been nearby all day. If there'd been an emergency, I could have been here in ten minutes."

"You should have called me! Isn't it important to talk to me? I'm her husband!"

"I did call you. I spoke with your secretary as soon as I was finished with the surgery."

"I assumed you'd call me back," he snapped.

"I'm sorry if there was a misunderstanding," Kylie said, "but we're both here now. Let me go take a look, and then I'll come back and talk to you."

He glared at her, and after a tense few moments, she walked into the room. The man didn't follow her, instead starting to pace up and down the hall, his grating voice disturbing everyone near. "Incompetent woman," he growled. "I've been waiting for hours." He glowered at the nurse on duty and said, "I told you to page her. Why didn't you?"

"There was no emergency, sir," she said, barely controlling her temper. "Doctor Mackenzie saw your wife at noon, and she said she'd be back this afternoon. I told you that earlier."

"Everybody's supposed to sit around and wait for the great Doctor Mackenzie. Well, I'm a busy man, too, and I don't have time to wait for her to take her sweet time." He turned and walked down the hall, not even waiting for the nurse to answer.

Eyes narrowing, face flushed with anger, Blair started to follow him. He was obviously heading for the visitors' lounge, and she was about to launch into a thorough tongue-lashing when she felt a pair of hands on her shoulders. "Hold on there, sparky," Kylie's voice sounded in her ear. "Where do you think you're going?"

"I'm not going to let him talk about you that way!" she whispered loudly. "Stupid asshole!"

Kylie physically turned her in the opposite direction and said, "Go to the nurses' station and tell them you're with me. They'll let you sit down in their lounge. Go on now."

"But—!"

"Go on. I can take care of myself."

Letting out a deep breath, Blair followed orders, sparing one last look over her shoulder. Kylie was standing right where Blair had left her, pointing in the direction of the nurses' station.

About fifteen minutes later, Kylie returned with the nurse who'd accompanied her into the patient's room. "Would you write a scrip for a sedative…for me?" the woman asked. "That man is about to make me lose my mind."

"I think I calmed him down," Kylie said. "He's going home now."

"God, at last!" the nurse said.

"Are you all right?" Blair asked Kylie, her concern evident.

"Sure. I'm fine. Things like that happen all the time."

"They do?"

"Yeah. This kind of surgery is usually elective. Many of these people have to pay for this—and all of their other fertility treatments—out of their own pockets. To afford this kind of thing, you have to be a pretty successful person, and I'm sure I don't have to tell you that many powerful people are major pains in the ass."

"What was he so mad about?"

"You heard him." Kylie shrugged. "He wanted me to be here all day. He's used to having people jump when he tells them to, and it pissed him off that he had to wait for me to return. Funny thing is his wife said he didn't get here until 4:00. He put in almost a full day at the office."

"Doesn't it bother you to be yelled at like that?"

"Mmm…no, not anymore. It's the result of either frustration or fear or the person's being a real jerk. Not much I can do about any of those things. The ones who reach me are the men who cry their eyes out when I tell them I couldn't fix the problem I went in to fix. That gets me right here," she said, tapping over her heart.

The nurse gave her a smile and said, "Doctor Mackenzie is everyone's favorite surgeon. She really cares about her patients, not just her reputation."

Blair got up and gave her friend a robust hug. "That's because she's got such a kind heart. You're a very special woman, Doctor Mackenzie, and if those jerks don't know that, it's their loss."

⌐

"Hey, as long as we're here, let's stop down in the obstetrics area and get you signed up for your Lamaze classes."

"Aren't those kind of a crock?" Blair asked, whispering the word *crock*.

"Why would you say that?"

"I don't know many women who want totally natural childbirth anymore," Blair said. "Anyone I've ever known says that the breathing techniques only work if they're accompanied by a nice epidural."

"Well, let's go see," Kylie said. "Maybe they have a short course for drug addicts."

To Blair's surprise, they did have a nice, short class that met on three Saturday mornings. During the class, the instructor would be discussing the breathing techniques, but the overall focus was more of an introductory parenting and childbirth class. Blair filled out all of the forms, her pen poised over the spouse/partner/coach box for a moment while she gave Kylie a pointed look.

"Like you could talk me out of coming," the doctor scoffed. "Heck, I might sign up for the six-week course, too, so I don't miss anything!"

⌐

Blair stopped for Chinese food on the way home, but even with her stop, she was still the first to arrive. She had fed the dogs and set dinner out on plates before the doctor finally entered the house, and Blair called out, "What took you so long?"

"I had to make a quick stop," she said. "Let me change, and I'll be right in."

Later, over dinner, Kylie said, "I've been thinking about what Monique asked you today, and it dawned on me that you've been in extraordinary spirits for quite a few days now. Are you really feeling that good?"

"I am," she said. "It feels so wonderful to be able to eat and hold food down. And it's no small deal to sleep through the night. I'm not nearly as tired as I was, and my hormones even seem to be taking a rest."

"Well, the progesterone has slowed to a trickle," Kylie said. "That's what causes most of the nasty symptoms in the first few months."

"I've started to have those really vivid dreams," Blair said, smiling shyly. "I'm dreaming about sex more than a pubescent boy."

"That's really common," Kylie assured her. "Enjoy it while you can 'cause by the third trimester, you'll start having problems sleeping again."

"Well, I feel great now, and I'm going to revel in it."

"So, how did you think the visit with your parents went? Did you have enough alone time with them?"

"It went well," Blair said. "I got to talk to my mom about David when we were out shopping. She was surprised by how well I'm taking the whole divorce thing. But then, she didn't see me when I was at my worst."

"Well, you have bounced back awfully quickly," Kylie said. "You know, if I didn't know better, I'd think you'd been expecting a divorce."

"I had been," Blair said. "When I saw the look on his face when he said he didn't want the baby named after him—I knew."

Kylie looked down at her plate. "I didn't know that was something you fought about." Her head shook slowly, and she looked like she was holding back tears. "How could a man be that callous? How could you not be thrilled beyond belief to have your wife want to honor you like that?"

"I guess he's like the people who yell at you sometimes. He's either scared or confused, and he doesn't know what to do with his fear. I feel sorry for him, Kylie. I really do."

"Do you still love him?"

"Not like I did. If he changes his mind and wants to help raise the baby, I'd love to have him, but he'll never be my spouse again." She looked at Kylie for a moment. "I've lost the respect I had for him. That's not something you can get back."

"He's lost more than he realizes," Kylie murmured. "Women like you are hard to find."

"Maybe," she said, "but maybe he doesn't need a woman like me. Maybe he needs someone who can pump up his ego more than I did. Not all men really want an equal partner, and I would never settle for less. Maybe it was time that we moved on."

"I don't know about that, but I do know that I'm impressed with how well you're doing."

"It's what's best for the baby. It's not good for him to have me moping around and crying. I've been doing that for weeks and weeks. Now it's time to get on with my life." She gazed at her friend for a moment and said, "I wouldn't be in nearly this good shape if it weren't for you. If I were living alone in a little apartment, I'd probably drown in my tears. Having you and the dogs has been such a blessing, and I hope you know how much this all means to me."

"I think I do, but it means a lot to me, too. I love having you here. Uhm, after dinner, I'm gonna go see Julie. Is that okay with you?"

Blair gave her friend an aggrieved look. "I'm not the housemother of The Mackenzie Home for Unwed Mothers, pal. You can go wherever you want."

"I know, I know, but I'm usually home with you."

"And I love having you here. But you're supposed to be hooked up by the end of the year, and I'm not doing a very good job of making that happen. So, you've got to work twice as hard!"

❧

After dinner, Kylie put up a very feeble argument about doing the dishes. As soon as Blair started running water in the sink, the doctor went to her room and emerged a few minutes later wearing a fresh shirt and a crisp pair of shorts. "I'm gonna get going now," she said.

"Have fun," Blair said. "I'm sure I'll be in bed when…and if…you get home."

"Why wouldn't I…oh, right." Kylie gave her a sheepish look and said, "I think I'll be home. I don't wanna rush things."

"Well, have a good time, even if you don't have sex."

"Oh, we'll have sex," Kylie scoffed. "It's just too soon to have sex all night long. Gotta pace yourself." She placed a soft kiss on Blair's cheek and added a pat on the belly. "See you two later. Bye, puppies!"

As she walked out the door, Blair stared after her. *I can never tell if she's kidding about things like that!*

❧

Kylie rang the bell at Julie's condo, her heart rate a little accelerated. The door opened, and Julie gave her a smile that made her knees weak. "Damn, you look fantastic," Kylie said and then reminded herself that she had a functioning brain, which was equipped to filter her thoughts before they became words.

"You're not so bad yourself. Come on in." The doctor walked into the nicely decorated space and let Julie take her on a tour. She was watching her former employee's ass more than the decorating scheme, but she was unable to control herself. "I just got home from work," Julie said. "Wanna go for a walk? I've been cooped up all day. I haven't even smelled the air."

"Sure," Kylie said. Julie grabbed her keys, and they walked outside, pausing when they reached the sidewalk.

"Side streets, Santa Monica, or Wilshire?" Julie asked.

"Let's cross Wilshire and go north. It's quieter."

"Good choice." They started off and spent the first few minutes talking about the past few days. Once they were both up to date, Julie took Kylie's hand, making the doctor smile. "Is this okay?" the redhead asked.

Kylie looked up at the night sky, giving the matter her full attention. "Well, holding hands on a first date is a little risqué, but I'm game."

"Are...I can't..." Julie stopped and looked at Kylie for a second. "I can never tell if you're kidding. Your expression doesn't change a bit. You always have a kinda half-smile that looks like you're teasing, but you look like that when you're perfectly serious, too."

The smile left Kylie's face, and she adopted a more earnest expression. "Of course, I was teasing." She bit her lip for a second and then decided to be completely frank. "Sometimes, I sound like a smart-ass when I'm not in control of a situation."

"Are you nervous?"

The doctor looked adorably shy. Her eyes roamed a little, never meeting Julie's directly. "I want you to like me."

"I like you already," Julie said. "I'm nervous 'cause I want you to like me."

"Well, I like you already," Kylie said. "So, let's not be nervous anymore."

"It's a deal." Julie took Kylie's hand again, and they walked down the street, exchanging small talk and details of their personal lives, neither one nervous in the least.

⟶

They got back to Julie's home at 9:30, and Kylie stopped at the door. "I should get home," she said. "I've got to be at the hospital by 6:30."

"I understand. I go to work early, too."

Kylie smiled at her and said, "Do you mind if I summarize the information I've gleaned tonight? I want to make sure I have it all right."

Julie leaned against the doorframe and crossed her arms over her chest. "You are awfully adorable, Kylie. I mean that."

The doctor smiled back. "I noted that you're adorable, too, so that's one thing off the list. I also learned the following: you've been single for about the same amount of time I have; you're looking for a relationship, not a fling; you like to spend your free time attending cultural events, although you have a fondness for the L.A. Sparks women's basketball team; and you're a runner, but you're not a fanatic about it." She had been ticking the items off on her fingers, and when she finished, she looked at Julie and asked, "How'd I do?"

"Very well," Julie said. "I learned that I attend more things at LACMA than you do, but that you do go to the major exhibits."

"Yeah, I'm more a live event kinda girl. But I spent a couple of weeks in Italy two years ago, and I was in one museum or another every day. So, the art museum is definitely something I could get into."

"I also learned that you're a very nice woman to go on a date with," Julie said. She leaned close and touched Kylie's cheek, barely pressing her fingers against the skin. Then her lips brushed across the same spot. "I had a very good time tonight."

"I did, too." She put a hand on Julie's waist and pulled her close, holding her still and watching her pupils dilate. With a smile pulling at the corner of her mouth, Kylie kissed her, holding her tightly for several seconds, breathing in her pleasing scent.

When she felt Julie begin to collapse against her, Kylie pulled back and set the woman on her unsteady feet. "I like you."

Julie was still staring at Kylie's lips, her eyes a little unfocused. She busied herself by straightening Kylie's collar, and the doctor was pleased to feel trembling hands against her skin. "Can I see you again?"

"Definitely. How about Sunday?"

"Afternoon or evening?"

"Yes," Kylie said. She gave her one more light kiss, turned, and walked down the sidewalk, feeling confident and sexy. "I'll call you."

"I'll be waiting."

⌒

Kylie returned home early—a little after 10:00. Blair was asleep on the couch with both dogs sprawled over her. The dogs opened their eyes, but didn't move, and Blair didn't even do that. The doctor tried to tiptoe into the room to turn off the TV, but the sound woke her friend, who let out a little cry.

"Are you all right?" Kylie asked, walking over to her.

"Yeah. Yeah." She lazily wiped her eyes with the back of her hand and asked, "What time is it?"

"Ten o'clock. Wanna go to bed?"

"I think so. Help me?"

Kylie gave her a hand up after moving both dogs onto a cushion. Blair leaned against her, walking like a drunken sailor. When they reached Blair's room, she sat on the bed and then fell backwards, too exhausted to move. "You can't sleep like that," Kylie said.

"Bet me," Blair muttered.

"Come on. Take your clothes off and use the bathroom. You'll feel better." Blair let herself be pulled to her feet, and she stumbled a little when she started to walk to her bathroom. "I'm gonna wait here," Kylie said. "You look like you might fall asleep in there."

Blair muttered something as she went into the bathroom, and a few seconds later, Kylie heard a bang and then a string of profanities. "I hit my funny bone," Blair called out before Kylie could throw the door open.

"You sound more awake."

"Very helpful."

When she emerged, Blair collapsed on the bed once again, not bothering to pull the covers back.

"Can I cover you with something?" Kylie asked. She paused as Nicky and Nora got into position. "Besides dogs?"

"No, I'm..." Kylie heard the first soft snore, smirked at her friend, and left the room, amazed at Blair's ability to fall asleep.

The doctor went into the living room to read the paper, something she hadn't had time to do that day. She was about halfway through when Blair walked into the den. "Hey, Kylie?"

"Why are you up?"

"Backache," she said, a dramatic pout in place. "I forgot to ask if you had a good date."

"I did, thanks. I'll tell you about it tomorrow."

"'Kay. I don't remember when I put the dogs out. Will you let them out before you go to bed?"

"Sure." Blair started to head back to her room, and Kylie asked, "Want a backrub?"

"You don't have to. It probably won't help."

"I'd like to," Kylie said. She got up and followed Blair into her bedroom, taking some lotion from the bathroom. When Blair was lying on her side, Kylie started to rub the lotion into her friend's skin, working powerful fingers into the stressed muscles. Blair didn't say a word for a long time, but she let out many moans and groans of appreciation. Her voice was still alert when she finally said, "Kylie?"

"Hmm?"

"How does this feel for you? Is this clinical?"

Kylie's hands stilled, and she hesitated a moment. "Uhm, no, it's not clinical. It...makes me feel very close to you and to the baby. It calms me down at the end of the day. I really like doing it."

"Good," Blair murmured. "That's how I feel, too, and I didn't want to think you were dispassionate about it."

Kylie started to rub Blair's back again, working on the muscles while thinking aloud. "I have to be in my usual business setting to feel businesslike about it—like today, during the ultrasound. The hospital is my office, and I feel very detached around medical equipment."

"Good thing we don't have a lot of medical equipment lying around, then, 'cause I like having you present when you touch me."

"I like it, too."

"So, nothing personal today, huh? You couldn't identify me if all they found was the lower half of my body?"

"Gosh, you come up with the most optimistic scenarios."

"You know what I mean. I can't believe you didn't notice anything."

Kylie laughed. "I didn't say I didn't notice anything; I said it was clinical. Part of my job is to look at things and see if they look right. I looked at you, and you looked right."

Blair couldn't let go of the issue. "What did you notice?"

The doctor grinned at her. "I noticed a Caucasian woman, obviously pregnant, somewhere in her second trimester. I saw a faint linea nigra on your belly, along with some visible veins. When the technician opened you, I saw what I assume was Chadwick's sign. I didn't notice any abnormalities on your vulva. Everything was just like I would expect."

"Linea nigra? What in the hell is that?"

"A little darkening on your belly from your navel to your pubis. It usually starts in about the fourth month. Yours isn't very pronounced yet, and with your coloring, it might not get much darker."

"Great. I've always wanted a dark line down my belly. And what's Chadwick's sign? I know I read about it, but my memory is shot."

"That's a bluish tint to your vagina and cervix."

"I have that? I'm blue?"

"Not blue. Bluish. Nothing severe."

"You tell me my pussy is blue, and I'm supposed to be reassured by 'bluish'?"

"You're fair-skinned, Blair. Your skin is more translucent than some women's. The increased blood supply shows through a little bit."

"And it's on my belly?"

"Uh-huh. I assume it's on your breasts, too."

Blair sat up and yanked her T-shirt up. "Is it on them?" she demanded.

Kylie gave her a half-smile and nodded. "Yep. The veins show through, and they're definitely bluish."

"Oh, fuck me. Every good part is blue!"

"Hey, it's no big deal. It'll go away after you have the baby. The linea nigra might stay, but it's very faint."

Blair got out of bed and turned the overhead lights on. She went into her bathroom and pulled her T-shirt up, standing on her tiptoes to be able to see her belly. "Why aren't there any full-length mirrors in here?"

"They're not recommended for pregnant women," Kylie said, only partially kidding.

Blair came back into the room and pulled her shirt up. "Tell me the truth. Swear you'll tell me the truth."

"I swear," Kylie said gravely.

"How bad do I look?"

With a full, warm smile, the doctor said, "You look wonderful. One of the prettiest women I've ever seen."

Her eyes closed a little when she spoke, and even though Blair was completely sure it was the truth, she was still astounded. "How can you say that? I've got a big line down my belly that makes it look like I was attacked by a sadist with a black Magic Marker, my tits are blue and swollen, my belly bulges out and has blue lines all over it, and my pussy's blue!"

"Well, you're wearing panties, so I can't see everything," Kylie teased. "But I didn't say your vulva was blue. I saw the blue tint on your vagina."

"Big difference!"

"I'm just trying to be precise."

"I'll check the whole disgusting thing out as soon as I get a mirror installed on the floor."

"Hey, you're entitled to your own opinion about your body, but there's nothing disgusting about it from my perspective. You look absolutely wonderful. You're like a beautiful meadow right before all of the blooms burst into color."

"I don't wanna be a meadow," Blair sulked. "I wanna be hot." She fell onto the bed again and tossed her arm over her face. "I want men to swoon when they see me naked, but not because they're ill!"

Kylie leaned close and spoke softly. "I'm not a man, but if I saw you lying in my bed, waiting for me, I'd...well...you'd learn how hot I thought you were."

Blair's arm moved just enough to show one eye. "Really?"

"Cross my heart. This is the first time that a straight friend ever begged me to tell her she was sexy, but I'm telling the truth. You are sizzling hot in my not-so-humble opinion." She leaned even closer and kissed her friend on the cheek. "And I have to tell you, I love natural blondes."

Blair took her arm away and stared at the doctor. "You looked!"

"Intellectual curiosity," she giggled, scampering out of the room before Blair whacked her with a pillow.

A minute later, the doctor knocked on the door. "I got you a little present today. Want it?"

"Of course." Kylie walked in, and Blair smiled at her. "I'm not mad at you, you know. I would have looked, too, but I know your hair's naturally dark."

"I didn't mean to let that detail register, but it did, and I thought I'd better come clean."

"Where's my present? You owe me one for sneaking a look."

"I'll show you. Close your eyes and lie on your back."

"You're not gonna look again, are you?"

"Nope."

When Blair lay down, Kylie pulled her friend's shirt up, exposing her abdomen, and placed something in her ears. "Headphones?" Blair asked.

"Sh...gotta be quiet for this to work." Suddenly, Blair felt something cool and smooth on her belly and concurrently heard her baby's heartbeat, thrumming rapidly.

"Oh, Kylie!" Her eyes flew open, and she saw her friend grinning at her, moving the stethoscope around to various parts of her abdomen. "Is that your stethoscope?"

"Nope. It's yours. You need a special kind to hear the heartbeat at this stage. I picked one up at a medical supply store on the way home. You said this morning that you'd sleep better if you could hear him."

"Kylie Mackenzie, I'd gladly give up men *and* sex to keep you in my life. You constantly touch my heart."

The doctor leaned over and placed a gentle kiss on her friend's belly. "Well, you won't let me touch your heart the fun way, so I have to get at it through your emotions."

"Lean over here and put these on, wise guy. I want you to hear Baby Spencer."

Kylie did, and the delighted look on her face remained in Blair's heart, soothing her to sleep minutes later.

⌒

On Saturday, Kylie spent much of the day at the hospital, tending to a woman who continued to have unexplained bleeding and pain nearly twenty-four hours after her surgery. The doctor called Blair several times, keeping her apprised of the changing schedule. "It's okay, Kylie. Get home when you can. If your little doctor friends get here before you do, I can keep them entertained. Actually, I'll spend the time finding out which one of them might be in the market for a new home."

"But I won't have time to cook," she said. "I hate to order pizza."

"I'll handle it. I'll go to the gourmet market and buy all sorts of goodies. Don't worry about it."

"Okay, I guess I don't have much choice. I think I have this patient stabilized, but I want to stick around for another hour or so to make sure."

"You do what you have to, Doc. Everything's under control on the home front."

⌐

When Kylie got home, she stopped in her tracks as she entered the kitchen. The counters, bare when she'd left, were now filled with attractive, silver-colored serving platters, trays, and bowls. A dozen appetizer plates, a dozen matching glasses, and a set of vividly colored linen napkins were neatly displayed, along with silverware that matched the Southwestern-themed serving ware and plates. "What's all of this?" she gasped.

"You didn't have anything appropriate for a party," Blair chided her. "You're not in college any longer, Kylie. You have to act like an adult."

"But…it's only my turn to have my buddies over for cards once or twice a year. Other than that, I never entertain."

"Well, I do," Blair said. "I have to entertain clients, and I have one or two big parties a year. We need things to serve people."

The doctor picked up one of the platters and hefted it in her hand. "This stuff must have cost a fortune!"

No more than one month's rent in a decent apartment, Blair chuckled to herself.

"Is it silver?" Kylie asked.

"Of course not. I'd never buy something I had to polish. It's…well, I don't know what it is, but it's not silver. It's great stuff, though. It retains heat beautifully, and it's got a real Southwest look, which is great for this style of house."

Kylie looked at her for a moment and then asked, "Do you like to decorate? You sound like you know what you're talking about."

"No, not really," Blair said. "I called a buddy of mine who dresses homes for me, and we went shopping together."

"Forgive my stupidity, but how does someone dress a home?"

"Oh. Well, when I have a house that isn't up to par because of how it's decorated, I make the owners put their own things into storage, and I have Walter furnish the place with things he rents or keeps in his warehouse."

"People don't mind having to do that?"

"Well, of course, they mind," Blair said, looking slightly puzzled. "But that's part of the deal before I'll agree to list the house. I'm not going to waste my time trying to sell a dog." She patted Kylie on the side and said, "Walter was going to dress your condo if I'd had to list it. I would have squeezed another $25,000 out of your unit if I'd had it spiffed up. But I didn't even suggest it since you would have had to move out." She was showing her usual confident grin, and Kylie realized that she wouldn't have complained a bit if this determined, charming woman had ordered her to clear out of her own home.

"You're good at what you do, aren't you?" Kylie asked rhetorically.

"You betcha. Now, go put on something nice. We're having company."

Blair didn't spend much time in the living room while the doctors were actually playing cards. She did her best to keep the dogs entertained in the den, but the little devils kept dashing into the living room, hoping someone would drop a scrap of shrimp or some guacamole, which, Blair discovered quite by accident, the puppies adored.

The card players took a break for dinner at 8:30, and Blair joined them, drawing a chair up next to Kylie. The food was a big success, and after everyone had eaten, Blair started to get up to return to the den. "Hang out for a while," Kylie said. "You might like playing cards."

"No, I really don't," Blair insisted. "I never got the bug."

"C'mon," the doctor urged. "Watch a hand or two. You can help me."

Unable to say no to her, Blair tucked her chair right behind Kylie's and leaned over so they could whisper. They were having such a good time that Eileen finally said, "C'mon, Kylie; let's move."

Giving her an outraged look, Kylie said, "I'm instructing my friend. Patience."

Another few whispers, several more giggles, and Kylie finally asked for two cards. Perhaps because everyone else was bored to distraction, Kylie won the hand, and Blair gave her a hug and a kiss on the cheek. "Good job," Blair said. "That's enough excitement for me. Have fun."

As she walked away, Monique couldn't help but notice the furtive glance Kylie shot after Blair or miss the mild look of disappointment on the surgeon's face.

When the game broke up at 11:00, Kylie said to the group, "I'll go tell Blair you're leaving." She returned moments later, saying quietly, "She's asleep on the couch. She never makes it past 9:00 anymore."

"It's good for her," Monique said.

"Oh, I know. She usually sleeps while I watch TV at night. I make sure she's getting her rest."

"I'm sure you do, Shakes. You're quite persuasive when you want to be."

On the way to their cars, the doctors gathered near the end of the driveway to gossip. "What in the hell is going on here?" Jocelyn asked Monique. "Are they lovers or what?"

Monique wasn't going to reveal anything she'd learned from Blair, so the obstetrician shrugged. "Not to my knowledge."

"Well, Kylie acts like she's in love—big time," Jocelyn said. "I've never seen her act so considerate and caring. She smothered Stacey less."

"Well, I don't know what's going on, but I think Blair's a doll," Monique said. "I'd love for Kylie to have a family, no matter how she gets one."

"Yeah," Jocelyn agreed, "we'd all like for her to have that. But I sure hope she isn't trying to get it from someone who can't give it to her."

Chapter Seven

*O*n Sunday, Blair was scheduled to meet with clients for both brunch and an early dinner. When she finished dressing, she went into the den to tell Kylie of her plans. She found the doctor outside, reading the *New York Times*. Both dogs were lying in the sun, with Nora on her back, tanning her belly. "This is such a lovely picture of domestic bliss," Blair said. She kissed Kylie on the top of her head and played with her curls for a minute. "I'm gonna be gone all day. Can you man the fort?"

"I think I can handle it. Julie's coming over around noon, and we're gonna hang out for a while. Then we're going to the Bowl to hear the symphony." Kylie turned so she could face her friend, and Blair noted a look of disappointment on her face. "I wish you were gonna be here. I'd like you to get to know her a little bit."

"This might surprise you, but some women don't like to have a third person on a date. You have to concentrate on her, not on letting your roommate get to know her." Blair sat on the edge of her friend's chair and handed her a silver necklace. "Will you put this on me?"

"Sure." Kylie hooked the piece and settled the clasp at the center of Blair's neck. "Pretty necklace."

"Thanks." She stood up and modeled a little. "How do I look?"

"Is this new?" Kylie reached out and fingered the material. "Did you go shopping?"

"Yeah. I had to buy a couple of skirts. I can still wear my blazers, but my skirts were nasty looking."

"You look great," Kylie said. Her eyes closed slightly, and she looked her friend up and down. "This new look is gonna take some getting used to. Your short skirts were part of your style."

"Yeah, nothing better looking than a short, tight skirt that's partially unzipped. I had to beat guys off with a stick."

"Your legs look great." Eyes still partially closed, Kylie regarded Blair for another few moments. "You know, the style for pregnant women is to show off their bodies. You don't have to cover up if you don't want to."

"I want to," Blair said, her tone leaving nothing in doubt. "I'm no Demi Moore. I don't wanna be nude on the cover of *Vanity Fair*."

"I wasn't suggesting nude. I was simply saying that your body's nothing to be ashamed of. Everyone will know you're pregnant; why not be proud of how you look?"

"If I could get away with it, I'd wear a heavy wool poncho that covered me to my knees. Actually, the Victorian idea of keeping women out of the public eye when they're pregnant is starting to sound pretty appealing. I wonder if I could buy a fashionable burqa…"

"You're obviously feeling uncomfortable in your body right now, buddy. But all I can do is tell you that you look fantastic. You don't have a thing to hide."

Reaching down and ruffling Kylie's hair, Blair said, "I wish everyone were like you." She started to hum and then sang as she left the house, "I see trees of green…red roses, too. I see them bloom…for me and you. And I think to myself…what a wonderful world."

⌁

Around 4:00, Blair stopped at the house to freshen up before her dinner. Nicky and Nora didn't run to greet her, so she assumed they were outside with Kylie and Julie. When the dogs were outdoors, they couldn't hear people come and go, a condition that distressed them to no end.

She went to her room and tidied up, reapplying her lipstick. She still had half an hour to kill, so she decided to go offer Kylie and Julie something to drink. When she got to the sliding door in the den, she stopped abruptly, amazed at how quickly Doctor Mackenzie could get to work when she had a mind to.

The pair had taken the cushions from the lounge chairs and put them by the edge of the lap pool. Julie was lying on her stomach, and Kylie was straddling her. It looked as if the doctor were applying suntan lotion to Julie's back, but after a moment, it became obvious that Kylie was giving her guest a massage. Julie's top was off, and Blair found herself staring at the women, unable to move. Kylie was laughing, her lips open and perfect teeth gleaming, making her all the more radiant. She bent over and started to kiss and nibble at Julie's neck, and that's when Blair decided that this wasn't the best time for a visit. Still, she didn't leave immediately, even though she felt guilty for peeking.

There was something so different about Kylie that she couldn't stop herself from observing her for a moment. The gentle, sweet concern that was always present in the doctor's touch seemed completely absent. The kisses she lavished on Julie had a sexual, sensual quality that Blair had never felt from her friend. Kylie appeared possessive and determined when she took Julie's hands and spread them out, rendering the woman absolutely helpless against the barrage of kisses that rained down on her.

For her part, Julie looked as if resisting were the last thing on her mind. Still, Kylie looked like she was in complete control, and Blair found this new facet of her roommate's personality absorbing—and arousing. The unintended voyeur felt a definite tingle between her legs, and by the time she tore herself away from the display, her clit was swollen and sensitive. *Okay, I might have been puzzled before, but now I know there's no earthly reason that Kylie's single. I thought she might be shy or ungainly around women, but if she'd been any more gainly, I'd be on the floor right now!*

Blair got into her car and started to leave the property. But once outside the gate, she killed the engine and sat for a few minutes, thinking. *Well, this pregnancy has produced a wealth of surprises. A divorce, blue body parts, swollen ankles, and now I find that I'm totally aroused by a woman. What's next? Maybe I'll join the circus!*

She laughed softly when a little voice reminded her of something. *Yeah, as if that's the first time in your life you've ever been aroused at the sight of two women making love.*

Well, it is! she said, defending herself. *This is the first time I've ever seen a woman I know making love, and that's a completely different thing. Watching a movie with your husband isn't the same as seeing your best friend get it on in the yard. And in the movies, there was always a guy involved, too. Yes, I got aroused when I watched those movies, but the dynamic of the group is what made me hot. Today was different—very different—and I'm not even sure why, but I know it was!*

Blair got home from dinner at 8:00, kicked off her shoes, and sank into the couch. It was a warm night, and her clients had chosen an outside table at the restaurant. She felt sticky, bloated, grouchy, and unreasonably jealous…of Julie.

She'd been on a rant for the entire time it had taken her to drive home, and even though the dogs were giving her the usual royal welcome, she couldn't stop herself from continuing it. *I don't want another woman to come in here and try to take Kylie from me! We have such a nice thing going, and I don't want her to be gone at night. And I certainly don't want Julie over here. If I have to watch them make out again, I might jump in and join 'em!*

She knew she was being ridiculous and that Kylie was doing exactly what she herself had encouraged her to do. But Blair was unable to quell her jealous feelings, even though she knew she was on the verge of scratching Julie's eyes out. The phone rang, and she was barely paying attention when she agreed to Sadie's coming by for a talk. She hung up and opened the sliding doors to let the dogs out. It wasn't until the heat of the early evening hit her like a furnace that she realized what she'd done. *Have I lost my mind?*

Sadie arrived in short order, and Blair knew that her mother-in-law must have been in the area when she called. *She was probably in the driveway two minutes after she hung up,* Blair thought to herself while waiting at the door. She had both dogs on their leashes because Sadie was no fan of pets in the house—much less, pets that jumped on her. The dogs cried and whined to get to the new human, but Blair was firm with them, and they obeyed better than she expected.

"Well. This is certainly an impressive house." Sadie stood on the walk and looked around for a moment, shaking her head when she turned and saw the lights of the Westside. "Some view!"

"Yes, it is nice, isn't it? Little did I know I'd be living in it when I sold it to my friend."

Sadie stepped onto the porch and enfolded Blair in a motherly hug. Even though they'd had their difficulties, there was always something reassuring in one of Sadie's hugs, and Blair was in no rush to terminate the embrace.

Eventually, they walked into the house together, and Blair led her mother-in-law to the den, with Sadie exclaiming over every room they passed through. They sat next to each other on the sofa. "My lord, Blair, who is this friend of yours?"

"Her name's Kylie, and she's a surgeon."

"A girl with this kind of house, and she wants a roommate?"

Blair's chin jutted out a little with her reply. "Yeah, yeah, she does. But I don't think you're here to talk about Kylie, are you?"

"No, of course not. I'm here to see how you are, sweetheart. When David told me that you were getting divorced, it took me a few days to call you. I couldn't...I honestly can't comprehend what would cause him to act like he has." She took Blair's hand and looked into her eyes. "I'm ashamed of my own son, and that's never happened before. Never! Not once in forty years has my David made me ashamed. But now...now..." She took a tissue from the pocket of her suit and dabbed at her eyes. "I don't know what's come over him, but he doesn't seem like the man I know. He acts more like the little boy he was."

"I'd have to agree that he's been a little childish throughout this."

"A little? Ha! He's been a complete child, and now he's turning into an infant!"

Blair smiled at the older woman. "He's having a tough time adjusting. I think he'll snap out of it at some point."

Sadie leaned back and let out a massive sigh. "Oh, my God. You can't imagine how relieved I am to hear you say that. I knew you'd be an adult about this."

Giving her a puzzled look, Blair said, "Uhm, thanks."

"David says there's nothing to do but divorce, but if you think he'll snap out of this—"

"Oh, no, Sadie." Blair put a hand up to stop her. "I think David will grow accustomed to the fact that he's infertile, and I hope that he's able to love this child or another. But I'm not going to wait around to see when and if that happens."

Sadie's eyes saucered. "But if you think he'll change, why would you divorce?"

Blair didn't really want to involve her mother-in-law in the details of her marriage to David, but she felt she had to be honest. "I don't love him the way I did. I've lost respect for him, and I can't be married to a man I don't respect."

"But you can get that back. He can earn your respect again."

Blair thought about that statement and then nodded her head. "You may be right. But David hasn't given me any indication that he wants me to wait for him. He didn't even comment when I said I was going to divorce him. He hasn't called; he hasn't even sent me an e-mail. He seems perfectly willing to move on. That's enough for me."

"Oh, Blair, he loves you so much. He does!"

"He may, but he hasn't *shown* that he loves me. That's the only thing that counts."

Sadie stood and began to pace in front of the sofa. The dogs were still on their leashes, and they looked at Blair beseechingly, desperate to follow this person in her purposeless path. But Blair shook her head and pulled them close to her, giving each of them a calming scratch behind the ears. "I don't have to remind you that you were married in a religious service," Sadie said. She was now in her lecturing mode, and Blair knew this could be a long night.

"I realize that. It was something I did because it was important to you and David."

The older woman looked at her, dark eyes flashing. "You took vows, Blair. You took a vow to remain faithful to David. You promised that he would be the head of your household...the king of your union!"

"I remember the crowning, Sadie," Blair said, still amazed that she'd consented to the traditional service. "I remember having our hands bound together. The entire service, even though it was in Armenian, was very meaningful for me. And I *have* been faithful. I've put up with more things than most women would to hold our marriage together. But things have changed. We're not the same people we were then."

"I know that! That's why it's your duty to stand by David until he comes to his senses. I can understand that you might have trouble living with him, but why are you in such a hurry to divorce?"

Blair was feeling a tightness in her neck and her stomach, and she wondered if she might have a bout of all-day sickness again. "Look, Sadie, this is between David and me. It's too personal to discuss with you. I know you care, and I know this is hard for you, but we've decided this is what we're going to do."

"You're both so unconcerned about this! David acts as if this were a weight off his shoulders, and you act as though you're totally disinterested in working this out. Don't your vows mean anything to either one of you?"

"I can't speak for David, but mine do...or did," Blair said, leveling a glare at her mother-in-law. "I honored all of my vows. But David has made it clear that he's not interested in working to hold our marriage together. And if he's not willing, I'm certainly not going to try to do it on my own. You just admitted that he feels it's a weight off his shoulders. He's ready to move on."

"Blair, your vows don't give you an out because things have changed. You promised to love, honor, and obey—till death parts you. Death!"

"I know what I promised, but we entered into a mutual contract, and he doesn't want to comply with the terms. I hate to sound so businesslike, but those are the facts."

Sadie stared at the younger woman and asked, "Why are you so unemotional? Have you met someone?"

"Yeah," Blair said, sarcasm dripping from her words. "Los Angeles is full of eligible, single men who're hot for pregnant women. I couldn't wait to get rid of David so I could have my pick!"

"I won't stand for this! Where's your respect?"

Blair stood up, both of her sentries flanking her. "I don't want to fight, but I've made my mind up, and so has David. You've got more control over him, so if you're going to work on anyone, he's your man."

Sadie picked up her purse and clutched it to her bosom. "I suppose you're going to try to keep me from seeing the baby once it's born."

Blair blanched. "Jesus! What kind of a woman do you think I am? You can see the baby as often as you want. David can see the baby as often as he wants. He can have joint custody if he wants to. You can have the baby at your house for visits. God *damn* it, Sadie, I couldn't be any nicer about this! So, count your blessings, but count them elsewhere!" The dogs saw how angry Blair was, and first Nicky, then Nora, began to growl. The hair on their backs stood up, and Sadie began to back out of the room.

"I've never been treated so shabbily!"

"You wouldn't be treated shabbily if you didn't insult me," Blair said. "The thought of my cheating on David is beyond ridiculous, and I'm not in the mood to defend myself against such unbelievable speculation."

"But you seem so calm. What am I supposed to think?"

"You can remember who I am," Blair said, her voice calmer. "I'm not the type to be emotional in front of people. I've cried my eyes out over this. I just don't do it for an audience."

"I'm not an audience; I'm your mother-in-law. You should be able to be yourself in front of me."

"I *am* being myself. And one of my traits is being direct. Now, we can have a good relationship or a bad one. It's in your best interests for us to have a good one." The dogs and she herded the older woman to the door, and Blair closed it behind her, ignoring the outraged squawk that followed.

⌒

Kylie got home around midnight and checked on the dogs before she went to bed. They were in Blair's room, and when Kylie pushed the door open, they both stood, shook, and stretched before jumping down. Their movement woke Blair, and she gave Kylie the usual half-scowl/half-"who are you?" look of which the doctor had grown inexplicably fond.

"Sorry," Kylie said. "Go back to sleep. I'm gonna let them out before I go to bed."

Instead of rolling over and beginning to snore, which was her habit, Blair continued to look at her roommate. "Did you have a good time?" Even though her question was pleasant, the look on her face was not.

"You okay? You look grouchy."

Blair moaned and fell back onto the bed. "No, I'm not okay. Sadie ambushed me."

"Ooh…didn't you screen your calls?"

"No. She asked if she could come over, and I said all right. I invited her! How stupid am I?"

"You're not stupid." She sat on the edge of the bed. "Wanna talk about it?"

"Not really, but I guess I have to. I won't get back to sleep if I start thinking about it without venting a little."

"Vent away."

"There's not a lot to say, really. She's on my side in a lot of ways. She thinks David has behaved abysmally, which was nice to hear. But she believes that I should stay married to him to give him every opportunity to change."

Kylie nodded a little. "You are moving quickly…"

Blair glared at her. "I thought you understood!"

"I do. I do." She reached out and stroked Blair's leg through the sheet. "That's not a judgment; it's an observation. I only meant that I could see Sadie thinking that you should slow down and wait, especially if you still love David."

"Kylie, I've told you. I don't feel love for him the way I used to."

"I know that, and I understand that. But maybe Sadie doesn't. I can see that she'd want you to wait until after the baby's born to divorce. There's really not much of a rush, is there?"

"Do you get this…or not?"

Fidgeting, Kylie said, "I think I get it. David's done some things and said some things that have made you lose respect for him. He's shown he's not very committed to you."

"Exactly! I'm not going to stay married to a man who isn't committed to me."

"Makes sense. But you *could* wait for a while before you start divorce proceedings. If nothing else, it would get Sadie off your back."

Blair thumped the mattress with both fists, looking as if she were about to have a tantrum. "There's no reason to wait. None at all. I don't love David any longer. And he doesn't love me. If he did, he wouldn't be going through the motions in therapy and spending his evenings with Kimmy. But there's no way I can convince Sadie of that. She thinks the sun rises when he tells it to."

"So, thank her for her concern, and tell her to butt out. You don't have to be nice to her anymore."

Blair sat up on an elbow and looked surprisingly guilty. "I did worse than that. I was really rude to her, and I feel sick about it. I never wanted to do that, but she made me so damned mad!"

Kylie gave her foot a pinch and said, "Don't feel too bad. I'm sure she deserved every word you said."

"She asked if I'd found a new lover," Blair said, looking ill at the mere thought. "And it took every bit of self-restraint I had not to tell her David's the one she should be questioning. I know he's either doing that girl or trying to. I know David, and he isn't the kind of guy who wants women friends. He wants women for sex."

"Ugh. That's awful," Kylie said. "You should be proud of yourself for not ratting David out. That must have been tough."

"It was. And Sadie *can* be a pain, but I still have to call her and apologize. Being pregnant doesn't give me the right to be an asshole." Blair lay down again and said, "Thanks for the dose of perspective. Now maybe I can get to sleep."

Kylie got up and leaned over her friend. She kissed her on the top of her head and started to walk away when Blair asked, "Are you wearing perfume?"

The doctor stopped, her hand on the doorknob. "No, why?"

"Mmm…my mistake. G'night."

When Kylie left, the blonde gave her pillow a good right hook, mumbling, "You *are* wearing perfume, you hussy. You're wearing Julie's!"

On Wednesday evening, when Blair went into her room to change, she found two packages resting on her bed. Sticking her head out the door, she called, "Hey, are these for me?"

"What's that?" Kylie asked, walking down the hall.

"There are packages on my bed. Are they mine?"

"Hmm…packages that I purposely put onto your bed. Are you sure you wanna persist in this line of questioning?"

"But the bags are from the Gap. They don't have anything that'll fit me. Is there a store called the Gulp? That'd be more my style."

"The Gap has clothes for you. I bought you a few things for Chicago. When I talked to my mom this past weekend, she told me they'd had very chilly weather lately."

"Really?" Blair asked delightedly. "You bought me some clothes?"

"Yep. You didn't get much in the way of casual clothes when you went shopping. My family is ultra-casual, and I didn't want you to feel overdressed."

"Ooh…I love new clothes. And more than that, I love new clothes that someone buys for me. It makes it even more special." She gave Kylie a robust hug. "Thanks."

"You're welcome," Kylie said, smiling delightedly. "Don't you want to open your presents?"

"I'm so excited about your buying me clothes that I can't decide which box to open first!"

"I'm gonna have to buy you presents more often. I haven't seen you this happy in weeks."

Blair gave Kylie another hug, this time holding on to her for a while. "Oh, I'm feeling kinda down these days," Blair said. "Don't mind me."

"Why are you down?" Kylie asked, placing a soft kiss on her hair.

"Wearing the new clothes I bought makes me feel so huge. I don't feel sexy or attractive anymore. I don't even flirt anymore." She released her friend and sat down on the bed. "This is all very puzzling for me. I was never the kind of woman who obsessed about her looks, but being pregnant has made me feel like I'm not even in the game. It's like I don't exist."

"Oh, come on. You get a lot of attention because you're pregnant."

"Yeah, but it's pregnant attention. Men hold doors open for you, but they don't look at you like you're a regular woman. I've really noticed it with clients. My male clients used to flirt with me, and I'd always flirt back a little bit. Now? Nothing."

"Boy, I'm glad I'm a doctor," Kylie said. "I'd never make it as a real estate agent; I'm the worst flirt in the world."

Blair started laughing, making her friend look at her curiously. "You flirt constantly," she insisted. At Kylie's stunned expression, Blair corrected, "No, that's not really the right term. You don't flirt like I do. I try to connect with the guy…to show him I notice him. You don't do it like that. You, Doctor Mackenzie, walk into a room like you own it. Your confidence oozes out of you. It's like you're flirting with yourself. That's it!" She giggled, saying, "You flirt with yourself! You give the clear message that you're way cool and that you're a lucky woman just to be with yourself."

"Jesus, Blair! You make me sound like an insufferable egoist!"

"You're not, though," Blair assured her. "That's your surgeon demeanor. You're not like that at home or when we're out in public." She thought for a moment and added, "Although you were flirting with the woman in the radiology department when you cut to the front of the line. That was definitely flirting."

Kylie thought about Blair's words and nodded her head briefly. "I guess I do put on my most confident demeanor when I'm at work. I mean, I'm trying to convince people that I can open up their bodies and make things work again. That takes a certain amount of chutzpa."

"You've got enough chutzpa for three women. Luckily, you leave most of it at work."

"It's on my checklist: take off stethoscope, wash hands, and drain chutzpa from over-inflated ego."

"I like it when you show a little of it at home," Blair said, looking at her pensively. "It's part of your charm."

"Thanks," Kylie said, giving her friend a hug. "I like to make you happy, and if I have to be charming to do it, I'll gladly comply. Now, try on your new clothes while I get your dinner ready. I want you to model for me."

"Okay. I can't wait!"

"I'll leave you to it," Kylie said. "Come on, puppies. Mama Blair needs some privacy."

⌐

Kylie was standing at the kitchen sink, rinsing vegetables for a salad, when a pair of arms slid around her waist. Blair pressed her cheek between Kylie's shoulder blades, nuzzling against her. "Oh, someone's feeling cuddly, eh?"

"Uh-huh. I haven't tried on my things yet. I had a nap."

"Do you like to cuddle after a nap?"

Blair was quiet for a moment, but then said, "I've been falling asleep so early that I haven't had time to…you know."

Kylie turned around and looked at her friend, giving her a puzzled half-smile. As soon as she saw Blair's slightly embarrassed expression, she said, "Ah…you had a productive nap."

"Yeah. I've been having those sexy dreams. I'm just too tired to make use of 'em." She walked over to a stool by the breakfast bar and flopped down onto it. "Is there anything better than having someone hold you after an orgasm? I miss that so much."

"I hardly remember," Kylie sighed.

"Really?" Blair gave her friend a surprised look. "I assumed you and Julie…"

Kylie scowled at her. "Jesus, Blair, we've only had one real date."

"You've had two. You went over to her house."

"To walk around her neighborhood after work one night. That's not a date."

Blair gave her a curious look. "Did I offend you?"

"No," Kylie said immediately. Then she stopped and thought. "Yeah, I guess you did. I told you I didn't sleep with women if I wasn't in love. I meant that."

"Shit, I'm sorry. That was presumptuous and rude of me. Not to mention nosy."

"'Sokay," Kylie said, her smile back in place. "I was tempted, to be honest. But I decided not to let my horniness do my thinking for me."

"That's why I like you. You're such an adult."

"Such a horny adult," Kylie said, smiling broadly.

"That makes two of us. Sex with a partner is purely a fantasy at this point in my life."

Kylie walked over to her friend and ran a hand through Blair's tousled hair. "It's good for the baby to keep everything in shape down there. And a good orgasm lowers your stress hormones, too."

"Isn't a 'good orgasm' redundant? Is there such a thing as a bad orgasm?"

"Not that I've ever had. They're all good."

Blair gave in to the soft crying that had been taking place below her since she'd come in. She fussed over the dogs and picked them up, cuddling them in her lap. "It doesn't bother you to talk about sex and masturbation and that kinda stuff, does it? I'd hate to think I was making you uncomfortable."

"Not a bit. Sex was a normal topic of discussion at the dinner table when I was growing up."

"Are you serious?"

"Totally. My dad's a firm believer in making sex a normal part of life. He's very antagonistic to the concept that it's something to hide and snicker about. I mean, he and my mom didn't leave their door open or anything, but they'd answer any question we had, and with the age range of the kids, someone was always on the verge of puberty." She chuckled and said, "I still remember going into my brother James's room to sleep with him when he was around twelve or thirteen. I woke up before he did one day and went running downstairs, telling my mom there was something horribly wrong with his penis 'cause it was sticking straight up in the air!"

Blair nearly collapsed with laughter, and Kylie had to scoop the dogs up to stop them from tumbling to the floor. "Oh, my God!" Blair gasped. "What did your mother say?"

"Well, she and my dad were having breakfast, and my sister Christine was there, too. My dad asked Chris to explain it to me, and she said that when boys got to a certain age, their penises started acting differently. She said it was no big deal, but that I probably shouldn't sleep with James anymore. I'm not sure how she put it, but I got the impression that he needed more room in his bed because his penis got bigger at night."

"That's so adorable," Blair said. "Was James embarrassed?"

"I'm sure he was, at least a little bit. Nobody wants his five-year-old sister to see his hard-on. But it wasn't a big deal. That's what my parents did so well. They made us all realize that sex was part of life, and that we'd all have different needs at different times of our lives. We only had five bedrooms, but they made sure that each kid had a private room by puberty—even though that meant that at one point, four kids were sleeping in the same room. But it made puberty seem like a good thing—like it was something to look forward to."

"Your parents sound great."

"Yeah, they are," Kylie agreed. "But you can make your own mind up this weekend."

⤺

When dinner was finished, Kylie offered to do the dishes while Blair modeled her new clothes. The doctor was about halfway through when she heard a discreet throat clearing. A wide grin settled on Kylie's face as she turned. "Now that's the Blair Spencer I've come to know and love."

"Do I look okay?" Blair's smile was tentative.

"You look a lot more than okay," Kylie decided, taking off the rubber gloves she wore whenever she handled glassware or knives. "You look like yourself. You've got your sexy smile back."

"I feel so much better. Funny what a pair of chinos and a T-shirt can do for you." She looked down at herself, ran her hand over her abdomen, and said, "The T-shirt's a little snug. Does that really look okay?"

"Yeah, yeah." Kylie nodded decisively. "It's supposed to be close-fitting." She walked all around the self-conscious woman, nodding the entire time. "Perfect. Really."

"My business clothes cover me up pretty well. I think I've gotten used to that. It feels kinda odd to display myself like this."

"Well, given that I think your developing body is a real work of art, I might not be the most impartial judge, but I think you look wonderful."

Smiling warmly, Blair said, "As long as you think I look good, that's enough for me. If you're finished, come to my room while I try on the rest of the things. No sense trying to be modest after that ultrasound."

"Good point. I've seen less of women I've seriously dated."

⤺

Kylie lay on Blair's bed with both dogs sprawled across her body while she watched the fashion show. "How did you know what colors I'd like?" Blair asked. "You did great, by the way. I look best in yellows and greens and browns."

"I'm not completely fashion challenged," Kylie sniffed. "I'm not a shopper, but I know what looks good on women. I thought warm earth colors would match your skin tone and hair color."

Blair held up a pink, sleeveless T-shirt, giving Kylie a doubtful look. "I don't know about pink."

"Try it. You've got a lot of pink in your complexion."

Blair did, and Kylie insisted they had another winner. "Go look. It makes your hair look blonder, and it brings out the pink in your cheeks. I like it a lot."

"You know, you're right," she said slowly, smiling at herself in the mirror. "I had no idea I looked good in pink." Blair whirled to face Kylie, hands on her hips. "Why have you been hiding your fashion genius from me?"

The doctor threw her head back in a laugh at this unexpected and affectionate accusation. "A girl's gotta have some secrets."

"Aha! I should've known. Well, do you like the T-shirt? I don't normally wear casual sleeveless shirts."

"Oh, yeah. You have nice arms. You should show them off."

"Swimmer's arms," she said, making her triceps muscles more defined. "I was on the swim team in high school, you know."

"No, I didn't. I must have had a premonition, though, 'cause I bought you a swimsuit, too."

Blair dug in the box and pulled out two pieces of stretchy black material. "A two-piece? Have you forgotten I'm pregnant?"

"Nope. The top is really quite substantial to give your breasts support as they continue to grow. But the bottom is a bikini. Rather than trying to cover your burgeoning belly, why not stay low? It makes sense to me, and since you'll be here in the yard, I'll be the only one to see you."

"I don't know," Blair said, giving the suit another doubtful look, "but since you're the only one who'll want to poke her eyes out, I guess I won't argue with you." She sat next to her friend on the bed and said, "Besides, who'd argue with someone who bought her an entire casual wardrobe? This was far too generous, but I truly appreciate every single piece. You've also given my self-confidence a nice boost." She leaned over and kissed Kylie's cheek. "Thanks."

"You're welcome. Now, put on something for company. Nick's coming over to get his dog-watching instructions." Turning to the dogs, she said, "Uncle Nick's coming over, puppies! He gets to spoil you all weekend!"

⤚

On Thursday afternoon, Kylie stood at the car rental counter at O'Hare, staring at the clerk. "That's not impressive enough," she said. "Don't you have anything hotter?"

The man gave her a bored look. "I told you what we have, ma'am. I can't make the cars sexy."

"Never mind. Cancel my reservation."

"Happy to," the clerk said, showing his first smile.

As they walked away, Blair asked, "What's that about? Your own car was boring in 1985, and age hasn't improved its allure."

"I'm not trying to impress my brothers when I'm in L.A. My sisters are rational, mature women—like me," she added. "But my brothers love to give me shit. If I rent a sexy car, that's one leg up since all of them have some form of boring SUV or minivan."

"But how does renting a car have much cachet?" she asked. "Anybody with a charge card can rent a nice car."

Kylie shrugged. "Don't know why it works, but it works. Trust me."

Blair bit her tongue, having little familiarity with large family dynamics. They had to take a cab to the proper car rental place, but Kylie was entirely pleased to score a bright-red Mercedes CLK convertible. Once settled in the car, she chuckled and said, "I've never had any desire to have a convertible in L.A., where I could have the top down all year. But here, I always lust for one. Makes no sense."

"I'd tend to agree, Doc, but then, I've come to expect that from you."

"Just for that, I'm going to leave the top on, and you won't get to have the wind blow in your hair."

"The Kennedy Expressway and an open top do not a magic mix make. I'll count my blessings."

"Actually, I need the quiet to question you on the family. We've been working on this for a week, and you're still not primed for hand-to-hand relatives."

"There are too many of them!"

"Too bad. This was your idea, bud. I don't care if you call them all 'pal.'"

"Okay, I started it, but don't ask me what I was thinking. First off is Christine. She's, uhm, fifty-three, and she's a mathematics professor at the University of Wisconsin."

"Very good," Kylie said, giving her a grin.

"Even before you told me about your family, I had a feeling that no one worked at a minimum-wage job."

"Nope. We're all yuppies, or at least, we were. We're clearly not all young anymore."

Blair took a breath and said, "Paul's next, and he's a doctor. He's fifty-one, and he'll take over your dad's practice when and if he ever decides to give it up."

"Excellent!"

"By the way, how old is your dad?"

"He'll be seventy-five on October 30. We're having a huge party. If you have fun this time, I'd love to have you come back with me."

"I might do that. I could have an early Thanksgiving with my parents to boot." She concentrated for a minute and said, "Next is Alan. He's the one you called when you were buying the house. He's a real estate lawyer. I think he's…forty-seven or forty-eight, right?"

"Right either way," Kylie smiled. "He'll be forty-eight in two weeks. Good job!"

"He's the guy I'm gonna look for. We're about the only people who aren't doctors. I understand real estate law—a little."

"We don't have little, tiny Mackenzie family AMA meetings. We're really pretty normal."

"That remains to be seen," Blair said. She wrinkled her nose at her friend and added, "You're not very normal, so your perspective might be skewed."

"Good point. Now, stop stalling. You've got some names left, you know."

"Oh, all right. James comes after Alan, and he's yet another doctor. He's forty-six." She thought for a moment and then asked, "Why isn't he a gynecologist?"

"I think internal medicine suits him pretty well. He has the mind of a detective. He loves to figure out what's wrong with people." Kylie gave her a sly smile. "But to be honest, I don't think he wanted to work with Dad. He's happy to be on his own."

"Gotcha. James is a bit of a rebel."

"Well, I wouldn't go that far," Kylie said. "He didn't want to always be the most junior Doctor Mackenzie in the practice. He wanted to be his own man. He isn't even affiliated with the same hospital as Dad."

"Huh. Probably smart if he wants to make his own reputation. Now, let's see. After James is Claire. She's a lawyer, too, like Alan, but she hasn't practiced for years. She's a homemaker, right?"

"Right," Kylie said, "but don't call her that, or she'll deck you."

"Duly noted," Blair nodded. "Next to you is Chuck. He's the baby boy. He's forty-three and an engineer."

"Absolutely correct," Kylie said. "Now, he's the rebel—at least our family's version of one. He bummed around after school, traveling in Europe for a couple of years. He didn't really settle down until…oh…four years ago. He's been married three years, and his wife's pregnant with their first. You'll like him; he has the best sense of humor of the group."

"So, everyone is married…except you?"

"Rub it in, why don't ya?" Kylie asked, feigning hurt. "Doctor Baby Sister comes home for her fortieth birthday, still unmarried and with no prospects."

"You've got prospects. You just have to exploit them."

"Maybe. But yes, to answer your question, everyone is married and has kids or at least one in the oven. They all live relatively close by, except for Chris, and she's only as far as Madison."

"Are you kidding about that Doctor Baby Sister thing, or do they really call you that?"

"Well, my mother used to tell the boys to keep an eye on their sister or call their sister to dinner, and there had to be a way to identify us. Since Chris was out of the house by then, Claire was referred to as 'your sister,' and I became 'your baby sister.' The name had fallen into disuse, but when I started medical school, good old Alan resurrected it."

"I think it's adorable," Blair said. She looked at Kylie's profile, seeing the calm, alert expression that usually graced her face. "You know what I can't tell?"

"Unh-uh. What?"

"I can't tell how close you are to your family. I mean, except for Alan, I've never heard you call any of your siblings."

"Mmm…it depends on what you mean by that," Kylie said. "I call my parents every week or two, but I only speak to my sibs when I need something." She gave Blair a guilty look and said, "That doesn't sound too awful, does it?"

"No, it doesn't sound awful, but that's not what I expected. I thought big families would stay close."

"Well, they're all married and busy with their lives, and I am, too. I'm always happy to see them, but I'd say we keep up on each other's lives mostly through our mother."

"That's funny," Blair mused. "I always dreamed about having sisters who'd be my friends for life."

"It might be that way for some people, but not us. We get along fine, and we like to see each other a few times a year, but I confide in my friends in California, not my siblings. When you have a family as large as mine, you tend to fight each other to get attention from your parents. I didn't have it too bad, since I was the baby, but some of the boys were very jealous of each other growing up. Alan and James were always knocking the snot out of each other. And Chris and Claire barely spoke. They still don't seem to care for each other."

"Were you close to either of them when you were younger?"

"Mmm…not close in the usual way. Chris was thirteen when I was born, and by the time I was in first grade, she was in college. So, it's almost like we didn't grow up in the same family. Claire's five years older than I am, and that's a pretty big gap, too. She was nice to me, especially when I was real young—always let me sleep with her and would comfort me when there was a thunderstorm—but by the time I was in third grade, she was getting ready for high school, and I was a pest." She looked a little sad and said, "Even though I had a huge family, it was lonely sometimes. Having a bunch of people in the house doesn't do you much good if none of them want you around."

Blair shook her head, murmuring, "I never thought of that. I guess I assumed it would be like *The Waltons*."

"Nope. Not by a long shot. I love my family, and I really wouldn't trade them, but I like being an adult much better than I liked being a kid."

"I like being an adult, but I had a great childhood. I basically had three parents: my mom, my dad, and my grandmother. I was my parents' only child and my grandmother's only grandchild. It was a little disappointing when I grew up and realized not everyone thought I was special."

Kylie smiled at her, "I loved being in college and having someone get my name right the first time. My mom used to be so confused. She'd go through three or four names before she got to mine: 'James! Claire! Chuck! Lancer! Kylie!' I can still hear her sputtering through the list."

"Who's Lancer?"

"The dog," Kylie said, giving her friend a "poor me" look that quickly dissolved into a warm smile. "Well, we've done our best to study the Mackenzie family in the time we had, and I guess we've scratched the surface."

"Scratched the surface?" Blair sputtered, "I feel like the Amazing Kreskin! I got all of them."

"Uhm, technically, yes, but…" Kylie winced. "Don't forget: they all have spouses and kids."

Blair made a sound, which Kylie could only have described as whinnying, as she threw herself limply over the armrest that separated them.

"Aw, don't worry, buddy. You've got me as backup," Kylie said, smiling and patting the back of her stricken companion.

—

In Blair's view, the reception at the Mackenzie house was underwhelming at best. The front door of the impressively large brick and ivy-covered home was unlocked, and Kylie opened it without bothering to knock. She called out, "Mom, Dad, I'm home."

"We're in the kitchen, honey; come on back," a woman's voice rang out.

"We'll take our bags upstairs first. Be right back down."

"Okay," the woman agreed.

Kylie hefted the bags, refusing to allow Blair to carry anything more than her body pillow, which Kylie had insisted Blair pack. The doctor's insistence had forced her to make a late-night visit to a discount store the night before to find a nylon duffle bag large enough to hold the pillow, but she seemed happy to do it, so Blair was loath to complain. "I'm not sure where Mom will put you," Kylie said. "Hmm…I'll drop your bag in my room."

Blair looked around the space, seemingly decorated as it had been when young Kylie left for college. "Valedictorian, Doctor Mackenzie?" she queried after noticing her friend's high school diploma.

"Yeah. I worked hard in high school. Grades mean an awful lot when you know you want to go on to be a doctor."

Nodding, Blair continued to look around. "I don't get a feel for you here. There's nothing really personal. Just books."

Looking contemplative, Kylie said, "I didn't have many interests. I wasn't in many clubs, and I didn't play sports. Heck, I probably couldn't get into med school if I were a kid now. They really emphasize a well-rounded candidate these days, and I was far from well rounded. I didn't start coming into my own until I got to U of C, and even then, all I really did was learn that I was gay. I guess I'm a late bloomer. But that's not odd for scientists. Medicine is more than a career for many of us; it's an obsession."

"You don't seem obsessed to me," Blair mused. "You're really pretty moderate about it."

"Yeah, that's true, but I had to work to be that way. When I had to pick my surgical specialty, I was on the verge of being a transplant surgeon. If I'd gone that way, my whole life would have belonged to my patients. It's what I really wanted to do, and I know I would have been good at it, but in retrospect, I'm thankful that I changed my mind."

"What appealed to you about that?"

Kylie gave her a wry smile and said, "You don't get much closer to playing God. If you do your job properly, the patient gets a second chance at a healthy life; improperly…" She shrugged. "The stakes are incredibly high, and the pressure is mind-blowing. An operation might take thirty-six hours, and if your attention flags for a second or two, you can wind up with a ruined organ and a dead patient." A grin creased her face, and she said, "It's a bigger high than you could ever imagine."

Blair gave her a hug and said, "I'll never understand what gives you that drive, but it's nice that there are people like you. Medicine wouldn't have advanced very far with a bunch of self-effacing people who didn't want to rock the boat."

"I guess you're right. But I'm glad I have a fairly normal job. I deserve it."

"You do. But was it hard to make your choice?"

"Oh, yeah, very hard, but I looked at the transplant guys who had a reputation at UCLA. They were tops in their field, and they loved their jobs, but they had no time for anything else. I thought I'd have a baby at some point, and I wanted my child to know his mother." She gave Blair a wistful smile and said, "Given how my life has gone, maybe I should have gone into transplants."

"Hey! Will you stop that! Your life isn't over, Doctor Mackenzie, and you still have time to find a spouse and have a few kids. Just because you don't pop them out, it doesn't mean they don't need you around."

Kylie gave her a hug and said, "Sorry. I get a little maudlin around my birthday. Especially a big one. Makes me take stock a little bit."

"Your stock is sky high," Blair insisted, "and it's only going to go up."

⤚

They went back downstairs and found the Mackenzies in the kitchen, enjoying what looked to be a homemade cherry pie. "Hi!" Kylie said brightly.

"Welcome home, honey," Mrs. Mackenzie said. She got up, gave Kylie a very quick, very brisk hug, and then turned to Blair. "You must be Blair. Kylie speaks of nothing but you and the dogs these days, and let me assure you that you always come first."

"This is my mom, Dorothy," Kylie said, and Blair shook the older woman's hand. "And this is my dad, Kyle."

At that, Blair's eyebrow rose, and the senior Doctor Mackenzie extended his hand, which Blair shook. "After six children, I finally convinced my wife to allow me to have a junior," he said. "Kylie ruined that, but we're glad to have her, anyway." He reached out and clapped his daughter on the shoulder, but that was the full extent of the physical affection offered at the Mackenzie house.

"I made a cherry pie for you, honey," Dorothy said. She looked down at the partially eaten dessert and said, "I suppose we should have waited for you to get here, but we got hungry."

"No big deal," Kylie said. "I'd love a piece. How about you, Blair?"

"Sure," she said, thinking that dinner wouldn't be a bad idea, either, but not wanting to whine. She sat down at the generously sized table, and within minutes, Kyle was peppering her with questions about her pregnancy. It was the first time in memory that one of her friends' parents had reminded her to make sure to do her Kegel exercises, so she didn't have incontinence after delivery, but she quickly got over thinking of him as Kylie's father and put him in the doctor category.

As Kylie ate two pieces of the wonderful pie, her father turned his attention to her. In mere seconds, Blair was lost, and though she had no way to access or understand what father and daughter spoke of, she enjoyed witnessing the discussion. In all the months she'd known Kylie, this was the first time Blair had ever seen her actually try to impress anyone, and Blair found it touchingly dear. The younger Doctor Mackenzie was talking about the recent surgeries she'd performed, and before long, she started to provide her father with details of the work she'd done on the man who'd accidentally mutilated his penis.

Either Kylie had been very self-effacing when she'd told the story to Blair, or she was exaggerating now, and knowing Kylie, Blair was certain it was the former. Kylie explained to her father that one of the vascular surgeons had lost focus and made a mistake that outraged the head of the trauma team. She described how he had called her in specially, not that she'd just been hanging around when one of the doctors grew tired, as she'd explained to Blair.

As she watched Kylie speak, Blair saw how animated she became. Her eyes sparkled as she clarified that the head of the trauma team was an internationally known surgeon and that he'd gone out of his way to find her to replace the vascular surgeon whose work had displeased him. Kyle had heard of the trauma surgeon, and he beamed with pride as his daughter spoke. "Well done," he said, giving her an enthusiastic pat on the shoulder. "I knew you'd make a great surgeon, Kylie. You were always the one." He nodded at his prescience, and Kylie tried unsuccessfully to hide her grin. "Were you written up in the paper?"

"Well, the local news mentioned the accident, mostly because it was so gruesome, but they did the usual 'team of doctors' thing," she said. "But the UCLA Medical Center had a nice mention in their newsletter. They noted that I was a med school grad, of course. None of the other guys went to UCLA, so it was kind of a 'local girl makes good' story."

"Well, there's gonna be another one when I call the editor of the *Lake Forest Times* to tell him he missed the story. I'll make sure the local folks know how well you're doing."

"Okay," she shrugged, looking enormously pleased. "If you want to."

"Of course, I want to. I'm proud of you, Kylie."

Blair thought her friend's cheeks might actually burst, she was grinning so broadly. Dorothy reached over and patted her daughter, as well. "I don't know half of what you two were talking about, but I caught some of it. I'm proud of you, too, sweetheart. Of course, I'm proud of you for being such a nice woman, as well."

"Nice women are a dime a dozen," Kyle decreed, and Blair did a double take when she realized he was being entirely serious. "Being a topflight surgeon is an accomplishment. Your brothers are good doctors, Kylie, but you're the only one in the group who has what it takes to hold a vital organ in your hands."

Gee, I wonder why she went into medicine, Blair thought wryly as she watched Kylie bask in her father's acclaim.

⌒

After the few dessert dishes were washed, Dorothy said, "Chris should be here soon. She's driving down, and she said she'd leave by 3:00, at the latest."

"Cool," Kylie said. "I assume that Willow will be the only one to make the trip?"

"Yes. Aaron started school almost two weeks ago, and Chris says he's having a tough time adjusting to being away from home. She thought it best to wait for Dad's birthday to upset his routine. And Carly's in some band competition in a week or two. They're practicing all weekend. You know how it is, Kylie. Once you're in high school, you never have time for family functions."

"Yeah, I remember." She filled Blair in. "My nephew started his freshman year at Princeton. I told him not to go so far from home, but you never listen to your aunt."

"Oh, I forgot: Chris said she's going to stop by Paul's house and pick up Jared and Jessica. If she's unlucky, she'll have to bring Kevin, too."

Alarmed, Kylie's eyes grew wide. "They're coming tonight? Where will they sleep?"

"Well, Chris will have her old room, and Jessica and Willow will bunk together in Claire's room."

Kylie gave her mother a pointed look, but the older woman continued. "I suppose Jared and Kevin will have to take Chuck's room, won't they?" she asked rhetorically.

"Uh-huh. I assumed Blair would take Chuck's room, Mom. That's gonna be tough with two boys in it."

Dorothy furrowed her brow and then made a dismissive hand gesture. "Oh, don't worry about it. Jared and Kevin can sleep down here on the floor."

"No, no, that's not necessary. I can sleep with Kylie," Blair said. Turning to her friend, she added, "Unless you're opposed to that."

"No, I don't mind. I can't imagine you'll be comfortable sharing with me, though. It's probably been a while since you've had a sleepover, hasn't it?"

"Yeah," she said, "it's been a little while, but I always enjoyed them. No reason to think I won't still like 'em. Can we tell ghost stories?"

"You're a trouper," Kylie said. "Troupers do well around here."

⟶

Blair was exhausted by 10:00, and even though the other guests hadn't arrived, she decided she needed to turn in. Kylie got her settled and started to head back downstairs, promising to be quiet when she returned. "Don't bother," Blair said. "If I'm sleeping well, I won't hear you, and if I'm not sleeping well, I'll hear you breathing when you're still outside the door."

Pausing, Kylie looked at her for a moment and asked, "Are you really sure about this? Maybe I should sleep on the sofa downstairs. I hate to think of waking you if you've just gotten to sleep."

Blair propped herself up on an elbow and smiled at Kylie, shaking her head. "Please don't let that bother you. I won't sleep at all if I'm lying here feeling guilty about throwing you out of your bed. It's really no big deal."

"I wish I'd known Mom decided to let the kids come over. I remember you wouldn't stay at my condo when I didn't have a second bedroom. You said you were too old for a sleepover."

"Please! I just didn't want to put you out."

"We should have stayed at a hotel," Kylie muttered, almost to herself. She rolled her eyes and said, "Of course, that would then subject us to the 'Kylie needs special treatment since she lives in California' lecture."

"Kylie, please don't let this bother you. I swear that it doesn't bother me in the least." She could see that the doctor wasn't convinced. Smiling brighter, she said, "I'm looking forward to bunking with you. You know how lonely I get. Having a nice, warm body next to me is a treat!"

Looking slightly skeptical, Kylie cocked her head and said, "Really?"

"Really. I'd ask you to sleep with me all the time if I didn't feel like such a baby."

Approaching the bed, Kylie sat down and said, "You can ask me for anything you need. Anything at all." She put her hand on Blair's cheek and stroked it, smiling when Blair moved into the touch. "Do you believe me?"

Nodding slightly, Blair said, "I do. Next time I'm lonely, I'll shuffle down the hall to your room, sucking my thumb."

Finally letting out a laugh, Kylie said, "I'd pay money to see that."

"You just might. Now, go wait for your sister and the kids and have fun."

"All right." Kylie got up and shrugged her shoulders, looking young and a little embarrassed. "I guess I should have warned you, but I get kinda grumpy when I visit. I like being here, but it brings up old slights and bad feelings from thirty years ago."

"Well, I don't have any bad feelings, so I'll keep you happy. Promise."

"It's a deal. Now, sleep tight."

❦

It was after midnight when Kylie cracked the door to her room, and she blinked in surprise when she saw Blair doing what looked like pushups against the wall. "Are you going out running?"

"I wish. Those were the good old days. I think I'll start running again after I have the baby."

"So…what are you doing?"

"I was sound asleep and having the nicest sex dream when I got this horrible cramp in my leg. Monique warned me, and she showed me how to stretch to avoid them. I'm supposed to stretch before bed, but I forgot."

"Why didn't you come get me?"

"I don't need to cause a scene every time I have a little ache or pain. I'm sure I can get this worked out."

"How long has it been bothering you?"

"I don't know…about fifteen minutes, I guess."

"Too long. Let me put my pajamas on, and I'll massage it for you." She got into a pair of red plaid flannel pajamas, while Blair continued to stretch, and then retrieved a bottle of moisturizing lotion from her bag and got into bed. "Let's go, pal."

Blair climbed in and lay in the opposite direction so her feet were at Kylie's head. Blair propped herself up on the huge body pillow and tried to relax her muscle, but she was unable to. "Wow, this really hurts," she said, grimacing.

"Just lie still and take a few deep breaths. Breathe through the pain." Kylie started working at the cramp, her touch gentle. "This is awfully tight. You must be hurting."

"Not too bad. I have pretty good pain tolerance."

"You must. This is like a rock."

"Did your sister get here?"

"Uh-huh. They stopped and picked up not two, not three, but five kids. All three of Paul's and two of Alan's. So, we have three girls, each around eleven, and two boys—seven and five. I can't guarantee they won't keep us up. The girls have a tendency to giggle uncontrollably."

"It'll be good practice. Someone's going to be keeping me up most of the night in a few months, so I might as well get into shape."

"We'll take shifts with the baby. It won't be so bad if you only have to get up every other time."

Blair chuckled softly and said, "How do you plan on breastfeeding the baby?"

"With the milk you express earlier in the day. We'll get you a breast pump. That'll allow you to be away from the baby for hours at a time."

"I would have thought of that if my brain hadn't turned to mush, but you're smoking dope if you think I'm gonna let you get up at night with the baby. You don't have the kinda job where you can be half-asleep, buddy."

"We'll argue, I mean, discuss that later. And don't worry about your brain. You'll be intelligent again one day. This is pregnancy-induced stupidity. It's a common symptom."

"I'm getting dumber by the minute, but the cramp's getting better." She sighed and stretched like a cat. "Much better."

"Want me to stop?"

"I hate to stop. It feels fabulous. But I'd better turn around, or you're going to have my feet in your face all night long."

"I don't mind. You have cute feet."

Blair got settled in the proper position and let out a massive sigh. The body pillow bisected the large bed, and she tossed an arm and a leg over it, a satisfied smile on her face. "This is sweet. I feel good now."

"This reminds me a little of being in bed with my older sisters when I was a kid. Brings back nice memories."

Blair's sleepy voice asked, "Why didn't you sleep with your parents when you were scared?"

"Not allowed. Dad believed that kids had to learn how to sleep alone. I wouldn't even have asked."

"But...they had to know that you slept with your siblings..."

"Mom did, for sure, but she never commented on it. She'd have to go from room to room looking for me most mornings 'cause sometimes, I'd kick my bedmate and get thrown out. I'd go from brother to sister, looking for comfort."

"Wow. I didn't do it often, but my parents always welcomed me when I was scared. I'm really glad you had siblings, Kylie. I'd hate to think of your being afraid and forced to be alone."

"You know, I'm sure I wouldn't have been so needy if my parents had let me snuggle with them once in a while. But my dad was really rigid about his child-rearing ideas. He's loosened up a lot in the last twenty years or so, but he was quite autocratic when I was young. I don't think my mother agreed with a lot of what he did, but she never openly disagreed with him."

"Well, I think I'll let Baby Spencer cuddle with me whenever he needs to."

"If you can wrestle him away from me," Kylie said. "I'll probably sneak into your room and steal him in the middle of the night."

"Remember, Doc, I can show a house when I'm half-asleep, but your patients need to have you bright-eyed and bushy-tailed."

"I've operated on people after being up for thirty-six hours straight. I won't even notice if I miss a few hours. I'm battle-tested."

"This argument will be continued. Right now, I'm going to sleep. Oh…I didn't listen to his heartbeat."

Kylie jumped out of bed and found the stethoscope Blair had packed. Listening carefully, she softly tapped her friend's thigh, illustrating the cadence of the baby's heartbeat. "Strong and steady," she pronounced. Turning her head, she kissed the abdomen and said, "'Night, Baby Spencer. Sleep soundly and don't wake your mommy up. We've got a big day planned for tomorrow."

"Yes, Baby. It's your godmother's birthday, and we get to go to the symphony to see your grandfather perform. I think you're gonna like it."

"I know I am," Kylie said, smiling sleepily. She got back into position, and by the time her body had stopped shifting, she was asleep.

"I've gotta learn how to do that," Blair mused quietly.

～

Kylie woke early, as usual, but Blair looked so peaceful and content that the doctor forced herself to go back to sleep to avoid waking her bedmate. It was after 8:00 when Kylie heard the door creak open slightly and Kevin, her five-year-old nephew, whisper loudly, "They're still asleep." Lifting her hand, Kylie made her index finger and thumb into an imaginary gun and pulled the trigger. "She's up!" The boy came running into the room, a gleeful look on his freckled face. "I wanna see your girlfriend!" he cried while trying to climb onto the bed.

"Hey, tiger, slow down. Blair's not awake yet. You have to be gentle with her, or she'll be grouchy all day."

"Will not," a grouchy voice grumbled into her body pillow.

"See, she's grouchy already."

His bright blue eyes barely peeked over the top of the bed, and they grew wide when Blair opened her eyes and growled at him. He squealed, more from amusement than fear, and then started to giggle when Kylie reached over and tumbled him onto the bed.

He got comfortable by sitting on his aunt's stomach, but then grew shy, leaning against Kylie and looking everywhere but at Blair.

"That's Blair, Kevin," Kylie said. "Do you know what she's got growing in her belly?"

"Uh-huh," he said soberly, peeking at Blair when he thought she wasn't looking. "She's got a baby in there. Gramma said."

"That's right. Right around your birthday, the baby's gonna come out. Cool, huh?"

"Yeah. Gramma says Uncle Chuck's gonna have a baby then, too."

"Well, Gramma's full of information, isn't she?"

"Yeah. Gramma says Blair doesn't have a daddy, and I'm not supposed to say so."

Kylie glanced at her friend, but Blair seemed not to be offended. "I have a daddy, Kevin, but I don't have a husband. The baby's all mine," she said, trying to put a spin on the situation that a child would understand. "I don't have to share him with anyone."

"'Cept Aunt Kylie, right?'"

Blair gave her friend a smile filled with affection. "Except your Aunt Kylie. I have to share the baby with her, but I won't mind a bit. She's my very best friend, you know."

"She's your girlfriend. Like Laura."

"Not exactly like Laura," Kylie said. But deciding that she had neither the time nor the ability to explain the difference between friends and girlfriends, she added, "Blair's really special to me, Kevin, and I'm very excited about the new baby."

"Me, too! Can I see him?"

Deciding to be a good sport, Blair rolled onto her back, pulling her T-shirt up a bit. She displayed her slightly protuberant belly for Kevin's inspection, and he regarded it curiously. "Looks like Grampa Jerry's."

Kylie broke into a laugh, telling Blair, "That's his maternal grandfather. He has a bit of a gut." Turning to Kevin, she said, "Blair's tummy is different from Grampa Jerry's. She has a baby inside hers, and I'm pretty sure he doesn't."

"I wanna see it!"

"Well, I could show it to you, but Blair's all skittish about scalpels," she teased, her joke going over Kevin's head. "If Blair doesn't mind, I can let you hear him."

"Can I?" Kevin asked, his strawberry-blonde hair falling into his eyes as he looked quickly from Kylie to Blair.

"Sure. I don't mind."

Kylie showed him how to place the stethoscope against Blair's tummy, and he was very quiet for a moment, listening intently. "You tap on my back and show me how his heart's beating, okay?" Kevin was too engrossed to speak, but he nodded to his aunt. Kylie was dangling off the bed, but she finally maneuvered her long body around until she was in the same position as Kevin. As agreed, he started tapping on his aunt's back, matching the rhythm of the baby very well. "Good job, buddy!" Kylie exclaimed. "If you like to listen to babies, maybe you'll grow up to be an obstetrician."

"Maybe," he said soberly, clearly not having any idea what she was talking about. "Oh! Gramma said breakfast is ready, and you have to come down right this minute!"

He scampered off the bed and started running, but then stopped and raced back to the bed, tossing his small arms around Kylie and giving her a sloppy kiss. "Happy birthday!" Then he was gone again, his small feet hitting the stairs in moments.

Kylie looked at Blair and asked, "You sure you want the baby to be born? They're so much easier to deal with when they're enclosed."

"Well, I thought he was adorable, but given that his breakfast message was so delayed, we'd better get moving. Shower first?"

"Yeah. We're casual about many things, but pajamas at the breakfast table are strictly forbidden. That's probably why I'm in my pajamas until lunchtime most Saturdays."

"You're a rebel," Blair teased.

◠

"Did you sleep well?" Kylie asked as Blair blew her hair dry.

"You know, I don't know if it was the bed or if I was extremely tired or if I slept better because I was with you, but I feel very well rested. I have a whole new outlook."

"You look good. And that outfit is adorable on you."

"Thanks again, bud. I feel my age in jeans and a turtleneck. And it feels so nice to have a stretchy panel covering my belly. Trying to jam myself into my old pants was getting ridiculous."

"You and Emily, Chuck's wife, can exchange fashion tips tomorrow. I think she's at nineteen weeks now."

"That'll be cool. I don't know any other pregnant women."

"Wait till we start our Lamaze class. You'll think the whole world is pregnant."

◠

When they reached the kitchen, everyone had eaten, but there was a spoonful of scrambled eggs, a piece of cold, dry toast, and a box of cornflakes sitting on the table. The kids were nowhere to be seen, but Dorothy and two women sat at the table. The woman who looked a great deal like Kylie stood and offered a hug. "Hey, Doctor Baby Sister, happy birthday!"

"Thanks, Chris. It's nice to be home for my birthday for a change." Turning to Blair, she said, "This is Blair. Blair, this is my sister, Christine, and her partner, Laura."

Blair blinked in surprise, but managed to shake both hands. "Good to meet you both."

"Likewise," Chris said, her grin nearly identical to Kylie's. "Come have a seat."

Blair sat next to her, and Kylie snuck around the back of the table. She poured a glass of juice for Blair, got a cup of coffee for herself, and proceeded to make small talk with her sister for a few minutes. Soon, the doctor picked up the piece of toast and started to munch on it. Blair eyed the cereal box and wondered, *Is this really all we're going to eat? No wonder everyone is so thin! They're starving!*

Chris turned to Blair and said, "Mom tells me you're due in December. Are you still excited, or has terror crept in?"

"I'm still mostly excited. I'm feeling really good, I'm sleeping well, and the birth feels like it's a long way off."

"That won't last," Chris said, and both Laura and Dorothy nodded agreement. "I had one, but Laura's had two, and Mom's obviously had seven. We're living proof that you can get through it."

"Pregnancy's the easy part," Dorothy decided. "It's the next twenty years that are tough."

"I have a feeling that's true," Blair agreed. "So, I guess I'd better enjoy the enjoyable parts while I can."

"Well, you look great," Chris said. "You hardly look pregnant at all."

"You know, I look less pregnant in these clothes. For some reason, properly fitted maternity clothes are much more flattering than trying to jam myself into my old stuff. Kylie bought this for me. I think she did a marvelous job."

"Good work, Baby Sister," Chris said. "Hey, Willow pointed out that sexy convertible in the drive. It has to be yours. Can I take a look?"

"Sure. We actually have to get going soon. We're going to spend the day with Blair's parents and go to the symphony tonight. I'm stoked!"

"Well, let me see your car before you take off, then."

"Blair, would you get my hanging bag from upstairs?" Kylie asked. "I packed everything I'd need for tonight in there."

"Sure. I'll get my things together and meet you at the car."

Kylie walked out with her sister, and it quickly became obvious that the older woman wasn't as interested in the car as she was in Blair. "So, what's up with your friend? Mom says she's in the process of a divorce."

"Yeah. It's been horrible for her, but I'm so impressed with how she's handling everything. She and her husband tried to have a baby for nearly two years, and not long after she got pregnant, he decided he wasn't able to be a father. I think he's gonna regret it and try to get her back, but I don't think Blair's the type to be burned twice. It's a damned shame." Shaking her head, she said, "Not only is he making a massive mistake in letting a wonderful woman like Blair go, how could you turn your back on your baby like that?"

"Don't look at me. I know a lot less about men than you do." She walked around the car, noting its sleek lines. "She's lucky to have a friend like you."

"I think I'm the lucky one. She's become my closest friend, and I'm more excited about the baby than she is."

"Knowing you, you're not exaggerating. I hope she stays in your life for a long time, Sis. She seems good for you."

"We're good for each other."

"So...how's your love life?" Chris asked, wincing a little when she heard how blunt her question sounded.

"Nothing much to report. I've had a couple of dates with a woman I used to work with."

"Really?"

Chris sounded so shocked that it brought Kylie up short, and she looked hard at her sister. "Yeah, L.A. is big enough for even me to find a date."

"Hey, that's not what I meant. I didn't know you were seeing anyone."

"Well, like I said, I've had a couple of dates. I'm not ready to pick a china pattern yet."

"But that's good, Kylie. That you're dating, I mean. It must feel good to get back in the game."

Kylie crossed her arms over her chest and gave her sister a scowl. "You make it sound like I've been sitting in a little bare room, feeling sorry for myself, for the past two years. You know, just because things didn't work out with Stacey doesn't mean that I'm lonely. I have a very fulfilling life."

"I'm sorry. This isn't turning out like I intended. I wanted to make conversation, Sis. Not start a fight."

Kylie nodded, slightly mollified. "It's okay. I get a little testy around my birthday. Don't worry about it." Kylie suddenly brightened, and her smile beamed when Blair came out the front door. "Let me get those bags," she ordered, nearly sprinting to stop Blair before she tried to negotiate the stairs.

"She treats me like I'm made of porcelain," Blair said, rolling her eyes at Chris.

"Take it while you can get it," Chris said. "All too soon, you lose the special status being pregnant gives you."

Kylie said, "Nah, Blair's naturally special." She held the door open for her friend and made sure she was settled before closing it. "See you late tonight or tomorrow," Kylie said, giving her sister a pat on the back.

"Have a nice birthday, Baby Sister. We'll see you tomorrow." Chris waved and then headed back into the house.

⌒

When Kylie got into the car, Blair was staring at her, wide-eyed. "You didn't tell me your sister was a lesbian!"

"I didn't? Really?"

"No, you most certainly did not! I was caught completely flat-footed, and I almost blurted out something stupid."

"Nah. I've never heard you say one stupid thing. You're not gonna start now."

"Thanks for the vote of confidence, but I almost said not one, but two embarrassing things this morning."

"What was the other?"

"I almost asked if anyone at your house ever ate a meal! I'm famished!"

Kylie looked chagrined and said, "That's my fault. My family eats a normal amount, but only at scheduled meal times. If you miss the time, you have to scrounge for yourself, and given that you're subject to the lecture about the house not being a twenty-four-hour diner, I always choose to wait for the next meal." She scowled and grumbled, "You're probably starving from last night, too, aren't ya?" At Blair's nod, Kylie continued, "I'm sorry I didn't take better care of you. When I realized that we'd missed breakfast, I assumed we'd stop to eat on the way to your parents', but I forgot to mention that."

Reaching over to pat her thigh, Blair said, "It's no big deal. It was probably good for me to eat light last night. Heck, maybe that's why I slept so well. How'd you sleep, by the way?"

"Good. I hardly notice when I have someone in my bed. I feel good today. That extra couple of hours sleep really perked me up."

"Would you mind waiting until we get to my parents' to eat? My dad would love it if he could make us breakfast."

"No, not at all. I stocked up on that piece of dry toast," Kylie said, winking.

↩

Chris hadn't been back in the house for two seconds when her mother asked, "Is there something going on between those two or not?"

Giving her mother a wry smirk, Chris said, "Gee, who'd have ever thought it would be a benefit to be a lesbian around here? Have you rendered your learned lesbian opinion yet, Laura?"

"I have, but I don't want to influence your vote."

"Okay," Chris said thoughtfully. "I don't think there's anything going on between them. But Kylie wants there to be; I'm sure of that." She looked at her mother for a moment and said, "But that doesn't mean Kylie knows it. She's notoriously clueless when it comes to herself. It took her three years to figure out Stacey wasn't right for her when we all knew it the minute we met her."

"I hope she knows what she's doing," Dorothy said worriedly. "She couldn't bear to have her heart broken again."

"Happens to the best of us, Mom. She's not immune to heartbreak—even though she *is* the spoiled baby girl."

↩

Werner was happy indeed to be able to make a meal for his daughter. "Your appetite is very healthy," he said. "That's good."

"Actually, my family tried to starve her to death," Kylie said. "We didn't get dinner last night, and we missed breakfast this morning. I'm surprised Blair wasn't lightheaded."

Werner gave Kylie a speculative look. "Your people don't like to cook?"

"No, not really. My mother's competent, but after seven kids, she feels she's paid her dues. If you're not at the table when the meal is served, you're on your own."

He nodded, looking as if he didn't really understand her point, but he was obviously too polite to voice his surprise. "In my family, my mother offered food to anyone who entered the house. Delivery men, the mailman, men who came to repair the washer." He chuckled and said, "She never understood why the mailman wouldn't come in for tea and a little cake."

Kylie laughed and said, "My mother figured out how to entertain without having to cook at all. She and my father used to have cocktail parties, starting at around 5:00 and lasting until 7:00 or so. Their poor guests would leave at dinnertime half-drunk with nothing but cheese and crackers in their stomachs."

"Every family has its own traditions," Werner said. "Luckily, we like to feed company constantly, so when you miss a meal in Lake Forest, you can come down here and let us fill you up."

"When do you have to leave, Dad?" Blair asked. "I don't want you to be late."

"Today, we're rehearsing from 11:00 until 1:00. You're welcome to come watch, but that would probably bore you. You could also go watch a run-through of your mother's new play. I think she said they're going to start after lunch."

"Well, since I won't get a chance to see the play, I'd like to do that, but I'm sure I know what Kylie will choose. Do you mind splitting up?"

"I'd really love to watch the symphony rehearse, but I'll go with you if you don't want to be alone."

"No, I'm fine. I'll grab a cab."

Kylie gave her a concerned look and asked, "Do the cabs have seatbelts in them? I don't want you riding in one if you're not belted in. I'll go with you if that's the case."

"See what I mean, Dad?" Blair asked. "Kylie fusses over me as much as you do."

"That's why I like her so much," Werner said, giving Kylie a smile that reminded her a little of Blair's. "It's nice to know I have an ally in California."

⟶

After going outside with Blair to make sure the cab did, in fact, have seatbelts, Kylie and Werner left for rehearsal. As soon as they were in the car, he turned to her and said, "Okay, now tell me the truth: how is Blair—really?"

Giving his question some thoughtful consideration, Kylie said, "She's honestly very good, Werner, and believe me, I'd tell you if she weren't. Blair has an ability that I envy. She's able to compartmentalize things to carry on with her life. I mean, I can't imagine how devastating it must have been for her when she realized that things weren't going to work out with David. But rather than focusing on her grief, she shut it away to concentrate on the more important issue—making sure the baby wasn't affected."

He nodded, his expression still filled with concern. "How's her mood? Does she laugh?"

"Yes. Definitely. Her spirits have been remarkably good, and she honestly seems content and happy. I still don't know how she manages, but I know for a fact that she's eating well and sleeping well and getting her exercise."

"And her health?"

"Very good. Her blood pressure is low, and she's not eating junk food or doing any of the things I do when I'm stressed. As I said, I don't know how she manages, but she's in very good shape."

"She's like my mother," he said, smiling. "I don't know how it happened, since they aren't related by blood, but she's so much like her that sometimes, it startles me."

"Blair told me she had three parents. She was obviously very close to her."

"Oh, yes. My mother lived in Rogers Park in the same apartment I grew up in. We had Sunday dinner with her every week until the day she died. I think Blair was a freshman in college when her grandmother passed unexpectedly. Well, I say unexpectedly, but she was eighty-five and had a bad heart. Blair took it very hard," he recalled. "They had a very special bond." He gave Kylie a look out of the corner of his eye and asked, "She doesn't talk about her much, does she?"

"No." Kylie shook her head. "She doesn't. She's only mentioned her once or twice."

Werner chuckled and said, "That's how my mother was. She didn't believe in talking about things that made her sad. She kept the things that hurt very private, always presenting a sunny demeanor."

"That is like Blair. She's more emotional now, of course, but still...when she cries, I know it's a big deal."

"Does she cry often, Kylie?" he asked softly, sounding as if he were worried to hear the answer.

"No more than your average pregnant woman. She had a few tough weeks at the beginning, and it was very hard on her when she moved out of the house, but she's good now. Her hormones have settled down, too, so she's much more herself. It was hard on her when she was going through so much turmoil at home and having a gush of progesterone racing through her. She's a strong, determined woman," Kylie said, "and I'm confident she'll get through this."

"She is strong," he agreed, "but my personal opinion is that she was too strong and too determined when she was with David. She's so independent, Kylie, and she tried to have a marriage where she retained every bit of that independence." He shook his head. "It never seemed so much a marriage as a partnership. She didn't depend on David, and I don't think he depended on her, either. Yes, I think they loved each other, but they didn't risk much." He looked at her briefly and asked, "Do you know what I mean?"

"I think I do," she said thoughtfully. "I haven't looked at it that way, but I see what you mean. It's hard to love someone if you aren't willing to risk everything for them."

"It is," he agreed. "I think that Blair's in the process of learning what real love is. She'll never be able to accept anything less once she knows it."

"She knows it already, Werner. Not long ago, she told me that if she had to choose between her own life and the baby's that she wouldn't hesitate for a moment to save the baby. That's a mother's love."

"That's exactly it," he said. "I learned how to better love my wife by loving Blair. I hope that's true for her."

"I think it will be. She has a lot of love to give, but she needs to let her barriers down to let someone love her as well."

"Very true, Kylie." He glanced at her. "You know my daughter well."

"I try to," she said quietly. "She means a lot to me."

"I'm very glad she has you in her life. I worry about her less since I met you. I know you'll make sure she takes care of herself."

"She does a good job of taking care of herself. I just provide some friendly reminders."

⌒

Blair and Eleanor returned home at 3:00, and the moment Blair walked into the apartment, Kylie nearly leapt upon her. "Why didn't you come with us? I got to sit up on the stage and play percussion!" She turned quickly to Eleanor and said, "Forgive my manners, but I'm so excited I'm faint!"

"Tell me all about it," Blair said, taking her friend's hand and leading her into the living room. "How did it happen? Do you know how to play?"

"I do now," she beamed. "I can play the vibraphone and the timpani and even the triangle!" She giggled and added, "I can't play any of them better than a three-year-old, but I can say that I stood on stage and looked like I could play 'em!"

"How did it happen?"

"Well, your dad took me on a long tour while the other members were getting set up, and we stopped at the percussion section last. The percussionist was a really nice guy, and we hit it off immediately. We started talking about repetitive strain injury, and I looked at his right hand, which has been giving him trouble."

"Always a doctor," Blair teased.

"Hey, the Hippocratic oath doesn't apply to business hours only," she sniffed. "Anyway, I told him I'd talk to somebody I know at UCLA and see if I can find out who the top hand doc is in the Chicago area."

Blair smiled and asked, "So, since his hand hurt, he decided to turn over the sticks to you?"

"Not hardly. He said I could pull up a chair and sit with him. Damn, Blair, you have no idea how wonderful it is to hear that music when it's being performed right in front of you. I was tapping my feet and squirming around on my stool so much that he could see what a fan I am, and when the rehearsal was over, he asked me if I wanted a lesson on his instruments!"

Blair laughed at the expression on her friend's face. "I can't imagine what force could have compelled you to refuse."

"Exactly! He showed me the triangle, and once I mastered it, we moved on to the big boys, and I got to bang on the kettledrums for a while. Those babies are a lot harder to play than they look!"

"Oh, I wish I'd been there," Blair said. "You must've been in heaven."

"I paid one of the union guys a ridiculous amount of money to run out and buy a disposable camera. Then he took a bunch of pictures for me, so you can see me grinning like a madman."

"Where's Dad?" Blair asked. "I want to give him a hard time for never letting me play."

"Oh, he's taking a nap. Which is what you should be doing. We'll be out late tonight, you know."

"What a slave driver," she said. "It's rest, rest, rest."

"I'm so excited for you, Kylie," Eleanor said. "What a thrill to get to do that."

"You have no idea," the doctor enthused. "This is the best birthday I've ever had."

"It's only gonna get better," Blair said.

‑

"I'd give anything to be able to wear my new jeans tonight," Blair said when she woke from her enforced nap. "I like my dress-up clothes well enough, but they're so businesslike."

"You know, I had a feeling you might feel that way," Kylie said. "That's why I brought something cute for you."

"You did not!"

"I did, too. Take a look in my hanging bag." Blair scampered off the bed and quickly unzipped the big bag. She removed Kylie's black pantsuit and then an ivory satin blouse that didn't look familiar. She held it up, but Kylie shook her head. "No, that's mine. Keep looking."

Reaching inside once again, Blair pulled out a stretchy black velour jumpsuit with a scoop neckline and no sleeves. "This is awfully...sexy for a fat woman." She was holding it out at a distance as if it might combust.

"You're so far from fat it's not even funny. All you have is a little thickening around your waist and a roundish tummy. From the front, you don't look pregnant at all. I have to look at you from the side to see the baby."

"I feel fat," she said. "It's been hard for me to lose my waist. I hate to be so vain, but all my adult life I've been very careful to avoid putting on weight, and this is really hitting me in the ego. These twelve pounds feels like fifty."

"I can understand that, but I want you to know that I'd never lie to you about anything—even how you look. You don't look fat in the least, pal, and I'm sure you're going to look decidedly non-maternal in that outfit. But if you don't like it, I'll take it back. No pressure."

"It'll show everything," she said, eying the garment.

"Yeah, it will, but there's a little more in the bag." The other piece was a filmy white shirt, generously cut. The shirt was nearly transparent and bore an attractive, Indian-inspired print. "I really like the blouse," Kylie said. "You should keep it even if you don't like the jumpsuit."

"It's positively gorgeous!" Blair exclaimed. "Help me put it on, okay?"

"All of it?"

"Yep. Might as well hear the screaming here rather than on the street."

Blair started to pull the snug jumpsuit on, and Kylie helped her smooth it in place. Blair added the blouse, and the doctor stood back to inspect. "Wow," Kylie said softly. "I'm speechless."

Grinning shyly, Blair moved to stand in front of the mirror, her smile growing as she looked at her reflection from every angle. "I hate to sound vain, but *wow* is the right word," she said. "I haven't looked this good since well before I was pregnant."

"Again, I'll disagree. I think you routinely look great, but you look particularly fabulous tonight."

Blair wrapped Kylie in a tight hug. "Thank you! Thank you for making me feel like a woman—not a pregnant woman, just a woman."

"A beautiful woman," Kylie insisted, "who gets more beautiful every day."

⟶

Eleanor had to leave for the theater at 6:00, and Werner had to leave by 6:30, so they were unable to join Kylie and Blair at dinner. They agreed that they'd all meet for dessert after the symphony. Riding down Lake Shore Drive in a cab, Kylie leaned back against her seat and stared at the lake. "I remember driving down here when I was a kid, thinking that one day, I'd live by the lake. The water was always such a draw for me."

"Is that why you picked California?"

"Yeah, pretty much. I loved the lake, but there was something so appealing about a body of water that stretched all the way to other continents. I don't go in the water much in L.A., but having it nearby really calms me down."

"Is that why you walk me up and down the Palisades so often?"

"Yep. I figure that if it calms me down, it'll calm you down, too."

"It does. Walking along the ocean is one of my favorite parts of the day. I'm definitely hooked."

"Will a stroll down Michigan Avenue do instead? We should have time for a little walk after dinner."

"Sure. For a change, I can walk down a fashionable street and feel like I fit in. My new outfit is très chic."

⟶

They dined at one of Kylie's favorite restaurants—a venerable Chicago institution her parents had taken her to when she'd graduated from college. "This place hasn't changed a bit," she said, deeply satisfied. "I haven't been here since I was twenty-two, but it's as fabulous as I remember."

"Special dinners must have set your family back a fortune."

"Not really. My parents established a tradition that you got to go out to a restaurant with them alone for important milestones. It seems silly, but it was always a big treat not to have all of the siblings around. It really made you feel kinda special."

"You're making me feel happier and happier about having been an only child."

"No, I don't mean to do that," Kylie insisted. "There were plenty of times I wished I were an only child, but there were some things about having siblings that were really great. When I was young, there was always someone to play with—even on a rainy day. And it was nice to have someone who'd just learned a concept in school help you with your homework. Yeah, I had to be the guinea pig sometimes," she chuckled, "but generally, we had a lot of fun together."

"I guess there's something to be said for it, whatever size your family is."

"Oh, and I'm glad that I had an older sister who was gay," Kylie said. "Chris had a hellish time, but things were really easy for me."

"You know, you've never told me what it was like for you. Wanna talk about it?"

"Sure. As I said, it was a piece of cake for me, but not for my poor sister. Chris came out to our parents when she was a senior in college, and they did everything but send her to a deprogrammer."

"Really? What was their issue with it?"

"I'm not sure. I mean, I was only nine, so I didn't understand half of what was going on, but the older kids gave me their version of events. Chris and I have never talked about it at length, but to be honest, I think she resents me a little because I had it so easy."

"She seemed very fond of you—" Blair began, but Kylie nodded emphatically.

"Oh, she is. I'm closest to Chris out of all my siblings. But she really did have to blaze the trail, and I got to walk it. My parents were pretty awful to her. They forbade her to come home until she got it out of her system, and they refused to support her financially. Luckily, she went to U of I, and the tuition wasn't too high, so she didn't have to drop out."

"That's awful!"

"Yeah, it really was. There was a strain on the family that lasted quite a while. Thankfully, I didn't know what the real issue was. If I had, it probably would have screwed me up when I was coming out to myself. All I knew was that Chris did something that made my parents really mad and couldn't come home until she stopped whatever it was."

"What did she do?"

"She had to work for a couple of years until she saved enough money for grad school. We didn't see her for almost two years. But not long after she started school again, my mother decided that she wasn't able to stand the distance any longer. It was a big deal—probably the only time I ever heard my parents argue. Mom got in the car and drove down to Champaign, and she and Chris worked it out. Chris came home for Thanksgiving that year, and over time, my parents got more and more comfortable with it."

"So, did they support her while she was in grad school?"

"Nope. They offered to, but she didn't trust them not to pull the rug out from under her again." Kylie shook her head and said, "She'd always wanted to be a doctor, but she changed her mind and got her Ph.D. in math instead. I always felt she did that to spite my dad. He really wanted her to follow in his footsteps."

"Damn, that must have been a horrible time for your family."

"It was. But in a way, her suffering allowed the rest of us to have an easier time. My parents really loosened up a bit after that happened, and I think my mom started standing up for herself a little. Like I said, I was pretty young, but the change was noticeable even to me."

"So, when you decided you were gay, your parents were pretty blasé about it?"

"I need to sit Chris down and ask her about this, but I've always had a sneaking suspicion that she told my parents even before I knew. They were entirely too matter-of-fact about the whole thing. They acted like I told them I was going to move to a different apartment or something equally innocuous. They could have been the models for a Parents and Friends of Lesbians and Gays advertisement."

"Lucky for you, but I could see that Chris might well be a little resentful. Especially since you got to go to medical school and all."

"Yeah, it makes sense, but she's had the last laugh in the relationship department. She and Laura have been together almost twenty years, and I think they're very happy."

"You'll get there," Blair said. "If I get you hooked up this year, you'll only be seven years behind her."

"I love your optimism," Kylie said. "It's one of your most wonderful qualities."

"I'm not optimistic; I'm confident. There's a small but critical difference there. You're a sure thing, Kylie, and the woman who snares you is gonna be one lucky babe."

⌒

They had some extra time, and since they needed to take a cab at some point, they decided to take a boat up the Chicago River and then grab a cab to Symphony Center. The night was warm and calm, and the trip from Michigan Avenue to Wacker Drive was very short—ten minutes or so—and Blair thought it would be a nice treat for Kylie's birthday since she loved the water so much. They sat alone in the open stern since the other passengers all chose to stay inside. "How can those people resist sitting out here with the wind in their hair?" Kylie wondered.

"Oh, they look like businessmen. They probably do this every day. They're jaded."

"Well, I'm not. I haven't been on one of these since I was in high school. Thanks for thinking of it."

"I think about you a lot," Blair said, suddenly serious. She reached into her purse and pulled out a card and a small, gaily wrapped package. "Especially lately. I spent a lot of time thinking about what I could buy you for your birthday, but I had a really hard time. I know you buy yourself whatever you want, so it didn't seem like it would be special to buy you a thing. Besides," she said, smiling warmly as she placed her hand on her abdomen, "I wanted to show you what you've come to mean to us."

Kylie's mouth grew dry suddenly, and she had to struggle to ask, "What have I come to mean to you?"

"More than I can express. No matter what happens to us in the future, I want you to know how much your friendship has meant to both me and the baby. We'll never forget you, Kylie, and we want you to know that. I want to guarantee that we think of you every day."

She handed her the package, and Kylie quickly tore off the paper and stuffed it in her pocket. Opening the box, she found a dark-blue velvet jewelry container. She smiled at Blair and opened it, pulling out a beautiful, plump silver heart on a thin chain. "This is gorgeous, Blair!"

"Turn it over."

Kylie did, and as she read the inscription, her brow furrowed in puzzlement. In a delicate script, the text read, "To Kylie: Love always, Mackenzie." She read the inscription again and was about to say that the engraver had made a mistake when her friend handed her the card and said, "Read this, too."

Kylie's expression was completely bemused, but she did as she was told. Inside the card, Blair had written:

> Dear Kylie,
>
> I want my baby to grow up to emulate the most generous, thoughtful, caring, and compassionate person I know. I couldn't think of a better way to ensure that would happen than to name him after her. I love you, Kylie, and I want you always to know that Mackenzie and I care for you deeply.
> Happy birthday.
>
> Love,
> Blair and Mackenzie

The expression on Kylie's face was so impossibly precious that Blair longed for a camera. But the look in those eyes was so heartwarming that she knew she'd never forget it. "You...you're...you're naming him after me?" Kylie asked, her voice thin and weak.

"Yes. I'd be happy if he had just a few of your wonderful traits. I hope that naming him after you inspires him to model himself after you."

"Bu...but..."

"Does this make you happy?" Blair asked, placing her arm on Kylie's shaking shoulder.

"Yes! But..."

"But nothing. This means a lot to me, and I don't want to hear any of the reasons you're going to come up with for why I shouldn't do it. I've thought about this for a while now, and I wasn't going to tell you until he was born, but I thought it might mean something to you on your birthday. It seemed like a good time to show you how much of an impact you've had on my life and how very glad I am that you were born."

Wrapping her arms around her friend, Kylie sobbed against her shoulder. "This means so much to me. I can't begin to tell you."

"You've had a pretty nice day, huh, Doc?" she cooed into her ear. "Playing percussion with the symphony and having a baby named after you. Not bad at all."

"Thank you," Kylie said, placing a soft kiss on her cheek. "It's gonna be hard calling a tiny baby Mackenzie, but I guess he'll grow into it."

"I know he will," Blair said. "And if, by some chance, my prediction is wrong, Mackenzie is a very nice name for a little girl, too—thank God!"

The orchestra was halfway through the second movement of Brahms's *Symphony Number Four* when Kylie felt Blair jerk in her seat. Suddenly, the doctor's hand was gripped and placed firmly against her friend's abdomen. "I felt him kick!" Blair whispered excitedly.

Turning to face her, Kylie saw the excitement in Blair's eyes and desperately wished that she'd felt it, too, but she knew it was too early for that. "He likes the symphony," Kylie whispered. Her hand slid up and down Blair's belly, rubbing her gently for a few moments. Soon, Blair placed her hand atop Kylie's and rested her head on her friend's shoulder, listening to the rest of the symphony without moving a muscle.

⬳

The Schneidhorsts were elated that the baby had finally made his presence known, and Kylie could see the disappointment in their faces when she informed them that it would probably be a few more weeks until anyone but Blair could feel the kicking. "I think I've talked Blair into coming home again for my father's seventy-fifth birthday party at the end of October," Kylie said. "I'm certain you'll be able to feel him then."

"Will you be able to travel then, Blair?" her mother asked.

"Yeah, I should be. That'll be my last trip until the baby comes, though. I'm sure my doctor will restrict me after that."

"Well, I've already told the theater that I'm taking my vacation in December. It doesn't look like your father will be able to come, but wild horses couldn't stop me from being there for the birth." She paused a moment and said, "I…I assume that's all right with you, Kylie. Lord, how presumptuous of me!"

"I took for granted that you'd come, Eleanor. Blair will need you to be with her."

"Yeah, Mom. Kylie asked me just the other day how long I thought you'd be able to stay. We've been talking about it like it's a given."

"Great," Eleanor said. "You tell me when you want me there, and I'll make my reservations."

"You know I obviously want you there for the birth, but I'd really like you there beforehand. I won't be working, and I won't be able to drive, so I'll be bored to death sitting around the house alone."

Kylie said, "I thought I'd take time off after the birth so that Blair can get some sleep at night while I handle the nighttime feedings. If you can be there beforehand to keep her entertained, we should have all the bases covered."

"I have a feeling I'm going to fall in love with that baby so fast I'll never want to leave," Eleanor said.

Blair smiled warmly and said, "That works, too, Mom. Then I won't have to hire a nanny."

"Don't tempt me, honey. I can't imagine anything I'd rather do than help you raise your child."

"Hey, I'm not kidding in the least. I'd love to have you both retire to California."

"Let's see how things go," Werner said. "One little earthquake and your mother will be on the next plane out of town—no matter where it's going!"

"Kylie?"

"Hmm?" the doctor asked sleepily.

"Did you have a nice birthday?"

Forcing her eyes open, Kylie focused on her friend for a moment and tried to clear the cobwebs out. There was enough moonlight coming in the window to be able to make out Blair's features, and Kylie smiled gently when she saw how brightly the other woman's eyes were shining. "Ya know what?" Kylie asked.

A grin settled onto Blair's face when she said, "Unh-uh. What?"

"If you took all of my birthdays and added them all together and multiplied them by ten, you know what you'd have?"

"No, what?" Blair asked, her smile growing.

"You'd have a really, really old doctor!"

By the time Kylie had started to laugh, Blair had already walloped her with a pillow, making the doctor laugh all the harder. "Pillow fight!" she cried a little too loudly.

Suddenly, the door to their room popped open, and three young girls ran in, each bearing a pillow of her own. "No!" Kylie cried, covering up as all three started pounding on her.

Blair was helpless with laughter, holding on to her stomach so she could catch her breath. The assault continued until Kylie wriggled around enough and got to her feet atop the bed, her height now putting her well above the range of a young girl. She swung her own pillow fiercely, and soon, the girls were forced to retreat. "We didn't get to see your girlfriend last night," one of the trio sulked.

"Well, you can see her now," Kylie offered. "Blair, meet the great triumvirate. This is Willow, Jessica, and Carrie. Willow belongs to Chris and Laura, Jessica is Paul's, and Alan is responsible…I mean, lucky enough…to be Carrie's dad. Girls, this is my good friend, Blair."

"Hi, girls," Blair said, smiling broadly. "Good job on knocking some sense into your aunt. She needs it."

"Yeah, she does," Willow agreed. "So, can we hang out with you guys for a while?"

"A very little while," Kylie said. She lowered herself to the bed and sat cross-legged, providing as much room as she could. "Come on up for a few minutes. But I really do mean a few minutes. Blair has to get her rest. She's having a baby, you know."

"How'd ya do it, Aunt Kylie?" Willow, the obvious ringleader, asked. "Sperm bank?"

Blair's eyes were nearly as wide as Kylie's at this question. "What do you know about sperm banks?" the doctor asked. "You're eleven!"

"My moms have their friends over, and they all talk about getting pregnant. Everybody knows about sperm banks." The other two girls nodded uncertainly, making it fairly clear they didn't have any idea what their cousin was talking about.

"Well, let me clear up a few of your misconceptions," Kylie said. "I didn't do anything at all. Blair's my friend, not my girlfriend. She got pregnant all on her own, and I don't think she cares to tell you little goofballs exactly how it happened." She wrapped an arm around the closest two girls' necks and gave them a rough tumble. "You guys should learn about sex in the alleys, like I did."

"What's an alley?" Carrie asked shyly.

"That's my girl," Kylie said, kissing the child on the head. "I knew there was still a bloom of innocence on these little flowers."

"In school, they tell us we should be absta—absti—abstinet until we have a husband so we don't get pregnant. Were you abstinet, Blair?" Jessica asked.

"No," she said, trying to avoid laughing. "No, I wasn't, Jessica. But I have a husband, and he's the father of my baby, so I didn't have to be abstinet. I mean abstinent."

Willow gave her a very dubious look and asked, "Well, if you have a husband, why are you in bed with Aunt Kylie? She's a lesbian, you know."

"Big mouth," Kylie whispered loudly. "Can't keep a secret to save your life."

All three sets of eyes went to Blair, and she slapped playfully at Kylie. "I know she's a lesbian, girls. And I'm not with my husband because he and I are getting divorced."

"Oh, so now that you're getting divorced, you can be Aunt Kylie's girlfriend," Willow decided.

"Not every one of my friends is my girlfriend," Kylie told the girl. "I'm a lesbian, but Blair isn't."

"Oh," the child said. "That's too bad. Aunt Kylie really needs a girlfriend. It's been ages since she's had one."

"Thanks, pal," Kylie said, smiling thinly. "Good thing Blair's not my girlfriend. She'd think I was a big loser."

"You're not a loser," Carrie said, smiling up at her aunt. "You're lonely."

Something about the tone of the child's voice got to Kylie, and she felt like she was going to cry. Blair saw the look on her face and tried to bring a smile back to it. "She's not lonely, girls. And after I have this baby, she's not going to have a minute alone. Kylie's so important to me that I'm naming the baby after her."

"You're gonna call it Kylie?" Jessica asked. "What if it's a boy?"

"Nope, I'm gonna call it Mackenzie," Blair said.

"That's my name!" each girl cried nearly simultaneously.

"It's mine, too," Kylie said, playfully leaning against each girl in turn. "Don't any of you tell people the baby's named after you 'cause it's not!"

"Do you live together?" Willow asked, still trying to make this situation fit into her worldview.

"We do," Blair said. "Kylie owns the house, and I'm her roommate."

"What's a roommate?" Carrie asked.

"Well," Blair said, trying to think. "When two people live together, but they're not in love with each other, they're called roommates."

"But if you're not a lesbian, why do you want to live with one?" Willow asked. "Shouldn't you live with a man?"

Blair gave her a thin smile and tried to think of a tactful way to answer her. "I'm not even divorced from my husband yet, Willow. I'm not ready to look for another one."

"But you will, right? You won't be Aunt Kylie's roommate forever, will you?"

"I…I guess not," Blair said. She looked at Kylie who wasn't giving anything away with her expression. "I guess that your aunt will find a girlfriend, and they'll live together."

"Cool! I want Aunt Kylie to have a girlfriend. I want her to have babies, too," Jessica said

"She's gonna help me raise my baby," Blair informed them.

All three girls looked at Blair, but only Willow had the nerve to say, "That's not the same. That's kinda like helping. It's not really hers."

"No," Blair said, feeling surprisingly sad. "It's not the same. But it's as close as we can get."

That answer satisfied the trio, and they moved on to a more pressing topic. "Can we come visit, Aunt Kylie?" Jessica asked. "We can fly without our parents next year, ya know."

"Wow, that's…that's something to think about, isn't it?" Kylie asked brightly.

"Yeah, we can all go and see movie stars!" Carrie said.

"And the dogs!" Jessica added. "Can we see pictures, Aunt Kylie?"

"I've got a bunch in my suitcase," Kylie said, "but I'll save them for tomorrow. I've got one in my wallet, though." She got out of bed and grabbed her wallet, taking out the picture that she carried.

"They're so cute!" all three squealed. But Willow wasn't through with her interrogation yet. She looked at the picture, observing Blair grinning widely, one dog held up to either side of her face. "Are they your dogs, too?" she asked.

"No…" she began, but changed course when she saw the hurt look on Kylie's face. "Well, kinda. I bought them for Kylie when she bought her house, but now they think I'm their mama, too."

"Is the baby gonna call Aunt Kylie Mama?" Willow asked.

"Uhm, we haven't discussed that," Blair replied, "but maybe the baby will call her Aunt Kylie. How would that be?"

"But she's not really the baby's aunt," Willow said. "You'd be making that up."

"Well, we've got time to work that out," Blair said, giving Kylie another quick look. "Right now, I've got to get to sleep. We can continue this discussion in the morning, girls."

"All right," they grumbled, heading for the door slowly. "Wake us up if you have another pillow fight, okay?" Carrie asked.

"You'll be the first to know," Kylie promised. "'Night, girls."

"'Night, Aunt Kylie. 'Night, Blair."

They closed the door, and Blair collapsed against the mattress. "My Lord, that group keeps you on your toes!"

"They sure do. They're old enough to hear their parents talking about me, but not old enough to get the nuances of my life. Well, Willow does," she corrected, "but her moms treat her like she's twenty, and they always have. That kid is way too mature for eleven."

"Uhm, did any of the things they said bother you?"

"Bother me? No. Why?"

"I don't know," Blair said. "When they started asking if we'd always be roommates, it made me kinda sad to think that we wouldn't…"

Kylie sighed and lay down, remaining quiet for a few moments. "I've decided that I'm not very good at predicting the future," she said. "A year ago, I met you at the Getty, and if someone had told me that you and I would be living together a year later, I would have told him he was nuts. All I know is that I'm happy with the way things are. Remember, we have a deal: if either of us isn't happy, we reassess."

Blair nodded and tried to smile. But inside she was thinking, *What if only one of us wants to move on? How does the other one not get hurt?*

Kylie shifted around until she was comfortable and then said, "Hey…before, when I said you could take all my birthdays and multiply them by ten?"

"Yes," Blair drawled.

"What I was going to say was that all of those birthdays couldn't come close to topping this one. The symphony rehearsal, going out to dinner, learning you were going to name the baby after me…" Her voice trailed off and grew quiet. "But as wonderful as that all was, do you know what the best thing…the very best thing of the whole day was?"

"No, tell me," Blair whispered.

"Seeing your face when you felt the baby kick for the first time," Kylie said quietly. "I'll always remember that."

Blair blinked away tears as she moved her pillow to her left side and snuggled up against it. Reaching behind her, she took Kylie's hand and tucked it around her waist, placing it against her belly. "He likes it when you touch him," she murmured. "He told me to tell you so."

"A perfect end to a perfect day," Kylie mumbled sleepily, patting the baby good night before she turned over onto her other side, her breathing evening out immediately.

"Happy birthday, Kylie," Blair whispered to her friend's back, "from Mackenzie and me."

⁓

To Blair, Kylie's party seemed more like an open house than a traditional party. People dropped in throughout the day, sometimes just for a few minutes. Actually, it seemed as if Kylie's siblings used the party as an excuse to get a day of free babysitting. Her brother Alan dropped his kids off at 10:00, and he and his wife didn't return until evening, and Claire wasn't far behind Alan in the drop-off line. But no one seemed to mind, and the unstructured atmosphere was actually rather refreshing.

The Schneidhorsts showed up at noon, and they tried their best to learn everyone's name, but it was a struggle. Young Kevin had taken a shine to Blair, and it was clear that he'd been away from his parents a little too long. He climbed onto her lap not long after Blair's parents arrived and refused to relinquish it, cuddling against her with his small hand on her abdomen. "I heard the baby," he informed Eleanor.

"Oh, did you?"

"Kylie let him listen to the heartbeat with the stethoscope," Blair said. "It was cool, wasn't it, Kevin?"

"Uh-huh. Like this." He patted Blair's knee rapidly with the flat of his hand, watching Eleanor carefully to make sure she understood.

"Maybe we can do that again later," Eleanor said. "I'd love to hear the baby, too."

"Okay. I'll show you how."

Kylie approached and asked if anyone was ready for some lunch. "Yeah, I'd like something," Blair said. "Wanna get up and get some lunch, Kevin?"

"No, let me," Kylie said. "I just wanted to make sure you were hungry."

"Ha!" Blair snorted.

"Oh, yeah, look who I'm asking," the doctor said, giving Blair's shoulder a squeeze.

Werner got up and offered to help Kylie, and Kevin decided he'd assist, too. The threesome went over to the buffet table that had been set up in the hallway, and soon, Kevin shouted, "Hey, Aunt Blair, you want turkey or ham?"

"Turkey's good, Kevin!" she called back.

Eleanor leaned over and teased, "I think someone has a crush on you, Aunt Blair."

"Seems that way," Blair said. "He latched on to me at breakfast and hasn't been far since. Mostly, I think he misses his mom. He's been here since Thursday."

"I think he's picking up on the maternal vibes. You positively radiate 'mom,'" Eleanor said. She looked at Blair and then, with a sudden disappointment showing, took her daughter's hands in her own. "I wish we had had more time alone. I have so many things I wanted to talk to you about, and now the weekend's gone."

Blair didn't get a chance to reply as Kevin returned, walking carefully as he held the paper plate in both hands. "Here's your sandwich, Aunt Blair." She accepted the plate with one hand and pulled him back onto her lap with the other. He nestled there contentedly while she ate, occasionally swiping a potato chip.

Chris came by, stopping to tease, "Get used to it, Blair. You'll forget what it's like to eat without someone on your lap."

"I'm looking forward to it. Besides, it's a good way to lose weight. Kevin here is eating at least half of my food."

As the party continued, more and more people arrived, and Blair finally gave up trying to associate kids with parents. She was able to identify each of the Mackenzie siblings, figuring that gave her a good basis on which to build in the future. She decided that her accomplishments were rather impressive when Kylie leaned over at one point and said, "Ask that little blonde girl what her name is, will you? I get Taylor and Darien mixed up, and I don't want them to know it."

"So, that's why you wanted me to come!"

"Nope. I wanted you to come because I love to be with you, and I'd be worried about you the whole time if you were back in L.A."

Blair pinched her pink cheek and asked, "Are you always this disarmingly honest?"

"Uhm, apparently not," she said thoughtfully. "Stacey used to say that she could never really tell how I was feeling."

"She must not have been trying very hard 'cause you're an open book, Doctor Mackenzie."

"Don't say that too loudly around here," Kylie joked. "Four people will think you're talking to them."

←

The Schneidhorsts had to leave at 5:00, and Blair walked them to their car. She kissed and hugged her father and watched him open the car door for his wife before continuing around to the driver's side. Blair took her mother's hands in her own and said, "I'm really disappointed we didn't have any time alone, Mom. This weekend got away from me."

"It didn't help that I have a new play opening." She laughed softly. "But I suppose I've nearly always got a new play at some stage of development."

"You love your job, Mom. It takes up a lot of your time, but that's how things go."

"I know," Eleanor said. "But I wish I could take a leave of absence and be with you until you have the baby. I feel like I'm missing so much."

Blair leaned in and kissed her. "I'd love to have you. But I have a suspicion that you're gonna be even more tempted after I have the baby. A cute little baby is a lot more tempting than a grouchy pregnant woman."

"You're my cute little baby, sweetheart. That will never change."

"Aw." Blair let herself be enfolded in a hug, and she relished the warmth she felt in her mother's arms. "You're making me cry, Mom."

"That's what mothers are for."

"I'm gonna come back in October unless I'm not allowed to travel. We can catch up," she said smiling as she pulled away. She kissed her mother again and closed her door for her, waving as her parents drove off.

←

Dorothy came up behind Kylie and asked, "Hey, birthday girl, how about sneaking outside with me for a while? I haven't had one minute alone with you."

"Sure, Mom." The pair started to wind their way through the house. They managed to get to the backyard without picking up any wayward children, which was quite a feat. Settling into a chair, Kylie asked, "What's up?"

"Nothing," Dorothy said. "I wanted a chance to relax with you for a few minutes. It's so rare that we have time alone when you're at home; I really think we consciously have to carve some time out. After you leave, I always regret that we didn't get to sit and chat."

"Quiet talks are at a premium, aren't they?"

"They always have been," Dorothy said. "You know I love you all, but if I had to do it over again, I wouldn't have more than four children. I often think about how little of our time each of you got."

"Well, I guess you have a point, but if you'd stopped at four, you and I wouldn't be having this discussion, would we?"

Laughing softly, Dorothy shook her head. "No, I suppose we wouldn't, and I wouldn't have missed being your mother for the world. I'm very proud of you, Kylie, and I fervently hope you know that."

"I do. I know how proud you and Dad are of what I've accomplished. It feels really good to know that."

"Of course, I'm proud of what you do, honey, but that's not what I meant. I'm proud of who you are. When I see how you are around Blair, it makes my heart swell with pride. You're such a generous woman; that's so rewarding to see."

"Thanks, Mom," she said, clearly touched by her mother's words. "You've never said anything like that to me. It means a lot."

Dorothy looked at her carefully, making Kylie fidget a little under the unusual attention. "Are you happy?" the older woman asked.

"Happy?"

"Yes. Happy. I know it's been hard for you to find the right woman to love. Are you…getting what you need from Blair?"

"We're not lovers, Mom," she said quietly. "I didn't want to announce that, but we're just friends."

"I guessed that, sweetheart. You would have told us if you were together. What I mean is will you be happy with this relationship, given that it's platonic? It's obvious that you're entirely devoted to Blair, but what's your future?"

Kylie looked at her mother for a few seconds, feeling her hackles start to rise. "You've never asked me where my friendship with Nick is going. Why is this so different?"

Dorothy reached for her daughter's hand and looked at it for a moment. She rarely touched Kylie in this way, and the doctor felt a little uncomfortable. Dorothy touched the visible veins on the back of the hand, then turned it over and brushed her fingers down the palm. "You have such beautiful hands. So soft and gentle." She looked into Kylie's eyes and said, "Like your heart."

Kylie was mystified by her mother's behavior, and she didn't respond to her observations. She cocked her head and met her gaze, waiting for more.

"What do you see happening with Blair?"

"Well, I guess I see us remaining close friends. She's gonna stay at my house for the indefinite future, and I'm gonna help her with the baby in any way I can."

"And that's what she wants?"

"Yeah! I'm not forcing myself on her."

Dorothy squeezed her daughter's hand and soothed, "I'm sorry, honey. I'm not trying to upset you. I don't know much about your life right now. I'm interested."

Giving her mother a long look, Kylie said, "Tell me what you're really worried about, Mom. You're not saying something."

"I'm worried about you. I'm worried that you'll invest a few years in helping to raise this child and then have your heart broken if Blair falls in love again. I know sex isn't the most important thing in your life, but it's a very strong drive, honey, and two young women like you and Blair both have that drive. I worry that it isn't wise to get so entwined with her when she can't give you the kind of love you need."

"But she does," Kylie said earnestly, sounding as if she were trying to sell her point. "I've never felt closer to a woman than I do to Blair. What's wrong with that?"

"Nothing, honey. Nothing at all. But you need to be honest with yourself."

"I am, Mom. At least, I think I am. Blair's straight, and she's probably going to meet someone at some point."

Dorothy gave her a penetrating look and asked the question that had been on her mind for weeks. "If you could have anything you wanted, would Blair be more than your friend?"

Frustrated, Kylie raised her voice unthinkingly. "Yes, of course! I wish she were a lesbian and that we could—" She stopped abruptly and shook her head to clear it. "Damn, I've never had that conscious thought."

"That's what I'm worried about," Dorothy said, placing her hand on Kylie's arm. "It seems as though you're blithely moving along as if you're committed to one another— but you're not. I'm sure Blair will always be your friend, but I can tell that's not what you want. If she started dating a man, you know as well as I that she'd have much less time for you. And you should know that very few men would want their wife's lesbian friend to be an integral part of their family. I'm so worried that you're setting this up in a way that will only cause you heartache."

Leaning her head back, Kylie gazed up at the darkening afternoon sky. "What can I do, Mom? I care for her so much, and I'm so excited about the baby I could burst." She blinked slowly and said, "She's naming the baby after me. I can feel that she cares for me as much as I do her. Do I give up something that means so much because we can't have sex?"

"I can't answer that, Kylie. I only want you to promise that you'll go into this with your eyes open. As much as you care for her, there will always be the threat hanging over you that one of you could fall in love and have to pull back."

"It makes me sick to think about it," the doctor grumbled. She shook her head and added, "I think she's more realistic about this than I am." Pulling out the heart that Blair gave her, she said, "Blair gave me this when she told me she was going to name the baby Mackenzie."

Dorothy took the heart in her fingers and turned it over, reading the inscription. "That's very touching, honey."

"Yeah. It blew me away," she said. "But when she gave it to me, she said something like no matter what happens between us, she wanted me to know how much it's meant to her to have me help her through her divorce and pregnancy." Looking up and staring blankly, she said, "In retrospect, it feels like she was saying, 'I know this might end at any time, but it means a lot while it lasts.'"

"It does sound like that," Dorothy said, wincing at the pained look on her daughter's face. The older woman took Kylie's hand again and chafed it gently. "What do you want, sweetheart?"

"Damn, Mom," she said, looking terribly confused, "I don't think I can have what I want."

"You want Blair, don't you, honey?"

"Yeah. Yeah, of course, I do. I wish I didn't, but I do." She couldn't stop a few tears from rolling down her cheeks. "I don't even know when my feelings changed...but they have."

"It crept up on you, didn't it?"

Kylie looked at her for a moment and then nodded. "I guess so. I swear...I swear I didn't have one single thought of her as anything but a friend when she moved in with me. But we've gotten so close." She shook her head briskly. "We just kind of tumbled into a deeper relationship." She looked so fragile when she met her mother's eyes. "I know she feels the same way. She asks me to hold her and cuddle her when she's sad. I rub her feet every night. Damn," she said, looking disgusted, "I shouldn't have let us get so close. I should have been more in control."

"Honey, you didn't do this alone."

"No, but I'm the one in danger of wanting more." She looked at her mother, her eyes darting back and forth as she thought, *It's like a woman having a straight man as a good friend. If she asks him to hold her and touch her and share everything with her, he's gonna start wanting more...even if she doesn't.*

"Shouldn't Blair have known that, too? I don't think I'd feel comfortable with any of my women friends holding me."

Kylie couldn't help but smile, knowing her mother didn't seem to feel comfortable holding her own children. "People in California are a lot more tactile than they are around here. It's not odd for women to be pretty physical. But I should have known better. I told her I didn't think of her as a sexual partner, and I should have kept some barriers up to make sure that didn't happen. I've dug my own grave."

"Oh, honey, don't make it sound so horrible. Can't you try to pull back a little and remind yourself she's not available?"

"I'm trying, Mom; I'm really trying. I've had a couple of dates with a woman I used to work with, and she's perfect for me—on paper. She's cultured and literate and funny, and she's fantastic looking."

"She sounds promising, honey."

"I know, Mom. I know. She's the woman I've been looking for. I'm very attracted to her, and I think we could be great together. She's independent, but in a good way— you know what I mean?"

Dorothy shook her head. "No, I don't, Kylie. Tell me more."

"Well, she isn't clingy or anything, but she wants to spend her time with the woman she loves. She has her own interests and her own friends, but she'll make time for me if I want to see her. She told me that she's looking for a best friend and a lover, and that's what I want, too."

"It wasn't like that with Stacey, was it?"

Surprised that her mother would have noticed that, Kylie said, "No. Stacey wanted a lover; the best friend part was optional. But Julie's not like that. I swear that if I were to write down all of the attributes I want in a partner, Julie would come the closest of anyone I know."

"Closer than Blair?"

"Yeah. Yeah. I think so."

"But…" Dorothy said, leading.

"But when I'm with Julie, I keep thinking of Blair. I'm with a beautiful woman who really seems to like me. I'm at her house, kissing her, and I look at my watch to make sure Blair will still be up when I get home." She stood up and curled her hands into fists. "That's insane!"

Dorothy reached out and touched her leg. "Calm down, sweetheart. It's not insane. But it's clear you've fallen in love with Blair. The question is what do you do about it?"

Kylie sat down on the chair, hitting the seat hard. "There's a part—a big part of me—that would give up sex to keep Blair in my life, and I know that's not smart…for either of us."

Patting her gently, Dorothy said, "No, I don't think it is. I know I don't think exactly like Blair does, but I would've loved to have had a woman friend help me raise my child—if that was my only option. But I wanted a husband. I wanted a man, not only to help raise children, but to fulfill me in ways that my women friends could never do."

"But I make her happy, Mom. I know I do," she said earnestly.

"That might be enough for her. But I want you to see how she feels about this before you jump in with both feet. If you know she's planning on dating, you might be able to hold back enough to protect yourself."

Her head shook slowly. "It's too late, Mom. I'm already in over my head." She gave her mother a wry look and said, "Let's skip the sensitive chat next time, okay? I can only handle one of these a year."

Chapter Eight

"Glad to be going home?" Kylie asked Blair once they were airborne on Sunday afternoon.

"Yeah. I had a great time, but it'll be nice to have a little time to relax and reconnect with the doggies before we have to go to work tomorrow."

"Yeah, I need some time to unwind. Being with my family is always emotionally draining. And I never get enough sleep when I'm there. There's always someone coming in to wake me up early or cuddle with me."

"That's because everyone loves Aunt Kylie." Blair tucked her hand under Kylie's arm and gave her a rough squeeze. "You're too cute for your own good."

"That's always been a cross I've had to bear," she said, looking stoic.

"You bear it well. So, how would you rate our trip? I got the impression that some of your siblings thought our living arrangement was a little odd. Is it a little too California for them?"

"Maybe a little, but they didn't pry or anything. They tend to keep their comments to themselves, which suits me just fine."

"Your brothers were the most puzzled ones. I don't think most men can understand why you'd share a house with someone you weren't sleeping with—unless you needed the rent money, that is."

"Yeah," Kylie nodded, shifting uncomfortably when she thought of her mother's comments.

"Well, it doesn't matter to me what people think. You don't care, either, do you?"

"No, of course not. I've been a little concerned about that for you, though. I know people at your office will gossip about you when they find out you've left your husband and moved in with a woman."

"I don't give a damn about what people say. All that matters is that this is the right situation for me. I love living with you, and I know you'll be a wonderful person to help me raise Mackenzie."

With a furrow settling between her eyebrows, Kylie gathered her courage and asked, "Will that be enough? Will you be happy living with me long-term?"

"Yes, I will," she said emphatically. "I mean, when I look at the big picture, I have to admit that I hope my sex life isn't over at age thirty-five. But if it is, I think I'll be able to live with that." She chuckled and said, "I never thought that comment would come out of my mouth. Just shows how your priorities change when you have a baby. What about you? You don't have a baby making you less attractive to eligible men."

Kylie smiled gently. "I hope mine's not over at forty."

"No, I want to know if my being at your home is gonna make you hold back. Remember, you *promised* me that you'd try to find a partner. That's something you have to do. You can't let Mackenzie and me take away your possibilities."

Kylie compelled herself to smile, but she was only able to manage a weak one. "I promise I'll try to ensure that the best years of my sex life are ahead of me."

⟶

When they got home, Nick was lying out in the sun, both dogs sharing his chaise. "Mommies are home!" Kylie called out. Eight little feet came running, and Kylie and Blair spent a long time petting the dogs while Nick regaled the humans with tales of the dogs' exploits over the past few days.

"Stay for dinner, Nick?" Kylie asked. "I'll make your favorite."

"If you really want me to, but if you're both tired, I can just take off."

Blair said, "We'd love for you to stay, but I desperately need a nap. You don't mind, do you?"

"Go right ahead," Kylie urged. "I'll tell Nick all about the symphony."

"See you in a little while. Who wants to go with?" Blair asked.

Both dogs followed her down the hall with Kylie shaking her head as she watched them go. "She's stolen my dogs from me, you know. I'm gonna have to steal her baby's affections just to pay her back."

"Tell me about the trip," Nick said. "I wanna hear everything."

They were outside for nearly an hour, chatting companionably. The sun was beginning to set when Nick asked, "What's troubling you, Kylie? I know something is."

She was poised to sidestep his question, but she decided that she needed to vent a little. "I had a talk with my mom yesterday, and it's really been on my mind. She asked me if I was prepared for how I'd feel if Blair remarried."

"Remarried? She's not even divorced! Is she seeing someone seriously?"

"God, no! But my mom sees how close we've become, and she's worried about me. I never thought I'd get the 'straight girls will break your heart' lecture from my mom, but that's essentially what she said."

"Oh. Well, how *would* you feel?"

"Shitty," she admitted. "Damn, Nick, I don't know what I want. I think I can be happy with just Blair and the baby in my life, but we clearly don't have any long-term commitment to each other. I'd feel like hell if I spent the next five years raising the baby with her, only to have her leave me for some guy. Even though we're not lovers, it'd feel like being dumped."

"I can see that. But what are your options?"

She looked contemplative and said, "Damned if I know."

On Tuesday, Kylie and Julie had dinner together, spending most of the time talking about Julie's sister, who had unsuccessfully been trying to get pregnant. Julie picked Kylie's brain, trying to come up with enough information to direct her sister to the proper care. Kylie had a nice enough time, but it was a little like being at the office. She had surgery scheduled for early the next morning, so they had to part by 10:00, leaving both of them feeling as if they hadn't had much time together. "You know, I'd really like to have a full day with you," Julie said. "Are you busy on Saturday?"

"No, I don't think I have anything planned. What would you like to do?"

"Nothing," Julie said. "I want to know more about you. Right now, I know that I like you, but that's about it."

"You're right. As a matter of fact, you read my mind. I think we need some quantity time. Saturday it is. Let's have breakfast together and hang out until we're sick of each other."

Julie grasped the fabric of Kylie's light jacket and held on, looking at Kylie expectantly. Waiting a beat, Kylie pulled her close and kissed her hungrily, not letting go until Julie began to feel limp in her arms. Smiling that enigmatic smile, she grasped Julie's shoulders and propped her up against the wall.

Looking slightly drunk, Julie murmured, "I think it will take me a long, long time to get sick of you."

Blair came home from work on Friday evening, feeling as if she'd been up for twenty-four hours. She'd had a morning meeting and then shown a couple around the Westside, taking them to see seven houses. After spending a little time at her office catching up on paperwork, she met with a new client for dinner, nearly nodding off during dessert. Kylie was already home, and Blair walked into the living room with the dogs to greet her.

"Tough day?" Kylie asked when Blair dropped her briefcase from a height of two feet.

"Day? This was only one day?"

"Yep. I saw you this morning."

"Can you just point me in the direction of my room? I'm sure I could find it on my own, but it might take me a while since my eyes will be closed."

"Come on, pal," Kylie said. She put her arm around Blair and kissed her on the forehead. "Time for good little real estate agents to go to bed."

They walked into the room together, and Kylie helped her out of her dress, reversing the process they'd gone through that morning to put Blair into the outfit. The blonde put her arms under her breasts and pushed them up a little, saying, "The straps of this bra dig into my shoulders so much that sometimes my arms feel numb."

"Maybe you've got it adjusted too tight. Let me take a look."

Blair hesitated for a split second, but then realized that Kylie was the last person with whom she should be shy. She faced her and watched the usual look of intense concentration settle onto the doctor's fine features. Kylie lifted one strap, giving it a good tug, and then did the same to the other. "This is way too tight. You have grooves in your skin where the straps dig in. That's not good." She adjusted each strap until it was looser and then stood back. "How does that feel?"

Blair shook her shoulders and smiled, saying, "It feels better on my shoulders, but I'm gonna bounce around more. I've been trying to keep them reined in."

"Breasts are supposed to move when you walk. It's a fact of life for you full-figured women."

Pinching her on the arm, Blair laughed at her friend's outraged expression. "Don't call me full-figured, or there'll be more where that came from."

"So touchy," Kylie said, smiling warmly. "Go put your pajamas on, and I'll give you a nice backrub."

"There's no such thing as an unpleasant backrub," Blair decided. She took her pajamas into the bathroom and emerged a few minutes later, finding Kylie and both dogs waiting for her.

"They want to help, but they hate to get massage oil on their paws," Kylie said. "Big babies."

"You two stay up by my head," Blair instructed. "Your other mommy has work to do." She lay face down, propped up by the mounds of pillows Kylie had already put in place for her.

Kylie warmed the oil in her hands and started to work on Blair's lower back—always a sore spot. The doctor used her thumbs and the heels of her hands to probe the tight muscles, drawing groans of pleasure from Blair. After a long while, Blair asked, "Could you go a little higher? I'm stiff between my shoulder blades tonight. Probably from being at my office for too long."

"Sure." Kylie's hands were oily, so she asked Blair to assist. "Will you pull your top up or take it off?"

Blair looked at what she was wearing and decided that she didn't want to risk getting oil on her new pajamas. She whisked off the top and lay back down, waiting for Kylie's gentle hands.

The doctor worked on the rest of her back and shoulders with such expert care that Blair refused to fall asleep. Kylie worked on her for a long time and was a little surprised to find Blair was still awake and grunting with the pressure. The doctor put her warm hand on the small of her friend's back and asked, "Anything else? You're usually asleep by now."

Blair propped herself up on her elbows and pointed to the muscles at the top of her chest. "These little monsters are giving me fits. Would you mind doing them, too?"

"No, of course not." Kylie grabbed a towel from the bathroom and helped her friend roll over. It was quite a production, especially with the addition of the towel. Pillows had to be adjusted several times, and some body parts had to be moved by hand. Blair was a bit like a beetle that had rolled onto its back. She wasn't going anywhere without a little help.

When she was properly positioned, Kylie ran her fingertips from the base of Blair's ear down to her elbow. "I bet you get sore here, too," the doctor said. "Your heavier breasts pull on these tendons."

"Yeah. I guess I'm used to them hurting all of the time, but these muscles just started aching today." She put her hand on the sore muscles that lay just above her clavicle.

"Hmm…I wonder why?" Kylie pressed on them lightly with her fingers, and Blair winced. "Are they that sore?"

"Yeah. They're really tight."

"Let me start higher up and work my way down. I'll work on your shoulders and arms for a while and then get to your pectorals."

"You're the boss." Blair had placed her pajama top over her breasts to allow for a little modesty, but it was clear that the garment was going to be in the way.

"Want me to get another towel?"

"You can if you want to, but I don't really care. It doesn't bother you, does it?"

Kylie smiled impishly. "Nope. I've seen 'em before, you know. Remember the 'blue' night?"

"How could I forget?" Blair took her top and tossed it aside. "Why should I have secrets now?"

Kylie took a quick look and said, "They've really filled out. I think you've gained half of your weight in your breasts."

"I assume you're kidding, but that's what it feels like. Wearing a bra puts stress on nearly every muscle in my upper body and back."

"I know; it's no fun," Kylie said. "I'll try to loosen you up." She started working again, and Blair soon felt the taut muscles start to relax. Kylie had such a knowledgeable touch that she managed to work the proper muscles in the proper order, making the spasms disappear as if by magic. She worked down Blair's arms, causing the blonde to giggle when Kylie touched the inside of her friend's elbow—always a sensitive area. The doctor worked back up the arm, soothing the muscles once again, and then moved on to the pectorals.

Blair wasn't sure when the sensation began, but she slowly became aware of a warm tingling in her breasts. It was a sensation she'd never had before she was pregnant, but it had started not long after she was inseminated. She'd felt it frequently, but this was the first time she'd noticed it during a massage. She almost mentioned it, but it continued to grow until she realized it wasn't just a twitching nerve. It was the insistent sign of sexual arousal.

Holy crap! Kylie's fingers are inches from my breasts, and I'm throbbing like I think I'm gonna get lucky! Blair tried to calm herself down, but was wholly unsuccessful. Any way the doctor's fingers moved stirred Blair's desire until she was consciously trying not to squeeze her legs together. Her clit was swelling noticeably and began to feel hard and tingly. Kylie was working all around her ultra-sensitive breasts, and it was all Blair could do not to grab her friend's hand and clamp it onto her flesh.

"Am I doing this too hard?" Kylie asked. "Your body feels like it's tensing up."

"No, no, it feels great. I guess I'm just a little ticklish there."

"Here?" Kylie smiled at her, tickling just in front of her armpit.

"Yes, there!" she squealed. She grabbed the doctor's hand and rolled away, taking Kylie with her. Blair was lying on her side with Kylie plastered against her back and a hand wedged between Blair's breasts. The blonde's heart was beating so wildly she knew her skin must be flushed, and she felt a slight sheen of perspiration cover her body. "I'm very ticklish," she mumbled into the pillows, mortally embarrassed.

"I promise I won't tickle you again," Kylie said softly into her ear. "I was a baaad little doctor."

Blair couldn't keep from laughing at the silly voice her friend had used. "It's okay. But I think I've had enough excitement for one evening. I feel much better, by the way." *Much wetter, too!*

Kylie rolled off and then helped Blair lie on her back again. "Let me get a warm washcloth and get the oil off your skin," she said, heading for the bathroom. She was back in a moment, and Blair had to grit her teeth while Kylie's tender touch played over her sensitized skin.

"Ooh, that's cold," Blair lied. "Give me my top before I freeze."

Kylie handed it to her and then leaned over, giving Blair a soft kiss. "Sleep well, buddy. I hope you feel better tomorrow."

"I will," she said. She grasped Kylie's hand, held it for a few moments, and then kissed the back of it. "Thanks," she said. "I appreciate you more than you know."

Kylie gave her a fond smile and then left, turning off the light as she went. Blair turned onto her side and cuddled up to her body pillow, trying to sort out her feelings. *That could have happened with anyone,* she reasoned. *My breasts are so sensitive they'd probably tingle if a complete stranger touched them.* She fidgeted and shifted her weight, trying to find a comfortable spot. But she wasn't able to stop her vulva from making its needs known. *Look,* she said, addressing the body part directly, *you're not allowed to get all hot and bothered from a simple massage. Life is complicated enough without masturbating every time someone touches me.* The tongue-lashing did no good at all, and her vulva kept twitching.

Blair rolled onto her other side and threw a leg up onto the pillow. *Oh, all right, but just a quick one.* She slid her hand down and started to touch herself, her mind nearly blank. She often fantasized about a particular sensation or a person who she thought was hot, but tonight, she just let her tingling body have its way. She was so swollen and sensitive that it didn't take long to drive herself to a tension-relieving orgasm, and seconds later, she was sound asleep.

⤚

On Saturday, Kylie walked into the kitchen while she was still drying her hair with a towel. "Hi," she said when she spotted Blair at the breakfast bar. "Didn't know you were up."

"Yeah. I have an appointment at 9:00. I'll probably only be gone for about an hour. How about you?"

"I'm having breakfast with Julie; then we're gonna hang out. Do you mind if we come back here at some point?"

Blair stuck her finger out and signaled for Kylie to approach. When the doctor was right in front of her, Blair leaned over so they were nose-to-nose, grasping Kylie's earlobe. "This is your house. You don't have to ask my permission to do anything in it or with it. Is that clear?"

"Yes," Kylie said. She crossed her eyes, mostly to drive Blair crazy, and laughed when her ploy seemed to succeed.

"Didn't your mother tell you not to do that?"

"Yep." Kylie walked over to the refrigerator and took out a bottle of juice. "Even though I don't have to ask permission, I think it's only polite."

"I don't mind, Kylie. I swear," she said, even though she was lying a little bit. She had had several long talks with herself about her jealous feelings concerning Julie, and she had been fairly successful in talking some sense into herself. But she still felt a twinge when Kylie made a date with the woman. Unable to contain her curiosity, Blair cocked her head and asked, "How's it going, anyway? You haven't talked about Julie much."

"Mmm...I still don't know her well enough to know if this can go anywhere. I guess I just don't have much to say yet."

"Well, have fun and please, please feel free to use your own damn house any old way you want."

"I'll try, but my natural politeness will probably rear its ugly head again."

⌒

Blair spent most of the afternoon lying by the pool, and by 6:00, the dogs seemed restless. She forced herself to get dressed, and then she put them in the car to take them to a big dog park in Encino where she and Kylie had been meaning to go. "We'll go check this place out and see if it's worth it for Mama Kylie to come with, okay?"

The dogs were all in favor of a trip, and the trio set off on their adventure.

By the time they reached the driveway gate, Kylie and Julie were starting to pull in. Blair lowered her window. "Hey, we're going to the dog park."

Kylie put on a pout. "I wanted to go with you guys!"

"Hi, Julie," Blair said, waving. "We'll do a little investigation and see if we like it. We'll take you next time, if you're good."

"I never get to go anywhere," Kylie said, lower lip sticking out.

"Kylie, please don't act like yourself in front of Julie. You have to keep up your 'normal' front for at least a month."

"I think I know she's a little off," Julie called out.

"You have no idea," Blair said, smiling at the outraged expression on Kylie's face. "Bye now." She waved and raised the window while trying to calm the dogs down. They hated to have their people apart, but it was much worse when they saw one of them actually leave. That was an affront to the pack, and they had no idea how to convey the egregiousness of this insult to their humans except by barking out their dismay.

⟶

Blair wanted to give her roommate some time alone, so she was determined to stay at the park until it was time to close. The pups immediately set off to meet every other dog in the enclosure, and they were pretty successful in their mutual quest. They ran themselves silly, going from dog to dog, spending just a few seconds with each one. Blair walked around the five-acre space, chatting with other owners while keeping an eye on her charges.

The dogs ran up to an Italian greyhound that jumped into a woman's arms to avoid the wild-looking terriers. Blair rushed up to her to assure her that they were only exuberant, and another woman walked over at the same time. Seeing a pregnant sister, Blair smiled at both women and said, "They're very nice dogs; they're just enthusiastic."

The woman holding the greyhound said, "Oh, don't worry about Piccolo. He's afraid of the wind when it blows a leaf around."

"Sometimes, I wish mine would show a little bit of fear. They'd chase a cheetah if there were one in Brentwood."

"Maybe they think there's safety in numbers," the pregnant woman said. She was less pregnant than Blair and was able to crouch down and pet Nicky and Nora. "Oh, they're sweet. What are their names?"

"Nicky and Nora. Nicky has on the black collar, and Nora's is brown."

"I assume they're brother and sister," the woman said, her face now being enthusiastically licked.

"Yeah. They don't know it, but they're gonna have another member of the family soon. I don't know how they're gonna feel about that."

"I know what you mean," the other pregnant woman said. She started to get up, and her friend immediately placed a hand on the woman's back, letting her know she was there to help if needed. The woman stood without difficulty and said, "I know Piccolo is going to be freaked out when the baby's born. He might hide under the bed for a few months."

"I'm worried that mine will be sitting on the baby's chest, waiting for him to get up and play."

"Oh, you know you're having a boy? We don't know yet."

"Well, I don't know for sure, but he seems like a boy, so that's what I've decided he is." Blair laughed. "I don't think my vote counts, but I've got a fifty-fifty chance at being right. When are you due?"

"Not until March. How about you?"

"Around Christmas. We're hoping he's not born too close to the holiday. I think kids hate that."

"Is this your first?"

"Yeah. Yours?"

"Uh-huh."

"That's nice to hear. Whenever I meet a woman who's had one or two, she's always ready to tell me how horrific her labor and delivery was. I swear I'm not gonna do that after my baby's born, but I probably will."

"I avoid women with kids," the other woman said. "I'll talk to a pregnant woman, but only if she's alone."

Blair squeezed the woman's arm and gave her a big smile. "That's a good idea. I think I'll adopt it. See you around," she said. "I've got to keep a close eye on my babies."

She walked away, thinking, *She seemed like a nice woman. She's lucky to have a friend to walk around with. God knows it's easy to get into an awkward position you can't get out of—especially when you try to squat down.* She thought about the day she had to yell for Kylie when she squatted down to give the dogs water and couldn't get back up. Kylie ran into the kitchen and thought Blair had thrown out her back, but it was just the weight of her belly throwing off her equilibrium. She could probably have gotten up, but she knew there was a slight chance of falling, and she would never take that chance when Kylie was around.

During her walks around the park, she passed the women with the Italian greyhound another couple of times, but the dogs were no longer interested in Piccolo. They knew he was a mama's boy and not up to their roughhousing, so they acted as if he didn't exist. "Snots," Blair whispered to them after they'd ignored the little dog for the second time.

It was nearly dark when Blair tried to herd her pair to the gate. They weren't ready to leave yet, and she cursed herself for not having an able-bodied person help her with their leashes before it got dark. Deciding to see if they'd follow her if she got out of their comfort range, she walked all the way to the gate and stood there, hoping they'd come. It was too dark to see where they were, and she was terrified that she'd have to call Kylie and have her drive all the way to Encino with a flashlight to find them. Luckily, the two women were just leaving, and the non-pregnant one walked over to her. "Do you need some help?"

"Yes," Blair said, exasperated. "My dogs have never been in a park this big, and they're not ready to leave. I thought I could freak 'em out by walking away, but now I can't see them."

"They probably can't see you, either," the woman said. "Give 'em a call."

Blair faced the open field and gave a yell. "Nicky! Nora!" In a flash, the pair came running, appearing out of the gloaming with their eyes wide and tongues hanging out. They leapt on Blair, whining and crying, obviously very distressed at having been left behind. "Oh, God, who feels like an asshole?" She raised her hand, and the woman laughed at her.

"Let me help you with their leashes," the woman said. "I know it's hard to bend over."

"You're a lifesaver," Blair said. "I couldn't go home without them."

"Your husband is attached to 'em, huh?"

"No, my…roommate and I, uhm, share them." She looked at the woman and said, "Our relationship is kinda hard to explain."

The woman laughed and said, "That's why we moved to California when Annette got pregnant. Same-sex parents don't go over big in our hometown."

"Oh…" Blair said, nodding. "My roommate's a lesbian, and she tells me that it's pretty easy to be gay here in L.A."

The woman gave her a slightly puzzled look and said, "Yeah, that's what we're finding." She handed Blair the leashes and gave her a little wave. "Good luck with your baby. Maybe we'll see you here this summer."

"That'd be nice," Blair said. "Our babies could play while our dogs ignore each other."

"See you." The woman went out the gate and trotted over to her car where her partner waited for her.

Blair watched them drive off and then made her way across the parking lot to her own car. She got the dogs into their crate, and after a few seconds, they settled down and fell asleep. But Blair's mind was very active. *Boy, they didn't seem like lesbians. I really couldn't tell! I wonder what in the hell that woman thought about me when I started blathering on about sharing the dogs with my roommate and how our relationship was hard to explain.* She thought about that for a minute and finally decided that the woman had probably assumed she and Kylie were lovers. Blair laughed softly. *No, even though I sometimes get wet when she touches me, we're just friends—who love each other dearly and are going to raise a child and two dogs together. I wonder where that category fits on the census form!*

⌒

Kylie and Julie had dinner at the house, and after cleaning the kitchen, they went into the den to relax. They'd had a very busy day, visiting a few art galleries and going for a long walk by the beach, and both of them were tired. Julie sat very close to Kylie and leaned against her, sighing audibly. "I'm beat."

"Mmm…me, too."

"Maybe we should take a nap."

Kylie put her arms around her date and pushed her to the seat of the sofa, smiling at the surprised look on Julie's face. "Sleepy?" Kylie asked.

"Uhm, less so now." She smiled up at Kylie, staring at her lips. "How about you?"

"No, I like lying down, but I don't think I want to sleep. Hmm…what can we do? We're lying down and don't want to sleep. I know!" She gave Julie a sexy smile and pressed their lips together. They kissed for a few moments with Julie shifting around to get comfortable. Without breaking the kiss, Kylie managed to get her legs on the sofa and then pulled at Julie's until their bodies were pressed together. The doctor felt her body revel in the glorious sensation of being held and kissed.

God, I've missed this, Kylie's muddled brain managed to think. *Having a woman hold me and kiss me like she wants me is one of the most wonderful feelings on Earth.* The kisses rained down on her unceasingly, and soon, she and Julie were grappling on the sofa, hands roaming everywhere at once.

Julie got Kylie on her back and started to unbutton her blouse. Kylie just looked up at her, watching her work with an almost abstract interest. As soon as the blouse was open, Julie gave Kylie a sexy leer and grasped a breast, giving it a healthy squeeze. Kylie wrapped her arms around the redhead's neck and pulled her down. Holding her tight, Kylie kissed her possessively while Julie rolled her hand around the breast, making Kylie shift to trap one of Julie's legs between both of hers.

⌒

Blair almost had to carry the dogs into the house, but they finally jumped out of the crate on their own. She always put a leash on them for even the shortest trip, and this was no exception. When they walked in the front door, all she heard was the stereo. She was about to call out a warning, but she decided to take a quick look in the den first. Keeping the dogs on their leads, she walked into the living room, just able to peer through the kitchen to see the sofa. When she didn't see anyone, she went into the kitchen, assuming Kylie and Julie were outside. It wasn't until she opened the refrigerator that she glanced into the den and saw Kylie being manhandled by a very determined redhead. She nearly screamed, making just enough of a cry to reach Kylie's ears. The doctor's eyes shifted, and she met Blair's startled gaze. Her own eyes grew large, but all she was able to do was hold up one hand in a "sorry about this" gesture. Blair tried to smile, gave her a quick wave, and spirited the dogs off to her own bedroom.

"Jesus! Did you two see that?" she asked once the door was shut. "You're too young to see that kind of thing! *I'm* too young to see that kind of thing! Jesus!" She got ready for bed, muttering to herself the entire time. The dogs were not nearly as traumatized as she, and they quickly took their places on the bed, beginning to snooze lightly.

⌒

Damn it! Damn it! Damn it! Why wasn't I more careful? I don't want Blair to see me rolling around on the sofa like I'm in heat! Shit! Kylie's mind wouldn't stop. Julie was still kissing her passionately, her hands roaming all over Kylie's body. But the doctor felt more like she was being frisked than made love to, and she found herself unable to think of anything but Blair.

Julie lifted her head and asked, "Are you okay? It feels like you've checked out."

"I'm sorry," Kylie said. "Blair came home a couple of minutes ago and saw us. It...I guess it freaked me out a little. Kinda like having your parents catch you necking."

Julie pushed her hair out of her eyes and looked at Kylie for a few moments. "Seems like you're not in the mood anymore."

Kylie gave her an apologetic smile and said, "I guess I'm not. Maybe it's not a good idea to be here when Blair's home. I mean, it's her house, too."

"Yeah," Julie said, giving the doctor a curious look. "I guess it is."

"Why don't we spend the day at your place tomorrow? Then we won't have any interruptions."

"All right," she said, looking unsure of herself. She crawled over Kylie and got to her feet. "I guess I'll see you tomorrow."

Kylie got up and put her arms around Julie. "Hey, I'm sorry for the way this turned out," Kylie said. "Tomorrow will be better."

Julie gave her a half-smile and said, "I hope so, Kylie. I really hope so."

⚊

Blair got into bed and spent a good ten minutes tossing and turning, feeling embarrassed, a little pissed off, and a lot turned on. Annoyed with her libido for firing in Kylie's direction, she refused to give in to its insistent desires. Finally, she drifted off into a troubled sleep.

⚊

After driving Julie home, Kylie went to her room and closed the door—a rarity for her. The dogs liked to go from room to room during the night, spending a little time with each woman, but Kylie knew she needed a good release, and she didn't want to be disturbed. She got into bed, incredibly turned on and frustrated. She started to satisfy her need with the help of electricity. The vibrator thrummed against her vulva while her mind replayed scenes from the evening's activities. *Oh, that was good when she pushed me down and climbed on top of me. When she grabbed my breast, I almost went off like a rocket! I guess that's what two years of abstinence can do to a woman.*

Spreading her legs wider, she eased off on the pressure, trying to make it last. *Boy, I would've loved to have sex tonight, but I can't let my clit make my decisions.* She started to fantasize, picturing the type of body that most appealed to her, imagining her mouth latched on to a ripe, full breast, her cheeks straining to suck in all of the tender flesh.

She dropped the vibrator to the bed and started to touch herself with her hand, easing her fingers into her wetness. "Nice," she purred.

The fantasy body was now face-down, and Kylie kissed the round, womanly hips, continuing to explore as she reached the generous cheeks of her ass. Kissing up and down the shapely legs, she turned the woman over and noticed a patch of blonde hair. Looking up, she saw Blair's desire-infused face and cried out, "No, not Blair! Not Blair!" But her body was determined to fantasize about Blair, and it flew into orgasm, stunning her with the intensity of the feelings. "Oh, my God," she moaned. "Not Blair."

⚊

Not long after falling asleep, Blair began having one of her vivid sex dreams and partially woke up in the middle of it. She gave in to the feeling and began to touch herself, forgetting her earlier pique. Sighing, she felt the tingles start immediately, and it began to feel like an extension of the dream. *This feels so good. But I desperately miss kissing and touching someone to turn him on. Damn, that's the best part of sex. The slow seduction—feeling like you want to rip his clothes off, but taking it slow and making him work for it to make it last. Feeling his hands slip under your shirt to unfasten your bra.*

"Mmm...yeah," she said aloud when the sensations started to build. *The way his hands feel when they caress your breasts for the first time. Damn, that must feel fantastic! To have that creamy white flesh just spilling over your hands and feel her heart beating when you squeeze them just enough to make her squirm.*

Shifting her hips, she started to tug on her breast, trying to imagine the sensation. *Mmm...to hold those nice, full breasts while her tongue's in my mouth. I'd suck on it while I flicked at her nipples with my thumbs, making them hard.* "God, yes," she gasped, pushing hard against her hand. Like a speeding train, her orgasm hit her, forcing the breath from her lungs. Both dogs ran to her and began licking her face, concerned by her vocalizations.

"Not really what I was looking for, guys," she said sleepily. She got her pillow into position and cuddled up to it, murmuring in satisfaction. *Nothing, but nothing, feels as good as having a warm body curl up against you after you come. Mmm...she'd stroke my body, soothing me to sleep while she kissed my neck and shoulders. Ooh...and those warm breasts would press against my back. Damn, it wouldn't take too much of that to make me forget about sleep. I'd turn over and grind myself against her, feeling every one of those womanly curves mold against my body. Mmm...once I started to kiss her again, I wouldn't be able to resist. We'd be at it for hours, just moving against one another, our sweat making us glide against each other until I'd move down and taste her. God, I bet she tastes divine! Oh, yeah, I bet she does...just divine...*

↩

After composing herself, Kylie disgustedly tossed the vibrator to the floor, where it made a surprisingly loud thump.

The noise startled the dogs, and they both woke, running to Kylie's room to investigate. When they saw the closed door, they ran back to Blair and leapt into bed with her, staring at her to tell her about the strange noise. Blair had been sound asleep, but their restlessness woke her. "Oh, no," she groaned. "I was having the nicest dream." Swinging her legs off the bed, she decided she might as well get up and pee since there was no sense in wasting a wakeup call. Getting back into bed, she sighed. *Okay, where was I? I was moments from orgasm—that's where I was*, she chuckled to herself. *Let's see...someone was just about to go down on me. Yeah, that's it. Kylie had just settled down between my legs, and...KYLIE!*

Shooting into a sitting position so quickly that her head spun, Blair's hand flew to her chest, trying to stop her pounding heart from breaking through her chest wall. *Kylie? Oh, fuck! Now I'm fantasizing about her? I have never fantasized about a woman!*

She got to her feet and started to pace, with Nicky and Nora watching her for a moment before tiring of the view and letting their heads drop to the mattress. *Okay, you need to analyze this. She's a very beautiful woman, and she's sexy as hell when she wants to be, but she's been that way since the day you met her. What's different?*

Continuing to pace, she tried to think the issue through. *The first thing you should do is put this into perspective. Just because you fantasize about her doesn't necessarily mean you want to do anything about it. You had that racy dream about the kid who used to cut your grass, and you'd stick your arm under the mower before you'd touch a sixteen-year-old boy! Fantasy does not equal reality.*

Her heart started to calm down, and she continued to go over the dilemma in her mind. *She's sexy, you're horny, and you saw her practically having sex on the couch. How could you avoid having sexual thoughts? You're only human. It was a very sexually charged situation, and you'd have to be the straightest woman in the world to ignore her allure. This is no big deal.*

Deciding that she'd given the matter as much thought as it deserved, she climbed back into bed and snuggled into her pillow. *Hey!* She sat up and ran her hands through her hair. *This isn't like fantasizing about a kid. That's morally wrong! But there's nothing wrong with thinking about Kylie like that. You're a very open-minded woman, and just because you haven't slept with another woman doesn't mean that you won't.*

Hmm…could I have sex with Kylie? She scooted around until she was resting against the headboard. *Well, I don't know why I couldn't. I mean, I love her deeply, I'm planning on living with her for the indefinite future, I like her better than anyone I know, my parents like her, and her family likes me. Why wouldn't I want to sleep with her?*

I can't think of a better person to be in love with. She's the kindest, sweetest, funniest, most clever person I've ever met, and she's so moral and kind. Yes, ideally, she'd be a man, but that can't mean all that much in the scheme of things, can it? All the experts say that sexual orientation is on a continuum. I know I'm not gay, but I'm not straight as an arrow, either. If I were, I wouldn't always have gotten hot when David and I watched movies with two women having sex. And I wouldn't have gotten aroused when she rubbed my chest if I wasn't at least open to the idea. I've had plenty of massages, and I've never gotten aroused during them. There's definitely something about Kylie. Some…magnetism that's pulling me toward her.

She got up and started to walk around the room again, letting her hand gently trail over familiar objects as she moved. *But why now? That's the question.* She thought as she paced, and finally, it became clear. *It's that damned slippery slope the televangelists are always yapping about! I hate to admit it, but they're right!*

She paced around the room, letting herself think about the slow progression of their relationship. *Neither of us was very physical when we met, but after I got pregnant, Kylie started to touch me more. I liked it, and it made me feel like she was excited about the baby, so I didn't give it a second thought. But when we moved in together, things started to progress. She touched me much more often, and pretty soon, we were kissing each other on the head or cheek when we'd come home or leave. And not long after that, we started kissing each other on the lips. Not big, wet smooches, but they were definitely loving, caring kisses.*

Walking slowly, she recalled when the next barrier was broken. *Having her go with me to doctor's appointments and for my ultrasound was a big jump. A very big jump. That's when I started to think of her as my partner. And that's continued until now. I treat her, and she treats me, just like those women at the park—but we don't have sex! That seems like a raw deal—for both of us.*

Blair lay down again, rested her head against the headboard, and let her imagination go. Thinking of how Kylie's eyes gleamed when she talked about sex and her mouth quirked into that adorable grin. Considering how attractive her body was and how nice it felt when Kylie held her close. She let her mind wander to Kylie's breasts and tried to imagine what they'd feel like if she held them in her hands or put one of the nipples into her mouth. *I've never even seen her breasts! She's practically seen my cervix, and I've never seen her undressed! Well, there's one way to remedy that,* she decided. *Ooh...but would she be interested in me like that?* Now her inner voice answered unequivocally, *Yes, Blair, she would. You know it, and you've known it ever since your mother put the idea in your head. She loves you, and she'd love to be your lover.*

Look, she reasoned, *you love her, and that's just a stone's throw from being in love with her. Yes, you've never made love to anyone who didn't have a penis, but that shouldn't automatically stop you from thinking about being her lover. Damn! It'd be worth being her lover if all you ever did was kiss each other. Ooh...I bet she's a fantastic kisser. No newsflash there,* she reminded herself. *She was kissing Julie's lips off!*

For the third time, she got to her feet and started to pace. *She was kissing Julie like mad, and knowing Kylie, she wouldn't do that if she didn't have feelings for her. Damn! If Kylie can make a life with Julie or another woman, I have to let her...no, I have to encourage her! If she can find love with a woman who knows she's a lesbian, that would be so much safer for her. I'd be like a science experiment, but Julie's a sure thing. It's completely unfair to expect her to turn down a chance to be with Julie on nothing more solid than the fact that I've started to have sexual feelings for her. It sounds incredibly lame now that I think about it. She'd probably laugh at me if I even suggested it. It's ridiculous to consider.*

She got back into bed and punched her pillow a few times, making Nora grumble a protest. *You can't have everything, Blair. Having her as a friend is all you're going to get, so get over yourself!*

⌐

Waking up in an incredibly bad mood, Blair stumbled into the shower, lambasting herself for agreeing to meet Walter at the ridiculous hour of 8:00 on a Sunday morning. They were trying to get a house dressed for the brokers' open house on Tuesday and had very limited time since the homeowner couldn't get his things into storage before Saturday.

She put on her chinos and one of the stretchy, horizontal-stripe, knit T-shirts that Kylie had bought for her and then pulled her hair back into a haphazard ponytail, which stuck out through the opening at the back of her baseball cap. Wearing no makeup, she looked like a pregnant teenager. Her belly was very prominent in the tight T-shirt, a look with which she was still trying to grow comfortable. *Oh, well, Kylie insists that I look cute like this, and she swore she'd never lie to me.*

Walking down the hall, she saw that Kylie's door was closed. *Oh, goody! Julie's here!* Forcing herself to refrain from kicking the door, she quickly fed the dogs and kissed them goodbye, instructing, "Be nice to the other lady in there. She might be your new stepmother. We have to like her as much as Mama Kylie likes her, get it?"

⌐

Walter saw to it that Blair didn't have to do any lifting or carrying, but that necessitated her staying at his warehouse storage space for most of the day, instructing the crew he'd hired on which pieces went and which stayed. The space was hot and dusty, and she had little to do between pickups other than walk to the mini-mart for water, which she drank by the quart, and for the use of their bathroom. By the end of the day, she was tired and grimy and felt as if she weighed a ton. All of the water she'd taken in made her feel bloated and heavy, and for the first time, she felt as if she were waddling more than walking. She'd spent most of her free time kicking herself for her dreadful timing in realizing just now that she was sexually interested in Kylie. *If I had done this a few weeks ago, she wouldn't be interested in Julie!*

⌐

Blair pulled into the driveway at 4:00 and spent a few moments trying to appear as if she were in a good mood. She had a smile pasted on her face when she walked into the house, but her smile fell when she got to the den. Kylie was lying on the sofa, her arm draped over her face, and Blair was certain she was crying.

"Kylie?" she asked, walking over to stand by her friend's side. "Are you okay?"

"No," the doctor mumbled. "I had a really bad day. Can I have some time alone?"

Stung, Blair tried to keep the hurt from her voice. "Sure. I'll go outside and play with the dogs for a while. Come on, guys; let's give Mama Kylie some time to herself."

She made it outdoors without crying, but as soon as she was away from the door, she felt the tears start to flow. *Damn, I hate this constant crying! It's the worst part of pregnancy so far. I've cried more in the last few months than I have in my entire life!*

The dogs were used to her rather frequent bouts of crying, but they'd never seen Kylie cry. Neither of them wanted to be outside without her, and Blair didn't, either. She was about to suggest that they sit on their haunches and scratch on the door and look pathetic, but Kylie saved her the humiliation by coming outside a few minutes later.

"Hi," Kylie said, wiping her eyes with the back of her hand. "I'm sorry for being so antisocial."

Blair walked over to her, putting her hand on Kylie's side. "What's wrong? Did something happen?"

"Yeah." She nodded, looking glum. "I went over to Julie's and told her I didn't think we should go out anymore."

"What? Kylie, why?" Her heart started to beat, hoping with all of her might that Kylie would say it was because she was falling for Blair.

The doctor shrugged, looking uncomfortable. "I don't know. Lots of reasons." She scratched her head and looked everywhere but into Blair's eyes. "I need something to eat. How about you? You probably haven't had a good meal today."

Blair gripped Kylie's arm and held on. "Hey, you're clearly upset. You don't need to tell me what's bothering you, but don't just blow it off. You're entitled to be upset once in a while, too."

"I, uhm, I really don't wanna talk about it. I think I'll make dinner."

"Let me." Blair put her arm around Kylie's waist and walked into the house with her. "I'd love to make dinner for you for a change. You go sit down and put your feet up. No matter what happened, you're obviously upset. So, let me take care of you this time, okay?"

Kylie gave her a hesitant smile and then nodded, spending a moment looking at her. "You look like you've been playing in a dirt pile. What've you been doing?"

"Oh, I had to help Walter get a house ready for Tuesday."

Kylie grasped her shoulders. "Were you lifting anything?"

"No, no, I was the one who sat at the storage room and told the movers what to do. It was hot and dirty, but I didn't do any work."

"You must be exhausted," Kylie said. "Let me take care of you."

Blair was exhausted, and she craved a shower, but she held firm. "I'm fine. And I'm going to cook dinner for you. So, go relax before I have to wrestle you onto that couch."

A smile settled on Kylie's face and stayed there. "All right. I'll put some music on and relax a little."

"It's a deal. Would you like me to make you a drink? A little Scotch on the rocks?"

Now Kylie nodded more decisively. "That'd be nice. Just a little, though."

"You've got it. One mini-Scotch coming up."

Blair made dinner and insisted on cleaning up afterwards. By the time she went back into the den, Kylie had finished reading the Sunday paper and was once again lying on the couch. She started to get up, but Blair touched her shoulder. "Stay there." Kylie was halfway up, and Blair sat down next to her, urging her to put her head in her lap. "You know," she said, looking down into Kylie's bright blue eyes, "you pamper the hell out of me, Doctor Mackenzie, but I never return the favor. Tonight, you look like you need a nice head rub. Any objection?"

Kylie gave her a warm smile, her eyes lingering on Blair's for a moment. "Do I look stupid?"

"Nope. You look bright and quick and a little sad tonight. So, just relax and let me try to make you feel better."

"Okay." She gave Blair a bigger smile and said, "I haven't had a head rub in years. Have at it."

Blair started to slip her fingers through Kylie's curls gently and lightly, being careful not to make any tangles. Occasionally, the doctor made a small sound expressing her pleasure, but other than that, she was completely silent. Her eyes were closed, letting Blair observe in a way she'd never been able to do.

Kylie's skin was almost completely unlined, a fact that didn't surprise Blair now that she'd met Kylie's parents. Even though they were in their seventies, they looked a decade or more younger. Her parents also had a good bit of dark hair left, giving Kylie a good prognosis for retaining her black hair for some time to come. *Very good genes these Mackenzies have,* Blair thought.

The doctor's dark brows were a little irregular with a hint of a scar in the middle of the left one. *I guess you can't grow up with that many brothers and sisters and not have a few battle scars,* Blair chuckled. Long, dark eyelashes were sinfully thick—a trait Blair had always envied. Her friend's lovely eyes were hidden, but Blair knew them well and gladly sacrificed looking into them for this chance to study her.

Kylie's lips were among her best features, Blair decided. They were well formed, and each lip was nearly the same fullness. Kylie wore lipstick, but the color she chose was so close to her natural shade that it simply highlighted her mouth's natural beauty and gave it a very attractive sheen.

The doctor's jaw was square—squarer than would typically suit a woman. But it worked perfectly for her, giving her face a substantial strength that was quite impressive.

Kylie's lips parted, and Blair thought she was going to say something, but a quiet snore came out instead. Blair smiled, so taken by her that she wished she could bend over and kiss her. *Poor thing had a very tough day. I'm glad I was able to comfort her a little bit. But it was so strange to have her refuse to talk about what was bothering her. I hope Julie didn't hurt her…but it sounded as if Kylie told Julie she didn't want to see her anymore. Obviously, it wasn't about me, or she would have said something. I guess I'll just have to wait and see if she wants to talk about it later. All I know is that Julie must have been devastated. No sane woman would let Kylie get away.*

She gazed down at the sleeping woman, and a jolt of panic hit her. *My God, what if Kylie doesn't really want a partner? She might think she does and say she does, but if she really did, she'd have one by now! Hell, she'd have women lined up taking numbers if she made herself available. Maybe it is her. Damn! She's only been out with Julie four or five times, and she's already broken up with her. She barely gave Amanda a chance, too. Maybe her words and her actions just don't match.* She put her hand on Kylie's forehead and lightly rubbed the soft skin. *What's going on inside that head, Doctor Mackenzie? Do you want to be loved or not?*

⌒

Kylie got home late on Monday, and she'd barely made it into the kitchen before Blair could tell she was in a bad mood. "Hi," the doctor said, her usual joie de vivre completely missing. "Did you eat yet?"

"No, I was waiting for you. I thought I'd make some penne with fresh tomatoes and sautéed vegetables."

Tilting her head, Kylie said, "Really?"

"Yeah. There was a farmer's market in Brentwood today, and I was lured in by the smell of the popcorn someone was cooking in a big kettle. While I was there, I decided to atone for having popcorn for lunch by having veggies for dinner."

"All right," Kylie said lethargically, not commenting on the rest of Blair's story. "Need help?"

"No. Why don't you go change and then sit in the yard with the dogs? You look like you could use a little time to relax."

Kylie nodded and then walked away, going to her room.

Boy, she's grouchy tonight! That's so unlike her. This thing with Julie must really be bugging her. Blair walked over to the doorway and watched Kylie enter her room. *God knows it's bugging me!*

They ate in front of the television, which was a little odd for them. But Kylie suggested it, and Blair readily agreed since she was determined to pamper the doctor. The usual weeknight game shows were on, and for a change, Kylie didn't shout out ridiculous answers to the questions. She stared at the screen, very little emotion registering.

Blair got up to collect their dishes, and Kylie didn't even offer to help clean up. She picked up the paper and started to read it, seemingly engrossed in current events.

When Blair walked back into the den, she turned on the stereo and looked through the CDs. She chose Bach's *Goldberg Variations*—Glenn Gould's later recording and one of Kylie's favorites. When the music began, Blair picked up a magazine and sat down on the end of the sofa. The doctor had her back against the arm of the couch, and her feet rested on the middle cushion. After a while, Blair reached over and tugged on a foot, pulling it until it was resting in her lap. Kylie lowered the paper and arched an eyebrow. Blair smiled at her and said, "I have an overwhelming desire to give you a foot rub. May I?"

The first hint of a smile lifted the corner of Kylie's mouth. "You know I can't say no to you. Go ahead if you must."

"I must."

The omnipresent bottle of moisture lotion was on the side table next to her, and she started to rub the aloe-scented cream into Kylie's foot. Blair wasn't sure if her efforts were appreciated until she noticed that a page hadn't been turned for quite some time. Finally, Kylie dropped the paper to the floor and stretched out, putting both of her feet onto Blair's lap. The doctor sighed heavily and said, "I had one of the shittiest days I can remember. This is just what I needed."

"Tell me what happened?"

"No, I'd rather not go through it again. Suffice it to say, it sucked on every level. I wish I hadn't gotten out of bed."

"Okay, you don't have to talk. Relax and put your head back. Foot rubs can relieve every kind of stress." Kylie did as she was told, and after a few minutes, she closed her eyes. Not long after that, she was asleep, not even waking when both dogs climbed onto her stomach and thighs. *Damn, I hate it when she won't tell me what's bothering her! Now I'm worried that something horrible happened in surgery. Why can't she give me a little synopsis so I don't have to think about it?*

Even though Kylie was asleep, Blair continued to rub her feet and legs, thinking about how helpless she felt. *Dear God, it must have been horrible for Kylie when I first moved in. I was so shut down! I wouldn't tell her anything that was going on in my head, even though she was clearly worried about me. What an asshole I was!*

She looked at the peaceful face, so lovely in slumber. *I don't know if I'll be able to change, Kylie, but I swear I'll try to be more communicative when things are bothering me. Feeling like this really sucks!*

⌐

On Tuesday, Blair had a dinner meeting, and she didn't get home until a little after 10:00, which was Kylie's bedtime. The doctor was in good spirits and seemed like her old self when she said hello. "Have a good night?"

"Yeah. How about you?"

"Nothing special. We missed you, though. The dogs have been asking after you for an hour."

Blair swooped up the dogs from the sofa and cuddled them for a few minutes. "I missed you, too," she cooed. Looking at Kylie, she said, "You seem like you're in a much better space today. Feeling better?"

"Yeah. I feel fine. Sorry I've been cranky."

"Hey, no problem. I'm still the cranky queen. You've got a long, long way to go to wrest my crown from me."

"I have my moments, too."

"Yeah, I guess you do. So…" She put the dogs down and sat on the sofa. "Feel like talking about what's been bothering you?"

Smiling, Kylie shook her head. "Not really."

"I thought it might be what happened with Julie," Blair said, unwilling to give up without a fight.

Kylie stood and stretched. "Yeah, sure, that's part of it." She bent over and kissed Blair on the head. "I'm feeling like myself again. Don't worry about me."

"Well, I'm not exactly worried. I just thought you liked to talk about things that were troubling you."

"Sometimes, I do; sometimes, I don't. This time I don't." She rubbed each dog's head and said, "I've gotta go to bed, guys. Mama Blair will take over now." She gave Blair the same head rub and said, "I'm glad you're home. See you tomorrow."

"G'night, Kylie." She turned to watch her soft-spoken roommate walk away.

Blair sat in the quiet room, trying to figure out what was going on. She desperately wanted to tell Kylie about her sexual discovery, but she didn't want to do it if the doctor was still smarting over her breakup with Julie. Not knowing what was going on in Kylie's mind was driving Blair nuts, but she knew she had to bide her time until the opportunity presented itself.

⌁

Even though Kylie acted largely like her old self the rest of the week, Blair could detect a distance that had not been there before. Kylie was being a little glib, acting more like she had when they'd first met. The change wasn't dramatic enough for Blair to comment on, but she was sure something was different, and she didn't know how to figure out what had caused the change or how to reestablish the easy familiarity they had managed to build.

⌁

On Thursday afternoon, Blair showed a house to a couple in Malibu. She didn't normally go that far north, but the people she was working with were only interested in having a house on the water, and very few properties in Santa Monica and the Palisades met their criteria.

The couple drove their own car to the house since they were heading up to Santa Barbara after the showing. Luckily, they loved the house Blair showed them, and she thought the odds were good they'd make an offer after they'd had some time to think about it.

Because of their immediate response to the place, they hadn't spent nearly as much time at the house as she'd budgeted. So, finding herself near the ocean with an hour to spare, she decided to go to one of her favorite quiet places. Los Angeles wasn't a haven for quiet unless one went up into the mountains, but her little sanctuary was only a couple of miles from Santa Monica and was nearly at the ocean.

She pulled into the parking lot of the Self-Realization Fellowship Temple, turned off her car, and sat quietly for a few minutes, letting the small stresses of her day float away. When she felt peaceful, she got out of her car and walked to the entrance of the temple grounds.

The site was fairly large, about ten acres, and the focal point was a lovely, natural, spring-fed lake. It was the only natural lake she'd ever been to in Los Angeles, and being near it gave her the sense of peace she occasionally craved. The past week had been so unsettling for her that she had a nearly physical need to commune with her inner self, and the temple seemed the perfect place. She'd never been so sure of something she wanted yet unable to move forward, and it was beginning to make her anxious.

She found a nice, shaded bench and sat down to think. While her eyes followed a pair of snow-white swans, her mind roiled with conflicting thoughts about Kylie. She knew in her heart that Kylie had very deep feelings for her, and there wasn't a doubt in her mind that the doctor wanted to be intimately involved in raising Mackenzie. But these outward signs of merger only served to confuse her.

Kylie has to wonder what I want from this relationship, but she's never specifically asked. Maybe she doesn't want to analyze it too much, or maybe she's afraid of what I'll say. Is she afraid? It's impossible to tell. I can't tell where Julie fits into this, and it doesn't make sense that Kylie won't talk about her! Why won't she talk? Is she embarrassed about something? Did she get dumped? Wait a minute, she thought. *If she'd been dumped, she would have told me! I'm her best friend, and she wouldn't be ashamed to admit that Julie didn't care for her. That's not like Kylie. The only reason that makes sense is that I'm involved in some way. But what way?*

Blair got up and walked around the gardens, finding them rather sparse now that it was fall. A few crape myrtle trees were still colored with their pastel pinks and purples, but everything else was nearly spent. *Maybe I have to look at this from Julie's viewpoint. How would I feel if I dated a great guy who had a roommate he did everything with? The guys owned dogs together, and they were planning to jointly raise a baby that one of the guys was adopting.* She started to laugh out loud, causing a man walking by to sneak a quick look at her. *God, I've never heard of anything so ridiculous! I'd be sure the guy was gay and using me as a beard. Well, Julie knows Kylie's gay, but maybe she didn't like where I fit into the puzzle.* She started to smile, feeling lighter on her feet than she usually did. *Maybe Julie said she wouldn't go out with Kylie as long as she had such a close relationship with me.*

Finding another spot to sit, Blair stared out at the lake for quite a while, gazing at the architecture of the temple, which rose up in the hills above the lake and gardens. *That makes perfect sense. It would make Kylie feel as if she hadn't been totally honest with Julie, and it would make her unable to talk to me about it. Perfect, perfect sense.*

She smiled at having figured out the problem, but simply finding the answer didn't get her anywhere. She had to find a way to get Kylie to talk about it, and that was proving difficult to do. *Come on, Blair,* she reminded herself, *you spend your days talking people into doing things they're ambivalent about! You can handle one recalcitrant doctor! All I have to do is have an evening alone with her. The little drama hound is going out with Nick again tonight.*

❦

When she got home the next evening, Blair decided she had to put her plan on hold for a while. She'd had a rotten day, and she wasn't in the mood to talk to Kylie or anyone else at that moment. *Maybe I'll feel better in a while*, she thought. Kylie came home shortly after Blair had gone into her room. The doctor assumed her friend was changing and knocked lightly on her door, walking in upon hearing a reply.

"Hi. Hungry?" Kylie asked.

"Not really. I had a sandwich when I got home. I didn't get lunch." Blair sat up and tried to smile, creating a reasonable facsimile. "I'm gonna rest for a few minutes, and then I'll be out, okay?"

Kylie ventured further into the room. "Are you all right? You look...sad or down."

Blair wanted to beg for her privacy, just for a while, but she remembered her promise to be more open with her feelings. "Really wanna know?"

"Of course, I do."

"Come sit down, then. But don't look at me. I don't want to see your face when I tell you what a baby I am."

Kylie smiled and sat on the edge of the bed. "I'll look out the window, okay?"

"Okay." Blair took in a breath and said, "There's a guy at work who's only been with the firm a year or so. He knows I'm a good seller, and he knows the managers like me. He's one of those idiots who thinks that women gobble up compliments like there's no tomorrow."

"Ugh," Kylie said, making a face. "What's this guy's name?"

"Mike. Mike Alexander."

"Got it. So, what happened with old Mike?"

"Well, he's always flirted with me whenever he gets the chance. I don't know what he thinks it'll get him, but he's really obnoxious about it. He comments on my clothes, and he always notices when I've gotten a haircut."

"Maybe he really likes you."

"No, it's not that. He does it to any woman he thinks he can get something from. He's new to the business, and he'd really like to work with me; that's the only reason he's interested."

"Okay, I get the picture. So, what happened?"

"Nothing!" Blair said, looking as if she were on the verge of tears. "I was alone with him in the breakroom today, and he treated me exactly like he treats the guys whose coattails he wants to latch on to. He was entirely professional. No comments about my body or my clothes or my hair. He didn't tell me that he knew I was coming into the room because his heart started to beat faster or anything!"

Blair was staring at Kylie, waiting for her to commiserate, but the doctor looked puzzled. "Uhm, isn't that good? Don't you want to be treated professionally?"

"No! I mean, yes, but not by him!"

"I don't get it. I'm sorry I'm not catching on, but I don't understand."

"Kylie, he didn't do it because he doesn't think of me as a woman anymore! Don't you see?"

Kylie gaped at her for a moment and then said, "No, that can't be it. No way!"

"Yes, that is it. And I've been noticing it more and more, but I've tried to shrug it off. None of the guys treats me like a woman anymore. They treat me like a...like a...mom!"

"Oh, sweetie." Kylie scooted over and tucked her arms around her friend. "You *are* gonna be a mom. That's not such a bad thing, is it?"

"I'm not gonna be their mom! They treat me like a matronly old aunt, Kylie. I'm only thirty-five, but guys act like I'm geriatric!"

"And this really bothers you?" Kylie asked, still a little puzzled.

"Yes! I told you it was stupid and that I was a big baby, but it does bother me. I don't feel sexy or attractive anymore. I guess it'd be different if I were with a guy who continued to tell me and show me that he was into me, but now..."

"Aw...I guess that does make a difference, doesn't it?"

"Yeah. I feel like this sexless creature all of a sudden, and it sucks!"

"Look, I can't say for sure what Mike was thinking or feeling. But I do know how you look, and I know that you're not just pretty. You're incredibly beautiful. I mean that with every bit of my heart."

"You're prejudiced," she grumbled.

"Yeah, I am. I'm prejudiced in favor of luscious-looking strawberry blondes with pale-green eyes. Guilty, guilty, guilty."

"I'm not luscious looking," she scoffed. "No one has ever called me luscious."

"You know, just because you've dated people who haven't appreciated your beauty doesn't mean it's not there. I'm an impartial observer, and I swear you're the prettiest woman I've ever held in my arms."

Blair gave her friend a swat on the back. "Liar. I'm nice looking...in the right light...if you've had a couple of drinks, but that's it."

Kylie gave her a half-smile and said, "Look, buddy, you can't tell me who is and who isn't pretty. It's subjective. There's something about you that I find very, very appealing."

"You do...really?" Blair's heart started to race a little, and she tried to give Kylie her best smile. But the doctor was still holding back. There was something almost sisterly—a certain distance and impartiality—about the way she was complimenting her that was driving Blair crazy. It wasn't even Kylie's words as much as her expression. But it was enough to make the compliments sound theoretical.

"I see a lot of pregnant women on any given day. I don't ever deal with them professionally, but I have colleagues who do genetic testing and things like that, so they're around the office all the time. Now, I find most pregnant women attractive. There's something about them that works for me. But I'd honestly say you're in the top 5 percent of the women I see. All women…not just pregnant women."

Suddenly, Blair knew this was the perfect opportunity to get Kylie to talk. Gathering her courage, Blair broke the silence to ask, "Would you do me a big favor?"

"Anything."

"Would you tell me *why* you find me attractive?"

Kylie cleared her throat and looked at Blair with a mixture of curiosity and doubt. "Are you sure you want me to do that? I mean, I will, but it might be embarrassing."

"Yes. You won't embarrass me."

"That takes care of one of us," she said, chuckling. "But you're the boss." She sat up straight and looked at Blair for a moment, eyes roaming from her head to her feet. Kylie's lips were pursed, and she looked as if she were contemplating a work of art. Finally, she smiled and said, "I'd say that part of what I find attractive is your hair. It's gotten prettier and prettier. It's a lot fuller than it was before, and it has a lot of…body to it. Is that right?"

"Yes, that's right. You have a good memory."

"I really don't think I'd heard of hair having body before you grilled me about Amanda. I'm kinda dopey about a lot of topics."

"Focus," Blair said. "Back to me."

Kylie grinned. "Okay. Your hair's grown really fast, too. I'd say it's grown four inches since you've been pregnant. It looks great at this length. I really hope you don't cut it."

"Thanks! This is fun."

"There's more," Kylie assured her, warming to the subject. "Your eyes sparkle a lot of the time. There's actually a scientific reason for that, but I ignore it and let them catch my eye. Very appealing."

"Thank you again."

"Your lips are a little fuller…almost pouty. If I didn't know better, I'd think you'd had a little collagen injected." Kylie playfully touched the tip of Blair's lower lip with her finger. "They're slightly darker, too—very luscious."

"There's that word again."

"Well, they are. Just being scientific." She shifted a little and said, "Here's where I start to feel uncomfortable." Letting her eyes linger for a moment on Blair's chest, she said, "I don't want you to think I walk around all day leering at you."

"I don't think that, Kylie. Believe me, I don't." *I wish I did, but I don't.*

"Okay," the doctor said. "Over the last couple of months, your breasts have become absolutely perfect in my book. They're substantially fuller, and they sway a little bit when you walk." Grinning impishly, she added, "I love that. And by the way, I love how I can see your cleavage in that V-neck sweater I bought for you."

"So, that's why you bought it!"

"Hey, might as well get some personal benefit from keeping you clothed."

Blair had to force herself to pay attention to what the doctor was saying and less to the way her lips moved when she said it. Blair had never noticed how adorable the tip of Kylie's tongue was, but now she found herself staring at her friend's mouth, hoping it would come out again when she said another word that began with "th."

Kylie met Blair's eyes and said, "Being a breast woman, I'm sure I devote more attention to that area than most."

"Got it," Blair said, nodding.

"I also like a good tush, and you've added just enough weight to get a nice curve there. Really, really nice," she said emphatically.

"Okay. Good to know."

"Now, I admit you've lost your trim little waist, but you've added a little volume around your hips. That still gives you a good curve, and that's important to me. I'm all in favor of curves."

"Anything else?" Blair asked, feeling that she had to kiss Kylie or leave the house.

"Mmm...nothing specific. I'd say that the overall effect I get from you is one of lushness and ripeness. You look like a juicy peach with that adorable blush you have on your cheeks."

"Well! This is all quite...revealing," Blair said. Her head was spinning, but she didn't want it to stop.

Kylie looked down and mumbled, "I told you I was embarrassed to tell you everything I'd noticed."

Blair lifted her friend's chin with her fingertips and asked, "Do you want to know how I feel when you talk about my body?"

"Uhm, sure. I'd like to know."

Leaning close, Blair kept her face mere inches from Kylie's. "I feel attractive and desirable, like I don't have anything to be ashamed of. I feel like a very beautiful woman."

"You are," Kylie said softly, her breath warm against Blair's cheek. "You're a very beautiful woman."

Reaching out, Blair pushed some of the tumbled curls back from Kylie's face so that she could see her eyes. Hesitantly, with more shyness than she'd felt in her adult life, she asked, "Do you find me desirable?"

The dark head began to nod, and Kylie said in her most enthusiastic and confident tone, "Absolutely. Very, very much so. I thought you were very pretty the first time I saw you, and you've grown more attractive since you've been pregnant."

Blair's heart fell, and she knew she was going to cry. Kylie's words were so soothing, so comforting, but her eyes weren't sparkling the way they did when she was genuinely excited about something. Blair believed her words. She was certain Kylie wasn't just soothing her ego, but it was almost as if her father or mother were telling her how attractive they found her. Not only wasn't she not getting a hint of a sexual vibe from her friend, there seemed to be an emotional distance that Kylie was intentionally trying to create. Something was off; Blair was sure of it. But she didn't know how to get back on track. "Thanks, pal," she said, trying to look happy. "I could probably manage a little bit of dinner. If nothing else, I'll keep you company. How's that?"

"Excellent. Dinner for three. You, me, and Mackenzie." She gave Blair a big smile and reached over to pat her friend's tummy.

On Saturday night, Kylie and Nick had tickets to a play, but he asked if Kylie would mind if he took a date instead. She wasn't set on seeing the production, so she gladly let him have her seat. Blair called Kylie on the way home, and when she learned that she wasn't going out, she stopped at the video store to pick out a couple of DVDs. When she got home, she walked into the den and dropped her selections on the table. "Your pick: drama or action."

"What's this?" Kylie asked, looking up at her.

"Your date got cancelled, so you should at least get to see something kinda special."

"Aw…you're awfully thoughtful."

"I'm learning from the master."

After dinner, they settled down to watch one of the movies. Kylie didn't know much about either, so she flipped a coin, and they watched the drama. It was a tearjerker, a much sadder film than Blair would have chosen if she'd known the plot. But it was a well-made movie, and it touched her deeply. It told the story of a love never fulfilled—of lovers who longed for each other all their lives—and Blair could hardly fail to notice the parallels between the film and her relationship with Kylie.

Blair dabbed at her eyes with a tissue and was surprised to hear Kylie sniffling, too. "Why did I rent such a sad movie?" Blair asked. "I wanted to have fun tonight."

"It was sad," Kylie said, her voice breaking a little. "So damned sad." She kept crying with only a few tears spilling out every couple of moments, but she was obviously very upset.

"Hey," Blair said. She scooted next to her and put an arm around her shoulders. "What is it?"

"Nothing. It's nothing."

Blair couldn't bear to let the wall that had built up between them stand. She gathered her courage and said, "Kylie, something *is* wrong…between us."

"Huh?" Confused, watery blue eyes looked at her.

"Something is…different between us. Ever since you broke up with Julie, you've been acting differently. I'm not sure what it is, but it's definitely not my imagination."

Kylie looked as if she were going to speak, but she obviously changed her mind. "It's nothing. Nothing. I…don't want to talk about it."

"Is it me? Did I do something to upset you or hurt you? Are you having second thoughts about living with me?"

"No, no, don't be silly. How could you have done anything? This is between Julie and me."

"But if it's not about me, why are you treating me differently? I swear there's a barrier between us that wasn't there before."

The brunette looked as if she wanted to leave the room, but she stayed right where she was. Blair could see the inner struggle her friend was going through and could tell that Kylie wanted to talk, but was fighting against something. "It's not you. I swear, it's not you," Kylie finally said. "It's…something that Julie made me aware of, and I'm having a hard time figuring out how to deal with it. It's my problem, not yours."

Blair felt tears sting her eyes. "It's my problem if it affects you." She put both of her arms around Kylie and hugged her close, feeling a little reassurance when she hugged her back. "I love you so much that I feel your pain when you're hurt. It's so hard when I don't know what's bothering you."

"I'm so sorry," Kylie said. "I swear I didn't know this was on your mind."

"It is, it has been, and it's gonna be until you're acting like your old self. I can't bear to have a distance between us."

Kylie pulled back just enough to focus. "There isn't much distance now," she said. She gave Blair her usual crooked smile, but her eyes looked so sad that Blair couldn't stand it.

"Why are you sad?" she asked, gently stroking Kylie's cheeks with the tips of her fingers. "Please, please tell me."

"It's…it's nothing bad. I'm trying to deal with some hard realities. There are some things I'm never gonna get, and I have to face up to that."

Blair gazed deeply into her eyes and said, "Tell me. Tell me what you want. I'll do anything I can to help you get it."

"Oh, Blair," she said. She dropped her head onto her friend's shoulder and cried softly. "I wish I could ask you for what I need. I wish I could."

Blair put her hands on the sides of Kylie's head and lifted it. She stared into her eyes for almost a minute, trying to see inside her…to read her mind. The energy between them was crackling with both women desperate but unwilling to speak. Finally, Blair summoned the courage and said, "I might regret this, but I'm going to ask you for what *I* need." She held on to Kylie's head and pulled it closer, seeing the blue eyes widen as she was drawn towards her. Blair closed her eyes and pressed her lips against Kylie's, hearing her friend let out a startled mew. Blair held her tight, and almost immediately, Kylie's arms wrapped around her, and they kissed again—longer and deeper and sweeter than before. Blair pulled back and looked into the fathomless depths of Kylie's eyes and kissed her once more, opening her mouth to Kylie's tentatively probing tongue.

Just moments of the exquisite sensation was enough to leave Blair breathless, and she moved her lips a bit, kissing all around Kylie's mouth, panting softly. Suddenly, Kylie's hands were on Blair's shoulders, pushing her away. Kylie stumbled to her feet and stared, asking in a loud voice, "What in the hell are we doing?"

Blair grabbed her friend's hand and pulled her back down, gazing at her with an inner sense of peace she hadn't felt in weeks. "We're kissing," Blair whispered. "We're kissing because we care for each other so much." She put her hand behind Kylie's head and drew her close again. Their lips were only an inch apart, and Blair could see the beautiful pink lips quivering with fear and anticipation. "Let me show you how I feel." She kissed her again, holding Kylie so tight Blair was afraid she'd hurt her. But Kylie looked so frightened that Blair felt she had to hold on to her to keep her from bolting. Blair slipped her tongue into Kylie's mouth and savored the warmth found there, letting herself explore and tease.

But once again, Kylie pulled away, staring at Blair with a stunned look on her flushed face. "Why are you doing this? We don't do this! We're friends!"

Blair stroked Kylie's cheek, feeling the heat radiating from it. "We can be more. I want to be more. Don't you?"

"Yes! Of course, I want more! That's what's been driving me crazy! But we can't have it. You're not a lesbian!"

"Where are the rules for kissing? 'Cause I didn't know you had to take an entrance exam. I thought you just kissed the person you loved."

Kylie looked at her exactly like Nicky and Nora did when asked if they wanted a treat. Her head was cocked at an uncomfortable-looking angle, and she asked, "You love me?"

"Of course, I love you. Is this a surprise?" She placed a soft kiss on Kylie's lips and then another and another. "I love you, Kylie." She kissed her again, urging her mouth open and probing the soft, moist skin with her tongue. "I love you."

Wrenching away again, Kylie insisted, "I know you love me, but you can't *love* me. You're not gay—at all!"

Blair reached for her again, gently stroking her shoulders. "I'm gay enough to be very, very attracted to you. Isn't that enough?"

This time Kylie wrestled out of her hold and moved away from her. "No, that's not enough. You can't…I can't…we can't…this isn't right for you. You're confused or something."

Blair's brows shot up. "Pardon me?" She glared at Kylie, and the doctor knew she'd made a mistake.

"Uhm, that's not what I meant. I…I don't know what I meant, but I know you're not gay!"

"Kylie, you're being ridiculous. I'm a thirty-five-year-old woman, and I know exactly what I want and what I think. I'm falling in love with you. I know that's not something I'm supposed to do, but it's happening. And don't you dare tell me that I'm confused! I'm pregnant, not delusional!"

"Okay, okay. *You* might know what you think, but I'm totally confused here. Up until about ten minutes ago, you were my straight friend. Now you're kissing me…" She gave her a goofy smile, and Kylie's voice grew soft and sweet. "Kissing me so very, very well. But no matter how well you kiss, this isn't you, or at least, it wasn't you before we watched that movie!"

"Do you think that a movie changed my sexual preference? Who are you, Pat Robertson? A movie can't make a straight woman have sexual feelings for another woman, you big goof!" Blair moved closer, wrapping her arms around Kylie's waist and looking up into her eyes, saying, "I've loved you for months, and a couple of weeks ago, I started having sexual feelings for you. It was a surprise to me, too, but it's true. I was only waiting for the right moment to tell you."

Kylie reached up and grabbed the top of her head. "I feel like my cranium's gonna blow! This is too much for me to process all at once. You've gotta go easy on me, please!"

Blair looked at her, trying to see if she was kidding, but Kylie looked deadly serious. There was a deep furrow between her brows that Blair had never seen, and Kylie's jaw was clenched so tightly that tendons in her neck stood out. Taking pity on her, Blair moved back, giving Kylie room to breathe. "Okay, you're right. This is a lot to absorb."

"A *whole* lot. A whole big lot."

Blair smiled at her, wanting to kiss her again because of the adorable look on her face, but not wanting to upset her. "Do you want to talk about it? Want me to tell you how my feelings for you have changed?"

"Yes," Kylie said. "I definitely want to hear everything—tomorrow."

"Tomorrow?"

"Yes. Tomorrow. I can't take any more tonight. I swear I'll have an aneurysm if we keep talking."

"Are you being serious?" Blair asked, frankly astonished. "You, of all people, don't want to talk about something this important?"

"I *do* want to talk about it," Kylie said, looking as if she were going to cry or scream, "but this is too much for me. I need some time to let this sink in. I'm sorry, but that's how I am. This is too important to just react to."

Blair stepped back another foot, holding up her hands. "Okay, okay. But I feel like I'm standing out here on a ledge. I told you something that could change my entire life, and you say you can't talk about it. I'm feeling a little exposed."

The doctor took a deep breath and gathered her wits as best she could. She moved close to Blair and put her arms around her. "Give me a few hours to calm down." Kylie hugged her tightly and whispered, "You know how much I care for you. Don't worry."

Feeling how Kylie trembled made Blair feel very protective of her. "Hey, it'll be all right. It's just me. You and me."

"I know," Kylie said, her voice shaking, "but this is so overwhelming. I can't even think straight."

Blair looked up at her while stroking her back. "Can we sleep together? I'd feel so much better if we could be close."

"What? No! We can't sleep together!"

"We've slept together before. It's no big deal."

"It is once you start kissing me! It's a very big deal!"

"All right, all right. I'm sorry I asked."

"Don't make this any harder on me," Kylie said, her eyes showing fear. "This isn't some little thing. It's life-changing."

"I know that, Kylie. It's life changing for both of us. I just thought you were the type to wanna talk about something this big."

"I do. But I have to calm down first. I don't do well under pressure."

Blair gave her a blank look, wanting to remind Kylie that she was a surgeon and worked under incredible pressure every day. But Blair realized that Kylie didn't consider surgery pressure. She reveled in the demands it put on her. However, she didn't ever seek out emotional risks—and this was a big one. "You're right," Blair said. "I'm sorry for pushing you. We'll talk about it tomorrow, but I have to leave the house at 9:00, so it'll have to be when I get home. Okay?"

"Okay," Kylie said, mollified.

"Can I kiss you good night?"

"Uhm, sure."

Kylie presented her cheek and scampered down the hall as soon as Blair delivered the kiss, leaving her to look at the dogs and sigh. "Here's a lesson for you two: if I'd been trying to lure a man to bed, we would have had sex—twice—and he would've been asleep by now. A woman wants to do a background check on you before she'll even give you a kiss!"

⟝

Blair was gone most of the next day, and she returned home when Kylie was preparing dinner. The dogs ran to greet Blair, but Kylie stayed at the sink, washing a few dishes. "Hi," she called out.

Blair walked into the kitchen and saw the tense set of the doctor's shoulders. *The poor thing. She's probably been stewing over this all day.* She went up behind Kylie, slid her arms around the doctor's waist, and then rubbed her face against her back. "Hi. I missed you," Blair said.

"I missed you, too." She rested her hands on the rim of the sink, and Blair could feel her friend's body relax a little bit. "Did you have a good day?"

"No. I wanted my clients to stay in their old house so I could be with you." Kylie let out a nervous laugh, and Blair tightened her embrace. "I have to tell you something."

The doctor slid out of Blair's hold and looked at her with a startled, nearly frightened expression. "What?" she asked, her voice a little high.

Blair placed her hand behind Kylie's neck and pulled her down. "Another day's passed, and I'm still falling for you," she said and then kissed her tenderly. "I thought about you all day and couldn't wait to get home so I could kiss you." She kissed her again, holding her close and reveling in the feel of Kylie's body. "I thought about your lips more times than I can count."

Kylie gave her a pleading look and then stood up straight. "I missed you, too, and I thought about *you* all day, but you promised we could talk about this. I thought the implication was that you'd stop kissing me until we did."

Blair stepped back and stared at her for a moment. "Does my kissing you bother you that much?"

"Yes. Yes, it does. It'll bother me more than you'll ever know if you…stop," she said, looking very vulnerable.

"Oh, Kylie, I'm not gonna stop. You know how much I love you!"

"I know you love me; I don't doubt that a bit. But I don't know that you'll be happy being my lover. I think...I think that you might be..." She looked into Blair's eyes, showing raw fear. "Settling."

Blinking slowly, Blair stared at Kylie for several seconds and then blew out an audible breath as she started to leave the room. "I don't want to snap at you, so I need a few minutes to think of a response that isn't profane. I'm gonna go change clothes."

Kylie watched her leave, wincing as the bedroom door slammed shut.

↩

It took Blair about ten minutes to calm down, and Kylie was on pins and needles the whole time. She was sitting outside, sipping a tall glass of what looked to be watered-down Scotch, when Blair sat next to her and said, "I don't even like Scotch, but I'd like one now. My nerves are twitching."

Kylie gave her a doe-eyed look and said, "I'm sorry I hurt your feelings. I didn't mean to. Really."

Blair reached over and took her friend's hand, kissing the back of it and holding it over her heart. "Don't apologize. I've obviously been pushing you too hard. I'm not being sensitive enough to the things that are bothering you."

Giving her a charming smile, Kylie said, "No, it's my fault."

"Unh-uh. My fault. I have to recognize how important this is to you and that you're not as sure of me as I am of myself. I promise not to get angry with you again. You're entitled to ask me anything you want."

"Thanks," Kylie said, her expression one of immense relief. "Uhm, do you understand what I was getting at before?"

"Yeah," Blair said, letting out a wry chuckle. "You want to know if I'm using you because I don't think I can get a man."

Horrified, Kylie gasped, "That's not true! That's not what I think! You'd never use me...consciously."

Blair took a playful bite of the doctor's hand. "Ooh...so, you think I have pregnancy-induced lesbian tendencies, huh? I have to find a mate to help me raise the baby, and I'm acting on such unconscious primal instinct that I've convinced myself you're the one for me."

"Well, that sounds harsh, but it's kinda close to what I was thinking."

"Yeah," Blair nodded. "It does sound harsh. It also doesn't sound like me." She threaded her fingers through Kylie's and rested their linked hands on her thigh. "Let's look at the big picture. I'm perfectly capable of raising Mackenzie on my own. I'm also sure that you'll be a lot of help even if things don't work out between us as lovers. You're just that kind of friend." She squeezed Kylie's hand, shaking her head, a frown narrowing her eyes. "How about this? Why don't I start at the beginning? I'm gonna tell you exactly what my thought process was when I started to have feelings for you. If it sounds like I'm settling, so be it."

She got up, walked over to the lawn, and then started to move around in no particular pattern. She walked with her hands linked behind her back, looking like a professor lecturing a small class. "I love you, and I have for months. But I never considered that I might be or could be *in* love with you. It should have been obvious, and probably was to everyone we know, but it didn't occur to me because I've never had sexual feelings for a woman."

"Never?" Kylie shouted.

"Sh! We have neighbors. Now, calm down, and we'll get to that little detail later. I have to do this in order."

Giving her a chagrined smile, Kylie nodded. "Sorry," she whispered.

"Okay," Blair said, looking thoughtful. "When you had Julie over to go swimming, I saw the two of you making out by the pool."

"Oh, shit, why do I always get caught?"

"'Cause you're a forty-year-old woman who has a roommate," Blair teased. "Anyway, I couldn't stop myself from watching you, and after a couple of minutes, I realized I was totally turned on."

Kylie brightened. "You were?" Then an eyebrow shot up, and she asked, "Did you say 'couple of minutes'? You watched for a *couple* of minutes?"

"Yes, hot stuff, I did. I couldn't tear my eyes away. I tried to shrug it off, but I couldn't. So, I made a conscious decision to think about what had happened. I realized that I used to get hot when David and I would watch porn with women having sex with each other. There was always a guy in the scene, too, but I sure didn't mind watching the women do things together."

"Sounds promising," Kylie said, giving her a big, bright smile. But her smile faded, and she looked puzzled. "I thought you'd never fantasized about a woman?"

"I haven't," Blair said. "I've gotten turned on watching them make love, but I've never consciously thought about women while I'm having sex."

Kylie's eyes widened. "Sounds like a fine line to me."

"Details, details," Blair said, waving the point away. "So, I realized I was aroused by you, and then it dawned on me that I was ridiculously jealous of Julie. I knew I was being an idiot, but I couldn't stop feeling that she was taking you away from me."

"That's what Julie thought, too," Kylie said, looking at the ground.

"Mmm...that was on my shortlist of reasons you two broke up. It just hit me the other day, but I had a feeling, especially since you wouldn't talk about it."

"Yeah, she feels pretty used. I feel like a huge asshole."

Blair walked over and sat on the edge of her chair. "You didn't do it on purpose, did you?"

Looking even guiltier, Kylie nodded. "Kinda. I knew I was falling for you, and I wanted to make myself fall in love with someone else so I could keep you in my life without pining away for you."

"Ouch," Blair said. "No wonder she's pissed."

"She has every reason to be, even though I wasn't as diabolical about it as I make it sound. It was mostly subconscious until we got back from Chicago. My mom made me admit that I was in love with you." She snickered and muttered, "Bitch."

Blair couldn't help herself; she had to lean over and give Kylie a kiss. But she made it a quick one to spare the doctor any more anxiety. "So, you knew you were falling for me, huh?" Blair asked. "That's pretty good news from where I stand."

Giving her an adorably shy smile and nodding, Kylie said, "Yeah, you know I'm crazy about you. You're too perceptive to have missed all of my not-so-subtle signals—the ones I tried like hell not to send out."

"I noticed some of them, and I was able to rationalize most of them. But the important thing is that Julie and I were right about you and your feelings. I realized that we were more than friends, and I liked it. I started thinking about it, and I finally decided it was silly not to let our relationship progress. I know I don't have lesbian street cred, but everyone has to start somewhere, right? You dated guys before you decided you wanted a woman."

"Yeah, but I was seventeen, not thirty-five. You've been putting up a very good front as a lesbian trapped in a marriage, having to perform despicable acts with a…" She put her forearm over her eyes and whispered, "Man!"

"Funny," she said, giving her a pinch. Blair got up and started to walk again, pacing slowly. "I love having sex with men. But I'm also a very sexual, very open-minded person. I don't see why I wouldn't love having sex with you. I think you're sexy as hell, and kissing you has been very, very arousing."

"Wait till I start kissing you," Kylie said, a little of her usual teasing personality starting to emerge. "My lips haven't gotten out of the starting gate."

Blair stopped and stared at her. "I can't wait," she said, giving Kylie a look that made the doctor's heart start to beat faster.

Kylie swallowed and tried to get back to the topic. "Are you finished?"

"For the moment. What do you think? Am I delusional?"

Kylie leaned back in her chair, finally relaxing her coiled posture. She linked her hands behind her head and gazed up into the sky for a minute or two with Blair raptly watching her face for a clue to her thoughts. Finally, Kylie said, "Well, if I had to write this script, I would have preferred you to say that you've always been attracted to women, but David came along before you could act on it. I'd feel much more comfortable about this if you felt you were bisexual. But it doesn't seem like you do."

"Well, maybe a little," Blair said. "On a scale from one to ten, with one being totally straight, I'd say I'm a two or a three. You're the only woman I've ever wanted to kiss, much less do anything more with."

"Hmm…I'm about a nine. I could have sex with a man, but I'd have to fantasize about a woman to be able to enjoy myself." She looked very thoughtful and asked, "The question is, can a three and a nine find happiness together?"

"Twelve's my lucky number," Blair said, beaming a grin.

"Twelve's not anyone's lucky number. What is it really?"

"Two. But I like twelve a lot. There's a two in it."

Kylie got up, approached Blair, and then put her arms around her, asking, "Can we take this slowly? I need to think about it and get all of my questions resolved before I can jump in."

Blair looked up at her, the setting sun forming a golden halo around Kylie's dark hair. "Do you love me?" Blair asked.

"Yes, I do. I love you very much, and I'd give anything to have this work out. But I'm not gonna do it just because I want it. I have to make sure that you want it, too. I can't risk your changing your mind and breaking my heart. I can't let that happen."

"I understand. But I don't know how you can know what's in my heart. How can I convince you?"

"I'm not sure. Maybe…maybe I just need a little time to let this sink in."

"Okay. I can give you a little time. But what did you think of my thought process? Did it sound like I was settling?"

Kylie shrugged her shoulders. Her brow was a little furrowed, and she seemed very thoughtful when she spoke. "It sounded more logical than emotional, but that's the way you are. I think you added up all of the positive things and decided this could work. I don't think that's settling, but it's not mad love, either."

Blair shook her head. "I'm not a 'mad love' kinda girl." She put her hands on Kylie's waist and said, "But if you need a 'mad love' kinda girl, you should have one. I'd hate to lose you, but I'd understand—in a decade or two."

Kylie kissed her on the head. "I'm pretty logical about things, too. I think I could live with a logical lover." She hugged her tightly and asked, "You're not logical all the time, are you? I mean, do you get emotional when you're…you know…" She looked charmingly embarrassed, and Blair had to kiss her once again.

"I'm like you are," Blair said. "I only have sex with people I love. And I have sex to show my feelings. I promise you'll know how I feel about you when we touch."

Kylie smiled at her and brushed a few strands of hair from her forehead. "I thought that's how you'd be. But before we go any further, I have to know that you've considered all of the negative things about loving me. That's a big deal."

"Oh, Kylie, I know you have a million faults, but I can overlook them for love." She giggled at the nonplussed look on Kylie's face.

⌐

After dinner they went outside as they often did on a warm evening. "So, start telling me all of the pitfalls of lesbian love," Blair said.

"No, not tonight. I know I'll get all worked up, and I have to go to bed early. I've got a hellacious day in surgery tomorrow, and I've gotta chill a little bit." She gave Blair a half-smile and said, "I was a nervous wreck all day, and I still feel tense."

Blair took her friend's hand and chafed it tenderly. "You poor thing. I'm sorry I had to work all day, but it couldn't be helped. I should have called you when I had a chance, just to see how you were doing."

"That's okay. I still would have been nervous."

"Tell me what makes you so tense? Isn't this what you want?"

Kylie looked at her to make sure she wasn't joking. "Of course, this is what I want! How can you even ask that? It's just that I want it so badly I'm afraid to let myself think it's gonna happen. I'll be devastated if this doesn't work out."

"Oh, Kylie, don't think like that." She got up and indicated that she wanted Kylie to draw her knees up to make some room. When she did, Blair sat on the foot of the chair and rested her arms on the doctor's knees. After gazing at her for a moment, Blair said, "Can I tell you what I want—big picture?"

"Sure."

"I want someone to spend my life with. I'm self-sufficient enough to be able to have a very good life alone, but I think I do better when I'm in a committed relationship. I also think it would be better for Mackenzie to have two parents. But even if I weren't pregnant, I'd still be falling for you. I'm not just looking for a co-parent. I'm looking for a partner, and I think I've found her in you. So, the only reason this won't work out is if you vote no."

Kylie's entire body was shaking, and Blair wrapped her arms around her friend's legs to try to reassure her. "How can you be so sure?" the trembling doctor asked.

"I know what I want in a lover. I want someone who's kind and thoughtful and intelligent and funny and cultured and sexy. And now that I'm pregnant, I need someone who wants to have children and wants to co-parent with me. It didn't occur to me that I'd find what I wanted in a woman, but I have. The fact that you're a woman isn't a big deal for me, Kylie. Those other qualities are non-negotiable, but much to my surprise, the sex of the person isn't."

"This is…I've…" Kylie shook her head, clearly flustered. "How can you say that? I've never known anyone who just decides that the sex of her partner isn't a big deal. I mean, I know that's true for bisexuals, but I've never heard of anyone figuring out she's bisexual when she's thirty-five years old!"

"Kylie," Blair said, her voice low and soothing, "it's not my fault I didn't meet you until now. Don't hold that against me. I was married for ten years, and I was happy with my husband. I wasn't exploring my sexuality then. I am now."

"That's part of the problem. You're not sure you can be happy in a lesbian relationship. You're exploring this! What if you find out that you can't do it?"

Blair gave her a puzzled look. "What would make me decide that?"

"See? This is what I mean!" She patted Blair and said, "I've gotta get up." As soon as she did, she started pacing. "Now I'm all worked up. I'm trying to relax, and you've got me in a lather!"

Blair went to her, holding her in her arms. "I'm sorry. You're right. We shouldn't have started talking about this again. I know it's hard for you." She hugged her tightly and said, "Go get ready for bed, and I'll give you a nice backrub. That'll help you relax."

Kylie gave her a slightly doubtful look and then said, "I'm not sure I trust you to rub my back. The last thing I need is to be all turned on. We'd better stick with a head rub."

"A head rub it is." She watched Kylie walk into the house, musing, *The supremely confident Doctor Mackenzie is nowhere to be found tonight!*

When Kylie was ready, Blair went into her friend's room and lay next to her on the bed. Blair started to thread her fingers through the doctor's soft curls, speaking to her in a soothing voice. "It's gonna be all right. Everything will work out. We're gonna be one small, happy family." She kept up her ministrations, until she felt Kylie's body relax, and then slowed down and finally stopped. Kylie was sound asleep, and Blair couldn't resist staying right where she was. She nestled her cheek against Kylie's back, listening to her strong, sure heartbeat and the steady intake of breath. *It's gonna be so nice when I can sleep with her*, she thought. *Just lying here with her calms me down.* She noticed that Mackenzie was unusually calm, too, and whispered, "Mama Kylie calms you down, too, doesn't she, Mackenzie? All we have to do now is convince her that we're gonna love her as much as she loves us."

⸺

Kylie and Nick went to the symphony the next night, and by the time she came home, Blair was sound asleep on the sofa. The doctor gently woke her and helped her to her feet. "But I wanna stay up and talk about being a lesbian," Blair mumbled, her words sounding comical given her tousled hair and sleep-suffused voice.

"We can talk about being lesbians tomorrow." Kylie scratched the back of Blair's neck, knowing that a good scratch was as effective as ether. By the time they reached the bedroom, Kylie merely had to urge her onto the bed and cover her with a quilt. "That's my girl," Kylie said. She sat down and ran her fingers through Blair's hair for a few minutes, reluctant to leave. Kylie had hardly noticed it at first, but Blair was slowly scooting closer, and in a short while, she was curled up against Kylie, holding on tight. For an instant, she was jealous, assuming Blair was unconsciously seeking David's familiar warmth. But when Blair nuzzled her face against Kylie's knee like a kitten and mumbled, "I love you, Kylie," the doctor smiled broadly.

She leaned over and kissed Blair's cheek. Keeping her lips right there, she continued placing tiny, soft kisses around Blair's ear, not stopping until the sleepy woman started to giggle. "Sleep tight," Kylie whispered. She gave Mackenzie a pat and bent to kiss him. "I love you, too, Mackenzie. Be nice to your mommy tonight."

Blair was asleep immediately, and the doctor stayed for another few minutes, feeling content and peaceful just to be next to her.

⸺

Blair was home when Kylie arrived the next night, and as soon as the doctor walked into the house, Blair called out, "Get changed! I brought carryouts for dinner. We're gonna spend the whole night talking about the dangerous world of lesbianism."

"I have a feeling that someone's not taking my concerns very seriously," Kylie said when she walked into the kitchen.

Blair gave her a hug and said, "I take you and your concerns very seriously. But I'm confident that I've thought of the repercussions, and I know that once I convince you of that, we're gonna be fine." She gave her a dazzling smile and said, "Is it okay if I'm happy about that?"

"I suppose so," Kylie said, trying but failing to look aggrieved. She wrapped her arms around Blair and playfully tossed her back and forth. "You're so darned cute that I can barely stand it!"

"Oh, you haven't seen half of it. Just you wait. I'll confound you with cuteness."

⌒

They went outside after dinner, and Blair was surprised to see that Kylie had a notepad with her. The doctor looked at her agenda and nodded, obviously satisfied with her script. "Okay." She tapped her bottom teeth with a mechanical pencil and said, "I think the biggest thing I'm worried about is how you're gonna deal with coming out as an adult. People are gonna treat you differently, and that might be very hard for you."

"For example?"

"Well, people in your office are gonna find this strange. What if your boss has problems with it?"

"Oh, he's as gay as they come. Real estate is full of gay men, and I can't imagine that people would be more tolerant of gay men than they would be of me."

Kylie scratched her head. "Well, no, they probably wouldn't be..."

"My clients don't need to know, although I doubt any of them would have a problem with it. You've got to remember that this is the Westside, Kylie. This is one of the most gay-friendly places in the world. Besides, you're a professional, and you don't have any problem with prejudice, do you?"

The doctor shook her head. "No, not really. I don't tell my patients that I'm a lesbian, but I certainly don't hide it, either."

"That's the way I'll be, too. I don't normally talk about my home life with clients. And when I have a client party, I'll just let people assume what they want."

"I could make myself scarce when you had people over."

"That's ridiculous! I wouldn't dream of asking you to leave when I entertain. I might not introduce you as my lover, at least not at first, but I would never be embarrassed by you. Never!"

Kylie smiled at her. "I'd hate it if you asked me to leave."

"You big goof! Why would you make an offer that'd make you feel bad?"

"'Cause I'm nice?" she offered tentatively.

"It's never nice to propose something that can hurt you or our relationship. Life's hard enough without asking for trouble." She sat on the end of the chaise and put her chin on Kylie's raised knee. "I know there'll be an incident or two where someone says something snotty about my being with you. But nothing anyone says or does will change how I feel about you. My feelings for you are genuine, and they run very deep. Can't that be enough?"

Kylie tenderly ran her hand through Blair's hair and then smoothed a thumb across her cheek. "Yeah, that can be enough," Kylie said. "But you can't forget that other people are gonna be affected by this."

"I assume you mean my parents."

"Yeah, they're important players."

"They are. And I know they would have been very supportive if I'd told them I was gay when I was a kid. But now…now…they're gonna wonder about it. I'm not sure which one of them it'll bother more, but I know they'll have some trouble adjusting. That won't bother me much—really. Over time, they'll see that this is what makes me happy, and they'll be fine. It's just…at first, they'll think you tricked me into this." She giggled at the stunned look on Kylie's face and then gave her bare knee a kiss. "They won't say that. They might think it, but they won't say it."

"It sounds funny now, but they could say something that really hurts you. I'd hate to have that happen."

"I'm sure you're right. Some people I love might hurt me. So, what's the answer? Give up someone I love so that I don't ever get my feelings hurt? You've gotta admit that doesn't sound like a fair tradeoff."

"No, it doesn't. But there are some people in your life who won't be so supportive. I can't imagine David or his mother will think this is a cause for celebration."

Blair's eyes closed, and she slapped herself on the forehead. "Oh, God, Sadie!"

Kylie cocked her head and asked, "You're more worried about Sadie than David?"

"Sure. Sadie's gonna be in my life. She wants to have a relationship with the baby. But odds are I won't see David much, if at all. Besides, what's he gonna do? Divorce me?" She made a dismissive motion with her hand. "His opinion doesn't matter to me anymore. He obviously doesn't care if I live or die. Fuck him."

Kylie smiled at her, always enjoying it when feisty Blair reared her head. "I know you don't care about his opinion, Blair, but you don't wanna hurt him, do you?"

"Not intentionally, but I'm not gonna ask his permission to do what I want."

Gently scratching Blair's neck and shoulder, Kylie asked softly, "Don't you think he'll be hurt when he hears about this? Someone *will* tell him, you know."

"Oh, fuck me!" She put her forehead on Kylie's knee and growled. When Blair lifted her chin, she pretended to gnaw on the doctor's leg. "I don't wanna be nice. I want him to find out in a public place and wet himself."

Kylie stroked her friend's hair, smiling at the fire that sparked in Blair's eyes. "Nobody would blame you if you didn't tell him," Kylie said. "He really doesn't deserve much consideration."

"But you know I'll tell him now that you've brought it up." She pinched Kylie's thigh, and when she yelped, Blair said, "I owe you about twenty more, but I won't deliver them all at once."

"Admit it. You're a nice person, and you don't want to cause him pain or embarrassment."

Blair laughed wryly. "I'm not sure that's true, but I will tell him. Besides, it'll make me feel superior to be adult about this."

"That's my girl. Selfless to a fault."

"So, are we done?" Blair asked. "I don't wanna have to contact my friends from high school, but I will put an announcement in the Northwestern alumni magazine if you want me to."

"Oh, like people necessarily know how to read when they graduate from Northwestern." That comment earned a much harder pinch this time. "Ow! Hey, don't bruise me!" She rubbed her leg and said, "Now we have to talk about the person who could suffer the most by your being in a lesbian relationship."

"I've already thought about the single men in Los Angeles who'll never get a chance to be with me. They'll just have to chase someone else. I'm yours." She crossed her arms upon Kylie's knees, resting her chin on them, and then gave the doctor a sickeningly sweet smile.

"I mean Mackenzie. This is gonna have a massive, lasting impact on him. You can't just shrug it off."

"I've thought about this—a lot. There are really only two options. Mackenzie can have two parents, or he can have one. I think it's better for him to have two. Yes, I know he'll have some tough times, and I know he'll be teased and maybe even shunned by some kids. But I think the benefits of having two parents outweigh all of that. I really do."

"So…you want me to co-parent with you? That's a huge step. Really huge!"

"I know," she said, gazing into Kylie's eyes. "And I realize that I'm asking you to skip some really big steps—like dating." She smiled back at the crooked grin Kylie was giving her. "Do you mind jumping from friends to co-parents in one big leap?"

"No, I guess not, although it does sound a little crazy when you put it like that."

"It does. And it *is* a little crazy. But this will work out. It can work out for all of us."

The doctor nodded, her expression very thoughtful. "It wouldn't bother me to jump right into being a parent. But I would like to have a little time where it's just the two of us. We're not just gonna be co-parents. We're gonna be…well, we're gonna be whatever we call ourselves, but our relationship has to be rock solid for us to be good parents. This is a lifetime commitment."

"I know that," Blair said, looking equally contemplative. "There's another thing we should discuss."

"What's that?"

"Even though I know this will work, I can't make another 'till death do us part' vow. I promised that to David, but now I realize that the vow doesn't mean anything. If things turn really bad, you break up. That's the reality, and I want to be completely honest with you. All I can promise is that I'll try to be the best partner I can be. I hope to God that we're together for the rest of our lives, but to promise that just isn't realistic." While she spoke, she'd been rubbing Kylie's leg, and Blair could feel the muscles begin to twitch before she was finished. "You don't look like you feel the same way."

Kylie gazed at her for a few moments. Then the doctor closed her eyes and started to stroke Blair's arm. Kylie was obviously deep in thought, and Blair didn't say a word. She simply waited with her stomach in knots, watching Kylie try to make a decision that would affect all three of them. "From a logical standpoint, you're right. Things change, and no one expects a couple to stay together if they grow to hate each other. But this is a big concession for me. A very big one."

"I can see that, just by the expression on your face. You look very conflicted."

"Yeah, that's what I am," Kylie agreed. "I want you, and I want Mackenzie. But I want to make a lifetime commitment to both of you. It might just be words, but they're words that mean a lot to me."

"I understand that," Blair said, "but if you made that commitment, and I robbed you blind and cheated on you, you might just want to break up."

Kylie gave her a half-smile and nodded. "Yeah, I might. I guess it depends on whom you were sleeping with."

"Mmm...your sister, Claire. The straight one."

"Yeah. We're done," Kylie said, her smile growing. "Okay. I see your point. But I've got to know that you *intend* to be with me forever. Can you promise that?"

"Yes. Absolutely. No question. I fully intend to be with you for the rest of my life. I promise you that."

"Are you sure?" Kylie asked, giving her a deadly serious look. "This is a very big decision."

"I'm sure. I'm 100 percent sure that you're the person I want to be with. And I'm 100 percent committed to being a very good partner to you."

"I guess there's only one thing to do," Kylie said.

"What's that?"

"Go to bed and worry about the things I'm sure I've forgotten. You know, I shouldn't admit it, but I'm starting to get used to this idea, and it makes me so happy I feel like dancing."

"Come on," Blair said. She pushed off, using Kylie for support, and then held out her hands to the doctor. "Dance with me."

"Now?" Kylie looked around as if she expected music to start playing.

"Yeah, now. C'mere and hold me." Blair grinned sexily. "You know you want to."

"I do." She put her arms around Blair's waist and shivered when their breasts pressed against each other. "Feels wonderful," she said, threading her fingers through Blair's hair and gently holding her head. Kylie started to move, just shuffling her feet across the stone patio. Blair followed her lead, moving slowly with Kylie's body. "It feels so good to hold you," Kylie murmured. "I love having the baby press against me, too." As if he'd been cued, Mackenzie let out a good one, and Kylie's eyes popped open. "I felt him kick!" She held Blair by the shoulders and squeezed her. "I felt him! I finally felt him!"

Blair hugged her tightly, overcome by the look of radiant joy on Kylie's face. "I could never have picked a better person to fall in love with. You're the woman I didn't know I'd been looking for."

Kylie closed the door to her room, her heart so full of emotion that she feared it would burst. She leaned against the door for a full minute, trying to get her mind around the idea that she and Blair would soon become lovers.

Kylie was a little lightheaded when she started to walk into the bathroom, but she knew it was just a symptom of the giddiness she felt. Her smile was so wide her cheeks hurt, but the magic of the evening was so overpowering that she knew it would linger in her heart for the rest of her life.

Damn, if Blair had told me she could only promise that she'd stay with me a month, I still would have agreed once I felt Mackenzie kick, she thought with a smirk. *I'm so in love with her that I'd risk my heart for one chance in a thousand to make a life with her.*

Instead of going into the bathroom, she opened her window and bent to rest her arms on the sill. Breathing in the early-fall air reminded her that Christmas was coming, and with any luck, Mackenzie would be at home with them to celebrate the New Year. Her mind was filled with an image of the three of them cuddled together on the sofa with her arms tucked around the most important things in her world.

Forcing herself to get ready for bed, she flossed and brushed her teeth, grinning at the goofy expression she couldn't erase from her face. The night was warm, and she pulled the bedspread and the sheet down to the foot of the bed. She climbed in, fluffed one pillow, and then molded the other to the perfect size, tucking her arm around it. Not surprisingly, she was too keyed up to even close her eyes, so she gave herself a pep talk. *You have a full day scheduled, and then you're gonna come home to Blair. You're gonna need every bit of energy you can summon if things go according to plan, so you'd better turn off that brain and get some sleep.* The talk did the trick, and in minutes, she was sound asleep, the goofy grin still plastered across her face.

⤚

Next door, Blair was also wound up like a top. When she entered her room, she didn't even consider going to sleep. Instead, she turned on her CD player and lay down on her still-made bed. Her head was resting on her arm, and with the other hand, she stroked and patted her belly, communing with Mackenzie. "I think everything's gonna work out, Mac. Mama Kylie's gonna take a chance on us. I don't know about you, but I feel awfully lucky," she said, speaking in the soft, soothing tone she used just for him.

Her body felt as if a weak electric current had been passed through it and she was still jittery from the jolt. Her hands shook noticeably, and she had to force herself to refrain from her insistent impulse to go next door and climb into bed with Kylie. It had felt so incredibly wonderful to be held and caressed while they danced that she still couldn't believe Kylie had the fortitude to go straight into her own room. "I guess that's how people get to be doctors, huh, Mackenzie? Commitment and determination."

She smiled, thinking about how adorable Kylie had been when she'd felt the baby kick. It was a moment Blair knew she'd remember for the rest of her life, and her heart ached with tenderness for the gentle woman she loved. "No matter what, she'll always be there for us, Mackenzie. If there's one person in the world you can always count on, it's your Mama Kylie."

With the thought of the smile that had become fixed to Kylie's face, Blair found herself drifting off, still lying atop the neatly made bed, music playing softly in the background.

⤚

The next night, Kylie called Blair from her car. "Hi, sorry I've been tied up, but I'm finally on my way home. Do you need me to stop at the store for anything?"

"No, I bought you a great vegetable salad. We're waiting patiently for you."

"Damn, that sounds nice. Where have you been all my life?"

"I've been a confused straight woman, Doctor. Do you think there's any hope for me?"

Kylie laughed. "Yeah, I think I can help turn you into an even more-confused straight woman."

"Hurry home. I'm ready to start."

⌐

Kylie got home a few minutes later, and upon seeing her, Blair knew Kylie'd had a tough day. Meeting her by the front door, Blair had her arms around her before Kylie could put her briefcase down. "First, I love you," Blair said. "Second, you look beat. Go put on something sinfully comfortable and come back here so I can spoil you."

Giving her a squeeze, Kylie said, "I need a shower first. I would have taken one at the hospital, but I wanted to get home sooner. I'm just afraid I'll starve to death if I don't get something to eat in the next thirty seconds."

"Pretty dramatic today, aren't ya?" Blair patted Kylie on the butt. "Go put on your robe and have some dinner. Then you can take your shower."

Kylie looked indecisive, but then nodded. "Okay. I'm getting a headache from hunger, and that's just dumb when there's a salad waiting for me."

"A vegetable salad," Blair said, "with all of your favorites."

"Poppy seed dressing?" Kylie asked hopefully.

"Yep. Now scoot!"

⌐

Kylie walked into the kitchen just as Blair was sitting down. "Well, this looks delightful," the doctor said. She sat and gave Blair's shoulder a squeeze. "Is there anything better than coming home from a hard day and having someone tell you she loves you...*and*...that she has dinner ready for you?"

"Yes, there is," Blair said, smiling sexily, "but we're not at the point where I can greet you at the door stark naked with a pizza in my hands, ready to worship your body *while* you eat. But if I get this girlfriend job, I promise I can think of ways to make you never want to leave the house."

"So..." Kylie leaned back in her chair a little and pointed the tines of her fork at Blair. "You're still interested in the girlfriend job, huh?"

"Oh, yes. I need this job desperately." She leered at her. "I'll do anything—and I do mean anything—to get it."

"You know, I've never had a pregnant woman look at me as if she wanted to chew my clothes off." She nodded thoughtfully. "I like it."

"If I get the job, I promise to help you fulfill every possible fantasy you've ever had about my pregnant sisters."

"You were never in the circus, were you?"

"No, but I took gymnastics all through high school. Will that do?"

"Close enough," Kylie said, smiling. She reached out and took Blair's hand. "What's got you so cheery and playful tonight?"

"Well…" Blair let her gaze shift down, lingering a while on the doctor's body. "I thought you might be ready to make up your mind about the girlfriend thing. And if you did, I thought we could…celebrate."

"You're certainly a girl with initiative," Kylie said, tingling a little at the look in Blair's eyes.

"You have no idea." Blair leaned forward and pressed her arms against her breasts, making them nearly pour out of the V-neck sweater she wore.

Kylie's eyes looked as though they'd fly from her head. "I've got a few more questions for you, and then I guess I'm ready." She swallowed, and Blair could see her throat constrict with anxiety.

"More questions? I think I can make you forget your questions. Isn't a hands-on demonstration worth more than a few theoretical questions?"

"I…I have some worries," Kylie said. She shifted in her chair and tried to concentrate on her salad. "Uhm, I think I'm convinced that you've thought of all of the practical realities of being in a lesbian relationship, but there are a few…more down-to-earth issues."

Blair took her hand and noticed it was trembling a little. "What is it? You can tell me."

"I'm…I don't mean to make this sound crass, but how do you know you'll enjoy having sex with a woman? I mean, it's a very different kinda thing."

Blair blinked at her. "Have you ever had sex with a man?"

"Yeah…kinda."

"How do you kinda have sex with a man?"

"It's…not that difficult. I was in high school, and a guy named I.V. talked me into it."

Blair giggled and put up a hand. "No, wait! You had sex with a guy named Ivy? Kylie, that was a girl!"

"He was not! His name was Chapin Danforth Hollingswood IV, and everyone called him I.V., like the Roman numerals."

"Lake Forest," Blair said, shaking her head. "Go on, tell me about I.V."

"We were in his car, and I was turned on out of my mind. He had a Porsche, which isn't the best car in the world to have sex in, but he put the top down, and that gave us a little room to maneuver. Anyway, he climbed on top of me, and I somehow managed to get my legs up, and he…couldn't get in."

"He couldn't get in? Was it his first time?"

"I guess so. I mean…I didn't ask him, but he acted like he'd never been there before."

"Ooh…he gave you a clue."

"Not knowing if he was inside was a pretty big one. Anyway, I was so wet I'm sure he had a hard time figuring out exactly where to go, so he just kept poking at me and sliding around. It started to hurt like hell! He kept asking if he was in, and I finally said yes just to get him to stop ramming into my labia."

"Let me guess the happy ending," Blair said. "As soon as he thought he was in, he…finished."

Kylie acted as if she were pulling the trigger of a gun. "You got it. A night to remember."

"I hate to tell you this, but you haven't really had sex with a man." She smiled at the doctor and took her hand, kissing it tenderly.

"Why does it matter?"

"It doesn't, really, but I was trying to make a point. This might not be true for most women, but for me, it took a lot of work to figure out how to be sexually satisfied by my male partners. I properly trained every man I ever slept with, and if I do say so myself, I helped each of them become better lovers."

"So, you think you can do the same for me?" Kylie asked, looking not only confused, but slightly offended.

"No, no. That's my point. I'm certainly not an expert, but I think it'll be easier to have good sex with you. You have the same parts I do, and you know how to use them." She raised an eyebrow and asked, "You *do* know how to use them, don't you?"

"Expertly," Kylie nodded, smiling confidently.

"That's my point. I know how to touch myself, and I can't imagine it'll be that hard to figure out how to touch you. You already know how to make love to a woman, so with your experience and my initiative, we should be set."

"It's not just about technique, Blair."

"I know that. Technique is the least important thing. But if that's an issue for you, you shouldn't worry about it. I'm sure you'll be able to please me, and I think I'll figure out how to please you. Sex for me is all about touching and stroking and rubbing and finding the things your partner likes. It doesn't matter if it's a man or a woman. It's using my body to show my feelings. And I have very strong, very loving feelings for you. This will work out."

"Are you sure?" Kylie asked, her blue eyes fixed on Blair.

"Yes, I'm sure. Now, finish your salad, and let's get busy!"

⌐

After dinner, Kylie took a shower, and when she emerged, Blair was lying on the doctor's bed, looking about as good as Kylie had ever seen her look. She was wearing a simple white terrycloth robe, and she'd obviously showered as well. Her hair was a little damp, and it clung to her creamy white neck, which looked long, lovely, and very kissable. Her cheeks were pink and freshly scrubbed, and her eyes were clear and alert. She was smiling at Kylie, not in a lascivious way, but in a way that made the doctor feel welcome and wanted. "Hi," Kylie said. "You look fantastic." She sat down on the edge of the bed and put her hand on Blair's smooth leg. "I've said it before, but I have to say it again: you are an uncommonly beautiful woman."

"You'd better not say that to all of the uncommonly beautiful women you find in your bed."

"You're the first. I told my exes they were marginally attractive. That's as high as I've ever gone."

"Such a good liar." Blair ran the tip of her finger along the neckline of Kylie's top, causing a riot of goose bumps to follow. "You're gonna get overheated. Maybe you'd better take off your outer layer of clothes."

Kylie looked down at herself. She was wearing a white tank top and a pair of blue scrub pants. "I only have one layer on."

"I know."

Now Blair was giving her "the look," and Kylie had to force herself to stand up to escape Blair's magnetic pull. "Don't be mad," Kylie said, "but I still wanna talk about a few things."

"Come here," Blair said, gesturing. Kylie sat down again, and Blair started to stroke her friend's leg. "I don't care if we sleep together tonight or tomorrow or the next day or the day after that. I want you to be sure about this. I never want to push you into anything you're not ready for."

"Do you understand why I'm concerned about having sex?" she asked, looking so earnest that Blair wanted to kiss her until her eyes crossed.

"Yes, of course, I do. You're obviously not very talented in this area, and you don't want me to find out how inept—"

"Don't you even suggest such a thing! I'm very, very capable in this area, and you're gonna eat those words!"

"I certainly hope so. But if you're not worried about yourself, you must think that I won't be able to please you."

"That's not it at all! I want to make sure this is something you're really drawn to. What if you don't respond like you think you will? What if you can't get turned on by my body? I'll jump out a window if you don't enjoy our lovemaking."

Blair lay down and pulled Kylie with her. Kylie's dark head rested on her shoulder, and Blair started to stroke her hair. "You've got to relax about this. I'm sorry I'm being flip, but I don't have a concern in the world, and it puzzles me that you do."

"I know, I know. I'm not usually a worrier, but…"

"But why now?"

"'Cause this means so much," she said plaintively. "We're making this huge jump from friends to lovers and parents and partners. Life partners. Life, Blair. It's such a big leap that I'm afraid you're assuming things that might not be true."

"What am I assuming?"

Clearly frustrated, Kylie's voice rose into a near whine. "You act as if everything will be fine. All of a sudden, you're this huge optimist, and that's not how you usually are."

Blair ran her fingertip all along Kylie's jaw, feeling the muscles there tense and release. "We might have a few problems, but it won't be anything we can't work through. I know how important this is, but you can't just ask questions and have all of your fears evaporate based on my answers. You have to trust me. You have to put your trust in me and in my knowledge of myself. I'm asking you to take a leap. A leap of faith."

"Blair, I'd leap off a cliff for you." Kylie grasped her tightly and hugged her. "I'm just afraid."

"I know. I know that." They hugged for a long time, the room filled with their silence. Finally, Blair said, "It'll be all right. I know it will." She pulled back and looked into the deep blue eyes. "I've been fantasizing about you for a while now, and every time I do, I'm so turned on I could burst. I'm ready to stop imagining and start acting."

The doctor's eyes opened wide. "You fantasize about me?"

"Of course, I do. Every night." She cocked her head. "Don't you fantasize about me?"

Kylie actually blushed, forcing Blair to stifle a laugh. The doctor's eyes shifted, and she looked like a felon being shown the lie detector test she'd just failed. "Sometimes."

"Only sometimes?" Blair stared at her lips and slowly drew near. "Only sometimes?" Kylie could feel the warm breath on her mouth, and she squirmed with desire. "Who else do you fantasize about?"

"No one! I think about you every minute of the day. I can hardly concentrate at work anymore. I've got to make love to you or take a leave of absence!"

Soft kisses greeted Kylie's declaration, and as the kisses continued to flow, her body started to relax. They kissed for a long time—lazy, soft kisses that made Kylie feel loved and very desired.

"God, I love you," Kylie whispered. Her head was resting on a pillow, and she pulled back just enough to look into Blair's eyes. "I know I have to jump in, but I'm so afraid of being hurt."

"I'm afraid, too, but loving you is worth getting past my fears. It's worth anything, Kylie. Anything."

"That's the nicest thing anyone's ever said to me." Blue eyes welled up, and Blair kissed the soft lids.

"It'll all work out. I promise. We'll work at this, Kylie. We'll have problems, like any couple does, but we'll work through them because we love each other."

"Promise?"

"I do." Blair took Kylie's hand and pressed it against her breast. "With all my heart."

"Will you sleep with me tonight?" Kylie whispered, her fingers gentle on Blair's breast, feeling her heartbeat.

"Yes." Blair kissed her again, turning up the heat while Kylie softly moaned.

The kiss lasted a long time, and Kylie was nearly senseless, but she managed to say, "I really need to sleep. It's past ten, and I have to be up by five-thirty. I don't wanna rush this. I wanna spend all night loving you."

"Call in sick?" Blair asked, looking like a hopeful truant.

"You know I can't do that, even though I wish I could. But tomorrow's Friday, and I don't have one thing to do on Saturday."

"How about Sunday?"

"Free as a bird."

"Not anymore, you're not. You're mine. All mine."

❧

The next night, Kylie came home to a house that looked like a set for a romantic movie. Soft, mellow jazz played on the stereo, and she smelled something delicious coming from the kitchen. She went in and opened the oven, finding a crown roast of lamb and some rosemary potatoes.

The dining room table was formally set, and she knew she didn't own any of the things that adorned it. Tall, pillar candles were burning, imbuing the room with a slightly spicy scent. "Blair? Where are you hiding?" she called out.

"I'm not hiding. I'm getting ready for dinner."

Kylie walked by Blair's room, slightly surprised the door was closed. "Should I be in formalwear?" the doctor asked, only partially kidding.

"No need. Just be comfortable."

"Do you have the dogs with you? They're awfully quiet."

"They're at the babysitter's."

"The babysitter? The dogs have a babysitter?"

"They do now. I didn't want them to bother us, so I hired someone to take them to the dog park. The sitter is gonna keep them at her house until we come get them."

"You're full of surprises."

"Lucky for you. Now, go get ready for dinner."

Kylie walked into her room and blinked at the remarkable number of large, burning candles, each inside a hurricane globe. In the middle of the bed, Blair had mounded a pile of red rose petals and shaped them into a heart. The entire room was suffused with their scent. Kylie changed into a comfortable pair of jeans and a cotton shirt and then walked back to Blair's door. "I promise I won't expect this every night, but anytime you feel like it—"

The door opened, and Blair smiled, the mere curve of her mouth making Kylie's legs a little wobbly. Blair was wearing her dressy outfit, the one the doctor had given to her on the trip to Chicago, and looked even more beautiful in it than she had that weekend. "I wanted to make this a special night. God knows we've waited long enough."

Blair laughed, and Kylie bent and kissed her tenderly. "You look almost perfect. Just one little thing's missing." She reached into her pocket and took out a necklace, quickly fastening it around Blair's neck.

Her hand went to her throat, and then Blair stepped over to the mirror so she could see her gift. "Oh, Kylie, it's beautiful." She fingered the small heart, outlined with diamonds. "Thank you." She stood on her tiptoes and kissed Kylie, murmuring, "Thank you so much."

Kylie made sure the clasp was at the exact center of Blair's neck and then nodded. "Perfect. Diamonds suit you."

"Why has no one said that to me before?" Blair asked, laughing. "I've always thought diamonds were my best stone." She kissed Kylie again and then gave her a robust hug. "I didn't buy anything for you. You need something sparkly, too."

"The way your eyes sparkle when you look at me is all I need. That's the greatest gift I'll ever receive."

Blair looked up at her. "Are you sure you were a science nerd? You sound like a poet."

"Well, that *was* my best material. Now, let's go eat that fabulous dinner you made."

"Fabulous dinner I bought. I'm not a great cook, but I can shop with the best of 'em."

They'd had a long, leisurely dinner with Kylie savoring a glass of the excellent Côtes du Rhône Blair had bought for her. "This was a very nice relationship kickoff dinner," Kylie said when they'd finished. She started to stand and gather the plates. "Wanna help me clean up?"

Blair gave her a deadpan look. "Now I know you're forty 'cause the very thought of choosing to clean the kitchen rather than make love is positively geriatric."

Kylie took Blair's hands in hers and smiled. "I don't care if coyotes chew through the door and come in here and eat the leftovers. I was kidding. Only kidding."

"I swear I can never tell!" Blair insisted. "You're just the type to want to clean up first."

"You don't know me very well," Kylie said, her voice dropping into a sexy timbre. "But you're going to."

"Now you're talking. Race you to the bedroom!"

Kylie caught her before she'd taken a step. "I'd like to take a shower. I guess we could do that together, but I'd like the first time I see you naked to be a little more romantic than stripping in the bathroom."

"You've seen me naked. Just not all the parts at the same time."

"Well, you haven't seen me. I'll take a shower and meet you in the bedroom. I'll be the woman lying on a bed of roses." She kissed Blair on the top of her head. "I love them, by the way. And you, of course."

"I've already showered, so I'll be waiting for you. Make it snappy, good lookin'." She patted Kylie on the butt, receiving a wink in return.

When Kylie was finished, she slipped into a blue T-shirt and a pair of print silk boxers. When she opened the bathroom door, Blair was lying on the bed, and Kylie stopped short. "I...I'm not sure how to react. I've never had my dreams come true."

Blair was lying on her side with one leg drawn up slightly. A hand supported her head, and her blonde hair shone in the warm candlelight. She drew her arm through the rose petals, and the scent wafted up to Kylie, making her smile when she breathed in. "I kinda thought you'd be...ooh...naked," Blair said.

"Unh-uh," Kylie said, shaking her head. "I'm not...shy exactly, but I was a little nervous about what to wear. But then I thought it'd be fun to have you undress me, so I put on my jammies."

"You think too much, Doctor Mackenzie." Blair was wearing a turquoise silk robe, which draped across the curves of her voluptuous body, and the visual stimuli were almost too much for Kylie's brain to process. "Come over here and kiss me."

Kylie did, sliding across the bed to nestle against Blair. They molded their bodies together as best they could, and Kylie rested a hand on Blair's hip. "From this day forward, I will never say no to that request," Kylie promised.

Blair's mouth quirked in a smile as she gently patted Kylie's cheek. "It's hard for me to believe that someone as wonderful as you wants to be with me," Blair said. "I feel so blessed."

Laughing softly, Kylie said, "Hey, I'm the one who feels lucky. I've wanted a woman like you in my life since I was in high school. You were worth waiting for."

"What about that kiss? You haven't forgotten your vow already, have you?"

Kylie didn't reply. She smiled gently and drew Blair close. With great tenderness, she brushed her lips across Blair's, returning again and again, barely letting their mouths touch, holding back until Blair started to move towards her. The moment she felt Blair move, Kylie slipped a hand behind Blair's head and pressed her forward. Her mouth opened, welcoming Kylie inside. The brunette started to explore, letting her tongue search and probe with a determined insistence.

After a very long time, Blair pulled away, resting her forehead on Kylie's chin and taking in some shallow breaths. "I've never had my breath taken away so thoroughly," Blair panted.

"Get used to it," Kylie murmured, trying to nudge her way back to Blair's lips.

Blair stroked Kylie's back, trying to slow her down. "I don't...I don't have my usual stamina," Blair warned. "I get out of breath pretty easily."

"Oops. I forgot. I guess we have to make some adjustments, huh?"

"Not many. I'm uncomfortable if I lie flat on my back for long, but that's about it." She put her hand on Kylie's cheek. "More kisses."

Kylie smiled at her, charmed by Blair's calm, casual demeanor. Holding her in her arms, Kylie kissed her softly and gently, forcing herself to go slower than her raging libido demanded. She spent a very long time memorizing Blair's delicate features with her lips, lavishing attention on the brow, cheeks, nose, eyelids, and chin. Then Kylie moved down to Blair's neck, so lovely and appealing. By the time the doctor had worked her way around to the ears, Blair was squirming and moaning softly.

"I like this. You can do this all night if you'd like."

"I just might." Kylie leaned over her and smiled broadly. "You have the most kissable neck in the universe."

Blair tilted her head and swept her golden hair up with her hand, exposing even more of the pale, soft skin. "It's all yours."

Kylie got back to work, kissing and suckling and taking soft nips of the flesh, feeling her heart start to pound harder as Blair's body began to move slowly, grinding against her own. "You're turning me on *so* much," Blair breathed. "My heart's racing."

Kylie pressed her lips to the silk that covered Blair's heart, holding still and letting the quick beat thrum against her lips. She moved slowly until her lips were nestled at the top of Blair's ample cleavage. Kylie's hand was on the tie of the robe, and questioning blue eyes peeked up, meeting Blair's. The blonde smiled and stroked the dark head. She nodded, her smile growing when Kylie's eyes lit up in anticipation.

Tugging on the tie, Kylie smoothed her hand along the fabric, spreading it open and revealing Blair's luscious body. The brunette stared, her mouth slightly open, taking in all of the wonders displayed before her. "You are so remarkably beautiful," she whispered. Then her hands were everywhere, stroking gently. She bent and kissed Blair's belly and then tapped on it with two fingers. "Go to sleep, Mackenzie. And don't worry when you hear your mommy screaming."

Blair grasped Kylie's shirt and pulled on it, with Kylie compliantly coming along. "Yes?" she asked, her head propped up on her hand.

"I feel awfully naked."

"You are naked, but there's nothing awful about it. Awesome, but not awful."

"I'd feel less naked if you were more naked."

Kylie immediately reached for her top to pull it off, but Blair stilled her hands. "I've been fantasizing about undressing you, but it feels so good to lie here and let you kiss me that I don't have the energy."

"How about a compromise?" Kylie sat up, pulled her top off, and then removed her shorts, revealing a lavender satin bra and panties. "You can take the rest off later."

"Such a brilliant mind," Blair said, patting her head. "It's sad you waste it on saving lives when you could be using it to have sex all day."

"I might change careers." She stood up and put her hands on her hips. "I hate to be so pragmatic, but we're gonna have rose petals...everywhere. Let me take the bedspread off."

"You are pragmatic, but pragmatic can be beautiful." She got up and helped Kylie carefully fold the bedspread so the petals stayed put. When they were finished, Blair lay on her side, facing Kylie, who quickly mirrored the position. Blair trailed her hand up and down Kylie's body, the experience made even more sensual by the deliciously smooth satin. "Ooh...a thong," Blair purred. "Let's see..." She reached behind Kylie and palmed her ass, giving her a hearty squeeze. "Yep, you've got the body for it."

"I don't like to brag," Kylie said, smiling cockily, "but I've been told it's one of my best features."

"What's your best?" Blair asked, giving her a long kiss.

"That decision will be yours. You've got the only vote that counts."

"I like the way you think. Now, where were you? Right about here, I think." Slipping her hand behind Kylie's head, she pulled it down until it rested between her breasts. "Was that right?"

"Good memory." Kylie placed a few dozen butterfly kisses on the fair skin and then gently rolled her partner onto her back. Kylie pulled Blair's arm from the robe and turned her onto her other side. Now they were back to front, and Kylie started to work on Blair's neck once more, smiling at the soft mew of disappointment. "Don't worry," she murmured. "I won't ignore anything. Promise."

"But my breasts keep telling me they want to be kissed. You don't wanna make 'em mad."

Kylie slipped her hand under one of the pale mounds, hefting it a little. "Poor breast," she said, fighting her desire to scramble over Blair's body and drown in the succulent flesh. "I'll get to you. I promise."

"Fine. Go ahead and worship the rest of me. I'll learn to bear it."

Kylie did just that, working slowly and patiently, covering Blair's entire back with gentle and not-so-gentle kisses. The doctor paid rapt attention, coming back to every spot that appeared particularly sensitive or ticklish. She didn't torture Blair, but Kylie did keep turning up the heat, making the blonde woman groan and twitch her hips in frustration.

She had a ferocious grip on the sheets, but Kylie could occasionally feel the muscles in Blair's arms start to relax. That's when Kylie would find one of those particularly sensitive spots and swipe at it with her tongue or bite it just hard enough to make Blair's hips buck. Kylie enjoyed the delightful torment more than she could believe, keeping Blair on edge the entire time.

Finally, Blair flipped over onto her back, staring at Kylie with desire-filled eyes. "The front is getting jealous of the back. There's gonna be trouble."

"Ooh…" She ran her hands lightly over Blair, touching every part, but not lingering anywhere. "Everyone's gonna be happy," she promised, speaking directly to the neglected body parts. "There are plenty of kisses for everyone. Just wait your turn."

Blair gurgled out another protest when Kylie scooted down to the end of the bed and spoke to her partner's feet. "I hear that you guys feel neglected," the doctor said, as if talking to small children. "Don't worry. Kylie's here, and you're gonna feel very well loved."

"It's not my feet that are throbbing," Blair moaned. "My feet aren't engorged with blood, swollen and pulsing and dying for attention."

"I need to make sure that doesn't happen." She sucked a toe into her mouth, grinning up at Blair. "Can't be too careful," she mumbled, her mouth very busy.

Despite Blair's earnest pleas, Kylie worked over the front of the blonde's body with the same single-minded determination, managing to keep Blair on the brink of madness for what seemed like hours.

After working her way up to the apex of Blair's thighs, Kylie lingered there for a few moments, reveling in the scent of her partner's desire. With great regret, Kylie moved up to kiss a pale shoulder and then quickly made her way down Blair's arm, spending extra time on the crook of her elbow and her pulse point.

By this time, Blair was weakly thrashing about on the bed, trying to position herself so that Kylie would finally love the parts that most needed attention. Finally, Blair asked, "Do you love me?"

"Yes. I love you."

"Then kiss my breasts! I ache for you. Don't make me wait anymore."

Kylie leaned over and kissed her hard, moving against Blair's body. When the brunette sat up, her face reflected rabid desire and true appreciation of the delights displayed before her. Her hands were steady as a rock as she brought them to rest just an inch above Blair's breasts, trailing her fingernails over the skin with the lightest touch imaginable. "You are so stunningly beautiful," Kylie murmured, continuing to slide her warm hands over Blair's breasts with an achingly gentle touch.

Her own hands were not nearly as steady as Kylie's had been, but Blair fought through her nervousness, placed her hands on Kylie's sides, and then brought them up to unfasten the front closure of her bra. The doctor's mouth quirked into a grin as she watched Blair struggle a little and then succeed in her goal. As the flesh spilled into her hands, Blair's smile quickly grew to match Kylie's. "Wow. Just…wow," Blair said. "My imagination sucks."

Kylie sat up, and her bra fell from her shoulders. She braced herself on one hand as she discarded it. Placing a hand behind Blair's shoulder, Kylie drew her up close— inseparably close—and kissed her, the passion flaring once again as their breasts slid together, rock-hard nipples pressing into pliant flesh.

Their kisses were so passionate that the women tumbled over, back to the bed, never breaking the contact. Blair's hands moved over her lover, feeling every delightful curve of Kylie's body. Returning again and again to her ass, Blair grasped it and stroked the soft skin. Unable to stand even the small strip of cloth that separated them, Blair stuck her thumbs in the waistband of the thong and pushed. Kylie helped by lifting her hips and then tugging the garment off.

Now two completely bare bodies rubbed against each other, both women thrumming with desire. Despite Blair's tenacious hold, Kylie started to move down, and when Blair realized her partner's destination, the blonde placed her hands on Kylie's shoulders and urged her along.

Kylie stopped and gazed at Blair's magnificent breasts. Pointing her tongue, Kylie flicked at the hard nipples until Blair threaded her fingers through her dark hair and urged her to open her mouth. As soon as Kylie did, her mouth was filled to overflowing with the alabaster flesh, both women simultaneously moaning in pleasure.

Cupping one of the breasts in her hand, Kylie looked up, her smile radiant and her eyes a bit glazed. "I've never been happier."

"Why don't you show me that you're a breast woman?"

Kylie managed a rakish grin and lowered her mouth, keeping their eyes locked. She pulled a swollen nipple inside and then laved it with her tongue, sucking and tugging on it, gently raking her teeth over it. Blair's eyes fluttered closed, and then her head dropped back against a pillow. Kylie continued to work, having to clutch her thighs together rhythmically to get some much-needed pressure on her aching clit. She suckled as if her life depended on it, filling her mouth with the tender flesh.

Blair squirmed under the intense ministrations, her soft moans the only sounds she uttered. Kylie moved from one breast to the other, kissing and suckling each with equal fervor, her desire for the writhing woman growing stronger with each passing moment.

As her need grew, Blair was unable to lie still, continually trying to force more of her throbbing breast into Kylie's hungry mouth. Blair stroked her lover's dark hair with one hand, while cupping one of her own breasts in the other, offering herself up to Kylie's voracious need.

The pair was in such a frenzy that Blair lost track of her position. After a while, though, she realized she was on her back and had been for some time. She raised her knees to take some of the pressure off, but she was beginning to feel the discomfort. Kylie sensed her distraction and looked up. The doctor's eyes were barely focused, and she asked thickly, "Okay?"

"Back hurts," Blair said, wincing a little now that she was fully aware of the rest of her body.

"Can't have that." Kylie looked around, trying to figure out how to solve the problem. "I've got an idea."

She helped Blair sit up and then asked her to scoot down the bed a little. When she did, Kylie sat behind her, wrapping her legs around Blair's hips. "Nice backrest," Blair said, sighing with pleasure as she settled back against Kylie.

"Nice view," Kylie countered. She ran her nails lightly up the nape of Blair's neck and into her hair, kissing the goose bumps in their wake, lingering here and there, trying to wait a few moments to make sure her partner was comfortable. When she started to squirm because of the kisses, Kylie knew Blair's back was feeling better and got busy once again.

She started using her hands to play with Blair's breasts, finding the experience just as enjoyable as mouthing them. They were so heavy and full and so exquisitely sensitive that the most gentle caress caused Blair's hips to sway sexily. Kylie was remarkably careful, but she was equally relentless with her explorations.

While Kylie continued to work, Blair's knees lifted until they were resting against Kylie's legs. The doctor saw a hand try to slip stealthily between open thighs. She grasped the wandering hand and brought it to her lips for a kiss. "That's mine," Kylie whispered. "No trespassing."

"I'll beg if I have to," Blair moaned pitifully. "You've got to touch me."

"I am touching you." She gave each nipple a pinch that made Blair squeal.

As she grasped Kylie's hand, Blair said firmly, "I want you here," and tried to force it between her legs.

Successfully resisting, Kylie buried her face in Blair's neck and nipped at her skin, marking her lightly all along the flesh. "I wanna be there, too," the brunette whispered. "I wanna make you happy. I want it to be *so* good."

Her hands slid down Blair's body, and Kylie smiled when a pair of knees lifted even higher, hips blindly thrusting toward her touch. Trying to soothe her partner, Kylie gently patted and stroked the fine blonde hair that covered Blair's mound. Blair groaned in frustration, but it was obvious that Kylie wasn't going to be rushed. She continued to touch Blair lightly and delicately in the gentlest way, letting her get used to the caresses before moving on.

When Blair settled down, Kylie gently spread her lover's outer lips and slid a finger down each side of her clitoris. "Ooh," Blair groaned. "Harder, please!'

Kylie suckled her earlobe for a moment, feeling the woman in her arms shiver roughly. "Don't you wanna take this nice and slow? I wanna touch you and touch you and touch you. Won't that feel better? We'll let it build up until you can't bear to wait another moment. Don't you want that?" Kylie's hands had remained where they were, holding Blair gently, but they were still.

"I can't bear to wait another moment now," Blair groaned. "Kylie, please, I feel like I'm on fire."

"Nooo..." Kylie soothed. "You're not on fire. We're just getting started. Relax against me, and let me touch you." She slipped her fingers up and down, caressing with the force of a whisper on the wind. Blair thrust her hips in vain and then let her head drop against Kylie's chest. "That's right...that's right...relax." Blair's brow was furrowed in frustration, but Kylie knew her partner's unhappiness was only temporary.

Kylie continued to gently rub the slippery flesh, sometimes using her fingernails to delve deeply into the folds. Soon, Blair's pleasure was evident in her moans, and she slowly moved against Kylie's fingers, riding a high that Blair never wanted to end.

The sensation built and built, but it escalated so smoothly and slowly that Kylie didn't realize Blair had wrapped her hands around the doctor's forearms and was squeezing her tight. Kylie was so engulfed by the pleasure of the experience that she wouldn't have known if time stood still. She was touching Blair in the most intimate way possible, and Kylie had never been happier in her life.

The quality and pitch of Blair's utterances changed, and Kylie knew her lover was close. Touching her wetness with slightly more pressure, Kylie increased the pace, moving faster and faster until Blair cried out in a loud voice and convulsed, thrusting her hips so forcefully that her ass slapped against Kylie's open legs. The orgasm seemed to last for a very long time, and Kylie held on tight, lightly stroking the quivering flesh until Blair finally relaxed against her—completely limp.

Kylie wrapped her arms around the exhausted woman and cuddled her tightly to her chest, murmuring soft, sweet words in her ear. The doctor held her for a long time, the only sign of life in Blair her still-rapid breathing. Finally, Blair stirred, stretching her legs and then her arms. After another cat-like stretch, she flopped back against Kylie's body. Blair draped an arm across her face and said, "I am dying, Egypt, dying." She craned her neck to look into Kylie's eyes. "What's the rest of it?"

Kylie laughed softly. "Uhm, something about not wanting to die until Cleopatra gives him a few thousand more kisses."

"Oh! Right! Let me think a second. I helped my mom when her theater company produced this one when I was in high school. I'm sure I know it." She lay still for a bit and then said, "'Only I here importune death awhile, until of many thousand kisses the poor last I lay upon thy lips.'" She snuck another look at Kylie and said, "I feel just like Antony. Only I don't really think I'm dying."

"You're the first woman who's ever quoted Shakespeare to me after an orgasm. Is this something I should expect?"

"Only when you deserve it," Blair said, smirking. "That one deserves the entire St. Crispin's Day battle speech from *Henry V*, but I only know a few lines from it: 'We few…we happy few…'" She looked up at Kylie and giggled. "This is fun, isn't it?"

Kylie kissed Blair's ears and her neck again, once more making her shiver. "It sure is," Kylie said. She leaned close and whispered, "You seem to possess some definite bisexual tendencies. I hope I'm not overconfident, but I think I flipped your switch."

"If I'd been any more turned on, my central nervous system would have shorted out."

"You know, that can't really happen. I mean, you could possibly have a stroke, but it's not technically the same as shorting out an electrical system."

"How long have we been lovers?" Blair asked in an apparent non sequitur.

"Mmm…about an hour, I'd guess. Why?"

"'Cause you've already used up your allotment of 'I'm a doctor, and I know lots of stuff,'" she said, laughing softly. "I picked you for your looks, not your brain."

"Aw…do you think I'm pretty?"

Blair swiveled her head around to look at her partner. "Are you kidding? Haven't I told you so a thousand times?"

"Uhm, I don't think you've ever told me. Do you?"

Turning onto her side as well as she could, Blair looked up with her mouth open. "God, yes! I think you're one of the most beautiful women I've ever seen! You're…you're fantastic looking, Kylie, and I can't believe I haven't told you!"

"I don't think you have. I'd remember."

Blair slapped herself on the forehead. "I feel like an idiot. You're always telling me how pretty you think I am. Why haven't I done the same for you?"

"I don't know. It doesn't bother me that you haven't. I was just wondering."

"You don't have to wonder anymore." Blair gave her a luminous smile and said, "I think you're absolutely gorgeous, and I promise I'll tell you every time it strikes me." She pondered the issue for a moment and said, "You know, I guess I'm used to lovers telling me what they think about my body and my face. Men don't seem to care what you think about how they look. As long as you tell them they have a fantastic penis, they're happy."

"Well, I'd like to think my vulva was the nicest one you'd ever had."

"I'm not the type to rush to judgment. I need to take a good, long look. Now would be good, I think."

"Now works for me," Kylie agreed, looking eager and willing.

"We just have to figure out how to get this ungainly body around yours. Got any ideas?"

Kylie scratched her head, looking a little embarrassed. "You know, in my fantasies, I'm always making love to you. I've never worked out the geometry."

"In my fantasies, I'm making love to you, but I'm not pregnant. I told you my imagination sucked!"

"This isn't a difficult proposition. Let's just do this the easy way. We can get more creative later."

"What's the easy way?"

Kylie climbed out from behind her and placed a couple of pillows down. "Lie on your side and rest against those. I'll be right back." She was back in a flash, carrying Blair's body pillow. "I'll put this behind your back to give you some support, and then we're good to go."

"Where do you fit?"

"Right in front of you." She lay on her side, facing Blair, sharing the same pillows.

"I like this," Blair said. "Looking at you this close up is a treat. So easy to kiss you, too." She put her arm behind Kylie and pulled her close. They kissed for a long time, slowly stoking the embers that had begun to cool. "Such beautiful breasts," Blair murmured, touching them with the backs of her fingers. "And sooo sensitive." The nipples popped up immediately, red and ripe like a pair of raspberries.

"I've been on the verge of orgasm for about half an hour," Kylie whispered. "If I'm not sensitive, then you were right about nervous systems shorting out."

"See? Everybody thinks laypeople don't know anything until a nervous system blows."

"You know, I think I need to protect mine. Why don't we get down to business?"

"I thought we were."

"I swear that I love to be touched and stroked, but I can't wait much longer. I'm in pain."

Blair ran her hand through Kylie's curls, looking concerned. "Are you really?"

"Well…maybe not exactly pain…"

"You big faker. You're not getting off so easily. You tortured me forever!"

"I know, but I was torturing myself at the same time. Can't you give me a little break?"

Blair gave her a facetiously scolding look. "Oh, all right, but not until I kiss those breasts."

Bending slightly, she started to reach, but Kylie scooted up to present them. "Always willing to help a good cause. Ooh…damn, I can't believe how sensitive they are."

Blair looked up, her mouth full of breast. "Too hard?" she asked once her mouth was empty.

"No, not at all." Kylie urged her lover's head right back where it had been. "I'm very good about saying what I need. I'll tell you if I don't like something, and you'll be able to tell how much I do like something."

Blair gave her a wry smile and said, "I don't know why I haven't guessed that. You're a gabby little thing." After wrinkling her nose at Kylie, Blair got to work. She wasn't tentative in the least, which surprised Kylie a little. Blair explored at her own pace, first licking the nipples gently, seeing how they reacted. She flicked at the hard tips and then ran her tongue around the areolas, watching Kylie's face to see if she reacted. Back and forth Blair went from firm, pebbled flesh to the softer, smoother surrounding skin, experiencing the differences in texture.

Using the flat of her tongue, she started to lick Kylie's breasts like ice cream cones, working all around the mounds. Kylie smiled down at her, one of her hands resting lightly on the back of Blair's neck.

Watching Kylie's face, Blair reached up, took one of the hard nipples between her fingers, and began to roll it back and forth. That got the doctor's attention, and she pressed her hips against Blair's belly while letting out a soft groan.

Intrigued, Blair increased the pressure and twisted the nipple a little roughly. "Yeah," Kylie growled, her voice low and sexy. Blair sat up so she could reach both breasts at once. Kylie rolled onto her back to present herself more fully, and Blair licked her lips at the mere thought of getting the doctor to make that sound again.

Blair plumped both nipples with her fingers and then squeezed each of them hard, her eyes sparkling when Kylie's hips thrust just as hard in response. Blair then bent over and took a rosy red nipple in her mouth, raking it between her teeth and then sucking on it with vigor.

"Just like that, just like that," Kylie panted, her voice sounding hoarse and raspy. She quickly and repeatedly tapped Blair on the shoulder, urging her on, the gesture seemingly unconscious.

Blair suckled one breast until Kylie winced in pain and then moved to the other, going back and forth until her tongue started to ache. Just when Blair thought she'd draw blood, Kylie raised her knee and planted her foot on the bed. In seconds, Blair could detect the scent of desire, and she licked her lips, ready to move down and taste her lover. But the doctor grasped Blair's hand and moaned, "Touch me, baby, please," as she slipped it between her legs.

Blair focused all of her attention on this new delight and touched Kylie's thigh, slowly starting to work her way up. But the doctor had an agenda, and she took over. "Suck on my nipples," she whispered. Blair blinked up at her, but did as she asked. "I need..." Then, instead of finishing her thought, Kylie took Blair's hand and grasped three of her fingers together. "Come inside me," she said hoarsely and pushed them against her opening. "In and out...yeah, just like that...perfect."

Kylie shifted her hips, opened her legs wide, and started to touch herself, rubbing her clitoris around in a circle with three of her own fingers. She started out quick and went faster and faster, desperately seeking relief. She got it when Blair sucked a nipple in and bit it, simultaneously pressing her fingers deep into Kylie.

"Yes!" the brunette cried out triumphantly. "Yes! God, yes!" Her whole body shook and rocked, and Blair watched in amazement as a pink flush slowly covered her lover's breasts and then her throat, her nipples fiercely erect. A rush of air flew from her pursed lips, and then she took in a few deep breaths. Softly, Kylie asked, "Can you hold me? I can roll over if you need me to."

"Oh, I can reach you."

Blair tentatively withdrew, trying to pull out as gently as she could. Kylie stopped her at one point, murmuring, "Wait...wait...just a second." Her muscles were still spasming, and Blair could feel the wet flesh pulse against her fingers. When Kylie had opened up, she took Blair's wrist and pulled the fingers out easily. Then the doctor rolled over and plastered their bodies together.

Blair held her fevered lover, stroking her damp skin and kissing her everywhere. They lay together in silence for a long while, Kylie's breathing changing from quick and short to long and slow breaths. When she had recovered, she rolled onto her back again and looked at Blair. "I swear I don't always have to take over," Kylie said. "But I was gonna die if I didn't get some relief, and I didn't want that on your head, especially your first time out."

Blair caught her partner's nose and gave it a good tug. "You can tell me what to do anytime you like. I enjoy working for an effective manager, and you sure as hell knew what you wanted."

Kylie looked thoughtful. "That was a little different for me. I'm not usually into pain, but I had to have you bite me today." She shrugged her shoulders. "Who knows?"

Blair cuddled up against her lover's shoulder and softly stroked her belly. "I had fun," she said. "A lot of fun. It was so cool to watch you and feel you get more and more excited. And when you came…with just a little stimulation, I could have come, too. It was sooo hot," she said, shivering at the thought.

"Huh," Kylie said. "Just watching me come could have gotten you off again. That's very interesting. I think we need to perform a little experiment."

"Such as?"

"Well, if you can almost come from watching, how much added stimulus do you need to come when you're not watching? This is something I need to know. Right now, as a matter of fact." She grabbed three pillows and pushed them against the headboard. "Sit up and rest your back against these," she said. Blair did as she was told, a smirk on her face. "Okay, now let me get into position." Kylie lay down on her side, her mouth exactly parallel with Blair's breast. The brunette sucked gently on a nipple while sliding her fingers into Blair's remarkably wet flesh.

"I love being partnered with a scientist," Blair sighed as her head dropped back onto the pillows.

⏤

Blair lay on her side, one leg and one arm thrown over her body pillow, her head resting on Kylie's arm. She was snuggled up against Blair's back, placing delicate kisses all along her shoulders. "I dreamed this," Blair murmured, her voice sleepy and soft.

"Dreamed…what?"

"That we'd just finished making love and you were lying behind me, kissing my back."

"When did you dream that?" Kylie asked, sounding equally enervated.

"The night I caught you and Julie groping each other on the sofa. I went to sleep, after masturbating furiously by the way, and I had erotic dreams about you all night long."

"You're such a little minx," Kylie said, her soft laughter making Blair's back vibrate.

"Yeah, I was in bed, dreaming about you, and you were next door having fun. I was more than a little jealous."

Kylie picked up her right hand and looked at it. "Hear that? She's jealous of you."

"What?"

"This is the only thing that got inside my panties that night," Kylie said, ruffling her fingers in front of Blair's face.

"Are you serious? I thought you and Julie were…well, I thought you were well on your way to bed that night."

"You…don't…listen…to…me," Kylie said, taking a playful nip of Blair's back to punctuate each word. "I make love to women I *love*. I didn't love Julie, so even though I was massively turned on, I kept my wits and stopped before we got out of control. Your coming home when you did was a great help, by the way."

"Anything I can do to help." She patted the bed in front of her. "Climb over me so I can look at you."

Summoning all of her energy, Kylie clambered over her lover and then settled down so they were facing each other. "Hi," Kylie said.

"Hi." Blair stroked Kylie's face and then kissed her tenderly. "I'm *so* glad you didn't sleep with Julie. I love the fact that you set standards for yourself and do your best to stick to them. Even though it must have been hard for you to refuse her that night."

Kylie hid her face by snuggling it into Blair's neck. "You have no idea. When she started playing with my breasts, I almost came! Two years is a long time to wait."

"We'll make up for lost time."

"If you want to make up for two years, you must have enjoyed your evening. Sure you don't have any complaints, criticisms…suggestions?"

Blair caressed her lover's cheek. "Not one. You, Doctor Mackenzie, are the most astounding of lovers. You made me feel beautiful and desirable and sexy. I felt absolutely idolized while you were touching me. You know, it's been half an hour, and I'm still having aftershocks from that last orgasm, so I'd say you beat my expectations by a wide margin." She kissed Kylie and grinned at her expectantly. "So, how'd I do for a rookie?"

Kylie wrapped her in a hug and kissed her repeatedly, touching Blair lightly enough to tickle her. "If the Cubs had a rookie like you, they'd finally make it to the World Series." Her expression slowly grew serious, and she said, "You know, I've tried to shut down quite a bit for the last two years so that I didn't think of sex much. But now that my senses have awakened, I don't think I'll be able to go two days! It felt so unbelievably fantastic to have you touch me with such love. That's what I've been waiting for, Blair. I've been waiting for the love." Kissing her lover slowly, exploring her mouth for a long while, Kylie finally lifted her head and murmured, "I felt so loved."

"You always will. Always."

⟳

Half an hour later, Kylie was standing in front of the refrigerator, shaking her head at the dearth of desirable foodstuffs therein. "Why do we never have any good junk food?" She turned to Blair and said, "Oh, well, I can live on love." She waited a beat for Blair to reply and then walked over to her, "Hey, what's wrong?"

Blair had her hand on her abdomen, and her face was tense. "My uterus is still pulsing pretty strongly, and it's starting to worry me."

"Is it like that time when you were first pregnant?"

Blair looked at her blankly.

"You were still seeing your gynecologist. You called me because she was out of town."

"Oh! No, no. That was a cramp. This isn't like that. This isn't painful. It's almost like I'm still orgasming. It's a strong pulsing. I think I should call Monique."

Immediately shifting into physician mode, Kylie said, "I have a disposable speculum in my bag. Let me take a look."

"Do you know what you're looking for?"

"Well, yeah," she said, slightly indignant. "I'm not a gynecologist, but I'd certainly know if anything was obviously wrong. I did a rotation in obstetrics when I was a resident, you know."

Blair pursed her lips and thought for a moment, but then shook her head. "No, I don't think I want you to touch me clinically. I think it'd be icky."

Kylie bit her tongue and tried to think of Blair's feelings rather than her own need to help. "That makes sense. I only offered because you look pretty tense."

"I am."

"I don't think there's anything to worry about. But if you're worried, you should talk to Monique. Let me give her a buzz. Then you won't have to go through her service."

"Kylie, I don't want you to impose on your friendship like that. She has the service for a reason. I simply want her to call me when she has a minute and reassure me."

The doctor sat down on one of the stools at the breakfast bar and drummed her fingers on the counter. "Are you sure you want to do that?"

"Why not? She's my doctor."

"I know, but she knows you're in the middle of a divorce. She might wonder…"

Blair touched her partner's shoulder and looked into her eyes. "Are you worried about what Monique will think of me?"

"A little."

"I think that's awfully cute. Why don't I just tell her the truth?"

"That you just had sex with a woman?"

Blair slapped Kylie lightly on the shoulder. "No, you dope! That I just had sex with *you*."

"Oh, Blair, you don't wanna do that. You don't wanna come out to anyone this soon."

"Kylie, I don't wanna argue about this. I just want someone to help me stop worrying."

A big grin lit up Kylie's face. "I'll call my dad!"

"Your dad? You don't want me to tell Monique about us, but you're willing to call your dad to ask him about the intensity of the orgasm you just gave me. Do you see anything wrong with this picture?"

"It's just a medical question. What's the big deal? I think he'd like it that we trusted his opinion."

"Kylie, you've obviously lost your mind. Now, I can either call Monique, or I can just worry until this stops." She put her hand on her belly and said, "You know...I think it *has* stopped." She put two fingers together and flicked them at the back of Kylie's head. "You wasted so much time the problem went away!"

"One of the first lessons I learned in med school: if you make someone wait long enough, he usually gets better on his own."

"Or dies," Blair grumbled.

"Well, there's always a slight risk of that. Stuff happens."

"Just for that, you have to go get the dogs from the sitter. And get some ice cream while you're out. I need mint cookies and cream, and don't even think about coming home without it."

Kylie shook her head, getting up from the stool. "I've been in a relationship for a day, and I'm already being ordered around."

Blair caught her before she could get away. "I'll only punish you when you're bad," Blair said. "Sadly, you're often bad." She kissed her softly and then turned up the heat a little when Kylie responded. "Thankfully, you're usually very, very good."

⟶

Kylie came home with two happy dogs and two pints of ice cream, the second one of another flavor, just in case. The dogs, as always, knew exactly where Blair was, and they ran, in tandem, down the hall to her room. Kylie followed along and saw that Blair was on the phone. The doctor blew her a kiss and then went and put the ice cream in the freezer.

Feeling a little at loose ends, she went into her office and spent some time on Medline, looking up information on the sexual response patterns of pregnant women. As always when she was searching for something in a database, other articles caught her interest, and she lost all track of time. It wasn't until her back began to ache from sitting in one position that she realized she'd been at her computer for over an hour. She got up and walked by Blair's room, finding her lying on the bed, talking to and petting the dogs. "Hi," Kylie said. "Uhm, do you need some alone time?"

"No. I'm just too lazy to move. Do *you* need alone time?"

"No." Kylie was leaning on the doorframe, looking very uncertain of herself.

"Come here." Kylie did, sitting down on the bed. "What's going on in that pretty head?"

"Nothin'."

"Ha! There's always something going on up there." Blair tapped the doctor's temple and said, "Come on; tell me."

"Uhm, I don't...I'm not...sure how we should be around each other now. You know what I mean?"

"Unh-uh. Not a clue."

"Aw, come on. You must feel a little funny."

"Nope. Not a bit."

"Blair," Kylie said in a voice that came perilously close to being a whine, "you just had lesbian sex for the first time. That has to bring up some kind of reaction. It *has* to. And don't try to tell me you're not feeling funny because you've been in here all by yourself for over an hour. That's not like you."

Blair stroked her lover's leg, smiling sweetly. "Where were you for the last hour?"

"On the computer. Why?"

"'Cause I was lying here, waiting for you to finish. You have to walk by my bedroom to go anywhere, so I knew I'd see you."

"Oh."

"I feel fine. Really, I do. But I don't think you do. What's going on?"

Kylie blew out a breath, the force making her lips flap. "I've met a lot of lesbians in my life, and all of them—every single one—had pretty strong feelings about the first time she had sex with another woman. I'm afraid you're not facing your feelings."

"Sweetie, I *am* facing my feelings. I feel loved and cared for and sexually satisfied and very, very happy. Those are my feelings. But I also feel a little boxed in by you. You seem to need for me to experience things in a certain way, and when I don't, you're upset."

"I'm not upset," Kylie said earnestly. "I'm worried about you."

"You don't need to be. I'm an adult, and I thought this through before I did it." She pinched Kylie's cheek. "In excruciating detail. I had no qualms before, and I don't have any now. I'm not that kind of person." She took the doctor's hand and chafed it between her own. "I told you last week that I wasn't a 'mad love' kinda girl. Well, I'm not a mad kinda decision maker, either. I don't do many important things impulsively, and I never have. I want to have a relationship with you, I want it to be sexual, and I want it to be permanent. I'm not going to change my mind."

"Are you sure?" Kylie asked, looking at her through thick, dark lashes.

"Yes, sweetheart, I'm sure. You're my love, and you're going to be until you're sick of me."

"Or you're sick of me."

"How could I get sick of someone who gets cuter every time I see her?"

Blair put a couple of pillows in front of her chest and urged her partner to lie down. Kylie did, facing Blair and nestling her face against the protruding belly. She pulled on the tie, letting the robe open, baring her lover's tummy. "Hi, Mackenzie," she said, patting the skin gently. "Did you have a nice evening? Your house got rocked tonight, didn't it? We're trying to acclimate you to earthquakes before you're even born. See how well prepared we are?"

Blair giggled, loving to watch Kylie talk to the baby as if he were looking right at her.

"Your house is gonna rock a lot, buddy, and I hope it doesn't bother you. But one day, you'll be outside with us, and you won't hear us making love. Well, you might hear us a little, but you won't know what we're doing for years and years, and by that time, your mommy will probably have killed me."

Blair rapped her on the head. "I meant that in a good way," Kylie said, looking up. "I don't know if my heart can take many more orgasms like I had today. Oh, speaking of orgasms, I did some research while you were on the phone. I read a study that showed uterine contractions can last for up to an hour after a strong orgasm and that it's nothing to worry about as long as they're not accompanied by pain."

"Far from it," Blair said, smiling. "They were accompanied by intense pleasure."

"So…did you really enjoy yourself tonight? Anything you wish I'd done differently?"

"Hmm…there is one thing."

"What?"

"You could stop asking me if I enjoyed myself! You know enough about the female body to know I wasn't faking it." She stroked Kylie's head and said, "You were so confident when we were in bed that I thought you were over your anxiety about this. But now you seem worried again. What can I do to reassure you?"

"Nothin'," Kylie said. "I just have to remind myself that you're not me and you're not a kid. Hell, you probably don't even think of this as a coming-out experience."

"No, I don't. It's a 'falling in love' experience. This doesn't change how I feel about myself."

Kylie stared up at her, unable to fully accept Blair's statement.

"It doesn't," Blair said, seeing the doubt in the concerned blue eyes.

"I don't get it, but I guess I have to learn to accept it. I don't have any option."

"Tell me how you felt after you kinda had sex with…I.V." She smiled and said, "I couldn't remember which Roman numeral he was for a minute."

"I felt stupid, I guess. I'd been dating him for a while, and I loved kissing him and having him touch me, but it didn't ever feel very, uhm…I guess…intimate. Yeah, that's it; it never felt intimate. It was kinda like masturbating with someone else's hand."

"Why'd you feel stupid, honey?"

"Because I didn't make him use a condom," she admitted, looking embarrassed. "Looking back, it makes me see how hard it is to convince kids to practice safe sex. I was a gynecologist's daughter, and I'd known about sex since I was a kid, but I still got into a position where I took a huge risk of getting pregnant. And I didn't even do it for myself. I did it because he wanted it so badly. When I got home, I lay in bed for hours, berating myself. I stopped going out with him after that. I didn't even want to have the temptation again."

"My poor baby," Blair soothed, stroking Kylie's head. "Everyone makes mistakes like that. It's hard to be in an adult's body, but still have a teenager's mind."

"I know. It was a hard time for me. I knew I was attracted to girls, but I didn't know it enough to do anything about it. I was in a strange place. I wasn't sure I was gay, and I wasn't sure I was straight. The fact that I got so turned on when guys touched me the right way only confused me more. I thought the fact that I could have an orgasm with them meant I might be straight."

"I understand what a tough time that was for you. You were trying to establish your identity."

"Yeah, I was."

"So, how did you feel when you had sex with a girl for the first time?"

Kylie smiled up at her, the sweet expression making Blair's heart melt. "I knew I was a lesbian," Kylie said. "It terrified me and made me face some things I'd been avoiding, but at least I knew where I belonged."

"That makes perfect sense. Tell me what was different about being with a girl?"

Kylie exhaled slowly, her breath warming the skin on Blair's belly, and said, "Gosh. So much. I really opened up with Nancy. I let myself be very vulnerable with her. With guys, I always had my guard up, worried that they'd be too aggressive. But with Nancy—I let her touch me any way she wanted. And it didn't feel like masturbation anymore, either. She made love to me."

Blair hugged her as well as she could, given her limited reach. "You must have been so happy."

"Yeah, but like I said, I was frightened, too. I knew I'd eventually have to tell my parents and my friends. I was pretty worried until I got that all out of the way."

"Now that I understand what it was like for you, let me tell you what it's like for me."

"Okay, but you'd better not say that this afternoon felt like masturbation," Kylie said, her eyes sparkling.

"I like masturbation as well as, or better than, the next girl, but making love is a whole different thing," she said while tweaking Kylie's nose. "A whole better thing."

"Whew," Kylie said, wiping her forehead dramatically.

"We'll talk about today in a minute. First, some history. The first time I had sex with a boy, I didn't feel different about myself. I felt a little more mature, like I'd moved into the adult world, but that's about it. I was in love with my boyfriend, we'd been dating for a year, and I was on the pill. It just seemed like the next step in our relationship, you know? Kinda like you must feel now."

"Yeah, that is how I feel now," Kylie said. "How old were you?"

"I was a freshman in college, so I was seventeen or eighteen."

"Why were you on the pill if you hadn't had sex yet?"

"Because I listened to my mother, you big goof! She knew Jason and I were serious about each other, and before I went to college, she suggested I get on the pill if I was going to have sex with him."

"Wow, your mom's cool."

"She is cool, but she also knows me. She could tell it wouldn't be long before I had the opportunity to sleep with Jason, and she wanted me to be prepared. And since I didn't want to get pregnant, like my egg donor had, I was ultra careful."

"Right. I'm sure that was an issue for you."

"It was. Even though Jason was a virgin, I made him wear a condom. There was no way I was gonna have a baby until I was ready for one."

"Hear that, Mackenzie?" Kylie asked. "You're the chosen one."

"Yeah, I probably could've whipped one out for nothing when I was eighteen. This little guy cost us a Mercedes. Luckily, I think he's worth every penny."

"So, tell me how you feel about today," Kylie said, getting back on topic.

"I feel a tiny bit like you did when you first slept with Nancy. I don't feel different about myself, but I do have to tell some people and face their reactions to my news. I'm not really looking forward to that, but I'm sure I'm not worried about it like you were. I'm an adult, and my parents treat me like one. Even if they don't like what I'm doing, they won't give me a hard time. They're just not like that. David and Sadie are gonna be hard, but again, what can they do? Sadie has to be nice to me just to make sure she gets access to Mackenzie. She's pretty powerless. And David can bite me! I don't give a damn about what he thinks."

"But you don't think you're gonna wake up tomorrow and look at yourself in the mirror and think, 'I'm a lesbian'?"

"No. I'm not gonna do that. I didn't wake up after I slept with Jason and think, 'I'm straight!' Why would I do that now? I'm the same person I was a year ago; I just know something about myself that I didn't know before."

Kylie gazed at her for a long time. "It's really that simple for you?"

"Yes, it is. If you'd tied me to the bed and made me call you Mistress while you spanked me, I would have learned something else new about myself—if I'd enjoyed it. But I wouldn't have pulled the covers over my head and worried about being a masochist. It just would have been something I didn't know about myself. You learn things about your sexual self when you have a new partner. From you, I learned that I love touching your body, and I love how soft and smooth it feels. I love knowing what you're feeling. When you come, I know just how it feels, and it makes me even hotter for you."

"It does?" Kylie's eyes were sparkling again, and there was a definite sexual vibe coming from them this time.

"Uh-huh. And you know, there is one tiny complaint I have about this evening. I didn't get to explore you enough. You were so turned on you couldn't wait—like I was forced to, I might add."

"Don't worry. You can explore anytime you want, as long as I'm not about to burst."

"I think I just have to get at you first. Before you're ready to explode."

Kylie smiled at her and then started thumping on various parts of her belly, trying to make Mackenzie respond. "I love doing this," the doctor said. "I always wanted to before, but I thought you'd think I was crazy if I asked."

"I would have." Blair laughed. "Now I know you're crazy."

"I'm crazy about you and Mackenzie. Uhm, do you mind if I tell my mom?"

"No, of course not. You can tell anyone you want."

"Really? You don't mind if I tell the guys at work?"

"Nope."

"My poker buddies?"

"Nope."

"David?"

"Yep." Blair caught Kylie's nose and gave it a tug. "He's my responsibility. I was gonna send him a letter, but I suppose that's the coward's way out."

"Hey, you don't have to be brave about this. A letter's plenty."

"Nah. I'll tell him in person. Then I know it's over. If I send him a letter, I have to wonder when he's gonna get it and then wonder how he'll respond. This way I'll know."

"Yeah, but you'll also be catching him without allowing time for it to sink in. He might be more upset if you do it in person."

"He might be, but I can't let that stop me. I don't have to think about it tonight, though. Unless a certain pretty woman keeps reminding me, that is."

"Sorry. I'm just keyed up."

"Then let's relax a little. Come up here and lie by me. I wanna see those lips."

Kylie tossed the pillows aside and moved up so she and Blair shared a pillow. "Here they are."

"Now, let me kiss them," Blair said, and Kylie willingly complied. Blair slipped her hand under Kylie's T-shirt, finding a soft, smooth nipple. "Not even hard yet," she murmured into a nearby ear. Sliding her thumb over the nipple just a few times had it plumped up and rigid. "That was fast."

"Uh-huh," Kylie whispered.

"I think this is a good time for me to explore a little, don't you?"

"Uh-huh."

"You're mine," Blair whispered into her ear. "And I'm ready to stake my claim."

Kylie put her hands over her head and crossed her wrists as if they were bound. "I surrender. Sweet, sweet surrender."

Chapter Nine

K ylie slowly emerged from a deep sleep, her body trained to answer the sun's call. She was hot and sticky, but when she tried to toss the blanket off, she had so little strength that it barely budged. Willing herself to wake up, she realized why she was both so hot and weak.

Blair's naked body adhered to her own like a second skin. Groggy as Kylie was, she smiled and hummed a quiet tune reflecting the pleasure she felt at her discovery. Once again, she tried to fling the blanket away, but this time it uttered a protest. Her eyes opened, and she saw two sets of brown eyes giving her a sleepy scowl. Nicky was lying between her legs, and Nora was on Blair's hip, the dogs' weight effectively holding the blanket in place.

She managed to push the blanket off her torso and pull a leg out, and in a few seconds, she began to cool down. Looking at the clock, she saw that it was 5:45, and she gave herself permission to stay in bed as long as humanly possible. The last time she'd seen the clock, she'd been burrowed between Blair's legs, exploring her body like an archeologist investigating the ruins of an ancient city. Kylie recalled weak entreaties to allow release, Blair insisting that her partner had been torturing her for hours. The doctor had glanced at the clock, realized it was after 2:00, and accepted that her lover had a valid point. Kylie had focused her efforts and brought Blair to a quiet, enervating climax, after which she'd immediately fallen asleep without so much as a good night kiss. But Kylie didn't begrudge the abrupt ending to their evening. They'd touched and talked and kissed and explored each other for six hours, and she realized they'd gone a little overboard in their enthusiasm. But she wouldn't have given up a moment of that time—no matter the price. Blair had thoroughly surprised the doctor on every level, and each surprise had been better than the last.

She heard a soft groan as Blair moved a little, peeling her neck and shoulder from Kylie's skin. Blair's eyes opened a few millimeters. "Hi," she said, her mouth curling into a slow smile. "Whatcha doin'?"

"Looking at you and thinking about how wonderful last night was."

Blair reached out and patted Kylie's leg, the blonde's movements not very focused yet. "It was wonderful, but as soon as I pee, we need to sleep some more," Blair said. "We've got a very busy day planned."

"We do?"

"Yep." After managing to wrench herself from her lover, Blair took care of her morning requirements. When she got back into bed, she smelled of toothpaste, and her body felt much cooler.

"What do we have to do today?" Kylie asked.

"First, we have to sleep until at least 9:00. Then we have to eat a little something. Then we have to start making love again. I thought of at least five things that I simply must do to you today, and I'm not gonna let these ideas slip away without trying them." She placed a soft kiss on Kylie's lips. "You inspired me."

Kylie gazed at her, blue eyes gone a little wide. "I guess we don't need to have that 'Are you sure this was the right decision for you?' talk, huh?"

"No, and if you ask me that one more time, I'm gonna find your scalpels and cut something off you. Something you like," she added, making as mean a face as she was capable of. "The only thing I'm wondering is why we didn't start doing this the day I moved in." She wrinkled her nose and giggled, making Kylie do the same in reaction.

"As I recall, you were kinda in a bad mood when you first got here."

"One more thing you need to learn about me: great sex always gets me out of a bad mood. Remember that for the future."

"It's in the vault," Kylie assured her. The doctor tapped her temple to underscore the point. Then she kissed her, delighted with the thought of making it the first of hundreds, or even thousands, of kisses they would share, if they could summon the stamina required for another day of lovemaking. She was confident Blair was up to the challenge, but Kylie had a few doubts about her own heart, given the way it was beating just because of the loving smile the beautiful woman in her arms was giving her.

⌐

The couple lazed around the house the next day as well, not straying far from the bedroom. But instead of making love, as they had on Saturday, they took three naps, managing a good one after breakfast, another after lunch, and a quickie before dinner. After watching a mystery on television that evening, Blair was almost horizontal by the time it was over, showing that their lovemaking had fully depleted all of her reserves.

They went to bed at 10:00, and at around 2:00 a.m., Blair blinked her eyes open and had a bit of a start when a pair of wide-awake eyes blinked back at her. "Hi," Kylie said quietly. "You feeling okay? You were grumbling a little in your sleep."

"I'm fine...fine." She smacked her lips together and asked, "Why are you awake? I'm not snoring, am I?"

"No, of course not," Kylie said, even though Blair had been. "I'm too wired to sleep. I'm just lying here watching you and thinking of how incredibly lucky I am."

"Hold that thought. I've gotta pee." She rolled out of bed, making both Nicky and Nora murmur their displeasure at being disturbed. "You're much more even-tempered than your dogs," Blair added as she departed.

"They've never been my dogs, and they never will be," Kylie called after her. "They've been yours from the start."

After a few moments had passed, Blair called out, "Hey, Kylie? Would you come here for a minute?"

Before the last word was out, Kylie was standing in the doorway, looking hyper-alert. "What is it?"

"Will you brush your teeth?" Blair had just finished doing the same thing, and even though Kylie thought the request a little odd, she took the new brush that Blair offered and did as requested.

"Is my breath that bad?" she asked, a little white circle of foam forming around her mouth.

"No, it's not bad at all near as I can tell. I just love the taste of a freshly scrubbed mouth. It's one of my…quirks."

"Okay," she said agreeably. "It's 2:00 a.m., and I'm brushing my teeth because my lover likes a squeaky-clean mouth. Works for me." After they'd both rinsed, they headed back to bed, and after some minor complaints from the dogs, everyone was comfortable again.

"You're too far away," Blair said, running the flat of her palm down her partner's long arm and taking her hand.

Smiling, Kylie scooted closer, now practically rubbing noses. "How's this?"

"That's good. I don't want to waste a nice, clean mouth. How about a little kiss?"

"Fine idea," Kylie said, her mouth immediately seeking Blair's. They kissed for a long time, and every time Kylie cranked up the intensity, Blair stayed right with her. The doctor felt a small, warm hand slip under her T-shirt and start to play with her breasts. "Oh, that's nice," Kylie sighed. "You have such a tender touch."

"Not always," Blair growled, adding a little force as she pinched a nipple. "Sometimes, I can be quite evil."

"I like evil women." Kylie's breath caught and then became slightly irregular under Blair's determined touch.

"Roll onto your side so I can cuddle up behind you," Blair said. Breathing a tiny sigh of disappointment that the game was ending, Kylie did so, giving her partner a final kiss good night. But as soon as Blair snuggled up, her fingers started to explore again, moving from Kylie's breasts, down her belly, and finally into her boxers. "Lift your leg for me, baby," Blair whispered, causing chills to chase down Kylie's spine. Immediately, the knee lifted, and the foot settled onto the mattress as Kylie waited for Blair's touch. The brunette gasped with pleasure when cool fingers spread her open and dipped into her wetness.

Blair wedged her arm under the taller woman's body, holding her tightly. When Kylie was fully under Blair's control, her fingers dipped and swirled across the slick flesh, playing the doctor like a fine instrument. With her lips so close to Kylie's ear, Blair took advantage of the position and whispered some decidedly wicked intentions, making Kylie squirm under the assault.

"Good God," the doctor gasped as her body shook and shuddered through an orgasm that caught her completely by surprise.

Blair lifted her head and kissed Kylie's neck, nuzzling against the warm, moist skin and delighting in the salty taste. "Mmm…nice," she murmured, holding Kylie even tighter. "I love the way your skin tastes." She delicately removed her hand from the swollen tissues, but didn't travel far. Staying inside the roomy boxers, she splayed her hand across Kylie's mound and felt the pulsing that continued for long minutes. "So nice," she breathed into her lover's pink ear. "Sleep now, baby."

"Don't you want…?" Kylie began, but Blair shushed her.

"I don't need a thing other than to hold you. Just close those pretty eyes and sleep with me. That's what'll make me happy."

"'Kay."

Blair could feel Kylie's body begin to relax, and before she could say another word, she felt the rhythmic breathing begin.

"I love you, Kylie." She kissed her neck once again, smiling to herself as she drifted off as well.

                        ↞

Blair was just getting ready to go home the next day when Kylie called from her cell. "Hi. I'm gonna be stuck at the hospital for a while. I want you to stop at C'est la Vie and pick up some dinner."

"Okay," Blair said, smiling fondly, warmed by just hearing Kylie's voice. "Any idea what I'm in the mood for?"

"Funny. But now that you ask, I think you should have two different kinds of vegetables and some of that good wild-rice salad with the raisins and citrus dressing. Gotta keep you regular."

"You will let me control my own digestive tract when I'm not pregnant, won't you? I mean, I've done pretty well on my own…"

"I'm not controlling you. You don't like to be controlled. I'm reminding you and making suggestions. I'm merely being helpful. There's a very big difference."

"Oh, I see. Sometimes, the difference is hard to detect. I'm glad you pointed it out to me."

"That's what I'm here for."

"Well, you do a good job. Now, how about you? Will you be home for dinner?"

"Doubtful. But buy enough for me, and if I don't eat it tonight, I'll take it with me for lunch."

"Is everything okay, honey? You sound a little stressed."

"I love it when you call me honey," Kylie said, obviously pleased.

Blair chuckled and said, "Why is it that, as soon as you sleep together, you start calling each other little pet names? I heard myself calling you babe and baby all weekend, and I didn't even realize I was doing it."

"I like it. I like being your honey."

"My honey didn't answer my question," Blair reminded her. "Are you all right?"

"Yeah. I'm a little worried about a patient. I reversed his vasectomy, and he's had some unexplained bleeding and swelling. I need to stick around until I'm sure we've got it under control."

"Well, make sure you get something to eat if you're there past dinner, okay? I worry about you."

"Promise. Give the puppies a kiss for me when you get home."

"Will do. Wake me if I'm asleep."

"Would you rather sleep in your room tonight? I hate the thought of disturbing you."

"Kylie, my sleep's gonna be disturbed for the next two or three years. It's no big deal. I want to sleep with you, even if it does mean that I'm woken up once in a while. Besides, I'm sure I'll wake you up twice a night with all of my bathroom visits."

"But I get back to sleep faster than you do."

"True, but irrelevant. I love you, and I love sleeping with you. So, get your cute little butt home as soon as you can."

"It's a deal. Me and my butt will be home as soon as possible."

⟿

She was agitated from a long night at the hospital, but Kylie got into bed as soon as she got home, hoping that she could calm down enough to sleep just by having Blair near. When the doctor was only halfway into bed, Blair woke groggily. "What time is it?" she mumbled.

"Just after 2:00. Sorry to wake you."

"Mmm...that's okay. It's time to pee, anyway. Be right back." She was gone for a few minutes, and when she returned, Kylie could smell the toothpaste on her. Blair cuddled up and nestled her cheek against Kylie's chest. "What happened? Wanna talk about it?"

"Nothing happened, really. It was one of those odd situations. He had a slight fever...seemed like he might have an infection. Then he had some bleeding, and after we got that controlled, his scrotum started to swell. We worked on him all day, trying to figure out what was going wrong, and then—poof!—he was fine." She shook her head and said, "I'm obviously glad that he's okay, but it's frustrating when unexplained things like that happen. My mind's racing from spending the evening with the internist I called in. We both just about sprained our brains trying to figure out what was going on, and we were getting ready to call in another doc when everything cleared up. Weird."

"You're all agitated, aren't you?" Blair pushed Kylie's hair back in order to gaze at the smooth, strong planes of her face.

"Yeah, a little. Maybe I'll get up and read or play some music."

"Let me help." Blair drew her into an embrace. "A little love will calm you down, won't it?"

Kylie's face lit up in a smile. "Well, it might. I guess it wouldn't hurt to experiment a little."

"That's what I love about you. Your total commitment to the scientific method." She pulled her even closer and captured her lips in a soft kiss that quickly grew to heated proportions. Kylie was hypersensitive due to being tense all day, and with just a few minutes of kissing and fondling, she was begging for Blair's touch. "Mmm...I don't want to touch you," Blair whispered. "I want to taste you."

"Damn, but you have great ideas. Where do you want me? I don't want you to be uncomfortable."

Giving her a fantastically sexy look, Blair urged her to come closer. Once she was kneeling upright, Blair put her hands on Kylie's hips, guiding her until she was poised over her face. "Come on," she urged, her leer making Kylie shake with anticipation. "I won't hurt you."

Returning her heated gaze, Kylie lowered herself just enough to allow Blair's tongue to reach her. "Oh, God!" she moaned, her whole body shivering from the delicious sensation. "Jesus! Yes—just like that, baby. Just like that!"

Blair's tongue slipped all around her heated flesh, investigating every furrow and depression, loving her thoroughly. The blonde kept trying to make the experience last, slowing and softening her touch. Kylie had her own timetable, though, and in a remarkably short time, she began to groan, her body unable to wait another second before it was engulfed in a shuddering climax. Immediately rising up a few inches, she held on to the headboard, her legs shaking under the strain. "Slide down and rest on me," Blair urged, stroking her lover's quivering thighs. "You won't hurt me."

Kylie did because she couldn't hold herself up for another moment. Still breathing heavily, she rested upon Blair's shoulders and chest, soothed by her tender touch. When Kylie was certain her legs would hold her, she swung one long leg over Blair and collapsed onto the mattress. "God, you're good at that," Kylie gasped, still trying to catch her breath. "Are you sure you didn't take some kinda class?"

"I'm sure. It's really not that different from doing the same thing to a man. You find the most sensitive spots and work on them until you get the reaction you want. Doesn't seem that tough to me." She smiled at Kylie and gave her a kiss on the nose. "It helps if you really enjoy what you're doing. And I do."

Smiling in return, Kylie rolled over and started to nibble on Blair's lips, thrilled by the taste of herself on her lover's mouth. Kylie quickly noticed, however, that her attempts to whip Blair into a frenzy were being met with soothing kisses, obviously intended to extinguish, rather than fan, the flames. Lifting her head, Kylie gave her partner a puzzled look and asked, "Not in the mood?"

"No, I'm satisfied," Blair said, smiling warmly. "I'd love for you to hold me, though. Maybe kiss my neck and back to put me to sleep?"

"Sure, if you're sure that's what you want."

"It is," Blair said, getting into position. Kylie began to kiss and nuzzle the skin across her shoulders, and in just a few minutes, Blair fell asleep, murmuring nonsense words as sleep overtook her.

After placing one more warm kiss right between her shoulder blades, Kylie fell asleep just moments after her partner nodded off.

The next afternoon, Kylie was at the sink peeling some potatoes when Blair snuck into the house quietly. The dogs ran to the door to greet her, but they didn't make much noise, so Kylie was unaware of her partner creeping up behind her. Not wanting to startle her, especially when the doctor had a potato peeler in her hands, Blair said quietly, "Don't move, you big, gorgeous hunk of woman."

Kylie stilled immediately, waiting for Blair to make a move. "Should I be afraid?" she asked, her voice growing deeper and taking on a sexy timbre.

"Depends." Blair came up behind her and formed her body against Kylie's. "Are you afraid of a very horny woman who's been dreaming of bedding you all day long?"

"No," Kylie said, chuckling softly. "That's never been a fear of mine."

"Just stand there and let me explore a little." Blair's hands started to move over Kylie, and soon, the doctor was pressing her butt against her partner. Determined fingers started to unbutton Kylie's shirt, and as soon as the third button was undone, short fingernails raked over her hardening nipples, making her squirm.

Kylie grasped the counter, needing some assistance to keep herself from turning to rip Blair's clothes off. Now one small hand held Kylie's belt, and the other started to lower the zipper on her chinos and then slipped inside. Blair's free hand tugged the shirt from the pants, allowing unfettered access to the sexy bikinis. "Damn, you wear nice underwear for a lesbian."

"You were expecting what, Jockey shorts?"

"No," Blair chided her, playfully slapping her butt. "I guess I believed the stereotypes, though. I thought you'd wear some sensible white briefs. Nothing too fancy."

"Au contraire, ma petite chou. The sexier the better. I love the feeling of silk and satin caressing my body. You'll never find me in sensible briefs."

"I love sexy undies," Blair murmured, biting Kylie sharply on her sensitive neck and making her yelp. "And I particularly like them on you. Your body is a total turn-on." Blair's fingers roamed from Kylie's navel down to the apex of her thighs, stopping to caress and tease at various points of interest.

The dark head lolled back and rested on Blair's shoulder, and Kylie's breathing became ragged and labored. Tilting her head just enough to be heard, she whispered in a surprisingly fragile voice, "Do I really turn you on?"

Blair's hands stilled. Then she wrapped both arms around the larger woman's body, holding on tight. "That's kind of a silly question. Why would I dream about you all day, rush into the house, and then start touching you before I even had my shoes off if you didn't turn me on?" She took another few nibbles of Kylie's neck, swiping her tongue along the path she'd just kissed. "I thought about how you taste and how deliciously soft and smooth you are." Holding even tighter, she rubbed against her lover's backside. "You make me wet. Hot and wet."

Unable to restrain herself another moment, Kylie turned and wrapped her partner in her arms. "Sorry. I'm feeling a little insecure today."

Blair pulled back so she could look into Kylie's eyes. "Why? Have I done something...?" Blair asked.

"No, no, it's me. I let myself worry about your making love to me two nights in a row and not letting me reciprocate. I let my imagination run wild and thought maybe you were having a hard time getting turned on enough to have sex."

Pulling back even more, Blair searched Kylie's eyes questioningly. "Sweetheart, we *were* having sex—and we were having it because I wanted to. I'm the one who made the overture both nights. Why would I do that if I didn't want you?"

"I know we've about beaten this to death, but we need to get a few things sorted out."

"Okay. Hit me."

"I want to eat soon, and you know you get indigestion if we don't eat pretty early. You go change your clothes, and I'll finish preparing dinner. Then we can chat while it cooks." She turned Blair in the direction of her room and patted her butt. "Go on, now."

"Back in a minute," she said. "C'mon, pups. You know you love to see me naked."

❧

When Blair returned, Kylie was sitting outside, the warm, late-afternoon sun on her face. She looked up and twitched her head to indicate the chair next to hers when Blair came out.

Blair sat down and, once she got settled, took hold of Kylie's hand. "Okay," Blair said. "Let's have another sensitive chat. But remember my threat about finding your scalpels."

Kylie squeezed her hand. "I know I'm driving you nuts, but I *worry* about stuff."

"I don't mean to make fun of you. You can tell me whatever you want. I promise I won't cut you."

Kylie smiled at her. "I don't think this is a big deal, but I want to understand how you're feeling about things and tell you a couple of things about myself."

"Okay, shoot. What do you want to know?"

"Well," Kylie said, clearing her throat as she realized she actually was a little nervous, "I guess I want to know what happened. It seemed like you were turned on and then lost it. I'm worried that I made you lose it."

"Bad supposition. Yes, I was turned on; that's why I wanted to make love. But I never 'lost it' as you put it. I was satisfied after loving you, so I stopped."

"But...what?" Kylie asked, befuddled. "How does that happen?"

"I had a really good sandwich for lunch today," Blair said, in what the doctor might have termed a dazzling non sequitur. "A little brie, some baby lettuces, tomato— heirloom, I think—and a touch of Dijon mustard. Really tasty. I only ate half of it though. Wanna know why?" she asked, her eyes twinkling.

"Sure," Kylie said. She'd remained patient throughout her lover's seeming tangent, knowing the point would be made clear.

"'Cause that's all I wanted. I could have eaten the rest and 'finished,' but that would have been too much, and the whole experience would have been ruined by my forcing

318

myself to eat it all. I'm like that about sex, too. I like a little sex quite often, and a lot of sex every couple of days."

"And making love to me is…?"

"A little sex," Blair said, smiling broadly. "I love the seduction and the buildup best of all. And it's so much fun to watch you get turned on. It's really fascinating for me. I mean, I never stopped to consider how easy it is to tell when a woman's aroused. I thought it was only patently obvious with men."

"No, we telegraph pretty well, too. At least, I do," Kylie admitted. "So…you really like that, huh?"

"Yeah," Blair said, grinning sexily. "It's very hot—makes me tingle in a good place. A favorite place, really."

"Okay, I think I understand that. That's not how I'm put together, but I can accept variations in an organism."

"So, last night, I felt like turning you on. I was awake, you looked all delicious, and I thought it would be fun to taste you for a while. It was, by the way. After I watched you get all hot and excited, I felt satisfied. I don't know why, but I was happy and content. I just wanted to be kissed and cuddled."

"Okay. I believe you. That will never happen to me, but I know we're not wired the same way. So, what happened on Sunday? Was that different?"

"Yeah, it was. I woke up in the middle of the night, and you were wide-awake. I knew I could make you sleepy with just a little touching, so I offered. It worked, didn't it?"

"Yeah, but you don't need to do that."

"I know I don't *need* to. I want to. When you have a backache, I want to rub it. When you have a bad day, I want to make you a nice dinner. When you're having trouble relaxing, I want to help you relax. That's one way to show how much I love you."

"I love you, too, and I want to make sure you don't feel obligated to do any of that stuff."

"Kylie, when I make the first move, you can rest assured that I'm doing it because I want to. I'm not the kind of woman who'd touch you because I thought it was my job. Actually, if I thought you expected it, I probably wouldn't do it at all." She laughed at the expression on Kylie's face. "I don't like to be controlled, remember?"

"Right. Right. I remember. I…I guess I was worried that you thought I expected sex every night. I mean, I've told you I like to have sex a lot, and I thought you might just be trying to please me."

"Well, I do want to please you, but I also expect you to ask for what you need. We're both big girls."

"I can do that. Although, I'll probably hold back a little while you're pregnant. I really am hypersensitive to not making too many demands on you while your body is going through so many changes."

"I don't need you to do that. I want to know when you want to have sex, and that includes after the baby comes. I'm not gonna want to be touched for months, but that doesn't mean you have to go without."

"Get real! I'm not going to expect you to service me when you've got a tiny infant suckling on you every couple of hours! I can take care of myself. I've had lots of practice."

Getting up from her chair, Blair sat down on Kylie's lap. "Not squishing you, am I?"

"Nope. Feels nice," Kylie said, nuzzling her face into the side of Blair's neck.

"Look at me," Blair said.

Kylie did, gazing at her partner for a few moments.

"Listen to me carefully. I hope we're gonna be together for a long while, don't you?" Blair asked.

"Yes," Kylie said decisively.

"It's important to me to ensure that we're both sexually satisfied, all during our lives together. Sometimes, I won't feel like being sexual; sometimes, you won't. But I want you to tell me when you have the urge. I can't guarantee that I'll always be able to summon the strength to take care of you, but I promise I'll always try. It's important that we take care of each other—in every way."

"I'll try," Kylie said. "I've never been in a relationship where I asked for everything I needed sexually, but I promise I'll give it a go."

"I want you to do what you need. If you want to please yourself, by all means, go right ahead. But if you want a little help from your bedmate, make sure to give me a nudge."

"I'll promise if you'll promise."

"Okay, it's a deal. I should warn you, though, that lately, my needs have been making themselves known in the middle of the night."

"Bring it on," Kylie said. "I can handle you any hour of the night or day."

⟳

Later that night, Blair lay mostly on her back, panting softly as she tried to catch her breath. "My God, woman, where did you learn to use your tongue like that?"

"Years of practice," Kylie said, snuggling up to her. "I'm gonna have to start wearing a football helmet to bed if you continue to enjoy my talents, though. I swear you're gonna snatch me baldheaded."

"Such a complainer. I never knew what a delicate little flower you were."

Kylie leaned over her, capturing her lips in a heated kiss. "I'm a hothouse flower. Emphasis on the hot." She bent to kiss her again, lingering for a long while and gently exploring Blair's mouth with her tongue.

As she pulled away, Blair looked at her for a moment and then smacked her lips together while she made a face. "Uhm, embarrassing question time: do you like the way I taste?"

"Oh, yeah," Kylie said enthusiastically, "most definitely. Why?"

"'Cause I'm not so crazy about it. I noticed it the other night, and I thought it might have been my imagination. But that's not it. I taste really different than I used to, and if it's unpleasant, I want you to tell me."

"Honey, there's nothing unpleasant about you. Your vagina undergoes a shift in its pH balance when you're pregnant. It's probably a little more acidic than it used to be. That's what you've noticed."

Blair rolled her eyes. "It's more than a little acidic. I used to taste kinda sweet. But now…" She looked down at herself. "God knows what's going on down there. I've got stuff gushing out of me nonstop!"

"It's perfectly normal to have some discharge. It's nothing to be worried about."

"I'm not worried; I'm disgusted!" She started to chuckle and then leaned against Kylie and said, "They don't tell you all of these nasty little secrets *before* you get pregnant. It's a conspiracy, I tell you!"

"I could tell you exactly what makes up that discharge if you're interested. It's nothing particularly gross."

"No, thanks. I like my non-medical diagnosis of grossness. And I want you to promise that if it starts to offend you, you'll touch me with your hands or the vibrator. I swear that when I get back to normal, you'll be suitably impressed with how sweet and clean I taste."

"Well, I think you're perfectly delightful now. No need to change."

"You win a free orgasm for making the pregnant woman feel better," Blair said. "When would you like to claim your prize?"

Kylie rolled onto her back and spread her legs invitingly. "Now. Right now."

⌒

On Friday night, the couple decided to celebrate the end of the workweek with dinner out. They chose a romantic northern Italian spot in Brentwood, and since Kylie had no one in the hospital, she indulged in a half-bottle of wine. When the server came over to take their dessert orders, Kylie asked for an espresso for herself and some steamed milk with a spoonful of honey in it for Blair.

As the server departed, Blair gave her a fond glance and asked, "What's next? A martini for you and a Shirley Temple for me?"

"Not a bad idea. I'll have to remember that next time I order wine."

Giving her a long, thoughtful look, Blair commented, "You seem very relaxed tonight. Are you feeling particularly happy?"

Reaching across the table, Kylie covered Blair's hand with her own. "I haven't had a bad day since you told me you loved me."

A delighted grin settled on Blair's face, and she finally nodded in agreement. "You have been even happier than normal. It's so nice to know that it's because of me."

"It is. Only because of you."

Blair ran her thumb across the back of Kylie's hand, looking contemplative. "During our friendship, there've been times when I thought you were as interested in the baby as you were in me. It's a relief to realize that's not true."

"God, no! I swear, I wouldn't feel any different about you if you weren't pregnant. You're the woman I love. The relationship we'll each have with the baby is an entirely separate thing. One doesn't depend on the other."

With love in her eyes, Blair looked at Kylie and asked, "Have you thought about what you want the baby to call you?"

The server returned with their drinks, and as he left, Kylie said, "No, I guess I haven't. Any suggestions?"

"Well, we could let him decide. I've read that most kids take the name you try to force on them and do what they want, anyway. It'll be a little harder for us since we need two variations of Mom."

"Huh?" Kylie asked, looking blank. "What…what do you mean?"

Now Blair looked puzzled. "Don't you want him to call you Mom or Mommy or Mama? I assumed—"

"Blair, that's your title!" Kylie's eyes were as wide as the saucer under her espresso cup. "You're his mommy!"

"Well, who the hell are you?" Blair asked loudly, causing a few heads to turn in their direction.

Kylie blinked at her and then cocked her head in thought. "I'm his…I'm his…" She looked at her partner with wide eyes and said, "We've always referred to me as Aunt Kylie. I haven't had time to think about this. I assumed you'd be the mommy, David would be the daddy, and I'd be…" She shrugged her shoulders, looking perplexed. "Kylie?"

"Is that what you want?" Blair asked quietly, looking more than a little disappointed. "Do you just want to be my lover? Is that how you want Mackenzie to think of you?"

"No, no…I…I want to do whatever you think is best. I need you to take the lead."

The server passed their table, making eye contact. Blair looked up at him and asked, "Do you have any biscotti?"

"Yes. We have a hazelnut and an almond dipped in chocolate."

"One of each, please." She raised an eyebrow in Kylie's direction, warning her not to even think of making a comment. She sipped at her steamed milk, waiting for the server to deliver her cookies. When he returned, she dipped the hazelnut into the milk, smiling in satisfaction when she took a bite. "I've only gained seventeen pounds, and I don't want to hear a word out of you."

"You're doing great. But you'll start to gain weight faster now. I know it's a pain, but every unnecessary pound will make you more miserable as you go along."

"I realize that, sweetheart, but I couldn't have wine with dinner, I couldn't have espresso, and I can't have my favorite aperitif. I've got to have some extravagances, or I'll go nuts."

"I know. I don't mean to supervise you. I know you hate that."

"I do," Blair said, "but I love you. Sometimes, ya gotta take the bad with the good." She held the biscotto up to her partner and instructed, "Bite." While Kylie chewed, Blair said, "We're having a failure to communicate. I was under the impression that we were going to raise this baby together. Remember that?"

"Of course, I do!"

"Well, why do you act surprised when I suggest he'll call you Mom? Isn't it obvious that he would?"

Kylie shook her head, looking thoroughly perplexed. "The way we've set this up is a little amorphous. It's clear that you're the mom, but we've just started to talk about my co-parenting with you. I didn't realize that you'd want Mackenzie to call me Mom. I'm thrilled, but I'm also a little surprised."

Blair cocked her head and stared at her partner for a few moments. "I think of Mackenzie as ours—both yours and mine—equally." Looking even more confused, she asked, "Don't you feel that way? Don't you want that?" She dropped her gaze, and her lower lip began to quiver as she whimpered, "Please, God, don't tell me you feel like David did."

"No!" Kylie said with alarm. "I swear that's not it!"

"Kylie, I'm divorcing him partially because he said he'd feel like a stepparent. I'm not going to raise this baby with you if you can't love him as your own."

"Oh, Blair, of course, I want that. I didn't realize that's what you wanted."

"How could you *not* realize that? Haven't you been listening?"

"Of course, I have. But the situations aren't the same. For the first four months of your pregnancy, I was just your friend, and David was clearly the father. Things got a little nebulous when you moved into my house and, even more so, when you decided to divorce, but it was still you and David. I haven't had very much time to adjust to my role here. Give me a chance."

"Are you sure this is what you want, Kylie? Do you want to be a parent to the baby?"

"Yes! With every bit of my heart, I do," she vowed, gripping Blair's hand tightly. "I didn't realize that you wanted me to share him so completely. I assumed you'd want to be the one calling the shots."

Blair let out the breath she'd been holding and felt her good mood start to return. "Are you sure that *you're* the lesbian?" she asked, wrinkling her nose. "I thought you people were into merging."

"You have a lot of stereotypes about my people. Where in the hell did you get them?"

"I dunno. TV?"

"Well, that explains it." Kylie reached out and captured Blair's nose between two fingers, giving it a tug. "I'll accept any name our baby chooses for me. I like all of the choices."

"I call dibs on Mommy."

"You picked that because the baby books say that's the easiest name for most babies to handle."

"There has to be some benefit to doing my homework," Blair said, playfully sticking out her tongue.

"You did a cool thing by deciding to name him Mackenzie. Now he'll have both our last names. That'll help people connect the dots that he's my son, too."

"Well, he won't really have my last name," Blair reminded her. "But there's no way I'm going back to Schneidhorst. Few women have ever been so elated to abandon their maiden names."

Kylie laughed along with her partner and then tilted her head, saying, "I haven't asked many questions about your divorce because you haven't seemed to want or need to talk about it. But now…I'm a little more invested in what happens."

Blair reached across the table and took Kylie's hand. "You're very involved now." She reached into her purse and took out her Palm Pilot. "Let's see," she said, scrolling through her files, "I filed a few days after Sadie came to visit me. Remember? The day I yelled at her and felt so crappy about it?"

"You did? I didn't know that!"

Her brow furrowed, Blair looked at her for a second. "I told you I was going to divorce him. Why would I wait?"

Kylie shook her head rapidly. "I thought talking to Sadie made you…slow down."

"Nope. I'm not the type. When I make up my mind, I act."

"I should count my blessings 'cause that's why I'm here," Kylie said, scratching her head with a half-grin on her face. "I tend to wait until there's no option. Heck, if I'd been the one who was married, I'd still be waiting for David to have that epiphany."

"Acknowledge your failures, accept responsibility for what you've done, and then move on," Blair said, her chin determinedly sticking out. "The sooner you let go, the sooner you can move on to something that works for you."

"That's my girl," Kylie said, smiling. "Your moving on has been the best thing that could've happened to me."

"Same goes for me." She looked at her Palm again and said, "David defaulted, so my petition was granted. But because I'm pregnant, we have to wait until the baby's born to determine child support and custody. So, in essence, I'm divorced. I'm only waiting for the final order."

"Wow, that seems like it was awfully easy. I thought he'd put up more of a fuss."

"No. We had a prenuptial agreement, and we didn't have any jointly owned assets. A divorce doesn't have to be devastating if you plan ahead."

Kylie stared at her head while Blair put her Palm Pilot away. "Do you want to…do something like a prenuptial agreement for us?"

"No. I talked to my attorney, and he said it wasn't necessary since we won't be legally married. We'll keep our assets separate, and everything will be clean."

Kylie stirred her espresso, staring into the dark liquid for a few moments. "I'm surprised you got around to doing that. It's only been a week."

Blair reached out and touched her lover's hand. "I think ahead. Don't over-think this. I was talking to him about my divorce, and while I had him on the phone, I asked about you and me."

Kylie held up a hand. "It's all right. I was only wondering."

Looking at Kylie until she looked back, Blair said, "I didn't plan on divorcing David when I signed a prenup, and I don't plan on leaving you, either. But if something does happen, and this doesn't work out, I wanted to know where I stand. Being prepared isn't a sin, is it?"

"No, no, of course not. I know it's important to you to have answers to these kinds of questions. No big deal."

"You sure?"

"Yeah," Kylie said, smiling. "I'm positive." *I'm positive I don't want you to know how insecure this makes me feel. But I know this is how you are, and I have to learn to accept it.*

‒

When they arrived home, they both put on their pajamas and went into the den to play with the dogs and watch the early news. Blair was wearing a pair of Kylie's flannel boxers and one of her T-shirts, and Kylie had on a nearly identical outfit. "It must be a woman thing," Kylie mused. "I've never had a lover who didn't wind up wearing my boxers and T-shirts to sleep in."

"It's a woman thing," Blair said, snuggling up to Kylie. "Your shorts are just big enough to fit comfortably over my stomach, and your shirts smell like you as long as I can grab one before you toss it in the laundry. Nice combo." They were sprawled across the sectional sofa in a new, more intimate configuration with Kylie stretched out and Blair with her back resting against her partner. This position allowed Kylie to wrap an arm around Blair's belly and feel close to the baby as well. "Mackenzie is really kicking up a storm," Blair said, patting Kylie's hand.

"I love feeling him. It's like we're really communicating."

"To me, he's communicating that he's so big he has to kick against my skin." She was quiet for a moment and then said, "Sometimes, it feels so strange. It's hard to get my brain to believe that there's another person inside my body. I…I can't explain the way it makes me feel."

"I don't think anyone can really understand it unless she's experienced it. Just like I don't think I'll ever be able to feel exactly like you do about Mackenzie. I mean, I'll love him with all my heart, but you have a hormonal connection that's uniquely maternal. Our species has survived because of that maternal bond. I truly think it's the most powerful force of love there is."

"I feel it. It's so powerful it takes my breath away. There's a little person, weighing less than two pounds, inside of me, and even though I've never met him, I'd give my life for him—without question."

Kylie tightened her hold and nuzzled her face into her partner's neck. "I know you would," the doctor whispered. "I can feel how intimately bonded you are. It's very moving for me."

"I'm so glad I have you," Blair said, her voice catching the tiniest bit. "It was so wonderful to be your friend, but to have this closeness is absolutely divine." Hugging her lover's arm tightly to herself, she added, "I'd just about convinced myself that I'd be alone for years, if not forever. It's not easy for single moms to find dates, and it would've been a lot harder for me since I'm so picky. You're a very unexpected, very welcome gift, Doctor Mackenzie, and I'm damned glad I have you."

"So, everything's good?" Kylie asked softly, her low, warm voice burring against Blair's ear.

"Yeah. Everything's very good. I'm happy, I'm happy with you, and I'm happy that you want to be a mom to the baby. We're gonna be great together."

Kylie spent a few minutes kissing Blair's neck, slowly working her way down to her lover's shoulders. She wasn't trying to arouse, merely trying to show how much she enjoyed touching Blair.

"Sweetheart, would you put some music on instead of the TV? Mackenzie much prefers music. Maybe he'll calm down a little if he hears his grandfather play."

Kylie did as she was asked, and when she returned, she urged Blair to lie down and put her head in her lap. She picked up the bottle of moisture lotion that had taken up permanent residence in the den and squirted some into her palm, warming it. Lifting Blair's shirt, she started to rub the lotion soothingly into her partner's skin, and in a few minutes, the combination of her gentle movements and the calming music resulted in significantly less fetal activity. "You're magical," Blair murmured. "He loves your touch as much as I do."

"I can't wait until I can hold him in my arms. I mean arm. I'm gonna have you in the other one. Thank God we're not having twins."

Blair snorted softly and then said, "While you were rubbing me, I started to think of my grandmother. Have I ever talked about her?"

"No, you haven't," Kylie said, thinking about the day Werner had said that Blair was exactly like his mother. "Tell me about her."

"She was my father's mother, my Gramma Lilli."

"Did she live in Chicago?"

"Uh-huh. Rogers Park. My grandfather died when my father was still in high school, so it was only the two of them for a while. Luckily, my grandfather had a successful business, and his partner bought out his share, leaving my grandmother enough money to live—not well, mind you—but enough to survive at a comfortable level."

"What did your grandfather do?"

"He was a watchmaker, and when they came to America, he went into a partnership with another man. They created a pretty successful jewelry store. It was down in the South Loop on Wabash."

"Came to America? Where were they from?"

"Germany," she said, lifting her eyes to meet Kylie's. "Didn't you know that?"

"No, I had no idea."

"With a name like Werner Schneidhorst, you thought my father's people came over on the *Mayflower*?"

Kylie chuckled softly. "No, of course not. I just didn't realize he was *born* in Germany. Why did they leave?"

Now Blair sat all the way up and looked at her confusedly. "How much wine did you have? There was a little thing called the Holocaust…"

"This is all news to me. I didn't know you were Jewish!" Shaking her head, she asked, "Are you Jewish?"

"Kinda…but not really."

"A little more detail would be helpful. Actually, any detail would help."

"Okay. My Gramma Lilli was Jewish and was observant when she was a girl. She was a bit of a rebel and started dating my grandfather against her father's wishes. He basically disowned her for dating a gentile, so she turned her back on her religion and her family."

"Wow. How hard that must have been on her."

"I'm sure it was, but she never talked about it. I only know the story because my grandfather told my father the whole scoop."

"So, what happened? Why did they leave Germany?"

"Well, they were really in love, and they got married. My grandfather's Lutheran minister wouldn't marry them, so they had to marry in the Hamburg City Hall. My grandfather's family wasn't happy about his marrying a Jew, so things were strained there, too. Gramma got pregnant with my father not long after they were married, and they struggled along while my grandfather served his long apprenticeship as a watchmaker. He had an uncle who had a shop, and he assumed he'd be offered a salaried position after he finished his apprenticeship, but that never developed. They were in bad shape, Kylie, but my grandmother had two brothers who really cared for her, and they managed to stay in contact against their father's wishes. They scrimped and saved and gave my grandparents the money to come to America."

"When was this?"

"Back in 1936. Good timing, huh?"

"Damn! How fortunate!"

"Yeah. Who would have guessed that being disowned by your families could wind up saving your lives?"

"How did they survive?"

"My grandfather had some acquaintances, and he got hooked up with this man—the one who became his business partner. Lots of hard work paid off, and they were finally able to open a decent store. And they did all right. Things didn't go as well for my Gramma's family, though. As far as she could ascertain, her entire immediate family was murdered." She said this very quietly, and Kylie could feel her partner's body start to shake. Pulling her closer, Kylie held her for a long while, soothing her with soft touches and gentle kisses upon her forehead.

"I'm so sorry, Blair," she whispered. "I'm so sorry she had to lose her family twice."

"Yeah, that's it," Blair said, sniffling. "She lost them twice. She was such a loving woman. I can't imagine how callous you'd have to be to cut off all contact with your child because she disobeyed you."

"Don't be too harsh on your great-grandfather. That was a different time and a different culture. I mean, in retrospect, it was wise for the Jews to be suspicious of gentiles."

"Yeah, I know you're right, but it's still beyond my ken."

"Was your father raised as a Christian or a Jew?"

"A little of both, I guess. They celebrated Passover, but they also celebrated Christmas. We went to Gramma's for Passover, but it was more of a cultural thing than a religious thing. I swear, I didn't know we were Jewish until I was in the sixth or seventh grade."

"Do you consider yourself Jewish?"

"I had a few years in high school when I tried to be a Jew. I think I was searching for a group to belong to. As I learned more about the genocide, I decided we had to claim our Jewishness so that our numbers were greater. I reasoned that if everyone who had Jewish blood claimed the faith, we'd have a real force." She smiled up at Kylie and said, "I went to a very progressive high school. Everybody had a cause."

"So, what happened? Why did you drop it?"

"Well, to be honest, I didn't get much support from my family. My dad didn't make a big deal about it, but the whole thing kinda confused him. He was technically a Jew, since his mother was, but he didn't feel like one. He identified more with the German side of his heritage. Probably because of the composers and conductors," she said. "Gramma liked retaining some of the cultural aspects of her faith, but she didn't see the point of my actually joining, either. I went to a couple of local temples, but they discouraged me, as well. I would have had to convert, since my mother wasn't Jewish, and when I told the rabbis that my parents weren't crazy about the idea, they didn't think it was wise to pursue it. They both said it was something I should look into when I was an adult."

"Have you had any urge to investigate again?"

"Well, I've had plenty of time, but I haven't done it."

"I'll support you if you're interested. Heck, I'll even keep a kosher kitchen."

"You're a good sport. I guess my only reason for wanting to do it is to make a political statement. My grandmother lost so many to hatred that it seems like I should replenish the ranks as much as I can."

"Tell me more about your grandmother. It sounds like she was a big influence in your life."

"Oh, she was. I think about her all the time now. She'd be so happy about the baby." She started to cry again, but forced herself to stop. Laughing softly, she said, "My dad says I'm exactly like her emotionally."

"Tell me how?" Kylie asked, already privy to Werner's thoughts on the matter.

"I think I'm most like her in my ability to move on. She lost her family, her faith, her country, and millions of her fellow Jews. But you would never have known any of that from seeing her. She had this incredible ability to be thankful for what she had and make the best of it. Every day she woke up, she was happy to see the sun in the sky. When I'd ask her to talk about growing up in Germany, she'd tell me the cutest little stories. She had hundreds of little tales, and she made it sound so idyllic. And I don't think she did that to humor me. I think that's how she remembered it. She talked about her father like he was the sweetest man on Earth, and he disowned her!"

"Remarkable," Kylie said.

"She was remarkable. She's the one who used to talk to me about being adopted and how blessed the whole family was to have me be a part of it. Honestly, she's the one who made me feel proud that I'd been chosen by my family, rather than being angry that my birth parents had given me away. It seemed like a good thing when she talked to me about it. She used to tell me that my parents had no other way to have children and that she wouldn't have had a grandchild if they hadn't been able to adopt. I knew how much she loved me, and I felt really great about being chosen to be her granddaughter." She sniffled a few tears away and then pulled back when she noticed her cheek was wet. "Are you crying?" she asked, turning around to see Kylie's red eyes.

"That's such a wonderful story," she said, her voice shaking. "I'll bet you made her very happy."

"You know, I did," she said, a note of pride in her voice. "I saw her every Sunday—at a minimum. When I was little, she watched me during the evenings when my parents were both at work. Then later, when I was old enough to ride public transit by myself, I'd hop on the bus, go up to Rogers Park, and see her in the afternoon. We spent a lot of time together, and it was wonderful for both of us." She looked thoughtful for a moment and then said, "You know, I really wanted to go away to college, but her health was failing, and I couldn't bear to be too far away. That's the only reason I chose Northwestern. I was ten minutes away on the Evanston Express."

"When did she die?"

"When I was a freshman in college. She started having heart palpitations, but by the time they got her to Evanston Hospital, she was gone. That was a very, very hard time for me." She blinked away a few tears and gave her partner a watery smile. "Still is."

"What was her family name?"

"Simon," Blair answered. "Lilli Simon."

"Well, Lilli wouldn't do for a boy, but Simon has some real appeal."

Wordlessly, Blair turned in place and buried her head against Kylie's chest, crying for a long time. Kylie soothed her with gentle touches, and finally, she was able to speak. "You know me so well. That would mean so much to me."

"It would mean a lot to me, too. We have to honor the woman who made you feel so special."

"Mackenzie Simon Spencer sounds very cool."

"Uhm, what would you think if we switched the names around a little bit?"

"What do you mean?"

"I don't think your grandmother should have second billing," Kylie said. "She means too much to you for that. I think the baby's name should be Simon Mackenzie Spencer."

"But...but...I want to name him after you!"

"Blair, I've never been more touched than I was on the night you told me that. I swear that's the truth. But I'm here, and I'm going to be here for him every day. Your grandmother won't be. Naming him after her will let him know that he has mommies who love him and grandparents who love him and a great-grandmother who would have loved him as much as we do, even though she'll never get to meet him."

Blair looked up at her partner and asked in a shaky voice, "Will you take me to bed and cuddle me all night long? I need to be close."

"Of course, I will. I'll cuddle you every night. I promise." She kissed her gently and then helped her up from the deep cushions, draping an arm around her shoulders as they made the short trip, eight tiny feet scampering after them.

⟶

The next evening, Blair was out late. Kylie tried to wait up for her, but found her eyelids closing at her usual bedtime, so she gave up. Blair tried to sneak into bed, but the dogs leapt up right before she pulled it off, waking Kylie. "Hi," she said groggily. "Just get home?"

"Yeah. I met some new clients for dinner. They want to list a very expensive house with me, but they both talk like they've been given truth serum. Do people really think I give a damn about where they grew up and what they think the stock market's going to do this year? I wanted to shake them and say, 'I want to sell your house so I get a commission! That's all I care about!'"

"Come here and let me calm you down, baby," Kylie said. "I think my mouth is still nice and minty."

"Aw...you're so sweet." Blair cuddled up as well as she could, and they kissed for a long time. Kylie's hands roamed up and down Blair's back, massaging her a little as they kissed. When she felt her lover start to relax, Kylie rolled her onto her other side and kissed her neck and shoulders, a surefire method for lulling her to sleep.

"Know what I like?" Blair asked, her voice a little groggy.

"Unh-uh."

"I like that sometimes you kiss me for a while and then stop."

"I love kissing you—for a few minutes or lots longer."

"You know what I mean. I'm sure there are guys who like to kiss, too, but I never dated any of them. They were always so goal-oriented. Kissing was a short stop on the way to fucking."

"Hey, I'm goal-oriented, too," Kylie said. "It's just that kissing you until I feel all warm inside is my goal."

"Oh, Doctor Mackenzie, you are such a catch." Blair cuddled a little closer and burrowed her butt into Kylie's lap. "I love you."

"I love you, too." Kylie placed a gentle kiss on her partner's neck and then patted her belly. "I love you, too, Mack...Simon. You get some rest so your mommy can, okay?"

"It's hard, isn't it?"

"Yeah," Kylie said, laughing softly. "I've been trying to call him Simon every time I think of him, but it's gonna take some work."

"Do you really want to change his name? It was incredibly generous of you to offer, but—"

"I'm certain. Besides, Simon's so much easier to spell. If he was Mackenzie, he wouldn't be able to spell his own name until he was in third grade."

"Don't tease. I really want to make sure you're okay with this."

"I'm absolutely positive, but you have to be certain, too."

"I am. I love the idea. Then he can have both of his mommies' names as last names. Hey, you know, we could hyphenate them."

"No, no. That's too much. I'm more than happy to provide his middle name. Let him decide how much of it to use. If he likes me, he might choose to be called Simon Mackenzie Spencer. Very formal," she said, smiling.

"They only refer to serial killers by all three names."

"Tell that to…Robert Louis Stevenson or Henry David Thoreau or Elizabeth Cady Stanton or George Washington Carver."

"Next time I see 'em," Blair promised. "Now, pat Simon to sleep."

Kylie did, and the baby calmed down after a few minutes. She leaned over and kissed Blair's belly, and the baby did one last somersault and calmed again.

"He likes your kisses, too."

"Just wait until he gets out here. I'll be kissing him so much his skin will chap."

"I wish I could take him out for a while tonight. I'd love to have my old body back. That's what you ought to work on—a removable uterus."

"I'll get right on it," Kylie said. "Remind me in the morning." She kissed Blair one last time, put a hand on their baby, and was asleep in seconds.

⌒

Kylie woke immediately when her partner got out of bed at 3:00 a.m. and then patiently waited for her to return. She was a little surprised when Blair walked over to her side of the bed and sat down. "You awake?" Blair asked.

"Uh-huh. What's wrong?"

"Nothing. I wanted to see if you're interested in fooling around a little." She pushed Kylie's hair from her face and trailed her fingers across her lover's cheek. "Had another sex dream."

"Sex dream?" Kylie asked, the room just bright enough to show her smile. "Tell me about it. Maybe we can recreate it."

"Ooh…that's a very good idea. It was really vivid—really sensual." She leaned over a little and took Kylie's hand, placing it on her breast. Her voice dropped into a low, sexy register, and she said, "I was straddling you while I was on my hands and knees…"

"I like it so far," Kylie said, her own voice taking on a sexy tone. Her hand started to compress the flesh it rested against, moving slowly and gently.

"You were propped up a little so I could reach you easily, and I'd lower my breasts down to your mouth, switching back and forth. You sucked on them so sweetly, caressing them until they started to tingle. Of course, every little suckle made my clit throb," she purred, sliding Kylie's hand downward.

"Mine's throbbing now," Kylie growled.

"So urgent," Blair said softly. "Slow down a little, now. Take it nice and easy. I need you to be gentle and tender with me tonight. Let me experience all of the sensations."

"Let me go brush my teeth," Kylie said, starting to sit up.

"Don't bother. I don't need a bit of foreplay. All I need is that sweet mouth on my breasts."

Kylie reached over, removed Blair's shirt, and then started to trail the tips of her short nails over her partner's skin.

"Perfect." Blair threw her head back, her golden hair catching the slight glow of the moon. "That's what I need—truly perfect."

After a few minutes, Blair pulled away and positioned Kylie as best she could, propping her up with several pillows. Standing, Blair pushed off her boxers and then climbed on top of her lover, straddling Kylie as she had in her dream. Kylie lifted her knees to provide a little stability, and then Blair leaned in close, letting one breast dangle just above her lover's lips.

Kylie looked up, her face flushed with pleasure. "There's no more arousing sight in the whole world." She took the breast into her mouth, tenderly laving it with her tongue. She didn't exert any pressure, knowing that Blair was still very sensitive. Surprised by her own satisfied growl, Kylie smiled when she heard another from her partner as the tender flesh was bathed with kisses.

As her breasts were being caringly loved, Blair began to urge her lover to suck a little harder, something Kylie did with great reluctance. "Come on, baby, suck me," Blair growled, making Kylie shiver from head to toe.

Kylie increased the pressure a tiny bit and then stilled completely, taking her mouth away. Reaching out, she grabbed the bedside lamp, drawing it close enough to switch it on. "What's wrong?" Blair asked in alarm.

Shaking her head while taking a tissue from the box, Kylie brought it to her mouth and then inspected it carefully. Nodding, she switched the light off and got back into position. "No big deal," she said. "It's only a little colostrum secretion."

Immediately, Blair climbed off and flopped onto the mattress, draping an arm across her eyes. "Oh, that was sexy."

"Hey," Kylie soothed, leaning over her. "Don't let little things like that bother you. It's no big deal."

"It must have been for you to stop and spit," she said, obviously on the verge of tears. "It must have tasted horrible!"

"That's not true! I'm a doctor—a scientist. When I notice something out of the ordinary, I look at it. It's part of my makeup, I swear. I thought that what I tasted was a little colostrum, but I wanted to be sure. I'm really sorry if I ruined your mood."

"I grossed you out," Blair mumbled, starting to cry.

"You did not! I swear I only wanted to take a look and make sure the fluid was clear. There was nothing gross about it! It actually tasted kinda good, and the next time you leak a little, I want you to taste it so you know how pleasant it is."

"I'm gonna do this again?" she asked, obviously alarmed. "Then we won't play with my breasts anymore."

"This is gonna happen every once in a while—with no stimulation at all. Your breasts are getting ready to work. They're making sure all systems are go."

"I hate this," she cried, rolling onto her side and turning away from Kylie. "Somebody else is in charge of my body!"

Cuddling up behind her, Kylie tucked an arm around her, curling a hand up under her belly. "Come on, now; don't let it get to you. Someone else *is* in charge of your body, but the one in charge is our baby in there. Little Simon's like a pilot in an airplane, checking all of the controls before takeoff." She trailed her hand up across Blair's abdomen and then hefted one of her breasts in her hand. "He wants to make sure there's plenty for him to eat when he gets here. That's all."

"I feel freakish," she sniffed. "My breasts are leaking, and there's always something going on with my vagina. It doesn't feel like my body anymore."

"Sure it is, but you have a boarder for a few more months. Once he moves out and gets his own room, you'll be back to normal in no time."

"Are you sure?" Blair's voice was shaking, and Kylie could hear how much she needed to be reassured.

"I'm absolutely positive. You're gonna be in control once again. Promise."

"It's so weird. There are so many changes. I really wasn't prepared for this."

"I know," the doctor soothed, "but there are some good changes, too." She gave a gentle squeeze to the breast she was still holding. "You tell me how your breasts tingle and react to the slightest touch. That can be good."

"Yeah, that's good," Blair agreed, sniffling.

"And you're extra sensitive down here, too," she whispered, tickling lightly between her partner's legs. "That's been kinda good, hasn't it? You get aroused so easily, and you have such intense orgasms. I know how good those feel."

Blair nodded, her tears now dry. "I'd like to keep the orgasms, even after the baby's born."

"We'll have to see what we can do," Kylie said. "Maybe I can do my job extra well." She started to move, rubbing her body against Blair's back. "Let me give you one of those nice, big orgasms. You know you want to."

Sounding tentative again, Blair asked, "Are you sure *you* want to?"

"Oh, yeah. I'm positive that I want to. If you're not in the mood, I'm gonna have to go solo. You've really got me going."

Blair rolled over to face her partner, giving her a decidedly sexy look. "Take off your shorts, sweetheart."

Kylie did and smiled as Blair snuggled closer and started to kiss her. Her hand settled on Kylie's leg, gently urging her to raise it. As soon as her fingers slid into the larger woman's wetness, Kylie pulled her mouth away to gasp in relief. "Oh, yeah," she panted, closing her eyes immediately to go back for more of the fiery kisses.

Urging Blair into the same position, Kylie's hand slipped down to nestle between her lover's legs. Murmuring against Blair's mouth, she growled, "You make me so hot!"

"Mmm," Blair moaned, holding on to Kylie with a rabid intensity. "Make me come, baby. Make me come now."

Slipping her tongue into Blair's mouth while her fingers slid through the copious wetness, Kylie tried to stay focused, keeping her pace even and smooth, even though Blair's questing fingers were about to drive her mad. She slid two fingers into her partner, as her breathing became labored, and then caressed the head of her clit with her thumb, making Blair's body jump and twitch. Just as the first spasms of her climax rolled through her body, Blair felt Kylie start to respond as well. The blonde thrust her tongue into her partner's mouth as her fingers slid into the doctor's hot, wet flesh, and soon, they were both crying out lustily, entwined in each other's arms.

"I love you," Kylie whispered, her voice shaking. "I love you so much."

"Hold me tight," Blair begged. "Cuddle me all night long."

Wrapping her in a snug embrace, Kylie smiled down at her as her lover lay her head on her shoulder. "Go to sleep, love," she soothed, the vibrations from her chest rumbling against Blair's cheek.

"Love you," Blair murmured before falling asleep immediately.

"I love you both," Kylie whispered, making sure that her hand was resting upon her growing child before she drifted off as well.

⌐

"Hey, Blair?"

"Yeah?"

"Can I invite Nick to go to the Bowl with us tonight?"

"Sure. By the way, you don't need my permission to invite people to do things with us."

"Well, I thought I'd ask this time," she said, "'cause he's a very perceptive guy, and he'll pick up on our closeness. I guess I'm asking if it's okay to tell him about us."

"What part of 'Tell everybody' didn't you get? I thought you told him already. He's your best friend, Kylie!"

"I didn't want to do it until you gave me the okay. I mean, you know him, too."

"Yeah, but I don't see why that matters. Who have you told, anyway?"

"Just the guys at work. I don't know why, but I haven't been in the mood to tell anyone else. It's like our little secret."

"Do you think your parents will be unhappy?"

"No, no!" Kylie's eyes brightened as she said, "My mom will be ecstatic! She really likes you."

"Not your father?" Blair asked, intentionally narrowing her eyes.

"He likes you fine. He's not the type to express his feelings verbally. But he spoke with you and was interested enough to ask you what you do for a living. That's a lot from him."

"Tough audience!"

"Well, I think I'll tell 'em tomorrow when I call. What about you?"

"Oh, I've got to tell mine in person. I thought I'd do it when we go to Chicago for your father's birthday."

"Dreading it?"

"No, not really. I think they'll be confused, and I think they'll worry about me, but that should be about it."

"I hope so," Kylie said, a sympathetic look on her face. "I don't want them to upset you."

"They're both exposed to a lot of gay people, and they're both very liberal in their views. Trust me, they won't blow a gasket."

"Nick might," Kylie admitted, chuckling to herself.

"What's funny?"

"Nothing," the doctor said. "Just thinking about Nick. I'd like to tell him in person, if you don't mind."

Blair approached her partner and grasped Kylie's hands, linking them behind herself. "Live...your...life. You don't need my permission to do things. Obviously, it's polite to tell me you're leaving the house, but that's all you need to do. I'm used to a lot of autonomy, and it makes me uncomfortable to think you feel that we have to ask permission to come and go."

"I don't," Kylie said, shaking her head. "I'm not usually like this, really. I'm trying to get a feel for how we should treat each other."

"We should treat each other like adults who have jobs and outside friends and interests. I want you to do what you want to do. When you're happy, you'll be a better partner, and the same is true for me."

Kylie dipped her head and kissed her, lingering for a moment to suck on her lower lip. "My problem is that you're the only thing on my mind. I'm sure the feeling will fade, but I love falling in love."

"I love it, too, sweetheart. Now, go see your buddy, and when you come back, bring us some lunch." She patted her firmly on the butt and ordered, "Don't rush home, either. Live your life, Kylie."

⟶

Before she left, Kylie gave Nick a call to make sure he was home and then took off. She arrived at his condo a few minutes later and gave him a sunny smile when he opened the door before she had the chance to buzz. Giving him a kiss, she went in and stood just inside the doorway, suddenly feeling a tiny bit uncomfortable.

He put his arm around her shoulders and led her out to his small but comfortably appointed balcony. "Get you something to drink?"

"No, thanks. I came by for a couple of quick things. One, we thought you might like to go to the Bowl with us tonight. Last chance for classical music, you know."

"Oh, I would have loved to, but I have a date. I'm seeing that flight attendant I told you about."

"Oh...the flight attendant, huh? Is she cute?"

"Yep. And she's bright, too. I really like her. I think you will, too. Maybe I'll have you over for brunch to meet her."

"Love to." She shifted a bit in her chair and cleared her throat. "The other reason I dropped by is to give you the bad news about Blair."

"Bad news?"

"Yeah. I know you've had a little crush on her since the night you met her, but it's not gonna get a chance to blossom. She's in love."

"Going back to her husband?"

"Nope. She fell in love with a really charming, good-looking, talented doctor. You know how they are," she said dramatically. "That's a tough person to go up against, Nick. The cards are stacked against you."

"She didn't!" he gasped. "She fell in love with you?"

"Hey, don't say it like she should be committed!"

"Oh, Kylie, you know that's not how I meant it. I didn't have any idea that she was…gay. It's no surprise that you care for her, but I didn't think you played on the same team."

"Surprised the hell out of me, too. But she's a very determined woman when she decides she wants something. And she decided she wanted me," she said, hitching her thumb at herself.

He reached over and grabbed her knee, waggling it enthusiastically. "I'm happy for you, buddy. I never guessed you'd wind up with Blair, but I'm very glad to hear it."

"Yeah, I've obviously been looking in the wrong places all these years. I should have been looking for pregnant straight women."

"So…she's not gay?"

"Not up until now."

"Huh. Any problem with that?" he asked. "I mean, I can't imagine this isn't a big adjustment for her."

"No, no problems. She doesn't seem to think the jump is a very big one. She's a very open-minded woman."

"Being open-minded is one thing; denial is another." He made a face and said, "I guess I shouldn't have said that aloud."

"It's okay. I know it's a…unique situation."

"Are you sure she knows what she's doing? I'd really hate to see you get burned here."

"I think she has both eyes open, Nick. I really do. She's a very decisive woman when she's chosen a course of action."

"Wow," he said, looking a little uncomfortable. "So…can I be the man of honor at your commitment ceremony?"

Kylie squirmed in her chair and gave him a thoughtful look. "I don't think she's at that point yet to be honest."

"Oh." His eyebrows lifted, and he cocked his head. "So, you're only dating?"

"No," she said, scowling. "It's more than that, but I don't know what to call it. We love each other, and we're gonna co-parent the baby, so it's a big deal…but it's a little vague."

"Wow! That's…you're right. It must be vague 'cause it sounds like a marriage, but you say it's not."

"Okay. Here's the truth. I'm ready for a permanent commitment, but Blair's…well, she's just divorcing her husband. I know she loves me, but she hasn't given me the whole 'I can't live without you' thing that I feel for her. That doesn't mean she doesn't love me," Kylie insisted. "She's cautious, and I don't blame her."

"You mean because of her marriage?"

"Yeah, that and the fact that she's pretty cautious emotionally, anyway. She's very logical, even about emotional topics. It's hard for her to really let go."

"But you feel loved, right?"

Kylie smiled a full, easy smile that made Nick smile back. "Oh, yeah. I know she loves me. Maybe not as much as I love her right now, but she'll get there. I trust her. I also trust her judgment."

"And I trust yours," he said. He stood up, and Kylie did, too. They hugged each other for a long time with Kylie squeezing her friend as hard as she could. "I'm sure this will work out. And I'm always gonna be jealous. She's, uhm, I guess I'd better keep my opinion of her to myself since she's your woman now."

Kylie grinned at him. "She's hot, isn't she?"

"Sizzling," Nick agreed, sharing her infectious grin. "If she hadn't been married at the time, I would have asked her out the first time I saw her at the Getty. She's *exactly* my type."

"Well, she's exactly my type, too, buddy. You snooze you lose. Meaning..." She jumped around in a circle, her head and curls bouncing. "I win! I win! I win!"

Chapter Ten

*O*n Sunday afternoon, Kylie tiptoed into the living room and spied her lover sitting on the couch. She walked up behind her and surprised Blair with kisses to both cheeks. When Blair turned around in surprise, Kylie pounced upon her lips, kissing her soundly. "I called every one of my poker buddies, and then I called my parents. Everyone is very, very happy to welcome you into the family," she said, beaming a grin. "For some strange reason, no one seemed very surprised. I think we might have been the last ones to know."

"No, I was the last one to know. You, Doctor Mackenzie, had a clue."

"True. Oh, my parents asked to speak to you, but I figured that might be a little embarrassing, so I said you were napping."

"Why would I be embarrassed? If anyone should be embarrassed, it's them. They're the ones responsible for creating you."

"You're such a funny woman," Kylie teased. "Lucky for me, I get your rather odd sense of humor." She sat on the floor in front of Blair and took her hand. Giving her a sober look, she said, "I didn't want to put you on the spot. I figured that if you wanted to talk, you could call them back."

"Thanks. I think I will." She leaned over awkwardly and kissed Kylie. "Will you call them back and then put me on? I feel a little uncomfortable cold-calling."

"Sure. They were leaving to go to Alan's for dinner. We can give them a buzz later this evening." She smiled up at Blair and said, "We can use my family as practice for telling the more difficult people on the list."

Running her hand through Kylie's hair, Blair said, "My parents will be fine. Really."

"I didn't mean your parents. I was thinking of Sadie and David."

Blair rolled her eyes and put down the book she had been reading. "I changed my mind. I don't wanna tell him," she said, sounding like a child. "I guarantee he's been boinking that girl I saw him with, and lord knows, I don't want him to call and tell me that."

Giving her a faint smile, Kylie pulled herself up and kissed Blair lightly. "Okay. I didn't mean to interfere." She picked up the discarded book and put it back into Blair's hands. "I'm gonna take the pups for a long walk. They're getting a little antsy."

"Let me come with you," Blair said, starting to get up.

"No, I'd...like to be able to let them go at a good pace. You and I can go out later for a more leisurely stroll, okay?"

"Kylie?" she asked, taking her hand. "Are you okay?"

"Sure." The taller woman bent down and kissed her partner on the top of the head. "Take a nap if you need to. We'll be out of your hair for a while."

"I like you in my hair," Blair said, still holding on to Kylie's hand.

"That's good to know," Kylie said, lifting Blair's hand to kiss it once more. "See you later."

Blair watched the dogs react jubilantly when their retractable leashes were taken from a drawer in the kitchen and then chuckled to herself as they immediately wound their way around Kylie's legs, forcing her to slowly unwind them. "Have fun, guys!" Blair called out.

"We will," Kylie said, blowing her a kiss.

When the door closed, Blair decided that Kylie's suggestion was a good one, and she curled up on the sofa in the living room. She lay there for a long while, unable to relax enough to sleep. She knew something was bothering Kylie, but she couldn't decide what had triggered it. She kept going over their conversation, wondering why Kylie would be upset by her reticence to tell David of their relationship. She tossed and turned for a few minutes, trying to recall exactly what she'd said. *All I said was that I didn't see why I had to tell him, and I made it clear that I didn't want to know about his personal life, either. What's wrong with that?*

She got up and went into the kitchen to get a glass of juice. Standing there, she recalled the exact words she'd used and then started to shake her head. *Oh, shit, that sounded like I was equating her with the bimbo David's screwing.* She set the glass down and grabbed her keys, heading out to look for her partner.

Their neighborhood was quite hilly, and they normally walked on the more level streets close to their home. But today, the good doctor had taken the pups on the street that led straight up into the hills behind the house. The trio was resting under a large Chinese elm near the edge of someone's property. It was hard to tell which of the three was most winded, but all looked grateful when Blair pulled up. Blair looked at her lover with an affection-filled gaze. "Somebody got carried away, didn't she?"

"Little bit. I was gonna have to carry 'em back. They lay down here and refused to go another step."

"Those are my smart puppies, right, babies?" Blair said to the jumping dogs, Kylie holding them back so they couldn't scratch the car. "Come on and hop in. You look like you need a cool drink."

"I won't argue." Kylie herded the pups into their crate and climbed into the front seat.

"Let's get a drink and go to the Palisades," Blair suggested. "I'd like to sit by the ocean and watch the world go by."

"Okay." As they took off, Kylie turned her head and gazed out the side window, lost in her own thoughts. Blair didn't try to make conversation, figuring they could talk more easily once they were outdoors. After buying a couple of Italian sodas and getting a cup of water for the dogs, they went over to Ocean Boulevard and found a bench along the cliffs above the Pacific. The ocean rolled rhythmically below them, and the air was sweet and clean there above the water. Each woman held a dog on her lap, and Blair reached over and took Kylie's hand. "I'm sorry I hurt your feelings."

Kylie didn't meet her gaze, continuing to look out at the water. "I didn't say you did."

"You didn't have to. You acted as if you were hurt, and after going over the conversation in my mind, I realized what I'd said and how it must have sounded to you."

The strong planes of Kylie's face were burnished with a golden hue in the late-afternoon sun. Her voice sounded stiff and formal. "I'm sorry if I was being overly sensitive."

"Tell me what you think I meant, and then I'll tell you if you were being overly sensitive."

Kylie frowned slightly. "I don't wanna."

"Come on; you can tell me."

"No. You'll think I'm being stupid."

"Will not."

"Will so."

Blair leaned over and whispered into her ear, "You're not stupid. I hurt your feelings, and I'd like to know what you thought I meant. Then I can tell you what I was trying to say."

"Tell me what you were trying to say," the doctor said, completely intractable.

Blair paused a second, but then conceded. "Okay. I was trying to say that I don't want to share my private life with David. He's gonna be pissy about it, and I don't wanna deal with that right now."

"Then why'd you mention the woman he's 'boinking'?" Kylie asked, her voice filled with hurt.

"'Cause *I'm* stupid. I meant to say that his private life isn't my business and hearing about it will piss me off. I'm sure hearing about mine will do the same to him. I didn't, in any way, mean to equate our relationship with some casual fling he's probably having. Nothing could be further from the truth." Lifting Kylie's hand and placing a kiss on it, Blair insisted, "I'm very proud to be your lover, and I'm sorry I made you angry."

"I'm not angry. I was hurt. It's no big deal."

"When I hurt you, it *is* a big deal. It'll always be a big deal, and I'll always try to apologize when I do it." She leaned in again and kissed her cheek, resting her head on Kylie's shoulder.

"Thanks. I'm better now." Blair felt the stiff set of her lover's body shift and relax, and she knew Kylie was telling the truth.

They sat that way for a long while, neither speaking, just feeling the cool breeze coming off the water. The dogs were in their semi-alert state—halfway dozing, but waking whenever another dog went by. First Nicky, then Nora, sat up and took notice of a cute Jack Russell terrier, and Blair sat up abruptly when the owner of the dog said, "Blair?"

"Hi, Daniel. How are you?"

"I'm good," he said, looking surreptitiously at Kylie. "Cute dogs. Are they…yours?"

"They're ours," she said without hesitation. "Daniel Carr, this is my partner, Kylie Mackenzie. Kylie, Daniel's one of the principals of the firm I used to work for." Kylie extended her hand and shook Daniel's, and they each mumbled a greeting. Turning back to the surprised-looking man, Blair said, "I have a couple of pieces of news. Kylie and I are having a baby this December."

"Wow," he said, looking truly stunned. "I had no idea…I hadn't heard that you'd gotten divorced."

She shrugged, unwilling to reveal too many details. "Yes, I have a new family now. A new spouse, two young dogs, and a baby all in one year. Just goes to show that you never know what tomorrow will bring."

"I guess not," he said, clearly trying to sound as if he wasn't flabbergasted. "Well, you look great. Pregnancy obviously agrees with you."

"It does," she said. Squeezing Kylie's hand, she added, "Being in love with a wonderful woman agrees with me, too. It's been a great year."

"I saw that you hit the $25 million mark already," he said, shaking his head. "I never should have let you get away."

Laughing wryly, she said, "I believe that's what I told you when I left."

"I honestly thought you were bluffing. I couldn't believe that you'd struck such a good deal with my biggest competitor."

"You know, Daniel, I'm one of the worst card players in the world. And it's all because I can't bluff. I was straight-up honest with you."

"I know that now," he said, giving her a chagrined look. "I assumed you were lying. Everyone does!" He laughed and said, "Having a $25 million woman on the staff would ensure me of a hell of a year."

"Daniel," Blair said, giving him the same smile she wore whenever she had Kylie dead to rights, "I was selling over $15 million when I was with you, and I'd only been selling for five years. It was clear that I was going to be a good earner."

"But I thought you'd peaked. I was sure you were too frank to really make it big in this business."

"Apparently not," she said, grinning at him. "I've got another $10 million booked that'll show up in the fourth quarter report."

"Ten million!"

"Yeah. I sold that vacant lot up on Mulholland in Brentwood a few weeks ago. It's amazing what people will pay for a quarter acre of land, isn't it?" Her tone was almost droll, but she didn't seem to be boasting, which seemed to exasperate Daniel.

"Well, if you ever need a change, you know I'd love to have you back. I'm sure I could improve on your current deal. I'd really like the chance to try."

"Thanks. I'll keep that in mind." She reached down and scratched his dog behind the ears while Nicky and Nora sniffed at him. "It was nice seeing you."

"You, too. Good to meet you," he said, shaking Kylie's hand again. "And congratulations to you both."

"Thanks," both women said as he walked away.

"That was interesting," Kylie said, watching as the man walked away. "How're you feeling?"

Blair sat in thoughtful contemplation for a moment. "Good. Very good," she said, looking quite content. "That's something that's been bugging me for years. It's nice to know he realizes he made a mistake. I was really insulted when he wouldn't even negotiate with me. I wasn't looking to leave, but when my current firm approached me with such a great deal, I had to listen to them. I tried to get Daniel to make a counter-offer, but he blew me off!"

Kylie nodded and found she couldn't help smiling at her partner. "How'd it feel to tell someone about our relationship?"

Blair looked at her for just a second and then smiled, her green eyes crinkling up when she did. "Huh. I didn't really think about that. I guess it felt fine since I didn't notice it."

"You are a woman of surprises," Kylie said. "Most of them good ones."

Blair reached up and tugged on her partner's ear, pulling until Kylie fidgeted. "Wanna correct that?"

"All of 'em. Every single one of 'em. Good, good, good."

The pups settled down again after the excitement of meeting a new dog, and Blair once again placed her head on Kylie's shoulder. "I could stay like this all night. I'm perfectly content."

"Me, too," Kylie said, gripping her partner's hand tightly. "Me, too."

⟶

Later that night, they lay upon the sofa in the den, sprawled upon one another as usual. "It was so cute listening to you talk to my parents," Kylie said, unable to control her enthusiasm. "You looked so adorable."

"They were really nice. Your mom especially. She's very sweet—kinda like you."

Kylie chuckled and said, "My dad has some wonderful qualities, too, but sweetness or sentimentality isn't one of them. My mom is pretty warm when you get past her reserved veneer."

"That describes her perfectly. She has a veneer that makes her seem a little stiff."

"Hey, we're WASPs. We're all about stiff. Now, my dad doesn't have a veneer. He's stiff all the way through."

"He's a nice guy. I think we'll get along fine. He was very interested in how my pregnancy's going."

"Shoptalk's his favorite thing. When we go to visit, he'll drive you nuts."

"Nah. I can handle him. As long as he doesn't try to examine me, everything will be cool."

"I defer to him on nearly everything," Kylie said, "but you can rest assured that I'd voice a complaint if he tried to get your clothes off."

"Only one Doctor Mackenzie sees me with my clothes off." She pressed a kiss to Kylie's temple.

Kylie slid her hand under Blair's shirt, tickling across her belly. "How ya feeling tonight? Need a backrub?"

"No, I feel good tonight. Lying around all weekend is really rejuvenating." She cuddled closer and said, "I'm mentally gearing up for work tomorrow. I wasn't really prepared to do it yet, but I'm going to have to tell my co-workers about us—if Daniel hasn't done it for me."

"Are you serious?"

"Oh, yeah, he's the world's biggest gossip. I guarantee he was on the phone thirty seconds after he got home."

"Are you okay with that? I mean, I don't know what your plans were, but I can't think you're happy being forced to tell people."

Blair shrugged. "It's no big deal. I haven't really wanted to get into it with people, but I can handle it."

"How many of your co-workers know you and David have split up?"

"None of 'em. I don't like to talk about my private life at work. Never have. There's a reason it's called a private life," she said. "I only wish some of my co-workers shared my philosophy. Some people tell you the most intimate details of their lives. I'll never understand that."

"You bring that out in people. You're not only easy to talk to, you seem interested. People pick up on that."

Blair said, "I *am* interested. There are just some things that I don't want to hear about. Just like there are some things I don't like to talk about. My sexual and intimate relations are definitely in that category."

Sitting up a little, Kylie looked at her partner for a moment and said, "Then don't tell them. You don't like to talk about it; other people obviously do. Let the ones who like it go ahead and talk. They'll probably like it even more if they can speculate and imagine all sorts of scandalous scenarios."

With a small smile on her face, Blair cocked her head and asked, "Do you think I should do that?"

"Why not? I told my partners, but that's only because I socialize with them occasionally. You don't see any of your co-workers outside of work, so you're obviously not very close to them. Why tell them intimate things if you don't want to?"

"You know, that's not a bad suggestion. My telling them won't make them gossip any less. Why not simply let the rumor mill handle this?"

"Exactly. If anyone gets up the nerve to ask you directly, you can confirm it or tell them it's a private matter that you don't care to discuss."

Blair nodded, her expression contemplative. "I'll tell the members of my team tomorrow 'cause they'll be hurt if they think I didn't trust them enough to tell them. Then I'll see what happens." She smiled and kissed Kylie tenderly. "Thanks for the suggestion. I feel calmer already." Adding another kiss to the tip of Kylie's nose, she said, "Now I only have to worry about telling David."

"But I thought…"

"Kylie, I spout off about things, but I'd never let David hear about this from someone else. Besides, no matter how he feels about it, he's Mac…Simon's father, and there's a chance he'll want to be involved in the baby's life in some capacity. I really want to maintain as good a relationship with him as possible."

"I think that's wise."

"I'm not ready to do it yet," Blair cautioned. "Maybe next weekend."

"Do it when you feel ready. You'll know when the time's right."

"I'm not so sure about that," Blair said wryly, "but I'll know when I'm able to gut it up and get it over with."

"I, uhm, noticed that you're having trouble with the switch to Simon. I am, too."

"We'll get used to it," Blair assured her. "We've been thinking of him as Mackenzie for so long that it's gonna take a while. It's like when I changed my name to Spencer."

"Are you sure you *want* to change it? It was just a suggestion."

Blair smiled at her partner and then reached up and tugged on her nose. "I hate it," she said, starting to giggle. "I love the idea of the change, but he's Mackenzie to me. I think he'll always be Mackenzie even if his birth certificate says Simon."

"I hate it, too," Kylie admitted, laughing. "And not just because it's my name—but that's a part of it. I really like the thought of his having my name and yours. Besides, I don't wanna have to have my locket engraved again. I'll do anything to save $20."

Blair tapped on her belly and said, "Hear that? You're back to Mackenzie. Your middle name will be Simon."

"Or Simonize if you're a girl."

On the following Thursday, Kylie came home from seeing a play with Nick. "Hey, sweetheart," she called out while trying to fend off the dogs, who were determined to ruin her nylons.

"I'm in the baby's room," Blair called out. Kylie walked down the hall and poked her head into the guest room, finding it empty. Next, she tried her office with no luck. Finally, she looked into Blair's room and gasped in surprise when she saw it filled with baby furniture.

"What in the hell…?"

"Hi," Blair said warmly, going to kiss her. "Do you like it?"

"Did I miss a meeting?"

"No. We haven't talked about which room to make into a nursery, so I had to make a quick decision when the furniture started to arrive."

"Why did you buy this stuff without consulting me?" Kylie asked, her confusion giving way to pique.

"I didn't buy it. Our neighbor gave it to us."

"Gave it to us! This stuff must have cost a fortune!"

"I'm sure it did, but he didn't pay for it. One of the studios gave it to him when his new baby was born. He claims that was their last baby, so rather than move it to the new house he bought, he thought we could use it."

"When did you learn about this?" Kylie asked, running her hands over the highly polished wood.

"This afternoon. I was talking to him about some last-minute details on his new house, and I said I could walk a few things over since I was living right next door now."

Kylie chuckled and asked, "Did he wonder how that came to be?"

"Didn't say so, if he did. You know how people in Hollywood are. You never know who's living with whom. Anyway, he noticed I was pregnant, and he asked if I wanted the furniture. I sure as heck wasn't going to say no to a whole set of hardwood cherry furniture, so he had his gardeners bring it over."

Looking disappointed, Kylie said, "But I was looking forward to buying our own stuff."

"Honey," Blair soothed, taking her hand, "this stuff is really nice, but Mackenzie will only use it for a few years. You and I can buy him something cool when he's old enough to appreciate what he has. Maybe we can get him one of those racecar beds."

"I want one of those. I wish they made them in a king-size."

"Don't feel left out. Please. I would normally have checked with you first, but he's very hard to say no to. He really would have been insulted if I'd refused."

Kylie nodded and then said, "I wouldn't have said no. I just don't like to feel left out of decision-making. This was a little bit of a shock—that's all."

"Well, do you want to use this room? I thought it made sense since it's the closest to our room. I can keep my clothes in this closet until we start filling it up with baby things. Then we can shuffle things around and maybe store some clothes in the office."

"Yeah, sure, that's fine," Kylie said, still a touch irritated. She walked around the room, looking at the furniture carefully. A smile began to grow, and she said, "Hey, I guess it's official now. You don't have your own bedroom anymore."

Blair looked slightly startled, but then smiled and said, "No, but if either of us needs some space, we've still got the guest bedroom."

"Yeah, I guess we do," Kylie said, her smile now departed.

"Hey, I've got an idea," Blair said, seeing that the doctor was still perturbed. "There's one extravagance I'd really like. This crib is great, but I've been thinking it would be nice to have a cradle, too. That way we could have him sleep right next to us. Why don't we buy a nice one? We could give it to Mackenzie when he has a family."

A pleased smile started to bloom again on Kylie's face. "Okay! Can I buy it?"

"Sure, if you want to."

"I do. I want it to be a special gift from me." She wrapped her arms around Blair. "I can't tell you how happy it makes me to think of having our baby in his cradle, sleeping right next to us. It makes my heart nearly burst."

"You have a sweet heart," Blair said, holding Kylie close. "You're gonna be such a good mom." She gave her a squeeze and said, "Now we only have to have the room painted or papered, and we'll be set."

"Ya wanna go look at colors this weekend?"

"No. Let's wait a while. I accepted the furniture because it was too good to pass up, but I feel a little funny about finishing the room. Let's wait until I'm at least in my thirty-second week. I won't feel like I'm tempting fate."

"Whatever you want. I don't want you to be uncomfortable."

"You must be uncomfortable still in your dress. Let's get you into your jammies."

"I have a better idea," Kylie said, giving Blair a decidedly lecherous look. "Let's skip the jammies. I have a compelling need to feel those pouty pink lips on all of the spots my jammies usually cover."

Blinking up at her with a faux-innocent look, Blair asked, "Why, Doctor Mackenzie, are you propositioning me?"

"You said you wanted me to tell you when I needed some lovin'. I warned you that you'd live to regret it."

"If you tried, you couldn't be more mistaken. There's nothing I love more than a woman who can ask for what she needs."

"Then it's no wonder you love me. I need it bad, and you're the only one I want to give it to me."

"The pleasure is all mine, Doc. Let's hit the sheets!"

⌁

On Saturday morning, Kylie had been up for four hours before Blair made an appearance in the den. "Hey," the doctor said, getting up to offer a hug. "Are you feeling okay? I was starting to worry about you."

"Yeah, I'm fine," she mumbled into the cotton of Kylie's blouse. "I decided yesterday that I'm going to tell David today if I can get hold of him. I think I was subconsciously trying to sleep the whole day so I didn't have to do it."

"This is really hard for you, isn't it?"

"Yeah, it is. I'd be hurt if he were engaged already. It's awfully quick."

"It is." The doctor placed a kiss on Blair's mussed hair. "Want some breakfast?"

"Sure. I'll take whatever's easy."

Kylie grinned wickedly. "Well, I'm the easiest thing around here, but you had me thoroughly last night."

"Hmm…that's a good idea," Blair said, capturing her in a hug. "If we stay in bed all day, I'll have a perfect excuse not to call David."

"Go shower, sweetie," Kylie said, patting her on the butt. "You'll feel better when this is over."

"All right. I doubt that, but I don't have many options."

Blair walked back into the kitchen quite a while later, showered and dressed for the day. She was wearing Kylie's favorite outfit: putty-colored corduroy overalls and a striped black, brown, and putty-colored turtleneck. "Oh, you look so cute!" Kylie said when she saw her.

"I found myself trying to look as non-pregnant as possible, but then I reminded myself that it doesn't matter what David thinks of me any longer. You're the person I dress to please now."

"That's a good thing to remember," Kylie said, urging Blair into a chair to eat her breakfast. "David doesn't have any hold over you."

"I know that, but I'm still very nervous about doing this."

"What are you planning? Are you going over to his house?"

"Mmm…I guess so," she said, looking unenthusiastic. "I don't really want to, but I don't want to cause a scene in a public place. I'm anticipating that he might raise his voice—at a minimum."

Kylie watched her eat for a minute, a look of deep concern on the doctor's face. "Have him come here," she said, making it sound more like an order than a suggestion.

"Why here?"

"Because I'll be worried about you if you go anywhere else. I know this'll be upsetting for you, and I don't like for you to drive when you're upset. If you insist on going to your old house, I'm gonna go with you and wait outside."

"Oh, Kylie, I'll be all right."

"I know you will, but you'll probably also be a little emotional. Please, Blair," she begged, looking at her intently.

"All right. I don't want to worry you."

Kylie looked down at the ground and shifted her weight. "I'm worried already."

"Already? Why? David won't be horrible about this. Really."

"That's not why I'm worried." She was frowning, and her jaw worked for a few moments. It was clear she had something to say, but equally clear she wasn't quite ready to speak. She finally made a face and said, "I'm really anxious that he'll change his mind and want to be involved with Mackenzie."

Blair put her arms around her. "Why does that worry you?"

"'Cause I'm afraid he'll take my place. If he's Mackenzie's dad and you're his mom, that doesn't leave much room for me."

"Wrong!" Blair said, her voice full of confidence. "Even if David has a complete turnabout and wants to be Super Dad, you and I are still gonna co-parent. Mackenzie might have two or three parents, but one of them is definitely going to be you. Period."

The doctor smiled, nodding her head, looking a little shy. "Sorry for that burst of insecurity."

"I have them every fifteen minutes. You were overdue."

"When David gets here, we'll stay out of your way. I'll keep the puppies outside with me."

"Okay." Blair looked at her for a moment and said, "To be honest, I'll be much more comfortable here in our home. Thanks."

"Don't mention it. We'll be right outside if you need us, 'kay?"

"I always need you," Blair said softly, watching Kylie pad across the kitchen and realizing, as she said it, how very true the statement was.

❧

Blair dawdled a bit over her breakfast, but finally felt ready to make the call to David. Her unconscious still managed a few last delays. She cleared her place at the table, went to the bathroom—though nature hadn't called—and carefully rearranged the flowers in a vase on the breakfast counter.

Blair took a deep breath and granted that she felt a little shaky. *Well, no way out but through.* She went to the kitchen phone, glad that Kylie was busying herself in her office, and dialed her old number.

David answered after only one ring. "Hi, David, it's me." Blair could almost hear the man's shock in the profound silence on the other end of the line. "David?"

"Blair. Oh…hi. Hi. I'm, uhm…" His voice trailed off weakly.

"David, I need to see you."

"Okay. That'd be fine."

"To talk," she said, wanting to be clear with him. "We need to. Can you come over to Kylie's at, say, 3:00?"

"Today? Sure! Sure."

"Thanks. I'll see you then. Bye."

Blair put the cordless back in its base, her feelings of anxiety still calling the shots.

❧

Shortly before 3:00, when David was due, Kylie took the soft Frisbee and a few squeaky toys and headed for the backyard, two enthusiastic playmates making mad leaps for the toys that, minutes before, had elicited nothing but boredom. Blair came out as well and kissed her partner after she had thrown the Frisbee for the first time. "Thanks for staying home. I'll feel better knowing you're here."

"I'll always be there when you need me. That's what partners do."

"Good partners," Blair said. She checked her watch. "I'll go keep an eye out so he doesn't ring the bell. I don't want the pups to get frustrated when they can't run to the door."

"Turn on the stereo in the kitchen when you go by. That drowns out a lot of noise."

"Okay. Classical music calms both me and the baby. Good idea."

Kylie wrapped her in a warm hug. "You'll do fine. I'm certain of it."

"Thanks," Blair said, her voice rather thin. "See you later." Her shoulders were slightly slumped as she went into the house.

A few minutes after 3:00, David pulled up, and Blair opened the gate to the property before he could roll his window down to buzz. Walking out to meet him, she found herself enveloped in an all-encompassing embrace that seemed to last for a very long time. They were both crying when they pulled apart, and she accepted his handkerchief to dab at her eyes and nose. "Seeing you again is so hard," she said wearily. "I never would have believed that this could happen to us."

He draped his arm across her shoulders, and she felt her head drop to rest against him. "I've missed you," he murmured, kissing her temple.

She didn't return the sentiment, unwilling to admit how infrequently she thought of him, especially now that she had Kylie. She started to head toward the house, and he stayed right with her.

When they got inside, he looked around and asked, "Are those dog toys?"

"Oh. Kylie adopted a couple of Norfolk terriers."

"Cool! Where are they? You know how I love dogs."

"Oh, they're outside. I didn't want them to disturb us."

He looked a little puzzled and said, "I've never seen Norfolk terriers. Can't I take a peek?"

"No. Kylie's outside playing with them, and they'll never leave us alone if they get to meet you. They're crazy for new faces."

He shrugged and stood there, looking a little uncomfortable. "Can I have something to drink? Anything's fine."

She nodded and went into the kitchen where she chose orange juice, one of his favorites, and poured a glass for each of them. "This is such a nice house," he said, looking around. "I didn't get to see much of it the last time I was here. Wanna take me on a tour?"

"Uhm, maybe later," she said, not in the mood to start off by explaining why there was only a crib in her room. "Have a seat."

He sat down and looked at her expectantly, a small smile on his face. "How've you been? You look really healthy."

"I am. We're doing very well."

"That's good to hear." His smile was stiff, and his body language reflected growing unease. "Uhm, did you want to talk about anything in particular? I don't remember your mentioning why you wanted to see me."

"That's because I didn't."

A warm, familiar smile settled on his handsome face, and he said, "I know. I just hate to admit that I'm clueless."

She looked to the floor and fidgeted for a moment, unsure of where to start. "I have to talk to you about something that's making me very uncomfortable, and I can't seem to make myself begin."

"Hey," he said softly, causing her to look into his eyes. "It's only me. You can tell me anything." His expression warmed even further, reminding her how deep their shared empathy and trust had once been.

She started to cry again, and he got up to sit by her, but she shook her head and put a hand up, warning him off. He sat down and looked at her with a bemused expression. "Is something wrong?"

"No, no. Nothing's wrong. This is just hard." She took a breath and let it out slowly. Then she looked him in the eye and said, "I've fallen in love, David. I wanted to tell you myself so you didn't hear it from someone else."

He looked as though he had been punched in the gut, actually leaning over a little as he tried to get a breath. Finally, after waiting for what seemed like the better part of the afternoon, he gasped, "You've fallen in love? Already?"

"Yes. I know it's awfully quick, but it happened."

"Wow." He ran his hand through his short hair and then shook his head roughly. He looked very confused, and when he met Blair's eyes, he said, "How did it happen? Is it that guy I saw you with?"

"No. Nick's my friend, but that's all."

He nodded again. "Well, I guess I should come clean and tell you that I've been dating the woman you saw me with."

"I thought as much," Blair said. "You've never been the kind of guy who likes to have women friends."

He gave her a melancholy look through half-lidded eyes. "I was lonely. I missed you so much, but I knew you'd never come back." His head snapped up, and he met her eyes. "But we hadn't slept together when I saw you. I really hadn't touched her up until that point."

The way he said that let her know that he'd probably slept with the woman fifteen minutes after he'd left Kylie's house that night, but she didn't want to dwell on the issue. "I hope you're happy."

"I was happier with you," he said, looking right into her eyes. "Much happier with you. We had a damned good relationship, and it was exactly the kind of marriage I needed. I wish we'd never tried to have a baby. That screwed everything up."

"Things would have been different." She saw no need to tell him she was very glad things had turned out as they had since she didn't want to hurt him intentionally.

He looked very uncomfortable, obviously not knowing what to do with his hands, self-consciously drumming his fingers on his thighs. "So, are you moving?"

"No. Why would I..." She winced, realizing why he'd asked. "I'm staying here. This is my home."

"Huh? What does that mean?"

"This is the part I've been uncomfortable about," she said. "I'm staying here because I've fallen in love with Kylie."

She paused, watching his face as the information finally reached his brain. His eyes widened, and his mouth dropped open. "You what?"

"I've fallen in love with Kylie," she said quietly.

"You're not gay!" He said this loudly, but he didn't seem upset. He seemed absolutely flabbergasted.

"I don't know what I am. All I know is that I'm in love with Kylie, and she loves me, too."

"Is *she* gay?"

"Yes. She's known she was a lesbian since she was a girl."

His brow furrowed, and he cocked his head. "Did *you* know that?"

"Yes, I knew that."

"Why didn't you tell me?" Now his tone was angry, and his cheeks were turning a dusty rose.

"I didn't think it was important."

"Not important? Your best friend—your confidant—the woman you spend all of your free time with—is a lesbian? And that's not important enough to mention to your *husband*?" He was shouting now, and Blair heard the sliding glass door in the den open very quietly. She knew Kylie was in the house and prayed she wouldn't interfere.

Blair could tell that David wouldn't be able to hear another word she said. All of their years together had made her very attuned to his moods, and when he was angry, he became as good as deaf. Nonetheless, she answered his question. "I didn't tell you because I thought you'd react exactly like you are reacting. I thought you'd assume she wanted something from me."

He jumped to his feet. "She did! And she got it! Jesus Christ, Blair! How stupid can you be? You let some woman talk you into getting divorced! Can't you see she wanted this all along?"

Blair stood up, having a little trouble getting her balance, as she often did these days. She walked right up to David and stared into his eyes. "If you want to know about my life, I'll answer any questions you have. But you have to go home and calm down first. You haven't called me once in the last couple of months, and it's too late now for you to play the wronged spouse. I want you to leave. Now."

He looked as if he wanted to argue, and for a fleeting moment, she felt a flash of fear. His hands were balled into fists, and his eyes were burning with such rage that she was afraid he might hit her. But he turned around, kicked the chair he'd been sitting in, and then stormed out of the house, leaving the front door wide open.

She followed behind him, shut the door, and leaned against it heavily for a few moments, feeling numb. Wearily, she forced herself to move, her natural instinct compelling her to head for the guest room to be alone. But halfway there, she stopped abruptly and headed outside. After she slid the door open, both dogs ran for her full tilt, nearly crashing into her. "It's nice to see some friendly faces." Out of the corner of her eye, she saw her partner, leaning against the house, her hands in her pockets.

"You heard me, didn't you?" Kylie asked.

"Yeah. Thanks for not coming into the room. I would have hated that."

"I'm sorry I came in, but when I could hear him even with the doors closed, I got worried."

"I understand. I probably would have done the same."

Kylie took Blair's hand, and they walked over to a chaise. The doctor sat and put a foot on either side of the chair. Then Blair sat between her legs and shifted around, trying to get comfortable.

"Let me lower the back a little," Kylie suggested. "That'll give us more room." She did, and Blair snuggled a little closer, rubbing her head against Kylie's chest and neck.

"I don't want to talk," Blair warned, "but I need to be close to you."

"You don't have to say a word. Lie here and relax." She started to run her fingers through Blair's hair, moving down to deeply massage the tense muscles in her neck and shoulders. Moving back to her head, Kylie lightened the touch, continuing to slide her fingers along Blair's scalp until her breathing evened out and her body grew heavy and still. Even though Blair was clearly asleep, Kylie continued to stroke her gently, trying to soothe her even when she wasn't consciously aware of her lover's touch.

—

Later that evening, they lay in bed together, Blair still clinging to Kylie like a lifeline. She had not said a word about the events of the afternoon, and even though Kylie wanted to know what was going on in her lover's head, she was loath to press her to speak. They'd been in bed about twenty minutes, and though Kylie would normally have been asleep in seconds, she fought her drowsiness in order to stay awake with Blair.

Despite her efforts, Kylie nodded off, waking with a start when she heard her lover sniffling. "Baby?" the brunette asked. "You okay?"

Blair nodded and then curled herself into a ball, crying just enough to make a soft sound.

"Tell me what's going on," Kylie urged. "You'll feel better if you talk about it."

"No," Blair whimpered. "Not tonight. Please."

"Okay, okay." She started to rub her partner's lower back gently, and after ten minutes or so, Blair was asleep. It took Kylie quite a while to relax enough to join her, the doctor's mind unable to erase the look of abject sorrow that had been on her partner's face after David left or the tears that lingered on her pale cheeks.

—

The next day, Blair left the house at noon, her afternoon and evening completely booked. Kylie hated to see her go since she knew how tired and drained Blair was from the emotional scene with David the day before, but Blair rarely let her personal life get in the way of work, and today was no exception.

Blair had dinner with a pair of gay men whom she'd worked with before. They were looking to buy a bigger house and sell the one they currently owned. They were a very pleasant pair, and they had been very easy to work with before, so she could relax and enjoy dinner instead of trying to impress them. Her mood was good when she drove up her street, but it soured immediately upon seeing Sadie's car in the drive. "God damn! Am I gonna have to throw *her* out of the house now?" She got out of the car and slammed the door, knowing she'd have a fight on her hands.

The dogs ran to greet her, and she spoke to them, too tired to get down to their level. She heard quiet voices coming from the den, and she kicked off her shoes and walked into the room, anxious to kick some ass and get it over with.

Sadie and Kylie were sitting in the den, both of them looking up rather idly when Blair walked in. "Hi!" Kylie called out, putting up her hand to give a poorly formed wave. "Come on in."

Blair stared at her partner and then looked at Sadie.

"You're so lucky you weren't home when I first got here," Sadie said, giggling like a little girl. "I was sooo mad at you!" She thought this statement was extremely funny, and Kylie was also caught by an attack of the giggles.

"You've never seen a woman so mad," the doctor chortled. "I thought she was gonna have a stroke!" She paused and then nearly went into hysterics when she said, "I'm a doctor! I could've saved her!"

"What have you two been doing?" Blair looked at the coffee table and saw an empty bottle of Scotch. She picked it up and pointed the neck of the bottle at Kylie. "This was half full the last time I made you a drink!"

"Not anymore!" Kylie laughed so hard she started to choke, and Blair pounded her on the back a few times.

"Kylie, I've never seen you drunk!" She turned to her mother-in-law and said, "Sadie, you don't drink!"

"I do now," she said and then looked at Kylie and laughed.

Blair flopped down onto the sofa. "Nothing better than coming home at the end of a long day and having a pair of drunken women in your living room. What am I supposed to do with the two of you?"

"You could take me to bed," Kylie helpfully suggested. "I'm tired." She rubbed her eyes like a small child, and Blair couldn't help but find her behavior adorable.

"I should make you sleep on the couch," she said, "but you'd probably fall off it."

"I could...I could fall off the floor." Kylie seemed determined to help.

"I would, too! I would, couldn't I?" Sadie asked the doctor, excitedly grabbing her hand. This selfless offer from Sadie sent the pair into a frenzy of helpless laughter.

Blair waited, somewhat in wonder, for this little episode to end and then snapped her fingers a couple of times. Sadie, wheezing to recover, blinked. "Yes?"

"Do you want me to drive you home?" Blair asked.

"No, I have my car here. I drove it," she said, just to be clear.

"You can't drive home. I'll drive you, or I'll have David come get you."

"Oh, no!" Sadie said, her eyes wide. "He doesn't wanna see you anymore. He's mad!" She waggled her finger at her daughter-in-law for emphasis.

"Fine. Then I'll drive you." She got up to put her shoes back on, muttering, "I get to haul your ass all the way to Glendale because my lover decided to play bartender tonight. That's an hour I could use for sleep, for the record. There'd better be a *really* good explanation for this."

Blair walked back into the room and found Kylie lying on her side, her feet still on the floor. "Pssht, pssht, pssht!" Sadie said, mangling what was probably supposed to be "sh" and pointing at the now-snoring doctor. "She's tired."

"Yeah. I can tell," Blair said. "I've made an executive decision. You're staying here tonight."

"Really?" Sadie asked. "Here? I don't have any pajamas." She looked around the room as if she expected her things to appear.

"I have something you can sleep in. I think we all need to go to bed now, or at least one of us is going to be very grouchy in the morning."

"Oh, Kylie's too sweet to be grouchy," Sadie insisted. "She's such a…" Drift had set in, and Blair put her arm around the older woman to get her up. Once they were moving, Sadie leaned in and whispered, "She's a doctor!"

"I've heard, Sadie."

"And funny," the sleepover guest added.

"Yeah, she's a pip," Blair agreed. "Full of surprises."

⟶

Blair woke up early—very early. The couch, such a luxurious place for a nap, was far less comfortable as a bed. Kylie came into the den to let the dogs out, and the light from the open door nearly blinded Blair. Kylie saw her stir and went to stand next to her. "How much trouble am I in?" the taller woman asked.

"You're not in trouble, but I've gotta go back to bed. Will you help me up?"

"I must be in trouble for you to refuse to sleep with me." Blair looked at her and saw that the doctor was near tears.

"I went to bed with you, honey, but you were snoring so loudly that I couldn't stand it. I came out here at around 3:00." She put her arm around her partner and said, "I swear I'm not mad at you. I'd like you to tell me why you poured Scotch down my ex-mother-in-law's throat, but that can wait until you get home."

"I can tell you now."

"No, I'm dead on my feet. I've got to get some rest. I feel like I've been awake for three days."

Kylie led her to their bedroom and then tucked her in. She grabbed each dog before eight wet paw prints could be left on the bedspread and then wiped each little paw dry with a towel. "I'll go get ready for work in your bathroom," Kylie said. "Then I won't disturb you."

"How's your head?"

"Not bad. My stomach's upset, but I don't feel as bad as I should."

"I have a feeling Sadie's not gonna say the same thing." Blair rolled over and cuddled her body pillow. "Thanks for taking off and leaving me with her. You owe me several."

"You still love me, don't you?" Kylie sat down on the bed and kissed Blair's cheek.

"I'm not even gonna dignify that with an answer," Blair said, almost smiling. "I love you no matter what. Now, give me a real kiss."

Kylie did, holding her breath since she knew she must smell like a peat bog. "I love you. Call me if you need anything. Can you sleep in?"

"Yeah. I had a staff meeting, but before I went into the den, I left a message canceling it."

"That's good. I'll put a note on your door telling Sadie not to wake you. I'll also make a pot of coffee and put out some Advil for her."

"Thanks. You don't have surgery today, do you?"

"No! I'd never drink the day before surgery."

"Just checking. I don't wanna have to call the AMA."

"I'll be home early—with something special for dinner. I'll wait on you hand and foot tonight."

"All week," Blair decided, scrunching her pillow into the perfect shape and falling asleep almost immediately.

⌐

Blair rolled out of bed at 9:00, surprised that she felt as well as she did. She took a long shower and then dressed for work. By the time she left her room, it was nearly 10:00, and she was famished. To her surprise, Sadie was sitting in the kitchen, fully dressed in yesterday's wardrobe, looking much like her usual self.

"You're quite the lady of leisure," she said to Blair. "Do you always sleep so late?"

"No, I don't," Blair said, a thin smile barely lifting the corners of her mouth. "Have you had breakfast?"

"Not really. Kylie left me some coffee and told me where all of the food was, but I'm not very hungry."

"I'm desperate for food. It won't bother you if I cook something, will it?"

"Why would it bother me?" Sadie asked, making Blair wonder whatever became of the good old-fashioned hangover. "You sit down and let me make you something. What would you like?"

Her instinct was to protest, but Blair had a fondness for anyone else's cooking, so she took a seat. "I've been in an egg mood lately. Can you make me some scrambled eggs? I need them dry, by the way."

"How about a little cheddar cheese in them?"

"Hmm…that sounds pretty good. Let's try it."

"Toast?"

"A bagel, I think. I won't have lunch today, so I need to stock up."

"Good. I'm glad to see you have your appetite back."

"Oh, it's back," Blair said, relaxing enough to laugh. "With a vengeance."

"When I had David, I gained forty-five pounds. I'm still trying to lose the last fifteen."

Blair had heard this lament many times, but she smiled and nodded. "I'm on target to gain about thirty. Kylie supervises me very, very closely. I think I've had junk food twice since I moved here. If I were on my own, I'd probably live on Big Macs."

"That's not good for the baby. You need to eat right."

"I do. I'm very careful, and so far, it's really paying off. I don't have a lot of the problems I've read about."

"You don't have hemorrhoids?" Sadie asked. "Oh, my God, mine almost killed me!"

"No, that's one part of my body that hasn't betrayed me yet, thank God. Kylie would consider it a personal failure if I got them, so I try to eat as much fiber as I can."

"Fiber!" Sadie was busily scrambling the eggs and moving around the kitchen, looking for what she needed without asking. "We didn't know about fiber. We didn't have all of the pampering you girls do. You went to the doctor a couple of times, and he took a look at you and sent you on your way. None of these big, expensive machines. I think my doctor bill was $400 when I had David."

Blair was feeling quite adult and was proud of herself for not saying, "You overpaid." Sadie got the eggs into the hot pan, and in a few minutes, she delivered them complete with a lightly toasted bagel.

"This looks delicious, Sadie. I think I'll start adding cheese on a regular basis. I like to have protein early in the day."

"Eat what you want," Sadie said, waving her hand dismissively. "Doctors don't know more than they did forty years ago; they only charge more."

She sat down and watched Blair dig into her breakfast. "You don't want anything on that bagel? Don't you have jam or jelly?"

"I like it dry. Butter's too oily for me in the morning. It's great exactly like this."

"All right. You know what's best."

Blair took another bite and then put her fork down and said, "Do you want to talk about yesterday? I know you must've been angry when you got here—before the resident mixologist got her hands on you—and I can't believe everything is fine now."

"No, everything's not fine, but you could have done a lot worse. That Kylie's a very, very nice girl."

"Uhm, yeah, she is. So, that's it? You're okay with my being in a relationship with her?"

"Oh, of course not!" Sadie said, laughing as she slapped Blair's hand softly. "But what am I going to do about it? You're not my daughter, so I don't have much control over you. I'm certainly not happy about my grandchild growing up in this environment, but it could be worse." She looked at Blair's empty plate and said, "You need another egg."

The younger woman was too stunned to speak, so she sat there for a minute while Sadie cooked. "I...know how you feel about gay people. I'm having a hard time believing that you're not more upset about this."

"Look," Sadie said, sliding the egg onto Blair's plate, "what do I do? David refuses to sue you for custody. I've got no chance of getting custody if I sue. I might be able to get visitation rights, but that would cost me an arm and a leg." Blair stared up at her, her jaw hanging open. "I want to see my grandchild, so I have to act like this is all normal. It's not, but I don't have any choice."

Slowly, Blair began to smile. "You know, you have some qualities I really admire. You're remarkably honest. Most people wouldn't admit they'd take your baby from you if they had half a chance. But you put it right out there on the table. I've gotta give you honesty points, if nothing else."

Sadie looked at her daughter-in-law for a few moments and then said, "I'm too old and too tired to raise a baby. And that girl David's dating doesn't have the sense to come in out of the rain. I wouldn't trust her with a hamster. You're going to be a good mother, Blair, and I'm very, very impressed with Kylie. Like I said, things could be worse."

"Well, I guess it's lucky for me that David's dating an airhead. Plus the fact that he doesn't give a damn about the baby, of course."

"I don't want to talk about that," Sadie said, turning her head away. "It's giving me an ulcer."

"Now *there* I can empathize with you. It almost drove me mad."

Sadie met her eyes, reached out, and took her hand. "I'm so sorry that David deserted you. I think I can understand just a little bit why you've given up men. I don't agree with it, God knows, but I can understand—a little bit."

There was a part of Blair that wanted to set Sadie straight, but a bigger part had no interest in it. She nodded, letting the woman believe what she wished.

When breakfast was finished, Blair put the dishes in the dishwasher and put her shoes on. After saying goodbye to the dogs, she walked Sadie to her car. The older woman hugged her tightly and said, "I love you, and I know you're going to do your best to be a good mother." She released her and asked, "Will you have the baby baptized?"

"I'm not sure, Sadie. We haven't talked about that yet."

"If you don't, I'll take him or her to my church behind your back. You know that, don't you?"

"Yes, I know that," Blair said, strangely amused by her mother-in-law's nerve. "It can't hurt to be baptized. Go for it."

"That's my girl," Sadie said, pinching her cheek. "We'll get along just fine."

"We will get along fine," Blair said, "and I'm going to be as honest with you as you are with me. I know how much having a grandchild means to you, and having my grandmother in my life was one of the greatest gifts I've ever received. I want you both to have each other, but…I want you to understand something. I don't ever—*ever*—want you to tell the baby how you feel about homosexuality. You have to keep those feelings to yourself. I'm going to have the kind of relationship with my child where he'll tell me if you say hurtful things about Kylie and me. If that happens, even once, you're cut off."

Sadie seemed to consider the issue for a moment and then nodded decisively. "It's a deal. Frankly, I'd prefer to never discuss the thing at all."

"Okay, we have an understanding. I know you're a woman of your word, and so am I." Blair gave her a hug, and then Sadie got into her car and drove away.

Too bad Sadie's got all the balls in the Spencer family.

⟿

Even though things had gone relatively well with Sadie, Blair had a very bad day at work. When she got home that night, she looked considerably worse for wear. "Did somebody put rocks in my pockets?" she asked grumpily, dropping her briefcase on the kitchen counter. "I feel like I weigh a thousand pounds. My back hurts, my legs ache, and those tendons on the side of my belly feel like they've been cut with razor blades."

Kylie got up, wrapped her lover in a warm embrace, and then pulled away, starting to undress her. "You probably feel crummy because of this outfit," Kylie said. "It must kill you to have to wear heels all day."

"Hey. These shoes were a major pregnancy concession. I had to put my Manolo Blahniks and Jimmy Choos away since my feet looked like a pair of bratwursts sticking out of the top of them. This is the lowest heel I've worn since I was in high school." She stuck her foot out to remind herself how much she hated the shoes. "They suck," she said with a touch of venom in her tone.

Kylie wanted to give her partner a lecture about wearing heels at all, since she could easily lose her balance, but the doctor knew this wasn't the time. She removed the dress and then reached behind her partner to remove her bra, the endeavor taking a minute since there were so many hooks to unfasten. "Boy, I bet it's really arousing to undress me," Blair said. "A nursing bra that could stop a pair of cantaloupes from swaying, the sausage-casing pantyhose, and the panties that I could dry my whole car with."

Kylie didn't say a word. She just gave her partner a wry smile, letting her voice her complaints without interruption. After helping her step out of the pantyhose and remarkably unattractive panties, Kylie sat on a kitchen stool and started to speculatively look Blair over. "Some of the clothes you have to wear are a little fashion challenged," Kylie admitted. "But the delights those clothes hide..." She shook her head while her eyes widened in appreciation. "They are truly works of art." With a look of intense pleasure in her eyes, Kylie started to run her hands over Blair's body, her smile growing wider and wider as she caressed her.

Standing naked in the kitchen while Kylie looked at her and touched her with such veneration made Blair start to feel uncomfortable. She placed her hands atop the doctor's and said, "I've got to get off my feet. Let me go put on my pajamas."

"I've got a better idea," Kylie said, taking her by the hand. She led her out to the backyard, having to tug on her a little to get her to follow.

"What in the heck are we doing?"

"I want you to lie in the pool and float for a while. I guarantee you'll feel significantly better to be relatively weightless."

"But it'll be cold!"

"No, it's not. I keep it at eighty-four degrees. I think you should start getting at least part of your exercise in the pool." She was retracting the cover as she spoke, and Blair realized that she wasn't going to get a vote in the matter. Kylie took her partner's hand and helped her into the lap pool, saying, "I'll go get you a towel. Be right back."

By the time she returned, Blair was floating on her back, a blissful smile already settled upon her face. Kylie was fascinated by the sight of her buoyant breasts and belly breaking the waterline, but she didn't think Blair would share her feelings, so she wisely kept her thoughts to herself. "The doctor is most definitely right," Blair said. "This feels divine."

"I'll leave the pups here to watch you," Kylie said. "I'll go finish dinner."

"Hey, Kylie?" Blair said, lifting her head. "I love you."

"I love you, too, my beautiful little mermaid."

⟿

During dinner, Blair said, "Given the discussion Sadie and I had this morning, I have an idea of what you two covered last night."

"Oh, yeah? What's your guess?" Kylie asked.

"I think you charmed her and let her know what a good parent you'd be to her grandchild, and I think you also let her know that she didn't have a legal leg to stand on—in a polite way, of course."

Kylie smiled and nodded. "I couldn't help being charming, but I did manage to let her know that the courts have held that grandparents don't have the right to visitation in California. That seemed to impress her."

"You did a good job, but I'm more than a little interested in why you both got stinking drunk."

"You'd know if you'd been here at 1:00. She was breathing fire!"

Blair covered her eyes. "You had to deal with her from 1:00 until 10:00?"

"Yep."

"I'm surprised you didn't inject her with a sedative."

"If I carried any on me, I would have. Scotch was the closest thing I had. We started off with very mild Scotch sours, and I kept pouring 'em into her until she stopped yelling and started listening."

"What was she yelling?" Blair asked, suddenly feeling very sorry for her partner.

"You don't wanna know. Trust me."

"I do trust you, but I want to know. I hate to be kept in the dark."

Kylie gazed at her for a second and then asked, "Where did you two leave things?"

"We decided we'd try to have a good relationship. She promised never to talk badly about our relationship or gay people in general, and I said she could see Mackenzie if she behaved."

"That's great. Really great."

"So…tell me what she said?"

"No." The doctor was shaking her head, looking as if she wasn't about to change her mind. "She was upset, and she vented for a long time. But there wasn't one thing she said that you need to hear. It would just piss you off, and you don't need the aggravation."

"*This* is what's aggravating me. I want to know."

"I'm not gonna tell you, so don't bother asking. You don't have to use too much imagination to guess. David got her all revved up about my luring you into being gay, and she has a load of her own negative stereotypes about gay people. Say everything in a very loud, abusive tone, and you'll have a complete picture."

Blair was frustrated, but also very unhappy that her lover had been subject to Sadie's wrath. "I hate to think of her abusing you," Blair said.

"It's all right. Really. I'd rather she do it to me than you. I could depersonalize it, given that she'd never met me."

"Still, it's not fair. I wish you would have called me and told me to come home."

"I deal with people like her all of the time," Kylie said. "It really wasn't a big deal. I'm just glad she was calm by the time you got home."

"She must have been like a charging rhino," Blair laughed. "You know, like on the nature shows when they have to keep shooting tranquilizer darts at 'em?"

"It was a little like that," Kylie agreed. "I was gonna have to go out for more Scotch!"

Blair reached out and took her partner's hand. "I appreciate what you did. I really do. I know you were only trying to protect me."

"I was," Kylie said earnestly.

"As much as I appreciate it, though, I don't want you to do anything like that again. Sadie's my problem, not yours. I can fight my own battles."

"But your problems *are* my problems. We both have to deal with her now."

Letting out a heavy sigh, Blair said, "I know you're trying to help, but this isn't the kind of help I need. If she makes another unannounced visit, either call me or don't open the door. Just don't try to handle her alone. Please!"

"All right," Kylie said quietly.

Blair gave her a chagrined look and said, "I'm sorry I'm being so pissy."

"You're not feeling well, are ya?"

"No, I'm not, but it's not anything in particular. I'm just tired and achy, and I feel like a walking sack of potatoes."

"You're a cute little spud," Kylie said, holding her grin until Blair joined her.

"Okay, you've spent enough time trying to cheer me up. Go relax while I do the dishes."

"No, you're not feeling well. You sit down and put your feet up. I had a really easy day."

"I can manage to do the dishes, Kylie. Now, go do something relaxing."

"But I'd really rather be with you. At least let me dry."

Giving her a decidedly perturbed look, Blair said, "No one *wants* to do the dishes. Go enjoy yourself."

Not wanting to start another tiff and recognizing that Blair was on a short fuse, Kylie did as she was told, even managing not to mumble under her breath. She went to her office and started to work on her bills for the month, getting everything organized by the time Blair walked in some time later. "Whatcha doin'?"

Turning in her chair, Kylie said, "Waiting for you to come in and sit on my lap." She patted her thighs, and Blair fulfilled her partner's wish.

Draping an arm around Kylie's neck, she asked, "What else are you doing—besides waiting to have your thighs crushed under my massive weight?"

"I'm getting ready to pay my bills."

"You pay your own bills?"

"Well, yeah. My dad stopped when I graduated from med school. Does some benefactor pay yours?"

"No, silly. My accountant does mine."

"Well, aren't we indulgent," Kylie said, immediately regretting her words when Blair's eyes narrowed.

"It's not indulgent. It's logical and practical. I have employees you know, and I have to make sure their tax issues are handled properly. I use my car and my cell phone and part of my home phone and fax for business, and I have to keep very careful records. The incremental cost for having her do my personal bills is next to nothing."

"Hey, I didn't mean that you were being indulgent. I was just teasing."

Starting to stand, Blair said, "Things don't seem very funny tonight. I'm gonna go watch TV."

Tugging on her arm, Kylie held her in place. "Tell me what's going on. You seem so unhappy tonight."

Blair sighed heavily, sat down, and rested her head upon the doctor's shoulder. "I was sitting at work for a couple of hours, doing paperwork and making calls between appointments," Blair said. "I'm always grouchy when I have to do that. My desk chair isn't very supportive, and those damned pantyhose are like tourniquets around my belly."

"Why don't you work at home? You can make phone calls from here."

"I know, but I've never wanted to have a home office. I wanted my home life to be separate from work. I've been able to maintain the separation so far, and I hate to merge the two now."

"I understand, but this might be the time to rethink that policy. What would you need to work from here?"

Scowling slightly, Blair leaned on the edge of Kylie's desk and thought for a few minutes, obviously creating a mental list. "I guess I'd need a desktop computer. My laptop is fine, but I intentionally bought a tiny one so I could carry it with me. I'd need a much bigger monitor to be comfortable and a fast Internet connection, and I'd need someone to configure the computer to let me get into the system at the office. Then, obviously, I'd need a desk and a good chair."

"There's a lot of room in here," Kylie said, waving her hand at the empty space in the generously sized room. "There's plenty of space for another desk. Let's get you set up with a home office. It might let you stay home for a couple of hours a day." Kylie gave her a curious look and asked, "What did you mean when you said you had employees?"

"I have employees," Blair said once again. "I have an administrative assistant and two agents who work for me."

"That's your team," Kylie said, looking confused.

"I know. They're my team. My employees."

"*Your* employees? Don't you all work for the firm?"

"No. They work for me. Who do you think does most of my paperwork and goes to the brokers' caravans on Tuesdays? Who does my floor duty? Who sits at my open houses nearly every Saturday and Sunday afternoon?" She gave Kylie a puzzled look and said, "Do you have any idea what my job is about?"

"Yeah, yeah, I do. I listen very attentively. You've just never told me this stuff before."

"Everybody who sells over $20 million of real estate has people who work for her. You couldn't possibly sell that much if you were tied to your desk or running around the Westside looking at a bunch of loser properties."

"But why do they work *for* you? Wouldn't it be easier if your firm assigned people to you?"

Blair would usually have smiled indulgently, but she was clearly in a bad mood. "Sure, it'd be easier, but they don't have to. Why should they do something if they can make me do it? Besides, if they didn't work for me, I couldn't have them do my floor duty. They'd have their own to do."

"Floor duty is…what?"

Sighing, Blair said, "You really don't know what I do, and it kinda pisses me off."

"I'm sorry! Really! But you never talk about the nuts and bolts of what you do."

"Fine." Wearily, she said, "If you work for the firm, you have to put in a certain number of hours sitting in the office. You have to handle all of the walk-in clients." Looking at Kylie drolly, she added, "Those aren't usually the multi-million dollar buyers. They're usually lookie-loos."

"Got it. Since you have employees, you can have them do whatever you want."

"Within reason, yes."

"Well, do you have to be in the office to supervise your team?"

Now Blair's look was even more puzzled. "Do you think I hire idiots? They're all independent and do their jobs well. I'm almost never with them."

"Okay, then there's really no reason not to work from home, is there?"

Blair looked unhappy, but was forced to agree. "I guess I have to. I know a guy who can get me set up with the computer. All I'll have to do is get the furniture and research the Internet connection."

"We can network. You can piggyback off my connection."

"Okay. I'll take care of the furniture." Kylie gave her a half-smile, and Blair amended, "Okay, I'll have Walter take care of the furniture. You're already on to my tricks. That's a very bad sign. We've been spending way too much time together."

"Oh, that reminds me. There's a medical convention in Chicago, and it starts right after my dad's birthday. I wasn't planning on going, but Joe Martini had to cancel. He asked me if I'd go in his place."

Blair just smiled. "Okay."

"Do you mind if I stay for a few days?"

With a look of true confusion, Blair asked, "Why would I mind?"

Kylie shrugged, trying not to look embarrassed. "No reason. I was just letting you know."

"Okay. Consider it noted. Have you changed your plane reservations?"

"Mmm…not yet. I'll do that now."

Blair got up and said, "I'll warm up a spot for you on the sofa. See you in a few."

Nodding, Kylie tried to swallow her hurt feelings. *I didn't change the reservations because I thought you might want to stay with me.* She shook her head, thinking, *She's not that kind of woman, Kylie. She has her own life, and she wants you to have yours, too. She's an adult, and she doesn't need to stick to you like glue.* Sighing, she started to change her travel plans, thinking, *I wish I hadn't told her about the stupid convention. Now I can't cancel or*

I'll look like a big, needy baby. Pouting, she admitted, *I can't bear the thought of being apart from her for three days—but I have to now.*

⟵

When they got into bed, Blair was already half-asleep. Kylie tried to curl up against her, but Blair mumbled, "I need some space tonight. I'm too grouchy to be close."

"Okay," Kylie said softly, scooting away. She lay there in silence, staring at the back of Blair's head, feeling terribly hurt.

Without warning, Blair turned onto her other side and caught the look in her lover's eyes. The scowl that was etched upon her own face faded, and she smiled and asked, "Can I hold your hand?"

"Of course."

Kylie extended her hand, and Blair captured it and nestled it between her breasts. "I can't sleep if I don't have a little part of you touching me," she said, staring right into Kylie's eyes. "No matter how grouchy I am, I still need you."

"I need you, too," Kylie whispered. She kissed her partner tenderly and closed her eyes, feeling some of the hurt disappear as if by magic.

⟵

When Blair came home the next night, she was still not in a very good mood. Once again, Kylie undressed her and sent her out to the pool, hoping that the water would buoy her spirits. The doctor went outside after a while and found her lover slowly kicking her feet just enough to keep her legs afloat. She didn't say anything since Blair's ears were underwater, but Kylie knew that something was wrong. And it was more serious than the minor physical complaints Blair had voiced the day before. Kylie sat on the edge of the pool, watching her lover. There were a few lines etched between Blair's eyebrows, and neither the weightlessness nor the relaxing, warm water was doing anything to wipe them away.

After a long time of merely floating, Blair started doing laps, gliding through the water with lovely form, even given her changing body. Kylie thoroughly enjoyed watching the muscles in her partner's arms and shoulders flex and extend through her stroke and the way just a few inches of her adorable ass stayed above the waterline.

Blair stayed at it until she became tired, and that was after only about ten laps. She stopped, and her head popped up as she gasped for air for a minute. "Jesus! That sucked!"

"What? You looked wonderful."

"Ten laps? Ten stinking laps? I used to do sets of two hundred, and I could do them for hours!"

"You haven't been swimming in a while, and your lung capacity isn't what it used to be."

Blair tried to get out of the pool the way most good swimmers do, but her arms needed to be at least a foot longer to allow her to propel herself up onto the coping. "Fuck me," she muttered, wading over to the stairs. "I haven't used the stairs since I was three!"

Kylie intercepted her on the way to the house and wrapped her in a big towel. The doctor held on tight and said, "Tell me what's really bothering you."

Blair tried to break Kylie's hold, groaning in frustration when she couldn't. "Let me go!"

"No, I won't," Kylie said, trying to sound soothing. "Something's really bothering you, and I want to know what it is."

"Let me go!" Blair yelled again, loud enough to rouse the neighbors. But Kylie wouldn't give in. She knew Blair was on the verge of exploding and wanted it to be sooner rather than later. Kylie got her wish when her lover started to cry, sobbing so hard that she almost fell. Kylie increased the pressure of her hold and guided Blair to a chair. She sank to the cushion and cried, great shuddering sobs wracking her body.

Kylie squatted down beside her and tried to hold her, but Blair wrenched her body away, crying even louder. "Don't!"

"Okay, okay." Kylie backed away and sat on the ground, watching her lover cry piteously while holding herself around her belly.

It took a long time, but Blair finally calmed down enough to get out a few words. "I feel so vulnerable!"

"Ooh…" Kylie stroked Blair's wet leg, glad that she didn't give her a swift kick. "Tell me why you feel vulnerable."

Blair looked at her as if she were dull-witted. Pointing to herself, Blair said, "I don't have my own body!"

"Sure you do. You just have a little more of it."

"I do not! When David was here, I honestly felt afraid of him for a second. I thought he might hit me, and I didn't know how to defend myself if he did. All I could think of was that I'd have to bend over so he couldn't hurt the baby! I would have had to let him hit me right in the head!"

Kylie's eyes grew dark, and her voice dropped. "If he had hit you," she said, enunciating each word carefully, "I would have killed him."

"Great! My husband leaves me, and my lover's in prison! That'd solve everything."

Kylie closed her eyes, angry with herself for such a knee-jerk reaction. "I'm sorry. That was a stupid thing to say. The best I could have done is tackle him. My mouth got away from me."

"You don't understand! I could defend myself before. I never felt small and defenseless. David's a big wimp. I could have taken him—easily—before I was pregnant. But now, I feel like I'm at everyone's mercy. I'm just an incubator for Mackenzie, and I have to protect him at all costs. I'm losing my identity."

Seeing that some of the fire had gone out of her, Kylie got to her knees and put her arms around her partner. Blair dropped her head to her lover's shoulder and cried for a long time. Kylie didn't speak; she just held and rocked her, letting her cry herself out. Finally, Blair picked her head up and looked at Kylie, eyes swollen and red. "Do you understand?" Blair's words were more a plea than a question, and Kylie nodded her head vigorously. Blair let out a breath and then put her head back down on the doctor's shoulder, finally calm. They stayed just that way for another few minutes. Then Kylie felt her partner shiver, so the doctor got to her feet and helped Blair up.

They went into Blair's bathroom, and Kylie stripped off her own clothing and got into the shower. She adjusted the water, helped Blair in, and then spent some time washing the chlorine from her lover's body, gently massaging her back and shoulders once she was soapy. When Kylie was finished, she turned Blair so her back was to the spray and held her while the water rinsed all of the suds away. "I understand," Kylie said softly. "I really do."

She turned off the water and gently dried first her partner and then herself. Naked, she guided Blair into their bed and lay down with her, holding her and stroking her softly until she fell asleep. Kylie stayed awake, patting her lover's belly while watching her sleep, trying to soothe the baby as well.

Blair slept for so long that she wanted breakfast when she woke. Kylie made a rather unconventional dinner of oatmeal loaded with fresh fruit, and that seemed to satisfy Blair's hunger. But she was still holding something back, and she didn't reveal what it was until just before bedtime. Kylie had been watching TV, but Blair was just staring in the direction of the set. She finally turned to Kylie and said, "Sadie said she'd tried to talk David into going to court and demanding sole custody of the baby. Because I'm in a lesbian relationship," she added, just in case Kylie didn't get the point.

Kylie dropped her head into her hands for just a second and then took a breath and held Blair. "We won't let him. We'll leave the country before we let that happen. There's no way in hell he's gonna get custody of our baby!" Blair could feel her lover's muscles tighten, and she let out a sigh of relief that Kylie really understood.

Blair patted her back, trying to calm her. "Sadie said he wasn't interested. Apparently, his girlfriend isn't interested, either. Thank God."

"I didn't know he had a girlfriend," Kylie said quietly.

"He's with that child I saw him with when you were in Maine. I knew it then. I'm not surprised in the least. He has to have a woman around to take care of him. I'm actually pleased that he sought out a sex partner rather than moving home to Mommy."

"But still…"

"Yeah, I hated to hear it. But if he didn't have her, Sadie probably would have talked him into trying to get sole custody, so I should be thankful." She put her head in her hands and then ruffled her hair. "How did my life turn into a soap opera? I was a happily married woman a year ago, and now I'm a pregnant lesbian with an ex-husband, his domineering mother, and his teenaged girlfriend trying to wrestle my baby out of my arms."

"We've gotta get a lawyer. Immediately."

"Can't Alan give us some advice? Or I could also ask the guy who's handling my divorce. He's competent."

"No. We need a specialist. We need someone who works with gay people. We need to find out what we can do to make Mackenzie ours—only ours."

"Sadie and I parted on good terms," Blair said. "She said she knows that David isn't interested."

"I don't care," Kylie said. "I don't want this threat hanging over our heads. It's not good for any of us."

"Okay. I guess you're right. Do you want me to look for a lawyer?"

"No, I can do that. I don't know a ton of people in the community, but I have a few contacts. It's time to call in some favors."

⌒

On Friday afternoon, Blair had an appointment to see Monique. Kylie had been in surgery all morning, and Blair had been unable to get hold of her. But just after Blair was shown to an examining room, her cell rang. "Hi, I can sneak over for a few minutes," Kylie said, "but I don't have much time. When do you want me?"

"How about now? Monique should be here in a few."

"Be right there."

Kylie arrived about five minutes later, and Blair blinked in surprise when she saw her partner. She was wearing bright-blue scrubs and a stunningly white lab coat with "Kylie Mackenzie, M.D." embroidered in red above the breast pocket. Her stethoscope was draped around her neck, and Blair noted that the rubber part of the instrument was a bright purple, adding a splash of color to her ensemble. Blair wasn't sure what it was, but she'd never seen Kylie look sexier and was unable to hide her obvious admiration. "Hi," she said, her voice a little low.

Kylie's head cocked a tiny bit in question, reading the subtle signals that Blair was sending out. The doctor leaned close and kissed her, lingering for a moment. When Kylie pulled away, she pressed her lips to Blair's sensitive earlobe and whispered, "Do examining rooms make you hot?"

"No," Blair giggled. "But gorgeous doctors do. I didn't realize until just this minute that I have a uniform fetish."

"I could tell Monique we need half an hour," Kylie purred, her lips brushing across Blair's neck. "Might be the first time you ever had fun with your legs in the stirrups."

"Who says it'd be the first time?" Blair asked, pulling Kylie down to plant a scorcher on her. Thankfully, Monique knocked before she entered, giving Kylie time to stand up, albeit on rather rubbery legs.

"Well, if it isn't the Mackenzie-Spencers," she said. "Or is it the Spencer-Mackenzies?"

"Either one," Blair said. "Actually, they both sound pretty good. Thank God I didn't go back to my maiden name. The Mackenzie-Schneidhorsts is horrid!"

"Oh, you poor thing," Monique teased, patting Blair's shoulder. "Aside from having a difficult maiden name, how are you?"

"I'm good. I've been a lot grumpier than normal, but Kylie's more affected by that than I am. Other than that, I feel good. I'm sleeping well, I'm eating right, and I'm getting my exercise."

"Sounds good," Monique said. "Any other complaints?"

"No, not really. The only other thing that's bothering me is my right hand and wrist, but that's not a part of the body you're interested in."

"Sure it is," Monique said. She took Blair's hand in both of hers and looked at it carefully. Blair noted that her partner tried to look over Monique's shoulder, but that the obstetrician moved just enough to block her view. "Looks a little swollen. Have you been using your hand in any repetitive motion lately? Anything new or unusual?"

Blair began to blush, and when Monique looked up, she caught her expression. Unable to resist, Monique turned to Kylie and said, "Damn, woman, give her a break, will you? You can't make up for lost time all at once."

"Hey, it's not my fault women find me irresistible," Kylie maintained, winking at her partner.

"Uh-huh. That's why you did without for over two years," Monique said. Looking at Blair, she said, "Your tissues are a little swollen, and they compress your carpal tendon a bit. Try to avoid a lot of repetitive motion for a while, and it'll calm down. I think I'll have you take a little extra B-6 for a while, too. That should help."

"Lord, is there any part of my body that isn't pregnant?"

"Nope. Every cell gets in on the act in some way. It's all good, Blair, even though it doesn't seem like it at times. Now, let's get you settled so I can take a peek and make sure the baby's as happy as you are."

Kylie helped Blair lie down on the table and stood by her head, holding her hand. "You really want to look, don't you?" Blair said, giving her partner a fond smile.

"Yeah, but I can control myself."

"You can peek if you want to, Kylie," Monique offered. "Everything looks perfect, Blair."

"No, thanks. Blair wants to reserve that view for you."

Monique nodded and withdrew the speculum, patting Blair's thigh to show she was finished. "Well, you're in great shape. I thought we'd do a glucose screening test to make sure you're not developing gestational diabetes. If anything looks suspicious, you'll have to take the extended glucose tolerance test but there's no reason to put you through that if we don't have to."

"Okay. What's the drill?"

"Do you like really sweet lemon-lime soda?" Monique asked in an overly cheery tone.

"I don't like soda at all. Never touch the stuff."

"Well, then you won't like this test. You have to drink a bottle of sugar solution, wait an hour, and then have a blood test."

"Golly, when can we start?" Blair asked, matching Monique's jolly tone.

"I have a couple of options for you. You have to do it after a twelve-hour fast, so obviously, you'll want to do it first thing in the morning. You can do it here or at the lab over at the hospital, and they open earlier than we do, so that might factor into your decision. I'll give you a bottle of the stuff, and you can chill it. Most women find it goes down better if it's really cold."

"Do I need an appointment?"

"No. I'd like you to do this within a week or two, though. Just pick a day when you feel good and your stomach's settled, gulp the drink down, and then show up an hour later. The lab opens at 7:00, and we open at 9:00."

"All right," Blair said. "My stomach's in good shape these days, so I should be able to do it."

"Great. Anything else?" Monique looked from Blair to Kylie.

"Oh, yeah. We're planning on going to Chicago next weekend. That's okay, isn't it?" Blair asked.

Monique thought for a moment and said, "Yeah, that should be fine. Just don't stay in one position for longer than an hour. Tops. Walk to the bathroom, stand up and stretch…whatever you want. Just don't sit still for too long."

"Are you sure it's okay?" Kylie asked.

"Yeah, it should be fine. But that should be your last flight until the baby's born."

"That's not a problem. We don't have anything else planned."

"Now, remember that your center of gravity is shifting, so your balance might be off. You have to be careful when you're moving around on the plane."

Giving Kylie a warm smile, Blair said, "I have a feeling someone will be right behind me, making sure I'm safe."

"Only on the outbound trip," Kylie reminded her. Looking at Monique, she added, "I have to stay for a few days. Medical convention."

"You'll be fine," Monique assured Blair. "I only bring it up to remind you to pay attention when you walk."

"I do," Blair said. "I'll be extra vigilant without my guardian angel."

"Never thought I'd hear anyone call you a guardian angel, Shakes. It's nice," Monique said.

"It's even nicer from here," Kylie said, giving Blair a look filled to bursting with love.

↬

Blair woke early on the following Wednesday and noted that Kylie was still home. "Sweetheart?" she called out.

Kylie poked her damp head out of the bath. "Yeah?"

"I think I'll go to the lab and have my test today. Can I page you when I'm done?"

"Sure. Go up to the second floor and talk to the nurses at station number three. They'll know where I am."

"'Kay. Gimme a kiss. I'm gonna go back to sleep for a while."

Kylie did so, tickling her partner's face with her damp curls in the process. "See you later. Call me if you need to. Good luck with your soda pop."

↬

At 8:30, Blair exited the elevator on the second floor of the hospital and made her way down the wide hallway. As she drew near the nurses' station, she spotted her partner, leaning casually against the counter and chatting with two nurses. Inexplicably, Blair felt her heartbeat start to pick up when she saw Kylie in her element, and by the time she reached her, Blair had a silly grin on her face. "Hi," she said, coming up behind the doctor to place a hand on her back.

"Hi." Kylie's face lit up when she saw her, and Blair's eyes fluttered closed as she considered how remarkably lucky she was to have earned Kylie's love. The doctor twitched her head in the direction of the nurses and said, "Let me introduce you. Marsha and Cathy, this is my partner, Blair."

"Good to meet you," Blair said, extending her hand over the counter to shake each offered hand.

"Congratulations!" Cathy said, her enthusiasm obvious. "Doctor Mackenzie was just telling us about the baby. We had no idea!"

"Oh, you know how she is. She likes to keep her little secrets."

"You won't have a minute's peace when you deliver," Marsha predicted. "Everyone's gonna want to see Doctor Mackenzie's baby." She looked up at Kylie with what Blair could only describe as a wistful look and added, "Everybody's crazy about her."

"How could they not be?" Blair asked, tucking her arm around Kylie's waist. "She's absolutely perfect."

"That sugar solution's gone to your head," Kylie said. "Let's sneak into the doctors' lounge. There's always something to snack on in there."

"See you later," Cathy said, and Marsha waved as well.

"Well, that doesn't surprise me a bit," Blair mused as they walked away.

"What's that?"

"That the nurses love you. Although old Marsha looked like she might like to love you in a more physical sense."

"Uhm, I've kinda thought that myself. I've just never allowed myself to date anyone connected with work. That's part of the reason my options were so limited."

"Well, I'm glad you're introducing me around. I want to make sure everyone knows I called dibs."

Kylie poked her head into the doctors' lounge and saw that it was empty. Blair walked in, spotted a tray of bagels, and nearly leapt for one. "If I don't get something solid in my tummy, I'm gonna start hallucinating." She cut a bagel open and stuck it into the toaster, giving Kylie an appraising look when she was finished. "Navy-blue scrubs today, huh? I like."

"Yeah," she said, looking down at herself. "We have several colors to choose from. I usually stick with the blues."

"They make your eyes look even bluer," Blair smiled, coming closer. She stared up into Kylie's eyes and said, "They're as blue as I've ever seen them. They look like the Caribbean today." She stuck her hands inside Kylie's unbuttoned lab coat and caressed her back. "You are so pretty," she sighed. Kylie bent to kiss her, and Blair smiled through the kiss, her eyes open. "You just brushed your teeth. Was that for me?"

"Yep. Ever since we became involved, I've been carrying a toothbrush with me." She reached into one of her large pockets and pulled out a small travel-sized brush with a tiny tube of paste. "I knew you were coming over, so I brushed after I had my last cup of coffee."

"I swear you're the most thoughtful woman on Earth. How did I luck out and snare you?"

"Must've been your lucky day," Kylie said, planting another soft kiss on her lips.

Blair's bagel popped up, and she shook her head as she went to fetch it. "If I don't watch myself, I'm gonna have you right on this table."

"I'm gonna get to the bottom of this. That's twice you've seen me in my doctor clothes, and twice you wanted to get frisky because of them. Now, what gives?"

"We can talk about it later," Blair said, giving Kylie a heated kiss. "I've got to go meet a client." She dropped a hand to her lover's ass and tickled along the bottom of her butt, feeling the bikinis she knew would be present. "Nice panties, even in scrubs. My kinda doctor."

"Kiss me goodbye," Kylie said, bending to investigate Blair's mouth thoroughly. "And be ready for action when you get home tonight." She placed the earpieces of her stethoscope into Blair's ears and held the diaphragm over her own heart. "You make my heart race."

⌒

When Kylie came home that night, Blair was in her former room, where she still kept her clothing, laying out what she wanted to take to Chicago. "Hi, snookums. How's my favorite doctor?"

"Good. How's my favorite real estate agent?"

"Good, also. I'm really looking forward to this trip."

"I am, too," Kylie said. "Dinner on Saturday is kinda dressy. Do you have anything to wear?"

"I'm bringing the outfit you bought me to wear to the symphony. Is that good enough?"

"That's perfect. I'll go start dinner."

"I bought something from the gourmet market. I knew we had a lot of things to do tonight."

"Cool. Have you had your swim yet?"

"Nope. I thought I'd swim after dinner. I want to get packed first."

"Okay. I'll do the same." Kylie gave her a gentle kiss and said, "Let's go to bed early tonight. I want you well rested 'cause traveling takes a lot out of you." She added one more kiss and decreed, "Doctor's orders."

⌒

The pool was only wide enough for one person to swim laps, but it was sufficiently large for Kylie to sit on the coping and dangle her legs in the warm water. She'd been using the pool as well, finding that swimming rejuvenated her body after a long day of standing. Neither was particularly fond of swimsuits, but Blair was forced to wear the top from her suit to support her breasts. Kylie had no such requirement, and she loved jumping into the warm water stark naked. While waiting her turn, she wore a T-shirt just to keep the evening chill from her skin, and that was her outfit on this night. One dog leaned against either hip, all three waiting for Blair to emerge.

Over the last week and a half, Blair had worked up to forty laps, and she pledged to be at a hundred by the time the baby was born. "You have such nice form," Kylie said when her partner finished her workout. "Can you help me improve mine?"

Blair shook her head roughly and then tilted it until a few drops of water trickled out of her ear. She gave Kylie a look and then felt her smile turn a little lecherous as she said, "Your form is absolutely perfect. Nice long legs, smooth as silk." She grasped one leg and rubbed her cheek against the skin. "Lovely cheeks, just waiting to be squeezed." Coming closer, she did just that, making Kylie squeal. "A sexy, dark triangle of perfectly groomed curls." Her fingers tickled along the edge of Kylie's mound, the doctor's giggle music to her ears. "I need to have a little nibble," she said, and before Kylie could say a word, Blair nestled her head between her legs and started to mouth her playfully.

Without further urging, Kylie scooted forward and draped her long legs across Blair's shoulders. Lying back on the grass, she relaxed and let Blair work her magic, gazing up at the twinkling stars in the indigo-blue sky. Sliding her fingers through Blair's hair, she sighed heavily as wave after wave of spine-tingling pleasure rolled through her body. "God, this feels so good I don't ever want it to end."

Blair's head lifted, and she rested her chin on Kylie's pubic bone, the moonlight causing her lips to glisten. "I've got all night. You just relax and enjoy."

"Oh, I'm enjoying. I'm definitely enjoying." She tried to hold off for as long as she could, but Blair was a very quick study, and she had learned most of Kylie's triggers. "Oh, God!" The long legs jerked upward until her feet rested on Blair's shoulders. Blair felt her partner begin to pulse against her mouth, grinning to herself at how easy it was to make Kylie come.

"You're such a pushover," Blair said, dipping into the water to rinse off. She kissed the delicate skin of Kylie's inner thighs and watched the goose bumps rise.

"I know," Kylie moaned, joining in her laughter. "I always think this will be the time I hold out and really make you work, but I have no self-control whatsoever." She slid into the water and grasped Blair around the belly, making her scream. Kylie started to kick, and Blair stopped struggling and let herself be dragged along after her. They played together for a long while, the dogs running along the side of the pool, yapping excitedly. After tossing Blair around like a doll, Kylie nibbled on her ear and said, "Let's go inside so I can return the favor."

"Don't you have to swim some laps, Doctor Mackenzie?"

"I'd rather lap you. I wanna see if I can make you come as easily as you do me."

"How can I lose in that competition? Let's go rinse this chlorine off and get moving!"

⌐

Kylie lost the bet, but she still felt as if she had won, resting with her head on Blair's thigh and a wide smile on her face. "Hey," she said, beginning to crawl up to lie next to her partner. "We didn't talk about your doctor fetish yet."

"I don't have a doctor fetish. I just found myself incredibly attracted to you—and only you—in your doctor togs. I assure you that this isn't a universal phenomenon. You're the only object of my affection."

Smiling, Kylie said, "I didn't get the impression that we were talking about affection. I thought we were talking about lust."

Returning the smile, Blair said, "I guess that'd be closer to the truth. You look hot. What can I say?"

"You can say a lot more than that! I want some details!"

Her brow knitting, Blair looked at her partner and asked, "Is this really important to you?"

Giving her an adorably shy look, Kylie nodded, her curls bouncing around her head. "It's important to know what turns you on. If there's a certain way that I look that works for you, I'll go out of my way to look like that. If you want me to wear my lab coat to bed, I'll gladly do it." She said this with a teasing tone of voice, but Blair didn't doubt her sincerity for a moment.

"No, it's not really the lab coat. It's just that when you're in your doctor clothes, you exude this sexiness that I find absolutely compelling."

"But what specifically appeals to you?"

"Mmm…I'd have to say that it's your demeanor. You seem forceful and kinda powerful. You honestly look bigger and more authoritative when you have on that white lab coat. It makes your shoulders look really broad and makes you look even taller than you are." She shrugged and said, "You just look impressive. Powerful and impressive. You're in full-tilt surgeon mode when you're at work." Smiling in remembrance, Blair said, "The first time I met you, I was taken by how you seemed to be the powerful one in a room full of doctors. I thought that was really cool."

Blinking, Kylie asked, "Were you attracted to me?"

"Yes, but not sexually. There was something about you that was very compelling—kinda like Bill Clinton."

Her brow knitted, and Kylie looked confused. "Bill Clinton?"

"Yeah. Everyone who meets him—whether they like him or not—agrees that he fills up a room with his charisma. You do that when you're at work."

"But not when I'm at home."

"Mmm…not as much. Oh, you're still charming, but you don't have the aura. At home, you're a little quiet and kinda self-effacing. You're really gentle and sweet and thoughtful when you're here. But at work, you're completely self-possessed. That's a turn-on," she said, shrugging her shoulders.

"Okay," Kylie said. "I think I know what you mean." She lay on her back and waited for Blair to curl up against her. She was almost asleep when she jerked sharply and said, "Would you like me to be more like that at home?"

"At home?"

"Well…at home…in bed," Kylie clarified.

"Oh, honey, you don't have to put on an act for me. I love you just like you are."

Rising up onto one elbow, Kylie quirked a grin and said, "I can be a lot of ways. I'm a very flexible woman, and I have a lot of facets to my personality."

"Really?" Blair asked tentatively. "You've never been very, uhm, forceful when we're in bed."

"No, I haven't been. But that's only because I've never gotten a signal that you want me to be."

Now Blair lifted herself up and matched Kylie's posture as much as she could, given her center of gravity. "What do you mean by that?"

"I mean," Kylie said, "that all I want is to please you. I read your signals, and I try to give you what you need."

Blair lifted her hand and scratched her head, her face set in a confused scowl. "I don't get it."

"Maybe this is a cultural difference," Kylie said. "Maybe it's the difference between men and women."

"I don't know. All I know is that I wasn't called on to set the tone before I met you. The guy did that."

"Okay," Kylie said, warming to the topic. "Tell me how it felt to have sex with a man."

"Really? You want to know that?"

"Sure I do, if it'll help us have better sex. My ego's not very fragile. I'm open to suggestions."

"All right." Blair lay back down and thought for a moment. "When I had sex with a man, it was mostly about power and a little bit of force. Not coercion—just a forcefulness to his need that I found really appealing. I liked having someone take charge and show me what *he* needed. I found it hot to have a man reveal how much he needed me and then be able to satisfy him. In a way, it was a reversal of power. He was stronger, and he was kinda dominating me, but I had to cooperate and work with him to allow him to be satisfied. I guess what I liked was the way the power shifted between us. That was hot."

"I can understand that," Kylie said. "Now tell me how you feel when we have sex."

"That's easy," Blair said, smiling warmly. "I feel loved and cared for. I feel like you're focusing on me to the exclusion of everything else in the world. I feel really precious, Kylie, like you practically worship me. You're gentle and sweet and so concerned with my pleasure and helping me reach orgasm." She shook her head and revealed, "David was pretty concerned with my response, but my previous boyfriends weren't. If I had an orgasm that was nice, but they certainly didn't lose sleep over it if I didn't."

Kylie nodded, taking in every word. "Are there things from your experiences with men that you'd like to incorporate into our sex life?"

"No, honey," Blair insisted. "I love feeling so connected to you and having you focus on me like you do. I don't want to give that up."

Drawing closer, Kylie looked into Blair's eyes and asked, "I love that, too, but it sounds to me like you might like a little change of pace." She tucked an arm around

Blair and pulled her as close as she could. "How would you like it if, every once in a while, I didn't spend any time at all worshiping you and a whole lot of time…" She placed her lips next to Blair's ear and whispered a few incendiary words.

Blair pulled away and blinked slowly. "You could do that?" she asked, eyes wide.

"Sure could. Have. Many times."

Starting to giggle, Blair wrinkled up her nose and said, "That could be fun."

"Oh, don't you worry," Kylie growled playfully. "It'll be fun."

"Why didn't you tell me this before now—when we have to leave for your parents' house? I can just see those little nieces and nephews of yours running into the room, trying to get in on the game."

"We can wait until we get home. But don't worry. I won't forget."

Blair cuddled up to her partner and joked, "I know what I'm gonna dream of tonight, and it isn't visions of sugarplums dancing in my head."

Chapter Eleven

S omewhere over the Great Plains, Kylie nudged Blair and said, "How about a
little stroll through the cabin?"

"Ugh. I hate walking around. I mean, it's not like there's anywhere to go."

"Come on. I'll go with you. We'll walk up and down the aisle for a minute, and then you can make a pit stop."

"Who says I have to go?" she asked, a tiny frown on her face.

Kylie leaned over and kissed her nose. "You always have to go. Now, come on; let's stretch a little."

Grumbling, Blair got out of her seat and started to make her way down the aisle. She followed Kylie's admonition to keep her hands at waist level so she could grab on to a headrest if the plane hit any turbulence. One of the doctor's hands was resting on Blair's shoulder, and even though she felt silly, Blair had to admit it was very reassuring to have her partner's caring presence beside her. As was so often the case, she drew more than her share of attention, the most vocal of her admirers being women in the grandmother age bracket. On their first lap, a few people smiled and nodded, but on the second, a couple of the women engaged her in conversation. One woman, probably in her sixties, stopped her and asked, "When are you due, honey?"

"December," Blair said. "I hope he's on time. I need that extra tax deduction."

The woman wasn't quite sure how to take the comment, but she laughed. "Is this your first?"

"Yeah. My last, too," she said without hesitation.

"Oh," the woman said, "are you having a difficult time, dear?"

"No, not particularly. I just don't see the point in stretching my body to ridiculous proportions when there are thousands of kids available for adoption."

"Oh, I'll bet your husband won't want to stop if you don't have a little boy in there," she said, patting Blair's belly without permission.

"My husband's the one who coerced me into this. He's the *last* guy who gets a vote. Besides, we're getting divorced."

The older woman's eyes widened so dramatically that Kylie was afraid they were going to pop out. Feeling sorry for the woman, the doctor urged her lover forward and then leaned over to whisper, "She's a little grouchy today. You know how it is."

Happy to be talking to a sane person, the woman nodded gratefully. "Oh, my, yes. I have six of my own. I never had to fly while I was pregnant, though. It's a good thing to keep her moving."

"Doing my best," Kylie said, dashing through the plane to catch her partner as she reached their row.

Blair was steaming. Her face was flushed, and she looked as if she could spit fire. "I'm finished. I refuse to have strangers pawing me today."

"They're trying to bond with you. They're welcoming you into the mom club."

"I don't wanna be in the fucking mom club," she groused, loud enough for their seatmate to hear and give Blair a startled look.

"What's wrong?" Kylie asked softly. "Tell me what's bothering you."

"Nothing," she snapped. Turning her head away, she pushed her seat as far back as she could get it and closed her eyes.

Kylie waited a moment to let her calm down and then reached over and took her partner's hand. Bringing it to her lips, she kissed it and then laced their fingers together. "Do you mind?"

"No."

Well, at least she didn't punch me when her fist was close to my mouth. I hope this mood lifts soon, or it's gonna be a long weekend.

⟶

The Schneidhorsts were at the gate to meet them, and Kylie wished she had a sign that read "Danger! Tread carefully!" Not only had Blair's mood remained sour, it had gotten worse, and Kylie fervently hoped that Blair's seeing her parents would serve to improve it.

"My God! You've gotten so big!" Werner said, and Kylie cringed, waiting for the explosion.

But it didn't come. Instead, Blair launched herself into her father's arms and cried piteously. Both Werner and Eleanor stared at Kylie, looking for an explanation, but she didn't have a clue as to why Blair was upset, so she made the "I have no idea" gesture.

Eleanor put her arm around her daughter's shoulders while Werner continued to hold her. It took a long time, but Blair finally stopped sobbing long enough to choke out a greeting.

"Tell me what's wrong, sweetheart," Werner said.

"I'm sick of people, and I'm sick of airplanes, and I'm sick of being pregnant," she sniffed. "I wanna go back to normal!"

"My poor baby," Werner said. "I know how hard this is for you. But it will all be over soon, and you'll be so happy with your baby that you won't remember one bit of the struggle."

"Is that true, Dad?" she asked, her tear-streaked face looking to him for reassurance.

"Yes, baby, it's true. I promise you."

"The day we brought you home was the happiest day of our lives," Eleanor said. "All of the struggles we'd gone through to have a baby faded away. All that mattered was that we had you. I guarantee you'll feel that way, too."

"I hope so," Blair sighed, "'cause right now, that seems like a long, long way off."

⌒

When they reached the Schneidhorsts', Kylie changed into a pair of jeans and a pastel flannel shirt and announced that she was going out for the evening.

"You'll have dinner with us, won't you?" Eleanor asked. "We're planning on eating in about an hour."

"No, but thanks. I have a friend from college who lives at the north end of the park. I thought I'd wander around the neighborhood a little and then head up there to meet her for dinner. I want the three of you to have some time alone."

"That's not necessary, Kylie," Werner insisted. "We'd like you to stay."

"She's antsy, Dad," Blair said. "She'll feel better if she's outside for a while. Now that she walks the dogs every day, she's finding that she actually likes to walk around and get some exercise."

"That's true," Kylie said. "I don't enjoy being a couch potato anymore."

"Well, I hope you know that we're happy to have you, Kylie. You really don't need to leave," Werner said.

"I know that. I'd like to be outdoors for a while. I haven't been able to snoop around the neighborhood since I was in college."

"Have fun," Eleanor said. "You have our number if you need it, don't you?"

"Yes. I have it programmed into my cell phone." Turning to Blair, she said, "Call me if you need me. I'll have my pager on just in case my cell doesn't work."

"Don't get lost," Blair said. "It's been a long time since you've been in the city."

Kylie chuckled, saying, "If I do get lost, I'll never admit it."

Blair walked her to the door and stepped out into the hallway with her. "Are you sure you don't want to be here for this?"

"No, I think you're right. This'll be easier if it's just the three of you. Besides, in case they're unhappy with me, I want to give them time to curse my name for a bit."

"They won't be unhappy with you."

"I hope it goes well," Kylie said, bending to kiss Blair gently.

"Sorry I'm so grouchy. You probably don't even want to come back."

"Yes, I do," Kylie said. "And you're not grouchy. You're pregnant. Your mood is all part of the pregnancy syndrome." She kissed her again and added, "I love you. I'll be thinking of you all evening—when I'm not boasting about how great you are."

"I'll page you with the all clear when we're done talking. I'll key in your birthday so you'll know everything's okay."

"What'll you put in if everything isn't okay?"

Blair thought for a second. "911. That means 'Come get me!'"

"It's a deal. Hope it goes well."

Blair watched her partner walk down the hall, wishing she could go with her and put off her talk for another year or two. Taking in a breath, she went back into the apartment. Her parents were sitting in the living room, both of them giving her a slightly puzzled look. "Is everything okay?" her mother asked. "Are you and Kylie getting along all right?"

"Oh, sure," she said, sitting down. "We're fine."

"You looked so bereft when you got off the plane," Werner said. "We're worried about you."

She shook her head. "I didn't like being on the plane. Normally, I don't mind flying, but I feel defenseless these days. When the steward was talking about how to evacuate in case of emergency, I had an image of people running over me to get to the exits. I'm not used to feeling vulnerable like this."

"That must be hard," Eleanor said. "I know how independent you are."

"But you had Kylie with you," Werner said. "She'd make sure you were safe."

"I know," Blair said wearily, "but sometimes, I get tired of having to rely on her. Not just her," she emphasized. "On anyone." She patted the part of her rib cage she could still find. "The baby's so big now that he's pressing against my diaphragm. It's hard for me to breathe when I exert myself the slightest bit, and that makes me feel so weak." A frown settled on her face, and she said, "I hate to feel weak, and sometimes, when I do, I take it out on Kylie. I know that's unfair to her, but it pisses me off that she's healthy and hearty while I get winded blowing my hair dry. I used to be in better shape than she is," she grumbled, looking petulant.

"Sweetheart," Werner said, "I know that you know this, but Kylie's gone so far out of her way for you that you have to try to be civil to her. Remember, she's only your roommate."

She hadn't planned on starting the discussion so early, but she saw the opportunity and took it. "This is gonna come as a surprise, but things have changed between us, Dad. She's not only my roommate. I've fallen in love with her."

"P...Pardon?"

"We've fallen in love, and we're going to raise the baby together."

"You're joking!" Eleanor gasped. "You're not gay!"

"I'm probably not. But it doesn't matter. I love Kylie, and I want to partner with her."

"And this is what Kylie wants, too?" Werner asked, still confused.

"Of course, she does, Dad. This isn't something I decided on my own! We've talked about it, and it's the right thing—for both of us. I've loved her for a while now, and adding a sexual component seemed like the next logical step."

"Decision? Logic?" Werner stood up and started to pace around the living room. "What kind of words are those to talk about love?" He stopped and stared at his daughter. "You sound like you're talking about a real estate deal."

Offended, she scowled at him for a moment. "I wasn't lucky enough to get the artistic gene from either of you, but I do feel love, you know. Maybe I don't express it poetically, but it's still real."

"Blair, your father didn't mean to hurt your feelings," Eleanor said, "but you do sound very dispassionate about this."

"Look, I'm not the most passionate person around. I never have been, and I never will be. But I love Kylie, and she loves me. Isn't that what matters?"

"But what does this mean?" Werner asked. "Are you making a lifelong commitment to each other?"

Blair sighed dramatically. "I made a lifetime commitment to David, and look where that got me. Kylie and I have an understanding. We're going to stay together until we stop loving each other. It's impossible to predict how either of us will feel in five or ten years."

Eleanor and Werner looked at each other, and Blair could see them silently communicate their shock and concern.

"This isn't a fling," she added. "I certainly hope we're together for the rest of our lives, but I can't predict the future."

"So, you're living together until you don't want to be together any longer," Eleanor said. "Is that right?"

"That's it exactly." Blair's chin had jutted out, and she began to feel very defensive. "How's that different from my marriage? We made a vow, and then we broke it. I don't see why the semantics change a thing."

"Is that what you'll tell your child?" Werner asked. "A child needs stability. He or she needs to know that both parents will be there."

"Dad, at the rate I'm going, this child is gonna be in therapy while he's still in diapers. I never should have agreed to have a baby with David, and I never should have had an artificial insemination. Now David doesn't want to have anything to do with the baby. So, before he's even born, he's lost his father. His crazy grandmother thinks I'm a pervert, and she'd sue for custody if she thought she could win. Wondering about the terms I use for my relationship with Kylie is gonna be way down on the list. He'll be in high school before he and his shrink get to that."

Both of the Schneidhorsts stared at their daughter as if she were speaking in tongues. "I don't think this is going very well," Blair announced. "I hate to be so demanding, but I've gotta have some dinner. All I had on the plane was a pack of almonds. Can we eat soon?"

Eleanor nodded, not saying a word. She walked into the kitchen, and Werner said, "Why don't you take a shower and change clothes? You've had a tough day."

"Okay. I'll be back soon."

She walked into her former room, and Werner ducked into the kitchen. He looked at his wife, and she returned his worried gaze. "I thought being a parent would get easier by the time she was nearly middle-aged," Eleanor sighed.

"What in the world is going on here?" he whispered. "Which grandmother is crazy?"

"God only knows," Eleanor said. "All I know is that I'd love some wine with dinner, and I'd like to start right now."

⌐

For the first half-hour at the table, Blair's contribution to the conversation was limited to "Thanks for making dinner so quickly, Mom."

Eleanor finally steeled her nerves and brought up the loaded topic again. "I know you're feeling very emotional, and I don't want to upset you, but I'm trying to understand everything that's happened."

"I know that," Blair said, "and I *am* emotional, but I wanted to talk to you both in person. I'm sorry it's going so poorly."

"Let's start over again, okay?"

"Okay."

"Can you tell us how and when this started?" Werner asked.

"A couple of weeks ago," Blair said, "Kylie had started to date a woman, and I realized I was jealous of her. I started thinking about it, and I discovered that I was sexually attracted to Kylie. I knew she was attracted to me, too. I mean…I knew." She giggled, blushing a little.

Eleanor nodded. "I saw that when we visited."

"I didn't see a thing!" Werner said.

Blair and her mother exchanged subtle, knowing looks. Eleanor asked, "Then what happened?"

"Kylie broke up with the woman, and a few days later, I told her I thought I was falling in love with her."

"Was she surprised?" Werner asked.

"Yeah." Blair laughed. "I told her after I'd kissed her. She was very surprised by the kiss *and* by what I said."

Werner's brows rose, but he didn't say anything.

"So, this dawned on you when you realized you were jealous," Eleanor said. "You weren't attracted to her before?"

"I don't think I've ever been attracted to a woman before, Mom, but Kylie's special."

"This seems so…convenient," Eleanor said, wincing as she spoke. "I know that sounds harsh, but you have to see how this looks from our point of view. You've always been heterosexual, but you move in with a lesbian who's a wonderful, generous person, and all of a sudden, you're in love with her, and she's going to help you raise your child."

Blair stood up and stared at each of her parents. Her voice was higher than normal, and her cheeks were hot pink. "Are you accusing me of using her?"

"I'm not accusing you of anything, Blair, but you've never shown an interest in being with women," Eleanor said. "This seems as if you're choosing Kylie simply because you need a partner."

"How dare you question my motives! I would never use Kylie or anyone else like that!"

"This is so sudden," Werner said. "We know you and Kylie are close, but this is a very big decision."

"Why is it such a big deal? We care for each other, she's always wanted to have a child, and we both want to have a partner. Can you think of anyone better for me to be with?"

"She's a lovely woman," Werner said, "and if this is really right for you, we have no objection at all, do we, Eleanor?"

"No, of course not. Kylie's a darling woman, but I'm not convinced she's the person for you."

"And how do I convince you of that?" Blair asked, the tone of her voice unmistakable. "Shouldn't *I* be the one to judge who the right person for me is?"

"Blair," Eleanor said, "I assume you had a reason for telling us this in person. I can only guess that it was so we could discuss it. Shutting me off with a sarcastic reply isn't very helpful."

"I apologize," she said stiffly.

"Please sit down," Werner said. "We have to be able to discuss this calmly."

Blair complied, staring at her folded hands.

"Neither your mother nor I think you're consciously using Kylie; you're not that type of woman. I think we're both worried, though, that you're falling into this relationship because it's the solution to a lot of your problems. It also sounds like it's giving Kylie a lot of things she wants, too."

"So, we're using each other, rather than only my using her?"

"Please stop being sarcastic," Werner said, raising his voice. "It's not helpful!"

"I'm sorry," she said quietly. "I thought you'd both be happy about this."

Werner looked at his daughter, paused to collect his thoughts, and said, "We can only understand what you tell us. We weren't around to see how this relationship developed. We don't see how you and Kylie act around each other. This is a very big surprise for us. A *very* big surprise."

"I know that," she said, "and I wish you were around us more. Then you'd see how much we love each other." She pursed her lips together and said, "Maybe we need to let this settle a little bit. I've got a throbbing headache, and I'd love to lie down with an ice bag for my head."

"Go lie down in the living room, honey," Eleanor said. "I'll bring you some ice in a minute."

"Okay." She stood up and held on to the table for a moment to adjust her balance. She walked over to her mother, kissed her head, and then did the same to her father. "I'm sorry for being so bitchy. I don't know what I was expecting, but this wasn't it." She laughed softly and walked out of the room, saying, "I don't know why I can't have normal parents who throw the Bible at me for having a woman lover."

⌐

Blair made a stop in her room before she went to the living room. She called Kylie's cell phone and greeted her when the doctor answered.

"Hi, are you okay?" Kylie asked.

"Yeah. You can come home whenever you want."

"Tell me what happened. You sound upset."

"No, I'm not…really. They were fine about the gay thing, like I thought they would be. They're not sure it's the right choice for me—or you, for that matter. But they're not angry with either of us. They like you."

"Sure you don't want me to come home now? I can see Janice some other time."

"No, you go on and see your friend. Stay as late as you want. Dad's always up until after midnight. I'll tell the doorman to buzz you right up."

"Okay," Kylie said warily. "I love you."

"I love you, too, Kylie." *No matter what my parents think.*

⌐

Kylie arrived at the apartment at 10:00, and Werner let her in. She stood in the entryway, noting Blair's absence. "Hi," she said, a bit of her nervousness showing.

Werner put his arm around her shoulders and gave her a squeeze. "Come sit with us for a while. Can I get you a drink?"

"Sure. Do you have any Scotch?"

"I do, indeed. How would you like it?"

"On the rocks." She started to walk into the living room, and Eleanor saw her eyes dart around the room.

"She's in bed, dear. I checked on her a minute ago, and she was sound asleep."

Kylie looked at her watch, saying, "It's only 8:00 in L.A. It's not like her to conk out quite that early."

"Today was hard for her," Eleanor said. Werner handed Kylie a glass and sat next to his wife.

Kylie sat, taking a tiny sip of her drink, trying to make it last so she would have something to do with her hands.

"Have you been in this situation often, Kylie?" Werner asked, a playful twinkle in his eyes.

"Uhm, which situation is that?"

"Talking with the parents," he said, smiling.

"No." She shook her head rather forcefully. "Actually, once before. I think that's enough for one lifetime." She quirked a grin at the couple, and they returned her smile.

"Blair's a little upset with us," Eleanor said. "We want you to know that we have no objections to your being together, Kylie. We're both very fond of you."

Lifting an eyebrow, Kylie asked, "What *is* your objection? I'm sensing that you have one—or more."

"Only one," Werner said. "This is such a major decision for Blair to have made so quickly. Over dinner, she admitted that she's not attracted to women in general and that she never has been. Choosing a lesbian relationship when she doesn't consider herself a lesbian seems…strange…to both of us."

Nodding, Kylie said, "I can understand that. It does seem a little strange, even to me. I've known many women who considered themselves primarily straight, but every one of them has had at least a glimmer of attraction for women. Blair's the first one I've ever met who swears that isn't true for her. But she's so loving and affectionate with me that I believe her."

"We don't want to question her decisions, Kylie, but we're both worried that she's making this decision based primarily on her circumstances."

Again, the doctor nodded her understanding of their position. "I think that's possible. I, uhm, I think that at this point, I'm much more head over heels than Blair is. But that's not necessarily such a bad thing," she said earnestly. "I know she loves me. She shows me in so many ways that she cares deeply for me. We love being together, we have lots of the same interests, and we share the same feelings about raising children." She polished off a bit more Scotch, looked contemplative for a moment, and then said, "She reminds me of how my brothers and sisters treat their spouses. They've all been married for quite a while, and they seem comfortable with each other. It's obvious that they love each other, but they're not all dewy-eyed about it. That's how Blair seems. I recognize that she's made this decision with her head as well as her heart, but I honestly think we can make a go of it, even if Blair's heart never skips a beat when she sees me."

"But don't you deserve that?" Eleanor asked gently.

"Well, I do see flashes of it. It's not consistent, though." Her brow furrowed. "She seems afraid to really let go."

"That's our girl," Werner said. "She's always been cautious."

"She has been," Eleanor said, "but it's hard to love with caution."

"I'll be frank," Kylie said. "I'd love it if Blair were wildly passionate about me. But of all the things that are important to me, that's the one thing I'd give up. I've had relationships where the woman was mad for me, but we didn't have the things that allowed us to grow together and work towards a common purpose. Blair and I have that," she said. "I think we have the elements that we need to have a very satisfying partnership."

"We trust the two of you to make the correct decision," Werner said. "I only hope you both get what you need out of this."

"I'm already getting what I need," Kylie said, a broad, confident smile on her face, "and I'm going to love Blair with everything I have for the rest of my life. She's a dream come true for me."

Werner looked at the earnest woman sitting in his living room and wished with all his might that his daughter had expressed the same sentiments for her. He went to Kylie and wrapped her in a hug, and then Eleanor did the same. "Welcome to the family. We're very glad to have you."

⌒

Sneaking into bed, Kylie lay quietly, knowing that if she lay still long enough, Blair would settle down and sink back into a deep sleep. She was quite certain that her partner was still asleep, but Blair turned over and draped both an arm and a leg over her, using her as a second body pillow. Kylie kissed the top of her head and tucked an arm around her, smiling when Blair snuggled even closer. She was almost asleep when Blair let out a whimper and woke abruptly. Blinking her eyes confusedly, she tightened her hold and shivered. "Kylie?" she asked, her voice shaking.

"I'm here. Go back to sleep. You must have been having a bad dream." She started to run her hand over Blair's back, trying to calm her.

"Kylie? Do you believe I love you?"

Sitting up halfway, Kylie leaned over her and looked her right in the eye. "Of course, I believe that. Of course." She bent her head and kissed Blair tenderly. "Do you believe I love you?"

"Yes."

"Then that settles that, doesn't it? Go back to sleep now. You've had a tough day."

"Are you sure you believe me?" she asked again, her voice sounding a little frantic.

Still leaning over her, Kylie's expression grew sober. "There isn't a doubt in my mind. You might not be all goofy over me, and you might not write me love poems, but that doesn't diminish the reality of your love. You don't have a thing to worry about. My faith in you is rock-solid."

Blair threw her arms around Kylie's neck, sobbing softly. "Promise me you'll always believe that."

"I promise," Kylie said, kissing her repeatedly. "I swear that I'll always believe in our love."

⚊

On Saturday morning, Werner and Eleanor gave Kylie and Blair a ride up to Lake Forest. Both of the younger women had insisted that they were happy to rent a car, but their offer was firmly rebuffed. "We really do appreciate how much you've gone out of your way for us," Kylie said, "but we probably should have rented a car. There's a good chance that no one in my family will want to give us a ride back downtown."

Werner blinked in surprise. "With all of those people?"

"Yes, we're united as a family," she said. "United in never going out of our way for one another. One good thing is that I have a couple of nieces and nephews who are just at driving age. I'm sure I can bribe one of them into taking us."

"I have a chamber recital tomorrow at 3:00," Werner said. "Anytime before that I'd be happy to come get you."

"I'm mostly teasing," Kylie said. "Someone will take us."

"What are your plans?" Eleanor asked. "I know you're here for a conference, but Blair didn't tell me the schedule."

"My conference starts on Sunday at 3:00," Kylie said, "and it's at a hotel on Michigan Avenue. Blair's flight is at 5:30, so we thought we'd go to the hotel together, and then she can catch a limo to the airport."

They arrived at the Mackenzie house at 10:00, and a group of the younger nieces and nephews came out to greet them and ineffectively help with the luggage. "See what I mean, Werner?" Kylie joked. "I'm sure there are quite a few able-bodied people in the house, but only the tiny ones try to help. It's survival of the fittest at the Mackenzie house."

Kevin came bounding up to Blair, but when he reached her, he turned shy and latched on to Kylie's leg. "Hey, Kev," his aunt said, picking him up. "Wanna say hi to your Aunt Blair?"

His little strawberry-blonde head nodded, and Blair leaned in and kissed him on the cheek. "Hi, Kevin. We missed you."

He held out his arms, and Blair gamely accepted him. Because of her belly, he rode so high in her embrace that he was as tall as his aunt, a fact he found entirely wonderful. After letting him cuddle for a moment, Kylie whisked him away and put him astride her shoulders, making him taller still. "I'm the biggest," he crowed to all.

"Come on in for a bit," Kylie urged the Schneidhorsts. "You can say hi to my parents."

"Not home," Kevin said. "Nobody's home but the big kids."

"Really?" Kylie asked. "Are you sure?"

The other kids agreed with Kevin, so Werner and Eleanor decided to take their leave. "It's been wonderful seeing you both," Eleanor said. "And I'm very sorry that I upset you, sweetheart. I know you always think things through carefully. There's no crime in that."

"It's fine, Mom," Blair said. "I was very grouchy when we arrived. It wasn't a good day to talk about a loaded topic."

"We're very glad that things are working out so well for you both," Werner said. "And we're elated to have Kylie in the family." He placed his hand lightly on Blair's belly and said, "Take care of our grandchild, sweetheart."

"We will, Dad," Blair said. "We'll see you both in December."

"I've never looked forward to a date with such pleasure," Eleanor said, hugging both of the women. "You two take good care of each other."

"We will," Kylie said, tucking an arm around Blair.

They watched the car pull away, and Kevin asked, "Who wants to play with me? The big kids just yell at us."

"We'll play with you, Kev," Kylie said. "We'll show those big kids a thing or two."

⌒

Later that evening, the entire group gathered at the local country club for the gala birthday party for Kyle. The affair was much larger than Blair had realized with most of the Mackenzies' extended family and dozens of their friends and colleagues in attendance. They'd been on their feet for hours, greeting family and friends, so when Kylie saw an opening, she directed her partner to a quiet corner and demanded that she put her feet up. Without argument, Blair did, sighing with relief when Kylie pulled her shoes off and started to rub her feet. "Oh, you're a goddess," Blair said. "The best hands in the world."

"Having fun?" Kylie asked. She took a linen napkin and scooped out some ice from a water pitcher, rubbing Blair's swollen ankles with the cold cloth.

"I am," Blair said. "Everyone in your family has made it a point to welcome me to the clan. They're teasing me like one of the group, too. It's nice."

"I thought Alan was a little out of line," Kylie said, scowling. "My dad even told him to knock it off, and he never gets involved."

"I thought it was funny," Blair said. "Calling you the world's laziest lesbian cracked me up. What did he say? Something like you're too lazy to even use your own turkey baster?"

"That was the gist," Kylie said. "I guess the good news is that he feels comfortable with you. He wouldn't have done that in front of Stacey, and she was around for years."

"Yes, Carly told me that everyone already likes me better than Stacey. She doesn't seem to have many fans around here."

"They never seemed to care for her. I'm not sure why, but they're going much easier on you."

"Oh, it's probably because I'm pregnant. Everyone has a soft spot for a big belly."

"I love your belly," Kylie said. She put both hands on Blair and smiled at her, their eyes locking together. "I love every part of you." She leaned over and kissed Blair tenderly, letting herself get lost in their embrace.

A loud throat clearing got her attention. "Oh. Hi, Chris," Kylie said, giving her sister a guilty look.

"That kinda stuff doesn't play in Lake Forest," Chris teased. "You two act like you're still in California."

"We're in love no matter where we are," Kylie said, looking at Blair dreamily.

"I hate to break the spell, but I've gotta pee," Blair said. Chris held out her hand, giving Blair a little help, and Kylie put a hand on her butt for added safety. "It's like hauling a car out of a ditch," Blair grumbled.

Kylie patted her ass and said, "Hurry back. I'll be right here."

"I'll keep an eye on her so she doesn't kiss anyone while you're gone," Chris said, taking Blair's seat.

Blair laughed and then went to the restroom. Chris put her arm around her sister's chair and said, "Inquiring minds want to know: how'd you lure her over to the dark side?"

"The usual. Charm, wit, good looks, money…a loaded gun."

Chris elbowed her playfully. "Come on; I really wanna know."

"Well, if you must know, she made the proposal."

"Are you serious?"

"Yep. Surprised the hell out of me. As I think the whole damn world knew, I was desperately in love with her, but I didn't think I had a chance. She thought differently, and she kissed me one night and told me she loved me."

"Wow. Are you really telling the truth? It was her idea?"

Kylie sat back and gave her sister a wry look. "Am I *that* unattractive?"

"You're gorgeous," she said. "You look a lot like I did when I was your age." She put her arm around Kylie's shoulders, gave her a rough hug, and then kissed her cheek. "I'm happy for you, Baby Sister. I hope that Blair knows what it's like to be a lesbian mom. It can be pretty tough."

"I know that," Kylie said, "but she's going into this with her eyes open. I know she loves me, Chris. We can work through anything if that's true."

"I guess you're right. But it's hard to picture you with a built-in family. I have this image of you as my little sister, the lesbian lady killer of Los Angeles."

"That was never true," Kylie said. Then she laughed and added, "Well, it hasn't been true for ten years. The truth is I've hated being single. Winning Blair's heart has been the best thing that's ever happened to me."

Blair walked around the corner as Kylie said this, and she leaned over and gave her partner a warm kiss. "Let's pay someone to take us home. You're too cute to share with all these people."

⌐

Twenty dollars and fifteen minutes later, they were back in Kylie's room. On the way home, Blair mentioned that she was a little worried about Mackenzie because he'd been unnaturally still all evening. As soon as they were in her room, Kylie undressed Blair so quickly that sparks nearly flew, and now she was on her knees, her cheek resting against Blair's stomach. Soft hands palpated the flesh, her face a mask of concentration. "Come on, Mackenzie, let me feel you," she soothed, her voice so gentle and sweet that Blair's heart nearly melted. She slid her hands through Kylie's waves, so intimately connected to her that she felt as though they were one. Kylie tapped gently, urging the baby to react to her touch. "Come on, baby boy. Come on."

Finally, the baby reached out and kicked with one of his feet, causing Kylie to jump. "Did you see that?" she beamed. "He reacted to my touch!"

"He loves his mom," Blair said, smiling down at her.

Kylie slowly got to her feet, staring at Blair as if she'd grown a second head. "I'm gonna be somebody's mom!"

"You sure are," Blair said, hugging her as tightly as she could. "And you're gonna be stupendous!"

⌐

"Aunt Kylie?" a small voice whispered, the sound accompanied by tugging on her shirt.

"Yeah." She turned over and spied Kevin, holding his pillow.

"Can I sleep with you? Just a little?"

"Sure, buddy." She reached down and swept him onto the bed, settling him between her and Blair. "You've gotta be quiet, though. Aunt Blair and the baby have to get their sleep."

"Okay," he whispered. "Is the baby sleeping, too?"

"I think so," she said quietly. "Tomorrow, we'll let you put your hands on Aunt Blair's tummy. I made the baby kick tonight. Maybe he'll do it for you tomorrow."

"He's inside Aunt Blair's tummy?" he asked slowly. "Doesn't the food hit him?"

Stifling a laugh, Kylie said, "It's not exactly her tummy. It's close by. There's nothing in the little space he's in except him. Nothing to worry about, buddy."

"Okay," he said. "Night, Aunt Kylie." He snuggled against her until he was comfortable, giving her a couple of good shots with his bony knees.

Kylie reached over the child and placed her hand on Blair's belly, sighing to herself. *Now, this is heaven.*

⌐

Blair woke groggily on Sunday morning, reaching down, with her eyes still closed, to pat Kylie's hands. Startled at the smallness of the hands, she opened her eyes and discovered Kevin sitting cross-legged between her and Kylie, his expression as sober as his aunt's had been the night before. His little hands pushed against her in various spots, and then he looked at her and whispered, "Is the baby still sleepin'?"

"I think so," she said. "Did Aunt Kylie tell you she felt him kick last night?"

"Uh-huh. Make him do it," he said, pressing a little harder than she liked.

"He'll do it when he's ready, honey. You can't make him."

He stared at her for a moment and then asked, "Why?"

"'Cause he's a tiny baby. He doesn't even know we're talking to him."

Looking at her dubiously, he said, "Aunt Kylie can make him."

"What can Aunt Kylie do?" Kylie asked, her voice sleepy and deep.

"You can make the baby do stuff."

"Hmm…" Kylie murmured, sensing a challenge. She scooted down and tugged Blair's shirt up, exposing her belly to Kevin's startled gaze.

"It's big!" he gasped.

"Thanks," Blair said, smiling thinly. "There's a lot of baby in there. He needs room."

"Put your hands on Aunt Blair," Kylie said. "I'll make him move…eventually."

"The landlord of baby manor has to go to the bathroom in the near future," Blair said. "Make it quick—and don't press anywhere, or I can't guarantee a dry bed."

Kylie pressed her lips close to Blair's skin and started to sing some silly song about ducks and frogs and catfish in a swimming hole. Blair had never heard her sing before, and while the doctor would clearly not win any contests, there was something terribly appealing about her deep, smooth voice. After a few lines, the baby seemed to take notice, and he kicked a good one, making Kevin squeal. "I felt him!" he cried.

"Bathroom break," Blair proclaimed, scampering off the bed.

"That was fun! Sing the song again."

Kylie lay back down, and soon, Kevin curled up against her, his head burrowed into the crook of her shoulder. By the time Blair came back to bed, Kevin was sound asleep. She looked at her watch and saw that it was just 7:00, so she got in quietly. Kylie was still singing softly, so Blair reached out and took her hand, asking, "Happy?"

"Never been happier," Kylie said, and Blair could see that it was so. "I'm gonna love bringing our son into our bed and cuddling with him in the mornings. I know how good it feels to be comforted like that."

"I know how good it feels to be comforted by you," Blair said. "Our baby is a lucky little guy."

⌐

When Blair woke again, she was cuddled up in Kylie's arms, and Kevin was missing in action. "How'd I wind up here?" she asked sleepily.

"Kev woke up and started fidgeting," Kylie said. "I plunked him out of bed, and the second he left, you started inching towards me like a little snail. It was cute," she added, dropping a kiss onto Blair's head.

"Hungry. How 'bout you?"

"Yeah. I'm starved. Go hop in the shower, and I'll strip the bed and get us packed."

"'Kay."

By the time they got downstairs, there was not a bite left to eat, but the table was still full of guests. "Well, here are the sleepyheads," Kyle said.

"Hungry sleepyheads," Kylie said, smiling at her father. Turning to Blair, she asked, "What would you like, honey? I'm sure we have whatever you have a craving for."

"Oh, don't go to any trouble," Blair said. "I can have some cereal."

"How about some shredded wheat?" Dorothy suggested. "The roughage is good for you."

"That's fine," Blair said, but Kylie was having none of it.

"She's not much of a cereal fan," she said. "How about some eggs?"

Blair took a breath, torn between playing by the Mackenzie house rules and letting Kylie do what she clearly wanted to do. Deciding that her allegiance should always be to her partner, Blair said, "If you really don't mind, I'd love a soft-boiled egg and some toast."

Kylie gave her a wide smile and said, "Of course, I don't mind. Anybody else?"

"I wouldn't mind an egg," Laura, Chris's partner, said. "We got up late, too."

"Chris?" Kylie asked, ignoring her father's narrowed glance. "How about you?"

She shrugged and said, "Can you handle sunny-side up?"

"For you? Definitely."

"This is turning into a regular diner," Dorothy sniffed. "I thought I could relax now that the dishes were done."

"We'll clean the kitchen, Mom," Chris assured her.

"That's what you always say." Dorothy, obviously miffed, stood to leave.

Kylie intercepted her and gave her a kiss on the cheek. "I promise we'll clean up properly, Mom. I'm sorry we got up so late, but I have to make sure Blair gets breakfast. It's my job now."

The older woman nodded and then gave her daughter a pat. "It's all right." She turned to the table and said, "Don't forget: we're going to church together. All of us," she emphasized, looking at Chris's children. "We leave at 10:45. Got it?"

"Yes, Grandma," the unhappy children grumbled.

Kyle's beeper went off, and he headed for his study to return the call. Now that the elder generation was gone, Blair leaned over and asked Chris, "What kinda church do we go to?"

Giving her a sly grin, she said, "We're Episcopalians, Blair. Do you mean to tell me that Kylie doesn't take you to services every Sunday morning?"

"I don't wanna go," Carly whispered harshly. "Why do we have to go to church whenever we come here?"

"It's important to your grandmother," Laura said. "It's an hour out of your week, honey. It won't kill you." She looked over at Kylie and said, "Besides, we've violated one of the sacrosanct principles of the Mackenzie family already today. I think that's enough revolution for one weekend."

⌒

The church was only about seven blocks away, so the entire group trooped over together. On the way back home, Dorothy took Blair's hand as they were leaving the church and urged her to stay behind and walk with her at the rear of the gaggle of Mackenzies.

"Well, you've been with us twice now, Blair. Having second thoughts about joining the clan?"

"No," she said, smiling warmly, "I think I might join even if I didn't love Kylie. I've always wanted a large family."

"We are that," Dorothy said. "I wanted to apologize for making a scene at breakfast today. I'm a little set in my ways, and sometimes, I forget that my children are all adults with their own families. I hope I didn't make you uncomfortable."

"No, not at all," Blair said, squeezing her hand. "Every family has its own rules."

"My ways might seem rigid, but honestly, having seven children would have driven me mad if we hadn't had order. Without set mealtimes, I would have been a slave in the kitchen. I had some predictability to my day when I knew that breakfast would be over and the kitchen would be clean by 8:00 when the school bus came."

"I don't know how you managed," Blair said. "Did you have any help?"

"You mean outside help? Goodness, no! By the time the little ones came along, the older children were mature enough to help out. I would have felt like a spendthrift hiring someone to do chores that my children should have been doing. Besides," she said, "it's good for a child to learn responsibility. They've all managed to be good spouses, so I guess we did something right."

"I can only speak for Kylie," Blair said, "but I can't imagine a better spouse."

"You do seem happy together," Dorothy said, a trifle dubiously. Turning her head slightly, she gazed at Blair for a moment. "Are you sure this is the right choice for you? I'd hate to have Kylie's heart broken if you found out you couldn't be happy with a woman."

Blair returned her gaze and nodded. "I can understand that you have doubts about me, Dorothy, but I truly love Kylie. Obviously, I can't guarantee that things will work out, but if they don't, it won't be because we're both women. That's not a big issue for me."

"I hope that's true," Dorothy said, "because I can see how much my baby loves you. She's never been like this about anyone, and I can't help but worry about her."

Blair squeezed her hand and said, "I worry about my baby, and I know exactly where he is at all times. I understand that you feel protective of her, Dorothy, but so do I. I swear I'll do my very best to take care of her precious heart."

Her eyes crinkling up from her smile, Dorothy said, "Forgive me for interfering. I know you're both adults and that you've thought this through. I'm sure everything will work out for the best."

"I'm sure it will, too, but I think you'd feel better if you spent more time with us. Is there any chance you'd consider coming out after the baby's born?"

"Really?" Dorothy asked slowly. "Have you and Kylie discussed this?"

"No, but I know she'd love to have you. I think it would be nice to get to know you a little. Kylie's planning on taking some time off after he's born, so we could all spend some time together."

Dorothy gave her hand a squeeze and said, "We'll see how you feel about it when the time gets closer. You might decide that you two want to be alone."

Chuckling, Blair assured her, "I think we'll be crying for help. A woman with your experience is gonna be in demand!"

⤳

It took a few phone calls, but Kylie finally found a nephew willing to give them a ride downtown—for nearly as much as it would have cost to take a limo. They reached the hotel at 2:30, and after a short wait to check in, they were shown to a very nice room. "Damn, I've never seen so much marble," Blair said while peeking at the bath.

"This is a nice place," Kylie agreed. She wrapped her arms around her partner and said, "Only one thing would make it nicer."

"A bigger minibar?"

"You. In my bed," Kylie said, her expression sober.

"Oh, you'll be home in a few days." She patted her partner and said, "I should get going. I have to check my bag."

"Leave it here. I don't want you walking through that huge airport with your bag. I want you to take everything out of your carryon that isn't essential, too."

"Kylie…"

"I insist," she said, giving her a no-nonsense look. "I hate the thought of your being at the airport alone. I'll feel better if I'm not worried about your having to struggle with your luggage."

Seeing a very determined look, Blair stopped arguing. "Okay." She went to her carryon and took out a few things. Kylie hefted it and pronounced it still too heavy. Rolling her eyes, Blair did as she was told and left only a few snacks, her book, and her MP3 player. "Better?"

Lifting the bag, Kylie nodded. "Good job." She cuddled Blair close and said, "I'd better kiss you goodbye now. We don't want to cause a scene downstairs."

"What are you planning on doing?" Blair asked, batting her eyelashes.

"I plan on showing you how much I love you and how I wish you didn't have to leave. I'm not sure I can say all of that with a kiss, but I'm sure gonna try."

Looking up at the tears welling in her partner's eyes, Blair tried to reassure her. "Honey," she soothed, brushing her hand across Kylie's cheek, "it's only a few days. We'll have lots of short separations through the years. You can't take them so seriously."

The doctor nodded, obviously trying to control her emotions. "It's…probably because you're pregnant. I'll toughen up over time." She was trying to sound flippant, but Blair could hardly bear to look into her eyes and see the sadness that suffused them.

"Come on, now. Walk me downstairs, and then you can go play with your doctor friends."

Kylie enveloped her in a hug, holding on tightly. "I'm gonna miss you so much," the surgeon whispered, her voice raspy and thin.

"You'll be home before you know it. Months from now, when the baby wakes you up six times during the night, you'll *wish* you were on a business trip. Store up some uninterrupted sleep while you can."

"'Kay." Kylie nodded and wiped at her eyes. She dipped her head and gave Blair one of the most tender, emotion-filled kisses with which Blair had ever been gifted. She could feel her lover's heart beating in her chest and knew Kylie was on the verge of crying again, so Blair pulled away and tried to lighten the mood.

"I hate to leave, but I've gotta go. The limo will be here."

Kylie picked up the carryon and slung it over her shoulder. Taking Blair's hand, she led the way out of the room, and they rode down on the elevator in silence. The limo was right on time, and the driver hopped out to take Blair's bag. "Is this all?" he asked.

"Yeah," Kylie said. "We'll be ready in a minute."

He nodded and took her cue, getting back into the car to give them a moment of privacy. The doctor placed a soft, light kiss on Blair's lips, squeezed her hand, and opened the door. Keeping her eyes locked on her partner, Blair got in and lowered the window. "Bye," she said softly.

Kylie didn't say a word. She bit her lip while she watched the limo pull away, standing there until she lost the big, black car in the heavy Michigan Avenue traffic.

⌒

Good God, if we have to go through that every time one of us leaves home… Blair looked out the window, watching the Chicago skyline pass by. After a minute, she dug into her carryon and found her book. She'd been in such a bad mood on the trip out that she hadn't read a bit, but she was determined to make up for it now. *Three days of reading and listening to music and going to bed at an obscenely early hour. I think I'll have ice cream for dinner tonight. Huh…maybe I'll have ice cream for breakfast, too.* With a sly smile she thought, *This is your last chance to revel in your baser instincts. No supervision for three whole days!* She patted her belly. *You're finally gonna know what junk food really tastes like, Mackenzie. You're old enough to withstand a barrage of fat and cholesterol for three days.*

She smiled, happily going back to her book, lost in the story. Before she knew it, they were pulling into the departures area for O'Hare. She tipped the driver and headed for her gate, feeling a little as if she were playing hooky. *Damn, why am I getting such fiendish pleasure from the mere thought of three days alone?* She considered the question for a moment, mulling it over while she waited. *God knows I love Kylie, but she does tend to hover. That was one nice thing about David. He realized that I was like a cat when I was sick or grouchy. I wanted to crawl under a piece of furniture and to be left alone.*

She let herself consider how Kylie treated her and couldn't help but smile. *She's so determined to make me feel better, no matter what's wrong with me. It's absolutely infuriating sometimes*, she thought, chuckling to herself. *No matter how grouchy I am, she can pull me right out of it. Hell, I haven't had a sustained bad mood since we moved in together.*

Boarding began, and she took advantage of her condition to get in line with the other passengers who needed special assistance. Without telling her, Kylie had upgraded her to business class, and she was in the first seat behind the bulkhead. She settled in and watched people start to pass by to get to coach. *Might as well plan my little vacation*, she thought happily. *Tonight, I'll have some ice cream, lie on the sectional, and watch TV.* Her smile faded when a troubling thought invaded her consciousness. *That won't be any fun. It's only fun when Kylie and I cuddle together. That sofa's too big for one person. Okay*, she decided, *maybe I'll lie on the sofa in the living room and read my book.* Grumpily, she recalled that reading was only satisfying when Kylie rubbed her feet. She thought about one night the week before, when they'd sat on opposite ends of the sofa to read and had wound up spending the time giving each other foot massages, which had eventually turned into something quite a bit more intimate. *Well, maybe I'll go for a swim*, she thought. But then she remembered their last swim and how they'd played in the water together after making love. *It won't be any fun to swim alone.*

She thought of her partner's face when they were in the hotel room, and suddenly, it hit her. Her chest constricted, and she struggled to take a breath. She couldn't *bear* the thought of leaving Kylie. Her heart raced, and her stomach started to spasm as she watched more passengers board. Her vision began to narrow, and her whole body was covered with sweat. She knew she was on the verge of panic, so she did the only thing she could think of. She grabbed her bag from under her seat and started to head for the door. The flight attendant gave her a puzzled look and asked, "Are you all right?"

Blair realized that she was crying, hot tears streaming down her cheeks. "No, I'm not," she sobbed. "I have to get off!"

"Pardon?"

"I have to get off!"

"You can't get off, ma'am. Once you've boarded, you have to stay on the plane."

Blair pointed to a stream of passengers still coming up the Jetway. "You're not ready to leave! I have to get off!"

"I'm sorry, but we have rules that can't be broken."

Thinking quickly, she stroked her belly and said, "I think I'm in labor. I'll never make it to L.A." Seeing the hesitation in the woman's eyes, she added, "What makes more sense? Letting me off now or helping me deliver this baby yourself?" The attendant still wasn't convinced, so Blair said, "I had my last baby after three hours of labor. My doctor says this one will come faster!"

The attendant got on the phone and called the gate, and a few seconds later, someone from the airline ran up the walkway with a wheelchair. Blair got in and let the man question her and check her ticket and her identification. A pair of officers from the airport security company came over and got into the act. They ensured that she hadn't checked any luggage, and then they searched all around her seat and those adjoining it.

The other passengers were buzzing about the event, and the officers questioned the few people who had boarded with Blair. When all of them agreed that Blair had only been on for a few minutes and that she hadn't moved from her chair, they allowed her to leave. "Would you like us to call an ambulance?" the young man asked.

"No, a cab is fine," she said. "I've got time to get to the hospital. I just can't risk a four-hour flight."

He put her into the first cab in line and stuck his head in the window. "Good luck, ma'am," he said.

"Oh, I'm a very lucky woman," she said. "I'm beginning to realize how lucky."

The cab deposited her at the hotel at 6:30. For once, Blair's charms failed her, and she couldn't convince the clerk to let her into Kylie's room. He did, however, agree to hold her bag while she searched for her partner. The conference didn't formally start until Monday, but there was a cocktail party to kick things off. Kylie had said she was planning on catching up with some old friends and hoped to have dinner with some medical school classmates afterwards. The cocktail party was scheduled until 7:00, and Blair fervently hoped that Kylie stayed until it was finished, or she wouldn't be able to find her for hours.

The fates were kind, and when Blair talked her way past the registration table, she was able to pick Kylie out of the crowd easily. She felt her heartbeat pick up and a fluttering in her stomach when she saw her. Her palms grew moist, and she actually felt a little lightheaded. Reminding herself that it was just Kylie, she stopped in her tracks and let herself feel how wrong it was to think like that. This wasn't *just* Kylie. This was the woman she had chosen above every other person in the world. This woman was the most important person in her universe, and she was determined to show her how true that was.

Marching over, she sidled up alongside her and put her hand on her lover's. The dark head whipped around, and Kylie gasped in shock. "Blair!"

"Changed my mind," Blair said, looking very shaky.

Blindly handing her glass to the man with whom she had been talking, Kylie threw her arms around her partner and squeezed her so tight she lifted her off the floor. "I'm so happy to see you," Kylie whispered fervently.

"Me, too," Blair sighed. "I couldn't leave you. I couldn't."

They held each other for a minute, drawing furtive glances from dozens of people. Kylie finally pulled away and said, "Were you frightened to fly alone?"

"No, no," Blair said, shaking her head. "I couldn't leave you!"

Kylie cocked her head, not understanding. Out of the corner of her eye, she saw a man shifting his weight from foot to foot. "Oh!" Kylie turned around and said, "Damn, Ethan, I forgot you were even here!"

"I assume this is the woman responsible for your talking my ear off," he said, "so I won't take it too personally."

"Ethan Levine, this is Blair Spencer. Blair, Ethan's one of my study buddies from med school."

"Nice to meet you," Blair said, extending a moist, shaking hand.

"It's a pleasure to meet you," he said. "I always knew Kylie would finally settle down. She obviously shopped very carefully, but it was clearly worth it." Clapping his friend on the back, he said, "You've done well for yourself."

"Not a doubt in my mind," she said, nodding, her eyes never leaving Blair's.

A few other people came up, and after meeting Blair, the group announced they were heading out to dinner. "I think we'll pass," Kylie said. "I don't think Blair's feeling well."

"I'm not myself," she agreed. "I'd love to go up to our room."

They said goodbye to the medical crowd and took the elevator to their floor, Kylie looking Blair over the entire time. When they reached their room, she grasped her shoulders and asked, "What's wrong? I know something is."

"Nothing's wrong," Blair said. But she was pale and shaking, and Kylie immediately went to grab her medical bag. "Kylie, please!"

That stopped the doctor short, and she walked back and put her arms around her partner. "Baby, something's wrong," Kylie said. "You look like you're frightened to death. You still haven't told me why you decided not to go home."

Dropping her head against Kylie's shoulder, she said, "I did." She looked up. "This afternoon it finally hit me. You're my home." Kylie was too stunned to reply, so Blair said it again. "You're my home," she repeated, a fiery certainty sparkling in her eyes. Linking her hands behind Kylie's neck, she tugged her down until their lips met. Pouring every bit of the emotion she felt into her kiss, Blair melted into her partner until she could feel own her knees weaken. "I love you so much. It…it frightens me, but I can't hold back."

"It frightens you?"

"Yes. More than I can tell."

"Don't be frightened," Kylie murmured. "I'll never hurt you, sweetheart. I swear!"

"I know," Blair said. "It's not that…it's…oh, I don't know what it is. I'm just scared."

"Don't let love frighten you. It's freeing. Trust me."

"I do. I do trust you."

"That's what love is," Kylie said fervently. "It's jumping out of a plane without a parachute, but knowing with every fiber of your being that you're safe. Your lover will protect you. No matter what. It's blind faith, Blair. Totally blind faith."

"I've never…ever felt this way before," Blair said, tears filling her eyes. "I'm so frightened, Kylie. Please, please don't hurt me." She held on to her lover with all of her might, sobbing so hard she felt sick.

"I'll always be there for you. I'll catch you. I promise I'll catch you."

⌣

Kylie undressed her partner with unflagging tenderness and then quickly discarded her own clothing. They lay together, wrapped tightly in each other's arms while Kylie smoothed Blair's hair and placed a stream of gentle kisses on her brow. "I was on the plane," Blair said quietly. "I was watching the passengers get on, and suddenly, I knew I couldn't leave you. Thank God I'm pregnant and the attendant bought the story that I was in labor, or I would have had to be sedated!"

"That must have been so frightening."

"No, that didn't scare me. I was doing something then. What frightened me was that I realized I can't keep trying to hold back. You've taken all of my defenses from me, and that scares me half to death. I've…I've never let anybody in like I have you."

"I haven't, either," Kylie said softly.

Blair lifted up a little and looked into her eyes. "You haven't?"

"No. Not fully. I always had to be sure the person I was with loved me as much as I loved her. I was always very cognizant of not giving too much—of not being taken advantage of."

"But you're not like that with me," Blair said, a little startled.

"No, I'm not. I'm not even sure why," she said thoughtfully. "From the start, something about you made me want to be unselfish. You make me want to give to you— without any desire to keep score."

"Luckily for me," Blair said, chuckling wryly. "I'd be so far in the hole I'd never get out."

"That's not true. You give me so much. I don't have a single complaint."

"I do," Blair said. "I want to show you more of myself. I want to really let you in—all the way in. I feel like I've been so withholding with you, and I'm so very, very sorry for that."

"You're cautious," Kylie soothed. "I know how you feel, even though I can tell that it's hard sometimes for you to show it."

"Do you know?" she asked earnestly. "Do you *really* know?"

"Yeah, I do. I've known from the beginning. Every once in a while, you really let it show, and that lets me see that it's there. That's enough for me."

"I wanna do better," Blair said. "I don't want to show you once in a while. I want to show you every single day. If I can't show you, I won't be able to show the baby, and I never want him to have to guess how I feel about him."

"Don't worry about that," Kylie said, rubbing her partner's belly and nuzzling her neck and hair. "That little guy's gonna be slathered with love. He'll never doubt you."

"I don't want you to doubt me, either. I'm gonna do my best to show you how I feel."

Drawing back momentarily, the doctor said, "You showed me today. Getting off a plane is a pretty dramatic demonstration."

"That's the most foolhardy—and the bravest—thing I've ever done," Blair admitted. "It felt great." She kissed Kylie, slowly sucking on her lower lip, and said, "It felt great because I was coming back to you. You know what else would feel great?"

Grinning sexily, Kylie said, "Uh-huh, but I'd rather hear it from you."

Blair wrapped her arms around Kylie's neck and pulled her close, whispering, "I'd love to have you make love to me. I want it slow and gentle and tender, and I want you to pack as much emotion as you can into it." Pulling away enough to look into her eyes, she asked, "Will you, baby?"

"No question," Kylie said, "but you have to do the same."

"I'll give it my very best," Blair pledged, "tonight and every night."

⌐

Kylie had to leave early and found her resolve severely tested by Blair's warm, naked body, which was plastered up against her own in such a delightful way. But the first lecture of the day concerned her specialty and was one of the main reasons she'd agreed to attend. So, she forced herself to rise, and she spent just a minute staring at her partner's beautiful body, only partially covered by the sheet.

Blair hadn't stirred, so before leaving, the doctor wrote her a note, urging her to order a good breakfast and eat every bite. The note rested upon the open room service menu, and Kylie mentioned a few of the choices she thought would be most healthful.

When Blair woke, she looked at the note, shaking her head at Kylie's supervision. "Not today, Doctor Mackenzie," she declared aloud. "I'm going out for pancakes!" Grabbing the phone, she dialed and waited for her father to pick up. "How would you like to take your favorite daughter out for pancakes this morning?"

"Blair?"

"Do you have another favorite daughter?"

"Well, no, but why are you here?"

"Long story, Dad. I'm gonna take a quick shower and hop in a cab. I'll be by to pick you up in an hour."

⌐

Werner opened the door to Blair's knock and blinked in surprise when she walked in, mumbling, "Everything was going fine until you and Mom had to get involved. Now I'm crazy in love, fighting my way off airplanes and making a complete fool out of myself." Turning, she faced him and demanded, "Happy?"

"Sweetheart, I have absolutely no idea what you're talking about! What's this about fighting in an airplane?"

She chuckled and said, "Let's walk over to Clark Street and get some of my favorite pancakes. I'll tell you all about it on the way."

"Are you sure you want to walk? That's quite a distance."

"After you see how many pancakes I eat, you won't question my decision."

When they reached the sidewalk, she tucked a hand around his arm and said, "What you and Mom said the other night really got to me."

"Honey, we're both sorry for that. You're an adult, and we have to stop treating you as if you're still our little girl—"

"No, no, I'm glad you talked to me. Just because I'm an adult doesn't mean I can always see myself clearly. You both made me take a look at the way I was behaving, and I didn't like what I saw."

"Really? What—"

"I got really freaked out that night, Dad, and when Kylie came home, I practically got down on my knees and begged her to believe that I love her." She laughed softly and said, "Of course, she said she didn't have a doubt in the world, but that's how she is. She's so careful never to hurt my feelings, even when they deserve to be hurt."

"She's a very kind woman, isn't she?"

"Yeah," Blair said. "She's the best. Anyway, I tried to pay more attention to her this weekend. I really tried to focus on how she is around me, and I realized that she's much more expressive about her feelings than I am. She made the baby move by touching me on Saturday night, and I was so moved by her joy that I almost wept."

"Oh, that must have been wonderful for her," he said, his eyes tearing up a little.

"It was magical—for both of us."

"You know," he said, "that's one of the things I missed being able to do with you."

"Oh, you'll have your chance. After I eat, he goes wild." She gave her father's arm a squeeze and said, "I felt really close to Kylie all weekend. Much more so than normal. Then, yesterday, we were saying goodbye at the hotel, and she became very emotional. I tried to make light of it, but it really got to me."

"I can see that it would have."

"Anyway, I went into my usual mode and started thinking about how cool it was going to be to have three whole days to myself." She laughed wryly and said, "But by the time I got settled on the plane, I realized that I didn't want three days to myself. I didn't want to be away from Kylie for three minutes—much less three days! I convinced the flight attendant that I was in labor, and after the airport police questioned me—and just about everyone who'd seen me—they let me go."

Werner's eyes were nearly round with alarm. "Honey! That's pretty drastic stuff! They could have arrested you!"

"I know it! But that's how focused I was on being with her! I've completely lost my mind, Dad, and I think you and Mom are to blame."

He smiled fondly at his daughter and said, "I don't want you to try a trick like that again, but I'm very glad you've decided to try to let your feelings show more. I know it will make both of you happier."

"I promised Kylie that I'm going to try my best to be more open and show her how I feel. It's not gonna be easy," she predicted, "and it scares me to do it, but I have to, Dad. I have to."

"It's uncontrollable, isn't it?"

"Yes! That's exactly it! It's uncontrollable."

He reached over and patted her gently, a wide smile on his face. "My little girl's in love."

⟿

Before they went to sleep that night, Kylie said, "This probably won't interest you at all, and I swear you won't hurt my feelings if you don't want to come, but I'm doing a little presentation tomorrow."

Blair sat up and stared at her. "You are? Since when?"

"Since they asked me to come. One of my partners was supposed to do it. That's why it was important for one of us to come and take over for him."

"Tell me more about this."

"Well, it's pretty technical," Kylie said, "but it's about this new technique we've been using. Normally, when a woman undergoes in vitro fertilization, we implant seven or eight fertilized eggs, hoping that one or two will attach."

"Yeah, I'm familiar with that," Blair said. "That's one of the big reasons I didn't want to have IVF."

"Exactly," Kylie said. "A lot of women are really worried about having quads or even quints."

"Count me in," Blair said, raising her hand. "What are you guys doing differently?"

"We're implanting fewer eggs, usually four, and we've varied the implantation technique a bit. We've been having a lot of success with it. Usually, you have a 15 percent chance of attachment to the uterine wall. With our method, we're getting about a 25 percent success rate. And if a couple is really worried about multiple births, we only implant three eggs. Most people are willing to risk triplets."

"That's really cool, Kylie, and I understood it," Blair said, beaming.

"Yeah, you did now, but you won't when I talk in doctor-speak. Anyway, I'm doing it at 2:00, so if you're not busy, you might want to drop by for a few minutes."

"I'll see what I can do, Doc. Are you nervous about it?"

"Huh? Nervous?" Kylie shook her head. "No, I don't get nervous when I talk to my peers. It's shoptalk." She gave Blair a little kiss and added, "But if you come, I might be a little nervous. You always make my palms sweat."

"Same goes for me. And you know how I get when I see you in doctor mode."

"I enjoyed having dinner with your parents tonight," Kylie said, "but it's room service tomorrow night. I don't want to be away from you for a minute."

⌒

The next afternoon, Werner and Blair made their way to the meeting room where Kylie was scheduled to speak. Blair was suitably impressed by the size of the crowd, and she and her father had to take seats in the last row. Kylie was standing at the front of the room, talking to a few people, and Blair commented, "Doesn't she look nice?"

"She's a beautiful woman," Werner agreed. "She knows how to dress."

"No, her personal shopper knows how to dress," Blair said. "She has a woman who picks out all of her clothes and sends her things on approval. This woman really knows what looks good on Kylie. She hardly ever sends anything back."

"Well, however she accomplishes it, she looks great."

Kylie checked her watch and strode to the podium, clearing her throat to get everyone's attention. "Good afternoon," she said, her voice ringing out clearly in the large room. "I'm Kylie Mackenzie from L.A. Reproductive and Fertility Associates, and I'm filling in for Joseph Martini. Doctor Martini is one of my partners, but he couldn't be with us today."

"She doesn't seem nervous at all, does she?" Blair asked.

"Cool as a cucumber," Werner said. "She's a natural."

Blair watched her lover perform, marveling at how effortless it seemed for Kylie to speak to several hundred people. The presentation was way over her head, but she didn't mind a bit; she enjoyed watching Kylie as much as listening to her. When the doctor was finished with her prepared remarks, she fielded questions from the audience. After a little while, it became clear to Blair that Kylie wasn't performing; she was teaching and learning at the same time. Her concentration was razor-sharp, and when someone asked an insightful question, she gave it her full attention, often engaging the other doctor in conversation, trying to work out an obscure issue. It was absolutely fascinating to watch, and Blair was struck by the thought that her lover could be an excellent teacher.

All too soon for Blair, the hour was over, and she and Werner stayed in their seats while many of the doctors gathered around Kylie to continue their questioning. The always-aware woman spotted Blair and Werner, and she dashed up the aisle to say, "I'm gonna be a while. I hate to have you wait until all of these guys are finished grilling me."

"We'll go down to the café," Blair said. "When you're finished, come find us." She stood and kissed Kylie's cheek. "You were awesome."

"Thanks," the doctor said, blushing under the compliment. "I'll see you soon."

After about half an hour, their server brought a phone to the table. "There's a call for you, ma'am," he said.

"Hi, honey," Blair said when she picked up.

"How'd you guess?"

"Call me lucky. What's up?"

"I'm still stuck here, and after this, I really should go to another talk. Is that okay, Lucky?"

Blair answered, laughing. "Sure, no problem. We only wanted to sing your praises for a while. We can do that later."

"I'm gonna be here until 7:00," Kylie said, "and then I'm free. I'm starving, though, so why don't you order some room service for us and have them deliver it around then."

"You've got it. Dad's got to go soon, so I'll keep myself entertained until you're done."

"Have fun, and thank your dad for me. Maybe we can have lunch tomorrow."

"I'll ask," Blair said. "My mom's gonna take tomorrow morning off so we can have a little more time together. Having lunch with you would work out well."

"See what you can work out. Talk to you later."

Blair hung up and shrugged. "I guess this is what happens when you're married to a doctor." She smiled and added, "It could be worse. At least, she doesn't play golf."

⌒

As soon as Kylie got back to their room, she quirked a grin at her partner and said, "I don't know where you've been, but I hope you go there often."

"I was at the spa. Do I look particularly beautiful?"

"Particularly. Your cheeks are pink, your eyes are sparkling, and you've got a healthy look that just glows." She came closer and sniffed, saying, "You smell like…cucumber…and avocado."

"Good nose, Doc. I had a facial, and that's exactly what they put on me."

"What else did you have done?" Kylie asked, looking for clues.

"A couple of things. Had a manicure and a pedicure."

"Nice," Kylie said, lifting Blair's foot and inspecting the pink nails.

"And I had a bikini wax."

"Yow!" Kylie clapped her hands over her vulva, recoiling in horror at the mere thought. "How can you stand that?"

"It's not that bad. Zip, zip, and you're done. Lasts for weeks and weeks."

"You don't have to do that for my sake. I don't mind if you're a little fuzzy."

"I like to be neat. The 70s are over."

Kylie pulled at the waistband of her partner's boxers and peeked inside. Drawing her finger down the neat blonde hair, she said, "I didn't know this was a fashion statement. But I'm very happy with the way you're groomed, so I guess I shouldn't complain."

"No, you shouldn't. But you should get out of your nice clothes and wheel that cart over here. I'm starved!"

—

On the way back to Los Angeles, Blair snoozed off and on, her head resting on Kylie's shoulder. They were nearly home when Blair woke up and stretched in her seat. She smiled up at Kylie and said, "This was the best trip of my whole life."

"Your whole life? Really?"

"Really. It was wild and scary and crazy, but so very worthwhile. I learned things about myself and about us that are probably the most important lessons I've ever learned. Things are gonna be different from now on, Kylie. You and Mackenzie are never, ever gonna have to guess how much I love you."

"We both know it," Kylie smiled, patting the baby gently.

"You're gonna know it, and you're gonna hear it," Blair promised. "That's as important as knowing it."

Chapter Twelve

$\mathcal{A}$ few days after returning from Chicago, Kylie sat down on the edge of the bed and gently scratched between Blair's shoulder blades. When she got no response, she leaned over and kissed all across the expanse of pale skin, smiling when she recalled the decadent number of kisses they'd shared the night before. But still Blair didn't flinch, and when the doctor started to run her short fingernails down her lover's flank, her efforts finally met with a giggle. "I thought if I held out long enough, you'd turn me over so we could get busy," Blair said, her voice low and sexy and raspy from sleep.

"You have quite an appetite, and I'd love to pick up where we left off, but duty calls. Sorry to wake you, but I forgot to tell you I'm going to stop for a drink after work. I'll be home a little late."

Blair rolled over onto her back and took Kylie's hand. "Steppin' out on me already?"

"Nope. I'm meeting with a guy who practices family law. He agreed to give us some advice if I bought him a drink."

"Gosh, he must be a great attorney. Is his office in the bar?"

"Funny girl," Kylie said, giving her a little tickle. "He's got a great reputation, and he does a lot of work with gay and lesbian couples. We're having a drink because we know each other a little bit, and we wanted to catch up, too."

"How do you know this guy?"

"He's on the board of GLBT Equality. I did a little volunteer work for them last year."

"GLBT. GLBT. Hmm…gay, lesbian, black…no, that can't be it. I can't guess," she said, giving up quicker than she normally did.

"Gay, lesbian, bisexual, and transgendered. You're a member now, so you should learn the initials of your peer group."

"I'll put it on my business card," Blair said, sticking her tongue out at her partner. "What'd you do for this guy?"

"Nothing for the guy, but I did some surgery on one of Equality's members. A guy had gone to Thailand for a sex change, and he had some complications. He couldn't afford to go back to the surgeon who'd done the job, so I fixed him up."

Blair's eyes opened wide. "What'd you have to do?"

"It's too early, honey. Trust me. I'll tell you later if you really want to know."

Blair pursed her lips and shook her head. "No, thanks. If it's gross now, it'll be gross later. But I'm proud of you for helping do...whatever you did."

"Thank you. I'll call you when I'm on my way home."

"I love you," Blair said, patting her partner on the cheek and then letting her hand slide down Kylie's body to rest on her ass. She palmed her butt and then gave it a squeeze. "You look pretty today," she said, obvious sexual interest coloring her voice.

"Thanks." Kylie bent and kissed her, lingering a little longer than she should have. She crossed her eyes as she sat up. "Gotta go or gotta be very, very late."

⌐

Kylie walked into the nautically decorated bar at one of the oceanfront hotels in Santa Monica and spotted Dave Robbins immediately. The large, redheaded man stuck out in a crowd, and he stood when she approached his table. "Kylie, good to see you again."

"You, too, Dave," she said as they shook hands. "How've you been?"

"Good. Nothing to complain about. Well, other than the fact that my lover's been out of town for three weeks."

"Ooh, that's a long time. Is he due back soon?"

"Yeah. Tomorrow. You'd think I'd like a little break after nine years, but I'm counting the minutes."

"I have a new perspective on being in love," Kylie said, smiling. "So I completely understand that 'counting the minutes' thing. Since I last saw you, I've not only fallen in love, we're going to have a baby in December."

"Congratulations! That's great to hear! Tell me about her."

"Her name's Blair, and she sells real estate here in Santa Monica. She's a wonderful woman, but she comes with a few unique issues, and that's what prompted me to call you. She got pregnant through anonymous donor insemination."

"Okay," he said, nodding. "Is there a problem?"

"Yeah. She was married at the time, and they performed the insemination through a doctor. Her ex-husband signed the consent form."

"Oh." He made a face and scrubbed at his chin with his fist. "And...you want to keep him on the hook or off the hook?"

"Off would be very, very nice. He has no interest in the baby. I'd love to be able to adopt, but I know I don't have a chance if he doesn't want out."

"Hmm...you're right. It won't be easy if he doesn't want to terminate his rights. Honestly, I don't think you'd have any chance at all."

She nodded. "That's what I thought. He's being an ass about our getting together, but I figure he might be reasonable and cooperate with us if he can make sure he's off the hook for child support."

"Yeah, yeah," he said absently. He was drawing designs in the condensation on his water glass, and after a moment, he looked at Kylie and said, "Are you familiar with the stepparent adoption provision in the family law code?"

"No. Never heard of it."

"Well, if the ex wants out, you're not gonna have a problem. The legislature passed a law allowing same-sex partners to be considered stepparents legally. You'd have all the rights and obligations of a natural parent."

"Are you kidding? We don't have to do that crazy second-parent adoption thing that people have been doing?"

"No, no, that's been over for a few years." He grinned at her. "You must not know anyone who's adopted recently."

"I'm remarkably out of the loop. But I'm gonna try to get into it. I know things will come up when our baby goes to school, and I want to make some friends who can empathize or advise us."

"That's a great idea. We'd love to have you at GLBT."

"I probably won't have much free time while the baby's an infant, but I'll go out of my comfort zone after that."

"Cool. I'm sure you can't wait to get home and tell your partner the good news about adopting."

Kylie sat back in her chair and smiled at the attorney. "I had no idea that could happen." Her smile grew, and she said, "Having the baby be mine legally is exactly what we both want. This is great, great news, Dave."

"It's been great for a lot of families."

"So, all we have to do is get Blair's ex to agree." She sighed and said, "Knowing him, he'll put up a fight to be spiteful. He's been a real ass."

"If you want me to represent you, I'd be happy to get involved. I'm very good at pointing out all of the detriments of being a non-custodial father."

Kylie nodded. "I'll have to talk with Blair first to make sure she thinks we should do this, and if she does, I think it would be best if she talked to him. She seems to know how to deal with him—most of the time."

Dave shook her hand and gave her a big smile. "I hope it works out, Kylie. I'm very happy for you and your partner. You're gonna be a great mom."

Kylie clapped him on the back and gave him a bright smile. "Thanks, Dave. I'm sure gonna try. Now, how about that drink I promised you?" She signaled the bartender. "What are you having?"

⟶

As soon as Kylie got home, she shared her news. "That's fantastic, honey!" Blair said. "I thought this would be a very long-drawn-out deal."

"It doesn't seem like it will be. As long as David agrees to terminate his rights, that is. Do you want to talk to him, or should Dave take a crack?"

"I'll talk to him. He wouldn't like it if a stranger approached him first. Give me a few days to come up with my strategy. I need to decide if I should get Sadie on my side first or if that would make things worse."

"I'm sure you'll come up with a plan. You're very persuasive. Heck, you made me fall in love with you, and I was sure I didn't have a chance!"

After dinner, the pair sat in the living room to read and listen to music. Kylie noticed that she hadn't heard much from her partner, and she lowered her book only to find a pair of eyes staring at her. "Yikes! It's kinda creepy to see you looking at me like that. Am I in trouble?"

"Hardly." Blair grasped Kylie's toes and tugged on them. "I was thinking about religion."

Kylie put her book in her lap and gave Blair a speculative look. "Religion, huh? Like 'what's the meaning of life, why am I here' kinda thing?"

"No, more like whether we should have Mackenzie baptized or…" She made a face and said, "Circumcised."

"Oh." Kylie looked at her for a moment and said, "I just decided I want a girl."

"Kylie, we can't ignore the issue. What do you think we should do?"

She sat perfectly still for a few moments and then met Blair's eyes. "If it means a lot to you, I won't complain if you want to have him circumcised and raise him as a Jew. But if that's what you want, we have to get involved, too. I don't want him to be the only Jew in the family."

"You'd convert?" Blair asked, her eyes wide.

"Sure. I think we'd have to. It'd be positively weird to tell him he was Jewish but nobody else in the family was. Heck, even your father doesn't claim his Jewish heritage. Mackenzie'll think he's a modern day Abraham."

Blair shook her head. "I'm not committed enough to have us both convert. I guess I'd like to incorporate some of the holidays into our lives, but that's about it. I really enjoyed having Passover with my grandmother, and I'd like to have that for us."

"We could do that, but I don't think it's fair to cut off a piece of Mackenzie's body so he feels Jewish. That's a big sacrifice, and he doesn't get a vote."

"Are you against circumcision?"

"Yeah. Very much so." She was wearing her most serious expression—the one she sported when she felt strongly about something.

"I haven't really given this a lot of thought. But won't he look different from the other boys?"

"Not really. It's not done routinely anymore, and of the boys born at my hospital, only about 30 percent are circumcised by doctors. I'm sure there are more done at home in a bris, but I'd bet no more than 50 percent of boys are circumcised now. Of course, that's in Southern California. I'm sure there are parts of the country where it's still routine."

"But you're against it."

"Yes. I already said that. I think it's unnecessary, and I don't like to perform unnecessary surgery—on anyone. There are risks with any surgery, and I don't want our son to be put at risk when he doesn't have to be."

"Yeah, but there are benefits, too, aren't there? I've heard circumcised men never get cancer of the penis," Blair said, making a face. "That's one place I'm sure he doesn't want to have cancer."

"That's true," Kylie agreed. "And if we removed his testicles, he wouldn't get testicular cancer, either. That sucks, too."

Blair raised her eyebrows and looked at her partner's expression carefully. "I'm surprised that you feel so strongly about this. And given that you do, why didn't you say something sooner?"

Kylie leaned back against the sofa and let her head drop for a few moments. "I'm sorry. I should have told you how I felt. This is an emotional trigger for me." She looked up at her partner. "When I was in my last year of residency, I assisted on a penile reconstruction for a two-week-old baby."

"My God!" Blair cried. "What happened?"

"The kid got a nasty infection from his circumcision. I won't go into detail, but they tried everything they could, and they weren't able to halt the infection. We had to remove a lot of tissue, and even though we saved his life, he was absolutely mutilated. I think about that little guy every once in a while and wonder how he's dealing with it." She took a breath, and Blair could see that she was struggling with her emotions. "Shit happens, and you can't prevent every freak accident. Nobody knows that better than I do, but I can't imagine how his parents feel. They thought they were having a little skin snipped off…" She reached up, wiped her eyes, and then said, "There's no such thing as minor surgery, baby. I don't wanna do anything invasive or permanent to Mackenzie that we don't have to do. It's his body, and if he wants to have his penis circumcised, he can do it when he's older and can make his own choices."

Blair scooted down and put her arm around her partner. "Okay. No circumcision. Besides, it's not like he's gonna have a daddy to compare himself to."

"None of my nephews are circumcised, so he'll look like his cousins. That should be good enough."

"I don't think he'll see his cousins' penises," Blair said, laughing softly, "but if he does, he'll be one of the guys."

"If you don't think little boys look at each other, you don't know much about little boys."

They cuddled together on the sofa for a few minutes, neither of them speaking. But there was a discomfort between them that Blair finally mentioned. "I have one of these moments every couple of days."

"What moments?"

"The 'I'm in complete control of another person's life' moments. It always scares the crap out of me."

Kylie laughed soundlessly, her chest bouncing against her partner. "We're not in complete control, but it's close—especially on things like circumcision. It's pretty awesome, isn't it?"

"That's one way to think of it. Sometimes, I feel like I'll wet myself it scares me so much."

Kylie patted her gently and then kissed her head. "We'll make mistakes, honey. Lots of them. We'll do things that screw him up a little bit. Every parent does. And no matter how good a job we do, he'll resent us for some things. Every kid does."

"I'm still mad that I couldn't get my driver's license until I was eighteen," Blair said, laughing.

"Wow, that's harsh!"

"Well, we didn't have a car at the time, and my school didn't offer driver's ed. My parents didn't want to pay a private company to teach me since there wasn't a car to drive. It made sense, but I was the only one of my friends who didn't have a license. I hated it."

"I hated never getting a new book. I longed for a brand new book without a dog-eared page or a pencil mark. I was so jealous of the older kids 'cause they always got new clothes and books."

"Damn, were your parents on that strict a budget?"

"Not really. But they didn't believe in wasting money. If there were clothes that fit me, I was gonna wear 'em. And someone had already bought every book I needed for school. It wasn't a big deal, but it always made me feel like I wasn't special enough to get something new."

"Ooh…you're my special girl," Blair said, hugging her tight. "You're finally the first in line for new stuff. And I love wearing your clothes."

"I noticed that you had on my new satin blouse today. Did you wear that to work?"

"Yeah. It felt great! I wore some black leggings with it. I thought it looked kinda cool."

"You always look cool. And I think you should dress as casually as you can get away with."

"I wasn't too casual. I dressed the blouse up with some gold jewelry and a scarf. I actually got a few compliments…from girls." She wrinkled up her nose.

"Well, girls are better than nothing."

"I'd consider it a good compliment if it came from a lesbian," Blair said. "It's just that straight girls don't really count 'cause they're trying to boost my confidence. But I don't give a damn. A day without pantyhose is a glorious day."

"You seem happy. And when you're happy…I'm happier."

"I don't wanna sour your happy mood, but do you mind if we get back to the religion thing?"

"No. Go ahead."

"What would you think of putting Sadie in charge of Mackenzie's religious upbringing?"

"Sadie? In charge?"

"Well, not in charge. That was a bad choice of words. But she's very involved in her church, and I know it would mean a lot to her. Since neither of us has strong feelings about organized religion, I thought Mackenzie could get a taste of it from her and bond with her at the same time. It might be nice to have a set weekly time with his grandmother."

"And you think it's important for him to have a religion?"

"Mmm…I don't think it's vital, but it'll give him something to rebel against later," she said, laughing.

Kylie gave a halfhearted nod. "I guess that's okay."

"But...? I know there's something you're not saying."

"Well, I kinda wanted to have him baptized in the Episcopal Church. It would mean a lot to my mom."

"But you don't wanna take him to church on a regular basis, do you?"

"No, not really. I was willing to go to a temple if you wanted Mackenzie to have a Jewish identity, but if he's baptized as a Christian, he'll be like all of his cousins."

"Then let's do it," Blair said. "We can take him to Chicago and have a big christening party. My family can come, too. It'll be fun!"

"So...we'd have him baptized twice?"

"Sure. What can it hurt? We won't tell Sadie we did it, of course."

"But Mackenzie will eventually be able to speak. He might spill the beans."

"He won't remember! He'll be a month old!"

"No, no, I meant that he'll tell my mom that he goes to church with Sadie."

"Oh! Yeah, that'll happen, but your mom isn't insane. She'll think it's nice that he goes to church. She won't care that it's Armenian Orthodox, will she?"

"No, I guess not. She thinks the world is easier for a kid to understand if he has a religious upbringing. I don't think she cares what faith it is, though."

"Something's still wrong," Blair said. "I see a little line here." She ran her thumb down the crease between Kylie's eyes.

The doctor nodded, looking contemplative. "How much do we know about this religion? I don't want Mackenzie to grow up thinking his moms are gonna go to hell for being gay."

"I'm not gay," Blair said, giving Kylie a hot, wet kiss. She was nearly cross-eyed when she pulled away, adding, "I'm a straight woman who happens to be in love with another woman. That doesn't make me gay. I can still go to heaven."

Kylie grabbed her and pinned her to the seat of the sofa, looking down at her with fire in her eyes. "You're gonna be good and gay by the time I'm through with you." She kissed Blair for a long time, thrilling at the taste and the feel of her soft, wet lips.

"I'll go wherever you go," Blair agreed after catching her breath. "You're nice."

Kylie sat up and pulled her partner up with her. "I was serious about the religion. I don't want him raised in some repressive atmosphere."

"I don't, either. But it won't hurt him to go with Sadie until he's in grade school. We'll pay close attention and ask him what he learns every week. If it sounds like he's getting a bad message, we'll put an end to it."

"You think it'll be that easy?"

"Yeah, I do. I've made it clear to Sadie that she's not allowed to make a negative comment about homosexuality ever. She knows I'll cut her off if she does."

"Okay. We can start him off with the Orthodox Church and see what happens. If it's not working, he can be a nice non-churchgoing Episcopalian—like all of his cousins."

"Sounds good to me."

Kylie squeezed her partner's hand and said, "One more decision made on Mackenzie's behalf. I hope he never finds out that we made two major decisions for him in the space of twenty minutes—with almost no deliberation."

"I won't tell if you don't," Blair said, crossing her heart with her finger.

The following Friday, Kylie was having lunch at her desk when the intercom buzzed. "Doctor Mackenzie, there's a man here to see you."

"I'm not seeing any salesmen today, Teresa. They have to make appointments like everyone else."

"I don't think he's a salesman. He said his name is David Spencer, and he's…well, I think you'd better see him."

"Great," she grumbled. "I'll come get him."

Kylie pushed her salad aside and put her shoes back on. Before she walked out of the office, she grabbed her crisply starched lab coat and shrugged into it. When she opened the waiting room door, she found David staring at her, his face blotchy and mottled from anger. He spoke loudly, gesturing at Teresa. "Does the receptionist have orders to keep all of your girlfriends' husbands away from you?"

Not saying a word, Kylie held the door open and waited for him to enter the corridor. Thankfully, it was empty, so no patient heard David's running commentary. "When you steal someone's wife, the least you can do is face him like a man."

Doctor Greene stuck his head out of his office before Kylie and David passed, and he gave Kylie a questioning look. She shook her head and waved him off. Then she walked into her own office and closed the door after David entered.

He didn't say anything, but she could see his eyes widen when he saw the size of the layout. Kylie was actually a little embarrassed by the size of her office, but today she was glad she had it. When her practice had moved to its present location, the doctors had drawn straws for best office and she'd won, something the others still held over her head.

The practice was located in a modern office building that was a few floors higher than any of the surrounding buildings. She had a corner office with six windows, three of them giving her an unobstructed view of the Pacific Ocean.

The room was lined with modern stainless-steel bookcases, and there was a glass conference table with four chrome and gray leather chairs surrounding it. Her massive desk and Aeron chair barely took up a quarter of the room, leaving plenty of space for a full-sized gray leather couch, upon which she'd spent many a night napping while monitoring patients in the nearby hospital.

She pulled a conference chair out for David, after standing nice and close to him so he could see that she was not much shorter than he was. She didn't normally play games like this, but she thought David might be the kind of guy who would be intimidated by them, and she wanted every possible tool at her disposal. "You know where Blair and I live. And I believe she told you she'd be glad to talk to you about her personal life. What makes you show up at my office?"

"I wanna know when you started fucking her," he spat, his eyes glowing like embers. "Was she still living with me?"

Kylie leaned back in her seat and gazed at him until he met her eyes. "I don't know what kind of person would talk about her partner behind her back, but I'm not one of them. I don't have a relationship with you. There isn't a reason in the world for you to ask me a question about your former wife. Unless you're afraid of her, that is." She spoke calmly and quietly, acting as if she were perfectly at ease.

He slapped at the table with his bare hand, making it ring when it vibrated against the chrome base. Kylie struggled to continue looking calm, but she was rattled by his obviously explosive temper. She wiped her clammy hands on her lab coat and kept them on the arms of the chair so he wouldn't see them shake.

"You're the one who stole her from me! You're the one I have a problem with."

"Fine. It doesn't matter who you're angry with. I'm still not going to talk about Blair behind her back. That's not the kind of relationship we have. You're welcome to come to our house and discuss anything that's on your mind."

"I don't want to come to your fucking house!" he said, glaring at her with a venomous expression. "I don't wanna see my wife shacked up with the dyke who stole her from me!"

"I didn't steal your wife. Blair isn't the kind of woman who could have been stolen, even if I'd tried." Kylie's mind was racing, and suddenly, she had an idea that came to her like a gift. She gave David as big a smile as she could and said, "You're gonna have to learn how to get along with me if you want to have a hand in raising this baby. If you and Blair share custody, we'll probably see each other every week. Maybe more."

"There's no way in hell I'll ever get along with you! You're out of your fucking mind if you think I wanna be involved in this! You two are gonna have that baby so screwed up there'll be nothing I can do to fix him!"

"I certainly don't think we're gonna screw him up," Kylie said, "but Blair and I are going to raise him according to our values. He'll be around a lot of gay people, and we'll teach him that he shouldn't judge people by their sexual orientation."

"He'll be ashamed of you two," David said, glaring at her. "Poor little bastard."

"Not if we raise him right," Kylie said, trying to control her temper. "Even though I'll be with him most of the time, you're the baby's father, and you'll have some influence. We both thought it would be nice if you could take him most weekends. We really haven't had much time alone—just as lovers, I mean. The baby's going to need an awful lot of attention, and we won't have time to lie in bed on the weekends like we do now."

David's eyes looked as if they were about to burst from his head, and his face was so red that Kylie thought she might have to perform CPR. The thought flashed through her mind that he might pick up a bookend and bash her brains in, but she soldiered on, knowing this might be her only chance to really get to him.

"We know that most of the day-to-day duties will be ours, but fair's fair. I'm not gonna have to pay one penny for his care, but you're on the hook for 50 percent, so you should get to visit him on a regular basis. We want him to grow up believing that a man can be a good parent, too. If you care for him two full days a week, he'll think of you as a real parent, not just the guy his mommy was married to when she got pregnant." She forced herself to laugh, and even though it sounded artificial to her ear, it got David's attention. "It's gonna be hard to explain all this to the baby, but someday, he'll understand that you weren't able to get his mommy pregnant. I'm sure he'd rather know his birth father, but I think he'll bond with you if you spend a lot of quality time with him."

He stared at her, his hands gripping the edge of the table. He was holding on to it so tightly she was afraid it might break off in his hands. He finally spoke, and each word was thrown at her like a dagger. "I don't want anything to do with you or that damned baby!"

She blinked at him, trying to act as if she were surprised. "But…what about the weekends? We were really counting on you."

He stood so quickly that his chair fell back onto the floor with a loud bang and the heavy glass tabletop rose an inch and slammed back onto the base. David leaned over the table, his face inches from Kylie. She knew she was shaking, but she tried with all her might to look as calm as she possibly could. "I don't ever want to see him! You two dykes can bleed me dry, but you can't make me be a father!"

"Are you serious? I mean, I know he's not really your son, but your name will be on the birth certificate. He's *legally* yours, if nothing else."

"If I had my way, that kid would never know about me."

"Huh. That really surprises me after all you went through to have him." Kylie paused for a second, acting as though she'd just thought of something. "You know, if you really feel that way, you can terminate your rights. I don't think you should, but you can if you really want to." Her heart was beating so loudly she was sure people on the sidewalk could hear it.

"I've already checked with my lawyer," he said. "I'm stuck. You two can stick it to me until the kid's eighteen. You'll probably run the bill up to spite me."

She scowled at him. "Hey, we're both busy women. We'll need a live-in nanny, and they aren't cheap."

"You fucking bitch," he sneered.

She leaned back in her chair and held her hands up. "Don't bitch at me. You're the one who wanted to have a baby, and now you're on the hook. You make a lot of money, and it costs a lot of money to raise a baby. Hell, one of the preschools we've looked at is $1,000 a week." She made a gesture of futility. "I don't think it's necessary to send him to a school with on-staff psychologists and movement specialists, but he should learn a lot with three teachers for every ten two-year-olds." Laughing wryly, Kylie said, "Blair wants to make sure he gets into an Ivy League school, and you've gotta get on track early in the game."

His voice was low and even, but the slight twitch in his eyebrow showed he was ready to snap. "If I could get away with it, I'd spend every dime I had to have a hit put on you."

"Temper, temper," she said, smirking at him even though she was afraid she'd wet her pants. "You don't have to get all dramatic about this. If you hate me so much, you ought to give up and get out of the way. There's a thing called stepparent adoption where I could take your place as the baby's parent. Check with your lawyer. That might be a way to get you off the hook—completely. Jesus, we don't want you around if you're gonna be an asshole about it."

His right eyebrow lifted. "Off the hook...including child support?"

"Yeah. I don't know much about it, but if you don't wanna be involved, you shouldn't be. Like you said, the baby's gonna have enough things to deal with. It'd screw him up worse to know that you wanted to have me killed."

He stared at her for a moment, looking as if he wanted to get the job over with right then. She didn't get up, mostly because she was sure her knees were too weak to hold her. "I'll talk to my lawyer," he said. He paused for a second, gave her a look filled with disdain, uttered a short, bitter laugh, and then walked out.

She managed to get up and watch him leave, standing in her doorway for a second, knowing Jonathan Greene would pop out of his office as soon as he heard the outer door close. Her prediction was correct, and Jon walked down the hallway. "What in the hell was that all about?"

Kylie gave him a weary half-smile. "One of the side effects of falling in love with a woman going through a divorce. I don't think he'll be back." She pushed off her doorjamb and said, "I'd better go talk with Teresa. She's probably a little freaked out."

"What did he say to her?"

"Nothing too bad. He asked if she had orders to keep all of my lovers' husbands out of the office."

"Does she?" Jon called out to Kylie's back, earning a discreet obscene gesture from the departing doctor.

⤙

"Hi, sweetheart!" Blair called out. Kylie slid the door open and watched her lover performing some lazy kicks in the pool. Blair was holding herself up on the coping by her elbows and had obviously already done her laps.

"Look at those pink cheeks!" Kylie exclaimed. "You've really been working, haven't you?"

"Yeah, I have. The feeling of being in the pool is so damned nice. This is the only time of the day I feel light. I don't quite feel like my old self, but it's as close as I get. Thanks again for persuading me to start swimming."

"I'm glad you enjoy it. Are you gonna stay in for a while?"

"Yeah. I thought I'd float around a little. It feels too good to get out."

"Uhm, I have something to talk to you about. Want me to wait?"

"Not with that look on your face, I don't," Blair said, her brow furrowed. "What's wrong?"

"Nothing's wrong. Really." She kicked off her shoes and then slid her hands up under her dress and took her nylons off. She paused a minute and then stripped the rest of the way, saying, "Why am I gonna sit here in a dress when that pool looks so good?" She walked over and got in, jumping around until her body acclimated to the temperature. "It looked warmer from out there."

"Come here, and I'll warm you up."

Blair put her arms around her, and Kylie tried to gain as much skin contact as possible. "That's better. You're a little heater, aren't ya?"

"I didn't used to be, but I'm a baby-making factory now. The furnace is always on. Now, tell me what's on your mind."

"David came to my office today."

Blair didn't say a thing. She pulled away and stared at Kylie, her mouth slightly open.

"Yeah," Kylie said. "It's wasn't a pleasant surprise for me, either."

"Why didn't you call me?" The tone Blair used was a little louder than it needed to be, and Kylie could almost see her blood pressure rising.

"I didn't call you because it didn't occur to me."

"David is my problem," she said, her voice still loud. "He's my soon-to-be ex-husband, and I want to be the one to deal with him. I wouldn't dream of talking to Stacey behind your back."

Kylie stared at her partner for a minute and then said. "Okay. What would you do if Stacey showed up at your office and started asking where the woman was who stole her spouse? Would you close your office door and dial my number? Or would you get your ass out to the receptionist before any of your clients heard her?" Kylie's voice rose with each word, and by the time she was finished, she was yelling at nearly full voice.

"Oh, Jesus, Kylie," Blair said, her eyes tightly closed. "I'm so sorry he did that. I'm so sorry, honey." She put her arms around Kylie's chilled body and hugged her tight. "You don't deserve to be treated like that."

"No, I don't," Kylie said, her voice soft and slow, "but that's the situation I was presented with. I had to act—right then."

"I'm sorry I made you angry. Of course, you didn't have time to call me."

Kylie pulled away and swept some of the wet hair from Blair's face. "Even if I'd had time, I wouldn't have called you."

"What? Damn it, why won't you listen to me? I want to be the one to deal with David. He's my problem! Mine!"

"No, he's not." Kylie was giving her partner her most intractable expression, which puzzled Blair completely.

"How can you say that? I was married to him. I'm the one who wanted to get pregnant with him. This has nothing to do with you."

"What part of the word 'partner' don't you understand?" Kylie asked, her eyes burning with intensity. "You tell me you love me and want to share everything with me. That means everything. The good and the bad. David's behavior affects our family— all of us. This isn't about you alone!"

"Kylie, I do love you, and I do want to share my life with you. But you can't expect to get into the middle of my relationship with David! There are parts of our lives we have to keep separate! I don't tell you how to operate on people, and you don't tell me how to sell real estate. This is exactly the same. My relationship—my problem. Now, if he ever contacts you again, I want you to refuse to talk to him. Send him to me. Do you understand?"

Staring at her for a second, the doctor said, "Yeah. I think I can comprehend a sentence or two. Especially when they're delivered in such a condescending tone." She stood closer to her partner and said, "Here's a message back: if David shows up at my office again, I'll handle it exactly like I did today. Do *you* understand?"

"Jesus Christ! Why are you being such a jerk about this?"

Kylie turned and hoisted herself out of the pool. She stood up and gave her partner a look Blair had never seen from her. "Thanks for the support. I'm very glad you had that revelation in Chicago. If this is how you let me in, I've gotta admit—it was warmer when I was outside." She walked toward the house, her naked body dripping as she padded across the stone deck.

Blair watched her walk away, stunned by her words and her demeanor. She wanted to chase after her and have it out, but something stopped her. She'd never seen Kylie so angry, and she thought she'd better calm down before they had a massive fight. She sank down into the water and started to swim again, hoping that the water would clear her mind and let her replay their very unpleasant encounter.

Half an hour later, Blair wrapped herself in a bath sheet and ran for the house. This was the part of swimming she hated, but she had to admit that it got her blood pumping. It was only about sixty-eight degrees that night, but after the pool, it felt like jumping into a snow bank. She walked through the house, listening for any sign of Kylie, but the only sound was the eight little feet scampering along with her. "Kylie?"

When she got no reply, she went to their room and found a note:

> I need some time alone, so I'm going to a
> movie to cool down. I'll be home by 10:00.
>
> Love, Kylie

"Jesus!" she said to the dogs. "I hate it when someone walks out on an argument!"
They looked up at her, but had little to offer in reply.

⟳

Kylie got home earlier than she'd predicted. At 9:20, she walked into the house and found Blair in the kitchen, writing something on a notepad. "Hi," Kylie said, her voice quiet.

Blair looked up and said, "I hate to have someone walk out on me. It makes me feel like I'm being punished."

Kylie nodded. "I'm sorry. But I was very angry, and I didn't want to stay here and let it escalate. I didn't feel like I was in control, and I hate that feeling."

"So, no 'I promise I won't leave during a fight, Blair'?"

She shook her head. "No, I can't promise that. I'll try not to, but I can't promise."

"What's gotten into you? I've never seen you so...I don't even know what to call it."

Kylie walked over to her and looked at the counter. "What are you writing?"

Blair tapped the paper with her pen. "We have to discuss this. There are things that we have to keep separate. I'm making a list. I know you might not agree, but I need to keep some of my autonomy."

Kylie took the paper and shook her head. "So…you want to keep our finances separate, you want me to make all the decisions about the house, you want to make all the decisions about your career, and you want me to make the decisions about my career. You want to have our prior relationships stay separate, and you want to pay the majority of Mackenzie's expenses." She gazed at it for another minute and then put it down on the counter. Without comment, she turned and walked towards their room.

Blair was off her chair as fast as she could manage. "Don't walk away from me! I'm talking to you!"

Kylie didn't stop. She went into the bedroom and started to take off her clothes, refusing to even look at Blair.

"Will you at least talk to me?" The words were neutral, but Blair's tone was sharp, and her voice was much louder than it needed to be. The dogs were obviously upset, both of them whining while they sat directly between the couple, looking from one to the other.

Kylie squatted down, picked both of them up, and then stared at her lover. "You wanna talk?" Kylie asked. "Fine. Here's my list." She put the dogs on the bed and petted them while she spoke. "I want to merge our money into one account. I want to pay for everything, including our son's expenses, out of that money. I want to put the house into joint tenancy. I will never make a major decision about my career without consulting you first. And while I don't want you to seek out my former lovers to chat about me, if you ever run into one of them, you're free to say whatever comes to mind. I trust you, and I know you wouldn't ever betray my confidences."

She started to walk towards the bathroom when Blair shouted, "Stop running from me!"

"Then stop hurting my feelings!" she yelled, whirling and facing her partner. "You've been treating me like shit all night, and I'm sick of it!"

Blair's hand went to her throat, and she gasped, "I've been treating you like shit?"

"Yes!" She was trying to control her emotions, but she couldn't do it any longer. Kylie broke down and started to cry like Blair had never seen her. She turned and held on to the wall for support as she made her way to their bed and then fell face-first onto the surface.

"Sweetheart, baby, tell me what I did to hurt you so badly." Blair was beside herself with worry, completely puzzled by Kylie's behavior.

"I had a horrible time with David, and you didn't even ask me what happened! You just got pissed that I talked to him even after I told you I didn't have any choice!"

"You told me you'd do it again. It was like you were trying to pick a fight." She started stroking her lover's back, wincing in sympathy when she felt how hot and wet it was.

"I had him in a position to get him to make some concessions about our son." She rolled over and glared at Blair. "*Our* son! Or do you get to make all of the decisions about Mackenzie, too? I guess that only makes sense since you want to pay all of his expenses."

"No, no," she said, trying to explain herself. "I only wanted to pay for him because you pay for the house. It seemed fair to me."

Kylie sat up and grasped Blair by the shoulders. Looking at her with fiery eyes, the doctor said, "A relationship isn't about being fair! I call you my partner, but you're not my business partner. You're my spouse!"

"I know that, honey. I know that."

"No, you don't! You say you understand, but you don't. You were more concerned about keeping David on your side of the ledger than you were with hearing how hard today was for me. He frightened me and made me look like a fool in my own office! Don't you even care?"

"Oh, fuck," Blair murmured, closing her eyes. "Of course, I care." She put her arms around Kylie and said, "Please tell me what happened."

"No. I'm too upset."

"Kylie, please don't shut me out like this. Please, honey."

The doctor pulled back a bit, wiping her cheeks. She looked at Blair. "I want to know if you really want to be my spouse. I'm not interested in a business partner that I have sex with. That won't work for me."

Blair looked stunned. "Of course, I want to be your spouse! How can you even ask that?"

"Because of that fucking list!" Kylie said, more hot tears spilling down her cheeks. "We're not going to re-create the kind of relationship you had with David. If that's what you want, you've come to the wrong place. If your autonomy is worth more than our merger, we've got big problems, and we'd better solve them before Mackenzie's born."

"But...you're asking me to do things I've never done in my whole life," Blair said, her voice shaking. "Why is it so important to you?"

"Because it shows our commitment to each other. It shows that we don't keep score. We share. What's mine is yours, and what's yours is mine. If I couldn't work, you'd support me. And the same is true for you."

"Of course, I'd support you. I can't believe that's even a question!"

"It is a question. It's one thing to support me and another thing to force me to ask you for money. Spouses shouldn't have to do that!"

"What about money we've saved? Do you want your name on my investments?"

"Yes," Kylie said, her blue eyes unblinking, "and I want your name on mine."

"But...what if things don't...work out?" Blair said, wincing on the last words.

Kylie stared at her for another few moments and then said, "You're either in, or you're out. You can't have one hand in a marriage and the other one preparing for divorce. You have to jump in. It's the only way." She took her by the shoulders and looked into her eyes. "I know this frightens you, but it's the only way it'll work. You have to trust me—totally."

Blair's eyes closed, and she started to cry, finally leaning against Kylie for support. "It's so scary," she mumbled. "It doesn't make any sense to me to trust someone that much. You could hurt me so badly."

Soothingly, Kylie stroked Blair's hair and peppered her cheeks with kisses. "I know that," Kylie whispered. "But you've got to let go of the notion that love makes sense. It doesn't. It's completely irrational. It's trusting someone with your most valuable secrets, your most personal thoughts...your entire future! I know it's scary. It scares me, too. But I truly believe that we have to lose our selves and form a new entity—our marriage."

Blair looked up at her, tears still filling her eyes. "You know...I told you...I can't commit to that again."

"I know you said that. But I can't live with that. I'm sorry, baby, but I can't. I can't give everything to you and not know that you give everything to me."

"But I promise to give everything...while we're happy."

Kylie released her and got up, the dogs dashing to run around her feet. She looked down at them and had to smile. She looked back at Blair and said, "What if we got tired of the dogs?"

"What?"

"You heard me. What if we wanted to travel more or not have to come home to feed or walk them. Would you get rid of them?"

"No! That's insulting to even have you ask that!"

"Right!" Kylie jumped onto the bed and slid a few inches on her knees. Her eyes were filled with passion, and she said, "You're in. For life. Even if you're tired of them or they chew up the couch. You're in."

Blair nodded mutely.

"Don't I deserve the same level of devotion?" She didn't say another word, but her nostrils were flaring from the emotion that was nearly flowing from her body.

Blair swallowed a few times and then quietly said, "Yes. You do."

"Will you marry me?" Kylie asked, tears rolling down her cheeks before the words were out.

Blair began to shake, and then she also started to cry. "Yes," she whispered. "Yes, I'll marry you."

Kylie wrapped her in her arms, and they held each other with a ferocity they rarely exhibited. After Kylie kissed her again and again, Blair said, "Is this why people are so nervous on their wedding days? I feel like I'm gonna faint."

"Yeah. The ones with half a brain, that is," Kylie said, managing a small smile. "Most people assume they'll walk away if things don't work out, but that's not me. I can't be that way. This *will* work out. We'll make it work. I commit every part of myself to having a happy marriage with you. 'For better or worse' isn't a stock phrase for me."

Blair sucked in a breath and closed her eyes, looking as if she were about to cry again. She didn't speak for a few minutes, but Kylie didn't say a word. She let her partner think. "It was for me," Blair said. "When I got married, I was scared to death, but that was mostly because I was afraid things would change a lot between us. I thought David might start trying to exert his will over me, and I knew I couldn't live like that. I would have left him if he'd done that. No question."

"Baby, I have no intention of exerting my will over you. I don't want to own you. I want to become one with you. There's a very big difference there."

"Is there?"

"Yes, yes, a merger takes all of the burdens and joys and spreads them around between the partners. It doesn't make one person the managing partner. We'll be completely equal. You'll still retain your free will. I mean, if you want to change firms and I don't think you should, you still have the final choice. I just want to be informed and allowed to offer my opinion."

"I can't tell you how big a change this will be for me." Blair shivered. "I've been pretty comfortable thinking you didn't need the 'till death do us part' stuff."

"I was fooling myself. I realized that today. I thought I could take it as long as you acted like you wanted to love me for the rest of your life. But I can't. I need to have you make a commitment. I need that, Blair. I'm sorry I didn't know it until now, but I need it."

Blair held her head in her hands, her eyes closed tightly. "I have to let this sink in. I need some time alone. Is that...okay?"

Kylie held her hands up. "Yeah. I'd prefer to celebrate, but I know this is hard for you. Let me know when you're ready to talk." She got up and went into the den, leaving Blair alone to think.

⌒

It was after midnight when Kylie walked back into the bedroom. Blair was nowhere to be found, so the doctor used her failsafe locating devices. "Nicky! Nora!" The dogs came running, and Kylie muttered to herself as she walked to the guest room. The door was open, but she still knocked before she entered. Blair was lying on her side, her knees drawn up in a semblance of the fetal position. "When you said you needed some time alone, it didn't dawn on me that you meant this alone."

"Don't be mad. But I can't think when I'm with you. This is a very big decision for me, and if you're next to me, I can't think."

Kylie gave her a dubious look and said, "Since when do I have that kind of effect on you?"

Blair looked at her for a long time, finally asking, "You really don't know, do you?"

"Know what?"

"How you affect me. How the whole world seems like a wonderful place when we're together. How everything—even the toughest thing—seems like it's possible when you're by my side." She reached out and took Kylie's hand, squeezing it to her breast as she closed her eyes tightly. "How very much I love you."

Kylie sat down on the bed, her weight making Blair roll towards her. She ran her hand through the silky blonde hair and said, "I guess I don't know."

"It's true. It's all true. Your presence is so powerful that I can't think clearly around you. Things I know are gonna be difficult don't look like that big a deal when you're here."

Kylie cupped her partner's cheek and let her thumb caress the soft skin. "And that makes you feel like you need to sleep in the guest room? Doesn't that seem a little silly?"

"Silly?" Blair sat up on one elbow and scowled. "Are you making fun of me?"

"No, not at all. But listen to what you're saying. You agree to marry me, and two seconds later, you have to be alone to think. You have to be alone to do this because when you're with me, you're too happy to be properly pessimistic and see the dark side of being together." She tilted her chin and narrowed her eyes. "Doesn't that seem a little silly?"

"No." Blair lay back down and put her arms around herself. "I have to think of the dark side. That's how I am."

Kylie put her hand on Blair's hip and then slowly lowered it until she could feel the baby. He was quiet, but after a few moments, he moved, and she patted him tenderly. "You don't have to be that way," Kylie said. "You can let yourself look at the bright side. You can let that unnaturally optimistic way you see the world when we're together become natural. I know this sounds childishly simplistic, but I believe it with all my heart. All that matters is that we love each other. I know there are a thousand things that could go wrong, but if we truly love each other, things will turn out all right."

Blair rolled onto her back and gazed into Kylie's eyes. They looked very dark in the lamplight, and she couldn't see the flecks of various colors that made them so vibrant in brighter light. But they still conveyed a boundless love over which she knew she was completely powerless. "That's all that matters? Are you sure?"

"I'm positive. Only our love matters."

Blair took in a massive breath and blew it out. She tossed her feet off the side of the bed and stood up. Standing next to Kylie, she held out her hand. "Let's go to bed. We've got a lot to do tomorrow."

"Like what?"

"Go to the bank and open a joint account. Find out how to add each other's names to our investment accounts. Figure out where we can get married. You know, stuff like that."

"Sounds like fun." She stood and put her arm around Blair's shoulders, and they walked down the hall together, heading to bed.

❧

The next morning, Kylie opened one eye, glared at the incipient sunrise, and closed it again. She put her hand out to reestablish contact with Blair and blinked when a wide-awake voice asked, "You awake?"

"Uhm...technically." Kylie's voice was low and thick with sleep, and her eyes closed again. She waited a moment and then opened her eyes a crack, hoping that Blair's would be closed. But the green eyes were staring at her, and her partner's face was somber.

"What's wrong?" The doctor rose up on one elbow and put her hand on Blair's cheek. "Everything all right?"

"Tell me what David said."

Her stare didn't waver, and Kylie resigned herself to the fact that they wouldn't be sleeping in. She rolled onto her back and then sat up, putting a couple of pillows behind herself. "Why do you want to know?"

Blair's brows drew closer together. "What do you mean? Why *wouldn't* I want to know?"

"Because all it'll do is make you angry."

"Don't think for me. I'm giving up an awful lot of my autonomy to make this relationship work, but I can't go that far."

Kylie looked at the fatigue evident in her partner's eyes and saw that her lips were drawn together tightly. "Having second thoughts?" she asked, her voice gentle.

"Second thoughts about what?"

"About merging our lives. You don't look like you slept well last night, and I thought our talk might have been on your mind."

"I asked a simple question about David. You don't have to look for an ulterior motive."

"I'm not. I'm not." She reached out and put her arm around Blair, pulling the slightly reluctant woman close. After placing a few tender kisses on her brow and cheek, she said, "Are you a little grouchy this morning?"

"A little," Blair admitted, shocking Kylie by so readily acknowledging her mood.

"You look exhausted." She started to rub her lover's side, smiling to herself when Blair sighed and draped her leg over Kylie's thighs. Increasing the pressure, Kylie started to bear down on all of the usual sore spots, her actions meeting with pleasured purrs. When she could tell Blair was starting to relax, she slipped out of bed and walked around the bed to get behind her. Now she could reach her lover's always-stiff lower back, and her touch was greeted with quiet appreciation. In a few minutes, Blair was still, and her breathing became heavy and regular. Kylie lay down behind her and molded their bodies together, sure that things would look brighter once her partner was a little more rested.

↤

It was 9:00 before Blair stirred again, and she forced herself out of bed immediately, heading for the bathroom. When Kylie heard the sound of teeth being brushed, she got up and joined her lover, sharing a wry smile with her over their morning habit. As soon as they were finished, Kylie guided Blair back to bed and went to let the impatient dogs out. A few minutes later, she was back, bearing a glass of orange juice.

"I was lying here wishing for a glass of orange juice to appear," Blair said. "To have it delivered by a gorgeous, naked woman is quite a bonus."

Kylie handed her the juice and slid in next to her. "I was walking around with a glass of juice, looking for a gorgeous, naked woman to hand it to. Quite a coincidence, huh?"

Blair put her hand on her belly and laughed. "I know that's a defensive compliment, but I'll take it anyway."

"Defensive?"

"Yeah. You're not dumb enough to tell me I look like a beached whale."

"And you're not looking at the world through my eyes, poopsie, so don't tell me who's gorgeous."

"Kylie, I know you love me, but by now, even you have to admit the truth. I'm gonna have a baby in a month, and my stretch marks have stretch marks."

"You're a beautiful woman, and your poor self-image isn't gonna change my mind. So, give it a rest." She took the half-empty glass and put it on the bedside table. "Now, come cuddle with me."

"Here we come," she said, inching towards her partner, a half-smile on her face.

Once Kylie had her arms tucked around her, she kissed her golden hair a few times, loving how the scent of Blair's shampoo lingered. "Now that we're starting our day over, can I ask my question again?"

Blair looked at Kylie and batted her eyes. "Sure. But I forgot what it was."

"Did last night's talk upset you?"

Blair's mouth opened and shut just as quickly. She paused, took a deep breath, and said, "It did upset me. I was up all night thinking of…stuff."

"Stuff? What kinda stuff?"

"Things that I want," she said, her voice sounding small and unsure. "Things that'd make this easier for me."

"Tell me. What'll make this easier?"

"Are you willing to compromise? Last night I got the impression that I had to give in or lose you, and there's no way in hell I'm gonna let you go." She looked at her lover, and the doctor saw the fear in her eyes.

"Oh, baby, I never meant that." Kylie held her tight, stroking her back and kissing her head. "I didn't ever mean for it to sound like I was giving you an ultimatum. I wasn't!"

"Sure sounded like it. Sounded exactly like it."

"I was upset. I was hurt. I told you exactly what I wanted. No, no," she amended. "I told you what I needed, but I don't need it all at once."

"Huh?"

Kylie pulled back and looked her partner in the eyes. "I need for us to merge, but you don't have to dive in if it's too much for you right now. What I need to know is whether you *want* to merge with me. If you'll agree to try to be closer than we've been before."

Blair gave her a suspicious look. "That's really all you want?"

"Yeah. I want to have our lives, including our finances, merged. That's what I need to feel that this is a permanent relationship. But I'm a very patient person. All I need to know is that you're willing to take some steps. Whatever you're comfortable with right now is enough."

Blair shifted and lay on her back, and in a few moments, she started to cry, silent tears skittering down her temples into her hair.

"What's wrong?" Kylie asked, hovering over her. "Why are you crying?"

"I was afraid. I need you so much that I'd do anything to make you stay with me. Even stuff that scares the shit out of me."

"Oh, Blair." Kylie lay down and buried her face in her partner's hair, stroking and kissing and caressing her until the tears stopped. "I'd never let you go. If you don't feel ready to get married, we'll look at it again when you're ready. Last night, I felt like you weren't even willing to try to make me comfortable. That really hurt." She lifted her head and felt the ache in her heart from the sadness in her partner's eyes. "We hurt each other last night, and I'm sorry for that, but things had been building up, and I had a meltdown." Kylie kissed Blair tenderly, feeling the trembling of her partner's lips. "I'll never stop loving you. I promise you that. We're a family."

"Promise?"

Blair's whole body was shaking, and Kylie wished she could have a second chance to start the previous day all over again. "I swear," she said softly. "I swear."

The dogs ran back into the room, their feet a little wet and their breath smelling like fresh kibble. Seeing that Blair had been crying, they flanked her and licked at her eyes, furiously trying to erase the traces of her tears. She laughed helplessly as the dogs' soft tongues tickled her face. Trying to fend them off, she pulled her knees up as much as she could, begging Kylie for help.

But the doctor merely watched the dogs for a moment and then scooted down and wedged in next to Nicky, swiping her warm, pink tongue across Blair's mouth, happy to hear her laughter again.

Finally, the captive pushed all three of her comforters away and sat up, gasping for breath. "I'm gonna have to start locking myself in the bathroom when I want to cry."

"We'll chew the door down, won't we, guys?" Kylie asked her compatriots, roughly tousling their coats while they panted their happiness.

Blair leaned over and kissed her lover, lingering for a long time. "I love you," she whispered. "I love you too much."

"Nah," Kylie said, full of confidence. "You love me exactly the right amount. You're not used to it yet, but it's the right amount. And we can skip our errands today. We'll think about this some more and see what we can agree on. The bank will still be there when we're ready."

"No, no, I want to open a joint account. I can do that."

"Really? You sure?"

"Yeah. I'm sure. I wanna give you what you want, and I know it'll be good for me to share. When I was thinking last night, I decided that the thing that bothers me the most is sharing the things we've accumulated."

Kylie cocked her head. "That's what bothers you? Not the marriage?"

Holding her close, Blair kissed Kylie's lips, then her cheeks. "I want to marry you. I'm afraid, but I want to. But I need to have my own money. I'll always need it. I want money for when I want to buy myself something silly or when I want to give you a present. I want money that only I'm responsible for. I've built my investments through the years, and I want to manage them my way—without compromise."

Kylie gave her a lazy grin and asked, "Sick of compromise already?"

"A little," Blair said, looking embarrassed. "Only kids don't have to share much, ya know."

"No, I don't know, but I can imagine that's true."

"Are you okay with that?"

"Sure. I'm easy," Kylie said, giving her lover a racy grin.

Blair gave her nose a tweak. "Let's settle this, and then we can see how easy you are."

"That's motivation to come to an agreement," Kylie said, wrapping both of her arms around her partner and nuzzling her breasts. "Can we stay in bed all day?"

"I might be convinced, but we have to spend some of the day napping. I can't keep up with you anymore."

"I love a good nap, too. What else do we have to settle?"

"Well, we'll have to talk to an attorney about how to do all of this, but I thought I could match your down payment on the house and use it to pay down your mortgage. That way we'd both have the same equity invested."

"You'd do that?" Kylie looked both pleased and surprised.

"Yeah, of course. It doesn't make sense to merge our finances if we don't equalize the equity."

"Can you afford that?"

"Yeah. If we hadn't moved in together, I would have bought a condo. I've got money set aside for a house."

"Great! Do you have a good attorney we can talk to about doing all of this?"

"Of course. I could populate a small city with the names in my PDA."

Kylie gave her a smile filled with love. "Our business affairs are officially tabled until we talk to an attorney. But our love affair's going strong."

⟶

After Kylie served breakfast in bed, she and Blair managed to spend the rest of the afternoon in a horizontal position. They napped and kissed and napped some more, the emotion of the night before having worn them out. Blair woke at one point and found Kylie wide-awake and staring at the ceiling. "What's going on in that pretty head?" She touched Kylie's face, slowly running her finger over her lover's features.

"I was thinking about David. Wondering what's going on with him."

"I'm wondering when you're gonna tell me what happened yesterday. Now seems like a good time."

Kylie turned and looked at Blair for a long time, with Blair completely unable to read the look in her eyes. "I don't think it's fair to tell you everything he said, but that's not because I'm trying to protect you."

"What other reason could you have?"

"Look." Kylie sat up and ran her hands through her hair, trying to keep the soft curls from falling into her face. "David was angry when he came to my office. I could see how angry he was, and I decided to make him angrier."

"What?"

"I intentionally tried to make him angrier. It might sound crazy now, but at the time, it made sense. I'm not sure I did the right thing, but it seemed like I could make him so mad he wouldn't want to have anything to do with the baby." She pursed her lips together and said, "I guess it worked 'cause he said he wanted to have me killed."

"He what?"

"He was steaming, and I kept making it worse. That's why it doesn't seem fair to talk about specifics."

"This is...surprising." Blair lay down and spent a moment thinking. "Okay," she said. "I guess it wouldn't help to give me any more ammunition to shoot back at him. Especially if you taunted him. So, what's the bottom line?"

"He agreed to do the stepparent adoption. He was so mad he would have agreed to move to a different planet to get away from me."

Blair blew out a breath while reaching out to touch her lover. She scratched the doctor's back for a moment and then said, "What a fucked-up day you had yesterday."

"It was pretty bad. That's why I was so touchy last night."

"Makes sense. I would've been, too." She was quiet for a minute and then asked, "Do you think he'll really give up his rights to the baby? Or was he only reacting?"

Kylie lay down next to her and ran her hand through her partner's blonde hair while she thought. "I think he'll give up his rights," Kylie said. "I don't know him at all, so I could be reading him wrong, but he only seemed to care about how much money the baby was gonna cost him. He didn't seem to have any real interest in Mackenzie."

"Or me," Blair said quietly.

"Still hurts, doesn't it?" Kylie said, her voice heavy with empathy.

"Yeah. It still hurts." She turned and faced Kylie, finally giving her a smile. "As screwed up as this year has been and as hurt as I've been, I'd do it all over again to get you in the bargain. You're my world. No one and nothing can keep us apart."

"C'mere and hug me," Kylie said, her voice choked with tears. "I wanna hold you until I have to go to work on Monday."

"It's a deal. But I wouldn't complain if you got up to make us a little dinner."

"Get out your PDA," Kylie said, smiling. "We're ordering in."

⌐

The next day, Kylie went out to do some shopping, not returning until mid-afternoon. "Where've you been all day?" Blair asked. "I thought you'd be home in an hour. I almost called you on your cell."

"Oh, I went to the grocery store and the pet store, and I made a little stop at a place on Montana. Nothing major. Did you have lunch?"

"Like I ever miss a meal. Can I make you something?"

"Sure. I'll have whatever's in the fridge. What did you do while I was gone?"

"Oh, I left another dozen messages for David on his answering machine. I know the little weasel won't call me back, but it's fun to know he jumps every time the phone rings."

"Honey, I think you should let it go. If we can get rid of him, I say good riddance."

"I know," she said, giving Kylie a half-lidded smile, "but it's fun to torture him."

"That's why I want to make sure we're together for life. I don't wanna know how you'd torture me if we broke up."

"It wouldn't be pretty. Or fast. Or painless."

⌒

They went for their afternoon swim, and after rinsing off the chlorine together, Kylie put on a thick Turkish robe and went into the kitchen. She headed back to the bedroom with a chilled split of champagne. "I bought a little wine to celebrate our engagement." She hadn't brought a glass, and rather than walk back to the kitchen, she opened it and lifted the bottle to her lips. "To us," she said, smiling brightly.

Blair was lying on the bed, and she gazed at her partner for a moment. Kylie was standing in the middle of the room, her robe open just enough to show a hint of cleavage. Her head was tossed back as she took a healthy swig of wine, and Blair decided that her lover looked like the very powerful executive of a major company, having an afternoon tryst in an elegant hotel while indulging all of her voracious appetites. "You're so damned sexy," Blair murmured.

Walking over to the bed, Kylie slid onto the surface, lying on her side and bracing her head on her hand. "Not trying to be."

Blair touched the tip of Kylie's nose with a manicured fingertip. "That's why you're sexy. It doesn't work for me when someone tries."

"I'll remember that."

"You don't have to. You're naturally sexy; it oozes out of you."

"You make lots of things ooze out of me," Kylie said, leering.

"Doctor Mackenzie, you beast!" Blair laughed and slapped at her lover.

"Sip?"

Kylie held the bottle out, and Blair nearly gasped. "You, of all people, are offering me wine? I can hardly eat a cookie without getting a frown."

"That's not true, and you know it. And a sip or two of wine at this point in your pregnancy won't hurt you a bit."

"Really?" Blair asked hesitantly.

"Would I encourage you to do something that could hurt the baby? Get a grip."

"Ah…good point. Gimme the bottle."

Blair took a small sip and let the wine roll around on her tongue for a few moments. "Ooh…I do love champagne."

Kylie retrieved the bottle, took another drink, and then handed it back to Blair. "Last sip for you, partner."

Closing her eyes, she savored the tiny sip and then scooted next to Kylie and gave her a long kiss. "Mmm…I love the way champagne tastes on your lips."

"I should have saved some," Kylie murmured lazily. "We could have discovered if you liked it applied to any other spots."

"Somebody sounds like she's in the mood for love."

Before the words were out of Blair's mouth, Kylie was hovering over her, resting on her hands and knees to allow for Blair's girth, a wickedly sexy grin on her face. "Count on it."

"Ooh…you know how to make my heart race," Blair murmured, drawing a hand along Kylie's cheek. "Let me run to the bathroom, and you can make me moan all night long."

Climbing off, Kylie got to her feet and extended a hand, pulling Blair upright. She tucked her arms as far around Kylie's waist as she could get them and said, "Sorry to break the mood. I promise that I'm much more spontaneous when I'm not pregnant."

"Don't worry about it. I'll still be in the mood in a few minutes." She patted her lover's butt and sent her on her way.

Minutes later, Blair was industriously brushing her teeth when the door swung open, a rakishly grinning Kylie filling the doorway. "Hi." She walked by Blair and set a glass of water down on the sink. Then she lowered the lid on the toilet and sat down. "Mind if I watch?"

Blair looked in the mirror and wrinkled her brow slightly. "You can watch me brush my teeth any old time you want to." When she was finished, she rinsed her mouth and started to turn around, but Kylie's voice stopped her.

"Stay right there," the doctor said, her tone commanding.

"Stay…here?" Blair looked into the mirror again, trying to figure out what Kylie had in mind.

"Yes. Stay right there. I like the view."

Playfully, Blair twitched her butt. "That view?"

"That's the one. Now, take your boxers off so I can see a little more."

"Really?" She started to turn around, but Kylie stopped her once again.

"Stay exactly where you are," she said, a little more firmly this time. "I know what I want to see."

Blair's hands went to her waistband and paused there for a moment, but then she slipped the boxers off and stepped out of them.

"Nice," Kylie said. "Now put these on." She held out her hand and Blair grasped a pale-peach G-string.

"You've got to be kidding! You'll retch!"

"I know what I want. And I want you in that. Now."

Kylie had never sounded so confident or sure of herself, and Blair found herself complying with her partner's wishes without further complaint. She stepped into the tiny garment and found that it was actually comfortable as long as she kept it under her belly.

"Nice. Very nice. Makes your ass look so curvy and voluptuous."

Blair didn't say anything, waiting impatiently for what she knew would be another instruction.

Kylie handed her another piece—a lace push-up bra, the flimsiest she'd ever seen. Her eyes widened, but she set herself to the task. Thankfully, the bra closed in the front, so she could exert all of her strength to wrangle her breasts into place and successfully hook the closure. It took her another few moments to adjust herself, but when she was finished, she glanced into the mirror and saw Kylie looking at her with an expression that could only be called feral.

"How does the bra feel? Touch your breasts and tell me."

Waiting only a second to comply, Blair lightly ran her fingertips across the material, feeling her nipples start to harden almost immediately. A tiny smile tugged at her lips, and she looked into the mirror, meeting Kylie's eyes. "Feels nice. Soft and sexy."

"Show me how big and full your breasts are. Put your hands under them and make 'em jiggle."

Her eyebrow twitched, but Blair forced herself to ignore the slight embarrassment she felt at fulfilling this request. She cupped her breasts and squeezed them in her hands, shaking each in turn and watching Kylie's eyes narrow at the sight. Feeling some of the power shift in her favor, Blair leaned over a little and put on a show, dropping her hands and shaking her shoulders, making her breasts dance before the doctor's dazzled eyes.

It was clear that Kylie wanted to regain the upper hand, and she gave a new instruction. "Reach back and caress your ass. Show me how nice all of that soft skin feels against your hands."

Blair's hands were resting on the sides of the sink, and it took a few moments for her to make herself comply. She was used to taunting men with her breasts, but she'd never caressed her own ass on command. She felt totally exposed and vulnerable, but there was something so sexy about Kylie that Blair would have put her hand over a burning flame if she'd been asked to. She started to run her hands over her cheeks, occasionally glancing in the mirror to watch the doctor's eyes.

"That's what I wanted to see," Kylie purred. "I want to see that you get as much pleasure from touching yourself as I do. It feels hot, doesn't it?"

"Uh-huh," Blair murmured, her voice a little shaky. "It feels soft and smooth and silky under my fingers." Her hands slid across the flesh, caressing herself tenderly.

"Now do it harder. Grab a handful and give it a squeeze," Kylie ordered, her voice dropping even lower. "A nice, sharp swat would be nice. Show me a pink handprint. Come on," she urged when Blair was slow to respond. "Look at me and do it."

Tentatively, Blair lifted her gaze to the mirror and met Kylie's eyes, seeing the fire burning in them. The desire that radiated from her partner emboldened her, and she reached back and slapped herself on the ass, the sting hitting her clit before her backside. She filled her hands with the flesh, squeezing it hard and offering her cheeks up to Kylie's fevered gaze.

"Perfect," Kylie growled. She shifted a little and spread her legs apart. Blair gave her a sexy smile, knowing that Kylie had to be throbbing as much as she was. A thrill raced through her body when she felt the power shift back to her.

"Go back to those delicious breasts," Kylie instructed. "Play with them through your bra. Look into my eyes while you touch yourself."

Locking her eyes on to Kylie's, Blair caressed herself softly, her breasts so hypersensitive that the slightest touch made her shiver. The lace was soft, but it gave her a little added stimulation when she touched her hardened nipples. Her self-consciousness was gone now that she could see how hot she was making her partner. Kylie's eyes were half-hooded and as dark as Blair had ever seen them, and after watching the display for a few minutes, she slipped her hand into her robe and started to play with her own breasts. Blair knew exactly what her lover was doing to herself, knowing that Kylie liked to have her nipples firmly pinched, and her suspicions were confirmed when the doctor let out a sharp gasp and tossed her head back, growling lustily.

"Now take an ice cube out of the glass and rub it against your nipples," Kylie said. Blair looked at her skeptically, but the doctor didn't flinch. "I want you to do that for *me*."

Blair picked up a cube, noticing that her hands were shaking. She got a good hold on it and barely touched her nipple through the bra, her whole body flinching from the sensation. "Come on," Kylie urged. "I wanna see you squirm when you rub those sensitive nipples for me."

Doing it for Kylie made it easy, and Blair barely noticed the cold. All she could see was the fire in Kylie's eyes. All she could feel was the pulsing between her own legs. Moving to the corner of the sink, Blair pressed against the cold marble, needing some kind of pressure against her vulva. Watching her, Kylie nearly leapt from her seat, but she controlled herself, clearly determined to have Blair precisely the way she'd fantasized. "Put your hand between your legs and show me how wet you are," Kylie said, and Blair rushed to comply. "Don't stay too long," she warned when it was clear that Blair was trying to get a little relief. "Just show me."

With a soft gasp, Blair slid her fingers through her moisture and then held up her shaking hand to the mirror, the warm lights revealing her glistening fingers to Kylie's satisfied gaze.

Suddenly, Kylie was pressed up against Blair's back, drawing the wet fingers into her mouth and sucking on them voraciously. Blair leaned heavily against her, groaning when Kylie's hands took command of her breasts, squeezing them to—and a little past—the point of pain.

Blair flung her free hand around Kylie's neck, pulling her down. Kylie released the thoroughly laved fingers from her mouth and then latched on to Blair's neck, sucking so hard she made her gasp. "Are you ready for me?" the doctor asked.

"God, yes!"

Kylie stepped back just enough to unfasten her robe and let it drop to the floor. She tucked an arm under her lover's breasts and drew her tightly against her body, making Blair's eyes fly open when she felt something cool and solid and firm press between her cheeks. Her hand flew behind her and slid up and down her partner's hip, her fingers finding a smooth rubber strap. "Are you sure you're ready for me?" Kylie asked again, nipping at Blair's neck and shoulder as she spoke.

"Yes! Yes! Yes!" She backed up against Kylie, pressing her ass against her.

The doctor grasped her lover's hands and placed them on either side of the wide sink. "Hold on tight."

Tilting Blair's hips, she pulled the G-string aside and slid into her all at once, making Blair cry out in surprise. "Jesus!" she gasped, her head snapping up, eyes wide.

Kylie gave her neck another lusty suck and then asked, "Too big?"

"No, no. Took me by surprise. Good surprise."

Kylie started to move inside her, holding on to her hips tightly. Her lips were pressed against Blair's neck, and she murmured, "We'll go nice and slow until you get comfortable." She pushed gently, filling her partner with the length of the phallus, and then pulled back until only the head remained. "Nice and slow," she repeated as she slid in and out.

"Ooh...that's good," Blair growled in a throaty voice. She reached back and held on to Kylie's hip, feeling the muscles in her ass contracting as she pushed. "That's it, baby...nice and slow. Fill me up."

Kylie started to rotate her hips as she slid in, making the phallus slide against every surface. "Oh, yeah," Blair groaned. "Hitting...all my...spots."

Kylie kept her pace slow and gentle, pistoning in and out, their movements so smooth and rhythmic that it seemed as if they were dancing. After a long while, Blair started to back up against her, their flesh slapping against each other's. "Harder, baby," Blair gasped. "Do it harder." Her head dropped, and she shook it roughly, feeling as if she'd go mad if Kylie didn't increase the pressure. "Come on; fuck me hard!"

Holding her tight, Kylie started to snap her hips sharply, making Blair moan with each thrust. "You are so damned sexy," Kylie panted. "It makes me so hot to watch your breasts bounce when I pump into you." Her eyes were fixed on the creamy flesh, and she was so mesmerized that she almost lost control.

With great difficulty, Blair lifted her head and stared at Kylie in the mirror, their eyes locked together. Again, Blair reached up and laced a hand around her lover's neck, pulling her down against her. "Bite me," she demanded. "Let me feel your teeth against my skin." Immediately complying, Kylie raked her teeth hard against the tender skin, marking Blair's neck and shoulder and back while she ground hard against her. "Don't stop, baby," Blair moaned. "For God's sake, don't stop." She dropped her head again while she held on to the sink with all of her might. "A little more...give me a little more."

Wrapping an arm around her for stability, Kylie lifted one of Blair's legs until her knee was resting on the sink. The new angle made Blair gasp, and Kylie slowed her pace, going in as deeply as she could, pressing hard against Blair's ass when she did so. Kylie reached down and grasped her lover's cheeks, pulling them open, varying the angle further still. "Yes!" Blair cried as the phallus entered her deeply. She bent at the waist and held on to the sink desperately, grunting with each smooth thrust. "So close...so close!"

Sliding an arm around her partner's hip, Kylie reached for her vulva and commanded, "Don't you dare come until I tell you to."

Blair's head lifted, and she stared at the fiery blue eyes in the mirror.

Kylie slowed her pace, moving in and out deeply, but leisurely. "You heard me. You come when I tell you to." Sucking a tender bit of skin in between her teeth, she tugged firmly and then released it, asking, "Are you ready?"

"God, yes, please, Kylie. Please make me come." She dropped her head again, and Kylie's eyes feasted on the swaying blonde hair and the full, ripe breasts that bounced with each thrust.

Kylie pressed her hips as hard against her partner as she could and held there, slipping her fingers into Blair's drenched sex. As soon as she began to manipulate her, Kylie growled, "Come for me!" Finally, Blair did, throwing her head back against Kylie's shoulder as she cried out.

Kylie held on tightly as her lover shook and panted out her satisfaction. Slowly, Kylie eased her partner's leg back to the ground and held still for a minute while Blair continued to pant. Then she gently withdrew, making Blair let out a startled gasp. "Hold me tight," she warned. "I'm shaky."

"I've got you," Kylie soothed. "Don't worry, baby." She kissed her neck tenderly, pressing gently against the same spots she'd marked so forcefully only minutes before.

"I'm okay now," Blair said, sighing heavily. "I think I'm stable."

Kylie kept a hand on her, but let her turn around. Blair leaned against the edge of the sink and shook her head, smiling gently at her partner. "I actually saw stars," she murmured. "That's a first." She reached down and tugged playfully on the bright-red phallus that projected from low on Kylie's abdomen. "You're still hard. Didn't you come?"

Chuckling, Kylie said, "No, I need some help. In the mood?"

"Indeed I am. Carry me wherever you want me, and I'm yours." She laughed and said, "Who am I kidding? I'm yours if you dropped me on the floor."

"No reflection on your weight, sweetheart, but if I tried to carry you, we'd both wind up in the ER."

"Near as I can tell, that's one of the few things you can't do," Blair teased, kissing her gently while she continued to play with the doctor's phallus.

"You liked my little friend, huh?"

"Sure did. If it were half an inch thicker and a couple of inches longer, it would be the world's most perfect penis."

"Half an inch?" Kylie nodded decisively. "I can do that. I have a blue one that sounds perfect. It has ridges up the shaft about every inch, too. They feel great when they pop past your opening."

Blair blinked up at her. "You have more than one of these little guys?"

"Uh-huh," she said. "I chose this one because it's small. I wasn't sure how much fullness you liked, and I wanted to make sure I wouldn't hit your cervix no matter how hard I pushed."

"So, this is the beginner model?" Blair teased, aiming a playful slap at it.

"After a fashion," Kylie said. "It's made for a smaller space." Blair gave her a slightly puzzled look, and Kylie turned her around and tucked the head between her cheeks, giving her a gentle thrust.

Blair grinned at her in the mirror and said, "Why, Doctor Mackenzie! You've led quite the racy life, haven't you?"

"I have a feeling it's only gonna get racier with you, sweetheart. I think I've met my match."

"I don't think this is an approved activity for these chairs," Kylie commented a few minutes later as they settled into place.

Blair lifted her head and wrinkled her nose at her partner. "I put a towel down before I sat, wise guy. Now put your foot up on this arm," she said. "You can hold on to the back of the chair for stability."

"What's wrong with the bed?"

"New rules," Blair said, grinning up at her. "If I have to come standing up, so do you." She trailed her fingertips along the edge of Kylie's mound. "I love this position. It's nice to have you so open. I can use my hands for other things."

She reached behind and held on to Kylie's ass, pulling her forward. As soon as her lover started to caress her, the larger woman let out a satisfied moan. "Nice. Very nice." Blair pulled her even closer and really dove into her, rubbing her entire mouth against Kylie firmly, trying to fill her senses with her essence. "I'm not gonna last long if you keep that up," Kylie gasped.

Thinking to herself that Kylie never lasted long, Blair did her best to slow down the pace, but as usual, Kylie dictated her own needs, pressing herself against Blair and making herself come noisily in a matter of minutes.

"Damn!" she grumbled, trying to catch her breath. "I've gotta learn how to slow down."

Blair got up and maneuvered her to the bed, letting Kylie rest against her body for a while. "Does it bother you to come fast?"

"Mmm…no, not really," she said. "I don't know why, but my body needs to be satisfied quickly. I guess I should just accept how I am."

"I love how you are," Blair said. "I get the best of both worlds. You've got a nice, firm dildo that's always ready, and I don't have to stay in an uncomfortable position for very long to make you come. I think you're perfect." She kissed her tenderly and spent a few minutes tracing the planes of her face with her fingertips, taking in Kylie's classically beautiful features. "You sure seemed like you knew your way around that little toy. Why haven't we played with one of those before?"

Kylie looked at her for a moment and said, "I've been thinking about it ever since that discussion we had before we went to Chicago. I wanted to use it then, but something stopped me."

Blair sat up and looked at her lover with a questioning expression. "Really? Do you know why?"

"I've been thinking about that, too."

Blair pinched one of her partner's cherry-red nipples, making Kylie squeal and clap her hands over both breasts, pre-empting another tweak. "You're so cute," Blair said. "I think it's adorable that you spend your time thinking about things like this. I love that you save a part of your busy brain for us."

"I spend half of my day thinking about us," the doctor said, laughing. "I have to force myself to concentrate in surgery! I've never had to do that before in my life!"

"You'll get over it," Blair soothed, stroking Kylie's arm while she inched closer to her breast.

Kylie grasped her hand and kissed it. "Don't pinch me again, or I'll get you back double. Remember, every kid in the family picked on me. I'm well trained."

"No more pinching," Blair promised, giving her partner a kiss. "I'll behave. Now, tell me what you've been thinking about."

"I've been thinking that I'm not letting loose—sexually."

"Really?" Blair blinked slowly. "I think our sex life has been great. Don't you?"

She was starting to look worried, and Kylie took her hands and looked into her eyes. "I love our sex life. But I haven't been showing you everything. Now that I know you're committed to me through thick and thin, I feel more comfortable being myself—all of myself."

Blair gave her a deep, soulful kiss and said, "I love your self. Every bit of it." She stroked Kylie gently for a few minutes, basking in the warmth and the scent of her body. "I'm so glad you showed me more of yourself today. I had a wonderful time."

"I'm sorry I didn't feel comfortable using my toys sooner. But we can keep 'em right in the bedside table. I'll always be ready."

Blair looked at her for a moment, and then Kylie's words sank in. "Do you think…? Are you saying…?"

Kylie's eyes went wide. "What?"

"I had fun playing with your toy, but that's not why I loved today."

"It's not?"

"No! I had such a wonderful day because you showed me more of your assertiveness—your forceful personality. That's what was so hot! The toy was fun, but I certainly don't need one. I like your fingers just fine. You know how to use 'em."

Kylie looked enormously pleased. "Really? You like the way I use my hands?"

Blair dramatically threw herself to the bed and moaned. "I constantly tell you what a talented lover you are! You make me come so easily it's remarkable! Haven't you been listening?"

"Yeah, yeah."

It was clear that Kylie was embarrassed, and Blair pulled on her to get her to lie next to her. "You're the most incredible lover I've ever had, Kylie Mackenzie, and I'm looking forward to a whole lifetime of being completely and utterly satisfied by you."

"I feel the same way about you."

Blair tickled the side of her lover's neck, making her giggle. "Would you like it if I used one of your toys on you?"

"Mmm..." Kylie reached down and ran her hand over the bulging belly. "I think you'd need the double extra long to accommodate Mackenzie."

Blair slapped at her playfully. "I didn't mean now, you goof. I mean in general. Do you like being on the receiving end?"

Kylie shook her head and then smiled slyly. "No, not really. I'm a giver."

"Yeah, you're generous to a fault. Is that the only reason?"

"Mmm...maybe not the only reason."

"I think—and this is a wild guess—" Blair said, "it might also be because you need to be in control."

Kylie grinned at her, holding her thumb and forefinger about an inch apart. "Maybe a little."

"When I'm back to normal, we can experiment a little. Who knows? You might feel different about my doing it."

"I'll try anything once," Kylie said. "And yes, you may take that as a challenge. You've had to make some changes for our relationship; I guess I do, too."

"One thing you don't have to change," Blair said, rubbing low on Kylie's belly, "is your quick recovery time. You come fast, but you can come often. Climb up here and give me another taste."

"Oh, gee, I don't know," Kylie said, already moving into place. "Maybe we should clean the house...oh, yeah," she growled, swaying her hips to make Blair's tongue reach every part. "Just like that. That's the spot, baby."

A week later, Kylie came home nearly bursting with excitement. She went out into the backyard and saw Blair swimming her laps. Rather than disturb her partner, she went into the house and changed into a pair of jeans and a fleece shirt to keep warm in the early-December chill. She was rolling up the sleeves when she walked back out, and Blair came up for air. "Hi," Blair panted, "I've been waiting for you. Aren't you gonna swim tonight?"

"Nope. Not in the mood. Are you about finished?"

"Yeah. I hate the thought of getting out, though. It's kinda cold." She looked longingly at the house, wishing she could pull it closer to the pool by telepathy.

"They said it was fifty-five. That's about normal for this time of year."

"True. But it's not normal to be outside and dripping wet at this time of year." Her face brightened, and she asked, "Hey, wanna hear how I humiliated myself today?"

Kylie sat on the pool surround, crossed her legs Indian-style, and smiled at her lover. "How could anyone resist that offer?"

Blair dunked herself, slicking her hair back off her forehead in the process. "Here's the sad tale. I was showing a huge old house. Two-story, Spanish. A big, rambling place. There was a bathroom on the first floor, but I snuck off upstairs and used the facilities. I hate to do that when I'm showing a house, but I figure that people would rather I used their bathroom than peed on their floors."

"Sounds reasonable," Kylie said, smiling. "That'd be my first choice."

"So, my clients really liked the place. We went back downstairs, and I could tell they were seriously considering making an offer. But they're the cautious sort and had to look at every nook and cranny, and there were a lot of crannies. I followed them along, watching them try every outlet…doing the things that an inspector really knows how to do." She wrinkled up her nose and said, "Clients. Gotta love 'em."

"Where does the humiliation come in? That's the good part."

Blair made a face and stuck her tongue out. "I'm getting there. They poked around for so long that I had to pee again. I was embarrassed, but I did it. I *had* to," she added emphatically. "I'd had two cups of herbal tea right before I left the office, and that tea had to get out!"

"You don't have to convince me. I swear you pee your body weight every day!"

"Ha, ha. Anyway, I excused myself and took care of business. They'd finally seen everything there was to see, and I locked up. Halfway down the front stairs, my pantyhose started to roll off my belly, and by the time I hit the bottom stair, they were stuck right under my ass! They were so tight I could hardly take a step!"

Kylie fell backwards, laughing so hard that she held on to her sides and rolled back and forth on the ground. "Dear God, why didn't I get to see that? My life would've been complete!"

"Yeah, well, it wasn't so funny at the time. I couldn't go back into the house again. What was I gonna say? I've gotta pee…again? So, I walked to my car like I had a stick—a big stick—up my butt, and then I had to get into the car and drive them back to my office. Getting my leg into that car was one of the hardest things I've ever done, Kylie! I swear! I had to use both hands to pull my foot up high enough. They must have thought I'd had a stroke!"

Kylie was crying with laughter now, unable to sit up even.

"The husband was standing behind me, and he looked like he wanted to help, but what was he gonna say? 'Do you need help pulling your leg up, Blair?'"

"Oh, for God's sake, stop! Stop, I'm begging you!" Kylie wheezed, pulling herself up and wiping her face. "I'm sorry for laughing, but that was just priceless."

"Oh, yeah, it was priceless all right. They wanted to make an offer, and I told them I had to run an errand first! What could they have been thinking? Other than I'd lost my mind, of course. So, we got to my office, and I didn't even try to get out of the car. I just sat there with the engine idling and told 'em to get out!"

"Did they?" Kylie asked, helpless with laughter again.

"Of course! They stood there looking at me like I was nuts, so I pulled a twenty out of my wallet and told them to go to Marmalade across the street and buy some coffee and something to snack on since it would take at least an hour to write up the offer. They took the money, and I waved and said I'd be right back."

"Where'd you go?"

"I came home, took off those demonic pantyhose, and put on a turtleneck and those black corduroy overalls you bought for me. They must have thought I'd wet myself at the house, but I wasn't even gonna try to offer an explanation at that point. I just acted like I threw clients out of my car every day while I went home to change."

"Good God, you must have been mortified!"

"Yeah, I was for a while. But then I thought, 'Fuck it!' I'm eight months pregnant, and shit happens."

"That's my girl. Besides, people give you a lot of leeway when you're pregnant. You're so cute in those overalls, they were probably blinded by your beauty."

"That's likely. Very likely." Blair grabbed the toe of Kylie's shoe and gave it a hearty tug. "All I know is that I'm not wearing pantyhose until Mackenzie makes his debut."

"I'll buy you some of those thigh-high stockings that the women in the Victoria's Secret catalog wear. You'd look sexy in those."

"Oh, yeah. Especially with the maternity panties. Woohoo!"

"Well, I always think you're hot. Even when you don't."

"I'm not hot now. I'm downright cold."

Kylie stood and held out a bath sheet. "Come on out. You're gonna want to hear the message on the answering machine, so make it snappy."

"Message?"

"Yep. He must have called when you were swimming."

"Who's he?"

"Come inside and hear for yourself. All I'm gonna say is that it's good news."

"God knows I love good news. I'm right behind ya."

Blair was wrapped in both the bath sheet and Kylie's arms when the doctor hit the play button on their answering machine: "Hi, Kylie and Blair. Dave Robbins. I've got good news for you. Mark Roth called me today and said that David is prepared to terminate his parental rights in favor of you, Kylie. Obviously, we can't proceed until the baby is born and the divorce is final, but it looks like this is going to work out just the way you want it to. Give me a call if you need any more information. Congratulations, you two!"

Kylie looked down at her partner, her smile nearly going from ear to ear. "Wasn't that worth coming in for?"

"Oh, Kylie, I can't tell you how happy this makes me." She burrowed into her lover's embrace, crying softly. But this time, the tears were made up of pure, unadulterated joy.

A week later, on December 10, Eleanor Schneidhorst arrived at Los Angeles International Airport, surprised to see only Kylie standing at the luggage carousels. "Hi," she said, giving the doctor a hug. "Is Blair in the bathroom?"

"Ah, she's told you about her new hobby. No, I convinced her to stay home. It's easier this way."

"Easier? Is she all right?"

"Oh, sure, she's fine, but I didn't want her to have to walk too far. She's pretty uncomfortable now, Eleanor, and when she's on her feet for too long, everything starts to hurt."

"Oh, my poor little girl. I bet she can't wait to have this baby."

Kylie laughed, her eyes crinkling up at the corners. "She keeps trying to get me to give her an injection of oxytocin. I don't carry it in my bag, but if I did, I'd get rid of it!"

"Oxytocin?"

"Oh. Right. I forget that not everyone is expecting a baby. Oxytocin is a hormone they give to stimulate labor."

"Is she that miserable, honey?"

As was her habit, Kylie took the question seriously and spent a moment considering her reply. "Yeah, she is. She's not sleeping well, and that certainly doesn't help matters. It's impossible for her to find a position that's comfortable, and believe me, we've tried everything." The doctor laughed softly and then shook her head, obviously remembering some of the things they'd tried. "The only place she's truly comfortable is in the pool. I'm sure the baby's gonna come out doing the backstroke."

"You've probably figured this out by now," Eleanor said, lowering her voice into a conspiratorial whisper, "but she's not the kind of girl who suffers in silence."

Kylie laughed and draped her arm around Eleanor's shoulders. "I've been very impressed with how stoic she's been. Honestly, she rarely complains. I can tell how uncomfortable she is, but she hardly ever makes a big deal out of it."

"She must have changed a lot since she was a girl. When she was little, the whole building knew when she had a cold."

"She has changed," Kylie said, her smile growing. "She's changed a lot."

⟶

Blair walked down the sidewalk to greet the car, waving happily at her mother and Kylie. "Oh, my goodness," Eleanor said. "How big is that baby going to be?"

"Looks like she's got a twenty-pound turkey strapped to her, doesn't it?" Kylie asked. "Uhm, I wouldn't say that if I were you, Eleanor. She's good-natured about it, but it hurts her feelings when people make a big deal out of her size."

Eleanor reached over and squeezed Kylie's arm. "I'm glad you're with her, honey. She's a lucky girl."

They opened their doors as Blair approached, her waddle nearly comical. She looked a little like a woman who'd been on a horse a very long time, but Eleanor, wisely, said not a word about her rolling gait. "You look wonderful!" she said, doing her best to get her arms around her daughter.

"Thanks, Mom. I've missed you and Dad. Being this close to delivering has really made me want my Mommy!"

"Aw…you haven't called me Mommy since you were in kindergarten. I forgot how much I loved that name."

"Well, I feel like climbing onto your lap and having you make this all be over."

Eleanor put her arm around her daughter, and the threesome started to walk into the house. "Only two more weeks until your due date," she said, trying to sound as if that were only minutes.

"My doctor says that most first babies are late," Blair said. "I keep hoping I'm the exception, but I have a feeling I'm not going to be."

"Let's keep a good thought," Eleanor said. "It couldn't hurt."

⌐

Later that evening, Blair floated in the pool while her mother sat on a nearby chair and watched her. The older woman was glad her daughter couldn't see her face since she was unable to keep from smiling when she looked at the pumpkin-sized belly breaking the waterline. After a while, Blair floated over to the edge and stood up. "You're not bored, are you?"

"No, not at all. Being able to sit outdoors in December is such a treat for me that I could sit here all night and not say a word."

"Oh, right. I've been here so long that I forget not everyone has weather like this all year round."

"Far from it. It was just starting to snow when I reached O'Hare."

"Brr! I hope it's warm when we bring the baby to Chicago to be baptized."

"I think it's so nice that you're doing that to make Kylie's mother happy."

"That's partially the reason, but it's also a way to have him officially be a Mackenzie. All of the kids and grandkids have been christened in that church."

"How are things going with that, legally that is?"

"So far, so good. When our divorce decree is final in August, we're going to file for a stepparent adoption. As I told you last week, David's attorney says he's ready to waive his rights."

Eleanor blinked and asked, "How long do you have to wait?"

"Until August," Blair said, looking unhappy.

"But that's so long!"

"Don't I know it," Blair grumbled. "There's a yearlong waiting period for the divorce to be final."

"Oh, honey, that's cruel to make you wait so long."

"It's gonna be hard. I keep thinking of all of the reasons the little snake could use to change his alleged mind, and it worries me to death. But there's nothing I can do about it."

Eleanor was quiet for a moment, and Blair could see the worry expressed on her face. "You're already going over the list, aren't ya?" she asked her mother.

Trying to make herself smile, Eleanor nodded. "I was thinking about Sadie."

"Yeah. She's the lynchpin in the whole thing. She has a lot of influence with David, and I worry that she could talk him into just about anything. She's supportive of Kylie at this point, but you never know how she'll feel when she sees the baby."

"Honey, I don't want to second-guess you, but are you sure it's wise to keep her involved?"

Blair considered her answer and then nodded. "I am. I realize it's a devil's bargain, but I'd rather try to keep her on our side. She's really angry with David, and she sees how devoted Kylie is—both to me and the baby. If she really cares about the baby, I think she'll stay on our side. And if she doesn't, we're screwed anyway. So, I think it's worth the risk."

"I see your point," Eleanor said, "but I wish there were another way."

"So do I, Mom, but I'm the one who made the mistake of marrying a self-absorbed adolescent. I can't blame anyone but myself for not knowing him better before I agreed to get pregnant."

"He doesn't know what he gave up," Eleanor said, giving her daughter a sad smile.

"No, he sure doesn't, and that's the best reason I can think of to divorce him. A guy who would give up a wife who loved him, as well as a baby, just because he wasn't the father, isn't a guy I wanna share a cab with, much less a life."

"I think you've found a woman who loves you very much, honey. Kylie acts as if she's the happiest woman on Earth. She talked about you and the baby so excitedly on the drive home that I was afraid she'd have an accident."

"It's a tie in the 'who loves whom more' competition," Blair said. "Most days we call it a draw."

"Is that true, sweetheart? Are you as crazy about her as she is about you?"

Blair looked at her mother for a few moments and then said, "I'm a little embarrassed to admit this, but I have a whole new vocabulary for love."

"Vocabulary?"

"Yeah. Take passion. I always thought that passion was a sexual thing. David and I had some very good, very passionate moments. But with Kylie…with Kylie, it's not just about sex. Do you know what I mean?"

"No, not really," Eleanor said. "I don't get the connection."

"I guess what I'm trying to say is that I feel passionately about Kylie whether or not we're being sexual. I mean, it's not every minute or anything, but I can look at her or think about her and feel so emotional." She wiped a few tears away with the back of her hand. "I have no control, Mom. None. I love her so much it amazes me. Sometimes, it actually takes my breath away. She was outside this morning, playing with the dogs, and when she came in, our eyes met. She gave me this look that showed all of her feelings—all of them! I started crying and went to her and threw my arms around her and cried for the longest time. Sometimes, it feels so fantastic that it's too much to bear."

Eleanor was crying by this time, and she smiled through her tears. "You've never said anything that made me happier. That's all I've ever wanted for you."

"Well, you've got it. I'm completely powerless against that woman. I just hope she never tells me to jump off a cliff—'cause I'd do it!"

"That part will pass. I felt the same way about your father at first, but now I'd need a little convincing."

"I guess that's true," Blair said, smiling at her mother. "But I'm gonna enjoy the hell out of this 'crazy love' period. It's too precious to waste a moment of it."

"Speaking of the love of your life, where is she? She doesn't think she has to make herself scarce because of me, does she?"

"Oh, no. She's been itching to do some research on the Internet, but she hates to leave me alone. She's in her element when she's in her office, being my cute little nerd, but we're both pretty clingy these days."

"I can understand that," Eleanor said. "Does she work at home often?"

"Oh, this isn't work. Her car failed its emissions test, and she's finally agreed to buy a new one. Her car doesn't even have air bags! So, I'm sure she's thinking about getting some sort of armored personnel carrier to protect the baby from safes and grand pianos falling from great heights."

"Sounds like your father. When you were learning to walk, he wanted to buy you a little bicycle helmet to protect your head."

"That'll be Kylie. She's like that with me now, so I can't imagine how she'll be with someone who really is helpless!"

⤳

Later that evening, the trio sat in the den with Kylie massaging Blair's belly. "I've been having these Braxton Hicks contractions for a long time now," Blair told her mother, "but they've gotten a lot worse in the last weeks."

"Are they painful?"

"Mmm…not really painful, but pretty annoying. Everyone tells me that I'll be able to tell the difference between these and the real ones, so the difference must be considerable."

"I wish I could help," Eleanor said, "but I don't have a clue."

"I'm glad you don't," Blair said, smiling. "You're one mother who doesn't have a horror story to tell me. I'm gonna punch the next person who tells me about being in labor for four days. I don't even ask these women questions! They see me at the grocery store and start asking me all sorts of personal things. I swear, it's like I'm wearing a sign that says 'Ask me about my uterus.'"

"It'll only get worse. When I used to push you around the neighborhood in your stroller, nearly everyone we passed stopped to take a look."

"I'm not taking Mackenzie out of the house until he can talk," Blair said. "If someone wants to know something, he can answer for himself!"

⤳

They spent the first weekend decorating the house for Christmas. Even though Blair's due date was December 25, they'd decided to plan on having a normal Christmas since it was their first together.

The first stop was a tree lot on Wilshire Boulevard. Kylie was drawn to the biggest trees they had, despite Blair's protest that they'd never be able to get any of them onto the car. "We deliver for only $15," the energetic young salesman said. "We'll even help you set it up," he added, casting a quick glance at Blair's belly.

Blair threw her hands up. "Go wild," she told her partner. "Just remember how tall the ceiling is."

When Kylie walked away to pay the man, Eleanor said, "We started out with huge trees, until the third time we had to have a maintenance man come up and cut a few feet off. Your father finally admitted that it was silly to pay $50 for a tree and then another $10 as a tip—or a humiliation fee, as he called it."

Blair nodded. "I have a feeling my beloved's eyes are bigger than our room, but I don't care as long as she's happy."

Eleanor smiled at her daughter. "That's how I felt until the third time in a row. By then, you just want to hit them on the head with the measuring tape!"

⟺

When the tree was delivered, it was apparent that Kylie had not recalled the exact dimensions of the room. But after the delivery boy cut off the gangly top branches and a substantial amount of the trunk, the tree finally fit in the stand. Kylie paid and tipped the young man and then stood back, admiring the goliath. "We always had a huge tree when I was growing up, and it doesn't seem like Christmas without one."

"We usually had one that sat on our piano," Blair said. "I'm used to a Lilliputian Christmas."

"That's the difference between growing up in the city versus the suburbs, but since L.A. is one big suburb, we can go big." She looked at Blair and asked, "Do you have any ornaments?"

"Unh-uh. David had some cool ones from his grandmother, and we always used those. I've got nothing. Where's your box of goodies?"

"I don't have any, either. I couldn't put up a big tree in my condo, so I never bothered. Besides, I always went home for Christmas, so it seemed like a waste of time."

"Well, I guess it's time to start our own family tradition. Time to head to Pasadena. Are you up for a road trip, Mom?"

"Pasadena? Don't they sell Christmas ornaments in Santa Monica?"

"Sure they do. But there's a huge Christmas store in Pasadena. Walter always goes after Christmas to stock up on ribbons and garland and all sorts of things he uses to decorate houses. He'd kill me if he knew I was paying full price, but we don't have much choice. We can buy just enough to get us through this year and then go back after Christmas to load up on the half-priced stuff."

"Yeah, that's just what you'll want to do on the day after Christmas," Kylie laughed. "Go wait in line to buy things on sale when you're nine months pregnant."

Blair nodded and said, "I'll give Walter my credit card and ask him to fix us up for next year. He has better taste than I do, anyway."

⟺

By Sunday night, the tree was attractively, if sparsely, decorated, and there were strings of lights surrounding all of the windows on the front of the house. Large, fragrant juniper wreaths hung on the doors, and the essential elements of a crèche, which they hoped to add on to, were arranged on the mantel. "It looks a little bare with just the baby Jesus, Joseph, and Mary up there," Blair said.

"Don't worry, folks," Kylie said to the holy family. "Once everything's on sale, you'll have some animals and some guys bringing you gifts. We'll hook you up."

Eleanor had already gone to bed, and the couple was sitting on the sofa in the den, cuddling before they turned in. Kylie looked at Blair and asked, "Is there anything unique about an Armenian Orthodox crèche? I wanna be authentic."

"Yeah. One of the wise men brings baklava," Blair said, giggling. She patted Kylie's side and said, "It's the same. Oh. Except for one little thing."

"What?"

"Well, the Armenian Church is similar to the other Christian churches, but they celebrate Christmas in January."

"What?"

"You heard me. They celebrate Christmas in January. And Easter's different, too. I think it's a week or two after most people celebrate."

"Blair! That's kind of a big deal!"

"No, it's really not," she said. "David's family celebrated Christmas with everybody else. They acted like December 25 was when Santa Claus came and brought gifts. They just celebrated Jesus' birth in January."

"Jesus' birth is kinda the whole point of Christmas. I think this is gonna be a problem. Mackenzie's gonna be confused."

Blair gave her partner a look, raising one eyebrow. "Honey, do you really think Christmas is gonna be the thing that confuses him? He'll have an unknown biological father, a legal father who's renounced him, two mommies, three grandmothers and two grandfathers who aren't biologically related, and dozens of aunts and uncles and cousins who all live far away. He'll be in high school before he figures out who his relatives are!"

"Still…" Kylie said, looking worried. "Maybe this religion thing isn't a good idea."

"Baby, I've told you: if this doesn't work out, we'll stop it. If he doesn't like it, we'll stop it. If he hears things at church that bother him, we'll stop it. Besides," she said, "Sadie will probably lose interest after a year or two, especially if she tries to take him for the entire service."

"Why would she lose interest?"

"'Cause the service is like…I don't know…two, two and a half hours long? Something like that."

"Two and a half hours? What do they do? Read the whole Bible?"

"I'm not sure. I've only been a couple of times, and it's all in Armenian."

"The service is in Armenian?" Kylie's eyes were comically wide.

"Well, yeah, it's the Armenian church. I'm sure the Greek Orthodox Church has services in Greek. What's surprising about that?"

"You're telling me that Sadie's gonna take our baby to a church service that's two and a half hours long and is in Armenian?"

"Yep."

"She won't last a year!"

"I think she might hold out until he starts to crawl, but by that time, I think she'll have had a bellyful. I think she just wants everyone to know she has a grandchild, babe. It means a lot to her."

Kylie nodded. "I think I'm beginning to understand why you're so calm about this. I should have known you had insider information."

"I always do," Blair said, smiling sweetly.

"One of the many, many, many things I love about you." She wrapped her arm around her lover and cuddled her tightly to her body. "You're the best Christmas present I ever got."

"I hope the best Christmas present we ever get makes an appearance before Armenian Christmas," Blair said, laughing. "'Cause if he doesn't, I'm gonna bribe Monique to induce labor!"

Kylie cuddled her partner even closer and said, "If anyone can do it, you can, baby."

Resting her head on her lover's chest, Blair said, "It's hard to believe that Mackenzie will be here before we take the tree down."

"Don't put it that way," Kylie said, her voice suddenly a little high. "It's too scary."

"It's starting to hit you, too, huh?"

"Yeah. I'm having really vivid dreams about our bringing him home and not having any idea what to do with him. He cries and cries, and we finally have to call Monique to teach us how to quiet him down. It's supremely humiliating."

Blair chuckled and then shook her head. "That's the difference between being normal and having hundreds of different hormones racing through your bloodstream. My dreams are horrific! There's always something wrong with him—or me. I had one the other night where they put me in a mental hospital because I was having a hysterical pregnancy! That was a surefire way to get me up to organize the spice rack—again."

"It'll all be over soon."

Blair looked up at her, surprised to see that she was completely serious. "It all *starts* when he's born. This is merely the warm-up act."

Kylie swallowed and looked at her partner for a moment. "Should we bother to go to bed or start organizing things right now?"

⌁

Kylie woke on Monday morning, looked at her sleeping lover, and wished she could call in sick. Blair never got up when she did, but there was something about knowing her partner wasn't going to work that made her jealous. Blair stirred and looked up at Kylie. "Getting up already?"

"Yeah. I don't wanna, but I have to."

"Oh, are you sad you have to go to work?"

Slightly embarrassed, Kylie nodded. "I feel like I did when the older kids got a school holiday and I didn't. You're not planning anything fun today, are you?"

"Mmm…what's your least favorite museum?"

The doctor thought for a moment and then said, "Probably MOCA. I'm not a huge fan of contemporary art."

"Good. Then we'll go to MOCA today."

"Yeah, but you'll go to good places later in the week."

"Yes, we will, baby, but I won't tell you about them. How's that?"

Kylie smiled and then gave Blair a gentle kiss. "I want you to have fun. The whole point of having your mom come this early was to give you someone to pal around with and to keep you occupied. I'll control my jealousy."

"I'm very glad she's here," Blair said. "I feel safer when my mommy's close by."

"And in two weeks, your daddy will be here, too. You'll be in a little cocoon of love."

"C'mere," Blair said, inviting Kylie to come close by making kissing sounds. The doctor leaned over, and they kissed gently for a few minutes. "I'm always in a cocoon of love when I'm with you."

"I *do* love you," Kylie said, the lovesick expression that Blair loved so on her face.

"And I love you. Remember that today, and think about it if you get lonely."

"You're nice," Kylie said with a charming, childlike smile.

"You're nice, too. Now, get in the shower, or your patient isn't gonna be nice to you. Go on, you little scamp."

Kylie jumped out of bed, both dogs jumping right behind her. "We love you," she said one last time as she went into the bathroom with her canine voyeurs.

Chapter Thirteen

Two weeks later, Blair was still growing, still gaining weight, and still ready to take the baby out by any means necessary. "When we met, all you talked about was operating on me," she complained when she and Kylie were lying in bed, watching the sun rise through some dark clouds. "Now I can't get you to take one little thing out. Easy as pie. Just one little incision…"

"I thought you didn't want me to touch you clinically." They were loosely wrapped in each other's arms, legs interlaced.

"There's an exception to every rule. Just this once, I won't mind."

"Tomorrow's your official due date. Maybe Mackenzie'll make a grand entrance on Christmas Eve."

"That due date stuff means nothing, and you know it. It's a crapshoot."

"Not when you're inseminated. I mean, every baby is on his own schedule, but at least you really know when the sperm started swimming towards that lucky egg."

Blair put her hand on her belly and then knocked lightly. "Come on out, Mackenzie. Your room's all ready, your grandma's here, and your grandpa's coming this afternoon. Don't be a divo."

"A divo?"

"If demanding, temperamental women are divas, then men should be divos. Makes sense."

"Can't argue with ya. What time are we seeing Monique today?"

"At four-thirty, same as usual. Mom wants to come with us. You don't mind, do you?"

"Heck, no. She'll see a lot worse when you actually deliver. If you want, you two can go alone, and I'll stay home and wrap your Christmas presents and then go to the airport and pick up your father."

Blair nudged her head against Kylie's chest. "I wanna be with you. Every single minute."

"Wanna go to the airport?"

"No."

"Want your presents?"

"Yeah."

"Then play along, sweetums. You go show Monique what's cookin', and I'll have your father here when you get back."

"That's the best present you could give me. Now, let's take a little nap."

"We just woke up!"

"You just woke up. I was up for three hours, alphabetizing our CDs."

"Blair! You did that last week!"

"I know, but I woke up at 2:00 a.m. and decided that I should categorize all of the classical ones by the orchestra, rather than the composer."

"I'm filled with empathy for you. Sorry I show that by sleeping through your nocturnal nesting frenzies."

"Try having a baby pressing against your diaphragm on one end and against your bladder on the other. Let's see how you sleep then, wise guy."

"I sleep best when you're pressing against me, so a nap sounds just perfect."

⌐

Kylie and Werner were making good time coming home from the airport, mostly because the doctor used her favorite shortcut—taking Lincoln Boulevard instead of the freeway. The freeway was unbearably crowded, but the surface streets weren't bad. Many of the stores on Lincoln had closed early because of Christmas Eve, and they were nearly home by five-thirty.

Her pager chirped, and Kylie crossed her fingers, hoping it wasn't the hospital. "Darn it," she said, looking at the display. "I didn't get paged once this week. Why now?"

"Maybe it's a mistake," Werner offered. "Most of the calls I get on my cell phone are wrong numbers."

"Mmm…they don't make many mistakes," Kylie said. "I'd better pull over and call." She found an empty space on Montana and opened the windows. Pressing the speed dial, she waited for a moment and then said, "Hi, it's Doctor Mackenzie. Someone paged me."

"Kylie Mackenzie?" the woman asked.

"Yes." Kylie rolled her eyes, thinking that Werner's prediction might prove to be true. "Is this the surgical nurses' station?"

"No. This is the obstetrics station. Blair Spencer asked us to page you."

"Blair's at the hospital? Why?" Her heart started to race, and she felt Werner's hand grip her arm.

"She's having a baby, right? Am I talking to the right person?"

"Yes, damn it! Is she in labor?"

"Of course, she is. Are you sure you're a doctor?"

"I'll be right there," Kylie said, hanging up while muttering a curse. She turned to Werner and said, "Either someone has screwed up royally, or Blair's in a labor room."

"Why wouldn't she call you herself?"

"That's why I'm so confused," Kylie said. "This doesn't make sense."

"I'm sure you don't want another false alarm," Werner said. "You're gonna get a reputation."

Kylie started to shoot him a look, but then her expression softened, and she tapped her forehead against the steering wheel. "Many, many people think they're in labor before they really are. I don't know what's going on in her uterus! If she says she's in labor, I take her to the hospital. I'm blameless."

"You're a good partner," Werner said, patting her on the back. "Why don't you call her cell phone to make sure this isn't a false alarm?"

"Good idea." Kylie called the number, grumbling when it went to voice mail. "Hi. Call me if you get this message—if you're not in the hospital, that is. If you are in the hospital, I'll see you soon." She looked at Werner and said, "Let's go. We might be having a baby!"

⌒

"One benefit of being on staff here," Kylie said, winking at Werner. "I can park close." They got out and walked into the hospital, going directly to obstetrics. Kylie was a complete unknown on that floor, and she didn't particularly like the feeling. She and Werner walked up to the nurses' station, and she asked, "Has Blair Spencer been admitted?"

The woman at the desk gave her a thin smile. "You didn't have to hang up on me. I was just trying to make sure you were the right person."

Kylie held back the retort she really wanted to use. She took a breath and said, "I apologize. I'm on staff here, and I don't have any patients in the hospital right now. I assumed the page was a mistake."

"When your…friend is nine months pregnant?"

Leaning over the desk, Kylie fixed the woman with a steely stare and said, "Look. I'm sure you don't like working on Christmas Eve, but quit fucking with me. I apologized once, and that's all you're gonna get. Now, has my spouse been admitted or not?"

"Delivery room six," the woman sniffed, turning her back on the doctor.

Kylie went barreling down the hall, leaving Werner in her wake. She noticed his absence and then slowed down, saying, "I'm sorry, but I'm really worried about her."

"Go ahead, Kylie. I'll be there…eventually."

She smiled at him and started to run, bursting into the room rather wild-eyed. "What are you doing here?"

Blair looked up from the magazine she was reading. She was lying in bed, dressed in a blue hospital gown, an IV in her arm and the wires from a fetal heartbeat monitor sticking out from under the covers. "Oh, Mom and I were bored, so we thought we'd check in. She's in the next room. Thought she'd have an appendectomy."

Kylie didn't blink, and Blair could see that her partner wasn't processing information at her usual rate. Werner walked in, and Blair gave him a beaming smile. "Dad! Give me a hug!"

He went to her and wrapped her in his arms, holding on tight. "How's my girl?"

"Fine," she said. "I guess you'd both like some details?"

"That'd be good," Kylie said. "Real good."

"We went to the doctor, and my mucus plug came out while Monique was examining me." She looked at her father and saw that he had blanched noticeably. "Sorry, Dad, but this is kinda gross."

"Oh, I'm fine," he said, looking anything but.

"What happened then?" Kylie asked. "Losing your mucus plug isn't that big a deal. You can go for days without going into labor."

Blair shot her father a deadpan look and said, "Easy to say when you've never lost one." She turned back to her partner. "I know that's not a big deal, honey, but when I was leaving the office, I had to pee. I went back in and started to pee, but when I started thinking the toilet would overflow, I began to worry."

"Ooh…your water broke, huh?"

"Yeah. It took me a while to calm down and remind myself that I've only been peeing a couple of ounces at a time. This was more like a gallon!"

"That sounds a little high," Kylie said, giving her partner an indulgent smile, "but I can imagine it felt like a gallon."

"It felt like two," Blair said, sticking out her tongue. "I was under-exaggerating."

Eleanor walked into the room, carrying a cup of ice chips. "Werner!" she said. She shoved the cup in Kylie's direction and embraced her husband. "It feels like months since I've seen you."

"Longer," he replied, giving her a kiss and holding her in his arms for a long while.

"Have you told Kylie and your father about our adventure?" Eleanor asked her daughter.

"I was just at the point where my water broke."

"Oh, the best part's coming," Eleanor said. She took Werner by the hand and led him over to a sofa, sitting right next to him while he put his arm around her shoulders to wait for the rest of the story.

Blair continued, "I grabbed some paper towels and stuffed them into my underwear, and then I went out and found a nurse. I told her what had happened, and she had me go back into an examining room. I'd been 70 percent effaced and two centimeters dilated when Monique examined me, and now I was three centimeters—and only about twenty minutes had passed."

"Damn!" Kylie sat down on the edge of her partner's bed, her eyes wide with amazement. "Where are you now?"

"The last time a complete stranger stuck her hand up me, I was four centimeters."

Her eyes closed, and she grabbed Kylie's hand and groaned softly, her whole body shaking with pain. Her face started to turn red, and Kylie stroked her arm and said, "Breathe, baby. Breathe through the pain."

One eye shot open and gave Kylie a murderous look. The doctor shut her mouth and grimaced in pain as Blair's grip nearly broke her hand. After what seemed like a very long time, Blair collapsed onto her pillow, beads of sweat covering her face. "If you value your life, you'll find the guy with the epidural and drag his ass in here."

Kylie hopped up and did as directed, determined to find the anesthesiologist or do it herself. Werner and Eleanor got up and tended to Blair, with Werner wiping her face with a cool cloth and Eleanor feeding her some ice chips. "I'd kill for a glass of water," Blair said. "Any chance of your sneaking me a bottle when no one's looking?"

"No, not me," Eleanor said. "The nurses were very clear that I should only give you a few ice chips at a time."

"Sadists," Blair decided. "They're all sadists."

Kylie came back a few minutes later, looking a little harried. "I hate not being able to tell people what to do!" She sat down on the bed and let out a frustrated breath. "The nurse said she'd page the anesthesiologist." She crossed her arms over her chest and pouted a little. "This sucks."

"Ooh, my girl's not top gun here, is she?" Blair soothed, giving her partner a tickle.

Kylie's lower lip stuck out. "No. I don't like being a civilian."

The nurse came in and said to Eleanor and Werner, "I need to examine Blair again. It'll just take a moment."

Werner was out of the room before the nurse reached the bed with Eleanor following behind after blowing her daughter a kiss. "Let's see how you're doing," the nurse said, pulling the sheet down.

"She needs an epidural," Kylie said, her voice low and firm.

"She'll have it as soon as she needs it," the woman said, giving Kylie a smile. "Are you Blair's partner?"

"Yeah. And she needs it now. There's no reason for her to be in pain."

"I know it's hard to watch her suffer, but it'll all be over soon." She started to perform a quick examination, but before she finished, another strong contraction hit Blair. She tried to pant her way through it, but wasn't able to. She held her breath for a few seconds, her face turning purple, and then cried out loudly, her anguish hitting Kylie like a blow.

When the contraction was over, Kylie took the nurse by the arm and led her out of the room. She'd obviously moved away from the door because the only word Blair could hear was a loud, firm "Now!" A few seconds later, Kylie came back in, accompanied by Werner and Eleanor. She took out her phone and dialed a number, waiting just a moment before she said, "Where are you?" Blair watched her partner talk, amazed at how tense and irritable she was. "Where's the fucking anesthesiologist, Monique? You know that no one's gonna bring him in here if you don't okay it." Her lips were pursed while she listened to Monique's reply. Then she said, "I know you're busy, but we've been friends for fifteen years. I thought you cared about me enough to go out of your way to make sure Blair gets the best care possible." She nodded and then said, "Fine. See you when you get here." She slapped her phone closed and then turned and walked out of the room, leaving three people staring at her in surprise.

Blair was in the middle of another contraction when Kylie walked back into the room, and Eleanor started to move away from the bed so the doctor could hold Blair's hand, but Kylie patted the older woman on the back and stood at the foot of the bed, rubbing Blair's feet while she watched her body contort with pain.

When the contraction passed, she moved up to the head of the bed, surprised to see Werner and Eleanor depart without a word. She sat on the edge of the bed and fed her partner some ice chips. "Guess I scared 'em off, huh?"

Blair looked up at her and shook her head. "They know you're worried about me."

Kylie nodded. "I am. This is a lot harder than I thought it would be."

"Just what I was thinking," Blair said, giving her partner a pointed look.

Kylie stroked her partner's face. "Oh, baby, I'm not minimizing what you're going through. I'm so frustrated! They're treating you like everyone else!"

"I *am* like everyone else. It's all right." Blair held her partner's hand and then brought it to her mouth and kissed it. "They're treating me fine. Don't be so stressed."

"But you shouldn't have to be in pain at this point. Monique should have her ass here so she can give some orders!"

"It's hard for you to give orders and have the nurses ignore 'em, isn't it?"

The doctor nodded, looking a little embarrassed. "Guess I didn't realize how much I enjoy being in charge. I think my favorite words are 'Yes, Doctor' or 'Right away, Doctor.' It's driving me nuts to have the nurses pat me on the head and send me packing."

Monique walked in while Kylie was still talking, and she gave Blair a knowing smile. She approached Kylie from the back and put her hand on her shoulder. "Sorry I wasn't able to get away until now."

Kylie stood up and gave her old friend a hug. "Sorry I was an asshole to you on the phone."

"Oh, I'm used to the fact that you're an asshole, Shakes. That's why I love you."

Gently jabbing her friend in the kidney, Kylie kissed Monique on the cheek and said, "Take a look at Blair right now, or I'm gonna have a tantrum."

The obstetrician still had her coat on, but she dutifully dropped her bag and her coat on a chair, then washed her hands, and put on a pair of gloves. She examined Blair with Kylie leaning over her shoulder like a vulture. "Wow, you're opening up awfully fast," she said. "You're almost six centimeters."

"Ten's the magic number, right?"

"Yep. Most babies need ten centimeters to make an exit." She covered Blair up and squeezed her knee. "Ready for a nice epidural?"

"Way past ready. Hook me up."

"I'll send the anesthesiologist in as quickly as possible." Monique picked up her things and looked at Kylie. "Come with me while I put my scrubs on. Maybe the nurses will treat you better if they see me talking to you. They all *love* me," she added with a superior grin.

"Funny," Kylie said. She'd assumed her friend was kidding, but Monique twitched her head in the direction of the door, and Kylie patted Blair on the leg and followed her out. Werner and Eleanor were just a few feet away from the door, and Kylie motioned to them. "Werner and Eleanor Schneidhorst, this is Monique Jackson, Blair's obstetrician." The threesome shook hands, and Kylie added, "I've already apologized for being a jerk, and Monique's forgiven me." She put her arm around her friend's shoulders and said, "She's used to me."

"I need to get changed. We'll be back in a few minutes," Monique said to the older couple.

"Keep Blair company for a few minutes, will you?"

"Sure, honey," Eleanor said. "Is everything all right?"

"Oh, yeah. Monique's gonna try to increase my status by letting the nurses know I'm a real doctor."

"You're not a real doctor," her friend teased. "You're a surgeon."

"Whatever." Kylie took her by the arm and led her down the hall. As soon as Werner and Eleanor went into Blair's room, she stopped and grabbed Monique's shoulder. "What's wrong?"

Monique made a face and said, "I think the baby's too big for a vaginal delivery. Sorry, buddy, but I think we should do a C-section."

"What?" Kylie's voice was a little loud, and Monique held a finger over her lips to shush her. Kylie quieted down and asked, "How can that be? Today's just her due date."

"You know it's hard to tell exactly how big a baby will be. I knew it was large, but I couldn't tell how large until I got my hand in there. She's six centimeters, and the head is nowhere near crowning. I'll let you two make the call if you want to wait and see what develops, but I think we're wasting our time."

Kylie fixed her with a penetrating gaze and asked, "Are you sure? I don't want her to have major surgery if it isn't absolutely necessary."

"Neither do I, Kylie. And no, I'm not absolutely sure. She's opening up faster than I want her to. That wouldn't be a problem with a small baby, but with a big baby…"

"What? You're worried that she might have some internal tearing?"

"It's a possibility," Monique said. "The baby might be able to make it out, but I think it's risky."

"So's a C-section!" Kylie said, looking terrified.

"Shakes, you're a surgeon. You know the risks of a C-section aren't that great, given Blair's health."

"I know, I know," she said, grumbling. She looked up quickly and said, "She wants to nurse him. Will she be lucid enough to do that tonight?"

"Yeah, yeah. I think we can get by with just an epidural if we crank it up. We shouldn't have to give her general anesthesia."

"Okay." Kylie hugged her again and said, "I'll tell her. Call the surgeon." When she pulled away, she said, "This guy had better be great 'cause I'm gonna watch."

"Kylie, stay at Blair's head and keep out of the way. No one likes to work with a family member watching. Behave!"

"Can't promise that," Kylie said as she walked away. "If the surgeon screws up, I'm taking over."

She had to walk up and down the hall for a few minutes, but by the time she entered the room, Kylie thought she looked calm and collected. Her belief was shattered when Blair took one look at her and asked, "What's wrong?"

"Nothing. Nothing's *wrong*," Kylie said, emphasizing the word, "but our little guy isn't so little." She stroked Blair's belly and said, "You were right, honey. He is a very big baby, and Monique thinks there's a good chance you won't be able to deliver vaginally."

"Oh, fuck," Blair said. She let her head drop back onto the remarkably uncomfortable pillows and said, "C-section, huh?"

"Yeah, that's what Monique thinks we should do." Kylie sat on the bed and chafed her partner's hand. "If we want to, she said we can wait and see, but she doesn't think the odds are good."

"What do you think?"

"Monique's the expert. If she thinks this is the safest way, then I believe her."

"Do I have to be knocked out?"

"No. She wants to do an epidural and crank it up really high. You won't feel pain, but you'll feel some sensation. It's hard to describe, but I promise it won't hurt."

"Damn! I really didn't want to have a C-section."

"I didn't want for you to. Your recovery won't be as easy as it would be if you delivered vaginally."

"True, but I won't have stitches in my—" She looked at her father and said, "I won't say it, Dad. You don't have to put your fingers in your ears."

"That's true," Kylie said, laughing at the look on Werner's face. "Let's face it. Either way sucks, but you could have a lot of tearing with a big baby."

"You know, there isn't a woman in the world who wants to think of tearing in that particular place."

"There isn't a man who wants to, either," Werner volunteered.

Monique came back in, attired in her green scrubs. "What's the verdict?"

"I never thought I'd say this with Kylie anywhere near me, but go ahead and cut me open."

"I think it's best, Blair, and believe me, I wouldn't advise it if I didn't think it was necessary."

"I know that, Monique. I'm not happy about it, but we might as well do it now while I still have some energy." She grimaced, another contraction hitting her. It wasn't as bad as the previous one, but Kylie still reached out and grabbed her hand, letting Blair squeeze as hard as she wanted to.

When the contraction passed, Monique said, "I think we should get moving."

A doctor poked his head in while she was talking and asked, "Is now a good time?"

"Oh, sure. Come in, Jake. Blair, Kylie, this is Doctor Marston. He's got a nice, numbing epidural for you."

He shook hands with Blair and Kylie and then said hello to Blair's parents. "Does everyone want to stay?" he asked. "These can be a little tricky."

"Another word no one wants to hear from a doctor," Blair said. "Mom, Dad, why don't you go get a snack? I don't want you to hear me cursing if this doesn't go well."

"We've been hearing you curse since you were fifteen," Eleanor said. But she kissed her daughter on the cheek and said, "We'll be down in the cafeteria. I love you, honey."

Werner kissed his daughter and gave her a hug, and then the older couple departed, leaving Blair with three doctors. "Let's do it," she said.

Doctor Marston said, "Let me ask a nurse to assist me, and we'll be set."

"I'll do it," Kylie said, drawing a scowl from Monique and a startled look from Doctor Marston.

"I'm a surgeon," she explained to the man, "I really do know how to hold a prep tray."

"She was a resident long enough," Monique jibed. "If there's one thing she knows, it's how to hand an instrument to a doctor."

"Kylie," Blair said in a very calm voice, "you're my partner. Now, come over here and hold my hand. Doctor Marston doesn't want you breathing down his neck."

"All right," she said, "I just wanted to get going. You know, we might not see him for an hour if we let him out of here." She looked at the man and said, "No offense. I just know that you can get sidetracked."

"Especially on Christmas Eve when I'm the only anesthesiologist on the floor."

Kylie gave Monique a look, and her friend stood next to Doctor Marston. "I know how to hold a tray, too," she said, giving him a thin smile. "If Kylie gets her way, I'll be down in the cafeteria, flipping burgers."

"Blair doesn't eat burgers," Kylie sniffed. "Too greasy. A vegetable salad would be nice, though."

All of this semi-good-natured banter took Blair's mind off the procedure, and she hardly noticed when the doctor gave her a local anesthetic. "Is that it?" she asked. She was sitting on the edge of the bed, bent over as much as she could so her back was exposed.

"No, that was just to numb you up a bit," Doctor Marston said. He waited a few moments and then took an ice chip and put it on the spot. "Feel that?"

"No. Nothing."

"Okay, we're ready to go." He marked the spot and advised, "Don't move. I know it might be hard, especially if a contraction starts, but it's very important that you not move."

"Got it," Blair said, bracing herself for the worst. She held on to Kylie's arms, closed her eyes, and tried not to even breathe.

The pain was bad, but she knew it would only last a moment. She was pleased when the doctor patted her back and said, "All finished. I added a little morphine to get you through the C-section, so you'll feel a little fuzzy. I've taped the catheter down so you can lie on your side or your back. Your choice."

"Then—" She grasped her belly as a terrific contraction began, squeezing the air from her lungs. This was, by far, the worst one, and she let out a howl that made Kylie's skin crawl.

Kylie held on to her, barely noticing that Blair's fingernails were digging into her arm. "You're doing fine, sweetheart."

Suddenly, Blair let go, her voice full of surprise. "It's gone," she said. "It's kinda gone."

"Kinda?" Kylie asked.

"Yeah." Blair looked at her for a moment, struggling to explain the feeling. "It's still there, but it's dull…really dull."

Kylie let out a sigh, happy that her lover was getting some relief. She tenderly wiped Blair's brow and neck, but scowled when she started to shake.

"I'm so cold. Especially my feet."

"Damn it," Kylie said. "We don't have your suitcase or your pillows or anything!"

"I know," Blair said. "All those nights of packing and repacking it—all wasted. But why am I so cold?"

"Common reaction to the epidural." Kylie went down to her lover's feet, held them in her hands, and then tucked them into her armpits to warm them faster. "Hey, where's Marston?"

"He left during the contraction," Monique said. "We're pretty busy tonight."

Kylie forced herself to widen her focus and ask Monique, "Are your kids home?"

The obstetrician checked her watch. "Yeah. There's no school this week, so A.J. and Keith are both with Keith's nanny until Anthony gets home."

"Who's cooking Christmas Eve dinner? Your sister?"

"Yeah. My guys know to leave without me if I'm not home when they're hungry."

"Do you have any other patients in the hospital?"

"Unh-uh. I can finally focus all of my attention on you two."

"Why don't you go home?" Kylie said, surprising both Monique and Blair.

"Home? Now?" Monique asked.

"Yeah," Kylie said. "I don't mean to diminish your role, but what do you do during a C-section?"

"Well, I used to perform the surgery, but since I've given that up, I stand around and assist if the surgeon needs me, and then I read the Apgar score and make sure everything's all right with the baby."

"But there's a pediatrician on call if there's a problem, right?"

"Of course. Alice Lipskind is on call tonight. She's one of the best."

"Then go home. It's Christmas Eve, Monique. Spend it with your family."

The obstetrician walked over to Kylie and put her arm around her. "I don't say this very often, but you're part of my family, too."

Kylie gave her a watery smile and nodded. "I know." She looked at Blair and asked, "Would you feel better if Monique stayed?" She lowered her voice and said, "She won't have much to do."

Blair smiled at her partner and then held her hand out. Monique took it and gave her a squeeze. "Please go home. We'll be just fine. The only thing I'm worried about is Kylie giving the surgeon a hip check and taking over."

"I could tackle her if I'm there," Monique reminded Blair.

"I'm sure one of the nurses will do it if I ask nicely." She let her head drop back onto the pillow and said, "At this point, I'm starting not to care what happens. I feel very, very good."

"The epidural is obviously working," Monique said. She leaned over, kissed Blair on the forehead, and said, "Thanks for letting me take off. This is the first Christmas that Keith's really aware of. He'd hate it if his mommy weren't there."

"Go. Have fun. Drink some water for me," Blair said. "I miss water."

"I will," Monique said. "I'm sure Kylie will call when the baby's all settled, but I'll congratulate you now. What names do you have picked out?"

"Just one. Mackenzie Simon."

"Nice name," Monique said, giving her friend a gentle punch in the arm. "But shouldn't you have played it safe and picked one for a girl? I know! How about Mackenzie Monique?"

"Get going, wise guy," Kylie said. "I know you know what sex the baby is, and I don't want you to taunt us if we're wrong."

"Me? Taunt you?" Monique asked, looking as innocent as she was able.

"Scram, Jackson, and give all of the men in your life a kiss for me."

Monique hugged Kylie and whispered, "I love you. Take care of Blair and that sweet little baby boy...or girl." She pulled away and giggled, sparing one last wave as she left the room.

~

Blair was vaguely interested in the flurry of activity going on around her, but in the main, she was largely unconcerned. The epidural was working, and she felt a little distanced from the concerns of the world, almost as if she were observing rather than participating. But she was awake, and she was very glad for that. The thought of seeing her baby as soon as possible was incredibly important to her, and she was trying to ignore all of the details that the people around her were so concerned with.

They were in a brightly lit operating room, and she was actually grateful for the light, given that it provided some warmth. After the epidural had really kicked in, she'd begun to shiver constantly, and nothing Kylie did helped. A pair of blankets didn't make any difference, but the hot light helped a little. Kylie was right by her side, explaining in a soothing voice exactly what the anesthesiologist and the nurses were doing. Blair didn't pay a lot of attention to what her lover was saying, but hearing her soft, calm voice helped a lot. Someone was putting some sort of vinyl boots on her feet and pumping them up, but she was more interested in watching the IV bag that hung right in her field of vision. She didn't know what was in the bag, but it was somehow reassuring to have some life-giving fluid dripping into her veins.

She looked up at Kylie and asked in mid-sentence, "Do you love me?"

The doctor leaned over and gazed at her for a second. "More than I ever have," she said, her eyes starting to fill with tears.

"Don't cry, baby. We'll be fine."

"I know you will, but it kills me to see you on the operating table. You look so small and pale."

"You look cute in your scrubs," she said in a bit of a non sequitur. "Promise you won't try and help?"

"I promise. I might watch, but I won't say a word."

"Don't do anything, either, okay? It's not your words that'll get you into trouble. It's your scalpel."

"I'm not gloved up, honey. Even I wouldn't operate on you without gloves. I won't offer a critique, and I won't move a muscle. I'll be right here, talking to you the whole time."

"Remember, you promised."

"I'll remember."

Kylie saw the surgeon scrubbing up, and she said, "Be right back. I wanna say hello to the doc."

"Be nice."

Kylie met him at the door and said, "Hi, I'm Kylie Mackenzie—"

"Doctor Mackenzie," the young man said, "you probably don't remember me, but I assisted you on a couple of procedures during my residency. Steve Haddad."

"Oh, yeah, I do remember you. That was about four or five years ago, wasn't it?"

"Yeah. Four years. You've got a good memory."

"Well, Steve, you're about to do a C-section on my partner, Blair. I'll do my best to keep my mouth shut, but feel free to tell your nurse to stick a wad of cotton in my mouth if I can't control myself."

"Don't worry about it. I've done more C-sections than I can count. I'm sure everything will go fine. Monique told me she was leaving, so why don't you scrub up— just in case."

"Just in case of what?" she asked, looking at him with surprise.

"Doctor Mackenzie, nothing is gonna go wrong, but it's always nice to have two surgeons in the room. I'm sure I won't need help. It's just insurance."

"Okay," she said, "but you have to tell Blair this was your idea." She went into the scrub room and got ready, seeing that Steve was talking to Blair.

When she came back out, Kylie walked up to Blair and said to Steve, "Would you mind if I explained what was going on to Blair? I think she'd like it if I was talking to her the whole time."

"No, not at all. Whatever makes you both comfortable is fine with me."

"Okay, let's go get that baby."

Blair made some polite sign of acknowledgment, and then she tried to relax and concentrate on Kylie's voice. They washed Blair's belly with Betadine, and Kylie stood up to look at the outline of the baby one last time. She was sure she could see his knees sticking out, and she wished she'd been able to get Blair to allow her to take a picture of her belly in the last week. But the only time she would have been able to get one was when Blair was asleep, and she felt that would be an invasion of her partner's privacy.

Steve made the first incision, and to her amazement, Kylie felt her knees get a little weak. That hadn't happened to her since she'd had to open a cadaver for the first time, and she immediately sat down on the stool by Blair's head. She did her best to control her voice and quietly said, "He's starting to work now, honey. In just a few minutes, he'll be ready to lift the baby out."

"I feel a tugging," Blair said. "I don't like tugging."

"That's normal. Perfectly normal. You still have some sensation, but you won't feel pain."

"Promise?"

"Absolutely. If you feel any pain at all, nice Doctor Marston will add something more to the epidural. Don't worry a bit. Just think about holding our baby in a few minutes."

"A few minutes? Really?"

"Yeah. It won't take long."

"Doctor Mackenzie?"

Kylie's head snapped up when Steve called her name. "Yeah?"

"Would you like to help deliver your baby? The head and shoulders are out now."

Blair squeezed her hand and looked into her eyes. "Bring him to me, sweetheart."

Kylie wished she'd never met Steve before in her life. She was sure she would faint or vomit, but she couldn't refuse Blair's tender request. She managed to stand and shuffle over to slip in next to Steve, but as soon as she saw the baby, her anxiety left her completely. She was mesmerized by the sight of their child and couldn't wait to get her hands on him. She heard Steve say, "Just reach into the incision a little bit and grasp under the baby's arms. I'll take care of the umbilical cord."

She nodded and then put her hands around their child, amazed at the feel of the robust body. She gently lifted, blinking in surprise when he popped out like a shot, covered with blood and a small amount of vernix, but the most beautiful little boy she'd ever seen in her life. Steve took him from her when it became clear that she was transfixed and wasn't going to hand him over.

The nurse's voice snapped her back to attention. "Would you like to cut the umbilical cord?"

Kylie managed to nod and then took the instrument in her shaking hand and snipped. Her brain managed to make her say, "We want to bank the cord. We signed some forms about it. Can you make sure—"

"Of course. It'll all be taken care of."

"We wanted to help someone who needed stem cells," Kylie continued, her diction not as crisp as it usually was. "If everyone would bank their baby's—"

"Don't you want to tell Blair that you have a son?" Steve asked gently, placing a hand on her back.

She looked at him blankly for a moment, nodded, and then managed to make her way back to her partner and put her mouth right next to Blair's ear. "Mackenzie's here. He's here, baby." Suddenly, she was crying so hard that her tears were falling onto Blair's face.

"How does he look?" Blair asked, sounding calm and tired and a little distant.

"He's beautiful. Just beautiful. Lots of black hair and a big pair of shoulders. Those must be from all that swimming you two have been doing."

"Can I see him?"

Just then, the baby started to cry, letting out a wail that matched Blair's earlier ones. "He has a nice big voice, just like his mommy," Kylie said, still struggling with her emotions.

The nurse brought him to Blair, letting her get a good look at him. He had a healthy pink glow to his cheeks, and he looked adorable in the little red Christmas cap they'd put on his head to keep him warm. He was still crying, and his entire face was scrunched up with his displeasure.

"Hi, Mackenzie," Blair said softly. "I'm your mommy."

Now Kylie really lost it, crying more than Mackenzie was.

The nurse said, "We have to take him for a few minutes, but we'll bring him back as soon as we can."

"Okay. 'Sfine."

Steve had already begun the somewhat time-consuming job of suturing Blair, and by the time he had finished placing the last staple, the baby was back. Kylie stripped off her mask, gown, and then her bloody gloves and held him, rocking him in her arms while Blair gazed at her, a happy, but slightly vacant look in her eyes.

"Congratulations," Steve said. He'd taken off his surgical gear as well, and he shook Kylie's hand. "I'm very happy for you both."

"Thanks for letting me help," Kylie said. "I'll never forget that moment."

"My pleasure, Doctor Mackenzie. I'm very glad I was here today."

An orderly sidled up to Doctor Haddad and said, "I have to take you to the recovery room for a little while, Ms. Spencer."

Blair looked at him with utter confusion. Then her eyes traveled to Kylie, where they spent a moment trying to focus. "What's happening?"

Kylie stroked her partner's forehead, a little concerned that it felt warm and clammy. "They want to keep a close eye on you for a bit. You won't have to be there long."

"You'll come with me," Blair said, not a hint of a question in her voice.

Doctor Haddad gave Kylie a quick wave and gestured for the orderly to leave the couple alone for a moment. "I can't come with you, honey," Kylie said. "I have to stay with Mackenzie. But it'll just be a little while. Promise."

"You'll stay with Mackenzie?" Even as she spoke, Blair's lids started to droop.

"He won't leave my sight."

"Okay." Her eyes opened again, and her gaze locked on to Kylie. "Don't forget me."

Through her tears, Kylie managed, "I'll be thinking of you every second."

Trying to compose herself, she nodded to the orderly, and he wheeled Blair away. Helplessly, she watched her lover depart, shivering at the sight of her looking so small and pale and debilitated.

"Okay!" a nurse with a remarkably cheery voice said as she put her hands on Mackenzie and tried to take him from Kylie.

Instinctively, Kylie stuck an elbow out, making the woman gasp. "I'm just going to put him in a cart," she said, looking rather indignant. "You're not allowed to carry him."

"Hospitals," Kylie muttered, watching the nurse like a hawk. She was so close to the nurse that she stepped on her heel as they were walking down the hall, but she wasn't about to break her promise to Blair.

"We'll take him back to the labor room. He can meet his grandparents," the nurse said.

"No! I mean, no," Kylie said in a calmer tone. "I want Blair to be there."

The nurse gave her a brief, indulgent smile. "I can't just walk around until she's out of recovery. This is what we always do." Her steps hadn't faltered, and Kylie was on the verge of shouting, "I'm a fucking surgeon! Will someone listen to me?" But she collected herself and tried to accept the fact that her credentials meant nothing on the obstetrics floor.

She dashed around to the front of the cart, nearly having to run to keep up with the nurse's pace. "Look, can't we go to the room they're gonna put Blair in? This is a very big event in her life. I know she'll want to be there when Mackenzie meets his grandparents."

Making a sharp right, the nurse wheeled the cart right into the labor room. "Look who's here!" she announced. Werner and Eleanor leapt to their feet and crowded around the cart, leaving Kylie staring at her, dumbfounded. The nurse turned and walked past Kylie, patting her on the shoulder. "Have fun!"

⌐

An hour later, Blair was wheeled back into the labor room. Attention was diverted from Mackenzie for a few moments as everyone gathered by the head of her bed. "We're so proud of you," Eleanor said, sniffling. "You were so brave and calm through all of this."

Blair looked at her, but merely managed a vacant half-smile.

Werner took his daughter's hand and kissed it. "We love you so much, sweetheart. And Mackenzie is the most beautiful baby in the world!"

"Good," she said, closing her eyes. "That's good."

Kylie met Werner's worried gaze. "She'll be out of it for quite a while. They were pumping a lot of drugs into her, and they take a long time to clear. Don't expect her to be like herself for another twelve hours or so."

"But she's all right, isn't she?" he asked sharply.

"She's fine," Kylie said. "They wouldn't have released her from the recovery room if she wasn't responding exactly like she should." Just to be sure, she handed Mackenzie to Eleanor and took Blair's chart from the foot of the bed. Seconds later, she was sitting in a chair, reading every notation with scholarly detail.

Shortly after 10:00 p.m., Monique cleared her throat, startling Kylie out of her investigation. She got up and threw her arms around her, picking the slightly smaller woman up off her feet. "He's here! My big boy is here!"

"Damn, I hated to leave," Monique said. "But Keith's little heart would have been broken if I hadn't been there for Christmas Eve."

Kylie released her. "Hey, I wanted you to go. You would have just stood around and watched me cry if you'd been there. But now you can check my boy out and earn your fee."

Monique took the baby in her arms and smiled so widely Kylie could almost see her molars. "Mind if I take a closer look?"

"Be my guest. Blair's out of it, so I guess I'm in charge."

Monique put the baby in his bassinet and took off his blanket and his diaper. "How were his scores?"

"Good. Very good for a C-section. I've been reading his chart while Eleanor and Werner hold him."

"He looks just great," Monique said. "I'm amazed at how big he is, though. What is he? About nine pounds?"

"Just under. Eight pounds, ten ounces. Twenty inches long."

"Boy, that's a big baby for Blair to carry. She never could have delivered vaginally." She looked at Kylie and said, "I'm sorry I didn't have a better idea how big he was. I could have prepared Blair better for a C-section."

"Don't worry about it. It was nice that she didn't have to worry in advance. Everything worked out just fine."

Monique wrapped the baby back up and handed him to Kylie. He started to cry, and she jiggled him in her arms, trying to soothe him. Monique was reading Blair's chart, nodding to herself as she did so, when the new mother started to stir. "Damn," Blair grumbled, "I feel like someone cut a baby right out of me."

"How ya doin'?" Monique asked. "There's a little guy here who sounds like he's hungry. Are you up to giving him a little snack?"

"I have a feeling that's gonna involve some massive pain, but I might as well get used to it, huh?"

"It shouldn't be so bad," Monique said. She showed Blair the button attached to her IV. "You have a little morphine in here, and you can control how much of it is added to your drip. So, don't be shy. If you're in pain, you can take the edge off."

"I'm not shy—at all."

"Let me call the lactation nurse. She'll help you get comfortable."

Eleanor walked over to the bed and said, "I think we'll leave you three alone now. You don't want us here while you're trying to feed the baby for the first time."

"You can stay, Mom. You'll see this a lot."

"I know, honey, and I want to see you feed your child, but not tonight. Tonight, you and Kylie should be alone with him."

"All right. Give me a kiss."

Eleanor kissed her and gave her a gentle hug. "I'm so excited about little Mackenzie. He's such a beautiful boy."

"Thanks, Mom," Blair said, now looking and sounding a little more like herself.

Werner started to cry again and wasn't able to say much more than "I love you" to his daughter.

The couple left just as Monique came back in with a cheery-looking nurse. "Blair, Kylie, this is Ellen. She's going to help you feed Mackenzie."

"Where's this Christmas baby who wants his dinner?" Ellen asked.

"Maybe we should have named him Nick," Blair said. Kylie smiled at her, seeing more and more of her normal personality emerging.

"Don't remind me of Nick," Kylie said. "I have about thirty people I have to call tonight, and I haven't even started."

Monique said, "Let me call our mutual friends, buddy. That'll knock a couple off your list."

"Thanks. That'll help."

"You can make some calls while I talk to the nurse," Blair said to Kylie.

"Are you nuts? I don't know a lot about this; I have a lot to learn."

Monique patted Kylie on the back. "I'm gonna take off. I'll make some calls on the way home. I'm sure this'll be a nice Christmas gift to everyone who loves you, Shakes. It sure was for me."

Kylie hugged her again and kissed her on the cheek. "Thanks for everything, Nique. And give my love to the boys."

"Will do. I'll check in with you tomorrow. Try to get some rest, you two. I know it won't be easy, but you'll be happier tomorrow if you can."

"We'll try," Kylie said. "See you tomorrow."

Ellen was busily getting things in order, and when the room was quiet, she helped Blair get into a good position. Propping pillows up created a decent platform on which to rest Mackenzie, and Kylie promised to go home before the next feeding and get the nursing pillow they'd bought. "Now, the most important thing is to relax. He wants to eat, and you want to feed him, but sometimes, one or both of you gets frustrated." She pulled Blair's gown aside and said, "Your nipples are a very nice size; he shouldn't have any trouble latching on."

She picked Mackenzie up and put her little finger into his mouth, smiling when he immediately started sucking. "He knows what to do. That's half the battle." Ellen guided the baby into position and said, "He needs to get your entire nipple into his mouth. Even the areola has to get in there for the tip of the nipple to touch the roof of his mouth. It's going to feel very strange at first, but just relax, and things will work out."

"Does he have an off switch?" Blair asked, her head starting to throb from the incessant crying.

"Once he latches on to your nipple, he'll be a happy little boy," Ellen said. "Guaranteed."

Ellen put the baby in a football-style hold, keeping him away from Blair's incision. "Now grasp your breast and tickle his lower lip with your nipple."

Blair tried to get Mackenzie to open his mouth, but he was so busy screaming that he didn't get the idea. Kylie was dancing around behind the nurse, acting as if she wanted to step in and help, but there wasn't a thing she could do. This was between Mackenzie and Blair, and they would have to learn to bond—on their own.

Ellen repositioned Mackenzie a few times, and he finally opened his mouth, but when he latched on, Blair's eyes popped open, and she gasped, "Jesus! Is it supposed to hurt this much?"

"No, no, it shouldn't be painful if he's latched on properly." She took her finger and broke the suction, and then Blair tried again. It took many attempts, and Kylie was about to jump out of her skin, but the baby finally found his way. Blair wasn't in pain, but it wasn't the most pleasant experience of her life, either. Having the baby so intimately attached to her, however, made up for the discomfort.

He started to suckle, but it was clear he wasn't swallowing. "Why isn't he swallowing?" Kylie asked.

"It'll take the colostrum a few seconds to let down," the nurse said. "He has to suckle for a little while to make it start to flow."

Blair looked up at Kylie and said, "You have no idea how weird this feels." She glanced at her IV and said, "Can you bump me up a little bit, honey? I'm starting to feel pretty bad. Sitting up like this sucks."

Kylie adjusted the drip and sat on the edge of the bed, watching her partner feed their child. Mackenzie started to swallow, and Kylie could see his entire jaw working to satisfy his hunger. She had an absolutely lovesick expression on her face, and Ellen started to walk away. "I'll come back in a few minutes and help you switch to the other breast. Enjoy," she said, smiling at the new family.

"My God," Kylie said when the nurse had left. "I've never been so awestruck. This is such a miracle."

"I'm still getting used to this," Blair admitted. "This is a lot to process in one day."

"You just take your time. You've been through an awful lot today. Most people don't start nursing a baby after major abdominal surgery. They tend to lie in bed and moan."

"That sounds good right about now. But someone's very hungry."

"It's so amazing," Kylie said. "A few hours ago, he was floating in amniotic fluid. Now he knows that he's supposed to latch on to your breast and suck for all he's worth. How in the hell does he know that?"

"Instinct, I guess. The whole thing would have stopped with Adam and Eve if Cain and Abel didn't know how to suck."

"Mmm…good point. Mackenzie sure has a good instinct."

"I think he takes after you," Blair said, giving her partner a loving smile. "You know how you like to get as much of my breast into your mouth as you can? He's the same way. Like mother, like son."

"Yeah, but I never get a meal while I do it."

"Don't count on one, either," Blair said, giving her a smirk. "The thought of having sex again is about as appealing as a root canal."

"You'll get the urge again. And we'll both be so tired for a while that neither of us will want to make love. Don't worry about it. Things will all work out."

Blair wiggled her finger, urging Kylie to come close. "Am I the worst mother in the world?" she asked quietly. "He seems like a stranger who's eating my breast."

Kylie smiled at her, giving her one of her high-wattage grins. "He *is* a stranger. The reality of Mackenzie is a lot different from the little guy we dreamed about. But don't worry. You'll fall in love with him in a few days. I'm sure of it."

"Promise?" she asked, her voice a little tremulous.

"Cross my heart. You're gonna love him with all your heart."

"That can't happen. You've got all my heart. You're gonna have to give some of it to Mackenzie."

"I'll be happy to share. Your heart's big enough to keep us both feeling very, very well loved."

⌐

Every time Blair woke during that long first night, Kylie was sitting in a chair, one hand on the bassinet that held Mackenzie, the other resting somewhere on Blair's body. There was something so comforting about having her lover so close—even though she was clearly asleep at several points—that Blair was able to reassure herself that the pain was temporary and they'd all soon be home.

When Mackenzie's crying woke her sometime during the night, she reached out and automatically felt Kylie's hand grasp her own. She opened her eyes and saw the sweetest smile she'd ever seen on Kylie's face. The doctor was holding little Mackenzie like a football in one arm, his tiny body wrapped snugly, and with her other hand, she stroked Blair, gently trying to rouse her. "Our guy's hungry. He says you're the only one who can help."

"He's lying," Blair mumbled. "There are dozens of women around here who could do it. Bitches."

"Nice to know you haven't lost your sense of humor." She gave Blair an empathetic look and said, "I know it's uncomfortable. I really do."

"You know, I hate the word uncomfortable. You guys use it for everything from a rash to third-degree burns. You really ought to come up with a list of words to use to show you have some idea of how this really feels."

"Uhm, agonizing?" Kylie said, trying to make her partner smile.

"That was labor." She pushed the button on the bed, getting into a more upright position. "Keep trying."

Kylie pulled her gown aside and then helped her get the baby into position. He didn't get the idea right away, and Kylie had to force his mouth open several times until he was properly latched on. After the second time, she silently prayed that Blair would curb her colorful cursing before Mackenzie learned to vocalize. She was very glad they had a private room as well, knowing that many new mothers might not appreciate Blair's frank critique of how it felt to have the baby latch on improperly. Finally, he managed to open his mouth wide enough, and the nipple was seated correctly. Kylie relaxed and sank back into her chair, very content to watch her child nurse.

Blair was obviously very tired, but she relaxed as well, and soon, she started to stroke his dark head, singing softly while he suckled. Kylie watched the pair and felt that her heart might actually burst with love. She started to cry for the umpteenth time that night, but this time, she didn't care. Only Blair saw her, and she had no secrets from this woman. They'd gone through an experience that had revealed depths and layers of fear and pain and joy, and Kylie was determined never to hide any part of her self from her partner again.

At 8:00 a.m., they were up feeding the baby again. Both women looked much the worse for wear, but they were in relatively good spirits. It was Christmas morning, and they'd both received a wonderful present—who was eating as if he'd been hungry for nine months.

Blair was ready to switch him to her other breast, and Kylie jumped up to help. She gently removed the baby, cooed to him while she turned him, and then helped him to latch on again. He did well this time, and Blair only flinched a little when he started to suck. Kylie covered her up, smoothing her gown in place, and then sat down and tickled Mackenzie's feet through the thin blanket.

At the sound of sniffling, both women looked up to find Sadie standing in the doorway, crying her eyes out.

Kylie blinked, trying to get her mind to work. She knew it was early, far too early for visitors, but the woman standing in the doorway was undoubtedly Sadie, dressed in a sedate, blue suit with a green and red print scarf around her neck.

"I'm sorry I'm here so early," she said, "but I haven't slept a wink all night!"

"But Sadie," Kylie said, stunned, "visiting hours don't start for…hours!"

"I know. I know," she said, edging closer to the bed, "but I had to see him! If you look like you know where you're going, most of the nurses don't get in your way."

"Most?" Kylie asked, already afraid for her reputation.

"Oh, one of them tried to stop me, so I waited in the stairwell until she left her station."

Kylie sighed, hoping no one would associate her with Sadie. She snuck a look at Blair, who looked strangely pleased to see her mother-in-law. "Come meet your grandson," the new mother said.

Sadie practically leapt for the child, and when she reached the side of the bed, she immediately put her hands on him, touching him everywhere through the thin blanket. "He's so beautiful," she cried, tears streaming down her face. "Oh, Blair, I'm so happy!"

"So am I," Blair said, a little of the sparkle coming back into her eyes. "My mom and dad were with us when he was born, but other than them, you're the first person to meet him." Her smile grew, and she added, "That's how it should be. Grandparents come first."

Sadie was still crying, and it took her a moment to get her thoughts together. "How are you feeling, honey? Your mother told me you had to have a Cesarean."

"I don't think anyone feels great after delivery. One thing or another's gonna hurt."

"I'll come over and help you with anything. Anything at all," she emphasized. "I can do laundry or cook or have my girl come over and clean." She shot a look at Kylie and said, "My cleaning days are over."

"I'd love to have you come over and make dinner for us," Blair said. "You know I think you're the best cook around."

"Your mother said they're leaving in just a few days," Sadie said. "I'll wait until they leave. I know they'll want to have some time alone with you."

Blair nodded and then gestured to Kylie. "I think he's finished. Will you help me?"

Kylie took the groggy baby from Blair's breast and wiped his mouth. Sadie was fidgeting, and the doctor took pity on her and said, "Let me get something for your shoulder, and you can burp him, Sadie."

"I can?" She looked as if she'd faint with pleasure, and the younger women were both touched by her excitement. Kylie put a diaper over Sadie's shoulder, and she tentatively took the child into her arms. By the time she had him positioned, she was crying so hard that Kylie was afraid she'd have to put her into a chair, but the emotional grandmother eventually quieted down and started kissing Mackenzie's dark head of hair. "He looks so much like David did when he was a baby."

Blair was prepared for the comment, especially since the baby's skin was a nice olive tone and he had a full head of black hair. She'd reminded herself that the donor had most of David's physical traits, but those reminders hadn't seemed to help. She cried along with her mother-in-law, thinking of the things she'd lost to gain Kylie and Mackenzie. She wouldn't trade for the world, but a loss was a loss, and a part of her still mourned David.

Sadie reached out and touched her daughter-in-law. "David forbade me to see the baby," she said. "He made me promise not to see you, either." She sniffed a few times and then said, "He's like his father. As hardheaded as Mt. Rushmore. But if he thinks he can tell me what to do, he hasn't learned much."

"I'm glad you're here," Blair said. She took her mother-in-law's hand and squeezed it. "I'm very glad."

Sadie looked at Blair and then turned to gaze at Kylie for a moment. "David told me about his run-in with you."

Kylie's eyes widened, and she desperately tried to think of a way to put a good spin on her string of lies.

"I'm not sure how much of what he said was true," Sadie said, her eyes narrowing, "but I don't blame you a bit." Her scowl turned into a jolly grin, and she added, "You didn't really tell him you needed him to baby-sit so that you and Blair could have sex, did you?"

"Kylie!" Blair's shout was so loud that Mackenzie's eyes opened and he shook all over.

Her face turning red, Kylie looked from one woman to the other. "I didn't really…precisely say that. I just…hinted…kinda strongly…"

"Why did you do that?" Blair demanded. "That's disgusting!"

"Disgusting?"

Making a dismissive gesture, Blair said, "Sex isn't disgusting, but telling him that is!"

Sadie moved closer and touched Blair's leg. "Don't worry about it. Kylie knew how to make him mad, and that's just what he deserved. She's one smart cookie, Blair."

"I'll give her a cookie," Blair mumbled. "I let you off the hook before, but you're gonna tell me everything that happened with him. I don't want any more surprises."

"I made up a bunch of lies," Kylie said. "I made it sound like we wanted him involved so he'd have to pay for half of Mackenzie's outrageously expensive upbringing."

"I don't want his money!" Blair huffed.

"I know that." Kylie perched on the edge of the bed. "But David didn't. I wanted him to believe that we wanted to use him when it was convenient for us. Then I told him that he could waive his rights in favor of me. It was…disgustingly coercive," she admitted, "but I don't feel guilty about it. After all the pain he's caused you, he doesn't deserve to be treated fairly."

Sadie stood behind Kylie and put a hand on her shoulder. "You know I don't approve of homosexuality, but you're the right people to raise this baby. David's proven he's not mature enough to be married, much less have a child. He's got a lot of growing up to do to get to that point, and it's not fair to the baby to make him into an experiment."

Kylie cleared her throat and said, "Thank you. It feels wonderful to have your support."

"You have it," she said decisively. "And if David tries to get in the way, I'll do anything in my power to set him straight. He should learn how to be a man, then how to be a husband, and then how to be a father." She raised and lowered her shoulders dramatically, gesturing defeat. "I don't think he's gonna get to step three." She pulled Mackenzie down so his face was inches from hers. "I think you're going to be my only grandchild, sweet boy, and you're all I'll ever need."

Blair reached out and took Kylie's hand, saying, "You did the right thing. And you thought on your feet. Sorry I was so bitchy about the whole thing."

"'Sokay. I should have told you everything. I was being too protective."

Sadie looked at the pair and said, "I don't understand the sex thing, but you two are gonna be a very happy couple. You're a good match."

"Not a doubt," Blair said, gazing into Kylie's eyes with a look that stopped just short of worship.

⟳

Two days later, Mackenzie and his entourage arrived home. The dogs were wild to see Blair again, and as soon as they crossed the threshold, she said, "Kylie, help me sit down. They've missed me."

It took a moment, especially since the dogs were jumping and whining, but Kylie successfully lowered Blair to a chair. The dogs' frantic cries woke Mackenzie, who started to cry, and Werner looked to Blair for direction.

Blair was trying to pet the dogs while keeping them away from her incision, but she managed to say, "Lower the carrier a little, Dad. I want the dogs to see him."

The dogs were completely puzzled. Werner lowered the baby carrier enough to let Nicky and Nora each take a look and a sniff, but they weren't at all sure what they were smelling.

Kylie and Blair had bought a CD of a baby crying, and they'd been playing it for a few minutes a few times a day in the weeks leading up to the birth. They'd also put some baby powder on the mattress of the crib, trying to make the room smell like it would when Mackenzie got home. But having the real thing in the house was very different from hearing a CD.

They backed up against Blair as they tentatively sniffed. They slowly got more interested as Kylie stroked their backs while keeping them away from Blair's belly. The doctor spoke to them softly. "This is Mackenzie, guys. He's gonna be making a lot of noise for…ever," she said, trying to be realistic. "He's gonna upset a lot of our routines, but we'll all get used to him in time."

"It's okay, babies," Blair said, also petting the pups. "His voice is kinda grating, but yours can be, too. One day, you'll like him."

They looked at her with suspicion. Then Werner lifted the carrier and took the baby into his room, Eleanor at his side. "I guess I'd better go feed him," Blair said. "He's a little overdue for lunch."

"He can cry for a minute," Kylie said. "Let's go get you into some comfortable clothes. I bought you a couple of big flannel nightshirts. They'll keep you warm and won't touch anything that's sore."

"Have I told you I love you today? 'Cause I sure do."

"I know it even when you don't tell me. That's the fun part of being in a relationship."

<hr />

At three in the morning, Kylie woke as Mackenzie started to cry. She held him in her arms and jiggled him a little, trying to get him to calm down before she handed him to Blair. The dogs hopped off the bed and left the room, deciding their sleep was more important than this troublesome new member of the family.

Knowing that only a meal would calm him, Kylie walked to the bed and sat on the edge, gently stroking her partner's frowning face. With her eyes closed, Blair said, "I don't like to get up in the middle of the night. I wouldn't like it if I had to answer the door to accept a gift at this hour. Imagine how much less I like it when I'm greeted by a screaming baby who wants to gnaw on my tender nipples."

"I'm sorry, honey. I wish I could help, but my nipples aren't as effective as yours."

"Oh, I'm just whining. I'm sure I wouldn't feel this way if the incision didn't hurt so damned much. It's hard to find a comfortable way to hold him, and my neck and arms are almost as sore as my nipples."

"Does the nursing pillow help?"

"A little. Will you give it to me?"

Kylie laid the baby on the bed and then helped Blair sit up. She got the pillow in place and unbuttoned Blair's nightshirt. When she handed Mackenzie over, he started to suck lustily, his cries dying out as soon as the milk hit his palate. "Our boy has a good appetite." Kylie gazed at her partner with loving eyes. She sat back down on the bed, stroking Mackenzie's back while he fed. "I love to watch you nurse," she said, her voice low and reverent. "It's so incredibly beautiful."

Blair smiled back at her, but Kylie could see the wistfulness in her eyes.

"You'll get used to this, Blair. I promise you will. You had major surgery just three days ago. No one feels well after that."

"But you seem so close to him already. You're really bonded, aren't you?"

"Yeah," Kylie said softly. "He feels like he's a part of me. You're the only person I feel closer to, and I've only known him for three days. It amazes me."

"You don't think I'm a bad mom?" Blair asked on her verge of tears.

"Absolutely not! It's different for me. I feel fine, and I'm not flooded with hormones. I also don't have to get used to another human using me as a food-delivery system. This is a lot of change for all of us, but most of all for you. I still guarantee you'll fall in love with our little guy, and I guarantee it'll be soon. You're not feeling depressed over this, are you?"

"No...not depressed, but I'm a little down over it. I feel really happy when I see you with him or when my parents hold him. I love all of you, and I see how much you love him. So, I get it, but I get it through you. It makes me cry every time I see my father hold him. He gets tears in his eyes every single time, honey. It's so touching." She started to cry just thinking about it, and Kylie swiped the tears away with her finger.

"You'll feel exactly like that. As soon as your body starts to adjust, your emotions will adjust, too. It's a big secret, and most women won't even admit this, but it takes a while for most of them to fall in love with their babies."

"Do you know that? Or are you just telling me that?"

Kylie smiled at her, cupping her cheek with her hand and looking deeply into her eyes. "I *know* that. I'm not making things up to make you feel better...although I would."

"I know that. I've always gotta double-check before I believe you."

"Well, I'm telling the truth. It takes most women a while to get comfortable being pregnant, too, but you were crazy about the baby from the minute you found out. Everyone is different. But you'll get there. I promise."

"Okay. I'll believe you," Blair said, smiling a little. "But right now, I'm about as happy as the dogs are."

"Those little brats have nothing to complain about," Kylie teased. "They don't have to feed him or change his diaper or anything! They're just pissed because they have to share us."

"We need to spend extra time with them so they don't feel left out."

"I'll carry the baby around, and you can spend time smothering the dogs with affection. And when my mom gets here, she can watch the baby, and I'll watch you. How does that sound?"

"Divine. I love being watched by you."

"And there's no one I'd rather watch, so we're in good shape."

⌐

After a week of lavishing Blair and Mackenzie with attention and love, Werner and Eleanor prepared to leave. They weren't nearly ready to go, and Blair had dropped a few not-so-subtle hints about their taking another week of vacation, but they both had demanding jobs to return to. So, after a tear-filled goodbye and enough pictures to fill Werner's new digital camera, Kylie drove them to the airport, leaving Blair and Mackenzie alone. There had been a short argument about the plans, but Blair refused all of Kylie's suggestions about having friends drop by during her absence. Blair knew a thinly disguised babysitter when she saw one, and she wasn't about to admit that she was slightly terrified to be alone with her own baby.

She and Mackenzie waved goodbye from the driveway and then went back into the house. "Well, Bruin, it's just you and me now." They'd taken to referring to the sturdy baby after the UCLA mascot. Kylie assured Blair that the dark hair on his forehead and back would fall off in a very short time, but Blair had her doubts.

They went into the den, and she put him in the wheeled bassinet that Kylie had adjusted so that Blair didn't have to bend to put him down. Her incision was very tender, and it had begun to itch, but Kylie was watching it like a twenty-four-hour intensive care nurse, so Blair was confident it would heal nicely.

As always, it took her a few moments to lower herself into a seat. She'd never realized how vital a person's abdominal muscles were during the sitting and standing processes, but she swore she'd never take them for granted again.

She'd nursed Mackenzie not long before her parents left, so he was full and content. Usually, he slept right after a meal, but he seemed quite alert today, probably because of the excitement of having the Schneidhorsts depart. "What's up, little guy?" She pulled the bassinet close and looked at him, and for the first time, he seemed to look back at her. There was a moment, just an instant, of true connection, person to person, and she blinked in surprise. Now he was looking around the room with his usual "where am I, who am I" expression, but she was intrigued and wanted to see if she could get him to look at her again.

She picked him up and put him on her lap. Kylie had come to the rescue in this department, too, having purchased a footstool, which let Blair elevate her knees enough to provide a nice angle. When he was fussy, the baby liked to lie across Blair's legs, and having her knees elevated made her feel as if he couldn't roll off—even though he didn't have the ability to roll.

"What's going on in that little head?" He looked everywhere but at her, so she decided to spend a little time investigating him. Kylie had gone over him with a magnifying glass, but Blair had spent most of her quality time with the infant nursing, rather than exploring. There had always been someone around, and she felt a little silly looking at her son as if he were a science experiment. But in a way, he was, so she took her time to check out her little creation.

She removed the thin, snug blanket in which they'd wrapped him. He loved to be all snuggled up in his little cocoon, and they'd reasoned it felt more like the womb to have his arms and legs close to his body. But he also responded when they rubbed him, and she decided a little massage was in order. They hadn't given him a full bath, partially because his umbilical cord hadn't fallen off yet. When he'd come home, he still had a little vernix in his skin folds, and Kylie had rubbed this into his skin. She'd read some research that maintained a baby's skin wouldn't peel off as easily if he was allowed to retain the skin's natural moisturizer. Privately, Blair thought her lover was being a little silly to think that rubbing in something that looked like mashed cottage cheese would help his skin, but when Kylie had a scientifically based idea, she was hard to dissuade.

Blair ran her fingertips up and down his legs, and they stretched out and shook for a second. His skin was unbelievably soft and smooth, and she found that stroking his little legs was very calming. She left his diaper on, having nearly broken her stitches laughing when her father got a very unwelcome sprinkling while changing his diaper for the first time.

Even though he was diapered, there was still a lot of skin to caress, and she let herself indulge in it. After rubbing him all over his chest and arms, she turned him over and touched his furry little back. "Who's my cubby bear? I guess we should have made sure the sperm donor was a human, huh? I wonder if the census has a box for half-ursine/half-human. Bi-racial is common, but bi-species might be a new one, Bruin."

The skin on his back was still as soft as the front, even with the furry covering. Actually, the downy hair made it a little softer, and she found that she really liked stroking his back with the flat of her hand. Mackenzie liked it, too, and he kept sticking out his arms and legs and shivering, a sign of pleasure she'd learned to distinguish from his "I'm cold" shivering.

She put him on his back again and played with his hands and feet, pleased that they were pink and healthy looking. At first, they'd been a dull grayish blue because his circulatory system wasn't in full swing, but now he looked healthy and vigorous from head to toe.

Though she hadn't been happy about having the Cesarean, Mackenzie had benefited by having a nicely shaped head. She'd been worried about his head becoming squished in the birth canal, but he'd come out looking about like he looked now. She was also pleased that she didn't have any stitches in her private parts, especially after having heard of women who'd had stitches in places that no one in her right mind would want. Of course, having a several-inch-long incision across the top of your pubic bone was no day at the beach, either, but she thought that being able to sit comfortably was a pretty good tradeoff.

She tried to make eye contact with Mackenzie again, even though she knew he could only see rough shapes at this point. "Mackenzie, Mackenzie, look at me, sweet boy. I'm your mommy. Yes, that's right. I'm the one who's gonna pay your therapy bills."

His head shifted around, and she felt as if he might actually be trying to track her voice, so she kept talking. "Here I am, sweetheart. That's a good boy; look up at me." He followed orders and seemed to gaze at her mouth, and then he locked on to her eyes for another second. She felt her heart start to pound, and before she was aware of it, tears were rolling down her cheeks. "I'm your mommy, Mackenzie. I'm your mommy." She was filled with such joy, such love, that she felt a little lightheaded. She'd never experienced such an overpowering depth of feeling, and at that moment, she had to have her baby close to her. She picked him up and cuddled him, ignoring the pain when his foot pressed against her incision.

Blair kissed his cheeks, his forehead, and his soft little chin. She nibbled on his ears and kissed the back of his neck, rubbing her nose between his shoulder blades. She couldn't get enough of his scent or the incredible softness of his skin. "You're my baby," she said again and again, filled to overflowing with joy. "You're my baby."

⸺

Kylie came home nearly an hour later, surprised to find Blair nursing. "At it again, huh? He's ahead of schedule today."

Blair looked at her and smiled one the most pleasure-filled smiles Kylie had ever seen. "No, he's not. I just couldn't wait."

With a small frown counterbalanced by a puzzled smile, Kylie sat next to her and put a hand on her partner's thigh. "What does that mean?"

"I'm falling in love," Blair said with a fresh round of tears to underscore her words.

Kylie gazed at her for a second and, for the first time, felt a twinge of jealousy. Normally, she would have ignored it, but today, she said, "I knew it would happen, but I didn't realize I'd be jealous when it did."

"Jealous?"

"Yeah." She leaned over and kissed her partner, lingering for a moment to show how much she loved the mere taste of her lips. "I wish I could feel what it's like to have that hormonal bond. It must be awesome."

Blair nodded and then leaned her head on her lover's shoulder. "It *is* awesome. When it hit me, I was minutes from eating the poor thing alive. I couldn't get enough of him."

Kylie slipped an arm around her partner, but didn't pull her close, always being careful of her incision. "I'm so glad you're starting to feel it. It'll get stronger and stronger."

"Uhm, I think it's plenty right now," Blair said. "I don't think I want it to be any stronger. Any more might stop my heart."

"Sorry, buddy. This is another one of those all-in kinda things. You're not gonna be able to hold back."

Blair let her head roll around while making a gurgling sound. "Whatever happened to having a nice, safe compartment to keep love in, huh? You know, control is underrated."

Kylie leaned in close and started to kiss Blair's neck, placing gentle, soft caresses all up and down it. She continued to move around, finally stopping by Blair's ear. "No chance. Mackenzie and I both love you with every bit of our hearts and souls. You've gotta do the same."

Blair sighed, playfully dramatizing the sound. "You two are so demanding. Love me, love me, love me! He wants to attach himself to my breast and…wait a minute…that's what you wanna do, too. You two are in some kinda conspiracy!"

"It's true," Kylie said, nuzzling against Blair's neck just like Mackenzie was nuzzling against her breast. "We've conspired to smother you with love, and there's nothing you can do about it."

Blair turned her head and kissed her partner, sucking the doctor's lower lip into her mouth and nibbling. She turned up the intensity until Kylie was moaning softly. "Then I guess I'd better enjoy it," she whispered, moving to a pink ear. "Thank God I enjoy it enough for all three of us."

"No, I do," Kylie whispered back, taking a healthy bit of Blair's skin into her mouth.

Blair leaned back and looked at the desire-filled face gazing at her. "I love you, Kylie, and I love our baby, too."

Kylie gave her a blazingly brilliant smile and said, "I told you your heart was big enough to love both of us."

"It is," Blair agreed, smiling back at Kylie. "Now that you've shown me how to love, it's the easiest thing in the world. Of course, it might help that I have the most wonderful lover in the entire universe."

"You know, cosmologists have discovered what might be an infinite supply of universes," Kylie said. "That used to be a great compliment, but now…"

Blair didn't say a word. She wrapped her free hand around Kylie's neck and pulled her close for a blisteringly hot kiss.

The doctor uncrossed her eyes and looked at her lover with a glazed expression. "On second thought, that's good enough for me. But I think you're the most wonderful lover in the entire universe."

Nicky and Nora, who had been sitting on the floor, looked at each other and rolled their big brown eyes. They'd seen this display many times before, and it had gotten old. The pair walked out the back door and lay by the pool, glad to feel the sun on their russet-colored coats. The dogs stretched out on the concrete, warming their bellies, while they dreamed up plans to teach the new puppy how to bark properly.

Chapter Fourteen

*D*orothy Mackenzie was in the middle of packing her suitcase when Kylie walked into the guestroom, carrying Mackenzie. "You're going to spoil that baby," Dorothy said, her expression showing that she wasn't entirely teasing.

Kylie sat on the bed and then put the baby next to her. "How do you spoil a baby?" Dorothy had been making very subtle comments all week about the way Kylie and Blair were treating the baby, and even though she didn't really want to have this discussion, Kylie thought this was a good time to get it out of the way.

Slightly flustered, Dorothy said, "You spoil him by giving him everything he wants."

"But all he wants is to be fed and changed and moved. He's not asking for anything out of the ordinary. He hasn't demanded a new teddy bear or anything."

Eyebrows narrowing, Dorothy said, "I know you'll do things your way, but I have some pretty hard-learned experience in this area. He'll run you ragged if you pick him up every time he cries. I don't think he's spending nearly enough time on his own."

It took her a second to keep herself from making a smart comment, but Kylie managed. "He's twenty days old, Mom. He can't even pick his head up yet. He has one way to communicate, and if I don't respond, I think he'll be anxious."

"I know there are a thousand new theories, but I put each of you kids on a schedule and didn't change it. And you all turned out just fine."

Kylie nodded, even though she had a fleeting desire to mention the fact that she got the majority of her comfort from her siblings when she was small. "We did turn out fine, but things were different for you. You had a house full of kids, and you had to keep your sanity. It's easier for us. We can adjust more to his schedule."

"That's a mistake. He'll start to think the world revolves around him."

"It does!" Kylie laughed, but her mother didn't join her. "At this point in his life, the world does revolve around him. Hell, he doesn't really know there *is* a world yet. But I think I understand your worry." Looking at her mother, she put her hand on Mackenzie's belly and rocked him a little bit. "We're not going to have one of those kids who bosses us around. Yes, we think he's the most unique baby in the world, but we want to raise him to be a good person. We'll set limits; he'll have rules. All of the

472

things that I had and that Blair had. We just don't want to make him do things he's not capable of doing. And right now, I don't think he's capable of manipulating us."

"Ha! If you feed him when he wants food, rather than when you want to feed him, he'll expect that kind of treatment from here on out."

"That's okay with us. Don't you think he's been a very happy guy so far?"

"Well, yes! That's the point! He has nothing to be unhappy *about*."

Once again, Kylie nodded while trying to keep her voice calm and even. "We don't want him to be unhappy. But that doesn't mean we're gonna try to keep him from *ever* being unhappy. I think we need to honor his development. Right now, that means following his natural schedule and responding to him when he cries." She picked her son up and stood next to her mother. "We'll make a lot of mistakes, but we have to do what seems right to us. If we followed your advice, we'd resent you if things didn't work. We're just gonna have to learn from our mistakes."

Dorothy sighed dramatically, but then gave Kylie a tiny smile. "Claire let me tell her exactly what to do. Why can't you be more like her?"

"'Cause Claire's a lawyer. They love to be told what to do. I'm a surgeon," she said, puffing out her chest. "We're leaders."

Reaching out, Dorothy took Mackenzie from his mom. "I guess I shouldn't worry that the baby will be difficult to manage. You're the one who's spoiled."

"Yes, I am," Kylie agreed. She kissed her mother on the cheek. "I'm the spoiled baby, so Mackenzie and I will always have a bond."

"Is it a little odd?" Dorothy asked. "Calling him by your name, I mean. It's taking me some time to get used to it."

"Yeah, it's...funny." The phone rang, and she moved to the desk to answer. "Hello?"

"Uhm, hi...this is David Spencer. Is Blair available?"

Kylie nearly dropped the phone. She was completely tongue-tied and only managed a "hold on" before she walked from the room like a robot.

Blair was dozing in their bedroom, and when Kylie walked into the room, Blair opened her eyes and blinked. "What's wrong?"

"David's on the phone."

"David? Fuck! What does he want?"

"I have no idea," Kylie said. She picked up the extension and handed it to her partner. "I'll go hang up the other phone."

Before Blair put the phone to her ear, she covered the receiver and said, "Come right back here."

"Like you could stop me!"

"Hello?" Blair said, her heart beating heavily in her chest.

"Hi," David said. "How...are things?"

"Fine," she said slowly. "Nothing new. Why?"

He paused a moment and then laughed nervously. "You haven't lost your sense of humor."

"Nope. I lost some weight, but the rest of me is intact. What's up?"

473

"I have…some…news, I guess. I…well, my mom thought I should call you myself."

"Your mom? I just talked to her yesterday."

"I know. Uhm, I just decided this yesterday."

"David," she said sharply, just as Kylie walked into the room, wide-eyed. "What's going on?"

"I'm nervous."

Her voice was louder than it needed to be. "About what?"

"What I have to say."

"Then fucking say it!" Dorothy walked into and out of the room during that sentence.

"I'm getting married."

Relief flooded through Blair, and Kylie began to relax when she saw her partner's body language. In a remarkably cheery tone, Blair said, "Congratulations! When's the big day?"

"Uhm, soon. As soon as the divorce is final."

"You don't sound very happy."

"Well, it was…unplanned."

"Unplanned? You're getting married, and it's unplanned?"

Kylie's eyes were wide again, and Blair patted her on the knee, mouthing, "It's fine. Not about us."

"Kimmy's pregnant."

"She's *what*? By whom?"

David's reply was sharper than Blair's had been. "By me!"

"Are you sure? I mean…"

"Thanks! Thanks for assuming my soon-to-be wife is cheating on me."

"Well, what do you expect me to think? You were the one who was so sure you were infertile."

"Lotta good that did me. Kimmy's not really ready to have kids, but she's against abortion…so we're stuck."

"Why don't you give the baby up for adoption?"

"What? Who'd do something like that?"

"Only someone who cared about the baby first," Blair said, sarcasm dripping from her words. "You wouldn't understand."

"Fine," he said, sounding as weary as he had when they'd been fighting constantly. "My mom told me to call you, so I did."

Blair noted that Kylie had left the bedroom. "Great. I don't know why she wanted you to tell me, but consider me told. And good luck, David. You're gonna need it."

He hung up without another word, and as she replaced the receiver, Blair sank into the bed. Kylie returned a few minutes later. "Upset?"

"About him?" Blair twitched her head towards the phone. "Hell, no. But I'm upset that those two idiots are gonna have a baby. I should call the state and make a preemptive complaint about poor parenting."

Kylie scratched her head, looking odd to Blair's knowing gaze. "Uhm, what's your blood type?"

"Huh?"

"What's your blood type?"

"O. Why?"

"What's the donor's type?"

Blair's eyes shot open. "I don't...I don't know. Why?"

"'Cause Mackenzie's B," Kylie said.

"No, he's not!" Blair was on her feet, shaking. "He is not!"

"Yes, he is. I read his chart at the hospital, and I recall thinking that he had a unique type. I meant to comment that night, but I forgot."

"David's B!" Blair was yelling at the top of her lungs. "David's B! Fuck! Fuck! Fuck!"

Kylie put her arms around her. "Calm down, honey. Calm down. Maybe the donor's B or AB. This could be nothing."

"He's not," Blair said. She dropped to the bed. "He's not. I don't remember exactly what he is, but it wasn't B. I think..." She closed her eyes, took a deep breath, and then looked up at the ceiling. "I think he's O. I kinda recall assuming the baby would be the same as me." She put her head in her hands. "Oh, fuck. The file's in my cabinet. Will you get it? My hands are shaking too badly."

"Yeah." Kylie got up and went into the office, returning several minutes later with the folder from the sperm bank. "It's O," she said, her lips pursed. "David is Mackenzie's father. Fuck me hard."

⌒

On the way to the airport, Kylie explained the whole situation to her mother, adding that Blair didn't usually swear like a sailor. Even though that last part was a lie, she knew Blair was trying to reform, so she didn't feel as if she'd told a complete lie.

By the time she returned, Blair was pacing back and forth across the living room, her face contorted into a grimace. "Sadie obviously had a feeling, or she wouldn't have told him to call me. But he's just dumb enough not to be able to put two and two together."

Kylie put her arm around her and forced her to stop walking. "We can handle this. It's gonna be all right."

"You don't know that!"

"No, no, I don't, but it doesn't change things legally. David's status doesn't change at all."

"It does in his mind!" Blair was glaring at her. "That idiot thinks his sperm is made outta platinum! Now he's gonna think Mackenzie is his! He's gonna want to see him now! He might want custody!"

"He might," Kylie agreed, "but that's not very likely. Hell, it's *less* likely now!"

"Less? Are you listening?"

"Sure I am. But think of it. He'll have his own baby by a woman he's married to. Why would he want shared custody of another one? Especially one he doesn't have much control over?"

"Oh, dear God, I hope he has a boy! If he had a son…he'd never want to see Mackenzie." As soon as she said the words, Blair started to cry. "I can't believe I'm happy about the fact that the man I loved won't want to see the baby we created." She fell into Kylie's arms and cried until she was nearly sick.

—

After a tense dinner and an hour of trying to calm Mackenzie down, Kylie took Blair by the hand and led her into the den where she cuddled her against her body. "We have to tell David," Kylie said.

"No, we don't. We don't have to do shit. He can go to court and demand to see the records. Might as well make him jump through a few hoops. The stinking bastard!"

"I think we should tell him," Kylie reiterated. "If there's a chance he's gonna want to assert his rights, we should be as cordial as possible."

"Cordial? You wanna be cordial?" Blair's body was tightly coiled, and nothing Kylie tried was convincing one muscle to relax.

"Yeah. I wanna be cordial. If he wants to have a role in raising Mackenzie, he's got every legal right. And…even though I know it's not what you want…I think Mackenzie would benefit from having David in his life."

"Have you been drinking?"

"No, of course not." Kylie shifted around so she could look into Blair's eyes. "David isn't a bad person."

"You've spent ten minutes with him!"

"I know that. But you spent ten years with him. You wouldn't have dated him for four years, and you wouldn't have married him if he'd been a jerk. I agree he's acted like a prize asshole, but I think that was the absolute worst you'll ever see him."

"What would be worse? Selling both babies to the highest bidder?"

Kylie cuddled her partner closer. "I know this is a shock. A terrible shock. But we've got to play it smart, and we've got to do what's best for the baby."

"What's best is to have you and I be Mackenzie's parents. We tell him about his donor, and at some point, I tell him I was married before. That's what's best."

"I disagree. There are too many people who know the truth. How would you feel if you'd found out things like this when you were old enough to understand them?"

Blair moaned and let her head drop back to rest on Kylie's shoulder. "I thought my birth family was fucked up. We're bringing our sweet little boy into a cheap soap opera."

"You can talk to some other people about this, honey, and we don't have to do it right away, but I truly believe we have to talk to David."

"Give me some time," Blair said. "I've still got to get used to the fact that half of Mackenzie's DNA comes from a motherfucking, shit-brained, jag-off."

"You're doing well on the swearing stuff," Kylie said, tickling her lover under the chin.

⸺

It took her a week, but after talking to her mother and father, Nick, Monique, Kylie's parents, their attorney, and a very prominent child psychiatrist—who charged her an outrageous sum of money for forty-five minutes of his time—Blair finally agreed that David should be told. She hadn't heard from Sadie, but she knew that her former mother-in-law was waiting to hear from her first. So, she got up the nerve to call her on a Friday afternoon.

"Sadie?" she said when the phone was answered.

"Hi, Blair. I was wondering how long it would take for you to calm down. Pretty big news, wasn't it?"

"Oh. Right. Well, to be honest, the marriage thing didn't even register. But the pregnancy thing got my attention."

"I'll bet it did." Sadie was quiet, and Blair was deeply touched by her control.

"David *is* Mackenzie's father."

Sadie gasped loudly. "Oh, God. Something you both wanted so badly. And now…"

"It's…something," Blair said. "I don't know what, but it's something. Do you think David's figured it out?"

"If he has, he hasn't said anything to me. He's very much into his own problems right now, honey."

"Problems?"

"Yes." Sadie sighed heavily. "I don't think he's really in love with that girl. She was just in the right place at the right time. And she's not happy about being pregnant. She wanted to finish college and—"

"Dear God, how old is she?"

"Oh, it's not *too* bad. She's twenty-two."

"Bad enough," Blair grumbled.

"A young lover is one thing. Being married to a girl who isn't ready for marriage or motherhood is quite another. I think David's gonna have his hands full."

Chuckling evilly, Blair said, "Maybe there is such a thing as karma."

"He probably thinks there is. He told me the other night that he realizes what an idiot he was to let you get away. I know it's too late, but I think he's beginning to get his head on straight."

"It's far, far too late for that. At least for us. But he's gonna have another chance. I hope he's happy about that."

"Maybe he will be as things develop. But he's not very happy now."

"I wonder if he'll be happy or more upset to learn about Mackenzie."

"Probably more upset. He'll feel like an even bigger fool."

"Well, that's one plus," Blair said, laughing demonically.

⸺

When Kylie got home that night, Blair was tucked into the corner of the sofa in the den. Mackenzie was lustily suckling on her breast, and a sleepy dog was lying on either side of her, each thigh serving as a doggy pillow.

Stopping just before she entered the room, Kylie stood for a moment, her expression gentling into a love-filled one. "It still takes my breath away to watch you feed our boy."

"This isn't an image I ever had of myself," Blair said, a slightly bemused smile on her face. "But I feel so ridiculously maternal!"

"Just seeing you four makes me want to crawl in there and let you comfort me, too. I'm jealous!"

"Go take that pretty dress off and join us. We can find a spot for you."

Kylie was off before Blair had finished her sentence. A few minutes later, she was back, clad in a T-shirt and scrub pants. When she sat down, the dogs jumped up and went to her, licking her face and giving her their usual ecstatic welcome. She leaned over and kissed Blair and then found a bare spot on her blanket-covered son and kissed his arm. "Where will I fit?"

"Let me move Mackenzie to my left breast. Then you'll have room." She gently disengaged the baby and switched him. He barely broke stride, latching on to the other nipple and beginning to suck.

Kylie put her head on Blair's lap, laughing when Mackenzie's feet were placed atop her head. The dogs climbed onto her hip and side, and soon, all five of them were entwined. "I'd love a picture of this," Kylie said. "We must look like a tornado hit the room."

"The dogs would jump up as soon as the photographer came in. They're not good subjects."

"Mackenzie and I are. I think we might just stay here all night." She gently nuzzled her head against Blair's belly. "Boy, it's comfortable here. I never feel better than I do when my head's in your lap."

Blair started to play with her lover's hair, taking a big curl, stretching it to its full length, and then letting it coil again. "Remember the old days when you used to like being a little more centered?"

"Huh?"

"In my lap. You used to like to be *between* my legs, not on them."

Kylie managed to get an arm around her partner's legs and give her a hug. "I'll get back there. I'm not worried." Blair didn't respond, and when Kylie looked at her, she could see that her partner didn't look convinced. "The baby's not even a month old. I bet there isn't a woman on Earth who feels like having sex this soon after giving birth."

"I'm just a little worried that it won't be the same."

"The same?"

"Yeah. That we won't...I don't know...I guess I worry that we won't spark like we used to. I don't just feel like a woman anymore. I feel like a mom."

"You're both, honey. And right now, the mom part is the big part. But that'll change as you get more comfortable. You'll feel like a sexy woman again. I'm sure of it."

"Will *you* think of me as a sexy woman again?" Blair's voice was a little quieter than usual, and she sounded tentative.

"Yes! Of course, I will. This is a period of adjustment for me, too, ya know. We're all going through changes. But we'll settle down. You don't have a thing to worry about."

"Do you miss having sex?"

Kylie laughed softly. "Haven't thought of it. I feel like I did when I was a first-year resident. I was just too busy and too tired to have it enter my mind."

"What if it's always like this?"

"It won't be. As soon as I got a week off, I was ready to go. It'll be the same with us. Once we get into a routine and your hormones have calmed down, we'll be going after each other like mink."

"Nice image." Blair tickled Kylie's nose with the soft blue blanket in which Mackenzie was wrapped. "Are we gonna have to take a week off? 'Cause I don't think we're gonna get one."

"No, probably not. But we can have a day to ourselves. Sadie would be happy to take over for that long. And all of my med school buddies have offered. I watched all of their kids at one time or another. They owe me."

"We'll see. There's no sense in thinking about it until one of us gets hot."

"Why's this on your mind, babe? You feeling insecure?"

"No, not really. Just a little, uhm…insecure." She laughed. "You know me too well."

"Anything in particular bring this up?"

"Just thinking about having to go talk to David."

"Should I be worried that you start thinking about sex when David's mentioned?"

"Yeah." Blair snickered. "I get all hot when I think about him." She grasped a lock of Kylie's hair and gave it a tug. "I just feel weird when I think about seeing him. We always connected on a very sexual level, and I don't feel like the me I used to be when we were married. It makes me…I don't know…worry about how to communicate with him."

"Let me do it."

"What?"

"Let me talk to him. I could do it with a lot less emotion than you could. And I had the last encounter with him. It wouldn't be a bad idea to try to smooth things over."

Blair looked at her for a second and said, "The mere thought of your doing this lifted a weight from my shoulders."

"Then let me."

"Oh, what the fuck. Go for it."

⟿

Deciding to return the favor, Kylie showed up unannounced at David's home on Saturday afternoon. She knew it was rude, but she also didn't want him to have the opportunity to build up his defenses, and after their last encounter, she knew he'd justifiably have some.

With butterflies flitting around in her stomach, she knocked on the door. A minute later, David opened the door and instinctively took a step back, his expression clouding over. "What do you want?"

"First, I wanted to apologize for the way I behaved when you came to my office."

"What? That's been months!"

"I know. But it's been bothering me. I didn't act the way I normally do. I don't want to have any bad blood between us."

He was still blocking the door, and her statement didn't seem to impress him. "Why?"

"Why...what?"

"Why do you care if there's bad blood between us? If it hadn't been for you..." He lowered his voice and then shot a look over his shoulder. Stepping outside, he quietly closed the door. "If it hadn't been for you, Blair probably wouldn't have started divorce proceedings. We might not have split up."

"Is this a bad time?" Kylie asked. "I could come back when you're free to talk."

He shook his head. "Now's fine. My...girlfriend is taking a nap. I don't wanna wake her."

"How about the backyard? This is kinda personal to be talking about on the front steps."

"Fine. Let's go around the side." They walked to the backyard in silence, and when they got there, Kylie took a seat, not commenting when David chose to remain standing.

He stared at her, so she replied to his previous comment. "I don't know what Blair would have done if we hadn't been friends. For all I know, you could be right. Maybe having support and a place to live let her call it quits sooner than she would have if she'd been living in a hotel. But that's not what happened."

"You wanted her from the start, didn't you?" David was glaring at her in a way that made the hair on the back of Kylie's neck stand up. If the dogs had been there, she was sure they would have started growling.

"No, I didn't. But I doubt I'll be able to convince you of that. Blair was my friend, and I wanted her to get pregnant and be happy. I didn't dream that she and I would end up together."

"You're right," he said. "You can't convince me of that."

"So be it. But that's not my main goal in coming here."

"That's not a surprise. I knew you had something else on your mind. What is it? Change your mind about the adoption?"

"Of course not! I want to be our baby's legal parent more than anything in the world. But...you might change your mind."

"We had a deal!" he said, his cheeks flushing.

"Yeah, we did. But you didn't have all of the information." She took a breath and spit it out. "You didn't know that Mackenzie was your biological child."

He sank into a chair as though he'd been thrown into it. "Oh, fuck." He slumped down in his seat, looking ill. "That can't be."

"Yeah, it is. The donor and Blair both have type O blood. You have B. The baby has B. You can have a DNA test done, but it seems pretty clear-cut to me."

"Christ!" He got to his feet and started to walk, moving nervously around his small yard. "What does Blair have to say?"

"She's…" Kylie thought for a moment and decided to tell him her true feelings. "I think it made her sad."

"Sad?"

"Yeah. I think it made the whole infertility ordeal and your divorce seem so unnecessary. She was really happy with you, David. No matter what's happened, losing you was a big, big loss for her."

"It was for me, too," he said. He sat down and ran his hand through his close-cropped black hair. "Damn, I feel like an idiot!"

"You must feel a little like Blair does." She didn't add that he should feel much more responsible. "It probably feels like you've lost something that you didn't have to lose."

"We could have had our own baby," he muttered, staring at the ground. "Our own damn baby."

Kylie looked at him, wondering how deeply hidden his good qualities were. She was certain he had some, but she'd yet to see any of them. "I still want to adopt Mackenzie. But the ball's in your court. I hope with all my heart that you honor our agreement, but you might think this changes things."

"It does," he said. "Of course, it does." He looked at Kylie for a moment and then said, "You didn't have to tell me."

"No, we didn't. But neither of us could live with that kind of lie. Especially when Blair knew how important it was to you to have a biological child."

He laughed wryly. "You'll never convince me that was her first instinct."

Smiling, Kylie nodded. "I won't even try. She lets her temper flare, and then she calms down and does the correct thing."

"Yeah. That's my girl," he said, making Kylie's heart ache. She knew how deep the bond between Blair and David had been, but she hated seeing evidence of it, especially from David.

"So…you want some time?"

"Yeah. I need to think about it. I'll have to talk to my…girlfriend. See what she thinks."

"Sure, sure. I understand. This is a big deal. And it'll affect you in a big way."

"Yeah, it will. I'll want to be involved…"

"Sure. Makes sense. You'll be paying for half of his care; you'll want a say in how he's raised."

His half-smile turned into a sharp look. "With as much money as you two make? You'll still sock me for child support?"

"Of course," Kylie said. "If he's not my child legally, I have no obligation to him at all. He's just a boarder."

"Blair makes as much as I do, if not more. She could raise a dozen kids and not be hurting."

"True. But that's not how it works. Actually, she's been thinking of cutting way back...maybe working part-time. She's really gotten into being a mother, and she's not sure she wants someone else caring for the baby."

"I should have known," he said, looking at her with venom in his eyes. "This is another fleece job. If I want to see my son, I've gotta pay."

"Nothing could be further from the truth." Kylie waited until he looked at her. "I think Mackenzie would love to have you in his life. You're his father, David, and every kid wants to know his father. We'll never ask for a dime from you if you let me adopt him."

"And if I don't?"

"Blair will sue you for child support."

He looked as if he'd love to wring her neck. "She won't get hardly anything once a judge sees how much she makes."

"She will if she quits her job. And if she puts most of her savings in trust for Mackenzie, she won't have much in the way of assets." She smiled insincerely. "Not that she'd necessarily do anything like that, but as you know, her temper can get the best of her."

"A good judge would see right through that!"

"Nothing to see through. My friend leaves her husband, and I take her in out of the goodness of my heart. She's worried about securing her baby's future, so she puts her money in trust for him. Then she decides she can't leave him with a babysitter. She'd keep her hand in real estate, just enough to pay for her expenses. But the baby...he's gonna be expensive. A judge would look at your behavior, too. I doubt he'd have a lot of sympathy for a guy who stated he couldn't love the baby he wanted his wife to have." Her smile turned even more devilish. "Especially when the judge sees that you immediately got another woman pregnant—while you were still married to Blair."

"So, I pay through the nose."

"Yeah. That's probably what'll happen. But only through college...or grad school."

"I've gotta call my attorney. See if there's anything I can do to keep you two from sending me to the poorhouse."

Kylie stood. "We both agree that we want you to get to know Mackenzie. You can take as active a role as you want. And we don't want a cent from you if you let me adopt. Other than that...it's game on."

"Thanks for coming," David said, sarcasm dripping. "It's always a treat to see you."

"Same here. A real pleasure."

❤

That night, Blair was on the phone with her former mother-in-law. "Can you try to pound some sense into him, Sadie? I don't want to be vindictive, but I will be. I swear I'll squeeze every cent I can out of him if he won't let Kylie adopt."

"Can't you understand his perspective...just a little?"

"No. Not at all. He ruined our marriage, and he started fooling around with that girl while I was still praying he'd come to his senses. He humiliated me and showed he didn't take his vows seriously. I'll never understand his perspective, and if he doesn't understand mine, he'll regret it."

"You're asking an awful lot. You want him to voluntarily give up his child!"

"He did that when he decided he couldn't love our baby. That's a done deal in my book. He can have a relationship with Mackenzie, he can call him his son, and he can take him to Father-Son Day at the office. He can do everything a real father would. All he has to do is let Kylie be his legal parent. That's not asking much at all in my opinion."

"You know David doesn't feel that way."

"You know, I have no idea how David feels. I thought I knew him, but...I didn't. So, feel free to tell him he can do this the easy way or the hard way. But the hard way is gonna cost him!"

⟿

A week passed, and Blair was edgy and irritable when Kylie got home. "I don't care what anyone says," she stated before the doctor had put her briefcase down. "We shouldn't have told dickwad about Mackenzie."

Having learned that "angry Blair" was not a good person with which to have a rational discussion, Kylie simply agreed. "You're probably right. I gave him too much credit." She put her briefcase down and put her arms around Blair, being careful of her tender breasts. "Where's Bruin?"

"He wanted to go for a walk. I'm surprised you didn't see him when you drove in. He couldn't have gotten too far."

"Wanna go out to dinner?"

"No." Blair made a face. "I hate it when people take infants to a restaurant."

"I wasn't planning on taking him. I thought it would be nice for us to be alone for a change. That darned kid is like a leech!"

That made Blair smile, and she looked up at Kylie with an impish grin. "Won't the neighbors hear him crying?"

"Not if we put him in your car before we leave. You have very good soundproofing."

Blair pinched her hard on the waist. "What's your plan? Besides criminal child endangerment."

"My plan was to take you out to dinner. I already made reservations and found a babysitter."

"You did?" A delighted smile lit up Blair's face, but it disappeared just as quickly as it had come. "I don't have anything to wear."

"Sure you do. You can wear your special pregnancy dress-up clothes one last time. I know you're comfortable in that outfit, and you look spectacular in it."

"Really? Even though I don't have a beach ball strapped to my belly?"

"I'm positive. You weren't showing much at all the first time you wore it."

"I guess my first question should have been who's going to watch the baby, huh?" Blair asked, looking a little guilty.

"Nick's gonna come by. With his girlfriend," Kylie added. "He wants to see how she is around babies. I think he's really serious about this woman."

"If he's giving her the baby test, he is! Does either of them know how to handle a baby? Not that I mind leaving our son with completely inept people, of course."

"Yes, dear. Nick has nieces and nephews, and he's watched them when they were young. Not as young as Mackenzie, but it's actually easier to watch a baby that can't roll over."

"Good point." With a spring in her step, Blair turned and headed to their room. "I'm gonna start getting ready. It'll take me hours to look halfway decent."

"You look three-quarters decent already!" Kylie called after her.

Blair twitched her butt in reply, and Kylie found herself appreciating the contours of her lover's ass for the first time in weeks. "Nice," she said aloud. "Very nice."

⌇

At midnight, Blair went to the bathroom to brush her teeth while Kylie sat by the cradle, waiting for Mackenzie to make some sort of mess in his diaper. "It's been ten minutes since you were fed," she said to the half-dozing infant. "Let's see some output."

He made a face and shivered, and she pulled his diaper away from his body and nodded. "Good job. I knew I could count on you."

Blair came out of the bathroom and watched her lover clean and change their son. "You're very efficient with that, you know."

"I turn everything into a science project," Kylie admitted. "I'm always looking for the fewest motions to give the desired result." Mackenzie was now clean and dry, and Kylie kissed him, tucked him in, and then disposed of his dirty diaper.

Blair heard her in the bathroom and called out, "You're not prepping for surgery. A simple hand wash will do."

But Kylie didn't like to be rushed. "I don't mind handling bodily waste, but I know what can be in it. And there's very little of it that I want on my hands. As God is my witness, I'll never contract gastroenteritis from Mackenzie."

"Come to bed, you weirdo."

"Ah…reminds me of my single days. That's one of my favorite come-ons." Kylie slid into bed and dramatically took Blair into her arms. "It makes me so hot to hear you call me a weirdo." She kissed her passionately and then pulled away, laughing.

Blair curled up next to her body and sniffed her breath. "I'm jealous of your being able to drink wine with dinner. My ravioli would have been even better with a nice glass of red wine."

"I had fun," Kylie said. "I'd forgotten how nice it was to be alone." She was quiet for a moment and then said, "That's the first time we've been alone since your mom got here—two weeks before Mackenzie was born."

"Damn! When you say it like that, it sounds like forever!"

"It's been too long. I know how crazy we are about the baby, but we've got to have some time for us—just us."

"I know. I miss having real conversations. I've forgotten that the world is still going on out there. Has anything happened?"

"Nah. Same old stuff. I'll let you know if I hear about anything important."

"You're important," Blair whispered. "You're very important to me."

Kylie turned her head, and Blair moved closer, starting to kiss her. For the first time in weeks, Kylie's libido began to awaken from its slumber, and she relished the feelings that coursed through her body. She didn't try to push Blair, though, thinking that it was best to let her partner make the first move when she was ready. They continued to kiss with Blair giving off signals that she wanted to keep going. Happily, Kylie showed her enthusiasm by opening her mouth and suckling on her lover's tongue. "I love you," she whispered, moving to kiss Blair's always-sensitive neck.

"I love you, too." She slipped her hand under Kylie's T-shirt and started to play with her breasts while latching on to her mouth for another heated kiss. The doctor responded enthusiastically, groaning a little while pressing against Blair's hand. "Can I?" Blair asked, her fingers breaching the waistband of Kylie's scrubs.

In a moment, the scrubs were off, and Kylie beamed a happy grin at her lover. "Can you what?"

"Can I kiss you until you're panting for me?"

"Yes. Most definitely. Pretty please." Kylie whipped off her shirt and lay on her back, ready to be ravished. "Take me."

"I love that you're mine. And I love that you planned a night out for us. I loved feeling like yours tonight…not just Mackenzie's mother."

"Did you feel like mine?"

"Uh-huh. Like when you held my hand when we walked into the restaurant. And the way you looked at me when I came back from the restroom. Your eyes lit up like you'd just seen Santa."

"You looked so pretty," Kylie whispered, turning onto her side to kiss along Blair's jaw. "Pretty and sexy and voluptuous. I know you're going to lose every pound you gained, but if I had my way, you'd keep ten of 'em."

"You don't have your way," Blair giggled. "But I'm gonna have my way with you." She pushed her onto her back and started to play with her lover's body, going over the familiar terrain as if it were brand new. "I've missed this," she whispered. "I've missed seeing how responsive you are…how your nipples get so hard so fast. You're such a beautiful woman."

"Your woman," Kylie said. "Yours."

"Yeah. My woman." Blair took a breast into her mouth and sucked a ripe-looking nipple between her teeth. After a few moments, she looked up at Kylie. "No milk?"

"Unh-uh. But other parts are getting wet."

"I like those parts." She captured the nearby breast again and let her hand slip between Kylie's legs, gently urging them apart. Kylie's breath caught when Blair's cool fingers touched her, and she shivered all over from the sensation. "Someone's excited," Blair murmured into her ear before nibbling on her earlobe.

"Uh-huh. Very excited." Kylie's voice was high and tight and a little tremulous.

"Open up for me," Blair whispered. "Let me in."

The soles of Kylie's feet were immediately on the bed, and her hands flew to her vulva, giving Blair unimpeded access. Just a few minutes of gentle stroking had the doctor panting and moaning, making Blair smile at her lightning-like response. Blair slipped two fingers inside her lover, and Kylie automatically took over, stroking her own clitoris until she blew out a whoosh of air, her flesh spasming around Blair's fingers.

"You've still got it," Blair murmured, kissing Kylie's hot, flushed chest. "You're still my Energizer Bunny."

"Damn, that felt good! How'd we go that long without?"

"We were busy. But you reminded me tonight that we have to make time for us. I love us."

"I love the 'you' part of 'us' very, very much." Kylie kissed her, lingering on her succulent lower lip.

But Blair didn't respond in kind. She patted Kylie's back and tried to roll her onto her back. "Let's sleep now, baby. Aren't you tired?"

"Unh-uh. Hot. Aren't you?"

"I don't...I don't think so. It still feels a little early."

"Early?"

"Yeah." Blair put her head on Kylie's shoulder. "I feel close, but I don't think I'm turned on. I just feel warm and cuddly."

"Sure?"

"Yeah. I don't think everything's back to normal yet. It's gonna take me a while."

"You know what you need?" Kylie asked. Without waiting for an answer, she scooted down the bed. "You need a professional opinion."

"I do?"

"Yep. I'd like to do a brief exam to make sure your head and your vulva are communicating properly."

"There's an exam for that?" Blair asked, chuckling. "I've never had that one."

"Good! 'Cause I'd be filing a complaint with the medical board. You have to have a special relationship to perform this exam. Sadly, I'm the only one competent to perform it on you."

"Go right ahead. Every other doctor in town's seen me. What's one more?"

"Good attitude." Kylie urged her lover to bend her knees, and then she settled down right between Blair's legs. "Let's see...there seems to be some clear fluid coming from the vagina. I'd better investigate."

"Is there really?" Blair asked, genuinely surprised.

"Yep. I think we might have a serious case of vulva-brain miscommunication." Kylie lifted her head and looked at her lover. "There's a cure, but it's a little...intimate. Do I have your permission to proceed?"

"What the hell? You're the doctor." Grabbing another pillow, Blair lay back and let Kylie work. Her soft, sure fingertip started to trace the very edges of Blair's lips, her touch so light that Blair could barely feel her. Then she slipped her finger into her lover, making her flinch. "I didn't know you were going there!"

"Just testing your reflexes." Kylie spread Blair's lubrication all around her vulva, making her sigh with pleasure. She touched her so gently that it was very soothing and calming.

"Nice," Blair murmured. "Like a really good massage."

"I'd better be the only one who massages you like this. Or I'll call...whoever you complain to about masseuses!"

"Just you, baby," Blair said, her voice low and soft. "Only you touch me like this."

Kylie kept up her slow, tender massage, eventually adding a little pressure. Blair's hips started to move, slowly twitching back and forth as Kylie worked. When she started to push her hips towards Kylie, the doctor moved just enough to be able to dip her head and capture her lover's entire vulva in her mouth.

"Whoa!"

"Mmm..." Kylie groaned, so very happy to have her mouth on Blair again. She grasped her partner's legs and lifted them a little, giving her a slightly better angle from which to dip her tongue into her lover, just the way she'd learned that Blair liked it.

"God, that feels wonderful!"

Sucking on her greedily, Kylie twirled her tongue around and across Blair's slippery skin, making Blair moan with pleasure. In far too short a time, Blair grabbed a handful of Kylie's hair and let out the beginning of a howl, which she somehow managed to contain. After nuzzling her tenderly for a few minutes, Kylie lifted her head to see her lover lying with a pillow over her face, completely spent.

Climbing up to lie next to her, Kylie took the pillow away and kissed Blair's open mouth. "Everything looks great under the hood."

Blair smacked her lips together. "Hey! That's closer to how I used to taste!"

"Works for me," Kylie said, grinning. "Of course, I liked it before, so it's all good."

"I'm not there yet," Blair said thoughtfully. "But definitely closer."

"I'll keep doing spot checks. We need to monitor the situation closely. Especially with your history of vulva-brain miscommunication."

"Is there really such a thing?"

"Got me!" Kylie grinned at her. "But it makes sense that it might take you a while to feel like you did before. Your body's been giving you some very confusing signals."

"Yeah. It sure has. Thanks for not going for my breasts, by the way. It's gonna take me a while to switch from feeling like Elsie the cow back to Blair the lover."

"I think Mackenzie's in charge of your breasts right now. I'll reclaim them— without doubt—but I'll let him have dibs for a while."

"One day, they'll be mine," Blair said rather wistfully.

"They're yours now. You're just very generously sharing them with our boy."

"I love feeding him. I really do. But I think I'll be done by six months."

"If you could keep it up for a year, it'd be ideal. But if you can only manage six months...that's good enough."

"A year, huh?"

"That's what current research says gives him the optimal immunities."

"We'll see. I wasn't breastfed, and I've done all right."

"I wasn't, either. My mom stopped after Alan."

"Really? She breastfed the older kids?"

"Yep. But she was sick of the whole thing after a few. She said it's just too hard with toddlers demanding attention all of the time."

"So…any attention we pay to Mackenzie's gonna be more than you got, right?"

"Probably." Kylie laughed. "Can you imagine how perfect I'd be if I wasn't the youngest?"

Blair stroked her cheek. "Say what you will, but your parents never cheated you on self-esteem."

⌐

On Sunday afternoon, Kylie was napping with Mackenzie, the pair lying in the shade on a lounge chair, Mackenzie nestled between Kylie's legs. Blair wouldn't normally have let her partner hold the baby that way, but she was outside as well, reading the Sunday paper for the first time since Mackenzie's birth.

Her cell phone rang, and she grabbed it before it woke either of the nappers. "Hello?"

"Hi. It's David."

"Oh. Hi." She knew she sounded cold, but Blair couldn't help it.

"Can I come over?"

"To my house?"

"Uhm, yeah. I want to, uhm, meet the baby."

Blair wanted to tell him to bring a court order, but Kylie had impressed upon her the importance of being as nice to David as possible. Of course, if David refused to allow Kylie to adopt, Blair was hell-bent on making her former husband's life a nightmare, but that was her trump card, and she wanted to hold on to it until she was forced to throw it. "Today?"

"Yeah. If that's convenient."

"I suppose it's okay. Are you coming alone?"

"Huh? Oh! Yeah, yeah, I'll be alone."

Blair thought it was a good sign that he didn't want Kimmy to accompany him. "He's napping now, but he usually likes to eat around 2:00. If you come then, he'll be awake."

"Okay. I'll swing by around 2:00. Uhm, can I bring him anything?"

"Like?"

"I don't know." He sounded a little irritated, like he often did when he was out of his element. "Like a toy or something."

"Well, he doesn't have a basketball," Blair said, trying to joke.

"Great! I'll bring him a basketball. See you later."

My God, was he always mentally defective? He must have been better in bed than I recall!

⌐

At 2:00 on the dot, David rang the bell. The dogs raced to the door, yapping their little heads off. Blair was in Mackenzie's room, getting ready to feed him after his nap. "I'll get it," Kylie said. "Want me to entertain him until you're done?"

"Uhm, if you don't mind, just send him in."

"Why would I mind?"

"'Cause I'm gonna be feeding Mackenzie." Blair looked up, searching Kylie's eyes. "I thought you might think this was too intimate for David to see."

"Nah." Kylie gave her a quick kiss. "He's seen 'em more than I have. One more time won't hurt."

She dashed down the hall, trying to shush the dogs. Opening the door, she saw a very nervous-looking David, carrying an official NBA leather basketball. "Hi," he said. "I brought him a present."

"Ah…" Kylie took the ball and looked at it for a moment. "He doesn't have one of these."

"That's what Blair said," he said, giving her a plastic smile.

Kylie opened the door the whole way, and the dogs ran out and in and out and in, flying around David's legs at least three times. "Black collar is Nicky. Red collar is Nora."

David squatted down and let them sniff and lick until they were satisfied. "They're fantastic!"

Unable to resist smiling when someone complimented them, Kylie grinned. "Yeah, they are. We rescued them."

"Really? That's…nice." He stood and walked into the house, looking around while trying not to look as if he were. "Blair home?"

"Yeah. She's in the baby's room. It's the first door on the right." Kylie turned and called, "Let's go, kids. Time for a little exercise." She walked towards the backyard, both dogs scampering after her.

David stood right where he was for a minute and then started to walk. When he reached the door, he knocked on the jamb. "Blair?"

"Come on in."

He swung around and entered, stopping in amazement when he saw her. Blair was sitting in a rocking chair with a very chubby, very happy baby nursing contentedly. David looked as though his legs might give way, and he grasped a stool and dropped to it. "My God! You look so absolutely beautiful!"

"He is pretty, isn't he?" she asked, looking down at her son.

"Yeah. Yeah. But I meant you."

Blair's head snapped up to look at him. "Me?"

"Yes," he said, his voice soft and seemingly filled with awe. "I've never seen you more beautiful."

"Uhm, thanks. Motherhood agrees with me."

"Your hair, your skin, your body…" His eyes were roving up and down, and she nearly told him to stop looking at her. But he looked so helpless that she cut him a break.

"I'm happy," she said. "I love the baby, and I love Kylie, and I love our life together. I'm totally content, and that must show."

"It does." He was still staring at her, and as the seconds passed, his expression changed, and he began to cry. "I can't believe how badly I screwed everything up." He took in a breath, his voice raw and shaking. "I'm so sorry."

"It's all right," she said soothingly. "Everything worked out in the end."

"I'd be so much happier if I still had you. I lost so much."

"I'm sorry, David. I really am. I wish you'd…I wish things had worked out better for you. But they still can. You and your wife can make a go of it if you work hard."

"But I *had* it with you. I had what I wanted with you."

"You didn't know it," she said simply. "You had to learn that the hard way."

"I did." He reached into his pocket and took out his handkerchief. "Can I…come closer?"

"Sure. I was just about to switch breasts." She tickled Mackenzie's cheek, making him open his mouth. David had turned away, letting her move the baby to her other breast and cover up. "Ready."

David squatted down and put his hand on Mackenzie. The look on his face was so sad that Blair could feel tears welling up. He stroked the baby's back and softly said, "My mom thinks he looks like me. Do you?"

"Yeah. I do. He's got your coloring and your eyes. He finally lost his back hair, thank God." She chuckled a little, sniffing away her tears.

He looked at her, and she felt a flicker of their old connection. "I'm so sorry," he said. Then he put his head on her knee and cried hard, sobbing like a child. She found herself running her hand through his hair, trying to comfort him in some small way. But she was just as sad as he was. Sad for the pain they'd gone through and the reckless way they'd created the baby she loved so much.

"Sh," she whispered. "It'll be all right. You and Kimmy can be happy. And you'll have a baby that you both can love."

"She doesn't want me to have a relationship with…" He nodded his head towards Mackenzie.

"Well, I wouldn't be crazy about it if I were her. The circumstances are a little strange."

"She's not happy about being pregnant. She blames me for telling her I was impotent."

"Yeah, that's a tough one. But she has to know you were pretty certain."

"I think she does, but she got mad when I told her I had a low sperm count. She thought I was shooting blanks."

"Ooh. That would make most women mad. Especially if they didn't want to have a baby."

"Her parents want her to give the baby up for adoption. I don't think she will, though."

Blair's eyes widened. "If you've learned one thing, it should be that you have to work through these things together. I know you don't like therapists, but you two had better get to one!"

"We probably should," he admitted. "She's really angry right now."

"That's not good for the baby. You need to sort things out. If nothing else, you should go see one of the priests at your mother's church. One of them might be able to help."

"Yeah. We might."

Mackenzie was slowing down, and Blair said, "I think he's finished. Want to burp him?"

His eyes saucered. "I don't know how!"

"It's easy." She removed Mackenzie from her breast, covered up as well as she could, and handed the almost-sleeping baby to David. He held him like a ticking bomb, but David was doing all right. Blair got up, put a diaper on his shoulder, and then showed him how to hold his son and pat him.

David got the hang of it and started to pat Mackenzie's back gently. "He's big, isn't he?"

"Yeah. He's pretty big. I was obviously pregnant for a few weeks before I was inseminated. That's why I felt pregnant so fast."

"Oh. That makes sense."

"Yeah, and if my doctor had known, she would have induced labor a couple of weeks earlier. Then I wouldn't have needed a C-section."

"It's not easy to screw up two pregnancies in a year," David said, rolling his eyes, "but I managed."

Mackenzie let out his usual robust burp, making David flinch. "He's got a good pair of lungs!"

Blair reached out and took the baby from David, holding him in her arms and rocking him. "He'll be asleep in less than a minute. Watch."

Mackenzie shook, yawned, held one little arm above his head, and nestled his face against Blair's breast. She stroked his head a few times, and he relaxed completely, sound asleep.

"God, that was...weird."

Placing him in his crib, she turned on the monitor and motioned for David to follow. They went into the living room, and she said, "All he does is eat and sleep and poop. Oh, and he can lift his head now. And once in a while, if he's really alert, he can follow a toy if we dangle it in front of him. He tries to reach for it, but he never gets close." She laughed. "Kylie swears he's right on schedule, but he seems a little slow to me."

"He takes after me," David said, looking down. "I just hope he doesn't screw up his life like I've done."

"You're having a bad year. It can get better."

"You're nicer to me than I deserve."

"That's me," Blair said, chuckling. "I'm a giver."

He looked at her and said, "I'm going to try to make up for some of my mistakes. I'm going to let Kylie adopt him."

Blair closed her eyes and took a few slow breaths. "Thank you," she whispered. "Nothing means more to me than that."

"I *would* like to see the baby," he said, "but I won't tell you what to do. He's yours."

Blair met his eyes and moved closer. "I've known you for a long time, and you've always been a man of your word. Do you swear you won't change your mind?"

"I do."

"What if Kimmy gives your baby up for adoption?"

"Separate issue," he said. "This baby is yours, and if you want to share him with Kylie…that's your choice."

"Please don't lie to me, David. I don't think I'd be able to stand it."

"I mean it. I swear on my life, Blair. I won't back out."

She put her arms around his waist and hugged him. "Thank you. This means more to me than you'll ever know."

He patted her back and then moved back when she pulled away. "I…guess I'll be going."

"Thanks, David," she said. As he turned to leave, she said, "You can't bring yourself to call him by his name, can you?"

He looked down guiltily. "I'll get used to it. It's a nice name."

"We call him Bruin. Would that be easier for you?"

His eyes met hers, and he smiled. "Much. Thanks."

"You're welcome." She touched his back as he opened the door. "I can be a very nice person when I want to be."

He smiled at her. "I know. That's why I love…d you."

"Take care. And feel free to come see the baby whenever you want. You and your mom can take him for a day if you'd like."

"That'd be great!"

"No problem. I want us all to get along. Like a big, strange family."

"It will be strange. But you never know. It might be fun."

"I think it will be." She smiled at him again, and he returned her grin. Watching him walk down the sidewalk, she shook her head, wondering how in the world things had turned out like they had. She was still standing there, lost in thought, when a pair of warm arms encircled her.

"Mailman doesn't come until tomorrow."

Blair leaned back, letting Kylie support her. "Guess what?"

"What?"

"David's gonna relinquish his rights. You're gonna be Mackenzie's legal mom."

Kylie wrapped her arms around Blair tightly. "Are you sure?"

"Positive. David promised, and his word is good."

"Let's go tell Mackenzie." Kylie took Blair's hand, ignoring the amused smile her partner was giving her. When they got to his room, Kylie leaned over and stroked his tummy, smiling when he shook in his sleep and tried to find her hand. "We've got something to tell you, buddy."

The baby went right back to sleep, but that didn't stop Kylie from delivering the news. "Here's the scoop. A long time ago…okay, about ten months ago, a beautiful princess and a handsome prince decided to have a baby." Blair looked at her partner, not surprised in the least to see a few tears in her eyes. "The baby started to grow from a tiny little seed." She held her hand up and moved her thumb just a hair's distance from her index finger. "Littler than this."

Blair hugged her and kissed her cheek, charmed by her story and the loving way she was telling it. Kylie continued, "But the prince was under an evil spell, and even though he wanted the baby very much, he got very, very confused. So confused that he told the princess to go away. The princess was very, very sad, but she was under a good spell, and she fell in love with another beautiful and talented princess-surgeon, who loved her with all of her heart." Blair let her head drop to Kylie's shoulder, listening to the soft, sweet cadence of her voice. "When the baby was born, the princesses were so, so happy. They were the happiest people in the whole kingdom. One day, the prince heard about the baby being born, and magically, the spell was lifted. He rushed to the castle where the princesses lived and said that he wanted to be a part of their family. That made the princesses very happy because they felt sorry for the prince when he was under the evil spell. So, that's why you, our little prince, have two mommies and one daddy. That's three people who love him and promise to take care of him every day of his life. The end."

She turned and took Blair into her arms, hugging her while they both cried from their shared happiness. "It's not the end," Blair whispered. "It's just the beginning. And we're going to live happily ever after in our kingdom by the sea."

The End